A RELATIVE INVASION

TRILOGY

ROSALIND MINETT

Uptake publications

Copyright © 2018 Rosalind Minett

All rights reserved.

The right of Rosalind Minett to be identified as the author of this work has been asserted by her in accordance with sections 77 and 78 of the Copyright, Designs and Patents Act 1988.

This book is a work of fiction. Historical events and named politicians or celebrities are accurate but otherwise the characters are entirely the product of the author's imagination. Any resemblance to actual people, living or dead, is entirely coincidental.

ISBN: 978-0-9927167-4-5

Uptake publications

TA4 2AR

PRAISE FOR ROSALIND MINETT

"Minett weaves a powerful and compelling narrative with strong and relatable characters, and offers an evocative portrayal of England's war-time home front... The mounting tensions between Billy and Kenneth parallel the rising agitation in Europe ... The author is deft in capturing that sense of tightly controlled emotions in the parents' characters ... and the sense of social and familial obligation. This and the war's tension is offset by the humour that comes through when seeing it all through Billy's five-year-old eyes – it foreshadows the violence about to erupt in Europe ... **Harper Collins editor**

"... I thoroughly enjoyed the book. The research is meticulously done with convincing historical detail ... the characters are carefully drawn and very believable as real people. **Historical Novel Society**

"The book is so beautifully scribed ... Very strong writing this, a book pleading to become a film. Rosalind Minett is becoming an upper echelon writer. Highly Recommended." **Grady Harp, Los Angeles, Vine Voice, Amazon Hall of Fame reviewer**

"... an enchanting trilogy by Rosalind Minett, a master of research. She has skillfully conjured scenes from the WWII era and the chaos and desperation of that time...seamlessly and effortlessly with clever interpretations from a five-year old mind. **CMT Stibbe, USA**

"Minett writes beautifully with a deep understanding of a troubled boy's journey through trauma, disruption and invasion...a remarkable boy whose story gradually unfolds and grips you from the very onset. I adore Billy's character ... and highly recommend this unforgettable and exceptional well written story to everyone. **C.R.Putsche, Austria**

"Minett's economic, yet powerful writing does a wonderful job at immersing the reader inside Bill's world. Her strength lies in the power of hints... The hapless hero, victim to forces he can barely fathom, let alone control. Even better is the underlying, parallel narration of the events unfolding in Europe, mirroring the invasion of Bill's life by Kenneth. Few capture so well (its) atmosphere…A masterful tale by an obviously very talented story-teller. **Nicholas.C.Rossis, Athens**

ACKNOWLEDGMENTS

I could not have written this trilogy without the BBC Peoples' War archive, online newspaper resources, predominantly *The Times*, but also local newspaper archives for valuable details of the difficulties and products current to the time. Further, the valuable wartime data held at Sussex University (where, incidentally, I gained my first degree).

My thanks to the following people:

Ron Large for interesting and useful information about post-war Wandsworth; all the Records Offices I visited, but especially Wandsworth Archives at Lavender Hill, and Surrey Archives at Woking.

My especial thanks to Louise Lawrence and Tessa Rivas for their dedicated editing, and to Alison and Kyle for their interest and support.

To all those who struggled to survive the emotional effects of the Second World War

FORWARD TO THE TRILOGY

When I began writing this story I had no intention of writing a trilogy, only to tell the tale of a young boy during the wartime years. However, it took the length of three books before I could reach the end I had planned.

The story was prompted by hearing an elderly man's experience of evacuation during World War Two. On September first, 1939, thousands of city children were transported by train to country villages. This man had been one of these evacuees from a school in London, arriving in a village, tired and hungry. Small, sweet and usually blond children were quickly accepted by volunteer foster families. The remaining children were marched around the village in a crocodile while the teachers knocked on doors and asked householders to take in a child as their war effort.

My informant was a tall child for his age, and apparently prospective foster carers feared he would cost more than the set eight shillings or so allowed for each child's keep. He spoke of being the last child chosen, his teacher being near despair. Eventually a housewife took him, but it was an unhappy situation for him, living with a resentful carer.

This anecdote made me wonder about the resilience needed by

such evacuated children. I decided my character would be a child of comfortably-off parents, and would be aged seven when the first evacuation began. Billy became a sturdy, well-meaning boy in my imagination. I wanted to show something of his life before war started, so I had the tale begin in 1937.

All begins innocently enough with Billy's parents preparing for a visit from relatives, the father's brother with his wife and son. Somehow, an antagonist for Billy emerged in the shape of the cousin, the frail, indulged, charming but devious Kenneth, smaller although a year older than Billy. The emotionally-charged relationship between these two boys became the focus of the tale, the war years serving as its background.

Billy is only five years old at the opening, and by the time I had written one hundred thousand words, he was still only seven. Evacuated during the phony war, Billy returns to endure a Christmas full of family tension. His school adapts with great difficulty to manage additional children whose school had closed down for the war, together with pupils returned from evacuation like Billy, while without many of its teachers who are either away with evacuated pupils or called up for military service.

Soon enough, bombing in London begins. That point was appropriate for ending Book One. Both Billy and Kenneth are about to be evacuated, together with both mothers and Billy's baby sister.

In Book Two, describing the disruption of such evacuation for each family member, the events and effect of real war, as well as Kenneth's continuing invasion of Billy's psychological space, was enough to fill a book length. It seemed appropriate for Book Two to end at the same time as War in Europe.

Billy was now twelve and Kenneth, thirteen. They return to ruined post-war London. Book Three had to bring both to adulthood. Before that, the climax I had planned would occur and its dramatic fall-out. In fact, the book became much longer than either of the earlier two.

It took the three books to achieve the story about Billy I had created. The ending still leaves interesting questions about what might happen to all the characters, for there are many.

Retribution is a compelling theme. Its potential may still simmer in the readers' mind when Kenneth and Bill begin their separate adult paths at the end of Book Three.

Some readers have asked that I write more in this series, and now I am beginning the necessary research for this.

BOOK ONE

INTRUSION

PREFACE

"In retrospect, though many were guilty, none was innocent."

The Origins of the Second World War
A.J.P. Taylor

CHAPTER ONE

October 22nd 1937. ***Today the Duke and Duchess of Windsor met Herr Hitler at Berghof***

Kenneth. Until now he'd been just a name on a Christmas card written by someone else. Kenn*eth*. Billy felt his tongue thick against his lips. It felt the same when he said 'filth'. 'Filthy' was the word Mother used when he'd got dirty knees playing outside.

He bent down to his hobby horse's hard white head. The furry strip along the top of its neck was nice to stroke. He whispered into the leathery ear, 'Do you know? We're really, really going to have a boy to play with *here*, in our house! He's called a cousin.'

The horse's wheel was shiny red like a ripe tomato and when its head was pressed down, the wheel squeaked. Really, that was the horse talking. Horsey always said it would be jolly good if Jim and Andrew could come over after school. But Mother said it would be too much to have a child here to play.

Now he would!

He smiled to himself. Yesterday, he'd felt really important at

News Time. Miss Peake was kind and sometimes wore a pretty blouse. He'd put up his hand.

'Billy? Do you have some news for us?'

'I've got a cousin and he's coming to my house.'

'My cousin lives next door,' said Sonia.

Dick and Mick shouted out that they had UMPTEEN cousins not silly old ONE.

'No such number, umpteen.' Sonia was clever, and she knew.

'Loads, anyway.'

'Yes, loads 'n loads.'

'Now twins, that's not very nice'. Miss Peake smiled, 'We're all happy that Billy has his cousin visiting, aren't we, children?'

'Yes, Miss Peake,' everyone chanted.

At home time, he'd told Mother, 'Miss Peake is ever so pleased that my cousin is visiting.'

Mother's mouth moved into something like a smile, only not as nice. 'Perhaps she'd like to entertain him, then.'

Now it was the very day the cousin was coming. He stroked Horsey's head. On Monday, he'd tell everyone what he and Kenneth had played.

'Billy!' Mother's voice calling upstairs made him start. 'Are you washed?'

He pulled Horsey away from the window where they'd been watching the children in the house over the road laughing and even shouting.

'Billy? They'll be here soon.'

He rode out of his bedroom and along the passage, past the big bathroom with its misty windows and the little lavatory with its long chain and white knob and down the stairs, being very careful not to catch the hobby horse wheel on the stair-rods as he went. At the bottom, it made a nice clickety-clack sound on the hall tiles.

Mother waved her arms. 'For goodness sake, child! Everyone can hear that for miles. People who live in Primley Road don't want your noise.'

The horse clattered into the hall-stand. Mother looked down with her *Don't* face. 'You'll have to behave when your relatives come, Billy. I'm sure Kenneth will, with that angelic face.'

A jelly face! He started to ask, 'Mother, why does—?'

'That horse in the umbrella stand, please. Look, here's your father home from Chambers.'

Horsey squeaked, 'Something big's going to happen.'

Father's shadow showed through the glass in the front door.

The galloping had made Billy's socks slide down to his ankles. They were a new pair but the elastic wasn't very strong. He pulled them up as neatly as he could before the front door opened.

Father came in with a whoosh of wintry wind, shaking raindrops from his gabardine. He shut the front door, leaving the dark outside with the empty milk bottles. 'Here I am, Marcia.'

Mother's shoes clippity-clicked forward as she went to collect his briefcase. 'You're quite late, Herbert. High tea is nearly ready. I'd have thought you'd be eager to entertain your relatives.'

'Indeed I am, dear. Family near at last. But what a day! Court sat late and then we were discussing this.' He tapped the newspaper under his arm. 'Ha! The Windsors' latest. Did you see it? I don't know what Frank's take on it will be. Judge Ware-Simpkins called it outrageous. I tend to agree.'

Mother nodded. She didn't answer but put his briefcase in its place and dabbed the raindrops off it. One dropped onto the hobby-horse's mane, but it didn't squeak.

'Swanning over to meet Hitler, Marcia. Bavaria. Huh! The King surely won't like that— his brother mixing with the ruddy Huns.'

Mother shrugged. 'They must know what they're doing, I suppose. We don't want any nastiness, after all.'

The wireless voice often spoke about Nasties. Mother was afraid that Nasties would come here. Billy looked at Father to see if he was frightened of Ruddy Huns, but he was twirling his umbrella into a swizzle stick like a barber's pole. Billy smoothed his hands round the damp folds and stood it in the elephant's foot, his most favourite thing in the house. Horsey liked it too.

Father hung his coat on the hallstand where two hooks were still empty and lit his pipe. 'So, Billy. You'll have someone to play with at last, now that Uncle Frank has brought Aunty and Kenneth to live in Balham. Just across the common, you know.'

'Yes, I know. Mother's told me. Goody.' Billy hopped on one leg and then the other. 'Father, I want to see Kenneth.'

'I know you do. It's not such fun being an only child, is it?'

Billy shook his head hard.

'No. A shame. I grew up with an older brother and Mother with a younger one. It will be good for you to have Kenneth around.'

Mother put her head on one side. 'I'm not sure whether it will be good for him...'

'Marcia!'

Father's eyebrows were so big, like untidy caterpillars, while Mother's were so skinny and small, just a couple of dark dashes.

'—or good for me. Isn't one boy enough trouble?'

'After her—' Father dropped his voice, '—women's trouble, it's the only child they're going to have. You can be such a support to poor Doreen. It's natural they should spoil Kenneth a bit.'

It was awful Kenneth was spoiled. Once Billy spilt tomato soup down his Sunday shirt. It was spoiled and was in the rag bag now. He'd got into terrible trouble.

'Boys can be such a blessed—'

'Children are a Blessing and Our Future.' Dad often said things to the ceiling or the sky. This time he talked to his pipe.

Mother's mouth gave that twisty smile again. She smoothed her apron, and flounced back to the kitchen. Perhaps she'd made those lemon cakes that had the squashy tops with a blob of cream.

'Will Kenneth bring his toys, Father?'

'I shouldn't think so. You must share yours.'

'I'm going to, Father. I've set out my farm upstairs and the small bricks for building walls.'

'Good boy. Now, listen. I've been thinking. "Father" is rather formal, these days. Uncle Frank would think so. You can call me "Dad" from now on.

Billy tilted his head up and looked carefully. Father looked like the same man. *Father.* That was his name. Was he really called "Dad"?

'So, Billy. You say "Dad", understand? Some of your friends at school probably use that name. So you practise saying it.'

It would feel ever so funny. "Dad" didn't feel like someone he properly knew. But Billy tried it, 'Yes—Dad.' It was like the *pretend* game. He'd been Teacher yesterday and swished his cane lots of times, and a fireman the day before. Now Father was joining in the game.

He scratched around his knees and up his arms. If only Mother hadn't made him wear his blue buster suit. It was a knitted one, and very itchy. She said it was dinky and he had to wear it for best. But it was worst! His hand couldn't get high enough to reach all the itches up his back.

'Stop hopping and wriggling, child. Go and sit in the front room until they get here.'

Billy looked at Horsey but thought he'd better leave it in the hallstand.

Dad's big hand moved him toward the front room door. 'You could get your new pencils and draw.' He pointed to the bookcase and the unopened pad and pencils upon it, Billy's birthday present.

'I don't really like drawing.'

Dad sighed and puffed at his pipe. A swirl of smoke rose up between them. 'When I was a boy, it was a treat to draw. Just sit then, and practise being quiet. Kenneth's a quiet child.'

'Yes, Fath— Dad.' Billy watched the smoky curl trapped in the closing door. The firm footsteps paced towards the kitchen.

The front room was like a foreign land, dark even on the sunniest days so the light had to be put on. It had a pale carpet to sail over and velvety seats with white clothy things which sat on their arms like silly gloves with no fingers. Billy perched on a webbing stool and bounced a bit, looking at all the things that might break or spoil. Mrs Donnington had been busy polishing in here all morning. There was a glass case with china teapots and vases, a picture of a sailing boat all alone on the sea, two low tables which shone and had a garden smell. There was a whopping great glass thing on one, a bluey-greeny ball with bubbles trapped inside it. When he'd asked, Mother said that colour was called turquoise. The word sounded like a special animal, so Billy always remembered it and told people it was his favourite colour.

He sat still watching for rain and listened to the Primley Road quiet. Until a huge knock on the door.

From the garden room, Mother's voice escaped. 'No question

that's Frank. He knocks hard enough to startle the whole of Wandsworth.'

Dad strode to the front door, saying over his shoulder, 'All right, Marcia. Don't start before they've even stepped inside.'

He let the knocking person in.

Uncle Frank's voice boomed out, 'Here we are.' And behind him, a trilling lady voice, 'Hallo, Bert, hallo.'

In the background, Mother was saying, 'Why, welcome all of you,' in her nicest voice. 'Do come in.'

Another boom sounded. 'Where's that boy, then?' and the front room door flew open.

Billy looked up with a start. The doorway was filled by this man with high, wide hair, bushy like a squirrel but more bristly. He didn't have a beard so the dip in his chin showed. When he spoke, a gap between his front teeth came and went as his lips opened and shut; bark, snap, bark, snap.

'Ah, there he is! Right, Billy. Remember your Uncle Frank? Last seen before you were two.' Uncle's moist lips widened into an alarming smile. 'Made a pudding of your mother before we'd finished the wedding cake, you did. Ha, ha, ha, ha, ha. Stand up and shake hands like a man.'

Billy looked at Mother to see if she was suddenly a pudding and whether he had to shake hands with Uncle but she was looking at the floor and her face was red. He took a slow step towards Uncle who grabbed his hand and kneaded it like plasticine.

'Look. I've brought your cousin for you. Here he is,' and he brought the silky-haired boy forward. 'This is our Kenneth.'

Billy looked. Kenneth didn't wear a buster suit but shorts, with a harsh crease down each leg. His calves, so smooth in the silky grey socks, looked like the visitors' bathroom soap. Aunty Doreen, in a green suit and squat hat, trotted behind. She held the cousin by his hand.

Mother said, 'Oh, smart little boy! What a lovely fair-isle v-neck you've made him, Doreen.'

Kenneth smiled, new front teeth gleaming under the bright electric light. His face was not like jelly at all. It was like the obedient boy on the castor oil bottle. People said it was good for boys, but it made Billy feel sick.

'Yes, here we are, everyone,' trilled Aunty on tippy toes. 'All moved in and snug as bugs.'

'I don't envy you the disruption, Doreen,' said Mother. 'It must have been a real headache.' She motioned to Billy, standing by the stool. 'Here's our one and only.'

Aunty let Kenneth's hand go. 'Ooh, Billy, you've grown big.' She bent to pinch his cheek. Her smell was like apple and custard. 'Can't call you Baba now,' and she giggled squeakily. 'So sweet, Marcia. You see, I told you it would grow on you, Motherhood.'

Mother fussed forward, her hand waving in front of her face like a fan. 'Yes, yes. Do all sit down, please,' she said in a funny voice and pointed to a chair for Aunty.

Aunty sat herself down and removed her hat, placing it carefully on her bag not to dent its curled front. Billy looked at her rolls of beige hair, her squashy knees. Would she be nice?

Dad was very polite to her and got a cushion from the settee.

She smiled. 'Your manners were always better than your brother's.'

Dad pushed his hand around the edge of his beard.

'Shhh, Doreen!' said Mother as she sat down beside Aunty.

'So, Bert. How are the great bewigged?' Uncle Frank boomed.

Bewigged. Billy had seen that wig. It had its own special box and sat on the dressing table when Dad was home. He'd never seen Dad wearing it.

Dad said, 'We peg along, same as always, with the same rogues popping up on a regular basis.'

'Funny old job, yours,' Uncle bellowed, rolling back on his heels. 'Not that you get to decide anything, just being the clerk.'

'Clerk to the Court,' Mother put him right.

'And,' Uncle's voice got loud, 'hardly worth sending 'em down if they just pop up again. Still, someone has to do it, I suppose.'

Mother stretched out her hands, showing her shiny nails. She looked at Dad sideways.

He blinked and motioned to the chairs but neither man sat down. Uncle Frank's head was even nearer the ceiling than Dad's. Billy didn't come up to his watch chain and Kenneth only came up to his belt.

Dad walked over and put a hand on Kenneth's shoulder. 'Well then, Sonny.'

'Hello, Uncle Bert.' Kenneth smiled upwards, head on one side. He had dimples.

Dad patted his shoulder again, then hesitated by the settee, waiting for Uncle to sit down. 'And how are things in the tax department, Frank?'

Uncle folded his arms over his wide chest. 'Magnificent.'

Aunty's eyes crinkled at the edges as she looked over at him. 'He's office-based now, you know. Such a nice varied job, mixing with the right people.'

Mother's eyes went hard. 'It's not as if Herbert mixes with the riff-raff, Doreen! He has such a responsible post, advising the judge of the law.'

Aunty didn't seem to hear. 'So, isn't it lovely that Frank's been transferred, just where he wanted, right beside County Hall? I reckon they think well of him!' She took off her scarf and folded it on top of her bag.

Mother said, 'I'll make some tea in a minute.'

'Splendid,' said Uncle, spreading himself on the settee, his long legs out straight before him. Dad sat down on the edge and rubbed his knuckles.

Kenneth leant against his mother's knee while everyone looked at him. His shiny hair curled over his ears. Aunty Doreen stroked it and smiled at them all, her chin high and her lips pressed together as if she was holding back a chuckle. Billy often had to do that when people were very fat or dressed funnily and he mustn't say.

Kenneth's eyelashes were so long and curved. They were like the camel's at the zoo where Billy had gone for his birthday. It wasn't just the eyelashes, but the lips with their edges turned up.

'Displays calm, the camel,' Dad had said, 'but they can turn nasty.'

Kenneth was standing very still, looking at the pictures on the wall. Billy watched him, remembering not to kick to-and-fro or fiddle with his fingers.

Aunty got out her knitting from a flowered bag. There were four skinny needles with grey wool hanging in the middle of them.

Dad leaned forward, 'At work already, Doreen? You've only just sat down.'

'Mustn't waste a moment. Gloves for my men', she said with a little sigh, smiling at Dad. 'Winter's pretty well here.' Mother didn't knit. She bought their clothes in Arding and Hobbs, where the buster suit came from, or from Allders in Croydon and Billy had to wait by the clothes hangers while she tried things on for herself. She'd asked him to choose between a green and a blue blouse last time. He'd chosen the blue. It had little tiny buttons from top to bottom and white dashes round the collar. It was much prettier than Aunty's yellow knitted top that had lots of holes as a pattern.

Mother was looking at Aunty's click-clacking fingers with her polite face.

'You're so clever with your needles, Doreen, and look at Kenneth's lovely jumper. I'd like Billy to have one like that if I could knit, but a size bigger.'

Kenneth turned his camel face towards Billy, one lip curled. Did he know that Mother couldn't knit?

'You're quite a big lad, Billy,' Uncle Frank said in a disappointed tone.

Mother sighed. 'Yes, and boisterous with it. Strange, isn't it, when he's nearly a year younger than Kenneth?'

Uncle leaned forward. 'Come here, lad, put your fists up. We'll do a bit of arm wrestling.' He showed Billy how.

'Frank!' said Mother.

Dad put his hand on her arm, his big fingers nested in her sleeve as though they were hiding.

Billy did his best, but Uncle Frank's muscly arm soon had his bang flat on the coffee table.

'Ouch.'

'Just so as you know who's Boss, boy. Can't have you bullying my little lad, even though he's a bit older than you.'

Billy stared. 'I wouldn't!'

'He wouldn't,' said Mother, but Fath– *Dad* didn't say anything.

'That's all right then,' said Uncle Frank, a glint of light shining on his front teeth. 'Now, Kenneth, my lad, your Uncle is my younger brother. You can remember that if Billy gets uppity.'

Kenneth's eyelashes flickered. 'Yes, Daddy.'

Uncle turned back to Billy. 'So, now that's clear, you can take Kenneth upstairs to play. He'll like to see all your toys. Mind you share them. Not that he hasn't got plenty of toys himself.'

Billy moved quickly out of Uncle Frank's reach. At last he and Kenneth could build the brick pens and line up the animals.

Kenneth gave his smile to Aunty and then to Mother.

'Come on,' Billy said, holding the doorknob until Kenneth followed him out of the room.

'Play nicely, you two. Leave this door open,' said Mother.

Billy led the way upstairs. This would be fun.

'There's lots of doors,' said Kenneth when they got half-way up.

They leant over the banisters and Billy told him what each room was, downstairs and up. 'And my room's round the corner upstairs.' He padded up to the top. 'I haven't had anyone to play with here before. I've got my toys out ready.'

On the landing, Kenneth said quietly, 'I'm six. Are you six?'

'No, five.'

'Thought so. So I'm Boss, right? I choose things.' Kenneth went to stand by Billy's open door.

'They're my toys, though.'

'Not if you give me any. If you give me something, that makes it mine.'

'Then I shan't give you things.'

'You will.'

'But some of my things say William Wilson on them because I take them to school on Fridays.'

'I'll cross out the William and put Kenneth, then.'

'Kenneth Wilson! That's silly. That'll be wrong.'

Kenneth's voice raised. 'No it won't, I *am* Kenneth Wilson.'

Billy's raised his more. 'You can't be. Wilson is my name.'

'It's mine, anyway.' Kenneth ran to the banisters and called downstairs, 'Daddy, Daddy, I am Kenneth Wilson, aren't I?'

Uncle Frank shouted up, 'Of course you are, son. THE Kenneth Wilson.'

Billy glared and Kenneth glared back. Mother came to the stairs, 'It's all right boys. No arguing. You're both Wilson. Daddy and Uncle Frank are brothers, so they're both Mr Wilson.'

Both Mr Wilson! Billy stamped back from the landing. They'd said to share his toys, not to share his name. Everyone at school had different last names, although some first names were the same. There were two other Billys. That was bad enough. And now there was another Wilson.

Kenneth shut the bedroom door behind them. He looked down at the bricks and animals laid out on the floor. 'Bricks! Haven't you got anything decent to play with?'

'There's all different sizes and shapes. We can make walls and sheep pens.'

'Ughh. Baby stuff. I don't want to.' He pushed the cows and pigs over with one foot.

Billy picked them up and made a pig sty. Kenneth would join in soon.

Kenneth looked around and touched the little yacht on the windowsill. 'Who gave you this?'

'Nanny and Grandad.'

Kenneth frowned. 'My Grandad gives me big things like a car which goes. Your yacht doesn't go. It just stays there.'

'Yes, but I like it. You won't like it.'

'I will. I want it on my windowsill. Give it to me.'

'No.' Billy ran to rescue it.

'Yes.'

Kenneth held the little yacht by its tip so that if Billy yanked on it, it would break. He played with it a little while, then gave Billy a smile and pushed out of the bedroom. He pattered downstairs with Billy close behind him.

'Give it back, Kenneth.'

'Mummy, Daddy! Look what Billy's given me! It's because I'm his best friend. Look after it for me, Daddy,' and Uncle Frank took it. His hairy check jacket had bulgy pockets. Were they full of things Kenneth had taken from people? Billy wanted to tell but Uncle Frank's face was raw-looking, with big bones for his nose and chin. Who could tell him anything?

'I think Nanny and Grandad might be upset,' Mother began just as Aunty Doreen said, 'How sweet, giving Kenneth his boat. They're such friends already. Kenneth's always so popular. Other children just give him things.'

Dad put in, 'I'm glad my boy can share despite being an only child.'

'So far,' said Aunt Doreen, and twiddled her fingers around her knitting.

Mother frowned at her and whisked from the room. She went down the hall to get the tea trolley ready. Soon, she called everyone into the garden room where there were little tables and not many ornaments. Billy led the way. Because of her dancing friends coming to tea, she'd taught him long ago how to hand round the plates and offer the cakes.

'That's nice, Billy,' Aunty Doreen said. 'Polite, like your father.' She spread a lacy napkin on her lap and put her head sideways at Dad.

Uncle Frank leant forward in front of her. 'What do you reckon to Halifax's trip, then, Bert?'

'Anything to avoid war. You know me.'

'You for appeasement! Where's your bottle? Lose it?'

Billy looked round but couldn't see it.

Dad said, 'Give the blighter what he wants. Then he'll be satisfied and stop grasping any new territory.'

Kenneth plopped down on Billy's special chair. He took three cakes and no-one said anything. He hadn't even had to ask first. Mother took her best apron off and tied it around him. 'We don't want you to spoil that lovely jumper, dear.'

Billy's wasn't lovely so she just said, '...and you be careful of your front, Billy.'

Uncle Frank was clicking his teeth and sighing. 'Impossible to have a conversation with nippers in the way.'

Although it was cold, the grown-ups sent the boys outside to get colour in their cheeks.

Billy rushed out. 'Topper. We can play football!'

Kenneth shivered. 'Rotten stuff. Boring. There's no outdoor toys.'

'Except my ball. Come on, catch!'

Kenneth missed but picked it up and threw it hard towards Billy.

'Ouch!'

'Your turn, dummy. Throw it, then.'

The ball kept going in Billy's face and it hurt.

'It's because you're only five. You don't know how to catch yet,' Kenneth said. 'Watch how high I can throw it.'

He threw it up higher than the fence and it came down the other side. He rushed indoors. 'Billy's thrown the ball over next door's.'

'Typical! How often have I told you to be more careful, Billy?' said Mother, in her annoyed voice. She flicked her black hair from her face like a piece of spare clothing. 'I can't face going next door to ask for it. I'll have to wait until I see them out shopping. You are a nuisance.'

'But I didn't!' Billy tried.

Dad said out of the side of his mouth, '*A lie never lives to be old*–Sophocles.'

Uncle Frank sniffed. 'So? I don't like the sort of lad that can't face up to what he's done. I'd give him the slipper if he was mine.'

Dad hesitated and turned a waxy face to Billy, his big hands hanging loose. They didn't look ready to grasp a slipper.

Kenneth stood close, his curls brushing Uncle's arm as he tipped his head on one side. 'It was an accident. Billy didn't mean to.'

The grown-ups made a soft murmur and Aunty put a hand on his curls, 'Bless him.'

Kenneth said, 'Billy, shall we play with your favourite things? We'll play nicely, Aunty. Upstairs. I think Billy wants to show me something.'

'Good boy, Kenneth. What a cherub you are,' said Mother in a breathy voice. 'Go along Billy, your father has let you off this time.'

'But it's not forgotten,' added Uncle.

Billy slid his fastest out of the door and up the stairs. Kenneth followed, humming.

Once they were in Billy's room, Kenneth stood with his back against the door. 'So. What are you going to give me for saving you from a thrashing?'

'You already took my yacht. And you threw the ball over the fence. I'll tell, I will.'

'So? They'll only say you're blaming me.'

Billy sat on his bed hard. He mustn't cry. He found a wind-up car that didn't go very well. 'This is my bestest car. I'll be g-glad when you go home,' and he threw it towards Kenneth.

Kenneth picked it up, looking pleased. 'I haven't got one like this. I'll let you off this time.' He put an arm round Billy's shoulder. 'I do like playing with you, Billy. What's in that drawer?'

He didn't answer. His aeroplanes were inside. Kenneth opened it.

'Be ever so careful with these. They're my special things.'

But Kenneth got the whole lot out, whizzing them up in the air, crashing them into each other. 'There's going to be an aeroplane battle. Wheeeee splatttt zooom— that one's hit— and RIGHT down into the sea. Smaaashed! Drownded.'

Dad put his head round the door. Kenneth's hand stayed where it was, grasped around the plane. Dad's hand closed around it. 'It wouldn't be fun at all to see planes crash.' He lifted Kenneth's hand until the little plane was safe on a shelf.

Uncle Frank loomed behind Dad. 'And it won't be fun for you, Billy, if I catch you besting my little boy.' He wagged a finger, fat and hairy. 'You know, Bert, I had an odd feeling when we were coming here that your boy might pose a threat to mine.'

'No, no, Frank, he won't. My lad's mild-natured, but I'll look out for your Kenneth, never fear.' He put one heavy hand on each of their shoulders. 'Now boys, we've had enough of wars and fighting. You stay friends, because you'll be playing together every Saturday from now on.'

CHAPTER TWO

March 13th 1938 ***Annexation of Austria! German troops march across the border***

'It's certainly been a long winter.' Mother was wearing the pinny for when no-one was visiting. She got butter from the larder and put all the cooking things on the kitchen table. 'It'll soon be Easter and I suppose I shall be expected to make a Simnel cake.'

'Does it have icing?'

'No. Marzipan.'

'Kenneth doesn't like that.'

'Well, he can just have sponge fingers. He can't come today, by the way, he's very off colour.'

'Yippee!'

She tutted. 'You're very lucky not to be a sickly child. Aunty's had Kenneth in bed off and on ever since New Year.'

Billy smiled and winked at Horsey. At last— a Saturday with no

Kenneth to hide his toys, break them or make him wait while he hogged them! 'M-Mother.' He'd better swallow so that the words would come out properly. 'Does Kenneth have to come S-Saturdays?'

'Yes he does.' She cracked two eggs into a bowl, 'and sometimes other days too because of Aunty's health. Since he's not here today, you can help me. Wipe up the breakfast things like I've shown you.'

While Mother bashed the butter and sugar like naughty children round and round the bowl, he wiped up the dishes, one by one, very carefully. He'd make sure Mother was pleased with him before he said anything. He piled up the plates just as she liked, humming the Hip, hip, hip hooray song.

'That's enough noise, Billy. You can play outside when you've finished the cutlery.'

He watched her sift the flour into the bowl, making a fairy snowstorm.

'Y-yes, Mother.' He swallowed as he picked up the first fork. 'I can play very quietly if I'm on my own. It's better when we don't have K-Kenneth.'

She didn't answer, so he pulled his jumper up to show the red marks on his side. 'Last Saturday, he t-trapped me in the Lloyd Loom basket.'

'You're both as bad as each other.'

'It jolly well hurt t-trying to get out.'

She looked at him over the bowl of creamy mixture. 'Don't you think it's a trouble for me, having two of you? But he's your cousin so—' she wielded the wooden spoon viciously round the edges of the bowl— 'we have no choice.'

Billy watched the nice sticky stuff as it went up the sides of the bowl then down into the middle where the spoon smashed it smooth. Sonia was allowed to lick the bowl after her mother made cakes. He watched until Mother scraped the sides of the bowl and spooned the mixture into the metal tin. Bits were left around the bowl. It would be ever so nice to taste it.

'What's Wehavenochoice?'

'It's Do What You're Told.' Mother plunged the bowl into the washing up water and ruined the scrapings.

He took Horsey into the garden, scuffing the toes of his shoes all the way down the path. 'She doesn't care. We'll ride right away, Horsey. Gee up.' He galloped to the end of the garden and pretended Kenneth was left far behind, like a slowcoach.

The back door opened. So Dad was home from his Conservative club.

'Billy! Come along indoors.' He was rubbing his hands in a pleased way. 'Bathroom. Now. We're going out. The Durbans have invited us over. Clean hands, knees. Jacket on.'

A quick, happy feeling squirmed inside Billy's tummy. He left Horsey by the big tree and ran indoors and up to the bathroom. He checked himself in the mirror and ran back into his room for his jacket. The Durbans were a father, a mother and a big girl. Mr Durban worked at Chambers with Dad and sometimes visited. He taught Billy the best way to catch a cricket ball and said he'd be a proper little sportsman. He let Billy sit on the arm of his chair to look at The Dandy together. Mr Durban was super-duper.

When Billy came downstairs, Mother had her red lips on and shoes with heels. She nodded to him. 'Good. We're all ready, Herbert.'

Outside, she held Dad's arm while Billy trotted beside them down to the end of the road where the trees were just stopping being bare and showing their green buds. There were three nice roads with flowers outside each house, then the horrid roads with no gardens, rickety bikes and fences squashed together. Children were shouting in the street, socks round their ankles and he wasn't supposed to look at them.

Dad was saying, 'So I thought we'd talk it over with the Durbans. It's not an easy decision.' They all walked more quickly until they reached the main road.

Mother held his arm closer to her, 'It doesn't really affect us, does it, Herbert?'

'It might. Hitler's amassing more and more power. That seems dangerous to me although the government is playing it down.'

Billy looked at Dad when he heard the Hitler word. Dad strode onwards, sucking at his pipe while Mother's steps got shorter and quicker.

'But the newsreel. All those Austrians waving and cheering, they're *glad* to have Hitler take over.'

'Hmph! I'm guided by Judge Ware-Simpkins' opinion. He has friends in high places.'

Billy was having to trot to keep up. They were passing high houses with great trees showing their tops behind the roofs. He knew someone in high places. Mrs Donnington had to go to even the top rooms when she worked in big houses, she said. It would be funny to see her behind a high window with her feather duster.

Dad halted. 'Stop staring into peoples' windows, Billy. That's very rude. Now, come along and mind you show the Durbans your best manners.'

Billy nodded. Mrs Durban was very nice too. There would probably be cakes for tea. 'Mother, if they say, "Would you like another cake?" can I have one?'

'May, not can,' Mother corrected. 'If that happens, look at me and you'll see what my face is saying.'

Billy looked now and it said, *what a nuisance you are.*

The Durbans had a house joined on one side to another house, just like at home. Their sideway was much wider, though. It had a gate to it the colour of chocolate, same as the front door. The lace curtains were not as fancy as Mother's and no-one was fiddling with them as they arrived. Billy was allowed to pull the bell. It went ding, dong, ding instead of just buzzzzzz. He wasn't allowed to pull it a second time because that would have been rude.

When Mrs Durban came to the door, they all went into the front room where the big girl, Angela, was sitting at the piano ready.

'How lovely, Angela,' Mother said as the tinkling began.

Billy hoped she wouldn't play for long. He didn't fidget with his feet through the tinkling music, or when the grown-ups were chatting about Huns but he did feel a sigh come out of his mouth.

Mr Durban said, 'We'll discuss this later, I think. These young things will want their tea and then Angela can take Billy off to play.' Mr Durban looked over at him and winked.

Soon, Mother and Dad were sipping tea. Mrs Durban gave him orangeade and a buttered bun from the tea trolley. Then he was allowed to choose a cake. It had a great big blob of brown icing on the top. He didn't drop crumbs, so it was all very cheery.

Mrs Durban said, 'Angela. Time for children to be upstairs.'

Angela left her music open on the stand. She was nine, much older than him and had yellowy ringlets that bounced on her back as she led him out of the room. She spoke to him in a very kind voice as if he was ill.

'Look, Billy.' On the landing shelf was her Japanese doll with its little hands and bobbles of feet. It was so different from all the people he had ever seen. She let him touch it.

'Their eyes are all slitty. Are there really people who look like that? How do they see properly?'

'Of course they can see. You are cute.' In her bedroom with fairy pictures on the wall, she gave him a hug. 'You'll be handsome when you're a man.' She pointed at his reflection in her mirror. 'Now I'm going to show you all my things, my special things. First, there's my Dutch Doll, Jane. Plain Jane, we call her.'

He looked at the hard wooden thing. Its arms swung to and fro and so did its legs but they didn't bend. You could see where all the bits were put together. Its lips were a thin red line.

'This is my box of handkerchiefs. They each have a different day of the week sewn on them. And here's my shell collection.'

He sat on the bed while she drew out one pretty treasure after another.

Angela nudged him after the last one. 'Do you like them?'

'Y-es. But they're girls' things. I like balloons and planes and swords.' He bounced up and down. 'Your bed's bouncy. Mine isn't.'

She looked at him. 'Shall I show you something really, really special? Something important?'

'Yes, please,' Billy jumped from the bed.

She took him downstairs again, creeping along towards a closed door. 'This is Daddy's study,' she said, 'so sshhh. And you mustn't tell. Promise.'

'Promise.'

Inside the room, shelves with lots of books went down to the floor as well as up high. There was a very big, shiny desk and a cupboard with shut doors. Angela opened these very slowly and carefully. 'Have to be careful or it'll squeak.' She put her hands inside and lifted out something very long and wrapped in rich brown leather.

He lifted a corner. 'I can see a red handle.'

'Hilt.'

He took a breath. 'Is that a sword inside?'

'A sabre, a kind of sword. Look, this is the scabbard.'

'Scabbard', he breathed. A wonderful word. It looked very old. Angela balanced the length of it on her outstretched palms and then pointed it to the floor. She held the magic thing in front of him so that he could see its full length, slightly curved. It was nearly as tall as he was, and everyone said he was tall. The handle was knobby, exactly right for fitting into a hand.

'Cor!'

Angela spoke just like a teacher, 'The knob and the hilt are silver and so are these studs down the sides of the scabbard.'

He touched halfway along where there was a circle of studded silver with a loop for hanging it on the wall, and the very tip had a silver sleeve.

After a few moments of stroking the leather scabbard, he asked, 'Can we take the sword out?'

'Sabre. Wait.' Angela put her head against the door, checking that the grown-ups hadn't moved from the front room. 'It's all right, they're still talking.'

She put the scabbard on the desk and waved Billy to stand away. Then, she slowly drew the sabre out. The metal was specky with brown, its grooved centre was softer, but its edges gleamed. Letters were dug along the length of the blade. Some were snake-like and others frilly. Billy's hand moved forward.

'No, you mustn't touch. It's very, very dangerous.'

His fingers itched to finger the blade and follow the pattern of the silver studs. Suppose it was out in the open in a battle, glinting in the sun, blinding an enemy! 'I do like swords, *sabres*. I haven't seen a real one ever.'

Angela said, 'It's foreign. Daddy got it when he was young. It belonged to a heroic Cossack soldier.'

'A Cossack.' The strange word sounded fierce. 'What's heroic?'

'Very very brave.'

'Was your father fighting him?'

'I don't know. I don't know how he got it. But he says this is the most valuable thing we'll ever have and it'll be mine when he dies. He was saving it for his son and we haven't got one. Only me.'

'Cor, Angela, you're so l-lucky. He could have had me for a son, then I'd have got it.'

'Shh. Don't be silly.' She carefully slid the sabre into its scabbard, then put it back in the cupboard. It was sad that such a thing, the most thrilling thing he'd ever seen, was hidden away. If he could have a sabre everyone would be careful of him, even Kenneth.

'I'm going to have one l-like that when I'm a man.'

Angela put an arm round his shoulders. He rather liked that, something his parents never did.

'You're sweet, so I showed you the sabre as a treat. Did you like it?'

He nodded so hard his chin hurt his neck.

She wagged a finger. 'Now, we've got to creep out and pretend we've been playing in the garden, so they won't know. Mind you don't say anything. Not ever!'

'No I won't. I won't tell anyone.' He really really wouldn't. Then when Kenneth was horrible, Billy could think, *I've seen a sabre,* and Kenneth wouldn't know.

'C-can I come and see it again?'

She grabbed his arm. 'Perhaps. Come on. Quick, while they're still talking.'

As they crept towards the back door, the voices streamed out into the hall.

Mrs Durban: 'We don't know the possibilities.'

Mother's upset voice: 'Herbert won't join up if it comes to war.'

Mr Durban: '—too old but there's bound to be home defence against the Nazis. I shall—'

Angela put her hands over Billy's ears.

'What's *defence*? What are they talking about?'

'Grown-ups' talk, Billy.'

'I heard them say *Nasties*. Is it nasty?'

'Probably. Come on.'

Billy was going to have a sabre like that when he grew up. He needed one. There were nasties. There was Kenneth.

'Billy, come on!'

They ran through the back door into the chilly garden.

CHAPTER THREE

March 18th 1938. ***Recruitment problem solved. 8,000 young men join the Territorial Army***

It was good having a secret, and it was very very good that he had seen a sword for real and it had been a sabre and belonged to a Cossack and fighting had happened with it. Now, when Kenneth got him into trouble and he was sent to his bedroom, he just practised being a Cossack,. He pulled out the sabre from its scabbard, held it and watched out for its sharp, sharp blade. It was a secret he wasn't going to share with anyone, especially not Kenneth.

On school days he didn't worry about big boys bashing him up. He ran round holding a piece of wood knowing it was really a sabre. He didn't even tell Jim, the friend he liked best, because he would tell Reg and Reg would tell all of the others and then there wouldn't be a secret and it would be like not having a sabre any more.

At home, he had a sword picture to look at. It was in the book he'd found in the Boots' library. An olden-times man was watching a sword stuck in a big rock.

'You won't be able to read that, silly child. Look at all the words!'

Mother had said, 'but borrow it if you want. I suppose it's something you can look at with Kenneth.'

Billy had it spread out on his small bedroom table.

'You can't read that,' said Kenneth. 'You only read baby words.'

Billy smiled to himself. He could look at the picture and that was all that mattered. Kenneth didn't know anything. He said, 'We're g-going to Nanny and Grandad's tomorrow. You don't go there.'

Kenneth stood on Billy's foot. 'We won't be friends.'

'Don't c-care. Ow.'

Kenneth pressed his whole weight down. 'Don't say anything or I'll tell Daddy you wouldn't share.'

'Ouch, ow, you're hurting my foot.'

Mother called up just then. 'Billy. Time for cubs. Uncle's going to walk you round.'

Kenneth got off quickly. 'Don't you dare say. I'm going to stay up here and draw while you go. Or I might play with your—'

Billy trailed downstairs. Uncle knew the cub master. They did Dib Dib Dibs together. If only Uncle didn't go to it, cubs would be fun.

Usually Sundays were happy, because they went to Nanny and Grandad's. Nanny's roast potatoes were crispy, not soggy, and she always found Billy interesting things to play with: buttons and conkers and coloured string. Grandad didn't go to work any more. He had a shed and a woolly waistcoat.

Billy skipped past Mother and Dad as they reached the green garden gate. He was going to tell Nanny and Grandad when no-one else was listening – not about the sabre, just in case they told Mother – but about Kenneth. Nanny sometimes gave Mother advice.

He was in his running position all ready, so Dad said, 'Go on, then.' Billy darted up the crazy paving path and patted the two friendly garden gnomes with their red caps. When Nanny had hugged him and given him a drink and biscuit, she sat down with Mother and Dad. There was lots of chatting. Billy swung his feet to and fro.

Grandad took Billy's hand. 'Come on. We'll go out to the shed.' It was a cosy place and smelled of old grass and sawn wood.

All the tools had their own special hooks. It was nice to take each one off, make a line of tools and hang them up again. 'See, Grandad, I know where they all go.'

Grandad was just finding a little hammer for Billy to bang a nail into a piece of wood, when there was a loud whistle outside.

'Uncle Ted!' Billy ran out to see his favourite person. Uncle Ted always laughed a lot and winked at Billy. He worked at an office in the West End. He didn't have a wife. Sometimes he had humbugs or a toy car, and he kicked a ball just right so that Billy could kick it back.

Today, Uncle was wearing his uniform. It was like soldiers wore, but Uncle wasn't one yet.

Billy jumped up and down. 'Uncle, Uncle, will you do that thing?' Uncle Ted could stand on his hands. 'Please, do that upside-down thing again.'

'Just a mo, then.' Uncle Ted took some things out of his pockets, then flipped his hands down on the ground and his legs into the air. It was very funny to see his face upside down and his trouser bottoms flopped back showing Uncle's very white ankles.

'Oh Ted!' Nanny laughed, leaning out of the lounge window. 'Come and see Bert and Marcia.'

Uncle Ted stood up again, 'Coming. Billy, you look at this.' He flicked a pack of cards between his fingers and shuffled them so fast you couldn't quite see them. 'See the King? Now. King's gone. Oh, look! King's at the front of the pack.'

'It's magic! Do that m-magic again. Please, Uncle.'

'Okey dokey, but inside. Time to see what's up in the kitchen.' He went ahead.

It would be jolly good to be a grown-up like Uncle Ted.

Billy walked behind him, trying to make his strides the same size. Uncle turned sharply, 'Bo! Caught you out.'

Billy couldn't help squealing.

Mother came out, 'For pity's sake, Ted, do you have to encourage his noise?'

Nanny bustled from the kitchen as Billy put his shoes alongside Uncle's huge boots. 'Just enjoying themselves, aren't you, my love? Your Uncle Ted was always a bundle of laughs.'

Mother's face looked hard as a plate. 'Always an excuse for the favourite child. He had a lot to laugh about, didn't you, Ted?'

Dad came to Uncle's rescue. 'Let's everyone move to the dining room.' He led the way. Inside, he took his pipe from his mouth. 'Enjoying territorials then, Ted?'

Uncle nodded. 'Doing my bit, Bert.'

'As long as it's only territorials,' Grandad muttered, following with a tray of glasses.

Dad sat down on the far end of the table and nodded slowly. 'Better to steer Ted into a career where he'll be exempt, just in case.'

That word again. 'What's X M-ed?'

Uncle slid into a chair and pulled Billy into the one beside him. He grinned at Dad. 'Exempt, Billy. Means you don't have to go, don't have to do something. Like you could be exempt from dinner.'

Billy knew he was joking. Such a meaty smell steamed out of the kitchen that he felt hungrier than he ever did at home. Nanny had laid the table with the snowy cloth that had shiny leaves on it. Now the big dishes came in with the joint and vegetables, steam rising off them.

When everyone was served out he ate everything Nanny put on his plate, especially the roast potatoes. He was so busy eating that he didn't listen to any of the grown-ups' talk. It was only as he dipped the last potato into his pool of gravy that he looked around.

Mother was telling Nanny about Kenneth's lovely knitted jumpers. 'I'm hoping Doreen will knit Billy one.'

Nanny said, 'Why don't you go to the Women's Institute meetings? Then you can learn to knit and sew like Doreen.'

'Good idea, Marcia,' Dad joined in, 'instead of your dances.'

Mother frowned down at the table.

Billy didn't like it when she wasn't happy. He said 'Mother likes d-dancing. She doesn't like knitting.'

Mother smiled. 'True. Knitting's a very poor swap.'

'Well, Sis, you'll be needing to sew and knit soon,' said Uncle Ted. 'You can't leave it at one nipper forever.'

'What do you know? You're fancy free as always, and probably will be for a decade more.'

'But he's right, Marcia dear,' said Nanny. 'We'd all like to see more young ones here.'

Billy squeezed his thumbs into the palms of his hands until it hurt. Was Nanny going to have another boy here? Did she mean Kenneth? He looked at Mother's face. It went tight and she opened her mouth to say something to Nanny, but then shut it again.

He waited until the spotted dick and custard was all finished and everyone went into the lounge, except for Nanny. He followed her into the kitchen. 'Can I help, Nanny?'

'You are a good little boy. Wait till I've stacked up these dishes.'

When she was washing up, Billy wiped up the cutlery and the small things that couldn't break. 'It's best having just one child in your house, Nanny, isn't it?'

'Oh I think you've been listening to your Mummy niggling about having a brother. It was only because she was quite a big girl when your Uncle came along. She doesn't mean half she says, Billy.'

Billy shook his head. He hadn't been thinking about Mother and Uncle Ted at all. Now that he and Nanny were on their own he could tell her about Kenneth.

Water splashed and china chinked as Nanny worked. It was easier not to have anyone looking at him while he talked about all the horrible times with Kenneth. There was a lot to say about it. He ended up, 'I d-don't really like playing with K-Kenneth. You'd h- hate having a b-boy like him here and s-so would Grandad.'

Nanny turned round, 'Dearie me.' She patted his head with damp hands. A trickle of water ran down his forehead. 'You're starting a bit of a stutter, Billy. You'll have to speak slower. Now listen. All children quarrel when they play. I expect having Kenneth is good for you. You always used to ask for someone to play with at home. Now you've got someone.'

'I p-play with boys at school. They're my f-friends. That's b-better. I've told M-Mother but she s-says we have no ch- choice.'

'Speak properly, love, and then perhaps your mother will listen to you. Come along to the lounge and let's hear Uncle Ted tell us all about his training camp.'

She pulled the back door to and shut out the sunlight.

CHAPTER FOUR

September 21st 1938. ***Nazis smash, loot and burn Jewish shops and temples until Goebbels calls halt.***

Dad disappeared with his wig box and suitcase taking the last of the summer with him.

'Is D-dad going to be away long?'

'The leaves might turn brown before he gets back,' Mother said with her lips tight. 'He'll be in Lincoln Crown Court for weeks.'

When Billy came away from waving to Dad through the window he heard her at the telephone arranging about dances with her lady friends. He always had to stay in his bedroom when those ladies came. Mother did a special tea for them in the front room and afterwards he came down to say *Hello*. They'd all pat his face and call him sweet, but never give him one. Then he'd go to bed while they whisked away in their frilly dresses, even Mother full of smiles. The lady next door popped in to check on him every hour, not that he heard her.

Mother was still on the telephone, giggling. He ran into the kitchen to make a whizzer. He used two cardboard milk bottle tops, and a piece of string off Dad's roll that hung outside the cellar door. When Mother came in, she let him borrow the sewing scissors with zig-zag edges. He used four different colours from his poster paints. It took ever so long but at the end it looked smashing. He cleared up and ran upstairs with his whizzer.

He'd just got it to whizz round so fast that all the coloured stripes went into a dark orange colour and the strings had that stretchy feel when he heard Uncle Frank rattle the letter box. 'Coo-ee!'

Billy jumped back against the wall.

Mother opened the door and let him in. 'Frank? Is everything all right, now Doreen's had the—?'

'Doreen's resting. She's not too bad, considering. Kenneth is drawing as usual, so I came to give you a hand, Marcia. With Bert away, your boy needs toughening up. I thought I'd exercise him.'

'Exercises? Well, I shall certainly be glad of some time to myself if you're offering to take him off for a bit?'

'I'll do it here. Keep you company at the same time, eh?'

Billy stayed very quiet, hoping they wouldn't call up for him, but they soon did. He dropped the whizzer and went slowly downstairs.

'Billy. I came over specially for you, boy. You'll have no time for that stuttering nonsense. I'll make a man of you. Toughen you up. Take off your shirt and vest.'

He put them on the banisters as Uncle waited.

'Ready? Outside with you.' He put a hand behind Billy's back and pushed him into the garden. He found a smooth patch on the lawn.

'Twenty knees-bend, twenty stretch-ups, then running on the spot till I say *Stop*. Right?'

The lady next door was hanging out her washing, but stopped to watch. It was very very embarrassing.

'Running, I said. Faster, faster.'

Afterwards there were arm wrestles, fisticuffs and heavy holds that Billy was supposed to escape from. Uncle taught him press-ups, roaring with laughter every time Billy collapsed onto the floor.

'Oh, Frank! You are a caution,' said Mother, coming out at that point. 'Come and have a cup of tea. Billy can stay in the garden with his ball, now.'

Billy caught his breath, 'I d-do like football, Uncle.' It would be much better if he could exercise at that. At school, he was one of the best at football. He and Jim, Reg, Danny and Andrew played every day. Kenneth couldn't play football much because he was delicate.

Mother said, 'Yes, he's mad about football. At least, it drives me mad.' She giggled.

Uncle Frank folded his arms. 'Football? I'll show him football. You wait till I get you on the football field, boy. You'll see football there. I'll give you football.'

'Goodness, Frank. You make it sound as if you'll kick football out of him,' said Mother.

'Hasn't Bert told you? I was the star player as a youngster. If only I could give the time to it now. Responsibilities come first. But,' he looked at Billy, 'I suppose I should give this lad a bit of a kick-around sometimes. Don't suppose Bert will, even when he's home. His head'll be stuck in a book, no doubt. It was always that way when he was a boy— reading or drawing.'

'Bert has to study his documents.'

'As I do the tax returns. But not after work! Not at the weekends!'

Billy stayed outside while they went to have their cups of tea, just in case Uncle felt like kicking him around. He pushed a ball around the back of the shed and pretended he was playing with Jim and Reg.

When Uncle had gone, Mother called Billy indoors. 'Put your shirt back on, do.'

'I don't want to do any more exercises, Mother.'

'Uncle Frank says it's good for boys.'

'Kenneth doesn't do them.'

'Kenneth's frail. Now then. Uncle has been here to help me with you. We must help him. We'll visit Aunty on Friday. She hasn't been well. She's in bed.'

'Ill?' He didn't want Aunty ill.

Mother nodded. 'Aunty's been in hospital for a few days.'

He felt a gulp in his throat. People died in hospital sometimes. 'Is Aunty dying?'

'Of course not. The doctors have— done things to make her better. Now she's resting. She needs time before she gets back on her feet.'

At Friday home time, Billy stood under the *Infant Boys* arch until he saw Mother's grey coat and silky headscarf between the umbrellas. It was pouring with rain.

'Ready to go, Billy? Pull those socks up, they're rumpled.' Although she let Billy walk close enough to be under her umbrella, its points dripped onto his hands because of 'no hands in pockets.' His raincoat didn't cover the bottoms of his legs.

It was difficult to keep up with Mother's swishing walk all the way down Nightingale Lane and several turnings afterwards. Now the houses were closer together and smaller and uglier. Kenneth's was one, and it only took three steps to get from the pavement to the front door. In the back garden, the square of concrete with a clothes-line doubled to make two rows was far too near to next door's to risk playing with even a little ball.

Mother let herself in with the key Uncle Frank had given her and propped her umbrella inside the entrance. She called out, 'Doreen, we're here.'

Kenneth came out with his hair not properly brushed.

Mother stroked it, then hung up her coat. 'Hello, Kenneth, dear. Billy, put your wet coat on the boiler rail in the kitchen. Play quietly with Kenneth in there while I sit with Aunty.'

He could just see Aunty in a pale nightgown with her feet on a stool before the front room door shut. Billy heard the word 'operation' again but he knew it was rude to listen. Mother's voice started gently, and there was the sound of coughing or hiccupping or could it be crying?

Kenneth was frowning, so probably he could hear it, but it was best not to ask.

Aunty had to use her front room for sitting in every day. Otherwise there was only the dining room. That was as dark as the school cupboard. The window looked out onto the fence of next door. The table took nearly all the space and the thick, furry cloth smelled like a rainy day. The chairs were hard with no squashy bits to sit on. Billy shivered. The bottoms of his shorts dripped onto the hall mat. He was so wet that he needed a towel.

'Ha-ha, wet dog, you are. Come on,' Kenneth led the way to the kitchen.

Billy put his coat on the boiler rail. The washing smells leaked from the scullery where he found a towel to dry his legs and hands. He used it until it was really damp all over, and he still felt wet.

Kenneth's head was bent over a picture of Blackpool Tower. 'We're doing a jigsaw, right?'

The oilcloth on the kitchen table was all one colour, like old blood. The jigsaw pieces slid around on it and wouldn't clip together easily but he sat down to help Kenneth.

'You do the sky and the pavement,' said Kenneth.

'I think j-jigsaws are really boring.'

'Boring like you. So there.'

'You're sickly.'

'I'm not. I'm frail.'

It felt like ages while they were doing the jigsaw. Kenneth was humming a song about a blackbird. It was annoying, but Kenneth's voice was rather nice. Billy did nine pieces of sky and he'd just seen a bit of tower when Kenneth slid the jigsaw to one side and put the lid on the box. 'We'll draw now.'

'I'm no good at it.'

'I know. You can just colour in.' He passed over a book. 'Don't go over the edge or I'll tell. You'll have to use the brown, I need all the others.' He worked away at a picture of a bird on its nest.

'Let's see?' It was ever so good. Kenneth was clever at drawing.

The brown needed sharpening but Billy didn't bother. He coloured as slowly as he could. The rain had stopped. If only they could play outside.

He was really pleased to see Mother when she came in to make the tea. 'Can I t-take the football outside while Kenneth draws inside, please?'

'In the road! Certainly not.'

He made a pleading face towards her but she didn't notice.

'Aunty, he's coloured over the edges on purpose.' Kenneth looked at Mother with a sad face.

Under the table, Billy's hands grasped the precious sabre. He closed his eyes and summoned up magic. Nothing came. He really needed to learn some special words.

'Billy! Can't you even play nicely when we visit?' He jerked forward as Mother buffed him on the back of the head five times. to match her words: 'Naugh-ty litt-le boy.'

Kenneth turned his sad face down to his drawings, 'Oh dear.'

At that moment, the front door opened and Uncle Frank loomed into the dark corridor. The rain had started again. He peered into where Aunty sat. 'How are we, precious one?'

Aunty sighed and Mother stepped forward. 'We're here, keeping her company, Frank. I'm just in the kitchen with the boys, putting on the kettle.'

'That's good, Marcia. Just what Doreen needs. Good companionship. I'm sure Bert would have a saying for that.'

'Indeed he would,' said Mother, with almost a smile.

Uncle put his hat on a hall peg and his umbrella beside Mother's. He put his head back into the front room. 'It keeps raining. You wouldn't want to be out in this today, my love.'

Aunty's weak voice came back. 'I don't suppose I shall ever feel like it.'

Mother clapped her hands. 'Nonsense, Doreen. You'll soon be on your feet. It's all over now.'

'Too right.' Aunty sniffed in the distance.

Mother stepped back into to the stove. 'Now, I'm making us all a warming cup of tea.' She put a hand on Kenneth's curls. 'After all, Frank, you've got this one. Much better to leave it at that, you know.'

'True,' said Uncle. 'No other kiddy could match Kenneth Wilson. No other boy can.'

Kenneth smiled up at him, and then over at Billy.

It was almost as if Uncle Frank had heard about Billy's colouring. He turned around fiercely and looked Billy up and down. He didn't seem to like what he saw. 'You, young man, need more training. I shall be coming round tomorrow to run you to the common.'

Mother's hand, which had been lifting the tea-pot, stopped mid-air. 'Oh would you, Frank? I shall have peace and quiet while you do. How wonderful.'

She finished pouring the stream of brown into the chunky cup with a monk's face on the handle. She passed it over the table with her little finger in the air. 'Here's your tea. I remembered your special cup.'

CHAPTER FIVE

September 29th 1938. ***Britain and France ratify proposals to keep Hitler from war***

They were all changing out of their plimsolls after P.T. when teacher handed everyone out an important note to take home. 'For your parents. And don't lose it or forget it.'

Now he was very nearly six, Billy was big enough to go to and from school on his own. He skipped along until he reached his gate. He was like a postman. 'I've got a note, Mother.'

Mother was leaning back on the garden room settee with a damp handkerchief on her forehead. Dad was already home, very early, with a pile of documents in his briefcase. He took Billy's school note and read it. 'Hmph,' he muttered to himself. 'The time has come.' Then he put Billy's cap on and said they had to get a gas mask.

'What's a gas mask?'

'You'll see.'

'As I did, Herbert,' said Mother. 'I went this morning, despite my condition. Most of the neighbours were there. It made me realize how imminent it all is. I feel quite sick. I don't know whether they disinfect the masks after fitting you. In the queue, I noticed a lot of Jews.'

Dad cleared his throat. He told her to sit quietly and keep calm. Then he prodded Billy forward, shut the front door and they walked down several streets to a brick building where Billy stood with other children and was fitted for his gas mask. It was a bit smelly in the room and it was nasty having something stuck over your mouth and nose, but you could still breathe. No-one made a fuss.

When he looked round, he wanted to laugh. The others' faces looked so queer squashed into the mask, their eyes all big and goggling against the see-through stuff. Afterwards, going home, several children he knew grinned and waved, holding up their square boxes. They shouted to each other across the street.

'Got mine.'

'Got mine too. My sister's having a Mickey Mouse.'

'Mine'll never wear that. Bet they won't get her to.'

'She'll get gassed, then.'

Billy was going to ask Dad what 'gassed' meant.

'I'm very glad you're not shouting across the road, Billy,' said Dad.

So Billy didn't ask.

Later, they had gas mask practices at school. Jim said that you had to wear a gas mask if the air got bad, full of gas. Enemies could do it to you. Two children got very frightened and had to sit in another classroom. All the rest of them opened their boxes and pulled out the masks. Teacher told them to spit on the glass thing so it wouldn't steam up, then fit the rubber bit round their head. It was quite exciting. There was lots of noise in the classroom and no work. Then it was playtime.

'What was it really like?' asked the frightened children who were still waiting to have the practice.

Billy told them, 'If you wear it too long, it gives you a headache. When you take it off you're ever so glad. You can feel how nice the air is.'

It was lots of fun in the playground, pretending to be gassed. Some of the girls played rescuers, running up and putting their hands over the boys' mouths saying they were putting their gas masks on.

All the teachers had a day off the following week for something important. Billy had to go to Kenneth's while Mother went to a meeting at the town hall. Aunty said it wouldn't apply to her.

In the back yard, Kenneth did a display of the Swedish Drill they did at his school. There was a lot of marching and turning sharply, hands up, down, bending, stretching.

'And all of us do this in time, smartly,' said Kenneth. 'Don't you do drill?'

'Not that sort. We have gas mask drill.'

Kenneth's eyebrows twitched. 'Course. So do we.' He looked around.

Uncle Frank had just gone back to work after his dinner hour and Aunty was lying down. Kenneth beckoned Billy as he crept out of the door and up to the landing cupboard. He stood on a chair and reached down his box.

'Now', he said, 'we'll have a drill.'

He got out his mask and put it on Billy's face, then flicked the rubber strap very tightly around his head. Billy couldn't breathe and started kicking. Kenneth moved sideways and pressed down on the mask so that no sound came out when Billy tried to shout. Billy flailed his legs wildly. Just as he thought he'd suffocate, Kenneth slid the mask upwards.

'Drill's over. I've saved your life. You didn't breathe any gas, did you?'

Billy lay on the bed taking great breaths while Kenneth neatly packed his mask away. 'Wait there,' he said, and Billy heard him slipping the box back on the cupboard shelf.

When his heart stopped thumping, Billy said, 'That was d-dangerous. I'm going d-downstairs. I'm not playing up h-here with you any m-more.' He ran out of the bedroom door before Kenneth could stop him.

Aunty was just getting up. 'What are those marks on your face, Billy?'

For once Billy thought he'd tell her, but Kenneth said quickly, 'How's your headache, Mummy? Can I get you a tablet and a glass of water?'

'My own little man. So thoughtful. Yes, if you could, dear. Run and get them from the kitchen.' She moved slowly towards Billy. 'I'm going to lean on your shoulder while we go downstairs, dear, is that all right? Such a strong boy.'

There were some semaphore cards on the sideboard. Billy picked them up quickly and asked to play with them so that he didn't get sent upstairs again. 'We can keep you company down here, Aunty.'

Kenneth glared, but he couldn't do anything about it with his hands around the glass of water.

Billy was watching Dad cut round the printed columns in several newspapers. Afterwards, he started sticking them in an exercise book. 'This will be history.'

'What will, Dad?'

He puffed at his pipe and didn't answer. He bent to turn on the wireless and spent ages tuning it.

The wireless had curly shapes cut out of its front as well as a big square, and there was shiny, bobbly material behind. When Billy touched it, it sometimes shivered, and the music or voice or hissing came out from either side of his fingers. He couldn't stop the sounds. Only the knob could do that but he wasn't allowed to touch any knobs in case the tuning went. Sometimes, it took Dad ages to get the voice back again.

'It's still whistling.'

'Shh.'

'Is it Children's Hour soon?'

'Shh. You've missed that. Tell your mother it's time, and then stay quiet.'

Mother came into the room before he could call her. She sat on the arm of the leathery chair that was usually Dad's and he arched his hand wide on her leg.

The doom voice came on, 'Radio 2LO. London calling.' That voice always made Billy feel a bit afraid. It said something about Munich again. He shut the door and hid behind the settee to read his comic.

Something was happening, but they hadn't said what. It didn't feel good. He got to the last page of Tiger Tim before he heard a loud 'Thank the Lord!' from Mother. Then she went to the telephone.

He heard her dialling but then she seemed mostly to be listening. When she put the telephone down he sidled through the door as she said, 'Herbert, Father thinks it's a let-down and it will only delay matters.'

'And I say Chamberlain's right and we should be grateful for one peaceful politician in Europe.'

'Well I'm sure I don't know. I'm just so glad it's not war here.'

At bath-time, Mother was smiley and humming to herself so he asked her what a let-down was.

'Little jugs have big ears,' she said.

He stared at her. They didn't have any ears at all. 'I know it's not war here,' he tried.

'Well, it's good news.' Then she explained that the government thought Britain had to go to war to save another country. That's why everyone needed gas-masks, but now there wasn't going to be a war in Britain after all. Mr Chamberlain had saved Britain from that. She was very, very glad because she didn't want to bring a child into a world of war.

'No.' He nodded. It was very good that she wasn't going to bring him into a world of war and gas masks. But it was rather sad for the country that wouldn't be saved.

CHAPTER SIX

November 21st 1938. ***Nazi forces occupy western Czechoslovakia and declare them German citizens***

Kenneth didn't get taken to the zoo for his birthday like Billy. He went to his Nanny and Grandad's and had his cake and presents there. The birthday was all over when Billy was taken to say 'Happy Birthday' and hand over the present.

'You'd have thought Doreen would have brought Billy back a balloon or a piece of cake even if Kenneth didn't think of it,' Mother said to Dad when they got home from Uncle Frank's. Billy went upstairs, but only as far as the landing. He hadn't thought about Kenneth bringing anything back until then. But he did now. He lay on the landing and waited for Dad to say what was right.

'Billy has a lot of everything. He doesn't need a share of Kenneth's few treats. Frank and Doreen struggle to do their best for their boy. I shouldn't think bringing cake for Billy crossed their minds.'

'No, indeed,' said Mother.

Billy lay still.

'Now, Marcia. We're not church-goers but I'll remind you of a certain catechism: *Not to covet nor desire other men's goods, etcetera, etcetera.'*

Mother slammed the parlour door then, so Billy didn't hear if she said anything back, but he did like the sound of 'Etcetera'. Perhaps it was one of Kenneth's goods— a board game. He could play Etcetera with him. He stopped lying at the top of the stairs, his favourite place, and wandered into his bedroom. Suddenly he wanted a piece of cake. But not Kenneth's.

Mr Durban had said that Hitler wasn't satisfied with the whole cake, but wanted a piece of everyone else's. No-one wanted to be like Hitler.

That 'being glad' Mother had talked about didn't last. Dad brought Mr Durban round for supper after work and they didn't look glad at all. Billy had to have his supper in the kitchen, not with the grown-ups.

'We need to talk in peace,' Dad said.

Billy pushed the kitchen door open once they were all in the dining room. He could hear a bit of the talk, and it wasn't about peace at all.

Jim rang the doorbell just then, asking if Billy could come round to play, and the grown-ups seemed very happy for him to go. The boys ran down the road, but didn't go to Jim's house.

'Guess what, Billy? There's men digging shelters right near the common. Come on. Reg is waiting for us.'

They ran on hard until they saw Reg jumping up and down and waving. There was a large, dark oblong hole nearby, men with large spades hard at work. It was very exciting watching the hole get deeper and longer. They stood at the side of the common as the entrance was bricked round and a doorway fitted. It was just like a secret passage.

Billy imagined its dreadful darkness. 'I can't wait till we're allowed to sit inside.'

Reg put his hands on his hips. 'It'll be scary.'

'We'll have to take torches.'

'And biscuits,' said Jim.

'Have you got blackout at home? We won't need it down that shelter, it's all black as black.'

Reg was bending so close to peer inside that they were all shooed off by the diggers. They ran off like aeroplanes, whizzing all the way home.

Next day, Mrs.Donnington made extra curtains with black material. Black curtains! They were to use as well as the ones they already had. Dad said they must close the blackouts carefully before ever putting a light on.

He stuck brown paper criss-cross over all the windows. It looked awful, like fearful kisses, but everyone else's windows had them too.

Mr Durban came round to talk about Safety at Home. He had a helmet, which looked funny with his suit. He did read Rupert the Bear Annual with Billy for a short while, but he soon wanted to talk about shelters and fire watch. Billy watched him hard the whole time.

'Good lad, you're listening well.'

Billy's face went hot because really he'd been trying to imagine Mr Durban as a young man, holding that sabre and fighting off Hitler and the enemy, not the today Mr Durban talking about keeping things safe at home. He so wanted to ask what a Cossack was, but that would have given the secret away, and Mr Durban had just been saying about Keeping Mum.

Dad took Mr Durban into the garden room, Billy and Mother followed. Both the men bent over to help Mother onto the reclining chair and she sank in with a sigh.

Then the grown-ups started talking about Billy having a brother or sister. He didn't listen to that much because everyone knew Mother wouldn't want two children.

'Just at the worst time!' she said. He'd heard her say ages ago that one was too much. 'And I feel so tired.'

'You should get away for a while, Marcia. Have some country air. Could you manage, Herbert, without her?'

Dad stroked his chin. 'There's our home help, Mrs Donnington. She could manage some extra hours, I'm sure.' He turned to Billy. 'You like her, don't you?'

Billy nodded. He remembered the time when Mother and Dad were so angry with each other that he'd been sent to the kitchen to sit with Mrs Donnington while they rowed. She was blacking the stove. She'd let him polish the little brass fire tools on their stand, each with a ship on the top of the handle. Behind him, the shouty voices spattered like coal dust from the hall into the parlour. He could tell that Mrs Donnington could hear it too because she stopped brushing away at the stove.

He said, 'They're really, really cross, aren't they?'

She shook her head until her hairpins fell out onto the hearth and put a black finger to her mouth. 'Shhh.' She gave him a barley sugar from the jar on the high shelf.

It was all right to eat it because it was wrapped. It was really sticky but he didn't lick the paper after he'd put it into his mouth because of the black on it. He took a long time sucking it and by then, the quarrelling had stopped.

Yes, it would be nice to be left with Mrs Donnington for a few days.

Dad shook his shoulder. 'Are you listening, Billy?'

He nodded, but he hadn't been.

'Billy?' Mother said. 'So, you don't mind if I have a little holiday, dear?'

Mr Durban bent down to him. 'I think your mother would benefit from some extra rest, young man. Perhaps you'll come and visit us a couple of times while she's away. Angela will like that.'

Billy could feel his mouth stretching into a grin. That would be super-duper, but should he say that in front of Mother? 'I'm glad you're going to have some rest, Mother,' felt much safer.

~

After Mother had packed and gone away, Billy waited for his visits. Annoyingly, it was Kenneth's that Dad took him round to first.

'Why, Dad?'

'Kenneth needs some company.'

'I need to see the shashka,' Billy muttered to himself as they marched through the smog. If they hadn't known the way, they'd have got lost as only the gates showed, the houses distant or disappeared, hiding behind the grey misty stuff.

'Have fun, you boys,' Dad said as he left Billy inside Kenneth's house.

'Of course, Uncle,' Kenneth smiled, smoothing down his latest knitted jumper, the colour of sick.

Dad waved and left for his club, becoming more and more mysterious as his shape became swallowed by smog.

Billy put one foot in front of the other to see how long he could be getting into the living room.

'Hello ducky. Kenneth's been longing for you to come.' Aunty was knitting as usual.

Kenneth would be mean as usual. The smile came. 'We two'll go to the kitchen to use the table, Mummy.' He pushed Billy into the passage.

Billy looked hopefully at the welsh dresser for signs of Kenneth's birthday presents. 'Have you g-got a new game, Etcetera?'

Kenneth laughed in a silly, high voice as if he was being tickled.

Billy put his hands on his hips. 'Well? H-have you?'

'No, stupid. "Etcetera" means "and so on." How could I have a game called that?' He went on giggling until Billy felt like kicking him.

Luckily, Dad had brought Billy's dominoes and Ludo over with them. Billy plonked them down on the table, hard.

'Oh, L-L-Ludo! I'll be r-r-red.' Kenneth set them out on the table.

Aunty brought her knitting in and sat by the boiler. 'Don't make fun of Billy's stutter, dear. We can't all have beautiful voices like you.'

Kenneth sighed sadly, his head on one side and his hands twiddling the red counters.

It would be so nice to stick out his tongue at Kenneth and as far as it could possibly go, but Kenneth would only get him into trouble. Billy took the green counters and willed them to win.

They played two games, and he did win both. Kenneth said 'Ludo's a game of chance. Anyway, I wasn't trying.'

Billy put the pieces back in the box slowly. 'Why weren't you?'

'Perhaps I had my mind on something else.' He nudged Billy and pointed at Aunty Doreen's knitting.

Billy stared at it. It looked all right, no stitches fallen off the needles. It was white, not grey or ditch green, that's all he could see. Kenneth stretched his eyes wide at Billy as if to say *you're stupid,* and pulled him out and up the stairs.

Billy stared at Kenneth's goggling eyes, 'So?' What was it to do with, his stutter or the Ludo? White knitting, so was it something rude, like a vest?

'What, Kenneth? What?'

'Not telling,' said Kenneth. He was giggling and jumping from one foot to another, up a stair, down a stair. It looked really silly.

'Tell me. I don't know.'

'Shan't. If you don't know, Billy, you're loony. And when she comes back home to you, Aunty Marcia is going to be FAT.'

Mother wasn't at all fat. Kenneth was really rude and if Mother could hear him, she wouldn't like him anymore.

~

Mr Durban didn't even ask Mrs Donnington if he'd been good when he came to collect him. At his house, Mrs Durban met them with a smile. 'Come along in, Billy. I've made those cakes you like so much.' She had a smashing tea all ready.

Afterwards. Angela was allowed to 'sit' for him while Mr and Mrs Durban went to the Town Hall to discuss the new National Service Handbook. They put on their coats and told Angela they trusted her to look after Billy well.

He watched them disappear up the road together. 'What is that Handbook, Angela?'

'It's to tell people if they're qualified to be soldiers or sailors, sort of thing.'

'My Uncle Ted is. He's got a uniform and black soldier boots and I've seen him practising his marching.

She didn't answer. He waited for her to choose something to do. She knew better than to get out her dolls but she did get him to play a board game with countries on it for a while. Billy couldn't really answer the questions, so they didn't get far. He looked longingly at Mr Durban's study door.

'All right. Come on. You can look at the sabre. We'll play knights and princesses.'

Angela put the sabre on the desk, then pretended to be frightened, and to need rescuing. It was ever such fun. Billy stood on Mr Durban's desk chair to be a knight, holding a cushion in front as a shield, fighting off enemy.

'It'd be more fun holding the sabre,' he said.

Angela bit her lip but held the sabre out. 'Just be very careful, mind.'

She wouldn't let him take it out of the scabbard, but she let him wave it and shout fierce words like 'Ahoy!' and 'Zounds!'

There was no-one to hear, so they practised shouting like people at war and then laughed as loudly as they could. It felt really dangerous.

Angela got worried. 'We'd better put the sabre away now.'

They went back into the lounge to bounce on the sofa.

'Do you mind your mother being away?' Angela asked.

'Not really. I like coming here. I'd like to come every day.'

Angela was going to be a real princess one day, and he'd be a real knight and protect her with the sabre. If only he could have it for himself, just once. After all, there might be a war and he might be a hero by then.

CHAPTER SEVEN

January 14th 1939. ***Hitler and Mussolini hand in hand. Dictators map out New Europe.***

It was a shame Christmas holidays were all over because there was snow, and Billy had seen people tobogganing on the common when his cub pack had been taken there for games. Tobogganing was the sort of thing Uncle Ted would do, but not Dad or Mother.

She'd had her little holiday, that was quite long, and come back in time to decorate the tree that he and Dad had dragged all the way back from the market. She was more smiley and she'd got so much weller she really was quite fat now, which she'd never been before. Kenneth was right. He always was. That was very annoying.

When Mother opened the front door and found Billy waiting by the Christmas tree, she threw up her hands and said, 'A tree. Marvellous.' Then, 'Were you a good boy, Billy? No trouble at Kenneth's?'

He shook his head. He hadn't got into any trouble at all, anywhere. Mother should be pleased with him. He said, 'Mrs Donnington came in almost every day to get the house ready.'

He thought of that now. She'd cleaned it out as though it was

Spring, and he'd told her, 'You won't have to do it when it is Spring now, Mrs Donnington. We shall have a very clean Christmas instead.'

She laughed her hair untidy. It was because laughing made her shake her head. He bent down to pick up her hairpins and she patted his bottom. 'You're a one, you are, Billy boy. You're quite cheeky with your mother away.'

It was true he could do forbidden things like slide down the banisters and wave to the children opposite from the front gate. Mrs Donnington didn't tell him off at all.

'If you were my child, you could go right over and play with them, but I know my place and it's not allowed.'

Billy screwed his eyes up at her, trying to imagine what it would be like to be her child. She had to clean other people's houses so she must be poor, and poor people didn't have books and wirelesses and new clothes and chocolate biscuits.

There was one thing she wouldn't let him do, and that was to follow her into the end bedroom. 'Now, now. I've got my work to do and soon there'll be a little person in there. You've got your very own room, lucky boy. Lots of children have to share. So in you go and play for a bit and I'll tell you when I'm done.'

Dad had talked about a little person too. Billy smiled at this fairy story thing they told him about; "little person" like Father Christmas's elves. Perhaps they'd pretend a gnome was leaving presents under the tree instead of a Santa. He'd worked out that probably all the presents were hidden in that bedroom. He wouldn't go in there and spoil the surprise.

Altogether, he hadn't been sad while Mother was away. Mrs Donnington's dinners were quite tasty. He got taken to Nanny and Grandad's twice, Mr Durban came for him three super times and he'd only had to go to Kenneth's that once. Dad said he was sick of seeing Billy's long face every time Uncle Frank or Kenneth was mentioned.

And now Mother was home and she was fat, at least round her middle. She also started talking about the little person 'in there' patting her tummy, which always made him giggle. The idea of Mother swallowing a little person like the old lady with the fly was ever so funny.

~

February was very cold. Mother said she couldn't possibly risk going out. There was quite a bit of snow. He wore his wellies every day and played snowballs every playtime. Mrs Donnington brought in the shopping and the greengrocer delivered.

One afternoon, Billy came home from school and a nurse lady in a hard white apron opened the door. Before he had time to feel hospital-frightened, she said, 'Be very quiet, there's a good boy. You've got a baby sister upstairs but your mother needs to rest in bed.' She hurried back upstairs as soon as he was in the door.

Billy stayed in the hall, trying to think what to do. Mother hadn't told him that she would be in bed when he got home, or that there would be a baby. She said she couldn't go out, so it must have been brought to her with the shopping.

He hadn't believed the talk about a brother or sister, or about a little person, but it wasn't a fairy story after all; it had been true! Mother must be very fed up that a baby had come and she would have to look after it. He'd better keep out of the way in case she wasn't smiley any more.

He sat down hard on the stairs. This was all a shock. He could use the phone and tell Aunty. First, though, he wanted to know what the lady and Mother were saying. He peered upwards to her bedroom but couldn't hear much, just footsteps and water running, and a bit of puffing and blowing. It was difficult to work out what was going on.

There was no answer when he telephoned Aunty, putting his finger in the right hole for each number and pulling it round as far as it would go. Number nine needed a pull almost a whole circle round. He was sure he'd remembered her number right. Would she already know about this baby? He certainly didn't want Kenneth telling him the news. *He* wanted to be the one who told it, and for Kenneth to be the surprised one.

He would try phoning again later. Meanwhile, he went in the kitchen and learned his spellings. He wrote them out so the grown-ups would know how good he'd been. Even when he'd finished them all, still no-one came, so he took a custard tart and a fairy cake from the larder without asking.

Dad arrived home before he got to telephone Aunty again. Billy ran to the door. 'Mother's in bed, Dad. A nurse has come to look after her baby, a girl one. Now Mother will have to look after two children after all.'

'A baby girl!' Dad was grinning. It made his face look very different, lumps on his cheeks and dimples showing through his beard. 'I must go up and see her for myself. Stay there, be good.' He didn't say anything about not touching the cakes. Perhaps it didn't matter today, so Billy took another. He was going to tell Mrs Donnington they were lovely, because she was the one who'd been cooking lately.

After Dad had been upstairs a long time, he brought down a white bundle to show Billy. He pulled back an edge of lacy shawl and there was a tiny face and weeny hand, very pink and squashy-looking. Billy looked hard in case it was some kind of doll, but then it turned up its nose and moved its fingers. It was the first baby Billy had seen up close. It was a funny feeling—not all that nice. 'It doesn't l- look as if it will be an-nother child.'

'You'll never have seen one this new,' said Dad.

'No. It's very s-small.' He nearly said 'smell' by mistake. It did have a funny smell, one he hadn't smelled before. He stood back and away.

Dad was still looking at the bundle. 'They soon grow.'

The baby mewed loudly and Dad hurried it back upstairs. He hadn't said what Billy should be doing, but it probably wasn't telephoning Aunty, so he went into the garden room and looked at books. He practised his reading. They'd be pleased when he showed them later. But no-one came for ages.

At last he heard Dad making a pot of tea, then calling out that there were sandwiches and milk on the table. Billy went in and ate them alone. Much later, Dad came down to tell Billy to get himself ready for bed and to do it very quietly.

It was all very strange and he felt somehow different. Things that people said wouldn't happen, did happen. So even when they didn't want them to happen, they happened. Would war? Everyone said they didn't want war to happen. For once there was no wireless on, no news to make Dad sigh. There was the newspaper Dad had left on the hallstand. He peeped at it, folded back to its third page. There was something about children. Jews coming on ships and an ever such long word beginning with 'kinder…'

'Are you getting ready for bed, Billy?' Dad called out.

Billy slipped upstairs quickly and quietly so that he could call from his bedroom, 'Yes, Dad.' He washed and slid into a freezing bed. He went right down deep below the blankets to get warm. It would be nice to have a soft one tucked round him, all cosily, like the baby's. He could hear mewing from Mother's room, and his feet were very cold, so he took ages to get to sleep.

The next day was Saturday but Aunty Doreen came alone without Kenneth.

'Dear little baby sister for you, Billy. Lucky boy,' and she crept upstairs where Billy heard her whispering and cooing. When she came down, Billy asked, 'W-will Mother ever be able to get up again?'

Aunty Doreen put an arm round him and said Mother would start getting up next week, but Billy could go upstairs to see her now if he wanted. He thought about it, but decided not to. He hadn't seen her in bed before and it didn't seem quite right.

It was a funny week with Dad putting out Sunny Jim cornflakes for him in the morning before he went to work and then Billy getting himself off to school. Mrs Donnington couldn't get in for long now that her husband was working nights. She came to do the cleaning and shopping, but she was gone by the time Billy got home. He felt like a man, going to work and coming back with no-one in charge of him. He wore the same socks all week and Dad didn't notice.

When Mother did get up again, she didn't seem quite the same person or perhaps Billy had forgotten her, or perhaps he hadn't looked hard at her before. Now, he noticed her dark hair hanging messily and her pink feet with lines like rivers and valleys. Her body wasn't so so fat, but thick and padded out, and she was more often in her dressing gown than in a dress.

'You'll have to be a quiet boy, now that we have a baby girl.'

'I'll be very quiet if I'm on my own, Mother.'

One lucky thing was that the girl baby took all Mother's time, so she didn't want Kenneth over. She didn't want any noise when Baby was sleeping, either, which was most of the time.

Dad took Billy over to see Uncle Frank (really, to see Kenneth, but when they got upstairs both boys put their fingers in their ears and didn't talk to each other).

Afterwards, Dad took him shopping. He'd never done that before, but Mrs Donnington had given him a list. They bought tinned peaches from the grocer and gripe water for the baby from the chemist and tobacco from a musty little shop he'd hardly noticed before, a man's shop, with pipes in the window and wooden tubs with different tobaccos in them. Each had its own smell, rich and fruity, dank and dusky. Dad knew exactly which one he wanted but there was a queue to be served. He lit his pipe while he waited. Everyone in the queue was smoking, with little trails of smoke coming up from each mouth and a big one floating out of the shop.

It would be nice to be a smoker like Dad. Billy was crouching over one tub, sniffing deeply when a man came up behind him and said, 'My word, is that tobacco-fancier Mr Billy Wilson?'

Billy nodded, grinning to see Mr Durban.

'Got a voice?'

'Yes, sir. Dad's got a b-baby now.'

'Has he indeed!' Mr Durban leaned over, all the folds in his face falling forward. 'And is that a boy baby?'

'N-no, sir, a girl one.'

'How nice for you to have a sister.'

Billy didn't know what to say. The baby was just a mewing thing in a bassinet.

'Well, now, you'll have to occupy yourself while your mother is busy with her. So you can keep yourself amused with these.' He passed over a bunch of little furry sticks that you could bend in all directions, pink, green, red, blue and brown.

'Thank you very m-much, Mr Durban.'

'Just a little something for a fine lad.' He clapped his hand on Dad's shoulder, who'd just been served. 'What a lucky chap you are, Herbert, a new little girl and this extra special son.'

Dad looked at Billy, his eyebrows like up-and-down arrows, and put his new tobacco inside his pouch. He started talking about ministers and policies, so Billy turned back to the barrels, rescuing one or two fronds of tobacco that were lying on the edges. He wanted to eat them, but probably it wasn't allowed.

When Mr Durban had finished chatting and gone on his way, Billy showed Dad the fuzzy things Mr Durban had given him. Dad said they were pipe cleaners and demonstrated how you could twist them together to make little men, bend their legs and arms and even make feet and hands. Billy put them in his pocket and kept his hand on them, all small and furry and ready to play with. It was funny, really. Mr Durban had given him these soft little sticks, when what he really wanted was the hard as hard big one that was the shashka.

CHAPTER EIGHT

March 15th 1939. ***Promises broken. Hitler seizes the rest of Czechoslovakia.***

Most of the baby things happened in Mother's bedroom, so Billy didn't see much of Baby. Aunty Doreen looked after her sometimes when Mother had to go out. Billy liked that because then Kenneth stayed behind with Uncle, and Aunty was nice and chatty when Mother wasn't around.

She'd just arrived, and was taking off her squashy hat.

'Do you like babies, Aunty? I don't think I do.' He swung to and fro on the hall chair, his legs going high in the air. He quickly stopped as Mother came downstairs, smartly dressed. Her hair was smooth and flicked over her shoulders. Her jacket was made of the same stuff as her skirt and her heels went clip-clop on the lino.

She said, 'Baby's just been fed and changed, Doreen. Sleeping peacefully. You shouldn't have to do a thing.' She looked at Billy sternly. 'Be a good boy for Aunty Doreen, I'm going out.'

'He's actually a very good boy for me, Marcia.'

'Boys!' Mother said.

He stepped behind Aunty, looking at the floor. He knew he was a nuisance. He'd been kicking the ball against the shed door, keeping out of the way but Mother had just told him her body had felt every thwack of the ball when she was trying to rest. The whisk of her skirt as she walked to the front door, showed how glad she was to be getting out and away from noisy boys. As the door shut, a blast of fresh air shot into the hall. Billy spun around, pretending to be a top.

Aunty beckoned him into the kitchen. She made herself a cup of tea and poured Billy some milk. She brought some biscuits out of her bag. They had jam in the middle. And she gave him three.

Then they went in the garden room and sat together on the settee. Aunty's face looked pink and powdery and kind. She asked him what games he liked to play when he was with other children. He knew she meant when he was with Kenneth, but he told her about playing horses in the playground at school. It wasn't Aunty's fault she had such a mean boy.

When Baby started crying, Aunty went upstairs and brought her down, walking up and down, patting her back. It seemed a funny thing to do, but Baby stopped crying and Aunty sat down again, the baby beside her on the settee.

He moved away from it. 'I d-didn't know I was going to have a girl baby in my house.'

'You're a very lucky boy, dear. Kenneth can't have a baby sister.'

He tried to imagine Kenneth leaning over a cot, looking pleased.

Aunty was rocking the baby in her arms, staring into its face. He thought there were tears in her eyes. He stayed very quiet, twisting his pipe cleaners. He made a tank instead of a person.

Aunty said, 'Babies need a lot of looking after.'

'How d-do you know what to d-do?' Supposing Mother went out and left him in charge!

'You have to know all their different cries. One is hunger, one's when they're uncomfortable and need their nappy changing, and this one, well, she just wants some company and comfort. She needs to be held and to know someone loves her.'

The baby just looked like a baby. How could she know what she wanted and things like love? 'Oh,' he said.

Aunty drew out a pack of cards from her bag and they played

Beggar My Neighbour for ages. He might be lucky to have a baby sister, but Kenneth was lucky to have a grown- up to play cards with.

When the baby started its cry again, Aunty put it on his lap while he sat far back on the settee. This funny, nice but dangerous feeling he'd never had before, especially when Aunty put his hands either side of the soft, woolly shape. It was smaller than his Donald Duck ball. The baby moaned a bit and he tried patting like Aunty had done and the moaning stopped.

'I s-stopped her from crying!' he said.

'That's it. You did. You're going to be a fine, loving brother and —'Aunty broke off suddenly and whipped the baby up smartly. Mother's footsteps were at the door.

Aunty jerked her head towards the garden, widening her eyes at Billy, so he scuttled outside.

Dad helped Mother with the breakfast, which was funny. Mrs Donnington was away, seeing her son off to the army.

'Will Colin Donnington be a soldier like Uncle Ted?'

Mother swept her head from one side to the other although there were no flies around. 'Just hurry off, Billy. Come on. Off to school.' She didn't look pleased.

Outside other people had long faces too, although a cheery new poster was up by the greengrocer's. Instead of *California Syrup of Figs*, this one said *AD 1939 will be brighter thanks to Sunlight Soap, Now only 4d.* So everyone should've been smiling.

At school, Mr Finlay said there was going to be another drill today, not just for gas masks but for air raids too. That would be fun. Everyone nudged each other and got into trouble for whispering.

The class hadn't done more than copy the date off the board, before a horrible noise sounded all around. It was scary and some people screamed.

Mr Finlay and the biggest boys walked up and down the corridors saying 'It's only a practice, don't panic.'

They had to line up quickly with no talking, then go to an underground place with long, fat pipes. They were squashed up close together and it was damp and dark. They had to stay there until another squealy sound came, then line up and be counted before marching back into school. Everyone missed mental arithmetic and the twins sniggered because they hadn't done their homework anyway.

Miss Spender, a thin teacher with a grey straggly bun and brown lace-up shoes with double bows, took everyone in the hall. She could play the piano. She practised *There'll always be an England* with all of the infants, and a row of the oldest juniors to lead them. It was difficult learning the words and some of Billy's class couldn't get the tune. The littlest children were too fidgety, and in the end Miss Spender said they could play quietly in their classroom with the door open so that they could listen. She said everyone must sing to show what a wonderful country they had; a wonderful country to be saved from War and by War.

Sonia, the cleverstick, whispered that you couldn't be saved by both.

The juniors told the infants what War meant: guns and fighting.

They played at War all the time in the playground and after school dinner they played again, the sound of the air raid warning still in their ears. If no-one liked a boy, he had to be the enemy and crouch behind the lavs and run away with everyone after him.

A few boys who were very new and couldn't speak properly because they were foreign, were just right to use as enemy. When they ran away, they really looked frightened. That was especially good. Billy, Jim, Reg and Andrew ran screaming after them, waving their arms, pretending they were holding rifles. Mr Hendrick, the top class teacher, was on duty. He came over and stopped them.

'But why, Sir? It was super fun,' Jim said. He was always the one who spoke first.

'Fun for you. Look at these boys you're using as enemies. It's very frightening for them.' He lifted a finger so that all of them looked up at him. 'Perhaps you need to know something.' He put his arms on the shoulders of two of the enemy boys. 'These lads had to run away from the German guns that were threatening their whole village. The Germans killed lots of their people and took their lands and homes.'

Several children gasped.

'That was wicked, sir. I don't like the Germans,' Andrew spoke up. Billy nudged Jim. Andrew liked things to be right.

'We hate Germans,' everyone chanted.

'Yes, Jones. Czechoslovakians have come to England to be safe. You must be kind to them.'

Czechoslovakians! They all tried, but no-one could say 'Czecho-slovakian'. Billy laughed so hard, he had to double over and lean on people. Now everyone was a stutterer.

After Mr Hendrick had gone to the shelter where the monitor had put his cup of tea, the boys crowded round the foreigners. It was very exciting.

'Did you really have to run in front of the guns?' Reg began. Two of the enemy boys nodded, the others didn't speak enough English yet. The bell went before they could be asked any more, but now Billy understood that the foreign boys were heroes and knew all about war.

At home time, Aunty Doreen collected him, bringing Kenneth. 'We thought we'd pick you up on the way, Billy. I want to see your Mummy about something.'

Billy walked behind in step with Kenneth. For once he had something to tell that Kenneth didn't know already. It was jolly annoying that Kenneth could say 'Czechoslovakia' the very first time he tried, but Billy could tell that he hadn't heard about the land stolen from them. Kenneth didn't have any foreigners in his school. Billy told him about the boys running from the guns.

Kenneth listened and was quiet for a bit. Then he said 'Now, if there's war, Billy, there'll be fighting all the time, everywhere. All the fathers will be soldiers and you'll have to fight the enemy in your house because Uncle Bert will be away at Assizes.'

Billy hopped forward to ask Aunty. Kenneth pulled him back. 'Stop! We don't frighten the women, stupid.'

When they got home, the two mothers went into the parlour to talk, but Aunty didn't stay very long. Kenneth had only had time to line up all the planes before he was called down to go.

'Think about it, Marcia,' she said as the door closed behind them.

It was a cold day and Mother had lit the parlour fire. Billy hunched by it imagining all of Wandsworth running away from enemy guns. Where would they hide? They'd have to run all the way to Grandad's Anderson shelter or to the one on the common, which might be crowded. He knew he shouldn't tell Mother but he needed to know what was happening, and he'd be in bed by the time Dad got home. When she came into the parlour, Billy just said quietly, 'There might be war and guns in England.'

She passed him the tongs. 'Put another couple of coals on the fire. Let's warm ourselves up. I don't want you to worry, Billy— the war's likely to stay overseas. Even if things happen in England, the government plan to look after all the children, mothers and babies, so that none of us will be near any fighting.'

He nodded. Governments were big, important people who could do all sorts of things. It was good they were going to look after mothers and children and make sure no fighting came near them. But governments didn't care so much about men. They made them turn into soldiers.

'What about Dad? Will they send him to be a soldier after all?'

'No. Your father's work is important. And he'll be out of London mostly. That's why we're not bothering with an Anderson. If the war comes, we just won't be here.'

She took up a book with trees on its cover, *How Green is my Valley*. She was smiling as she read.

The fire was fading. Mother took up the poker and dug it hard into the back coals. Flames licked up, orange and scarlet. Billy leant forward.

Mother said, 'Sit back. That's dangerous.'

CHAPTER NINE

May 22nd 1939. ***Italy and Germany sign friendship pact.***

The telephone rang and it was Billy who lifted the receiver. 'Southview 1281?'

'That must be Billy. How's that baby of yours?'

'Hallo, Grandad. Baby's got bigger and bigger. She fills up her cradle from top to bottom.'

'Does she now?'

'Yes, she spends much more time downstairs nowadays and her crying's got louder.'

'Well, I'm sure. Now I need to talk to your mother and father, so put me on, there's a good lad.'

He left the receiver on the telephone table for Dad and galloped to the kitchen to finish his milk and biscuits.

After a bit, he heard the receiver ting as it went on its rest, and Dad's voice talking to Mother, '—bad as each other. Grim news for us.'

He went into the hall to rock the pram. That usually stopped the crying. Mother seemed a bit grumpy. Billy hadn't done anything wrong so perhaps it was because Baby kept yelling. It was called *Teething*. He put a finger on Baby's cheek where a red spot showed.

'Leave her, Billy. Just take yourself off somewhere, will you.'

Dad put a hand on top of hers, 'Come along, Billy. Put on your blazer. You and I will take a walk.' That was nice, and it didn't often happen.

He walked along with a lilting walk to keep up with Dad's long strides. He practised whistling and nearly had the hang of it when Dad said to stop because it was common.

That was funny, because just then they stopped at the common. He couldn't remember Dad ever taking him there before. He was hot in his blazer. Would Dad buy him a bottle of pop? He didn't like to ask.

Overhead, a plane droned. Billy squinted upwards to see the propeller with two blades and the stumpy body sitting on its wings, the sun glinting on them.

'Cor, Dad. A smashing plane.'

Dad said, 'Not a nice sight really. Those wings have four Browning machine guns in them.'

Billy peered again to see if guns were pointing down at them, but it flew too fast.

The slides and roundabout were filled with children enjoying the sunny weather. It would be nice to have a turn, but he wasn't sure if he was allowed.

The park-keeper was doing his rounds in his brown uniform.

Dad said, 'He won't be doing that much longer.' Another low-flying plane nearly drowned his words. While Dad stopped at a news-stand to read and tut, Billy looked over at some boys kicking a ball. There were a few fathers too, joining in with their sons.

'Dad?'

'Mm.' He turned a page.

'Dad, did you play football when you were young?'

'I left that to my brother. He was the sporty one. Muscly, strong, full of energy, like you.' He turned back to his paper. 'Off you run and have a turn on the roundabout.'

Billy ran off and whizzed round fast leaving the thought of Uncle's muscles behind with Dad, who sat smoking his pipe and reading. Soon, Dad would be working away somewhere, taking his pipe with him as well as his wig in its special box. Mother wouldn't have his help. The baby would trouble her and Uncle Frank might come to do more toughening up. That would be rotten.

On the way home they passed Wandsworth prison. It looked wide, grand and frightening with brick walls all around it. The men in there must be very toughened up.

'D-do you have to be very, very bad to be in there, Dad?'

'Mostly. But not all. Men who won't fight in the war may end up there.'

'You d-don't want to fight. Will you have to g-go to prison?'

'No, no. I will probably be needed here given the job I do. But I'm afraid there'll be a lot of people who will have to fight although they don't want to, because prison will seem worse.'

Billy shuddered as they walked right close to it. 'Prison is the worsest, isn't it?'

'Worst. No. War's the worst. Best avoided. Small chance,' he took a big puff of his pipe. The smoke rose dangerously near to the barred windows of the prison. There were so many, and such long walls. There was room for hundreds and hundreds of men. A whole army could get in there. But inside they would be safe; soldiers wouldn't be, because Hitler would be waiting for them.

'Come along, stop staring. We must get home to your baby sister.'

Perhaps Mother would be in a better mood by the time they got through the front door.

Billy had just hung his blazer up and had a long drink when he heard Uncle arrive with Kenneth. Probably the whole street heard his bellow.

'Ah, Marcia, I've brought Kenneth to keep that son of yours out of trouble for five minutes. We thought we'd see how things are going on with the nipper.'

The front door closed behind them and soon enough, Billy was called into the hall. 'Play upstairs, boys.'

For once, Uncle didn't start on Billy's exercises or make him say sentences without stuttering, but took Baby from Mother and lifted her high into the air. 'Look at this little darling,' he said, and tickled her under her chin.

Billy and Kenneth stood side by side watching as he made a great fuss of her. Had Uncle magicked into another man? Mother was smiling and nodding.

Kenneth yanked at Billy's arm and pulled him upstairs.

Billy opened his bedroom door. 'What do you want to play, then?'

Kenneth didn't answer but climbed onto Billy's chair. He flipped the aeroplane hanging from the ceiling, to and fro, to and fro. 'I'm glad we haven't got a smelly baby.'

'She's not smelly. They have to have nappies when they're little.'

'Ugh. And they cry. And when she gets bigger she'll be a girl. Mummy and Daddy were saying that will make Aunty Marcia happy because she didn't want a boy.'

Billy felt his eyes fill, so he quickly picked up the King Arthur book that was open on his bed. He held the picture away from Kenneth and just stared at the sword in the stone until he almost felt his hand on the hilt.

In real life it wouldn't be King Arthur's sword in his hand, it would be the sabre and he, Billy the Cossack, would be the brave-as-brave warrior who no-one dared challenge.

CHAPTER TEN

August 25th 1939. ***Can Hitler's demands be met? His "horror" at idea of Germany and Britain at war.***

Billy spread himself out on the carpet by the open French windows with his book. It was so hot, and it had been hot for ages. All summer holidays aeroplanes had been droning overhead, like now. Dad said they were pilots, practising.

He had The Tales of King Arthur, illustrated, from Boots library again. The man in the blue tunic had his hand on the hilt of a sword. It was exciting, but not nearly as good as a Cossack sabre. He turned a page. There was no picture on it but some long words, so he went to ask help.

Mother and Dad were sitting in the parlour, with the wireless droning in the background. They always seemed to be listening to the wireless these days. The BBC man droned on something about Mr Chamberlain.

'What's this w-word, Mother?'

'Excalibur. Shh a minute...'

They were leaning forward, towards the wireless. Dad had sent

Billy out for accumulators that morning. 'Must make sure we always have reception. Best to have some spares,' he'd said to Mother, and then put them on the high shelf in a box wrapped in brown paper.

'And what's this word?'

Mother waved him away. 'Not now, Billy. We're listening to the news, so go in the garden or stay upstairs, but don't wake Baby with loud footsteps please.'

King Arthur was much more interesting than the wireless because he had Excalibur. With Excalibur anything was possible. Enemies could be vanquished— squish, like treading on a snail. He shut the door behind him and just caught Mother's murmur about armies.

When Baby woke, Dad said, 'Get ready to go shopping, Billy.'

'We're always shopping these days.'

'It's necessary, Billy.'

Mother had already brought back large parcels, which she put in the loft 'in case' as well as lots of tinned food until the larder was so full Mrs Donnington said she couldn't clean it out properly. Mother put a lock on the larder and said she needn't bother as it was Stores.

Now they were going to buy more stores. It felt funny, because Dad was coming too. Fathers didn't shop. Not unless they had a really new baby.

Baby sat up in her pram that was like a great carriage. Its wheels came up to Billy's thighs, and when he pressed on the handle, the whole thing bounced on its springs. Mother walked briskly talking to Dad about Preparations.

At the common, all the railings had been taken away for making ships and a whole chunk had been dug up and changed into allotments.

'What's allotments, Dad?'

'For growing vegetables, so everyone has enough food. Your Uncle Frank has one here.'

'He's welcome to it,' said Mother. 'Spoils the look of the park. But Battersea's much worse off, allotments all the way round, I heard.'

Billy slowed down to stare. It would nice to dig at the allotments instead of queuing outside the grocer's, the baker's, the butcher's and then the draper's. He needn't have come; he was big enough to stay home on his own, these days. He sighed.

'Don't sigh,' Mother said. 'After shopping we're going to Nanny and Grandad's.'

'While we can,' Dad muttered.

The shopping took ages, and then there was the long walk up Lavender Hill.

They found Grandad planting vegetables at one side of his garden. The Anderson shelter was on the other. It had a funny door with a curved top. Inside there were two bunks as well as two camp chairs. It was a wonderful new place to play. He scrambled in and felt safe and secret. Outside, Grandad was saying, 'I wish you'd get on with yours, Bert.'

Billy put his head round the shelter door.

'There's an old French proverb,' Dad looked to the sky where perhaps he could see the words. '*One meets his destiny often in the road he takes to avoid it.* It would be just my luck to slip a disc digging the foundations.'

'Cheerful soul, you are. Never mind about proverbs and we're not French anyway. What about protecting your family?'

Dad waved a hand towards Billy and Mother, heaving his shoulders and acting as if he was carrying a large weighty bag.

Grandad stared. 'What? Now?'

'Very soon, I think.'

Grandad looked down and nodded grimly.

He took Billy into the kitchen and gave him half a crown. That was so much money and he hadn't done anything good! He promised to put in his money box, but Grandad said, 'You can take it with you, in case.' Nanny nudged Grandad to be quiet and Mother also mouthed something silently.

Of course Billy would take the half-crown home with him, so he didn't understand what their secret was.

Suddenly he heard an aeroplane and took Baby outside to look up at it. 'Hurricane!' he shouted. All the boys at school knew a Hurricane and a Spitfire, but the girls didn't.

Nanny followed Billy and Baby into the garden looking worried, as if children weren't safe there. She always wore a little apron when she cooked and she kept twisting this in her hands. 'You're such a good little boy, Billy. We look forward to your visits so much. You won't forget that, will you?'

Why would he forget it? They always visited Nanny. He looked at the grown-ups' faces; all worried faces, but they didn't say anything about worry.

Then Uncle Ted came up the garden path wearing a soldier's uniform with huge black boots.

'Uncle! I want to tread on your boots. Walk me on your boots!'

Uncle Ted let Billy put one foot on top of each of his hard boots and they walked down the garden together. Billy couldn't stop giggling.

'Have you f-finished for today?'

He knew Uncle Ted had joined the Territorial Army ages ago and had to learn all about fighting. Billy pulled him further down the garden, while Nanny and Mother went inside to make tea.

'Can you show me all your fighting things? Have you got a gun, a sword or—?'

'Billy, I'm off to a training camp somewhere secret.'

'Ooh, su-per. Will you have tents? Are you c-coming back?'

'Of course, afterwards. Don't know how soon. If there's a war, I'll be called for, but I'll be training with chums I know. That'll be topper, won't it?'

Billy looked at the hard earth where he and Uncle had played kick ball. The war was Abroad. He didn't want Uncle Ted to go to it. It wouldn't be topper if he went away for a long time. 'I don't want you to go to the war. Can't you stay here and just practice war?'

Uncle Ted ruffled his hair. 'I've practised all I can. Come on, let's see what cakes Nanny's got for us. I can see she's bringing them out here.'

Dad was putting two wooden tables on the concrete part of the garden. Mother carried the tray of tea and Nanny followed with the plates and cake.

'Isn't it nice to be outside in the sunshine?' Mother said pouring the tea.

Grandad got everyone a deckchair and they admired the blue sky and warm weather.

'Has to come to an end sometime,' said Dad, as more planes

passed overhead. *Dost thou love life? Then do not squander time, for that's the stuff life is made of,* Benjamin Franklin.'

Grandad frowned and passed round the cakes. 'American, wasn't he?'

'Thought we were thinking of war, not loving life,' said Uncle Ted.

Then everyone turned to talking about his trip. It was a long time to wait while Uncle answered all their questions, but as soon as he could, Billy asked him to show him his marching, which he did, up and down the garden very smartly.

Mother giggled and Dad said, 'Ted, you'll soon be very sick of that! Come and eat your cake.'

Uncle Ted grinned. 'I'm nearly a professional, y'know, Sis.' He looked proud of himself, but Nanny turned to Mother with a sad, worried face. 'I don't know what I'll do if he has to go abroad.'

Grandad put his arm round Nanny and said, 'Perhaps it'll all be settled and over before Ted's finished his training. Storm in a teacup. The Hun won't want a go at us again, not really. Too busy where he is, the devil.'

'Chamberlain's got it in hand,' said Dad.

'We hope. Meanwhile we're off to proper camp,' said Uncle Ted, coming back for another cake. 'It won't be for long and makes a change from work.'

Dad nodded grimly, pulling Billy away from Uncle Ted's arm. 'Let your uncle eat his cake in peace.'

Uncle Ted laughed. 'Won't get this at camp, mother's cooking, eh? Or the taking it easy.' He looked at Mother and Dad on their deckchairs. 'I'm glad you were here for me to say cheerio, just in case we get sent straight off after camp to collar Hitler for you.'

Billy said, 'I've heard of H-Hitler. He's the war. He's got a horrid n-name, a hitting name.'

Dad put a hand over Billy's mouth and carried on talking to Ted. 'I'm not in favour of war but if it does come to it, I have to wish you all the best. *It's a great life if we don't weaken,* John Buchan.'

'You're a case, Herbert. Did John Buchan, whoever he was, face the Nazis? All your sayings! I'll try to remember some when I'm on the march, ha-ha. Now— time for the off.' Uncle Ted stood up and dusted down his smart uniform trousers.

'Good luck with camp, Ted,' said Mother. 'Rather you than me.'

'Hope the grub's good, that's all.' Uncle Ted went into the kitchen, where Nanny packed him up a fruit cake to go in his kitbag.

Billy followed. 'Do you want to take my half-crown in case you don't have enough food or guns?'

Nanny gave him a hug. 'The army will feed him well, Billy.' she said. 'That's the least they can do after your Uncle doing his drill three times a week all this time. No, your half-crown is to buy yourself something nice, if you— Well, for later.'

Uncle Ted said, 'You know what? That half-crown needs a shilling to go with it. But mind you don't spend it yet, Billy boy. Save it for some special time, good or bad,' and he pushed both coins into Billy's pocket. He took him by the shoulders. 'Listen, Billy. Whatever happens to you, make it fun, right? Keep your chin up,' and he winked twice. Billy tipped up his chin and tried to copy the wink, but Uncle didn't smile.

By then, the grown-ups were all standing in the hall. Billy stood where he was. He had a lot of money, for nothing. He hadn't done any jobs. Things felt important but not nice, not safe.

Grandad followed Uncle Ted out of the front door and pushed it behind him so no-one heard what he was saying.

Billy saw Nanny make a face at Dad. 'He takes it hard, seeing Ted go off at this point. Took him such a time to get over his own service in the Great War. You were lucky you just missed it, Bert.'

'I had the contemplation. And remember my father copped it.'

Billy hadn't seen Dad's contemplation. Where was it kept? It might be bigger than Mr Durban's sabre. He'd ask Dad when he could.

Nanny and Mother went out to Uncle Ted, and Billy waved from the window as he marched down the road with his haversack. It was ever so big.

After that, Mother spent a long time upstairs with Nanny. Grandad shook his head at Dad. He gave Billy some dinky cars to play with, while he and Dad listened to the wireless in the other room.

When Mother came downstairs again, Dad got up to go. Nanny

and Grandad gave Billy a specially hard hug, and Nanny said again, 'Don't forget us, will you?'

He shook his head. Nanny was a puzzle. Why would he forget them? It was only a week till next Sunday.

Then Dad wanted to go on to Uncle Frank's. They didn't normally do this on a Sunday. He shouldered a heavy bag he was taking with them. Mother put her felt hat on and sighed. Dad said, 'Look, Marcia. It's going to be the last time for one of us.'

'Indeed,' said Mother, pressing the long cruel pin through her hat brim.

Billy tried to look as if he hadn't heard. Who was going there for the last time? He pretended there was hop-scotch on the pavement as Mother and Dad walked along in front of him with the pram.

He heard Dad say, 'You mustn't worry, Marcia. Even apart from exemption, I reckon they won't call our age group up. They're taking all the youngsters first. And if they start on civil servants, Frank should still be all right. He's thirty-nine.'

Billy looked at his feet with a secret smile. Grown-ups didn't usually let you hear how old they were. And now he knew.

When they got to Uncle Frank's, Billy pretended Baby wanted to sit outside. He stayed by the front door, 'I'll watch over the pram while you're indoors, Mother.'

Kenneth usually stayed inside, drawing, so outside he'd be safe from Kenneth's jabs. It was best to be careful when the grown-ups would all be talking and not notice boys.

'Looking out for his baby sister,' Aunty said. 'Aaaah', and Mother looked pleased with him too, but Uncle Frank muttered to Dad that Billy wasn't normal.

Kenneth moved his mouth down like an old man, nodded hard and wiggled a finger at his head. He followed Billy into the yard, arms folded.

Billy turned on him, 'Your D-dad is thirty nine.'

'He's not.'

'He is. I heard D-dad tell Mother.'

Kenneth tried to give him a Chinese burn, but Billy ran to pick Baby up and held her in front of him. Mother looked out of the window to check on her, so Kenneth smiled at Baby and stepped away. 'You wait,' he muttered.

Billy said, 'This w-will be the l-last time here, for one of us.'

Kenneth looked at him, frowning. Billy knew he was cross not to be the first to know something. He opened his mouth, but they were called into tea just then. Billy let Kenneth take the best biscuits without saying anything. It didn't matter if today was the last time.

After tea, Dad collected the heavy carrier bag from where he'd left it in the hall. It was full of stores. 'I'm just going to fill a shelf in your Anderson, Frank.'

'Obliged, I'm sure,' Uncle sniffed, but looked pleased.

'That's kind of you, Bert,' said Aunty, 'but let's hope we won't need any of it.'

The side door swung to behind Dad and Uncle clapped his hands. 'Let's have a concert to brighten our spirits. Good practice for us. They'll be no singers on the wireless, you know, if we have a war. Those stage people'll have to go and fight like the rest. Then we'll have to do our own entertaining; no wireless programmes. There'll just be war announcements to listen to, I bet.'

Mother shuddered. 'There's not going to be a war. Stop it, Frank.'

Aunty said, 'We won't think about it now. I thought this was to cheer us up, Frank? I have to bear up over my own tragedies, without worrying over war. Come on, I'll go first.' She stood up and sang *Roses of Picardy* all the way to the end, until they felt better.

Then Mother did a lovely dance, the frills on her skirt flapping along with her sleeves.

'Ooh, hoo,' said Uncle, clapping his beefy hands, 'What a mover! Think what Bert is missing!' As he stood up, the table wobbled.

'Perhaps we should have waited for him,' said Aunty.

'He'll come in a minute. Now it's my turn.' He stood beside the glass-fronted cabinet, one hand on its side and started talking in a wireless voice. 'I will recite. I shall entertain you with *The Lion and Albert,* a cautionary tale for certain young people who go to the zoo.'

Billy sat still. That was him. He'd gone there last year. Kenneth hadn't ever been to the zoo.

Uncle started off in a very strange voice, so the mothers giggled behind their hankies, although it was a very sad tale and the boy got eaten at the end.

'Clever, clever,' said Kenneth. 'It all rhymed, Daddy. I liked it ever so. It was the boy's fault he got eaten, wasn't it?'

'It was, Kenneth. Quite right, sonny.'

'Your turn, sweetheart,' said Aunty straightening the points of his shirt collar. Take your slippers off and stand on the little table where we can see you best.

Kenneth stood in his socks with folded hands. He closed his eyes and began. He could sing lots of songs. He sang the first part of *Oh for the wings, the wings of a dove.* Some of the notes went up terribly high.

Aunty and Mother sighed with their heads on one side. 'Ohhh, Kenneth,' they breathed. 'Perfect. Such feeling.'

He sang again. Kenneth was a horrible boy, but his singing was ever so good. Everyone clapped hard.

'Billy next,' said Aunty.

He backed to the far wall. 'I c-can't.'

'What do you mean, boy?' said Uncle. 'We're all doing something. Right?'

'I haven't g-got anything.'

Mother said, 'I don't think Billy's good at that sort of thing. I can't think I've ever heard him do anything.'

'Then he'd better recite, and answer questions. Make him aware of his own voice. Or v-v-voice, ha ha ha.'

Kenneth tittered. Mother tutted.

Uncle Frank glared, 'Start!'

Billy managed a verse of *The Grand Old Duke of York,* but couldn't answer the questions, and all his Don't Knows were d-d-don't kn-knows. Kenneth turned his eyes up to the ceiling.

'Never mind, Billy.'

Aunty looked at him kindly. 'Why do you stutter, dear?'

Billy shrugged because *Don't Know* was a very stuttering thing to say.

Mother said, 'Ignore the stutter, I do.'

Aunty looked at his shrug. 'He doesn't really know why he does it, Marcia.' She sounded kind but looked across at Kenneth, smiling fondly at the boy who never stuttered.

Mother sighed. 'You're seven, Billy, not a baby. You can't talk like one.'

Uncle said, 'I've tried to toughen him up. Marcia. You want to take him in hand, you and Bert, with that stutter. Or he'll be hammered when he gets to—' Billy wandered into the hall before they said any more about him.

Kenneth followed. 'Stutterer!'

'Don't even know what it means.'

'Stuttering, Billy, is when you say K-K-Kenneth instead of speaking properly.'

'I d-don't.'

'You do. You're doing it now. And you've got to stop it. Daddy says so. You mustn't stutter. It sounds soppy and you might get thrashed.'

Billy stared at Kenneth's neat lips. He nearly told him he had a sabre, but that wasn't true. Yet. He had to get one, it was the magic he needed. 'I'm g-going in the g-garden,' he called to the grown-ups.

Before he could go anywhere, the side door opened and Dad joined them.

'We've just done a concert, Uncle,' Kenneth chirped.

Uncle Frank stretched out his long legs. 'Yes. 'fraid you've missed your chance to perform, Bert. But you need to take note. This boy,' and he leant forward to pat Kenneth on the head, 'sings like an angel,' but this one,' he poked Billy in the chest, 'can hardly get a word of a rhyme out without stuttering. Show him, boy.'

Billy looked over his shoulder at Mother in his most pleading way, but she shrugged.

Dad said, 'Don't you want to show me your rhyme, Billy?'

He shook his head.

'Seriously, Bert, listen.' Uncle Frank leant forward. 'Billy! Recite it again.'

Billy stared hard at Mother.

She tipped her head on one side and spread her hands on her lap. 'You'd better try, Billy.'

He looked at Dad, who gave him one brisk nod.

Kenneth was leaning against the cabinet, one foot crossed over the other. He put the tip of his tongue out.

Billy stared hard at the green zig-zags on the carpet. 'The g-g-grand ol' D-duke of York, he h-had t-ten thou-.'

Before he got very far, Dad said loudly, 'Stop that rubbish! Just slow down and speak properly.' He turned to Mother. 'You've got to see to this stutter before— the other.'

Another? Was there a stutter somewhere else?

Mother leaned back in her chair and stretched an open hand towards Dad. 'What am I supposed to do?Aren't there more pressing things,' and she pointed to something in the newspaper.

CHAPTER ELEVEN

August 28th 1939. ***Plea to country towns. Accommodation for thousands needed, should war not be averted.***

They were just finishing breakfast when the door-bell rang. Mother went out to answer it. Billy heard Mr Durban's voice.

'Good morning, Marcia. Sorry to come early. I wanted to catch Billy before he—'

Mother held up a flat hand. 'Thank you, Peter. That will be good if you have Billy for a bit. You can imagine how much I've got to do now. Billy, you'd love to go to Mr Durban's house for a bit, wouldn't you?'

Billy nodded hard. Soon he was skipping down the road with Mr Durban, counting the windows where the blackout looked torn.

'Hmm. I shall have to make a few evening calls, I see.'

When they got to his house, Mr Durban called Angela. Then they all sat round with fizzy lemon and Mrs Durban's nicest cakes. It was almost like a birthday.

Afterwards Mr Durban took Billy into the living room on his own. He pulled out a book with a green cover and gave it to him. It was about heroes. There was a strong-looking boy on the front cover pulling a boat ashore. 'You keep this. I read it a lot when I was a boy. A lot. It's all about people who have done brave things. Those stories made me try to be brave. Now you can read about them. I'd like you to have it, if you go away.'

Go away? Perhaps he would be a soldier one day and then he'd need the book. It was a super one. 'Th-thank you, sir.' He held the book carefully. 'I'd like to b-be a hero.'

Mr Durban put an arm on Billy's shoulder and said, 'You will be, in your own way. But not just yet, God willing.' He pulled him nearer. 'I'll tell you something. You know, Billy, I'd have liked a son. A boy just like you.'

'Really, t-truly, sir?'

'Indeed. Just like you. And if I had a son I'd share this secret.' He bent down with his face near Billy's. 'Our King has to speak really carefully because he has a stutter.'

Billy looked at him hard. 'The *King* has?'

'Yes. You see, you're not the only one. The king has to practise, you know. He has to think before each word he speaks. The trick is, you have to watch out for the words that make you stutter, and avoid them. Choose words which start with a different letter.'

That was such a good idea. But what words could be instead of 'Yes' or 'No'? Those were the words he seemed to say most. Bother. It was a nuisance. But the stutter didn't seem to come so badly when he was with Mr Durban.

Angela put her head round the door. 'Shall I play with Billy, Daddy?'

'Yes, off you go, you two. Have some fun.'

Angela shut the door behind them and took Billy upstairs. She leaned on the banisters, looking at him.

'I know what you want to see. The sabre.'

He could hardly breathe. 'Yes please.'

'You have to kiss me first.'

She was like the girls in the big playground.

'Ugh.'

'Go on, you have to, or I won't let you see it,' Angela leant forward.

He couldn't miss seeing the sabre again. He breathed in and kissed Angela on one soft cheek. Actually, it wasn't awful. It made him think of marshmallows and that's how she smelled. 'Right. I've done it. Can I see the sabre now?'

'We have to wait until they go into the kitchen. Daddy's going to put wood shutters on the windows.'

Once they heard the voices move, they crept downstairs and into Mr Durban's study. The curtains were closed against the bright sun, so the small room felt dark and mysterious. There was a musty smell from the velvety chair, which Billy crouched beside in case someone came in. Angela put one hand inside the cupboard doors and brought out the sabre. She pushed one curtain a little to the side. A shaft of golden light hit the blade as she drew it out and laid it carefully on the desk.

'Can I touch?'

'No, just look. I'll be for it if you cut yourself.'

'I want to hold it. Please. I'll be ever so careful.'

He turned and lifted the sabre by its knobbly handle, catching the light on its dangerous tip. A snaky shudder went through him and he put it down again.

He was going to tell her that Mr Durban wanted a son, but stopped himself. Angela might be cross. She couldn't help being a girl. He stayed staring at the wonderful thing. 'Did you tell your father he c-could leave it to me when he gets old and dies?'

'No! Why should I? I don't want him to die. Here, give it to me, that's enough.' She slid the sabre back and closed the cupboard doors.

They went back up into her bedroom and she talked about secret things. He kept his finger on his lips. Then she said, 'Now you can tell me boy things.'

Angela was nice, so surely she wouldn't tell on him. He told her all about Kenneth, the beastly things, the gas mask, the Chinese burns and the tale-telling.

She listened all through without fidgeting. 'He sounds a meanie. Never mind, Billy. You might not have to see him for some time. Come and see what's happening in our garden.'

They ran downstairs. The drone of voices filtered through the lounge door as they went out to the one square of grass. All the rest was turfed up into a heap ready for the Anderson shelter, which lay in pieces.

Billy put a foot on the sheet of corrugated iron. 'My G-Grandad's built one of those, but we haven't g-got one. What are they t-talking about anyway?'

'Evacuation.'

'What's that?'

'Haven't they told you?' She put an arm round him. 'Why do you think I let you see the sabre again? Why did I need a kiss? Evacuation means going away. Children have got to go. The government are sending us to the country, to be safe.'

Was she playing the pretend game? He didn't answer her.

When Mr Durban took him home, it was still warm, still nice and light. He talked about the heroes book, which made Billy long to read it. He didn't say anything about evacuation.

Was Angela telling him stories, like Kenneth always did? But perhaps she believed it. Girls might not always get things right.

CHAPTER TWELVE

August 29th 1939. ***Hitler "only desires Danzig and a small section of the Polish Corridor".***

A thin brown envelope came in the post. Mother showed it to Dad. Then Dad told Billy to get his gas mask out. It sat on a dusty shelf in the parlour. Everyone had stopped carrying them since spring.

'You'll need to carry this everywhere from now on, Billy.' Dad put an arm on Mother's shoulder. 'The time has come, Marcia.'

Billy looked at the cardboard box. No-one had been bothering about it lately. It would be a nuisance always having to carry it. School holidays were very nearly over. Would he have to take the box into the playground? How could they play football?

Dad walked him into the garden where they blew the dust off the gas mask box. 'You haven't forgotten how to put this on, Billy, have you?'

Billy shook his head. He waited while Dad filled his pipe. A train whistled in the distance. Dad struck one match after the other before his pipe got going. He didn't say anything. Perhaps he was choosing a saying.

Billy looked up at the sky. It had clouded over, but he could still feel the sun.

Then Dad told Billy about evacuation and it was just like Angela had said. There was going to be danger and children had to be kept safe by going away. Dad nodded at him, sucking at his pipe.

'Go away? On my own?'

'You'll go with the school. We've put your name down.'

'But what about you and Mother? And Baby?'

'Mother will be evacuated too, with Baby. They'll go together; not with your school. That's just for school children. The teachers will look after you.'

'But Dad, what about you? If Hitler comes, you'll have to fight, or you'll be sent to Wandsworth prison.' In his mind's eye he could see all the little windows with their criss-cross bars and he imagined Dad's face, peering from one of them.

'No, no, Billy. Other men are needed as soldiers, younger ones, like your Uncle Ted. I'm needed for my work here, well, various places just as usual. I'll hardly be in London at all.'

Billy remembered Mother saying they just wouldn't be here if there was war. They still didn't have an Anderson shelter.

They walked around to the side path, some way apart. Dad lit his pipe and leant on the front wall. A lorry trundled past the top of the road. It was full of soldiers looking out of the back, shaded by the canvas. There were rucksacks beside them stuffed full.

'Is Uncle Ted in a lorry like that? He hasn't come back from camp.'

'No, he's joined his regiment. He's more trained than other young men, so he'll be needed.'

'Nanny gave him fruit cake for his kit-bag.'

'I expect he had to pack all sorts of things. Like you will when you're evacuated. Quite soon now.'

Billy stood looking at the house, his bedroom window. So that's why they'd given him money. He was going away, just like Uncle Ted.

'What's quite soon?'

'Two days.'

'That's the day after tomorrow!'

Dad gave a nod and puffed at his pipe.

Billy's arms ached, although he hadn't been carrying anything. He rubbed them, his arms crossed in front of him. 'I'll take my heroes book. Can I take my toys?'

'One small toy.'

The smallest toy he had was his whizzer, but it would be better if he could have one of his aeroplanes to go with him. He waited for Dad to tell him more but the only sound was the drone of aeroplanes.

Dad puffed on his pipe again. A little wind blew the smoke upwards. Billy watched it go away to the heavens. Dad zipped his green ribbed cardigan right to the collars, although it was still warm. He sighed, then knocked the black bits out of his pipe onto the grass. He gestured to Billy to go on indoors.

Mother had made a Shepherd's Pie. They sat round the table and Billy passed the salt. There were tinned peaches afterwards with evaporated milk. It was ever so nice, but no-one was saying much except Baby, who was doing all the grizzling for them.

Dad had to say goodbye the following night. His holiday was over and the Courts would be sitting in Kent. He said he wasn't sure when he'd be able to see them next. Mother was in her prettiest dress. It went in at her middle and out lower down. It was the one she used to wear to her dances. Dad stroked his hand down her back. Mother put Baby in his arms, then her head on his shoulder.

Billy heard him say quietly, 'You're not one of these women who make a fuss. You're used to me being away, so this is not that different. Think, some time in the country will be good for the children's health.'

He hugged them, put Baby down to crawl around, then placed a hand on Billy's shoulder. 'You'll need to be brave and sensible, Billy. Remember that. Do as your teachers tell you and things will be all right. I'll see you Christmas-time, probably.'

'Christmas! Am I staying away right up until Christmas?'

Baby was hugging Dad's legs, but he didn't seem to mind.

'Nobody knows much of what's ahead, Billy. Evacuation is safest, better for you.'

Billy tucked his chin down, waiting for Dad to change his mind, but the large hand just came down on his shoulder twice more. Pat, pat. 'Goodbye, Billy. Be good.'

Mother stood beside him at the door, Baby holding her skirt. Dad had a suitcase and his briefcase. It was like he was going to war, but he was going away to work as usual. It was Billy who was really going away, Mother too.

Dad walked up the road, turning to wave once. The sky was red behind him. Planes passing in the distance looked like teacher's crosses when he got his sums wrong.

CHAPTER THIRTEEN

Sept 1st 1939. ***Germany Attacks Poland. Many cities bombed, including Warsaw.***

The next morning it was difficult to eat breakfast. Baby was quiet in her high chair. He whispered, 'Baby, I'm going away. Then you are too, but don't worry, you'll be with Mother.' He put her rattle in one sticky hand.

He knew it was time for school but hesitated on the front doorstep, in case the going away wasn't true. Mother handed him his gas mask and his case. 'When you get to — wherever they put you — there's a clean change of clothes inside for the day after tomorrow. Don't forget. There's a packed lunch in there, too. Now, don't worry about anything. The teachers will make sure you're all right, and you'll have some friends with you, I'm sure.'

He looked up and down the road. Surely Dad would come and stop this. Billy had never been away from home. Surely Aunty would never let Kenneth go.

'Is Kenneth being evacuated, Mother?'

'No. Not all children are going. It depends what their parents have decided.'

He scanned her face. So she had decided, and Dad had.

Several children passed his gate carrying their gas masks. 'Watcher Billy! Come on.'

He went towards the front gate. Mother suddenly got hold of him and kissed him.

That was startling. 'Goodbye, Mother.' His feet started moving after the other children. He felt the damp place on his cheek all the way up the road.

Jim caught him up. 'Billy. You got sweets in your bag?'

'Dunno.'

Jim's bag wasn't big. 'I'm staying,' he said.

When he got to the school wall, Billy looked in his bag and saw his heroes book and a bag of barley sugars under the clothes. He was wearing a cap and a mackintosh and he was too hot.

Inside school, everyone crowded into the corridor and there was an awful lot of noise. The tall teacher with long skirts, Miss Johnson, pushed forward to the middle. She clapped her hands. 'Now some of you are excited and others are jittery, but if you keep chattering, you'll miss the instructions when they come. Calm down everyone.'

'Where are we going, Miss?' said Mick.

'No-one knows where they're going, Miss,' said Dick.

Miss Johnson held her hands out wide. She told them that not even the teachers knew.

Mr Hendrick was staying behind. It was because had a stick and was very old. He had a moustache too and it quivered when he shouted at the class. Everyone was noisy until he banged the stick on the floor. The next door classroom quietened too.

In the pause, Mick called out, 'Sir? Sir? Are we going yet?'

'When are we going, Sir?' said Dick.

Just then, Mr Finlay came in and gave Mr Hendrick a big nod.

'Line up, those on the list for evacuation! Quick sharp! No talking!'

'Put your label on,' muttered Jim, 'or they won't know your name.' He stayed sitting down.

Mick had his wicked grin on. 'We're going to swap ours when we get there. No-one will know which of us is which.'

'That's stupid.' Sonia was always sensible. 'Both of you are going to need a home, whatever your name is. They're going to find us all homes.'

Homes! Billy hadn't thought of that, only about the going away. He scrabbled in his case and found his label. It had his name, school and address. Silly! He could have told anyone all that anyway.

When the register was taken and everyone checked again, they marched down to the local railway station. The ones with brothers or sisters were allowed to walk with them. Although Mr Hendrick and his stick had stayed behind with the non-evacuees, Mr Finlay from the top class was coming. He taught P.T. in a green vest with words on it, and black shorts so you could see his great muscles move like steam engines, but he told the class he had asthma so he couldn't be a soldier even if he wanted. Jim said he was forty-four, anyway. Forty-four! Too old, so it was good he wouldn't have to go to Wandsworth prison.

A few mothers had run down the road to wave, and some were crying. Some followed them all the way to the station and onto the platform. He knew Mother had to stay home with Baby. He looked around at everyone else. Jim had stayed behind, so had Reg and Andrew. Mother was wrong. His friends weren't with him.

After a while, the train chuffed in. A plume of thick smoke buffeted down the platform towards them. Some older boys cheered.

A guard opened a train door and held it open wide. Billy was going to say Goodbye to the mothers he knew, but they were busy hugging their children and telling them last minute things. A gust of wind blew some smut in his face. The label round his neck flapped up and then back.

He clambered on board alone. There was a great press of knees and suitcases, elbows and excited voices, the chestnutty smell of train smoke. The guard slammed the door shut. Billy was pressed against the carriage wall as heads poked out of the window shouting and waving Goodbye. He saw the hats and waving hands slowly and then more quickly left behind, then found himself sitting in a carriage with Sonia and the twins, John, who was in a higher class, and four girls.

'I'm the oldest,' said John. 'So toe the line, you lot.'

'We won't be gone long, will we?' one of the girls asked. No-one answered.

At first they all looked out of the windows and shouted every time they saw an army truck, some cows, and their first haystack ever.

It was the first time the twins had been on a train. They wanted to climb up to the luggage rack, then they wanted to see what everyone had in their greaseproof paper packages. Their mother didn't seem to have packed them up much. Bill shared his barley sugars with them and John gave them some lemon squash to quieten them down. But soon they were rolling and tussling on the carriage floor.

'It's a good job there's no corridors, twins,' Sonia said. 'Miss would be ever so cross with you and Sir might give you the cane.'

'So what!' said Mick.

'They can't see, so there,' said Dick.

The girls started playing cats' cradle and John buried his head in his comic. Billy waited for a little while in case John finished it and passed it on, but he didn't.

If only Mother had put a comic in his bag. The train was too jolty to read the fine print in the heroes book. The twins were too noisy to think about difficult words anyway and he was glad when John said, 'Let's have our lunch now. It must be time. Anyway I'm hungry.'

'Rath-er' said Mick.

'Grub. You bet.' said Dick.

They all opened their packages and peeped inside each other's. One girl had chocolate biscuits that had melted onto her paste sandwiches.

Sonia turned her nose up. 'Ugh, look at yours!'

'I can't eat them now.'

The twins looked at her, hopefully. They were always hungry.

'I will.'

'Let's have 'em.'

Sonia said, 'You'll have to eat them, Elsie. We're not having anything else for ages and ages.'

Perhaps he ought to give the girl a Bovril sandwich, but he didn't have many. John had lots in his paper bag, so Elsie had a share. Then everyone had to put their paper bags into one big screwed-up bundle, not to leave a mess.

One girl had a paper book and crayons so the girls took it in turns to colour in. The boys said that was cissy and started kicking the girls' seats so that the pencil jogged. The boys had nothing to do. They played paper, stone, knife but John kept winning and the twins said it was a rubbish game.

Some singing sounded from another carriage, *Ten Green Bottles* and *Fire Down Below* so they joined in for a while. Their singing petered out.

Mick said, 'I've finished my drink. Can I have some of yours?'

Dick wasn't having any. 'No-o. You didn't share, why should I?' Then there was more fighting.

'Shut up you twins,' Sonia buffed the nearest one. 'Just our bad luck to get you in our carriage.'

It seemed like a whole day had passed before there was a hoot and the train stopped. Mr Finlay came along the platform, telling them to get off. Billy swung his gas mask from his wrist and looked around. He'd expected fields for miles and miles but there were houses all close together, right by the station. 'Are we at the country, then?' he asked no-one in particular.

No-one answered. Everyone seemed dazed, and for once there was hardly any noise.

A coach stood outside the station. It took them to an empty church hall. It was made of pink brick with a slate roof like a Chinaman's hat. They filed slowly into the hall after Mr Finlay. Even the twins had gone quiet. Inside there were loads of ladies sitting waiting for them and one or two men with big brown boots and rolled-up sleeves. They were looking round at the children, some of them with screwed-up eyes. A few ladies gave out milk and some dull, dry biscuits.

Mr Finlay arranged the school on benches in groups. He told Billy to sit with the oldest children because he was tall. John squeezed up to make room for him.

A large lady with a blue flowery frock sat beside an old whiskery man. They had a list that they showed to the teachers. Miss Johnson was pointing to the smallest children.

'Why are they first, John?' Billy asked.

'That's so that any crying can be sorted out by someone else.'

The older sisters and brothers were allowed to sit and comfort the smaller ones. Everyone else kept still on the benches drinking their milk, while the village people walked around. Billy kept his eyes on them while they chose which child they wanted. He saw them point out little girls with pretty ribbons and small boys who were sitting cross-legged, quietly.

Billy was sitting quietly but he wasn't little. The older children beside him exchanged ideas between each other.

'She's chosen. See, you've got to look small and sweet.'

'But he isn't. I know him!'

'Let's pretend we're brothers and we've got to go together.'

But it didn't work. One of the ladies came past and John got chosen.

'Its 'cos he looks grown up,' said a large boy with messy hair and unlaced boots sitting next to him.

Billy sat up very straight and folded his arms, trying to look grown-up but then a fierce-looking man beckoned to the large boy, 'Reckon you'll put in a good day's work,' so Billy slumped down again to look as small as possible. Mother and Dad wouldn't like it if he went to work instead of to school.

When the village people had the children they wanted they took them off to their homes. It was mostly boys left, apart from two girls holding hands, one very tall and thin and a smaller one with lots of spots. Sonia had gone. He couldn't see anyone he knew, except for the twins. Billy looked at the dry biscuit in his hand. He might as well eat it.

Mr Finlay stood up and said in a loud voice, 'All remaining children line up.' He led the older children, younger ones copied, the twins doing a silly walk behind them. Miss Johnson walked nearby to keep them in order. Billy was left at the back.

They all marched out of the hall and alongside the church where the gravel on the path crunched under their feet. Pieces of pink and blue confetti were trapped between the stones. So funny that a wedding had been there earlier!

As their crocodile walked around the town, both teachers started knocking on doors to see how many children each house could take.

The first houses were strange, made of grey lumpy stones stuck together to make walls, not like brick at all. They were good houses with gardens round them, the soil around the flowers a gingery brown. One garden even had a swing. The door to that one was closed and no-one answered the teacher's knock, but at most of the others the ladies were standing by open front doors and some called out that they'd take one child.

Surely he'd soon be chosen because he was the smartest and had kept himself clean on the journey. The twins kept messing around and they already looked filthy because of rolling around on the platform and under the train seats. It would be ages before anyone chose them. But a farmer passing in his hay cart called over to the teacher, 'They two, Miss, they twins –they look as if a bit of rough won't hurt 'em. I'll take 'em off your hands.' And off Dick and Mick went, laughing as they scrambled up onto the hay cart.

'Yippee!' The cart moved off and they threw bits of hay back at the others.

The crocodile turned up the next road. There were some big houses here, followed by lots of small ones close together. The following road was the same. One after the other, children were taken. Billy watched the grey socks of the boy in front of him sinking lower and lower down his legs.

Then a lady nudged the teacher. 'I'll tak 'im. That ginger one. He reminds me of my son.'

The girl with spotty skin and her thin big sister, were taken up to the next gate. One of the women standing there said 'I suppose I have to take a child, Miss? All right then, but only one; the big one.'

The spotty sister started crying so Miss Johnson held her hand until some people at the house at the end of the road took her in.

'There, Mavis, you're not far from your sister,' Miss Johnson comforted her.

Billy thought how far he was from his sister.

When Mr Finlay led them into the fourth road there were very few children left, and soon there was only one.

Billy gripped his gas mask handle until his fingers hurt. Mother wouldn't like it at all if she knew he was the last to be chosen.

Mr Finlay took his own case into a large house where he was going to stay.

'You go on,' Miss Johnson said. 'I'll see to this last boy.'

'Thanks, Miss Johnson. Don't you worry, young fellow. It won't be long before you're settled in somewhere.'

The long road petered out into the country. They turned uphill to a line of brick houses. They'd already been there.

Miss Johnson sighed. 'We'll have to make the rounds of the streets all over again. I'm sorry. What's your name? Billy? Well, you need to look a bit more cheerful, I think, so that one of these ladies takes you.'

Billy's suitcase banged against his legs. If only he could dump that and the wretched gas mask.

At the bottom end of the town, several rows of very little houses were stacked so close to the pavement that they had no front garden. Front doors opened straight onto the street, but now they were nearly all closed.

'Someone will just have to take a second child,' Miss Johnson said.

And that someone was a girl in a flowered apron that tied all the way round her middle and back again, with a bow at the front. She was only standing at her door because she was minding two little children playing with sticks on the pavement. She didn't look up until Miss Johnson asked her, 'Excuse me, is your mother in?'

Then she blushed and twiddled the hair over her ear, 'I am the mother, Ma'm. Mrs Youldon, me.'

Billy was very surprised she was a mother because he was nearly as big as her and her hair was traily and curly like some of the girls in his class.

Miss Johnson said, 'Oh, I'm sorry. Of course.' Then, for the umpteenth time, she said, 'Good evening. I wonder if you can take this nice lad?'

'I've got a lad already, Ma'am.'

In the gloom of the house, a closely freckled boy stood behind her door, his hands hanging by his sides, his eyes bulging.

'But you can manage another?' She put down her bags and took out her purse.

'I suppose,' said Mrs Youldon, holding out her hand.

Miss Johnson placed some money in it.

Mrs Youldon looked at it. 'Oh.'

'It's only eight and six for the second child.'

'It's not a lot if they're going to need clothes too.'

'The mothers should be sending on any extra clothes the children need. This child has a mackintosh as you see.'

'More than my own'll ever have,' Mrs Youldon said.

Miss Johnson picked up her bags again. 'There now, Billy, so you're all right. Take your case indoors. I'll be off back for my tea, then.' Billy heard her sigh with relief as she turned away.

Mrs Youldon looked at Billy and then at Miss Johnson's back. It was a worried look but she said, 'Come in, then. I'm sure you're a nice boy. There's another here to keep you company.'

She must surely have the smallest home in the village. The front door opened straight into the living room where there was only a cupboard door with wooden slats, a bench and a battered easy chair, a hearth with a stove and a pot on it. A door at the back led into a scullery, and then out into a thin yard. Behind the easy chair was a twisty staircase. There were no mats on the slate floor, no carpets.

The other boy had gone to sit on the bench, his suitcase and gas mask beside him. He sat with round shoulders, doing nothing. Billy hovered just inside the door.

'Come on in, dear. What's your name? This is Alan, do you know each other?'

The boy didn't look up. Billy shook his head miserably. The two very little children scampered back in, then stood and stared at the newcomers. He remembered the Mary Mouse books at home, and all the tiny mouse children with their matching shorts and skirts and the stick legs beneath. He managed a wavery smile. They hung together and looked at their mother.

She put her arms round them and pointed. 'This is Billy and here's Alan. They're both going to live with us for a bit.'

The little children stared with big eyes. Billy fidgeted. He and Alan looked suddenly very big. The ceiling wasn't far off.

Mrs Youldon smiled. 'Billy, these are my little ones, Tim and Sally. They'll get used to you.' She set about folding some rags that were on the end of the bench. Billy saw that one of them was a sort of shirt. She went to the scullery and brought out a plate of bread.

'I'll have to get their tea now. I hope you've been fed at the centre, because I haven't got that much tea for you. We were told you'd have had your meal.'

Alan took out a tin of corned beef from his case and handed it over. Billy remembered his and got it out. He was starving. She beamed and put the tins on a shelf above the stove. She took a damp rag and wiped her children's hands, then perched them on the bench with a hunk of bread.

'You boys go up and put your cases away.'

They looked at each other carefully. Alan led the way up the narrow stairs. The room at the top had a double mattress on the floor and a large chest with Mrs Youldon's skirt on it. Next door there was a cupboard with a camp bed squeezed in it. Billy stared at it.

Alan plumped down on the bed. It made a creaky, metally noise and wobbled. He sat with his feet firmly on the floor. 'You shouldn't be here. This home was meant for just me.'

'Mm,' said Billy, wondering where to put his case. Alan was lucky he hadn't been the last child to be chosen.

They sat still for a bit, feeling their way into the silence. The room was so very small, there was nothing to look around at.

'Where's the bathroom?' Billy said after a bit.

'Don't know. Let's go and ask.'

Mrs Youldon was watching her children eat. She took the boys into the scullery where they passed a broom, a mop and a hip bath hanging on a peg, an airer swinging over their heads. She pointed down to the bottom of the thin yard. 'That's the privy,' she said, pointing to a little hut with a roof, 'and you can wash here.' A half bar of carbolic soap waited on the corner of the large sink. 'We'll need another towel out here. I don't suppose you've brought one?'

They both shook their heads. Billy realized there wouldn't be an airing cupboard full of them, like at home.

He hesitated, then went down the yard. There was a bit of grass on both side and a picket fence to divide them from the neighbours. Then there was a very little rickety shed thing. He looked back at Mrs Youldon.

'It's all right, dear. We don't have to share the privy with anyone.'

He swallowed. He hadn't even thought about that. He went in. It was nearly black inside. A large wooden seat had a bucket beneath it and a tin potty. That must be for the little ones. The floor was earthy, and damp. Strips of newspaper were looped on a string.

He came back, making a face at Alan, and washed his hands in the scullery sink.

A large tin bucket stood beside him filled with clothes. Mrs Youldon came to the doorway with her children's dirty plates.

'What ab-bout in the dark, Mrs Youldon?' He hadn't seen any light bulb in the privy. He looked up, and there weren't any light bulbs in the room either.

'I keep a torch by the back door, don't worry. Candles just blow out.'

'Candles!' said Alan.

'Candles for indoors. And I'll put a potty under the bed so you don't need to go outside at night.'

Billy kept his eyes on the floor. There was no way he was going to use a potty like a baby.

'Now then, cheer yourselves up. You both got long faces. Fancy some tea?'

'Yes please!'

She busied herself at a cupboard and enamel table top.

When her back was turned, Billy muttered to Alan, 'I haven't eaten anything since those biscuits at that hall place, have you?'

'No, and I didn't have much packed lunch. Teacher said we were having our main meal at tea-time.'

It seemed like days ago since Billy had opened the greaseproof paper for his cheese sandwiches on the train. Since then, he'd made the long walk round the town twice. He held his stomach and doubled over, looking at Alan, who began to grin. Now they were friends.

Mrs Youldon called out, 'Here you are boys. Come and eat up.'

But she just put the tail end of a loaf on the bench with a small tomato each. Billy nudged Alan and frowned. Alan frowned back.

After they'd eaten everything, Alan was the braver and asked if there was anything else. Mrs Youldon made a face and said she hadn't known she'd be having two extra and it was time to play outside.

They wandered out together and looked at the ginger hills far beyond the houses. There wasn't a wall anywhere to sit on, so they just stood. Billy twiddled his fingers. Mrs Youldon was very poor. She hadn't enough food. Her clothes didn't fit properly, there weren't any cupboards and the little children hadn't got socks on. Dirt poor, Dad would have called it. He remembered Angela's voice, 'Evacuation.' At first, he hadn't known what that meant, that he'd be in a dirt poor house, no garden, no table, no bedroom, no toys, not enough to eat and not even a bathroom. They hadn't said.

But late that night, squashed up against each other, it was Alan who was crying and wanting to go back home.

CHAPTER FOURTEEN

September 2nd 1939. *Outcry over Poland. German invasion forces penetrate further.*

The breakfast porridge was grey but they both ate every speck. Mrs Youldon cleared their plates and told them to play out.

'Out?' Billy started. She hadn't even told them where they were. How far could they go, and how would they find their way back?

'Is the park and swings near here?' said Alan.

'Park? There isn't that sort of thing. Not here.'

They both stared at her.

She laughed, 'Londoners! There's a field by the school. Up the big road and turn round right. And much further on there's some nice woods with a stream. If you're good, I'll take you up there one day. Timmy and Sally like that place, don't you?' She turned to the little faces, with their pink noses and bright eyes. 'You boys run about and enjoy yourselves. There'll probably be school Monday.'

'School!' Alan nudged Billy. 'Do you think we'll go together?'

Billy felt his tummy lurch. He looked at Mrs Youldon. 'Well, I don't know, dear. We'll be told by the billeting officer, I expect,' she said as she took the dishes to the scullery. 'The school's not far. If you want, take the ball.' It was a sad-looking rubber thing with nicks and scratches all over it.

Billy saw the little mouse faces looking at him and he smiled. Timmy smiled back, while Sally hung her head. She had wisps of pale hair that hung round her ears. Timmy pushed a little wooden car along the bench just a few inches. It only had three wheels. Billy wondered who would mend it. He might have a go himself.

'Come on,' said Alan. They nodded and made for the door.

'Just a minute, boys. Take Timmy and Sally with you. They'll want to play. There's some other boys and girls in this road, so you can make some new friends.'

Did she really mean the little ones could play outside without their mother? Shouldn't Sally be in a playpen? But Billy could see there wasn't anything like one here.

Mrs Youldon moved to the scullery and poured water and washing soda into the sink.

'Let's explore,' Alan said.

Billy frowned, but Mrs Youldon said, 'Yes, perhaps that's best this first time. Find your way round the village. You can play with the little ones later. She took Sally's hand as they went outside.

They wandered from lane, to road, then another road where one or two houses were bigger, some with nice gardens. One had a thatched roof, very strange, so they stopped to stare at it. A cat came down the path, then a small, nearly bald person.

Alan nudged Billy and whispered. 'Gosh, it's a girl with hardly any hair.'

She was waving. 'Billy!' she shouted out, almost joyfully.

He couldn't work out for a moment how this awful thing knew his name. But as she got near he saw it was Sonia. Sonia, with no curls or ribbon, just tiny stubs of hair like a convict in Desperate Dan. He gawped at her and she began to cry.

'They cut my hair off in case I had nits,' she said. 'I can't go to school like this.'

The boys both said, 'No.'

Billy said, 'G-go in, go indoors. St-stay in bed when it's school day and say you've got a headache.'

Alan didn't know Sonia but he added helpfully, 'Ask to go to bed early, so they'll believe you in the morning.'

She started to say something, but a large lady with her hair in a bun came to the door and called, 'Sonia! Are you talking to rough boys?'

They moved off, just in case the woman searched their hair. Billy risked a small wave to Sonia.

'Gosh!' he said to Alan when they were at a safe distance. 'S-Sonia looks awful. She's got curls really, you know.'

'She hasn't now!'

'We sh-should rescue her.'

'Not likely— we don't want to be caught! That woman might be a witch. Let's go back.'

They ran faster and round a corner back to their lane. The little ones were hovering at the door. It looked as if they'd been waiting for Billy and Alan all that time. Billy ran forward and took their hands.

'Swinging?' Timmy said.

Billy followed Timmy's glance and at the end of the lane, children of various sizes were swinging round a tree at the end of a short rope.

Billy and Alan stood watching, wondering if this was allowed. 'C'm on,' Timmy pulled at his hand.

'Coming?' Billy asked Alan. They wandered down towards the game. Timmy stood behind the line of boys and Sally sat down on the side of the lane on the hard mud. No-one stopped her. 'She'll get grubby,' Billy muttered.

'S'pose Mrs Youldon doesn't mind.'

'Vaccies, vaccies,' two of the bigger girls called over to the boys while the other children stared without smiling.

Alan rubbed one sandal against another. 'I'm not really keen on doing this, Billy.'

'You joining in, or what?' asked a large boy in tattered plimsolls.

They moved forward slowly.

One girl with her thumb against her lips, opened her eyes wide at them, especially at Alan. It was a rude look. She giggled. 'You, Freckles. D'you talk different? Say something.'

'Let's hear you,' said the large boy. 'Go on.'

'All right then. I'm Alan. He's Billy.'

There were shouts and laughter. 'Listen to 'um. Say some more. More.'

'It's you that talks funny,' said Alan.

'Tohks funnee. Yaw!' they all shouted as one, laughing and pointing. 'Vaccies!'

Billy bit his lips. They did sound different from these children. How could they change the way they talked? Suppose they got bullied at their school?

He looked back into Mrs Youldon's door. Did they have to play outside? Fancy allowing her little ones to! Dad would call swinging on the rope 'misbehaving'. You never saw such a thing as rope swinging in Primley Road. Probably a policeman would stop you. He hadn't seen any policemen here, none at all.

The set of four older children minced towards him and Alan, pretending to be them. 'Po-osh, po-osh. Look at youse, then, in youse London clothes.' They were laughing but not in a nice way. One of them had his fists clenched at the ready.

Billy couldn't run back to Mrs Youldon's because the little ones were ahead of him. He glanced at Alan as the four came nearer.

Alan took a step back. Before they could attack, Billy grabbed the rope and swung himself round as fast as he could. Whi-i-zz. It took the breath out of him. He could smell the grass, onions cooking, smoke as he swept past different doors and hedges. All he could see was a mash of children's heads, muddy road, and green banks with the twine of the rope in front of him. He staggered to a stop. The threatening boys had been watching him, but now were making steps toward Alan so he shouted, 'Come on, Alan. It's good fun.'

Alan shook his head.

'Yaw. Freckles can't do it. He's too namby pamby.'

'Alan, you do it,' Billy yelled urgently, throwing the rope towards him.

Alan grabbed it and swung round faster than Billy had.

'Ha! I'm faster'n that,' said the boy who'd spoken first, pushing the threatening four out of the way. 'I'm Big Ronnie, I'm ten. I live next door of yours. See how fast I go.' He swirled round, then pointed to Alan. 'Come on, Freckles, let's see you again then.'

Timmy ran towards the rope, Sally close behind him. She was too little but Timmy wanted to swing. Billy got ready to lift him up to the rope's end, Alan holding it.

This was quite a lot of fun, but it felt very wrong and he could see Alan felt bad about it. 'Playing out' wasn't the sort of play Mother and Dad would like at all. Did it matter, if it was all right with Mrs Youldon? Home seemed very far away.

'Look', said Alan, taking his hands off the rope. A neatly dressed lady rounded the corner and came towards them, holding her gloves. The other children ran off in a group, leaving the little ones squatting on the mud.

Billy stopped swinging the rope. 'Miss Johnson!'

'Billy, I've come to see whether you're all right. Yesterday was a hard time for you, walking all around the village. I'm sorry you were left till the very last.'

The awfulness of it rushed back like a swish of dirty rainwater. His eyes filled.

'But now you've got a new friend here. Is it Alan?'

He nodded.

'How is everything, Alan?'

'All right, Miss. Mrs Youldon is nice. But there isn't much to eat and we have to share a bed.'

'And there's n-no b-bathroom,' Billy choked back his tears.

Miss Johnson bent down to them. 'I'm afraid that's something you'll have to get used to. Not many of us have proper bathrooms down here. We're all somewhere very different from home. We have to make the best of things, boys. I know you'll try your very best. Now, I'll just go inside and speak to your foster mother. You can wait for me here.'

Billy kicked a ball lying in the mud, and ran after it so that Alan wouldn't notice his tears.

Miss Johnson came out again after a few minutes, a smile on her face. 'Good boys, you've made the right impression. I'm sure there'll be more to eat soon. Just be polite and fit in. We don't want this village to think badly of Londoners, do we? Now there may be church tomorrow, so make your way there when you hear the bells, all right?'

They went back to Mrs Youldon's just as a big girl stepped inside. She had a laughing voice, and a laughing face and a dress that only just covered her knees. 'H'llo, Joan. How is it? I heard you'd got vaccies. H'llo boys. Londoners, eh?'

It turned out that she was Mary, Mrs Youldon's older sister, but she had no children. The two girl-women chatted in front of the broken bit of mirror propped on the high shelf, doing each other's hair and giggling. Mary had a handbag with a lipstick and powder. They took it in turns putting it on. Timmy and Sally hung onto their skirts.

Alan felt in his pocket for his fivestones. He and Billy went through to the back yard and played three contests with their backs to the privy, waiting for the sister to go so they could have their meal.

Alan groaned. 'I'm awfully hungry, are you?'

Billy nodded. He felt empty and miserable inside, deep down. 'Miss said there'd be more food soon. Are you going to tell her?'

'I don't know. Mrs Youldon doesn't seem to have much. If she hasn't got it, she can't give it to us.'

'And it's rude to ask.'

'I'm never hungry at home, are you?'

Billy shook his head. Suddenly he longed for Mother's soggy potatoes and mince with gravy. There was always enough to eat and often he left some on his plate. He didn't tell Alan this because his throat was all achy.

They hovered at the back door and neared the bench when Mary went on her way. Mrs Youldon said, 'Ready for your dinner?'

They nodded hard. 'Yes, please.'

She went into the scullery and found a wet cloth, wiping her hands with it and then the hands of Timmy and Sally.

'Up on the bench, you two.'

'Shall we go in the back and wash our hands, Mrs Youldon?'

She looked a bit surprised, then nodded. They squeezed by the clothes horse which had damp washing on it, and ran the scullery tap. There wasn't any soap now. Alan looked at Billy and shrugged. The bit of towel on the peg was torn and damp. They shook their hands hard, keeping the water drops away from the washing, and squeezed back into the main room, turning hopeful eyes on Mrs Youldon.

She had cooked sausages and some potatoes and cabbage. There was one sausage each and two over. Billy tried not to look at them, but he did, even though his mouth was full of potato, and he saw Alan doing the same.

Soon, their plates were probably the cleanest they'd ever been. Billy put his hands by his sides, politely. He couldn't put his hands on his lap without sitting on a chair and there still wasn't one.

Mrs Youldon had stopped to cut up the little children's food. Sally didn't look as if she was going to finish hers. Such a waste! But no, Mrs Youldon took Sally's leavings onto her own plate. She ate on, so slowly. Then she looked at the boys and said, 'My, you've finished already? I don't suppose either of you would like a little bit more?'

She started at their quick 'Yes pleases', but Billy was almost past caring. She gave them half a sausage each and shared the last small potato between them. It seemed only fair that she had the last sausage herself. 'Keep my strength up, for looking after all you,' she said.

When it was bedtime, they didn't feel at all tired but without electric light it seemed later than perhaps it was. The candle was too low a light to read by although they both pored over Alan's comic.

'This is going to have to last a long time so you're not to touch it when I'm not here.'

Billy nodded. 'Okay. I wish I had some of my Wizards. We could've swapped.'

When Mrs Youldon called up to tell them to sleep they wriggled down sideways, one facing each way.

Alan was cross. 'Shove over, I haven't got room.'

'Neither have I.' He'd fall out if he moved any further. He put one hand on the crumbly wall.

Alan settled down after they'd given each other a few kicks.

Billy's knees pressed against the wall. If only he could stretch out in his own bed and look up at his aeroplane hanging from the ceiling. He thought of it all by itself in the empty room. And he'd never found out where Dad kept his contemplation, or what it looked like, or whether he'd even kept it after the Great War.

CHAPTER FIFTEEN

September 3rd 1939. *"War is declared, but win we will."*

They were playing out, but keeping clean because of going to church later.

Suddenly, Mrs Youldon called out, waving wildly at them. She was with the lady next door who shouted, 'Come here, you boys. It's important.'

Big Ronnie pulled Billy and they all ran forward. His mother pulled them inside her open front door. She had a wireless that was crackling on a sideboard. Faint church bells came from it. Ronnie bent down to tune it better and the bells pealed louder. When he stood up, his round face looked bigger than Mrs Youldon's white one, although he was only ten.

'It's the Announcements, boys,' said Ronnie's mother. 'The eleven o'clock news said we had to listen at eleven fifteen. I told Joan you'd better all come in to hear.'

Mrs Youldon's eyes were wide and her fingers fumbled with the dishcloth in her hand.

They stood looked at the wireless, waiting. Billy held his stomach.

It sounded deathly, the church bells ringing like that. Then the announcer's voice began, sounding like the pounding of a bell itself. Something about an 'ultimatum'. Then he said the country was at war.

A gasp. It was Billy's. It was everyone's.

The announcer was giving out lots of Don'ts. No sounding a hooter or whistle, because they were going to be used for air raid warnings. They'd hear rattles if gas was coming and then they must quickly put on their gas mask. They must always carry them.

Alan clutched Billy's shirt. 'Ours are under the camp bed!'

If they heard those noises, they had to go to the shelter straight away. And schools would be closed all week.

Ronnie let his breath out with a whistle. 'All ruddy week!'

'Shh! You heard the man,' said his mother.

When the announcements ended, the boys stayed standing exactly as they were. Timmy and Sally made no sound. Mrs Youldon put a hand on Alan's and Billy's shoulders. 'That's why you've come here, boys, to be safe from Hitler, see.'

Billy didn't answer. The voice had been so grim, nobody anywhere could feel safe, even in the country.

Ronnie was grinning and nudging Alan. 'No school for a week!'

Mrs Youldon moved to the front door, the little ones moving as one with her. Alan pushed Billy forward. 'Come on.'

Other mothers came out into the lane, saying it was awful. One of them was crying. 'Don't fret. It's not us down here that'll get bombed or gassed,' said another. 'It's them in London'll cop it. That's why we're lumbered with this lot,' and she jerked her head towards Alan and Billy. The women's eyes swivelled towards them.

Alan nudged him and they walked off down the road together. 'We didn't ask to come,' he muttered. 'I wish I was back home,' he turned around to squint at the groups of women sympathising and worrying with each other, 'and not with those lot.' He pulled out two barley sugars from his pocket. Here.'

'Thanks.'

They both sucked hard on the sweets. 'Have you got a brother?'

Billy shook his head. 'Have you?'

'No. We'll have to be like brothers then. Stick together.' He put his arm round Billy's shoulder.

It felt friendly. He said, 'I have got a c-cousin. He comes round my home a lot. But he's really m-mean. And he hasn't been evacuated because Aunty can't do without him. He's always t-taking my toys or giving me Chinese burns, and he b-blames me for everything.'

'Rotten luck.' Alan was on his side. 'But why don't you do something about it? He won't stop if you just put up with it.'

The church organ began distantly. It was quite a nice sound, like God trying to cheer everyone up.

'We've got to go to church,' said Alan. 'Remember, Miss said.'

Billy had forgotten. The barley sugar was all sucked away and he swallowed the last sugary drops. He stroked his throat. It was hurting. Everything was very scary. Surely, everything did have to be put up with?

They turned the corner. Some way down the road, there was Miss Johnson with several children hanging on to her hands or clothing.

'C-come on, Alan. We're all right.'

They ran up to her.

'You listened to the announcements, boys? Good.' She stood in the middle of the group. The faces of everyone turned to her. 'I know it's bad news, children. But, listen. We got you here to safety in time, didn't we? Now we all have to be brave and do our best. There won't be school for a bit because we teachers have to sort out how to fit everyone in.'

'When's air raid drill, Miss?'

'Oh, you'll be told exactly what to do and where to go if we have an air raid. But that's just in case. We're not likely to have one down here. That's why we've all come to the country.' She laughed in a long trill, like a person on the wireless. 'Come along, we're going to church now.'

They walked on in an untidy group as the church came into sight bit by bit between the trees. The bells finished chiming. Mr Finlay stood sternly at the church door. 'No talking.' He stayed watching until they were all inside.

The twins weren't there. John slid into a bench beside Billy and Alan. He'd been billeted in a cottage right by the twins' farm. 'Dick and Mick are milking cows, lucky beggars. They're going to get out of going to church and all sorts of things, I bet.'

Alan nudged him. 'Shh. Vicar's coming.'

The service began and although Alan helped by picking up the right book, Billy couldn't possibly keep up with the words of the hymns - great long words that no-one had ever heard of.

After the Vicar talked of War Being Declared and Being Brave, he talked of Evacuees and welcomed the newcomers, so then everyone began listening. He told them that Life would be difficult for them and for their foster families but that everyone had to get used to different people and different ways.

'We have to shake down,' he said, 'shake down and do our best. We're living in turbulent times. This terrible news that we are at War means we don't know what's coming, but we fear it. It's a time when we all have to make changes and stand together firmly against the foe. Remember, God looks after his own.'

He did go on and on, but he didn't use too many long words. Soon he was saying that he was sure the Evacuees would be good and do their best, and that the locals would be very kind and do theirs, before touching the bible and blessing everyone.

The vicar stood at the door, shaking hands with the grown-ups as they left church. Billy filed out with the other children, looking as holy as he could.

Outside the church gates, the local children thumbed their noses and made rude noises. 'We didn't want you'se here, anyways.'

CHAPTER SIXTEEN

October 18th 1939. *Nazis require all Jews to wear Star of David.*

Billy could hardly remember his old life. On this golden October day he was lying on his bed struggling to remember something, anything about home. He got as far as remembering his father's beard but not his face. He saw a green dress for his mother and the tip-tap shoes she wore for going out. There was a line going down the back of each leg. She'd say, 'Are my seams right, Billy?' and he'd have to put his finger on the line and trace it down to her ankle so that she'd be sure. Where was Mother now? And Baby; he could just about hear her crying and picture her curly hair and dummy.

Billy had written his postcard giving the address after the very first night he'd slept there, but he still hadn't had a reply. Mother must've forgotten him already. She would be busy with Baby and Dad wouldn't have seen any letters if he was away at work.

Other boys got letters in the post. At school, the 'vaccies' boasted about what they got from home, like clothes and paper books. Worst of all, they had food parcels and so did Alan. When Alan passed food over, Billy had nothing to offer Mrs Youldon. Mrs Youldon didn't hold it against him for not having food treats for her. 'It's not your fault, Billy.'

But having no comics or treats to share didn't help him at school. He'd already got thumped 'for speaking dotty.'

'An'when you don't go "d-d-d-", you got a posh voice,' the locals jeered.

But school wasn't really bad. Miss Johnson and Mr Finlay took the vaccies for nature walks when the locals had the classrooms for lessons. That was ever such fun, and afterwards they usually had a story.

It wasn't horrible in the billet. Mrs Youldon was kind. Tim and Annie did everything he said and always wanted to hold his hand and play with him. They made him feel important. Alan wasn't all that good at sharing, but otherwise he was all right. He wasn't mean like Kenneth so they didn't quarrel much at all, and Mrs Youldon didn't do any tellings-off or sendings-to-rooms. She seemed pleased to have big useful boys. They'd collect the wood for the fire, take the wet washing to the washing line, tear the newspaper into strips for toilet paper, empty the washing tub, wipe the little children's hands and keep them amused.

The main trouble was that he was always hungry. Alan was too. But Mrs Youldon was fair. They got the same as her own children and as she did herself. But the food wasn't enough and it wasn't particularly nice except when she opened a tin of corned beef. That came from Alan's mother.

All of this had taken his mind off home and family so far. But now he lay on the camp bed, back from school because of a sick headache, alone until Mrs Youldon got back from her ironing day at The Grange. Timmy and Annie would be playing in that lovely garden while they waited for her. They weren't much bigger than Baby, but she couldn't possibly be left to play on her own. She'd shriek the place down, or touch something dangerous. But perhaps Baby was bigger after all this time. Perhaps she didn't have tantrums any more.

Billy tried hard to remember what he could about 'Before'. He stretched out and waited for his headache to go away. It was a luxury to have the bed to himself. At home, he'd never dreamed that it would ever be different.

He thought about his toys and his bedroom, not just a whole bed but a whole room to himself. His row of books, comics and annuals stood on a bookcase. If only he had them here! They were no use on their own in an empty bedroom. Were his planes still safe in the boxes under his bed? Suppose Kenneth sneaked up there! But no-one was at home now.

If he was at home he wouldn't even mind bedtimes! He remembered Mother saying, 'Into the bath, Billy. Time for bed.' A bath! A bathroom! Here it was a 'sit down wash' on Sundays in the hip bath that hung on a peg in the scullery. He wasn't always the first to use the water, so he hated that too. He missed the bathroom and the lavatory. He'd never get used to the privy at the end of the back yard. And dinners! Home ones now seemed wonderful and he never remembered being hungry there. His stomach was rumbling right now.

He heard Mrs Youldon come through the door. He padded downstairs in his socks. 'I was sent home. Had a headache.'

She pulled raw-looking hands from her pockets to feel his head. 'Been lying down?'

'Yes. But please can I have something to eat? I missed school dinner.'

She turned her mouth down and said, 'That's a bother. I've got broth for tea but only just enough bread.' She felt his head again. 'You're hot. Lie down again. I'll find a bit of porridge, all right? It might make you feel better.' She put a saucepan on the stove and started stirring. 'I can't have you being ill. It's hard enough as it is. When did your headache start, love?'

He thought. It wasn't there when he got up. It must've started at school. 'Miss was putting the date on the board for us to copy and my head hurt then. October 18th, my birthday. I'm eight today.'

'Oh my! Eight! We'll all have to sing the birthday song then, when it's tea.'

His last birthday he'd had presents from everyone. He wouldn't think about that. He'd think about the sabre. He gazed into space and summoned it up. He saw it lying across Angela's open hands, ready for the rightful owner to seize it just as it had been for King Arthur. He could thrust the sabre into the nearest enemy when he was old enough to go to war. He would go instead of Dad.

Mrs Youldon spooned him out some porridge and gave him a spoonful of brown sugar from the bag Alan's mother had sent. 'There, that'll make it taste really nice.' She licked her lips at Billy, and he knew she was enjoying the treat at second-hand. He did that sort of thing sometimes too, like when a mother walked home with her boy from school, her arm around him. He spooned the porridge all up and his tummy stopped rumbling.

Mrs Youldon patted his shoulder. 'Can't have you hungry on your birthday. There. I reckon your headache'll go now.'

~

Saturday was a good drying day. Alan was helping Mrs Youldon hang out the clothes. Most of the children were playing hop-scotch. Billy and Ronnie found a good rut in the lane for rolling marbles along.

They were busy racing them when a slight rumbling noise made them stop. A car was rolling down their lane. They often saw the milk cart and the bread van, occasionally the coal lorry, but not cars. So when this one slowed down right next to him, Billy looked wonderingly at its shiny black wheel hubs.

Ronnie stood up to peer in the window. The driver rolled it down a few inches. 'Young man, do you know William Wilson?'

Billy looked up. 'That's me, sir. I'm William Wilson.'

The man looked down at him disapprovingly and turned to his passenger in the back. 'He's right here.'

She put her head out of the window and gasped, 'Billy!'

At the same moment that he recognized his mother, Billy realized how shocking it was that he was playing in the road, in the earth. He looked at his knees and sure enough they were dirty. His socks were wrinkled around his ankles, like every-one else's. He'd lost his garters long ago.

His mother got out of the car and he stood beside her. He didn't quite like to look up. His face was probably grubby.

It was a moment or two before she spoke, 'Well, Billy, here I am. I hope you've been all right. It's been a long time but now I know where you are.'

She'd come to collect him at last! 'Yes, Mother. Am I going back with you today?' He turned to run inside and gather up his things right away.

She stepped forward, 'No, wait.' She tapped on Mrs Youldon's door. Together, they went indoors.

Mother took just one step, then stayed still at the door. Billy remembered Angela's Dutch doll. Its wooden arms and legs swung forward and back but not sideways, and didn't bend.

She spoke to the back of the room. 'Good afternoon. I'm Mrs Wilson, Billy's mother.'

Mrs Youldon had her hands to her apron, then her mouth. 'My goodness, Ma'am, we didn't expect you.' She brushed the easy chair for Mother to sit down then scuttled over to pull down the washing from over the stove, looking small as a mouse.

'Please don't trouble yourself,' said Mother, looking around, her eyebrows lifted high. 'And you are—?'

'Mrs Youldon, Ma'am.'

'Mrs?' Mother sounded surprised. 'The foster mother?'

'Yes, Ma'am.' She fiddled with a pillowcase, its corners tucked in. Her cheeks had gone pink. 'And these are my little ones, Sally and Timmy.' The two little faces peeped round the scullery door.

'You have children too! My goodness, where do they all fit?' Mother turned her head slightly to one side and then the other, her eyes wide and shocked.

'Yes, Ma'am. But Billy and A-' she blinked a couple of times,'Billy is such a helpful boy. He's been wondering why he hasn't had a letter from you. I said it was probably lost.'

Billy stood at the door half out of sight, licking his handkerchief and trying to clean his hands while Mother explained to Mrs Youldon that sadly Billy's postcard had arrived after she had been evacuated herself with her baby girl. His father found it when he returned home from working away.

'He sent Billy's card on to me and I've come straight away. Such a thing! Baby and I have been living with a vicar's family not even five miles away,' Mother said with a slight laugh. 'Fancy, and all the time Billy was right here.'

Mrs Youldon gaped. 'I must offer you tea, Ma'am but I haven't enough milk. I could run to my neighbour's. It'll only take a minute.'

'Please don't worry. The vicar who kindly brought me is waiting outside.' She opened her velour bag and brought out some jumpers and underclothes. 'I expect you could do with a few more clothes for Billy,' she said.

'Ooh, they're lovely,' Mrs Youldon held them up. 'Shop clothes. They can go under his bed for best.'

'No,' said Mother, looking Billy up and down.

He felt very awkward. The shirt was tattered and the shorts were Ronnie's cast-offs. 'Worn-outs more like', Alan had muttered privately when they'd first been given them.

'These can be worn now. It's getting colder. He'll need them.' She eyed the shirt and baggy shorts. 'Erm— thank you for lending him clothes, but he can give them back now and wear his own. This green jumper is suitable for school and— '

Billy leaned forward, 'But aren't I going with you, Mother? Now you've found me. I can have a wash...'

Mother looked at Mrs Youldon. 'It'll be a while yet, I think.'

Mrs Youldon stood nodding and nodding, still fiddling with her pillow-case.

After giving him a jumper to cover up the shirt, Mother took Billy outside. 'I can't take you with me, Billy, I'm sorry. Safest for you to stay here; although not in this billet if I can help it. Outrageous!'

'I could stay at your billet.'

'But there isn't any more room where I am, there really isn't. The vicarage is overcrowded as it is. They have two teachers and an older child, as well as us. And Baby still has tantrums, so we walk a lot, to keep the noise out of the way. I don't know how I'd manage if I had to get you to a school as well.'

Her voice rose higher and she twisted her gloves between her fingers. 'It's very difficult, being away from home. Very difficult. I've just come to visit you, check that you're well. Now I know where you are, I can come again.'

She put a hand on his front to push the shirt collars under the jumper. 'Dear me, what a mess you look. I'm so embarrassed, but you'd better come over to the vicar and say How do you do.'

She looked all flying hair and worry lines as she went over to the car where the vicar, looking fairly patient, sat behind the wheel.

'This is my son. Forgive his appearance. You would have thought he would have been placed in a home like his own, not a hovel.'

Billy followed her. 'How do you do, sir.'

The vicar shook Billy's hand doubtfully and then looked at his own as if working out how long it would be before he could reach a washbasin. 'Mrs Wilson, let me visit my counterpart in the vicarage here while you and Billy go for a little walk together.' The car purred off, several of the children in the lane running after it.

Mother's eyes went wide and hard. 'I hope you wouldn't do such a thing, Billy. Now, where can we walk?'

'The Grange? It's the nicest place. Mrs Youldon does ironing there.'

'I see.'

'And we had a party there once, with balloons. A man played the piano, we sang songs and they gave us two sherbet dips when it was over.'

'Lucky boy! No such luck for us.'

'You could bring Baby next time you come, Mother?'

'No, dear. It's too difficult with her fidgeting and crying. I can't expect the vicar to bring us by car again. I shall have to come by bus and find someone who'll have Baby for the afternoon. As it is, the vicar's wife is very kindly looking after her this once, while I visit you.'

She looked down at his face. Then she said in a comfortable, strange-but-kind-lady voice, 'I've got an orange for you and some sweets.'

He went to take them, 'Oh thank you.' He hadn't seen an orange since his seventh birthday party. He began to tear off the peel.

'Not here!' Mother said. 'In the street? Eat them when you get back to the hou— to your billet.'

'But then I'll have to share them.' He stopped. 'Perhaps I should. I bet Sally's never seen an orange.'

She didn't answer.

They walked on. He saw his mother looking down at his legs and feet. It was no good pulling up his socks, they only fell straight back down. He could tell she was about to say something.

It was Mother's visit being so sudden that stopped his news from rushing out of him. Words seemed choked in his throat. He didn't even manage to say she'd missed his birthday, or that he was always hungry. He could tell she didn't like the way he looked, or his new home. He swallowed. He was guilty of getting to be a worse boy. He must find something that would please Mother. 'I came top in mental arithmetic,' he tried.

It was no good. Now that they were well away from any other people, he could sense that Mother was going to tell him off.

'Billy! It was such a shock when we drove up and saw you. What were you doing playing in the road like that? Why don't you play in a friend's garden? Where are your garters and where are your proper clothes?'

'Under Mrs Youldon's bed in a parcel. I wear them for best. I go to Sunday school in them. But I play in these.' He looked down at the plimsolls and tattered shorts.

She tutted. 'No more. And I can't have you playing in the gutter. I don't know what you were thinking of.'

'Mrs Youldon likes us to play out after we've had our food.'

'Out? She lets you play in the street, do you mean? Doesn't anyone around here have a garden?' She looked despairingly at the tightly terraced homes with their thin muddy strip at the back. Billy didn't dare mention the privy or the hip bath. It was all his fault for being chosen last. It would be awful if she found that out. And he didn't want her to be mean to Mrs Youldon. It wasn't her fault. Wasn't there really any room for him at the Vicarage?

'Do you have to share beds where you are, Mother?'

'No of course not! Do you?'

'I share with Alan. He's eight, like me.' Surely she'd remember she'd missed his birthday now.

'Alan? There's actually another evacuee in your billet?'

'Mm. He's nice. You'd like him.'

There was a pause as they marched on at a smart pace.

'I shall ask for you to be moved to another billet. It's totally unsatisfactory. And I'll send you some garters.'

They neared the school. Billy felt her looking at him.

She said, 'You look a bit peaky.'

'I get a bit hungry.'

Her face softened.

He rushed to take his opportunity. 'Mrs Youldon doesn't always have enough.'

'Oh dear. I'd see about a food parcel for her if I was at home.' She patted his hand, the one with the orange and sweetie bag in it. 'You can eat your sweets now, if you like, but don't throw the papers down, please. As I say, I shall have to get you a different billet.' She looked down, frowning, and stopped talking.

Now he'd found his voice again, Billy chatted about his new life while they walked past The Grange for her to admire the drive and the gardens, then around to the church and back down the narrow road to the lane where he now lived.

'The vicar will be back. I must go. Look out for his car. Now, keep yourself clean, Billy, or no-one will want to take you in.'

So that's why Mother wasn't taking him with her! But he had been clean when his school arrived in the village and no-one had wanted him anyway.

'I promise I'll keep myself clean, Mother.' He could find a rag to hang in the scullery ready for cleaning himself up when she visited.

They walked back, a fierce wind blowing from behind. Mother looked at her watch. 'We're nearly back to your lane, aren't we? Time for me to go, Billy.'

He felt around in his jacket pocket. 'I drew some aeroplanes, Mother. They can be for Baby, but I don't suppose she'll like them.'

'Oh, she will. She's kept all the ones Kenneth has sent her. He's a wonderful drawer, isn't he?'

'He's written to you, to Baby?'

'Auntie writes and puts his little drawings into the envelopes.'

He kicked at a stone. 'Is the war nearly over?'

'Not yet, dear, I'm afraid.'

'But there haven't been any bombs, have there?'

'Well not yet - but there might be.'

He breathed in and looked right up at Mother. 'Why's Kenneth not having bombs in London and he's not evacuated?'

She shrugged her shoulders. 'It's no good asking me, Billy. He's not my son. And perhaps Doreen was right to take the risk and keep him back. What do I know about war? I'm kept away from my home the same as you.'

The vicar's car reappeared in the lane ahead. Mother waved. Several children were running alongside it. Big Ronnie was standing outside his house, hands on his hips, waiting.

'Have you got to go, Mother?'

She bent and tidied his shirt collar. 'Now, keep yourself clean and tidy. I'll see you soon, Billy.'

'Will it be next Saturday?'

'No, but I will come when I can. Now, say Goodbye to the vicar, properly.' She looked meaningfully at him.

He went round to the driver's side, his hair blowing into his eyes. 'Goodbye, sir. Thank you for bringing Mother to visit.'

The vicar nodded. 'Remember your prayers, young man.'

Billy moved away quickly. He blinked his eyes hard. Apart from school prayers, he hadn't remembered them at all.

'Oof. Glad to be out of this wind!' Mother slid into the back seat where a magazine lay open.

'Goodbye Mother.'

She leant out of the window. 'Goodbye. Be good, and get your hair cut, do.'

Big Ronnie was sitting on his doorstep watching. He thumbed his nose at Billy and shouted 'Be good. Get your hair cut, dooo'. His face divided into an evil grin.

Mother didn't hear. She'd wound the window up. The car moved off. Billy kept waving until he saw her open her magazine to look at hairstyles and skirts. He shivered. The wind was so strong that if she'd brought him a comic it would probably have blown right away.

Billy turned his head away from Ronnie and ran indoors. He slipped upstairs to sit by himself to think about his family. He shut his eyes and 'saw' Baby, Nanny and Grandad, Angela, the Cossack sabre. If the war went on long enough, he'd be old enough to be a soldier, Mr Durban would be very old and die. Although that would be sad as sad, Angela would give Billy the sabre because he'd be going to war while she'd just be staying at home, a girl, a woman, being kept safe.

CHAPTER SEVENTEEN

November 29th 1939. *Many evacuees return to London against advice to leave children safe in the country.*

Billy kicked a stone to-and-fro outside the front door. Some of the Vaccies had already been collected and others had been put on trains back to London. Even Alan's letter from his mother said she was coming to take him home.

Alan danced around outside. 'Yippee!' Then he stopped and put his arm round Billy. 'You'll be next, don't worry.'

Billy shrugged. Mother hadn't visited for a while, so it didn't seem likely that she'd collect him, even though Dad had said 'Christmas' when he told him about evacuation.

Without Alan, it would mean more room, especially in bed, but it was miserable, him going. He and Alan did everything together. 'It won't be nearly as good here without you.'

'Cheer up! If Mummy brings me chocolate biscuits, I'll give you one.'

When the day came, Mrs Youldon had all Alan's clothes clean and ready packed. Alan stood on the doorstep for ages before his mother arrived, and then he gave her such a huge hug. His mother had lots of smiles on her face but wet eyes. She thanked Mrs Youldon many times and gave her a tin of biscuits. She was really kind because she gave Billy a bag of bull's-eyes before she took Alan away.

'I'll see you when war's over,' he called to Billy, and marched smartly down the road with one hand in his mother's and the other holding his suitcase.

Billy held a heavy hand up to wave back. When would that be?

At bedtime, having the bed to himself felt colder and sadder. Mrs Youldon found a second blanket but it was only thin.

Winter was deepening and it was very cold at night. It was dark soon after tea, now, so he played inside with Tim and Sally, making up games for them with all sorts of scraps.

Mrs Youldon was chopping onions again to make soup. It wasn't a horrible smell but it stayed around all the time. She wiped her eyes. 'Only onion tears, me. You're not sad, now, are you, Billy? Not fed up because you haven't got Alan to help with the jobs?'

He shook his head. It felt very comfy in other ways, being Mrs Youldon's big important boy. No-one nagged him about his stammer. Actually, he hadn't noticed whether he had stammered for some time.

'It's going to be Christmas ever so soon, Mrs Youldon. My father said I was here until Christmas.'

'Then your Ma will come for you, I'm sure. Perhaps things aren't quite ready at home yet. She'll come soon.'

He didn't believe it. Mother was probably very happy at the vicarage.

Mrs Youldon didn't have a wireless, but what Ronnie told him about the news was horrible, all about ships being sunk and planes being shot down. The only good thing was that Uncle Ted was a soldier and not a sailor or an airman.

Miss Johnson had the younger vaccies and village children together all day. Now the school wasn't so crowded they could all fit into the classroom, not have it for just half the day. That was good, because it was jolly cold for nature walks. She led sing-song classes, because it was important to *Keep Your Sunny Side Up*. They learned new songs, ones they could almost shout in, like *It's a Long Way to*

Tipperary. Singing was quite jolly and soon more singing went on in the playground than fighting.

They made Christmas decorations the last week of term. They couldn't get red and dark green, only pale green and pink. Billy managed to save some of the strips to bring home for Timmy and Sally, but Mrs Youldon hadn't any glue to make the chains. He was going to ask Miss Johnson if he could have the left-over glue when it got to the last day of school.

He was building a tower of his playing cards with Timmy when there was a bang on the door. Mrs Youldon stopped her sewing and went to lift the latch.

A deep voice said, 'Good evening. Mrs Youldon?'

She took a step back and let the man in. He had a beard. The man reminded him of Dad.

He looked at the face blankly until it said, 'Billy? Aren't you going to come and say Hello after all this time?'

Billy's hand was halfway in the air, ready to put another playing card on the tower he was building for Tim. He couldn't think, suddenly. Tim took it from him and the tower fell, flip flop flip off the bench onto the floor.

'Oh dear,' said Dad, stepping over the pile to put a hand on Billy's shoulder.

'Mr Wilson!' Mrs Youldon cleared the newspaper strips and offered him the chair.

'My apologies for the lack of notice,' he said as he sat down. 'I've been working just over the county border and I wanted to take the opportunity to collect Billy. It does seem safe enough in London for the time being. And Christmas is nearly upon us. A colleague with a car is kindly giving us a lift home. We're very lucky.'

With Dad's legs almost touching the bench, the room felt very crowded. Billy stayed crouched, very close to Timmy, staring at Dad's black shoes. They were the same. He remembered them.

'Have you lost your voice, Billy?'

He put a hand to his throat. 'Dad? Are you taking me home?'

Dad nodded. 'Indeed. No moss gathered here.'

Billy had left his at school on the Nature Table. That was a shame.

Mrs Youldon was still standing, pressing her hands together. 'I can offer you tea, sir - er Mr Wilson.'

Dad waved a no-thank-you hand. 'So. Billy. Are you going to get your things?'

'But what about Mother and Baby?'

'They've already gone. They went by train. Go and pack your suitcase. Bring everything.'

Sally sidled up to hug Mrs Youldon's knee, staring at Dad. 'Not go, Billy.' Her face puckered.

Timmy collected all the cards together in a pile, one by one. His hands hung loose on his lap.

Billy ran upstairs and packed very quickly, leaving all the play clothes on the bed.

When he came down, Dad was thanking Mrs Youldon for looking after him all this time. 'I'm sure you'll be glad of the peace with both boys gone. Here's what I think we owe you.' He handed over an envelope and a brown package.

She bowed her head. 'Really grateful.'

'Don't mention it. Now. Ready, Billy?'

Billy had changed into his school uniform with an extra jumper on top and then his mac and his cap. His socks were pulled right up. Mother had sent him garters after her first visit and he'd been careful not to lose them. He pulled his fingers through his hair. He felt fairly sure he looked all right. 'I'm ready, Dad.'

Dad looked him up and down. 'Where can he have a wash, please? I can't take him out to my colleague looking like this.'

'Oh dear.' She put the envelope and package on the bench. 'He looks all right to me, but I'll give him a rub. We weren't expecting you,' she said.

She took Billy into the scullery and found a towel. She wetted one end under the tap and scrubbed away at his face and knees. 'I shall miss you,' she whispered.

Feeling bold, he put his arms round her, and her shoulders were bony. If only he could bring her, bring all of them back with him to share all the food locked up in the larder at home. 'You're the bestest billet,' he whispered back.

CHAPTER EIGHTEEN

December 21st 1939. *Winter may be the worst for decades.*

That first night was lost in the long car journey. The man driving gave Billy a blanket to put over his lap and told him to stay quiet in the back so that he could concentrate on his finding the way. Dad soon seemed to be dozing.

The driver murmured to himself, 'Darn good job I know this route.'

It was jolly hard to see the way ahead with no lights. Billy was used to it in the country, walking around with a torch like everyone else, but last time he was on the road at night there were lights from all the traffic. Now car headlights and traffic lights were shielded with sort of folders. They drove through dark villages and then into a town. Even now there were no lights. The buses had lights inside dimmed to a glow, so were almost on top of them before Billy saw them. Once, the car almost bumped into a person crossing the road, and he cursed.

More countryside and almost invisible villages before a really big town where all the shop windows were completely dark. Then they reached the black of hills and woods. It was easier to nod off than to wonder about enemy hiding in them.

When Dad said, 'We're home,' Billy opened bleary eyes onto a sea of black. They could have been anywhere. Dad shivered, 'Certainly a bad fog tonight.' He thanked his friend and shut the car door quietly. The car slid away, becoming invisible within seconds.

Billy could see white rings gleaming faintly. They seemed to be swimming mid-air. 'What's them?' he muttered sleepily.

'So that you won't bump into the trees. Look out now.'

He saw that the nearest white ring was painted round the tree trunk, and round all the trees up the road. He stumbled forward to a ditch-dark doorway. When Dad tapped on it, Mother stood there in a blue dress he'd seen lots of times, long ago, but now it seemed like a fairy tale. The long hall yawned behind her, the doors and stairs a wilderness. He could hardly believe this was his home. No light showed until the front door shut.

'Took forever,' said Dad, as he put the bags on the hall floor and kissed Mother's cheek. 'You settled in then? Did you manage to light the boiler?'

She nodded, then looked at Billy. 'Good to be home, dear? We came back yesterday. Phew what a journey, my goodness! Straight upstairs, now, Billy. You're half asleep. It's so late. And quiet foot-steps. Don't wake Baby.'

It was Dad took him upstairs, which felt very odd. He put him to bed with a sheet over him as well as under, and long enough to tuck in. The blankets felt so thick and cosy. He lay in the soft bed, almost dreaming the voices in the room below him as sleep washed over him again.

When he woke, the bed felt wrong, too big and too bouncy, and the ceiling looked high and different. Then he saw his aeroplane dangling from the ceiling and sat up, excited. He'd really come home. He ducked his head underneath his bed and drew out his box of small aeroplanes. There was a film of dust on top. He smiled to himself. He'd play all morning with them.

He padded round his room reminding himself of all his things: planes, cars, puzzles, farm, bricks, shelf of books, even the wardrobe of clothes and the chest of drawers. He'd forgotten what loads of things he owned. The hobby horse leant sadly against the wall. He patted its head. 'Sorry, Horsey, too old for you now.' But he still liked looking at Horsey. He'd leave him standing there.

Hanging behind his door was his checked dressing gown. Suddenly he had more than a pyjama jacket for facing a cold morning. He slipped it on and the sleeves still touched his hands. He hadn't grown.

Outside the door a little voice called out, 'Mummy.'

Baby! He was curious to see her again. Did she still have tantrums? Would she still grab his toys? He peeped round his door. A small girl with a flushed face and a trailing nightie stood by Mother's bedroom. He tried to see Baby in her, but she was different. She stared at him with a wobbly lip, then Mother came out and took her hand. 'Look, it's your brother, Billy.'

'Hello Baby,' Billy said.

'It's Jill,' said Dad's voice deep from the bedroom. 'She's not going to be a baby forever.'

Billy shut himself in his bedroom again. Jill. He'd almost forgotten her name. Bill and Jill. How silly of Dad and Mother. Hadn't they noticed? He fingered his bi-plane for quite a while, until he was told to wash and dress.

As soon as he'd done, he ran downstairs and found them sitting at the dining table.

'My name rhymes with hers. Bill, Jill.'

'What a cross voice on your first morning back home. Jillian and William, not exactly the same.'

'S-sorry.' But they sounded the same to him, so he was glad Mother was still calling her 'Baby'.

'Sit down there and eat your bacon. We may not get much more of this from now on.'

Billy sat and ate his bacon and egg eagerly. Delicious! A long time since he'd had this! Any cooked breakfast was a tremendous treat and he knew all about not getting much any more. He felt each mouthful deliciously tasty on his tongue before he chewed and slowly swallowed. Looking across to the larder door, he saw it wasn't locked. Would it still be full of food, like before he went away?

Mother was wearing a red jumper with white fuzzy blobs and a little red scarf round her hair. She had lots more clothes than Mrs Youldon, as well as having bacon. Baby crashed her spoon onto her plate saying 'La, la, la-la.'

He smiled at her as he put in another lovely mouthful. Mother was cross. 'You are not a country savage now, Billy. Put your fork down between mouthfuls. And stop that infernal noise, Baby.'

Dad's voice sounded deep. '*A house divided against itself cannot stand,* – Abraham Lincoln.'

Billy looked up. It seemed very strange to have a man beside him. He'd forgotten all about Dad's sayings. What did this one mean? Bombed houses could not stand.

Mother placed a larger plate of breakfast in front of Dad and a cup of steaming tea. 'Wise words are all very well, Herbert. It's so difficult just being back. It took all my time yesterday getting the boiler going, doing the beds and queuing for food. I can hardly find anything clean in the house. It's so dusty after all this time. And no Mrs Donnington! The evacuation was all for nothing. I wish I'd never gone away.'

'Better safe than sorry. To me, it was worth it for peace of mind. But, by Jove, it feels nice to have you bring my breakfast again, Marcia.' He smiled up to her. 'I'm sure you'll adapt. We can't resent Mrs Donnington for doing her bit for the war. The buses need conductors.'

'I suppose I shall have to manage.' She was looking anxiously at Baby banging her spoon as if she'd never be able to manage her, or perhaps that Dad wouldn't put up with the noise.

'And wonderful for me to have the children here, of course,' he added, turning to say something to Billy, but Mother interrupted,

'You have egg on your chin, Billy. Where's your napkin?'

He'd forgotten about napkins, it had been so long since he'd seen one. He pulled his out of its silver ring and flicked it onto his lap. In Mrs Youldon's home this would probably be used as a towel except it was too smart. In the village right now she'd be sending Sally and

Tim to play out after their grey porridge. They'd have to run up and down the street without him.

Billy hadn't said Goodbye properly! The little ones had been huddled by the playing cards and paper strips as Dad had taken him to the car, Timmy's arm around Sally. He'd come away without doing their Christmas presents or making their paper chain. He should have used some of his Uncle Ted's shilling to buy pipe cleaners at the village shop and shown them how to make cars and little people holding hands. Now they might not have anything for Christmas because Mrs Youldon wouldn't have his billeting money any more. Could he could post his shilling? Was it right to ask? Mother was frowning over the teapot. Dad, he could see, was very busy eating, and thinking about work.

Dad said, without looking up, '*Silence more beautiful than any song*– Rossetti.' Probably he was practising what he'd say at work. It must be a funny place, Court, with people doing these sayings. After Mrs Youldon's home, Dad's voice sounded strange. And Dad was like a stranger after all this time.

Mother muttered, 'Well, Herbert, I should think you've had enough of silence without us.'

Billy nibbled a piece of toast. Christmas was only a few days away but no-one had said anything. Were there presents wrapped up and hidden under his parents' bed? Where was the tree, the decorations? He wanted to ask Mother about Christmas, but she might get cross. He couldn't tell what might make her cross now. He'd only seen her three times since being evacuated and she was wearing a skirt and jumper he'd never seen before. She was snappy even to Baby and her face was all sort of tied up.

His eyes strayed to Baby. To Jill, if he could get used to saying that silly name. Silly Jilly. No, it was "Silly Billy" people said when they made mistakes. Why did he have to be called *Billy*? It wasn't fair.

Jill's face was quite fat. He was used to Sally who was about the same height. Sally's face was thin and she had a shy little smile. Baby was cross and looked it. She didn't have a dummy any more but she did look as if she might still scream.

'You can play with Baby after breakfast,' said Mother.

'Jill,' said Dad, as he put his coat on. 'Jill, dear. You must use her name. She's walking. She's a child now. If she goes to a nursery, she can't be called "Baby", can she?' He went to the door. 'I'm afraid I must be off to Chambers. *No peace unto the wicked* – Isiah. I have to report in and look at the next listings. Judge Wiggins presiding. Everything must be just so. I'll be back by tea, Marcia. Don't forget to pin up the blackout properly. It's sagging.' He clucked at Jill, and said 'Be helpful' to Billy, before disappearing to his important work.

Baby, Jill, stared after him, then turned her plate upside down.

Billy asked, 'What does she p-play?' as he rescued it.

Mother didn't seem to hear him. She was clearing the breakfast things and looking at suitcases which needed unpacking. 'There'll be a lot of sorting out to do,' she was muttering, lines in between her eyebrows.

Billy knew what was wrong. Mother didn't like having to do Mrs Donnington's work, now she was back home.

She lifted Baby down from her high chair and stood her in front of Billy. 'There you are, Billy. Now I have a lot to do, so you keep her amused, please. And keep the toys to one side so that I don't trip over them as I come to and fro.'

A pile of her toys sat on a box ready for her to play with. It should be easy to amuse her.

Baby stood on chubby legs. Her pink shoes had a shiny white button on the side of each strap. He couldn't imagine her playing out and spoiling them. He picked a toy up and showed her, and put it down again. She did nothing. After a lot of staring at Billy, she showed that she liked putting her doll in a blanket and taking it out again. She wasn't interested in building houses of cards. When Mother came back into the room she toddled over and clung to Mother's skirt, although Billy was trying to play with her.

'Oh well,' sighed Mother, taking Baby's hand. 'You might as well play upstairs then, Billy.'

He went upstairs gladly. His own room now, all and everything to himself, and there was so much!

He'd just pulled his box of aeroplanes out from under the bed and organised some bricks to be aircraft hangers when Mother trilled up the stairs in a new voice.

'Billy! Guess what?'

Billy's heart started thudding. Dad might have hidden the Christmas tree in the garden. He rushed to his door. 'Is it a tree? Or fairy lights?'

'No, dear,' Mother said in a calming down voice. 'It's your cousin. So long since you've seen him. Look out of your window.'

His tummy seemed to turn upside down. He looked out, and saw the back of a boy going round their path towards the side door and Aunty Doreen, further behind, still on the pavement. He heard the door open and his mother's voice, friendly and welcoming, then Aunty's, excited and chatty.

The next moment, 'Bi-lly,' sang a familiar voice up the stairs, 'Coming to ge-et you.' And it was followed by the clip-clop of feet in heavy shoes. Billy shoved all his toys quickly under the bed and came out onto the landing. He started down the stairs and met Kenneth who was bigger, his hair longer, his camel face the same. He pushed his face forward so that Billy backed up the stairs.

'Hello, Chicken. Had to run away to safety? Evacuee. I stayed at home. Mummy couldn't do without me. Where did you go? To the country. With all the pigs and cows, Mooo-ooo.'

'Not with pigs and cows. It was a village. With country round.'

'There weren't any bombs here, anyway,'

'I know.'

'So it was a waste you going.' His hand came out from under his newly knitted jumper and pushed Billy backwards into his bedroom. 'I've been playing with all your friends.'

'You haven't! You're not even at my school.'

'I am now. My school closed because too many children went away. Our lot that stayed behind joined up with what was left of your lot and had your school. It's nice as pie. Reg and Andrew and Jim are all my friends now.'

'Bet they're not.'

'Bet they are. They've forgotten you, you've been away so long.'

Billy sat down on the stairs. This was awful. He could hear the chatty voices downstairs. Mother hadn't seen Aunty for ages and she was cooing about all the new things Baby could do.

'I'm going to say Hello to Aunty,' he said, pushing past Kenneth.

'She's busy. I want to play with your things. Come on.'

'Not now.'

'Yes. I want to see them all again.

'No.'

'I'll tell.'

Billy ran downstairs, as if he couldn't wait to see Aunty Doreen again, and perhaps he couldn't. He liked Aunty. He stood at the parlour door. She looked sort of fluffy, her hair very curled up and a frill on her skirt. Baby was clinging to Mother's knees and staring at Aunty whose hands were stretched out towards her.

'She'll get used to me soon enough, now you're back, bless her.'

'Hello Aunty—'

'Oh it's Billy! Hello dear. So grand to have you home.' She smiled and patted his arm. 'Long time, no see. Excited to see our Kenneth again, I'll bet.'

Billy twiddled one of the tassels on Aunty's chair cushion. 'Is Kenneth really with all my f-friends at school?'

'I expect so. Now the stay-behinds are put together so there's enough teachers. And you'll have made some new friends out there in the country, won't you?'

He nodded, suddenly remembering how awful it was not to have Alan any more.

Aunt Doreen drew him towards her and looked him up and down. 'The country air hasn't fattened him up any, Marcia. Look. His arms are quite skinny.'

Aunty wouldn't understand. She'd never have been in a cottage like Mrs Youldon's. 'Mrs Youldon hasn't got a lot of food, Aunty. She does share it and Alan's mother sends food parcels sometimes.'

Mother put her hands to her face. 'Oh dear, I just brought things when I visited. I didn't really think. Billy did say he got hungry, but then boys always say that. Baby and I were fed ever so well at the vicarage.'

'I must say, Marcia, both you and Jill look positively blooming.'

'Yes, we do enjoy the country food. I'd have thought Billy got the same. The billets do get an allowance for evacuees, after all.'

'She g-got eight and six for me,' Billy said.

'Do I cost eight and six, Mummy?' Kenneth pushed his way forward.

'And the rest! Whatever you cost, you're worth every penny, my little man,' said Aunty.

Worth every penny— Kenneth? Ugh! But he knew Aunty meant it. She poured herself another cup of tea from the second best teapot. There was no lump sugar on the tea tray for her. He used to take a lump, sometimes, when it was only Aunty around.

'You h-haven't got sugar, Aunty.'

'Learning to do without, Billy. Aren't we all?'

Mother said, 'The Simpkins, next door to you, Doreen, are they back from Wales?'

The mothers started to chat about all the people they knew and what they were doing. He needed desperately to tell Aunt Doreen lots of news so that they wouldn't be sent to play upstairs. The words wouldn't come out quickly enough. 'Aunty, w-when I was away we had n-nature w- walks and I –I've been m-making d-decorations at my n- new school. P-paper chains and— '

Aunt Doreen looked across to Mother with a sympathetic glance. 'He still has his little problem, then?' She turned to Billy.

'Yes, dear. Let's speak slowly. Paper chains? That's nice.'

'And I lived with a n-new friend called Alan.'

'Not A-A-Alan?' said Kenneth.

'Kenneth! That's not like you. Don't make fun of Billy's stutter,' Aunty Doreen said.

'I thought you'd lost that stutter, Billy,' Mother said in a disappointed voice.

'I had.'

'He can't help it,' said Kenneth lowering his lashes.

'That's right, dear,' said Aunty. 'He can't. You have to give him time to get the words out. Remember that when you're playing, Kenneth.'

'Of course, Mummy,' Kenneth lifted his lip at Billy and whispered in his ear, 'because he's so soppy.'

'Such a lovely smile, your Kenneth,' said Mother. 'Billy, I never see you smile like that. In fact, you don't smile much.'

Billy put his hands to his mouth to feel if it could stretch sideways like they wanted.

Aunt Doreen got out her knitting. It was long, a dirty sort of green. 'I've joined the WVS, Marcia. You'll have to. We can be ever so useful, turning our hands to whatever's needed. We don't have the formality of the services, you see.'

'Oh, I couldn't. I still can't knit.'

'It's not just knitting. There's the catering side.'

'Ugh. And I've got the little one.'

'Anyway you could knit while she plays. Of course you can learn. You could have learned at the Women's Institute before you were evacuated. I'd better teach you now.'

Mother looked doubtful. She glanced at her fingers with their long pink nails and then at Aunty's, which were flicking to and fro like machinery.

'These will be army socks,' Aunty said. 'The soldiers will be glad of them. If we're shivering in this bitter cold, think how it'll be in the trenches.'

'Is that where Uncle T-Ted is, in the trenches?'

'I'm sure he's fine,' said Mother. 'He would have said, if not. All his letters are very jolly.'

'And is Uncle F-Frank a soldier now?' Billy asked. It would be awfully good without him here, and the trenches might make him nicer when he got home afterwards.

'No dear. Tax Inspectors are exempt.'

Bother. He'd had just a tiny hope that the government had made Uncle go to war.

'Daddy's job is too important. He can't be spared to fight,' Kenneth said.

'Well, my D-dad's still here. So his is im-p-portant, too, isn't it Mother? He does Assizes.'

Mother raised her eyebrows at Aunty, who grimaced.

Kenneth said, 'And I'm still needed here, too, aren't I, Mummy? I can't be evacuated.'

'Oh yes, my little man. You're needed here.'

Billy squinted at Mother sideways. 'You had to take Baby away to keep her safe, didn't you Mother?'

She nodded.

'So there was no-one at home for me.'

Mother smiled with a little bit of her mouth. The lipstick was only on the front bits. She'd told him once it was a cupid's bow. 'That's right. We thought it was safest if you went away with the school.'

Kenneth put his head on one side and flicked his eyelashes at Mother. 'Are you and Jill staying home all the time now, Aunty Marcia? Then Billy can. We haven't had any bombs here. He can be back at school with me.'

'Oh, you missed your cousin, didn't you, Duckie? Such good fun you always have together,' said Aunty Doreen.

She turned to Mother, nodding her head. 'Work on Herbert, Marcia, so you can stay here. There's some lovely dances on. You know how you love dancing. Got to have some fun, war or no war. Nothing's really happened here after all. It's all happening at sea, or in France. You'd be better off here. And Billy will. He and Kenneth can go through the war together.'

Having the war AND Kenneth. That wouldn't be fair. Billy wanted Alan back and their country school, the nature walks and the shared lessons. He wanted Mrs Youldon and the little ones. He didn't want the war and Hitler. 'I can't stay home, can I Mother? I have to be evacuated.'

'We'll see. We'll learn what your father thinks. He'll know best.' She turned to Aunty Doreen. 'To be honest, I can't think straight. I'm just home. Mrs Donnington's left us to do war work. Everything's covered in dust. I haven't fully unpacked. There was nothing much in the shops yesterday. Baby can't understand where she is or who she's with and she's a handful at the best of times. Plus I've got Billy to look after now, too.' Her voice rose to a high pitch. 'It's so difficult, you just don't know. Christmas is almost on us, Herbert's busy at the chambers and I've absolutely everything to do.'

Aunty Doreen put her knitting down and placed a hand on Mother's knee. 'Don't worry about Christmas. That's all sorted. You're coming to us.'

Billy froze. With Kenneth for Christmas! He bit his lip to stop himself shouting out NO!

'Frank's got a goose,' Aunt Doreen went on.

'A goose! Never!' Mother giggled and let her breath out at the same time.

'Yes, really.'

'How wonderful. Goose! How on earth?'

'A manager at the Coop depot has a brother who's a farmer in Kent. He got it for us. Something tells me he doesn't pay that much income tax. Don't ask me if he owes Frank a favour,' Aunty spluttered.

The mothers both threw their heads back and laughed in a screaming sort of way. Kenneth folded his arms across his front and smirked.

'Doreen, thanks so much. It's a huge relief to have Christmas taken care of.' Mother took Baby's hands off Aunty's ball of wool and put a stacking toy on the floor.

Billy bent and started the pile for her. She put on the smallest piece. There was coal dust on the floor where the mat ended. Baby put her finger in it. He moved her further onto the mat. 'Is it just for Christmas D-Dinner we're going f-for, Mother?'

Mother's brow puckered threateningly.

Baby put on a larger piece and the stacking toy collapsed.

Kenneth said, 'Aunty Marcia, do you think we can play with Billy's aeroplanes? We could play upstairs, quietly?' His lips curled above his wide white teeth and his cheeks rounded.

'Of course, dear,' Mother said, smiling at Kenneth as if he was the angel for the top of the tree. She passed Baby another piece of the stacking toy. 'And mind you share nicely, Billy.'

'He will, Aunty,' said Kenneth.

There was no escape from two pairs of motherly hands ushering them away. It wasn't fair. Billy slouched off to the stairs, Kenneth close beside him. Upstairs, he quickly set to, searching out all Billy's toys and treasures.

Billy shouted, 'Leave them! I only got home last night. I haven't seen my stuff myself yet.'

'So?' Kenneth darted at the boxes under the bed, where Billy had shoved them when Kenneth arrived. He knew exactly which were Billy's best things. Some were easy to break, especially those Billy had made himself.

Kenneth got started with a fighter plane straight away. 'Whee-eeee! He zooms down and crr-aa-shh. He bombs the cars, and the cows in the field and all the cottages.' He acted as if he was really in a raid. 'Get out some more of the farm while I'm doing this. Let's have some casualties. I know you've got more. I remember everything you've got.'

Billy looked at his farm animals, some of them made of matchsticks and wool and the little cardboard planes that last year had taken ages to stick together. He didn't want them bombed. He hadn't had any of these to play with at Mrs Youldon's. Or anything else. He hadn't had Reg, Jim or any of his friends for company. He hadn't had his parents. Kenneth'd had it all.

Suddenly it was all too much. It was time to play out.

CHAPTER NINETEEN

December 23rd 1939 *Admiralty will lay mine barrage off East Coast as reply to German action.*

Billy pretended to go into the bathroom while Kenneth carried on whizzing and zooming planes into victims, then he slid out from behind the bathroom door and down the stairs. He crept out of the back door and was well down the road before anyone had time to notice. It was only like playing out.

There was one place that Kenneth didn't know, and one friend he'd never met, and one thing that was very powerful and was going to be Billy's and only Billy's one day. He remembered the way to the Durban's very well. Angela hadn't been sent away after all and she'd be pleased to see him. Before evacuation she'd been very nice to him and she was the one who told him about things.

He ran on, being careful how he crossed the roads. It seemed funny to have carts and vans to worry about. He'd almost forgotten about the big red buses that looked so huge on the main roads. There were new posters up outside the newsagents' and the metal fences all along the road had been removed. Otherwise, everything was the same as before the war.

Actually, it wasn't really Angela he was going to see, but what she might show him. He might have forgotten about buses but there'd never been a moment when he'd forgotten Mr Durban's treasure.

Billy started to run his hardest because he hadn't picked up his coat and it was bitterly cold. When he got to the house he reached for the ding-dong bell with a freezing hand, then put his head against the door. Suppose they were all out? He'd have to run home again and Kenneth would still be there. He'd be telling on him right now. But if the Durbans were in, Billy would stay as long as they'd have him. Afterwards, when he got home he'd just say he was very sorry and they couldn't do that much, surely, because it was going to be Christmas. He could just go to bed after the punishment. Spending Christmas Day with Kenneth was a real punishment anyway. He shivered and wished he'd brought his coat.

At last, the door opened. Mr Durban stood there wearing a maroon checked dressing gown. He stared for a moment, 'Wait a bit. Let me see, I know you, don't I?'

'Yes, sir. I'm Billy Wilson. I've come to see you all. I'm back from evacuation.'

Mr Durban smiled widely. 'Of course you are, I'm teasing you! Back for Christmas? That's very good. Well, you come on in. No coat! Better come near the fire.'

He led the way into their living room, where reddened coal flickered behind the criss-cross stove doors. Shabby paper lanterns dangled and tinsel glittered on a small tree.

'Sit you down, Billy.'

There was a Tommy helmet on the arm of the settee. Number 723 1939 was painted on the rim. It looked very heavy. Mr Durban sat by it. He moved a large pile of newspapers so that Billy could sit down beside him. 'I'm afraid Angela's at her friend's and Mrs Durban does war work most days. I've just got up. I'm on nights this week.' He patted his tommy helmet. 'So with the women out, it'll be nice to have another man to chat to.'

Billy looked round for the other man but then realized Mr Durban was making a little joke. He tried to think what another man might say back. 'Not much happening in London, after all, is there, sir?'

'Not much bombing, but a lot's happening all over London. Getting ready for the worst. Never fear, it'll all be sorted, one way or another, by the time you're of age.'

'Old aged?'

He laughed. 'You're good fun, young Billy. *Of age* is what I said. It means you're old enough to serve your country, go to war. Like I did in the last one.'

'Not now?'

'No. I'm an air raid warden after work. I don't go away with the judge like your father, I'm always in Chambers. Easy for me to do the midnight-to-four shift, looking out for the safety of everyone here. I'm too old to fight, so I'm serving my country that way, you see.'

'Will I have to serve my country?'

'Perhaps.That's a long time away for you, so you just make sure you enjoy yourself, meanwhile. Why aren't you playing at home, now you're back?'

'I want to.' Billy's voice rose and quickened. 'I was looking f-forward to getting out all my toys. But my c-cousin's there and he's got all my things and they've l-let him. And if I d-don't, he always gives me Chinese burns and g-gets me into trouble.' His voice trailed away again.

'I see, I see. You have a bit of a problem there, have you? So you've come over to see Angela instead, and now she's out? Shame. But I'm up and fancy free for a little while. What sort of toys do you like? I should look out some of my keepsakes. As long as they're not in the attic.'

Mr Durban's cheeks were pinky-red, quite different from Dad's longer, waxy-white face with its beard. There were little lines at the sides of his eyes and he always looked friendly. Billy took his chance.

'I'm very interested in swords, sir, especially foreign ones. I've got a wooden one but I'm too old for it now.' He looked up at Mr Durban hopefully.

'Swords, eh? Then I might have something to interest you. The women are out, so we shan't bore them with men's things. Mind, you can only look. It's a dangerous weapon.'

Billy felt his face go hot. He was breathing fast. He mustn't give the truth away. He'd thought of Mr Durban's dangerous weapon so often at Mrs Youldon's, and when Kenneth sneered at him, he wanted to see it more than anything, more than going to the zoo or even getting a Christmas present. Mother probably wouldn't have time to shop for one anyway.

Mr Durban was standing up and telling Billy to wait there while he went to get his 'surprise'.

When he returned, he was holding the Cossack sabre the same way the village vicar held the chalice and his face looked the same, faraway and solemn. He laid it on the coffee table beside Billy. 'There. See this treasure? This is the scabbard. Isn't it fine? One day, I'll tell you a foreign tale about it.'

Billy stroked it, remembering every last detail of the decorations.

'Inside this scabbard, is something very dangerous, as I said. I expect you can guess what it is, can't you, young man?'

He wasn't supposed to know about it so he said it wrong. 'Sir, it's a sword.'

'It's a sabre from Russia. Its proper name is a shashka.'

'Sha-ska,' Billy breathed. Angela hadn't told him that. Perhaps she didn't know. 'Russia? That's a very far away country.'

'Indeed it is. Now stay sitting there and I'll show you.' Still standing, Mr Durban drew out the blade very slowly.

Billy gasped. It looked even more shocking than the very first time he'd seen it, partly because of the slow coming-out. The curved blade glinted in the winter sun slanting through the window. Mr Durban held it up for some moments, moving it just a little from side to side.

'Sir! It's spiffing!'

Mr Durban placed the scabbard on one side of the coffee table and the blade on the other, the furthest from Billy.

'Is a sabre for something different than a sword?'

Mr Durban screwed his eyes up and stroked his face. Stubble showed. It would probably be scratchy. He looked as if he was thinking. 'I'm afraid they're both for killing. Let's talk about the technical side. The sabre's a very strong sword design and the shashka is a special type. The blade's hollowed out to make it light and stiff.' He slid it a little nearer to Billy. 'Put your hand over mine and you'll see it's not nearly as heavy as you'd guess.'

They lifted it up together. Billy's chest felt fluttery. It was as though he and Mr Durban were going to fight together against the enemy.

'It's still heavy enough to be used for work when it's not wartime.'

'Work?'

'In the fields, cutting crops. The design came from Persia or somewhere Eastern, but the Russian Cossacks found this shashka perfect for hacking, cutting and thrusting.'

'What's thrusting?'

'I'll show you. Sit back, right back.' He stood a little way from the settee and demonstrated with a wild empty arm: 'Hack, cut, thrust.' The air whistled. Although the shashka wasn't in Mr Durban's hand, hacking and thrusting, Billy couldn't help jerking away further.

Mr Durban sat down again and pointed to the hilt, with its closely patterned silver grip. 'You see the shashka has no guard? Sabres normally have them, but the Cossacks were such skilled fighters they reckoned they could fend off sword strikes with their bare hands.' He gave a grim laugh.

'Why don't they have a guard, Mr Durban?'

'Having no guard means better cutting. The cutting motion can begin closer to the hilt. You see how it's curved forward?' He pointed. 'This very small grip ends in the large pommel.'

'Pommel.' He whispered the new word. It was magnificent, much better than a sword, and surely the best sabre ever, a prince of sabres. Perhaps it had belonged to a prince in Russia. All those times he'd brooded over it, Billy hadn't thought of its real owner. He sat very still, his eyes hard and dry.

Then Mr Durban took several steps backwards into a space between the chairs and table. 'Can you keep very, very still?'

Billy nodded, holding onto the settee arm to make sure.

'Don't move then, not an inch, and I'll demonstrate.' His wide wrist grasped the shashka, flourishing it forward, left and right, twisting it beside, below and above him, swish, swish, swish. The cut air whistled against Billy's face bringing a faint smell of metal.

Billy flinched and curled back into the corner of the settee. His eyes hurt with stretching so wide. It was dreadfully scary to think of how terrifying it would be to face that curved blade! He hadn't remembered its awful sheen and cutting edge. The shaska would make such terrible wounds, no-one would be able to bandage them. They'd probably never stop bleeding.

Mr Durban, tall and proud above him, looked a bit like a foreigner, his dressing gown a strange uniform with a shiny corded belt. Would he be a dangerous enemy?

Mr Durban lowered the shashka carefully. 'I can't do it as well as the Cossacks do, but that's more or less what it looks like in action. Except, that they often did it with two. One in each hand.'

'Two!' Billy gulped, trying to think of a double swishing and thrusting through the air. 'I'd like to see that. Sometime.'

Mr Durban smiled. 'Enough excitement. Let's put it away safely.' And he did, the fearful point sliding into the scabbard where it, and the silvery blade could do no harm. Then he sat in the big leather chair at one side of the settee.

Billy let out a little sigh. 'How did you get it, Mr Durban? When did you meet Cossacks?'

'Ah, now, that is a tale. Do you like stories?'

'Sword stories. Yes, I do. I read about King Arthur lots of times before I was evacuated. I got a big book from Boots library. He pulled his sword from a big rock.'

'King Arthur is a famous myth, but this is a true story.'

'Like the heroes book you gave me, sir? They were true people. It would be really super to hear the Cossack story.'

'Now the shashka's safely back in its scabbard, you can hold it on your lap while you listen and imagine the man who once owned it.' He passed the scabbard across and laid it over Billy's bare knees. The leather was soft and hard at the same time, the thrilling weight of the sabre denting his skin.

'Did he kill anyone with it?'

'Probably many.'

'In front of you, sir?'

'No. If he'd used it then, I wouldn't be here to tell the tale. Shall I start?'

Billy nodded hard.

'Listen, then. This isn't girls' stuff. It's not to talk about with the women, mind.'

Billy shook his head. No way! And certainly not with Kenneth. He kept his hands lightly round the shaska so he couldn't harm it. His eyes felt hot, but he kept his gaze on Mr Durban's face.

Mr Durban sat back in his big leather chair and closed his eyes for a moment. 'Nineteen fourteen. I was seventeen, enjoying the summer before starting at University in the October. One of my school friends, Otto, invited me out to spend the summer with his parents in the far north east of Germany, near the border with Russia. At least it was, then. All the borders are different now, since the Great War.

'At first, we had a wonderful time, walking, riding – his family kept horses – and visiting his friends who were older and seemed very glamorous. The sea was not far off and the weather was beautiful. All the local men were in the fields getting in the harvest. There were lots of parties in the evenings and it was very cheerful.

'Everyone was shocked when we heard that the Archduke, Franz Ferdinand of Austria, had been killed by some wildcat Serb. Otto's father said there'd be an apology from the Serbian government.

'A lot of soldiers began parading smartly in full uniform in the streets. We saw armoury as well. I said to Otto, "It's like they're preparing for war." He made a face. "The German army's the strongest, the best in the world. They need to show everyone that."

'We carried on enjoying ourselves in the bright sunshine – world affairs no concern of ours! But there came a day soon enough, when Otto's parents seemed very panicky, speaking in German so that I wouldn't understand. Otto shrugged it off.

'That night Otto's friends came to warn me that now the harvest was in, the menfolk could be freed to be soldiers. Austria had declared war against Serbia. Russia was Serbia's ally so would fight with them. Germany backed Austria and soldiers had already started their damn raids before even declaring war. All the countries of Europe would be drawn in. An Englishman would be in great danger.

'Within an hour, Otto's friends helped me escape towards the

Russian border which was about fifty miles away, first sewing English sovereigns into the waistband of my trousers.

'I had never travelled alone in the dark even in my own country. I spoke no Russian, but the sovereigns bought me food from farmhouses and inns in the next few days. I hid when soldiers were on the road. Twice I was nearly handed over, but my sovereigns saved my skin.'

Billy thought of his half-crown that Grandad had given him 'in case'. It had seemed safe enough in a purse, but perhaps he needed a better place. After all, it was wartime here too.

Mr Durban was deep into his story. 'I saw German soldiers, drunk, rolling out of inns. There were killings, young and old people, children kicked aside, houses ransacked. This made me hate the German army. I vowed I'd fight them when I was no longer alone and unarmed.

'Eventually, I saw Russian soldiers and let them capture me. Their commander sent for an interpreter. When they understood that I was an English student, accidentally caught up in Germany and ready to fight beside the Russians, there was a cheer. The commander ordered the captain to give me food. It was the first proper meal I'd eaten for very many days. He found me a uniform and a rifle and taught me how to fire it.

'The Russians were disciplined, having sworn no wine or women until the war was won. I was proud to march along beside them, although I couldn't understand their language. I had no knowledge of where we were, or of the progress of the war.

'For our first battle, I fed ammunition to my comrade at the rear as the riflemen forged ahead. Each wave was shot down, but we fought for hours. The roar of the firing was deafening and the air thick and smutty. When the noise eventually died down, I climbed on a nearby truck to get a sense of what was happening.'

Mr Durban's eyes were dark. He swallowed. 'The fields were littered with bodies, dead or dying, all in our uniforms. I turned to the captain, dismayed, but he told me there were even more German bodies. I was appalled. This was my first experience of death and it was so massive.'

Billy screwed into the back of the settee, imagining it all. Mr Durban didn't seem to notice him. He sounded like a long-ago man, his eyes gazing far away.

'They were so brave, those Russian soldiers. The battles went on for weeks, until it was deep winter, thick snow on the ground. I was given a greatcoat and a cap with fur flaps. Just in time, for I thought my ears would drop off. Some men did lose fingers or toes.

'Every day was so terrible I stopped being shocked. In an icy trench without relief and under heavy fire, we couldn't move to right or left. Sometimes, there were several layers of bodies with a lowest layer of blood, shit and snow. Sometimes, uninjured men suffocated under the press of dead bodies above them, while below, the blood merged into one stench of filth.'

Billy stuffed one knuckle into his mouth to press away the very bad 'shi-' word as well as the truly awful scenes but Mr Durban spoke on.

'It was almost better to be under fire in the open, deep snow slowing every step. We kept on firing and being fired at, the waves of our riflemen mown down by the greater German force. Then, our Cossacks came speeding in, brandishing their sabres. Their faces were so fierce, I thought they would terrify all the Germans away. Our cannons gave the best cover they could, but the German machines had a better range. One after the other, the brave Cossacks fell, their horses writhing beneath them. As the sky darkened, it all became horribly silent. We had run out of ammunition and needed to retreat. The enemy had stopped firing too. We were told to rest as best we could where we were. I shinned up a tree to take stock.'

Billy opened his eyes a bit, he'd had them screwed shut. He saw Mr Durban's eyes were far, far away.

'The ground ahead was flat and in the bitter blue sky, I could see for miles. The sight was far, far worse than the first battlefield I'd seen. As far as the horizon there were bodies; not hundreds, not thousands, but hundreds of thousands, far-off splats of blue and brown with great splashes of red staining the snow. They filled the icy fields as closely as the corn had filled them in August. A few German soldiers were walking amongst the fallen, looking for survivors.

'Then I saw a Cossack, still alive in the midst of a pool of dead German riflemen. I ran over to pull him out of the snow and back to our lines. Before I reached him, a German had his rifle at his throat. I dived low at the German's knees and toppled him over. The rifle fire hit high into the sky. As he lost his balance, I threw myself at him, managed to get his rifle and shot him at close range. I turned to the Cossack, who pointed a weak finger to the shivering flank of his steed where his weapon lay trapped.'

Mr Durban picked up the shashka reverently. Billy turned his gaze to it, shaking all over from tensing his muscles rigid for so long. He'd never ever heard such a scary tale and it was true, really awfully true.

'I could see how old and how precious this sabre was. The Cossack pointed to it, murmuring urgently, "Shashka, shashka lixodaika" and gestured at his stomach which gushed dark blood. Rifle shots rained around us, but my comrade ran up and we carried the Cossack to lie beside our vehicles.

'He was so weak, but spoke rapidly to my companion, then glared intensely at me with his black eyes, pushing the shashka into my hands. He fell back, shaking his head as if to say he was all done. I knelt and thanked him for his most precious gift. I wanted to express my total respect. He understood, and put a finger on my forehead like a blessing, saying words I had no way of understanding.

'A shouted command just then meant I had to run, a German rifle on one shoulder and a Cossack sabre in my hand.

'When we got to base, my rifleman comrade took the story of my wonderful shashka to my friendly captain.

'"You saved the Cossack's honour if not his life," he explained to me. "His dying words to you were: Take this shashka, like a son of mine. Mind its path, protect it well. It will inflict the most terrible wounds."

'I was awestruck. The captain examined the shashka carefully. The fineness of the workmanship and engravings showed that it had once been the weapon of an important, perhaps even royal soldier. "You are honoured. The sabre which takes down a Cossack warrior is legendary in its own right, and is named shashka lixodaika."

'One of the Cossacks with us demonstrated how it should be used, with rapid cuts and thrusts above and about his body. The captain told me not to try to use it unskilled, for it was a fearfully dangerous weapon.

'After this, because I owned the shashka, the men respected me, and any German soldiers who set eyes on me kept their distance. I never had a chance to use it, and perhaps as well. I'd seen enough violence and death to last a man many lifetimes. I'd been just a schoolboy in the summer. My eighteenth birthday was still some months off.'

Billy took in a breath. Not eighteen? That was younger than Uncle Ted!

'We reached the port and the captain arranged for me to be taken onto a ship bound for Finland, saying from there I could get to England. I made my sad Goodbyes, knowing it was very unlikely that any of my brave comrades would survive long. The Germans had far more forces and machinery.

'In fits and starts, I did get home safely, much to the relief of my poor mother who'd had no means of contacting me. She said she should never have agreed to my holiday. I told her the Russians had looked after me. I couldn't tell her how dreadful things had really been, that I had fought deadly battles and seen thousands of brave men dying. I hadn't the heart to put such images into her innocent mind.'

Suddenly Mr Durban stopped short, blinked and looked down at Billy as if Billy had just appeared. He took a little breath. 'How old are you, son?'

Why did he ask that? Did he want Billy to be his son right now, one day to give him the shaska? Billy stood up proudly, hands straight by his sides, head up, just like a soldier and said, 'I'm eight, sir.'

'Eight! Lord, I thought you were much older.' Mr Durban leant forward and took the shashka from him. 'You are a big lad. Eight! I shouldn't be telling you stories like this. I'm afraid I've been in another world. Whatever will your parents think of me?'

'I won't tell them.' They might be cross if they knew how scared he'd been. He felt his hands to see if they'd stopped being so shaky.

'Mm. Perhaps best not. I'll go and put this away.'

Billy's legs felt light without the shashka resting on them. He sat down again. He didn't want to go home yet.

When Mr Durban came back in, he said, 'Sir, it was jolly good you did get back home safely. And with the shashka.'

'Indeed. My goodness, what a tale to tell you.' He looked at his watch. 'Just time for some fizz and biscuits, then you must scoot off home.'

Billy didn't rush his drink when it came and he took two biscuits with thick custard cream in the middle. He'd have missed his elevenses by now. 'Thank you, sir.'

'No, you tuck in.'

Billy really meant thank you for the story, but perhaps also, in advance, for the shashka. He nibbled and sipped as slowly as he could, but Mr Durban thought he should get back.

When they got to the front door, Mr Durban said, 'That problem with your cousin, Billy. Remember the heroes book? They had huge problems but they stood up for what was right. Remember? Think of Joan of Arc, or Spartacus.'

'I do. I have thought of them. All of them. I want to be a hero, but I'm not.'

'There's time. You're a good little lad. Just - always stand up for what's right.'

Billy bit his lip. that would be difficult.

'As for the shashka and its history. Not for others' ears now!' and Billy shook his head. He wasn't a tell-tale, and anyway, the shashka was his secret. His and Mr Durban's.

He set off home quickly but couldn't run fast, for all the scenes in his head seemed to weigh his feet down and anyway the street was now icy. He didn't know whether he was shivering from cold or from hearing about all the death and dying. There would definitely be punishment at home now, but that wasn't nearly as scary.

When he got to his road he could see there was trouble. Everyone made a big fuss. Kenneth and Aunty, holding Baby, were at the window. Mother was standing on the doorstep in her coat, looking around wildly.

Dad was just coming up the road as Billy reached the gate. He glowered. 'So. There you are! I've been looking for you in the school playground. Where have you been? You were supposed to be upstairs with your cousin.'

Kenneth called out, 'I searched downstairs and in the garden before telling.'

Mother's hands flew in the air. 'Going out without telling anyone! How was I to know where you were, please?'

'I wasn't far. I was just playing out.'

'You could have been miles away. Someone could have taken you.'

He was confused. They'd wanted him to be taken last September. Why wasn't it like being evacuated? 'But—before, I was miles away. Miles and miles away for ages. You let me.'

'That's different. Mrs Youldon was caring for you and it was in the country. She knew where you were. This is London, you can't just walk off when you like.'

Dad joined in, 'Completely out of line. You worried your mother. This simply will not do. Go to your room. Now.'

It could have been a lot worse. Dad hadn't gone for his slipper.

Billy went to his room and spent the rest of the day there with no dinner. It was meant to be a punishment, but he was really glad of the silent, safe space while he lay on his bed and thought about Mr Durban's terrible tale. The huge rank of cannons, hundreds of soldiers on both sides, the Russians thrusting forward, wave after wave against the constant cannon fire, the Cossacks riding up with their sabres against their hip. He especially tried to replay the moment when Mr Durban first saw the shashka under the dead horse.

When he imagined all the hundreds and thousands dead bodies he put the coverlet over his head. Then he thought of holding the shashka up high. He sat up and stared at the wall as if he were at the pictures. Although the war stuff was terrifying, when he had the imaginary shashka he felt braver and more able to face enemies. He practised swishing his arms in the air, like slashing with a shashka or two.

Down below, the sounds of home seemed suddenly silly: Kenneth being fussed over in the kitchen while Mother twittered about what cakes and biscuits to bring to Uncle Frank's on Christmas Day.

When he went to the bathroom he found that a plate of sandwiches and a drink of orange had been left outside his bedroom door. He was jolly glad to see them, and took them inside to eat and drink like a soldier after a battle.

CHAPTER TWENTY

December 25th 1939. *Olivia De Havilland enchants in 'Gone with the Wind'.*

Billy woke early. He put his nose around the blackout and saw a few flakes of snow drifting past. Christmas Day was still sort of exciting even though they had to go to Uncle Frank's. He hadn't been there since summer. Would Uncle be bigger and fiercer, or nicer because it was Christmas? Had Mother had been shopping for presents? Would Uncle Frank still want to wrestle, and would he have a tree? He'd better not ask anything, because everyone would still be cross with him.

Breakfast seemed to take ages because of Jill fussing about her porridge and then having to be wrapped up in all her pram clothes, but at last they were off walking down empty roads sprinkled with white. He remembered last year's twinkly lights inside houses that had curtains open to show the tree. That made things feel cheery at night-time. Everywhere now, windows were blind and if there were decorations behind them, it was secret. Everything had to be kept dark for war.

A bitter feeling was in the air and there was white on the top of hedges and bushes. His wellies made a crisp crunch when he stepped into the gutter.

'A great deal of frost, today,' said Dad. 'Any snow will stay put.'

He looked up at the low white sky. Billy expected a saying, but none came.

Mother and Dad strode along quickly. Billy hopped behind, watching their footsteps appear in the thin snow. The push-chair left its own little roads behind. They'd make marvellous marble runways if only he was allowed to play on pavements, but 'playing out' was probably gone for good.

Mother said, 'I do hope their place is warm, Herbert. I feel like ice right through.'

Billy counted to four-hundred-and-seventy-two before they turned the corner into Uncle Frank's road.

'Thank goodness, we're here.' Mother parked the pram inside the gate and picked up Baby with all the bedding. Aunty's hall had no room for prams.

Dad knocked and Kenneth let them in from the cold. He was wearing brown corduroy shorts and a jumper with a yellow tractor knitted into its front. It was such a dark day that the curtains were drawn and the light on.

Aunty Doreen, red-faced in a floral pinny, welcomed them in to sit beside the smoking fire. 'The goose isn't nearly cooked yet, so excuse me all of you. Sit yourselves down and Frank'll entertain you.'

There was a Christmas tree in the corner with little candles on the branches. Aunty had sprinkled talcum powder so that it looked snowy, but Dad said there might be real snow outdoors soon. 'It was certainly cold enough on the walk over.'

'I'm the Christmas Spirit. Treats to come.' Uncle Frank came round the door dressed in a Father Christmas suit, his beefy hands around a large sack. It was difficult not to look at him. 'And here's our little darling and her not-so-big brother, if I'm not mistaken.' His cheeks curved round and his range of teeth showed. 'Hello, kiddies.'

Kenneth fingered a set of dominoes. He looked at Billy from under his eyelashes, waiting.

There was a lot of grown-ups' talk about what had happened to them since War had been declared and whether both sides would have a cease-fire today. Billy put his head between the velvety curtains and watched in case snowflakes fell. He perched up on the windowsill making sure all of him showed, even his feet, so that Kenneth couldn't do anything sneaky without being seen. It was a good place to stay.

Every now and then Aunty popped her head in and out of the kitchen door, reporting on the progress of the goose.

Uncle said, 'Sit down, Doreen, for Heaven's sake. It won't cook quicker for you looking at it.'

'Oh all right.' She flopped into a chair. 'I wonder what'll be in the King's speech this afternoon.'

'Progress of the war, bravery, what else?' Dad said.

Billy wondered if he'd have to listen to the speech. It might be longer than a sermon. He and Kenneth might be sent upstairs while the grown-ups listened and by tea-time, he'd have bruised shins or worse. He couldn't stand up for what was right on Christmas Day.

Baby toddled about, touching everything.

'Not that, darling, it could break.'

'Don't touch. NO! Here, have dolly.'

After she'd explored the room and been passed from lap to lap, Baby got restless. Then Uncle Frank, not at all like Father Christmas, gave his toothy smile and lurched forward with his hessian sack. 'Ho ho ho. All little kiddies who have been good can have their toys from Rudolph the Reindeer's sleigh.'

There was no sleigh. Uncle knew Billy was eight and Kenneth was nine, so he must have meant this silly talk for Baby. Uncle held out the bulgy sack. But she didn't know what to do, and it was Aunty who had to lean forward and pull out a present for her. Kenneth showed her which one, and stayed close to the sack.

Baby pulled at the crackly paper and played with that, while Mother looked at the present, six blocks in a box.

Kenneth lifted his lip to Billy, his hands on the sack. 'You can have first dip, Billy.'

Billy hesitated, it was so surprising. Could Kenneth really be standing up for what was right, just like Mr Durban said to do?

Aunty pushed him forward. 'Go on, Billy. Kenneth's giving you first go, bless him. You can take three things each.'

Billy unwrapped a Bakelite dog with brown spots, a book about Jesus and his disciples, and a colouring pad. Than Kenneth pulled out a pop-pop gun, the Radio Fun annual, and a chocolate ball filled with fruit jellies. He displayed his goodies on two open palms. Billy stared at them and then at his own presents.

'They're what you picked out, Billy,' said Mother.

'Lucky boy!' said Aunty Doreen, nodding at the book of Jesus as she unfolded a pink petticoat Mother had given her.

Dad said, 'Who could guess which presents were on top?'

Billy saw Kenneth's lip twitching. Something wasn't right.

Then Baby pulled out a present, and it was the last one. Just a doll made of that hard stuff that cracked.

Mother handed Billy another parcel from the big pram bag. Kenneth looked over keenly as a striped spinning top came out of the brown paper. 'It's from Uncle Ted,' Mother said. 'He sent it from abroad last month.'

'Abroad!' Billy held it very close. It would never fit into Dad's coat pocket.

Aunty peered at it over the table and said, 'Kenneth got a wonderful train set from my parents. I don't know how they afford it. I reckon it came from Harrods. They know I get worn out going shopping. He's got it in his trunk.'

That meant Billy wouldn't get to play with it, for sure. He slid the top under the table between his feet as Kenneth opened the present Mother and Dad gave him. It was a set of drawing pencils and a sketch pad, really boring. But Kenneth seemed pleased. His lips curved upwards and he took out the first pencil very carefully. He drew a large T on the first page, and decorated it, then turned it into a fancy *Thankyou*. Billy knew that should be two words but none of the adults minded. They all clucked and admired what he'd done. It did look good.

'Good choice, you two,' Uncle Frank said, as he went towards the kitchen. 'Just the job. Our boy's like you, Bert. Always with a pencil in your hand, I remember.'

Dad grinned and pushed at his beard.

'Do you like drawing, Billy?' Aunty asked, nicely.

'No. I hate it.'

'He shows not a jot of interest in it,' said Dad, and bent over the drawing book as Kenneth started on a large bird.

Aunty handed over their present to Billy. She had knitted him a stripy scarf.

'That'll come in handy right now,' said Dad. 'Snow's on its way.'

'Thank you, Aunty,' said Billy.

'How nice,' Mother called over to Aunty, then turned her head to mutter to Dad, 'I was hoping for a jumper.'

'Now. I am On Duty,' said Uncle Frank coming back from the kitchen with a tea towel tucked into his Father Christmas trouser fronts. 'Do you want to see this fine bird before I carve?'

Everyone crowded round him in the kitchen. The browned carcass cowered on a carving board as Uncle raised a hairy forearm and offered the knife. Aunty put parsley on the stumps where feet had once been.

'Ooh,' squealed Mother.

'Superb,' said Dad.

'You all get sat down while I deal with this,' Uncle ordered, bending his muscly frame over the goose.

Everyone deserted the bird and went to the dining table which had its leaves pulled out so no-one could quite squeeze by the chairs. If only they'd had the dinner at home! There was plenty of space there, and it was a proper dining room.

Aunty came in and out with dishes of food. 'Are we all in?' She took her pinny off. Under it was a purple dress with red flowers mashed into it.

Dad looked at the dress a lot. 'Shall I turn the gas fire up? You've no sleeves.'

She shook her head. The shiny roll across her forehead slid forward. 'I'm warm enough with all that cooking, don't you worry. Now I'll bring the plates in. Help yourselves to greens, everyone.'

Aunty brought Baby's plate out first so that Mother could cut everything up and turn it into mush for her. Baby was already turning her head away and saying 'No, no.' But then when the other plates came out and they all started eating, she forgot and put her spoon in her mouth.

Billy got the darkest bits of goose. He found he didn't much like the meat, and Aunty's gravy was thick and lumpy.

Dad said, 'What a treat, Doreen. These potatoes!'

Mother said, 'So kind, all this work, Doreen. Hope you haven't worn yourself out. Lovely, isn't it, Billy? Tell Aunty how lovely it is.'

'It's lovely, Aunty,' said Billy before he put a sprout in his mouth. Kenneth put his napkin to one side of his face and mouthed a mocking, 'It's lovely, Aunty,' to Billy from behind it.

'And guess what I've brought! One can't come over empty-handed.' Dad bent down and brought out from under the table a bottle of ginger beer and two golden brown bottles with shiny corks. *A man hath no better thing under the sun, than to eat, and to drink, and to be merry.* Ecclesiastes.'

'You and your sayings, Bert! But that one'll do.' Uncle Frank rubbed his hands.

'Ooh, all that merry sherry,' giggled Aunty and rushed into the front room where the ornament cupboard was.

She came back with four glasses. Kenneth had already prised off the wire clip on the ginger beer bottle and poured himself a glass, and Billy half of one.

Uncle Frank poured the golden drink into the four glasses. Mother lifted a pale pink hand, then stood up.

'Wait everybody! A toast to those who aren't having a lovely Christmas dinner like us.' Her face was serious, so did this mean him, and was his Christmas dinner going to be taken away as punishment for playing out? His hand left his glass and landed on his lap rapidly. But then she said, 'To Ted, and all our serving soldiers. Let's pray they'll soon be home.'

Everyone stood up then and drank to Uncle Ted, and all soldiers. Billy felt a little shiver go through him. Was there fighting and bombing in places where Uncle Ted was right now? He wanted Uncle Ted to come home more than anything.

'Drink your ginger beer then, lad. It's meant to be a treat,' said Uncle Frank.

'I'll have it if you don't want it,' said Kenneth, his hand halfway across the table.

Billy drank it down with a gulp ready to ask for seconds, but the words got mixed up with the bubbles and he spluttered all over the table. Lucky the grown-ups were so busy talking and drinking themselves that they only tutted at him. He left it a minute before risking a sideways plea to Aunty.

'Seconds, dear?' she said vaguely as Kenneth's hand shot out and upended the bottle into his own glass. 'Oh dear, looks like Kenneth's beaten you to it.'

The adults' bottles lasted right through the goose dinner until the gravy had a skin on it. Then it was time for the Christmas pudding.

'It's Billy's first time with Christmas Pudding,' Mother said. 'So rich. We always thought it best to keep him to rice pudding.'

'This has been boiling away for hours,' said Aunty, as she took from the steaming pan a bandaged lump the size and shape of a bum.

She unwrapped the white cloth carefully. Billy was shocked to see that the pudding was black, but no-one said it was burned. It made him think of his bad knee being unwrapped by the hospital nurse. It had hurt because his skin was stuck on the bandage. Quite a lot of the pudding stuck to Aunty's cloth, but there was still enough to go round.

Mother had made the custard. She'd brought the Bird's Eye tin with her. 'Better to save the rest of this for special times,' she said. 'Harder times after Christmas is over, so it's said.'

'Now, Marcia! You're here to enjoy yourself, remember. Or do I have to help you have fun?' Was Uncle Frank tickling Mother? She certainly laughed a lot, in her way. It sounded like an owl 'Oo, oo-hoo, oo-hoo.'

Mr Durban always had pinky-red cheeks but today Dad had them too. The grown-ups finished the pudding and cleared the table. Aunty put her feet up for a moment because the others told her she'd done her bit, cooking the dinner. And anyway, she had the hiccups. Baby stood very close and watched Aunty's body jerk.

Then they all had a jolly game of musical chairs that ended with Dad being cross with Mother. 'Honestly, Marcia, you could move a bit quicker.'

She'd landed on Uncle Frank's lap, fighting for the chair he'd won. Dad pointed a finger at her. 'You're out, anyway. Out you stand.'

Aunty Doreen hadn't done too well either, as she had Baby by the hand. Luckily Baby was happy to plump down on the floor every time the music stopped and other times as well, so she didn't have a tantrum when the others got the chairs. Billy let Kenneth win so that he wouldn't get Chinese burns when they were sent off to play with their new toys. They soon were.

'Enough fun, you boys. Don't want you over-excited. Off you go upstairs with all this clip-clap,' said Dad motioning to their presents. Mother took Baby to have her sleep on the reclining chair in the parlour.

When the boys reached the little bedroom, Kenneth said, 'I've put all my toys away so I can play with my new ones. I can't share when they're new. You play with your spotty dog.'

Billy held the hard thing that was only any good as an ornament. It didn't even have a nice face. 'It doesn't do anything.'

'I know. I watched Daddy pack the sack.'

'He let you!'

'Through the crack in the door, soppy.'

Billy sat on the bed. It wasn't fair. Kenneth wanted him to be upset so he wouldn't let it show that he minded. 'I think I'll read,' he said, opening the Jesus book.

'I think I'll eat these jellies,' said Kenneth. He began to chew and suck. 'Oh, yum, yum.'

Billy turned a page, trying not to listen. There were no pictures, apart from the one on the cover.

'Now I'll try out my gun,' said Kenneth. 'See if this hurts,' and he tried shooting pellets against Billy's arm and then his leg.

Billy read about Jesus turning the other cheek but he wasn't going to let Kenneth try the gun on his. He put both hands up against his face.

Kenneth looked around the things on the bed. 'You don't like that spotty dog much, do you?'

'Not really. I might give it to Jill when she's older.'

'I don't like it either but it'll make a good target.' He put the dog on the chair against the far wall and knelt on the floor, shooting it.

With Billy reading and Kenneth's mouth full of gummy jellies, they were loads quieter than the grown-ups downstairs in the front room. A lot of shouting-out and laughing and hooting rose up the stairs.

Billy asked, 'What are they doing?'

'Playing housey-housey. Bet Daddy wins,' said Kenneth. 'He always does.'

Billy went to the landing and hovered near the stairs, trying to enjoy the game from above. The grown-ups didn't notice and Kenneth was busy behind him. Suddenly, Kenneth's arm curved round Billy. 'Something for you.' He was holding a folded piece of card.

Billy took it cautiously. Was there a spider or something inside it?

'It's all right. It's for you. I did it for you, for Christmas.'

Billy unfolded the card. There was a little picture in poster paint on each of its four sides: a boy snowballing, a holly bough, a present with a striped bow, and a smiling Father Christmas. The pictures were ever so, ever so good. On the back it said 'To Billy from Kenneth.'

Billy held it so hard that his fingers hurt. 'It's smashing.' He hadn't done anything for Kenneth. He hadn't even thought about it. 'I'm sorry I haven't done one for you. I'm no good at drawing.'

'I know. It's all right. I've got those pencils Aunty and Uncle got me.' He looked down at the pictures. Do you think they're good paintings?'

'They're really smashing. No-one in my class can paint like that.'

'Good. I'm going to be a painter, that's what.'

'Are you? Like pictures on the walls, painter?'

'Yes. Now you're supposed to say Thank you.'

'Thank you ever so. I do like it. I'm going to keep it.' It was suddenly the best present he'd had.

Now Christmas Day was all over and Billy was saying his Goodbyes and Thank yous. Aunty wrapped the new scarf around Billy's neck as Mother bundled Baby into the pram with loads of baby blankets. Then they were out in the bitter cold, feeling their way home in the unlighted streets and he was very glad of the scarf.

He hugged his new spinning top to his chest. Hiding it under the table had worked perfectly. But he felt mean, now. At least he could have shared spinning it with Kenneth when he hadn't made any present for him.

There were other people struggling home in the cold, heads down, a flickering torchlight in front of each of them. You could smell the frost in the air, a gritty, mean frost waiting for snow to blanket it.

'My word, I shall be glad when this blackout business is over,' said Dad.

Mother was shivering. 'And I never remember winter being this cold. I wish we could have stayed longer, Herbert. It was such fun.'

'You're fuelled up quite enough for one night, Marcia. High time we were home, given your carryings-on.'

Billy was behind them in the dark. All he could see was the snow, not even a chink of light from any building.

'Come on, Billy, one, two, one, two,' and Dad led the way, his big shoes faintly gleaming where that morning they'd been polished like a guardsman's.

Billy was sure the sky hadn't been so very big before the evacuation. There were so many stars and he could see nobbles and clefts on the moon's surface like never before.

'Why is the sky so big now?'

'Don't be silly. The sky's as big as it ever was,' said Mother. 'Hurry up, do, stop standing and staring. Aren't you cold enough? I know I am.'

He wanted to ask Dad, but he was striding ahead, his ears covered by his scarf, snowflakes on his trilby.

This is how it had been for the Cossacks fighting, fiercely cold, white and dark, field after field until they marked the snow with their blood. He wouldn't have been able to stand it, fight in it. He couldn't wait to get indoors to a fire right now. He wasn't a hero.

Dad turned back and started to pull him along. 'Come on, Billy. You'll freeze to death if you don't hurry up. Quick march, that's the way to get home.'

It was so good to feel some warmth when their front door opened to Dad's key.

'Better run straight up to bed, Billy. Very late for you.'

Billy took up his top and Jesus book and the painted card from Kenneth. He'd left the Bakelite dog behind on purpose, just to show it didn't count for anything. To help the shivers away, he counted while he undressed for bed – eleven, twelve, thirteen. The bedroom was always very cold and Mother had forgotten to put any hot water bottles into the beds before they went out, so when Billy slid into bed he felt like an ice sandwich.

He fell asleep dreaming he was a Russian soldier, a brave Cossack, dying in the snowy field that was splattered everywhere with blood.

CHAPTER TWENTY-ONE

December 26th 1939. *Londoners cheered by the King's Christmas Day Speech.*

Boxing Day seemed to begin very late. Billy felt very hungry before he could hear any sound from his parents.

He waited quite a while, but the house remained silent. Did he dare sneak down and find some food? First, he had to brave the cutting cold that lay between his bed and the door where his dressing gown hung. He rushed to snuggle into it and crept downstairs. There was an uncut loaf in the larder. It was best not to touch that. He cut a piece of cheese from under its white cloth cover and tried to make a smooth edge like it had before. There didn't seem to be anything else unwrapped or half ready.

Mother had brought the rest of the custard home in a jug. He lifted the edge of the skin and spooned up a few mouthfuls. The custard was set hard, so although he carefully replaced the skin, the curved dents in the surface showed horribly. He was scared, but Mother surely wouldn't look at custard until well after breakfast.

When they did get up, Mother and Dad didn't seem in a very

good mood and because he'd been so recently in trouble, Billy cleared the table without being asked and then went to play in his room, happy to have it to himself.

He tried out Uncle Ted's top, setting it to spin so that the stripes became one splodge of colour, just like his whizzer. It went ever so well and with a cheery whirring sound. If only he could thank Uncle Ted for such a lovely present. He wanted to see him; he wanted him home. He was a soldier somewhere and there were cruel Germans around. But at least Uncle Ted wasn't in Russia.

Kenneth must've messed with his home-made planes because there were breakages. He got out his glue and matchsticks.

Cross voices sounded downstairs. He heard Mother's snappy voice at Baby when she whinged. A freezing blast shot up the stairs as the front door opened extra wide.

Dad's voice stated, 'I shall go out to clear my head.'

'All right for some,' Mother said loudly before the door shut with a whoosh.

Billy kept out of the way, lost in repairing his aeroplanes.

Dad must have come back later, for wireless sounds floated up the stairs, but Billy had been too busy to notice Dad's return.

Lunch was silent and the dining room table seemed bare; only a sandwich of hard cheese with the custard to follow. Mother removed the cover and looked at it closely. 'Have you been at this, Billy?'

He hung his head and nodded. 'Sorry, Mother. I was hungry this morning.'

'You helped yourself? How dare you!'

Dad didn't look at her, or at Billy. Even Baby was quiet, eyeing each of them as she sat in her high chair, squelching mashed carrot between her teeth.

Eventually Mother said, 'Well you needn't try that again.'

She spooned the custard into the four dishes, splat, splat, splat, splat, the skin sliding silently into Billy's dish like a slice of dead body. It would be his punishment to have to eat it. Surely everyone hated skin?

Dad was looking at the dishes. 'I think I'll have a spot of jam with mine.'

Mother tutted and click-clacked into the kitchen. Dad swapped the dishes and put his in front of Billy, frowning as Billy gasped with surprise. 'Mouth shut, son.'

The click-clacks returned, and the jam pot with the lid like a flower, banged down on the table. Mother wagged a finger. 'You needn't think you're having jam, Billy.'

He lowered his head and ate up his skinless custard, gladly.

In the afternoon, Baby was dressed up and put in the push chair. Nothing was said, but they all wore their best clothes with extra cardigans on top and walked towards Nightingale Lane. Walking behind Mother, he saw her seams were a bit crooked but he didn't dare say so. He hoped Dad would notice and put them right, but he didn't. This road led to Grandad and Nanny's so his tummy had a happy butterfly feeling. It was ages since he'd come here. Also, Mother wouldn't want to show her crossness there. Dad walked forward and rang the bell.

Nanny and Grandad came to the front door with smiling faces that seemed as foreign as France. It was so long since he'd seen them. At last he had someone he could tell all about the evacuation: the playing out, the hip bath, the privy and running in the wood in old, torn clothes.

They both opened their arms and Billy ran forward. Baby had forgotten them and hid behind Mother's knees. In the end, Mother had to carry her inside.

'Well what a palaver, this evacuation,' Nanny began. 'And all for nothing, wasn't it? I've had your letters, Marcia, we've read them all so many times. Your kind vicar, the dear little village. But I don't know anything about how Billy got along. You tell us, dear. Come and sit here between us, and your little sister can get used to us gradually.'

As Billy opened his mouth he caught Mother's eye. It was narrowed by furrowed brows. There was a *Don't* message here. What was it he mustn't say?

'I was in a tiddly village with country round it.' He looked at

Mother. All seemed well. 'I can't say its name because it's secret.' He looked at Mother again for approval.

Grandad gave it. 'Learned your lessons well, bright lad. Now then, were they good to you, then, those people you stayed with?'

'Yes. It was just a lady and her little children and they didn't have—'

Mother pushed a flat hand towards him. 'I'm sure Grandad doesn't want to hear about someone else's children, Billy.'

He wanted to talk to Grandad. Was it just about Timmy and Sally he couldn't speak? He tried again. 'There was another boy there like me, Grandad. He was called Alan, only he wasn't from my school. I didn't know him before.'

'That was nice, then,' said Nanny. 'A new friend. Another boy evacuated like you to share your room.'

'Yes, and we had to share a—'

'That's enough, Billy. Go and find Nanny's old dolls-house for Baby, please.'

'You're not letting him talk, Marcia. We want to hear all his news. He's been away weeks and weeks, after all.'

'Best he doesn't think too much about it,' said Dad. 'If it comes to it again, we'll look for a re-billeting. It wasn't a suitable place.'

Billy didn't know what 're-billeting' meant, but he understood 'billet' and 'not suitable'. Was coming back home, 're-billeting'?

If only Mother and Dad would go in the garden or upstairs or something, so that he could tell Nanny all about the train, the crocodile around the town, even being left till last, as well as the forbidden stuff of Mrs Youldon's home, the little ones and everything.

As he came back with the dolls' house and set it down before Baby, Nanny leaned forward to Mother. 'You started your family late, Marcia. So you're slow to understand children, what they're needing to do or say.'

Mother's lips formed a straighter line. 'My goodness, Mother, I'm bringing up two. I do all right; *very well*, I'd say, under the circumstances. Billy's been allowed to run wild while he's been away. He needs a bit of correction, now he's back with us.'

Grandad turned to the mantlepiece, sighing. Then he picked up some letters and put them in Nanny's hand. She waved them at Mother. 'Did you hear from Ted as well? We've kept all his letters.' She held them out. 'He sounds cheery, but we dread what he might have to go through, now or later.'

'If it's like the last war...' Grandad muttered. 'I wouldn't wish that on anyone, let alone my son.'

Nanny looked over and Shh'd him. Mother was reading the letters closely.

Billy felt a thump in his stomach. Whatever it was Uncle Ted was doing, it must be horrible if Nanny dreaded it, and Grandad wouldn't wish it on him. 'Are there cannons where Uncle Ted is?'

Nanny quickly put the wireless on and there was Christmas music playing, although Christmas had ended. She turned to Billy. 'Know this one, pet? Jingle Bells, Jingle Bells.' She didn't sing in tune, but she waved her pinny in time to the music. Baby chortled and tried to copy. Nanny held out her hands, and with a little push from Mother, Baby took them. Nanny danced her around the room. The men went outside.

Looking through the lounge window, Billy saw them walk down the garden path together, smoking. It was very, very cold but they stayed there, talking with churchy faces. Grandad was tracing a sort of map on the bird table, jabbing his finger from time to time. Dad hunched his shoulders and rubbed his chin lots of times. The smoke from both of them made pretty twists in the air. It was ages before they came in again.

'Just as well to keep all that smoke out of here,' said Nanny following Billy's gaze. She'd never grumbled about Grandad's pipe before.

Mother was looking at a magazine. It was last year's. 'Now we're home, I just don't want to think about any of it,' she said. 'Anyway, it doesn't seem like war is going to be actually dangerous, here. Just think— we went all that way, had all that nuisance and here we are back at home. All for nothing.'

'Keeping your children safe isn't for nothing, Marcia, and now you're home, perhaps you can nag Herbert into seeing about a shelter.'

'Oh, we keep seeing notices about shelters. I see next door

haven't bothered. They say they'll go to the park one, if there is a raid. Herbert hasn't put in the Anderson yet, and just as well. It would ruin the garden.'

'Well, I wish he would. Think what's happening in other places. Try to persuade him, Marcia. Better be safe than sorry. It's quite a long way to the park shelter and you've got Baby to carry. I hate to think of how it would be.'

'There's our cellar if we really did get a raid. Sitting beside a heap of coal. That will be jolly! Anyway, we'll surely get warned if there's going to be bombing, so we'll worry about it then. The newspaper says Hitler's busy in Norway just now, and anyway Herbert reckons Britain's too tough a nut for him to crack.'

Nanny made a face. Was Mother right, or Nanny? Beastly Hitler. War and sheltering from it. It all seemed very gloomy.

The afternoon cheered up when Grandad came in and collected Christmas presents for them all from upstairs. Billy's was extra special because it was for his birthday too. They hadn't had an address for him. He opened the brown paper, letting it crackle to slow down the surprise. Inside was a large and shiny red car with opening doors. 'Super, super, Grandad! Thank you ever so much.' He held it on his lap to keep it safe until he was allowed to play with it somewhere.

'Let's have some tea, everyone.'

Mother went out with Nanny to the kitchen and brought back a tray with the teapot, milk and cups. Nanny passed round bread and butter, with a spot of jam on each slice. Then she brought in a jelly in the shape of a fat rabbit. It squelched loudly as it was spooned into dishes, which made him giggle. She poured on thin custard and it had no lumps or skin. Afterwards, there was Christmas cake for the grownups and little cakes with white icing smothered with coloured dots for him and Jill. Hundreds-and-thousands, Grandad called the dots. It was a good name because you really couldn't count them. Billy bit into his cake and watched the colours melt into the white, bit by bit, like little dead bodies in the snow.

'Good job that's not ice-cream, young Billy,' said Grandad, 'or it'd just be water, the time you've been gazing at it. Don't you like icing?'

'It's yummy. I'm just waiting for the hundreds-and-thousands to disappear like they've never been.'

'Funny little lad,' said Nanny. 'You take your time, dear. Enjoy it. And I've got another one for you to wrap up and take home.'

It was sad that there was no chance to say anything private before it was time to go home, but the great fuss his grandparents made of him made Billy feel the happiest he'd been for a long time.

CHAPTER TWENTY-TWO

January 8th 1940. *Finns make huge captures. Another entire Soviet division killed.*

'Guess what?' said Kenneth, standing on Billy's bed, one hand on the hanging aeroplane. 'We're not going to be able to have butter, or bacon and all sorts of things. There's going to be ration books so you can't just go shopping and get what you like, even with lots of money. There's a thingy— shortage.'

'No butter? What'll we have on our b-bread then?'

'P'raps we won't get bread. We might have to eat dog biscuits.'

'Aunty Doreen would never give you d-dog biscuits.'

'But your Dad might give them to you. Because you don't need building up. And Mummy always says I do. So if there's any butter, I'll get it. They'll probably give me yours.'

Billy bit his lip. This could be another of Kenneth's tales. He waited until they went down to tea, until Mother brought in the scones. No-one had ever stopped him from ladling on the butter. He did so now, waiting for a moment when Kenneth had his nose in his mug of milk.

'You won't be able to do that, in future, Billy.' Mother had her eyes on his knife. 'Put some back. Bacon and butter, and probably other things, are going to be rationed.'

'What's rationed?' Best to try to get the truth.

Kenneth brought his lips out of his mug. 'He already knows because I just told him upstairs. Why does Billy ask questions when he knows the answer, Aunty Marcia?'

'I d-didn't understand. I'm not as old as you,' said Billy, playing the game.

Mother's eyes swivelled between them. She took a breath and explained all about rationing.

'I knew that, Aunty. We're all going to have to be very careful not to take more than our share, aren't we?' said Kenneth, his eyes pointedly on Billy's scone.

'Yes, Kenneth, that's right. Let's hope you don't have to go without too much,' and there was a definite edge to Mother's voice.

Billy held his serviette to his mouth so that he could peer at her face without being noticed. Was she cross? With him or with Kenneth? He wasn't sure. It might be worth trying to tell Mother a bit more about Kenneth if he could just make her pleased with him. 'Shall I b-butter this scone for Jill, Mother? Jill, do you like scones?' He bent over her as she held her sticky hands above her plate. 'You like jam, don't you?'

'Yum yam,' she nodded.

'I expect jam will be rationed, won't it, Aunty?' said Kenneth.

'Perhaps. Put your napkins in their rings, when you've finished, boys. Then you can listen to Larry the Lamb on the wireless.'

Billy smiled. He always looked forward to that.

Kenneth muttered, 'That's just for babies.'

Mother heard. 'Kenneth, I've seen you listening to it before.'

When she went out, Kenneth made a little noise like a growl. Mother had caught him out and he'd hate it that Billy had been there to hear. Good.

It was six in the evening when the door-bell rang. Billy rushed to open the door before Mother could stand up.

'Put that light out!' bellowed the Air Raid Warden. But it was all right, because it was Mr Durban. Mrs Durban and Angela were standing behind him. Dad had invited them to spend a jolly evening.

Dad said, 'Next time, just wait until I say, Billy. Don't just take it on yourself to open the door.'

Mr Durban was wearing his ARP band but not his helmet. 'Never off duty,' he grinned.

'Oh, you gave me quite a turn,' said Mother bringing them all inside quickly and shutting the door tight behind them as a search-light swept up and lit the heavens. 'Happy New Year. Come right in. There seems no end to this icy weather.'

Mrs Durban put a hand on Billy's shoulder as the light went back on. 'Safely back, dear? And you, Marcia, you must be so glad to be home? Good evening, Herbert. Is it still busy at the Courts?'

'Still hearing miscreants. People don't change, war or no war, sadly. Let me take your coats.'

As they put their coats on the hallstand, Angela smiled at Billy. 'You can tell me all about evacuation.'

She was wearing a blue flowered dress and a little cardigan, fluffy like an animal. Billy went to stroke it.

'It's called Angora,' she said.

'Bit like you. Angora. Angela.'

She laughed and went down the hall after the women.

Mr Durban followed slowly, looking hard at Billy. He raised his eyebrows. Billy shook his head. He knew Mr Durban was asking if he'd told about the story. They were like two secret friends, men who knew the shashka.

'Good lad,' said Mr Durban, slipping half a crown into Billy's hand. 'A late gift. Go and post it in your money box. You can buy something later.'

Billy looked at it, and then at Mr Durban. The shashka story was thrilling enough, without a reward too. Angela was so lucky that he was her father.

'Th-thank you very much,' he breathed. But Mr Durban was

saying Shh at the same time, so the thank you got mushed up with the Shh and sounded like *shashka*.

He fetched the Ludo set to play with Angela while the grown-ups talked. He felt rather shy of her. It seemed a long time since she'd put her arm round him and told him about Evacuation. She beckoned him over to the little table at the other side of the room and they set out the board and pieces.

Mr Durban was saying, 'You are going to join us ARPs, Bert? You're a long time nailing your colours to the flag.'

Dad's face was grim. 'For defence, maybeI will. Not offence.'

'He's a bit of a pacifist, on the quiet,' Mother said.

'Even so, wherever I can, I shall do my part. Fire-watching, I expect.'

Angela slid her white piece towards Billy's row of blacks. 'I didn't go away.'

'I know.'

'So tell me about evacuation.'

No-one else was listening, so he told her about the village, the nature walks, Alan, Mrs Youldon and the party at the Grange.

'Like an adventure,' she breathed. 'I've just stayed here, knitting grey pieces for soldiers and sitting in the Anderson for practice. Some of our best teachers have gone to war and loads of my friends are still evacuated. I was sorry for you when you went, but now I think you had the luck.'

'Not really,' Billy said. In a whisper he told about being the last child to be chosen, the hip bath and the privy. 'But it's a secret like the— you know.'

'Sabre, yes. Sh.'

She looked over at the grown-ups but they were still busy with war talk.

'An outside lavatory? Ugh! Poor you. I'd hate that. I was supposed to be evacuated to my Aunty's in Wales, but I begged Daddy not to go. We were just going to start learning Shakespeare at school.'

'Shake spear?'

She laughed. 'Nothing to do with spears. It's a man who wrote plays long ago. I love English lessons and I don't want to miss any. The English teacher's quite old, so she won't go for war work. Daddy says even if there is bombing now, we're all staying or all going, and I think it'll be all staying because he's got to stick at his job and his ARP work. They depend on him.'

Mother called them over to the tea trolley. Billy handed round the plates and serviettes while she poured the tea. Angela passed the ham sandwiches and iced tarts.

Afterwards, Dad moved everyone to the front room where he'd pinned a white sheet on the far wall and set out the magic lantern. An open wooden box with white glass squares sat beside it. They had the special pictures on them.

It was so exciting sitting in the dark as the light flickered onto the white sheet, and scenes of iced mountains and great wide rivers and castles and jungles and Spanish dancers in long frilly dresses with black lacy fan things on their heads flashed up one by one. There were loads of scenes and by the time it was all over the scenes were mixed in Billy's head and he couldn't think whether the dancers lived in the jungle or the castle.

'That was a super show,' Mr Durban said as Dad collected their coats.

Mother turned off the hall light and opened the front door onto the freezing night. A searchlight swept right across the sky ahead and then everything went black. Billy gazed up at the stars in their strange patterns.

Mr Durban looked down at him. 'Star-gazing, my boy?'

Billy knew he wasn't Mr Durban's boy, not really, but he could ask him questions. 'Why does the sky look so big?'

Mr Durban didn't laugh or sneer. 'It's the black-out, no lights spoiling the view of the sky. I've never seen it like this in previous years, Billy.' A searchlight swept past again. 'Or those, I have to say.'

A light snow was falling as they walked away, smattering Angela's green school mac and pixie hood. She looked like a pine tree as she turned to wave. Mr Durban sent a smile specially at him. Billy felt the half crown in his pocket, all ready to join Uncle Ted's shilling. He knew where the ARP hut was. He'd visit it if he was sent to the shops and then he could ask Mr Durban anything, even about the shashka.

~

It hadn't stopped snowing for days. They all sat with their chairs close to the stove. *Bandwagon* was playing on the wireless. Mother took up some grey socks to darn and said, 'Early night tonight, Billy. School starts again tomorrow.'

Billy jerked his head up. 'Aren't I going to be evacuated then? Am I staying here?'

Dad said, 'While things are quiet in London. You can go to school, meantime.'

Billy rubbed his hands together. That was good, he'd see Jim, Andrew, Reg and everyone. There'd be games of football in the playground. He hadn't played since last term in the country school. 'I'll be able to see my friends.'

Mother stroked back a grey thread before plunging her darning needle back into the heel of the sock. 'Yes, you will. And Kenneth will be there of course.'

~

It was a funny feeling running towards school. He hadn't even thought about those roads for months and he knew them so well. The bitter morning made him rush along, the wind whipping round his knees like a punishment. He reached the dirty cement wall with *Wot no Dads?*chalked on it and followed a crowd of children through the school gate. He didn't recognize many faces.

He looked for anyone he knew. Sonia was back, and she waved, but there were loads of children he'd never seen before. When the whistle went, he moved towards his old class line and at last he saw Jim and Reg.

'Yahoo, I'm back.'

They grinned, but as he started over towards them an elderly lady teacher pulled him back in line. Wasn't he going to be in the same class?

Inside was different. The men teachers were all gone except Mr Hendrick. Miss Johnson and Mr Finlay were still at the village. The old pair of classrooms had its dividing doors open, so there weren't two classes now, but one big one. Mr Hendrick stood at the door waving his walking stick to anyone not walking in quietly. He looked greyer and couldn't remember Billy's name. That felt horrible.

The most rotten thing was Kenneth standing there at the middle desks, still with his gloves on. It was very crowded, three to a desk. Jim and Reg were in the back row with another boy, so there was no room for him. Mr Hendrick pointed to an empty seat by two smaller boys. One of them smelled like bad wee.

Billy looked all around. There was Andrew! They made silent signs to each other. There were so many in the class! Billy counted forty-two, and that was with some absent, as he learned when Sir did the register. They all had to call out their names and ages. Some children were younger than Billy, and others were more than two years older.

'Now settle down,' said Mr Hendrick. 'I know you've all got lots of news about Christmas. Welcome back, those children who were evacuated. We're very happy to have you here safe and sound. But we must work all the harder because there are lots more of us. Older ones help the younger ones; good readers help the strugglers. Understood? And no talking.' He handed out the exercise books, cut into three.

After everyone had written a page about Christmas, and chanted times tables that Sir had pinned on the wall, it was time for Reading. There were only six copies of the reading book and so everyone had to read from the same one, reading round the class.

The book was far, far too easy for Billy, but some children staggered over every word. It was very boring, so when it was his turn, he tried to make it more interesting by doing the voices of the different characters. Behind him, he heard a snort. It was Kenneth, nudging his neighbours and encouraging them to snigger.

'Don't be silly, boys,' said Mr Hendrick. 'Go on, Wilson, please.'

But now every word threatened to trip him up and the beastly stutter came back. Some of the girls tutted and sighed. Kenneth and the boys beside him snorted as loudly as they could without getting caught.

Luckily, the milk bottles were put inside the door at that point, so everyone lined up while Sonia handed out the straws. Mr Hendrick spooned out the cod liver oil and malt at the doorway before they drank their milk and went out to play.

Outside, he was just joining Andrew, Jim and Reg when Kenneth ran up with a crowd of boys. They surrounded Billy, calling him soppy and mimicking his reading.

'What ab-bout you then?' Billy complained. 'P-people might laugh when it's your t-turn to read.'

'M-m-my t-t-turn.'

'M-m-my t-t-turn.' The boys copied and laughed.

Billy's face got hot and he raised his fists.

'Don't,' said Sonia, her new hair tied up neatly with a pink satin ribbon. 'Sir'll come out and you'll be for it if you fight.'

'Can't fight, Weakie. Girls say so,' taunted Kenneth.

'He m-might get into t-t-trouble, s-so he c-can't f-f-fight,' joked a fat, toothy boy and the whole lot fell about laughing.

They all needed bashing. Billy looked wildly around for his friends. They were at the edge of the crowd, looking awkward. Jim took a ball from under his arm and nudged the others. They ran away down the playground, kicking it between them as they went.

It was freezing and many of the girls were huddled in their coats under the protruding roof. Sonia pointed to them as she ran off. 'Come up here, Billy, with us lot.'

He shook his head, miserably. He couldn't sit with the girls, and if he hit out at the teasers, Kenneth would tell and if he was hit, perhaps he'd be ill again. Then there'd be Uncle Frank's punishment. Why couldn't Uncle Frank be a soldier and go to war, and Uncle Ted come home again? Uncle Ted would know how to deal with Kenneth.

The boys jumped up and down around him making stupid faces and putting their tongues out. If only he had the shashka to whistle round their heads. That'd shut them up.

As soon as their attention wavered, Billy ran off down the playground to join Andrew, Jim and Reg. He'd always played football with them at playtime before. As he reached them, Reg kicked a whopper and it hit the sheds with a twang. Everyone cheered.

Kenneth put his foot on the ball.

'Kick it back, Kenneth,' said Jim. 'Give us it.'

Kenneth did, and so was then in the game. Jim gave Billy half a glance. Billy hesitated, then walked off. It was too risky playing any game with Kenneth in it. As the yards grew between Billy and the football, he heard Kenneth say, 'You weren't going to let old B-b-billy play, were you?'

This was too much, especially when the others, his friends, just shrugged. As Kenneth ran past, putting his tongue out, Billy grabbed hold of him. The school wall was nearby. Kenneth was backing towards it but Billy held on to his coat lapels. He pushed Kenneth against the wall, saw his beastly eyes with their long lashes and skinny throat all white and smooth. He hated him, his hands itched to squeeze and strangle the throat.

'You better not hurt me. I shall tell Daddy.'

'I feel like killing you. I could put Hitler onto you.'

A crowd of children ran up. 'A fight, a fight. Go on Wilson, bash him.'

They were both Wilson, so which of them was meant?

Kenneth smirked at him, looking confident that Billy would never dare hit him.

Billy pulled back his fist ready. He wouldn't think about Uncle Frank. He just wanted to bash Kenneth into the far away.

'Fight-ing, fight-ing,' the girls were chanting.

Billy held firmly onto Kenneth, who was looking hard at Billy's fist. The other boys closed round them in a ring.

'Go on, Wilson, get him,' someone yelled from the back of the crowd.

Kenneth leant forward with hard staring eyes. There was a spot of malt just near his stupid mouth. Spit came out of it, he spoke so fast, 'You're being sent away to the country. If you hit me, they'll give me your toys and you'll never come back home.'

Billy's fist went slack. Was it true? He'd been sent away before.

Kenneth wriggled out of his grasp and ran through the circle of children, punching the air as they yelled 'Aw, Kenneth! Fight him.'

'Not worth it, the soppy stammerer!'

Billy could have chased him, pushed him to the ground and pummelled him over and over. He knew he was stronger. But then Aunty would hate him, Uncle Frank would beat him and Mother and

Dad would send him away. Were they really planning it already? Or was it one of Kenneth's lies?

He leant against the wall, warm where Kenneth's body had just been, and folded his arms in front of him, holding the hate safely inside. The circle mooched away, leaving him alone.

After the whistle went, Andrew ran into school beside him. 'You should've fought him. Otherwise, Kenneth'll do it again.'

'You didn't stick up for me.'

Andrew hurried ahead.

In the classroom the ink-wells were being filled up. The teacher had chosen Kenneth as the class monitor because he was clean and reliable. Some inkwells had fresh ink. People who got those could write fairly neatly. Others were clogged with bits of blotting paper so that pens made blotches even with the most careful of writers. Billy knew he would get a clogged one, and he did.

Sir had been busy in playtime. There were loads of sums written up on the blackboard. There were some groans. Kenneth looked around and frowned, as if he was the teacher.

Everyone leaned over their desks, some with the tip of the pen in their mouths. Billy was one of the first to finish.

'You boys who've finished, help these boys on the front row, please,' said Mr Hendrick. 'I see you've not forgotten your lessons after all those weeks away, Wilson. Well done.'

'Well done,' mimicked a quiet voice. Kenneth's head wagged from side to side, a stupid grin on his face. Boys near him sniggered, and so did some girls. Mr Finlay didn't see. He had his head down trying to explain pounds, shillings and pence to the back row. Billy hunched his shoulders. It was a beastly day, and his knees burned ever so badly.

When Mr Hendrick paced down between the rows he noticed how red Billy's knees were.

'You've got chaps, Wilson. It's very cold weather, everyone. Turn your socks up so that they cover your knees when you go outside.'

Billy glared at Kenneth as they lined up, hoping to scare him but Kenneth just mouthed 'country' to him. Aunty always collected him at the school gate so Billy couldn't risk doing anything. He turned his socks over his knees and ran home.

He was out of breath when he got through the front door and it felt good to see Jill in the parlour with her toys.

He sat down to play with her and put his freezing hands and knees to the fire. The coals were red but his knees were even brighter. Mother put her head round the door.

'You're back sharpish, Billy. Was it nice to be back at your old school then?'

He wanted to tell her. 'I d-didn't like it with Kenneth in my class.'

'He's older than you, so of course he's going to be able to do everything quicker and better.'

'Not that. He's p-playing with all my friends, Jim and Reg and Andrew.'

'Of course, everyone's mixed in. You have to share, Billy. Share your toys, share your friends.'

'But he laughs at me and things.'

'That's nothing. Ignore it.' She wiggled a toy at Jill. 'Just poke the coals a bit, Billy. Put the poker back well behind the fire-guard, then go upstairs and wash your hands. I've got some jam sponge for tea.'

'And spam sandwiches?'

'Yes.'

'Goody.' Was she really sending him to the country? He'd test her. 'I was always h-hungry when I was evacuated, Mother.'

'That's in the past. At home, you can always have more bread.'

In the past? So Kenneth had been lying. Billy hadn't eaten much at lunch-time, that horrible pale mince and wet cabbage and ucky junket afterwards. It would be super to sling the lot at Kenneth.

He slid back from the fire, a bit warmer now, and put the hot poker well out of Jill's reach.

CHAPTER TWENTY-THREE

March 18, 1940. *Hitler meets Mussolini. Will Italy join the war?*

Billy was zooming in the garden. That meant being a spitfire, speeding across the sky.

He stopped when Kenneth arrived with Aunty and Uncle and followed them indoors. Mother had a flowered dress she'd finished with, and Aunty thought it would fit her.

'Will you excuse us, Frank, while Doreen tries this on?'

'Go on you girls. I'll take care of these lads.'

They giggled, went up to the bedroom and shut the door. It reminded him of Mrs Youldon when her sister Mary visited, except that they were young, more like Angela; Mother and Aunty Doreen were proper mothers.

Uncle Frank took Billy and Kenneth into the parlour. 'Stand back to back, you two.'

The back of Kenneth's head pressed against the top of Billy's neck. Uncle turned them both to face him. He was scowling. 'Put up your arms, Billy. No, roll up your sleeves first. Ha! Call those muscles! I've felt worms firmer.'

Kenneth leant against the wall, smiling quietly, although his arms were probably like threads of cotton.

'Now then, push against my arms, boy. Harder, try to get my arms down. No, no. Hopeless. Like this, like this,' and he pressed Billy's arms back until they felt they would break.

'Phew. Ow.'

'Take it like a man. Pain. Growing up. That's what it's all about. You wait till you get in the army. Sergeant Major'll make mincemeat out of you. You've got to toughen up.'

'W-what about Kenneth?' It wasn't fair.

Uncle removed his beefy hand from around Billy's arm and placed it gently on his son's curls. 'He's an artist. He'll be exempt. His paintings will be on the walls of every fashionable house in London, in Paris, everywhere. Ah, yes. You, though. You're no drawer, are you?'

'No.'

'You'll be infantry. Marching your boots off. Cannon fodder, no doubt.'

'What's that?'

Uncle laughed. It wasn't a nice sound. 'Secret. You'll find out if this war goes on long enough. Eight, aren't you? Only six more years, then territorials. My bet's that this war'll go on and on. You better build up those muscles. You want to be able to fight Hitler off when he comes, don't you?'

Hitler? Coming here! Dad should come home. Or Mother come downstairs. Now that Uncle had freed his arms, he could turn round. Kenneth didn't have a frightened face. He was looking at Uncle as if he was an ice-cream.

Uncle liked painters. Hitler might like painters, might save them, even.

Uncle Frank shook his sleeves down. 'I've got to be off, boys. I'm on blackout watch. Upstairs to play, now.' He poked a finger in Billy's chest, 'and I'll be back soon for your training, Sonny Jim.' and went into the hall. 'Back later, girls,' he bellowed upstairs, before shutting the front door behind him so firmly that the house shivered.

Billy led the way upstairs, rubbing his arms. Even playing with Kenneth was a relief.

Kenneth took his shoes off and stood on the bed, looking around. 'Hey, you've got a new car!'

'Grandad gave it me for Christmas.'

'So! Reg Parsons is having me to his party next Tuesday.' He bounced a bit on the bed.

'He's my friend; why hasn't he invited me?'

'Ha-ha. You're a left-out.'

'Why are you so nasty?'

Kenneth bent down. His face was so near that Billy could smell the cod liver oil spooned into him that morning. 'Because you've got everything.'

Billy stared at him. 'What?'

Kenneth stood up again. 'And you're never ill. Anyway, you don't live here any more and Reg is my friend now.'

'I do live here.'

'Not really. I told you, you're going back to the country. I heard Daddy say.'

Billy went to his window and looked out at the washing on the line. His trousers weren't there. Mother would have washed them if he was going away. Kenneth was jumping lightly up and down on the bed, his hands like palm fronds in front of him. He wanted to be annoying.

'It's not true', Billy said. 'One of your fibs. I'm staying here now, like you.'

'No. You're going back to that country place. Like before. And I'll stay here with all your friends and play with your toys.'

'I'm not going. I'm not!' Billy plucked his pillow from his bed and pressed it round his ears.

Kenneth bounced up and down higher, chanting, 'You won't have your toy-oys, you won't have your toy-oys, I will play with the boy-oys, I will play with the boy-oys.'

Mother's voice streamed from her bedroom, 'Billy! Don't you dare bounce on the bed! Stop it at once!'

Kenneth slid down rapidly and went to the window where three little planes stood on the window-sill. He was pushing them along sweetly as Mother opened the door.

Billy was smoothing the coverlet that Kenneth had rucked up.

'Billy! You know you mustn't bounce on the bed.'

'It was Kenneth.'

Kenneth looked up from the planes with a hurt expression. 'Billy!'

Mother took hold of Billy's arm and smacked his leg.'Naugh-ty-Boy-Pass-ing-The-Blame,' she said, in time to each smack.

Billy swallowed hard several times. 'Is that w-why you're s-sending me away?' he asked in a wobbly voice.

Mother dropped her smacking arm and glanced at Kenneth just as his smirks disappeared. 'I am not sending you away,' she said.

'Kenneth told me.'

This time it looked as if Mother believed Billy. 'Kenneth?'

'I thought I heard Daddy say he was going back to the country, Aunty Marcia,' Kenneth managed a bewildered expression.

'Only if the war steps up, that's all we've decided. And then you may have to go too, Kenneth.' She tossed her head as she shut the bedroom door again.

'And it was Kenneth bouncing,' Billy muttered as loud as he dared.

'Grrrrrrrr,' they both said, hunching their backs and going for each other, arms flailing, pulling hair, kicking and thumping. Billy put all his hate into it.

'Shhhhh,' they both said, not wanting the mothers to return and find them fighting.

Billy ended it by sliding out to the bathroom and locking the door.

When the six o'clock news started, they went downstairs. Kenneth hung about, half listening to what had been shot down or sunk.

Billy leant on the window-sill, peering through the coloured bits in the panes of glass. It was very dark. Enemies of all sorts could be out there, and no-one would know. He said, 'It'll be t-time for you to go home soon, Kenneth. No p-point in going upstairs again, is there? Shall we just play draughts?'

'All right. I'll be white. You're black, ha-ha.'

Halfway into the game, Kenneth said, 'Anyway, bet you do go back to the country soon. Then I'll take these draughts to school.'

Billy folded the board up with all the pieces inside, ignoring

Kenneth's outraged wail. He put the draughts in two piles, then pushed the black pile so that the whites collapsed in a heap. He pointed to them.

'That's you, that is. White. Black's vanquished White, see. Now I'm putting the draughts away and I hope you're ill in bed again soon, so there.'

It was only a week ago that he'd quarrelled with Kenneth and wanted him ill. Now Kenneth was ill in bed and it was Billy's fault for wishing it. This was scary.

He piled up Jill's bricks and let her knock them down again. She giggled. He liked her when she was happy. Her cheeks were like little bouncy balls, pink ones. Not marbly white, like Kenneth. He bent his head, pretending he wasn't listening to Mother and Dad talking about helping Aunty.

'It's little enough, Marcia.'

'But we've only just finished tea. Do we have to go now?'

Dad said, 'Doreen needs some support.'

'Doreen and Kenneth are a pair, always sickly.'

'Yes, they're very unlucky.'

The voices moved to the hall, Mother's getting a bit shrill. 'It is a nuisance, sometimes. We don't cause them any.'

'So I'm blessed with my healthy trio. Just go and relieve her for a couple of hours. You should be charitable to Frank's wife and child.'

'I am. Don't I have him here week after week?'

'He's a charming child.'

'Mm. He has the looks, those eyes and lashes, I'll give you that. But— there are things about him that aren't— oh I don't know. I just don't want the bother of looking after him so often, and really not now.'

'Just do your bit. *The only gift is a portion of thyself*— Emerson.'

'I do wish you wouldn't quote at me. All right, I'll take Billy to keep Kenneth company while I do my best to cheer Doreen up.'

Dad came back into the parlour and lifted Jill onto her chair. 'Looks like you're going to be a Daddy's girl for the evening, so none of your nonsense. Billy, Mother's going to take you to see Kenneth. Run upstairs for some books or games to lend him while he's stuck in bed.'

Billy went to his bedroom. First, he pulled out the Jesus book. That would do. He looked at its hard white cover, sniffing its horrid shiny smell. Jesus on the front was its only picture. He dangled the book in one hand. He'd never been ill for more than a day himself. It must be awfully boring to be stuck in bed. He got some Beanos off the bottom of the pile and a magic painting book.

'Time to put your coat on,' Mother called.

'Oh, am I pleased to see you,' said Aunty when they arrived. 'Kenneth will be thrilled, Billy.' She waved him upstairs straight away and took Mother into her kitchen.

He padded upstairs, one step at a time, and put his head round Kenneth's bedroom door. There were drawings all over his walls, people and buildings and aeroplanes and whole scenes with things happening in them.

'Cor,' Billy said. 'These are super. Just like the real dog fights. We lot've been watching them at school. Two of them flew right near. You should've seen them.'

The bedroom was stuffy and the windows misted over, so Kenneth couldn't even see the clouds let alone aeroplanes outside even when he was sitting up. His hands lay on the covers like pale seaweed. Billy hadn't noticed before that although Kenneth was smaller than him, his fingers were longer and very white at the tips.

A half-finished jigsaw of some horses in a stable, spread on a piece of thick cardboard, lay on the foot-end of the bed.

'Do you want us to do your jigsaw?'

Kenneth shook his head. 'You do some.' He leaned over sideways to turn on the bedside lamp. It was getting dark.

Billy did the sky pieces and the muddy ground so that Kenneth could do the horses and all the interesting bits. Kenneth put in a few pieces, slowly.

He looked over the picture. 'I'm sure pieces have fallen under the bed,' he said in a crotchety voice. Billy bent right down, but he couldn't see any.

'Put the jigsaw away. It's uncomfortable on my legs.'

Billy wandered round the bed. 'I've brought you some things to read.'

'My eyes hurt.'

Billy started to draw the curtains. 'Come to the window, Kenneth. See all the stars and the moon.' It had been hanging halfway out of the sky Christmas night. Now it was skinny and mean.

Kenneth said 'It's small, not worth drawing.'

'But you always draw.'

Kenneth slid back into bed and shut his eyes. 'Just talk to me.'

He lay back and Billy pulled the curtains to, crossing the blackout sheet over the middle. He re-told the best of what he remembered from his heroes book. Kenneth liked the stories and said 'More', even though he'd surely never ever do anything like discovering a new land, or bravely fighting the Normans like Hereward. It was lucky Billy hadn't brought the book with him, because Kenneth might want to keep it. He jolly well mustn't because the boy on the cover looked like Billy and Mr Durban had specially given it to him. It was a book to keep always, like the secret about the shashka.

When Aunty called him downstairs so that Kenneth could rest again, she said he was a life-saver. 'Kenneth needs you more than ever.'

Billy didn't say anything. He pretended to look at a ginger cat on her calendar.

Mother was looking at him with her head on one side. She picked up her hatpin and felt its cruel point before skewering her hat with it. 'Time to get back, Billy. Your father's probably going potty trying to put Baby to bed. Bye, Doreen. Let's hope Kenneth's fit again soon.'

CHAPTER TWENTY-FOUR

June 5th 1940. *Dunkirk rescue – Churchill defiant.*

The skies had been blue for some time and Kenneth had been well for ages. Sometimes he had to come home from school with Billy and stay for tea because Aunty did work at the Mothers' Union.

Everyone got very excited at school when Mr Churchill became Prime Minister. They were allowed to bring their flags and wave them and cheer after Mr Hendrick read them Mr Churchill's speech about having 'nothing to offer but blood, toil, tears and sweat,' and that Britain wanted 'Victory. Victory at all costs. Victory in spite of all terror. Victory, however long and hard the road may be, for without victory there is no survival.' They all wrote those words down and the top set learned them off by heart.

At home, Billy told Dad about it proudly because he'd been one of those to memorise the words.

Dad said with a long face, 'Mr Churchill may be a war-monger but at least he doesn't pretend the price will not be paid.' Dad didn't look to the ceiling or say a name afterwards so that must have been his own saying.

Today Mother had a special meeting at the town hall. Everyone was looking grim so it was probably important. 'I'd better go to it, Billy. You can walk to Nanny and Grandad's and I'll collect you from there.'

Nanny met him at the door and took him in for milk and fruit buns. 'I'm sorry there's no cake, Billy. I just haven't the sugar, you see.' She didn't chat and didn't bring out anything for him to play with. Mother had told Dad that the war was getting Nanny down. He ate up hungrily and looked round for Grandad.

'He's in the garden waiting for you, my dear.'

Billy ran out. It was warm and lovely, just right for playing ball with someone. But Grandad said, 'Come along, Billy. I'm going to teach you how to grow vegetables. It's very important now.'

He showed him all the planting in rows, then how to weed round the carrots.

Eventually he said he'd go indoors for a cup of tea and sit down. 'I'll see how Nanny is. You finish those last two rows yourself, now.'

Well past tea-time and still sunny, it was such a happy feeling. There was no Jill to whine or Kenneth to bully him and he'd just learned how to make a whistle sound. He practised as he pulled out the weeds and put them in a little wooden trug by his side. He did a whole row then held out his hands, really black with mud. All the fingernails were too. That was rather shocking but Nanny wouldn't mind and there was plenty of time for cleaning up before Mother came for him. Perhaps her meeting would be long, and she might ask Nanny if he could stay the night. That would be topping. He finished the last row and stood up to admire his work.

Down the road he could see someone dragging along. It was a sort of scarecrow man, all dirty and hairy in a big long coat and he kept coming nearer. Billy backed towards the house as he watched the boots all cracked and green, with only bits of lace, slop, slop, slop, coming right towards the gate. Billy scampered round to the back door.

'Quick, Grandad. There's a scarecrow man coming to your gate. He's going to come in. Stop him, stop him!'

Grandad pushed Billy gently towards Nanny, and went through to the front door. They heard him open it and start down the path. There was a pause, then hoarse voices.

Grandad put his head round the front door and called to Nanny, 'Send Billy next door for an hour or so. Then run a hot bath.'

Nanny looked confused, then gestured Billy towards the gate. But as he went he heard Grandad whisper to her, 'It's Ted, love. It's Ted.'

The neighbour had to give Billy a tin bowl to soak his black hands in, with a nailbrush and carbolic soap. There was something bubbling on the stove and it smelled horrible. 'Don't mind my cooking, duck. It's a pig's head. Hubby loves it, see.'

He shuddered. He didn't want to see.

The lady put gramophone music on for him while he sat there trying to work things out. *Uncle Ted?* Did he come after the scarecrow man, chase him away? He scrubbed at his nails. The dirt wouldn't come out. Was the scarecrow man Uncle Ted? It didn't look a bit like him. The man on the record sang on, *Nice work if you can get it*. It took ages for his nails to get clean and soon the needle was just scratching round the record. He didn't want to listen to singing anyway.

It seemed a long time before Mother came for him, with Jill in the push-chair. She didn't even look at his hands. She walked back home slowly, ignoring Jill's jabber. Although Dad said she was a late talker, Jill could say several words now, so she said them over and over, 'cup, dinner, dinner, cup, cup, mama, cup, cup, cup, cup, cup, mama, mama, cup.'

When they were well away from Nanny and Grandad's, Billy asked, 'Did Uncle Ted come home, Mother?'

She loosened her silky headscarf and shook her fringe from her forehead, looking to left and right as if she was going to cross the road, but they weren't near any crossing.

'Yes, he did. He's safe, isn't that good? He's back from France and needs to rest. So it may be a while before we see him.'

She wasn't going to say any more. He could tell.

As usual, it was Kenneth who told him more. At school playtime, Kenneth ran over to him. 'Your Uncle Ted's home.'

'Mm.' Billy didn't want him to know about the scarecrow man.

'Came home filthy. Nothing on except his underwear and a great-coat. I know all about it, Aunty Marcia rang Mummy last night. Then she told Daddy, and I was there.'

Billy hunched his shoulders so that his neck was hidden by his jumper. Why couldn't Aunty be like Mother and not say anything in front of children? He glared at Kenneth. 'Uncle Ted couldn't help it.'

'I know. Taken off the beach, like the others. Rescued.' Kenneth raised himself to full height, looking important. 'See, France has gone.'

'Gone where?'

'Nowhere, stupid. Hitler's fighting there and we've lost. Daddy says Hitler's won France now. He's doing Belgium and he'll come for England next. He'll bring thousands of soldiers and they'll all come to London.'

'They w-won't.'

'Will. Defeated, your uncle. De-feated by the Ger-mans.'

'Germans are ENEMY!'

Kenneth danced around singing tunefully. 'Defeated by the Germans, defeated by the Germans.'

Miss Keaton, an old teacher who had come out of retirement, was on duty. 'Lovely singing voice, Kenneth. It's good to see you have so much energy after being ill so often.'

Kenneth lowered his head, his eyelashes too. 'Thank you, Miss Keaton.'

Miss Keaton blew her whistle hard and Billy ran as fast as he could to sit in his desk far away from Kenneth at the front. The sums were easy, but he couldn't concentrate and for once he was nearly the last to finish instead of one of the first. He'd wanted Uncle Ted to come home so much and now he had. But he wasn't Uncle Ted, but some dirty man like the ones people put notices on their gates for; *No Hawkers*. He screwed up his eyes but couldn't get those greeny cracked boots out of his mind.

He ran straight home before Kenneth could get to him or shout out things to all of the others. This time, he was jolly well going to ask Mother. 'Mother. Was Uncle Ted on the b-beach? Was he d-defeated? Is England d-defeated?'

Mother sat down on the sofa in the parlour. She hadn't laid the table and Jill was still in her high chair from lunch, kicking the foot rest and banging a board book up and down on the tray, just like she'd done when she was a proper baby. Mother sighed and put her hands round her face.

'England isn't defeated yet. Our armies just had to withdraw. That means, get away for the moment. They'll go back again.'

'To France? Where the Germans are?'

She shook her head. Did this mean No, or she didn't know, or to stop asking her? 'Mother. Please tell me what happened to Uncle Ted.'

For once she didn't wave him off. She just looked tired. 'He was with his regiment but they got split up when they were fighting. He had to wait on the beach with all the other soldiers who needed to get back to England. Rescue boats came out but they were mostly small. He waited for his turn three days and nights standing in the sea. They had no food; he was exhausted. So he's resting now at Nanny and Grandad's. I told you that.'

'Is he a hero?' Billy could hardly hear his own quiet voice.

'Everyone's a hero who fights in the war. Or no-one is,' Mother said to herself, standing up at last. 'Jill, stop that banging.' She lifted her out and muttered, 'There's a nursery on the common now. I could sign up for war work, though I don't know what— make phone calls for the officer class?'

Jill trotted over to Billy and held up her book. 'Read me.'

'Do I have to, Mother?'

But Mother had gone out to the kitchen. He opened Jill's book. It only had six pages. It really was very boring. Cup. Doggie. Pussy. Chair. Bed. He could do much better if he wrote books for little children. He took Jill by the hand and went upstairs to his room with her. He found her one of his old books with a story about a bear who ran away to sea. He read it to her and she really listened. She was growing up, getting to be a proper person at last.

'Again, more,' she said.

He looked at her fat little face. Perhaps she'd grow up to be nicer than Kenneth. 'If you're good,' he said, 'I'm going to give you my animals.'

'Amimas.'

He found her a bear that fitted into her chubby hand very well and they went downstairs for tea. Mother only had bread and jam, no cake, but he didn't say anything. No-one said anything. If there had been cake, he'd have saved it for Uncle Ted.

After tea, he said he was going out for a run, just nearby. It was still light, so Mother let him. It was Jill's bedtime. He ran really fast until he got to Mr Durban's ARP hut. He was lucky, Mr Durban had just come on duty.

'My Uncle Ted's back,' Billy had to stop to take a breath, 'and he's resting. From France. Mother said he had to wait three days and nights to be rescued from the sea. I saw him come up Nanny's road all dirty like a tramp and his boots had no laces and had gone all green.'

'Now slow down, Billy. Thank the Lord our good lads are home safe from Dunkirk. Tell me, is your uncle all right?'

'He's resting and Kenneth says England was defeated.'

'Defeated? Never! Mr Churchill says the withdrawal was a masterful success.'

'Success?' Billy looked at him hopefully. 'Was it? But Kenneth says France has gone. Where's it gone?'

'It's still there, my boy, but the French let Germany take over. Our brave soldiers couldn't fight the Germans alone. They went back to the French beaches to be collected. Your uncle needs his rest now. A couple of days then he'll be back at the front.'

'Back! But he's done his fighting.'

'He's still needed. Britain needs all the soldiers she can get. But not your father, Billy. Don't worry. He's needed here.'

'What about my Uncle Frank?'

'Tax inspector, isn't he? Retained. So he stays.'

Why couldn't Uncle Frank fight Hitler? He'd be just right. Hitler needed bullying. It wasn't fair. Billy fidgeted with his feet.

'Sit yourself down.'

He sat on a wooden stool underneath the poster of Hitler looking sneakily behind some nice English people to hear what they were saying.

'Now, Billy. I was just about to have a bit of tea. I've got chocolate here that I won't be able to manage. Can you help me out?'

Billy nodded. Probably he could. 'Thank you,' he murmured with his mouth full.

There was a map of Europe on the table beside him. Mr Durban pointed out Dunkirk and where the Jerries were. 'Doubt if it'll be France your uncle goes back to, don't worry.'

Then another warden arrived and Billy had to scuttle off home.

Nanny would look after Uncle and make him clean and strong again. He wouldn't let Kenneth sneer about Uncle even if he had to bash him and get punished. If only he had the shashka he could wave it and Kenneth would shake. Or it would be magic, and in a moment Uncle Ted would be just the same as he always used to be, laughing and teasing him, even doing handstands. He had to be, otherwise, how could he be sent back soldiering?

Uncle had been five days resting when Mother said to hurry home from school so that they could see him again.

Jill was already in her push-chair when he got back. She waved a toy at him, smiling, because she didn't understand they were going to say Goodbye to Uncle Ted.

On the walk to Nanny's, Billy didn't try to tell Mother about school that day. It didn't seem important, even though on this air raid practice they'd all had to run their fastest and Andrew had tripped and fallen and blood came down and down from his knee. It couldn't be seen to until the pretend All Clear came. There'd been another Run Rabbit, Run game with teachers joining in too. It was like grown-ups growing down.

He watched Mother's feet marching along behind the push-chair. Her shoes weren't shiny and the heels rolled over at the sides. Everything was getting wrong.

Nanny gave Mother a special look when she opened the door and hugged Billy to her side while muttering something to Mother over his head. Jill was happy in her push-chair so they left her in the hall. 'It'll be quieter for Ted if she stays here,' Nanny said.

Grandad was in the sitting room with a pack of cards dealt out on the card table. Uncle Ted was sitting the other side of it with his back to them. Mother went forward and bent over him to say Hello.

He turned round slowly and then noticed Billy. 'Hello, Billy,' was all he said.

Billy stared. Although his shirt and trousers were clean and his face too, his face was hollow where his cheeks had been and the front of his hair wasn't right. A great chunk of it was white, whiter than Grandad's.

'Hello Uncle,' Billy muttered and quickly stood back by Nanny. When she went into the kitchen, he followed. He found lots of helping to do while Nanny put things on trays for tea.

She said, 'We're keeping things nice and peaceful for your Uncle Ted so he can set off in a calm way, you see.'

He nodded, then when Jill whimpered, went into the hall to keep her company until Nanny came to lift her out, one finger on her lips.

She put Jill up at the table on a big cushion to make her high and gave her an iced bun, which kept her quiet. She didn't seem to notice Uncle Ted and he didn't seem to notice her.

Grandad went on with the card game while they all had tea and cake.

As Billy was carrying the dirty cups to the kitchen, a snatch of conversation escaped from the sitting room. Mother was saying, 'Thank God you managed to get on a boat, that's what I say. You got back safely, and you will next time.'

And Uncle's low voice, 'I did. But some Frenchies with us didn't.'

Billy edged nearer the kitchen door.

'They wouldn't let them on. "Britons only," they said. We'd fought beside them a few days before, and we had to leave them. Just standing in the sea, bodies floating all around them, and the Jerries still coming over, plane after plane, kerchow, kerchow! None of us were firing, we weren't in a state to do anything. And they still bombed us. The Frenchies just left behind. I can't stop thinking about it.'

'You've got to put it out of your mind, Ted. There was nothing you could do.'

Billy rushed past for a wee. Grandad cleared his throat at that point and they all stopped talking. It was lucky Nanny was in the kitchen so she hadn't heard. She would've been very upset.

When he came back from the downstairs lavatory, she was collecting up the left-over cake from the table, saying, 'We're going to sort stuff in a moment, Marcia, so that Ted goes back with what he needs.'

Mother kept her hand on Uncle Ted's shoulder, shaking her head.

Billy sidled back into the kitchen. Nanny was muttering, 'Though I can't believe they're sending him back in his state.'

He piled the plates and saucers up neatly on the draining board. It was such a high pile that it would topple if he didn't stay there, holding it all up. Nanny took over. 'Good boy. You go back and sit down now.'

Grandad was holding one of Uncle Ted's arms as if he'd just fixed it on. 'See, they need you to get back, lad. The longer you stay, the harder it'll get.'

'I can't face it.'

'You can.' Grandad put a cigarette in Uncle's mouth and flicked his lighter. The flame caught the end of the cigarette with a little flare. In a moment, the end glowed and a line of smoke crept out of Uncle's nostrils. 'Stiff upper lip. We all have to do our duty. I'd go for you if I could, son, but I'm no use to them.'

Uncle drew again at the cigarette.

'Gee-up, son, let's stop upsetting the women-folk.'

They stayed by the spread-out cards, but not playing any more. Grandad puffed at his pipe. They were both looking down at the carpet.

Billy wanted to speak to Uncle Ted so much. He wanted to ask him what wild animals there were in France and see him do a cart-wheel again. But he couldn't. This was a strange man sitting and sending out puffs of smoke. He wasn't like the scarecrow, but he wasn't like Uncle Ted, either. Uncle didn't even see Jill wagging her doll up and down in front of him, and he didn't say anything to Billy.

When Mother said it was time to go, Uncle Ted stood up and she hugged him hard. 'Good luck, Ted, I'll be thinking of you. Stay safe.' She pretended not to, but she was crying. Grandad and Nanny stayed in their chairs, looking at the floor.

Billy opened his mouth but didn't manage to say Goodbye. Uncle Ted didn't seem to notice. His eyes were bleak and his lips gripped the cigarette.

Jill was bawling as they reached the hall. Billy opened the front door. Mother took the push-chair and moved away down the path quickly. She didn't talk all the way down St James' Rise. At last, he risked saying, 'Is Uncle Ted going back to France, Mother?'

She was a long time answering. Then she said, 'Not France. They're all coming out of France. I don't think his regiment have told him where it's to be next.'

Billy watched a soldier on the other side of the road go into a pub. Had he been rescued?

They crossed the big road and turned a corner. He wouldn't ask Mother any more. He'd go to Mr Durban's hut tomorrow and find out what other countries there were to fight in, now that France was empty.

When they got home, they found Dad was back from Lincoln.

'Thank goodness, Herbert.' Mother almost ran to put her head on his shoulder. She was going to tell Dad about Uncle, so Billy took hold of the push-chair. He heard her whisper 'Ted—' in a quavery voice.

Dad put his arms round her and turned her away. 'Ah, I feared that.' After a moment, he let her go. 'Let's see to these children first and then we'll go in the parlour.'

He came to help Billy with the push-chair. Jill was squealing with excitement to see him, so he picked her up and then patted Billy's back. 'You're a good helper.'

Mother sent Billy to bed right away, although it was early. He lay in bed and listened to her talking and talking and talking, and Dad answering.

The voices stopped when they put the wireless on. The last thing he heard was something about towns falling. That was a very scary thing to think about. At least Uncle Ted hadn't been in a falling town and perhaps he'd be sent to a country with no sea this time.

CHAPTER TWENTY-FIVE

September 7th 1940. *Luftwaffe target London. Civil Defence responding admirably.*

Dad's puffs of smoke danced down the hall as he went to the front door. 'Kenneth has been nervy since that air raid, Billy. I want you to be especially thoughtful when he comes today, please.'

Billy swallowed his last sweet. *He* hadn't been frightened in the air raid. There'd been a torch in the cellar. He'd always watched the coal falling through the hole when the coalman came. Now the coal hid behind shelves, and two camp beds filled the space. The air raid didn't last long and it was rather exciting, and it'd been fun everyone swapping notes on their first day back at school after holidays, especially as now he was a junior, not an infant schoolboy, and had to line up outside the Junior Boys entrance.

Luckily, Mother wasn't there to see the evacuation notices on the school gate. Perhaps she wouldn't know.

Now Kenneth was here. He watched him coming down the hall, white and thin in his short sleeved shirt.

It was flipping hot so Mother put out a tub of water in the garden for them. 'Yippee! Come on, Kenneth!'

They both pulled off everything except their pants and took it in turns to pretend they were swimming. It was even fun splashing around with Kenneth until water went on his hair.

'Stop it, Billy. I don't want my face wet. I'm getting out.'

'Cissy. You get scared of everything.'

'Don't. Anyway, air raids are scary.'

'I'm not scared.' Billy stood up and looked down at his bare chest. It was strong-looking besides Kenneth's body, which caved in round the ribs. He felt proud. Perhaps he was growing into a Cossack.

Kenneth pointed at him. 'You're stupid and— ignorant. Don't you know a bomb dropped right in the middle of London during that air raid? And it was on a church!'

Billy didn't know. Dad didn't tell him anything. He risked saying, 'Only one bomb. That's probably all the Germans have.'

Kenneth started dressing. 'Huh! Fat lot you know. Bombing's horrible.'

'We've got shelters.'

'I don't want to be buried in an Anderson, thank you very much.' Kenneth walked over to the french windows. They were wide open because of the heat. He called in through them, 'Uncle, I've brought my paints over.'

Dad came over and gave him half a roll of wall-paper. 'Here you are, Kenneth. I thought you might need this. Got it from the cellar. It's nice and smooth on the back, so you can paint on that.'

'Thank you, Uncle.' Kenneth set to work.

Billy stayed in the pool finding ants to plop into the water and then rescue out of it. He stayed in until his feet were all wrinkly.

Kenneth was still painting a long time after they'd eaten their stew and dumplings. Dad kept coming in and looking over his shoulder. 'Well done, Kenneth.That painting's worth finishing.'

Billy came to watch. He was no good with a paintbrush, the powder paint at school made a horrible mess when he tried it at school. Nothing of his ever looked any good, so he liked to see how Kenneth did it. The long white fingers gently swished up and down and soon there was a WVS canteen on the paper, sky behind it, and little figures in front.

Dad sounded pleased. 'Excellent, Kenneth. Very good composition.'

Kenneth only said, 'I'm nearly out of blue.'

Billy said, 'I haven't got paints.'

'I know.'

If he had paints, he would have let Kenneth have the blue so that the picture could be finished.

Dad went into the parlour and turned on the wireless. It must be time for the news.

The large jam-jar beside Kenneth was full of brown water.

'Whatever colours you paint with, Kenneth, the water ends up brown.'

'That's because it's a tertiary colour, stupid.'

Billy wasn't going to ask what *tirshy* meant. He'd ask Mother later, if he could remember the funny word.

Kenneth turned to him. 'You could get me some clean water. That'd be something useful.'

Billy took the jar out to the kitchen. Mother had finished making the scones. The lovely smell filled the room. The wireless, droning on in the parlour, got louder as Mother opened the door. 'Well, Herbert?'

'It's stepping up.'

That meant Hitler, war and bombing. He watched Mother flap her hands. 'Now don't mention the dreaded E word, please. I can't stand the thought of that disruption again.'

'Safety, Marcia. That's what I care about, for all of you.'

'Dal lalla, dalla lalla.' That's what Jill's babble sounded like as she put a block on the top of a tower, shakily. She chortled. The tower fell for the umpteenth time, and for the umpteenth time Billy built it again. 'Lally da lal-lal.'

The doorbell rang. Billy shushed Jill because he heard Mr Durban's voice in the hall. 'I'm here to give you the nod, Bert. Got your cellar more organised? The East End's been copping it and there's word of a convoy coming.'

Kenneth carried on painting. Tiny leaves decorated the border of his page and he was bending low over it.

Billy was just wondering if Mother would ask Mr Durban to stay for tea, when the air raid siren screamed out. Kenneth gave such a start that he knocked the paint water over, but Mother just said, 'Leave it, Kenneth. Come on, both of you.' She picked up Jill and made for the cellar.

Footsteps hurried up the hall and the front door slammed. Mr Durban was going out into the danger, like a hero.

'Quick sharp,' Dad shouted. 'Mr Durban says it might be coming our way.'

They scrambled down to the cellar. Kenneth sat himself on a little chair, saying nothing. Jill's eyes were wide and wet as she gazed around her. Mother started reading. Although the story was silly and only fit for a baby, Billy listened and kept listening until the rumbling started.

'It's some way off,' said Dad. Then it grew louder.

'Dad— Mr Durban's outside in it!'

'He's on duty, Billy. He'll be in the right place with his tin helmet on, don't worry.'

Dad brought a book out and some biscuits and a thermos flask. But before he could pass any over there was a huge thumping and thudding, and not so very far away. Kenneth slid forward and climbed into the bunk, covering his head with the blanket.

Remembering what Dad had asked of him Billy said, 'Isn't it lucky you're safe down here, Kenneth, and not in your Anderson?'

It was so good they had a cellar. Some people would be running for the underground station or the public shelter near the park. He hoped not anyone he knew. Then he remembered that Aunty and Uncle would be in the Anderson. Kenneth wouldn't like that.

They all sat waiting for the next thump. Billy could hear everyone's breathing, even his own. He kept his eyes on Dad's large hands gripping the sides of his chair. He put his own hand on his hip, pretending he could feel the hilt of the shashka there. He must be the one to protect the others.

When the All Clear sounded, Dad hurried them all into the

kitchen, then went out himself to find out the situation. Kenneth said he felt sick, so he was sent upstairs with a bucket to lie down.

Mother made sandwiches and tea, then saw to Jill. 'You read a book for a bit, Billy.'

Dad came back indoors and looked over at him as he had his tea. 'Reading. Good boy. Take your mind off. *What worries you, masters you* — John Locke.'

The air raid warning woke him with a start. He found he'd fallen asleep over the middle pages of his Wizard annual.

Mother was running down the hall outside, 'It's only two hours since the All Clear. Do you think it's a mistake, Herbert?'

Dad called down from upstairs, 'We won't risk it. Get Billy, I'm bringing the other two.'

This time no-one bothered with books or stories but just scrambled down the cellar stairs and sat waiting for the siren to stop wailing. As it did, there was a huge whooomph. Everyone jerked and gasped. Jill started whimpering.

'I should have got on with those arrangements,' Dad was muttering. He held a small torch over his notebook, making pencil ticks or crosses over his writing.

Thump. The house shook. Billy looked up at the black cellar ceiling. 'Is it a bomb falling?'

'Sit back, Billy.' Mother ducked her head and pushed Jill's into her chest. The whimpering went on and on. Mother couldn't stop her. She was all creased up herself. She said, 'Billy, I've got my hands full with Baby, look after Kenneth, please.'

Billy turned round and saw Kenneth on a little chair behind him, both arms wrapped around himself and shaking all over. He spoke in his nicest possible voice, 'We're safe down here, Kenneth.' But Kenneth didn't stop shaking so Billy moved beside him and put an arm round his shoulders. 'We've got a thick ceiling, look,' and Billy tipped his head back to have a good look himself. It was curved, like a cave, with thick beams running along it. Surely no bomb could bash through that?

Every time there was a thud, Kenneth shook, and Mother jumped, squeezing Jill tightly into her chest.

Billy imagined the shashka was at his hip, lashed onto a wide leather belt. No one could be scared while he had that.

Far away there was a fearful crash. Dad stopped his writing. 'Hope there's no-one under that, whatever it was.'

It wasn't like other times when they'd sat for a while and then been able to go back into the kitchen. This time the rumbling, whistling and thumps went on and on and on, so no-one could sleep even though Billy's eyes felt so hot and droopy. Every time his head jerked down to his chest, a bang or a whistling or a crashing brought him wide awake again.

Dad waved Billy and Kenneth towards the camp bed but it was furthest from the cellar door and it seemed safest to stay put. Dad leaned down a couple of times to unscrew the cap of the thermos. He must have made tea beforehand. He never quite got to pouring it. His hand would reach down, Mother would shake her head, the cups rattled and Dad would sit up again. It was truly a terrible noise outside, like hundreds of roofs crashing, loud aeroplanes too low down and a kind of roaring.

Billy wanted so much to sleep that he almost didn't care about the noise, but the rumblings and shakings kept him sitting up straight. Looking after Kenneth, and keeping his hand on his shashka, stopped him being scared for himself.

It was a long long night, but eventually they heard the All Clear. Dad spread his hands wide. 'It's over for now. Come on, boys.' He took Jill from Mother's arms. 'Thank the lord we're all safe.'

Mother pushed them towards the stairs and when the cellar door opened, the hall was still there and it was morning. She went straight to put the kettle on, Kenneth close beside her, while Dad took a quick look out of the front door. Billy took a few steps towards him. As the door opened, Dad was silhouetted against a distant blaze of red and orange going far up into the sky. It looked beautiful but there was a stink of brick dust and smoke.

Dad said, 'Stay inside,' and pulled the door to behind him. In a while he came back, grey-faced.

Kenneth whispered, 'What about Mummy and Daddy?'

Mother put four cups of tea on the table and a mug of milk for Jill. 'They'll have been in the Anderson, Kenneth, don't worry, but I'll ring them up. Look after Baby a moment. I'm going to check on my parents too.'

'Is Nanny and Grandad's house bombed, Mother?'

Dad sipped at his tea. 'We must certainly hope not. But some poor folks have been bombed, that's for sure.'

When Mother came back from the phone, her face looked relieved. 'No problems, Kenneth. They're all safe. Nothing came that near them.'

'That's good,' said Dad. 'Now, I think these children had better make up on their sleep.'

Mother bustled Billy and Kenneth back to bed, carrying Jill up too.

Kenneth was still silent. He looked so white and his eyes so sore that Billy gave him the best pillow for his camp bed, before sliding into his own bed. He tried to settle down, Dad's voice rumbling on down below and a strange glow outside seeping under his curtain. He pulled the blackout until it touched the windowsill so that not even a tiny plane could see in.

In the morning, Dad said the situation in London had got really serious. He was going to take Kenneth home and talk to Uncle Frank, and 'discuss matters with people.'

Billy went with them as far as the end of the road. He was surprised to see people going to church. Surely no-one had time to go today, even if it was Sunday. It seemed very wrong to be bustling along the in the normal way, but just everyone was going along the same as always.

'We don't want another night like that!' the lady opposite called to Dad as he passed.

'Indeed not! Let's hope that's the end of it for a while. I gather the Jerries lost twenty-two planes in it. Punishment enough, I should think.'

Billy waved Goodbye to Dad and Kenneth, then ran home to amuse himself in the garden for as long as he was allowed. He went to the far end of the garden behind the tool-shed to practice kicking and catching his tennis ball. He listened hard to the aeroplane sounds and whether they were turning into dangerous dronings, ready for the squeal that would mean rushing indoors and down to the cellar.

There was a thick soup for lunch, and Dad still wasn't home. 'Is that the end of the bombing, Mother?'

'How can I know?I hope so. I'll wait to hear what your father says. He's seeing several people and making phone calls. Go and tidy your bedroom the best you've ever done before. Then you can keep Baby occupied for me.'

He saw that Mother was twisting her hands and not really looking at him, so he didn't argue. Dad would calm her down when he got home. He wanted to run down to the warden's hut to see what Mr Durban thought, but he didn't dare.

After he'd done a really good job on his bedroom, he came down to the parlour to play with Jill. He piled up a few bricks and let her topple them down. She seemed happy doing that on her own, so he sat at the table and played patience. Uncle Ted had taught him last year when everyone was happy and safe. He turned the cards over slowly, wondering what was going to happen.

Bombs sounded again in the night, so they spent another night in the cellar. It was really fearful, like before. The noise went on and on, way past even Mother's and Dad's bedtime. Even though Dad wanted him to lie down like Jill, it was too scary to sleep.

In the morning, Mother was white and irritable, smacking Jill's hand when she grabbed things off the table.

He was going to get ready for school but Mother sent him to play with Jill, 'and don't come out until I call.' He heard the telephone go, the crackle of the wireless and footsteps up and down the stairs. When Mother did call, it was to send him for a bath.

'But I've only just washed!' Then he saw suitcases standing open in the front room. He screwed up his eyes. 'Are you going away, Mother?'

'We all are. Your father told you that you were only here while the going was good and now it's not. Aunty phoned. Kenneth's in a dreadful state, apparently, and you don't want to go through another night of bombing do you?'

'No.' Billy stood still, pushing a foot against the edge of the lino. There was going to be more going away. This was all Kenneth's fault. 'But I didn't make a fuss. Do I have to be evacuated again?'

He knew it was going to be Yes before he even looked at Mother. He pressed his hands on his tummy and twizzled around twice. He wasn't sure whether he minded dreadfully. He didn't like bombs. And Mrs Youldon would be happy to see him. 'Am I going back to the country?'

'Yes, but not to the same billet. We've been making the arrangements, so go and have your bath quickly. We need to get going and arrive well before dark.'

He went upstairs to run his bath, and had it slowly. It might be the last time he was in a bathroom. Tomorrow or the next day he might be shivering in a scullery, hunched up in a hip bath and it wouldn't even be Mrs Youldon's. He'd be with another stranger. Suppose he was put with that horrible woman who shaved Sonia's head!

He heard Dad come out of the parlour where he must have been making important telephone calls.

Billy dressed again and got his whizzer from the toy box. It would be 'only one small toy' again. He put a dinky car in his trouser pocket and picked up his whizzer, his heroes book and a comic. Downstairs he was able to push these inside the small case that was meant for him before Dad checked with Mother that everything important was packed. He was going to walk them to the train.

They had sardine sandwiches and jam doughnuts before putting on their coats. Jill was surprisingly quiet. He held her soft little hand, and found she had a tiny rubber doll squeezed in to it, as if she knew.

'Right then, everyone.' Dad put the gas masks out for each of them, then took two large suitcases.

Mother took a deep breath and looked around the room. 'I wonder how long we shall have to be away this time.'

She took the smaller case and the handle of the push-chair. Dad put Jill in it, where she sat very quiet, her mouth slightly open. The gas masks sat at her feet.

Billy held his small suitcase and a carrier bag of food. He hoped the new billet would be pleased.

Dad shepherded them through the door and locked it behind him. A light rain was falling. Mother pulled her scarf over her hair, and wrenched the push-chair hood up. Father couldn't use his umbrella because the cases needed both his hands.

They left their road behind, making for towards the railway station, the barrage balloons swaying in the damp breeze with no sign of sun shining behind them.

CHAPTER TWENTY-SIX

September 10th 1940. *Two waves of German bombers fly up the Thames. 28 downed by RAF.*

Kenneth was already on the station platform when they arrived, wearing his camel coat and hat as though he was going to a party. But it was his gas mask he was carrying, not a present.

'Hello Billy,' he called, like a best friend.

Aunty stepped out of the waiting room, where two large suitcases were standing. 'Frank says "God Speed",' she said to Mother. 'He couldn't come. He was needed at the first aid station for training. Heaven knows how I'll manage without him.'

Mother shrugged slightly and raised her thin eyebrows. 'And I'm having to do this all over again.'

Dad went down the platform to speak to the station master.

Billy pointed to Kenneth's hands holding a bag and the gas mask. 'Doesn't Aunty need you here?'

'Mummy's coming with me. We're right near the vicarage where Aunty Marcia stays.'

Billy looked quickly at Mother. 'They've got room for me at the vicarage this time?'

'No. It's too full.' She brushed away the wave of hair on her cheek. 'They've said they'll take me and Jill again.'

'But— what about me?'

'Your father has sorted somewhere.'

Kenneth put his head on one side. 'It was Daddy who phoned the vicar first. He found a lady nearby who could take a mother and child. We couldn't waste her billet on just you.'

Mother nodded. 'So then it was a decent billet for just one boy we needed to find.'

Aunty put a hand to her hair. 'Oh dear. It doesn't seem fair on poor Billy. I didn't mean it to work out like this.'

Billy looked at the floor. It wouldn't be Aunty's fault. Uncle was just quicker than Dad. 'Will my billet be near you, Mother?'

'It seems there's a nice one not far from where you were before.' She bent to rearrange Jill's curls.

Billy swallowed. So he wasn't going to be with any of them, or with Mrs Youldon. Bits of dust blew along the platform and he screwed up his eyes.

Dad came up to them again. 'Apparently, it doesn't make much difference where you wait on the platform. The station master said all the carriages are going to be crowded.'

'Purgatory.' Mother made a face at him and tilted her head towards Billy. 'I've told him about the billet.'

'Right.' He put a hand on Billy's shoulder. 'I'm sorry you can't be with Mother and Jill, son. It's not that easy to get billets, you see, especially arranging it privately. You were doing well at that village school and you'll go there again. I've found you a billet with your own room. It'll be much better than where you were before.'

'I was all right there,' Billy muttered. Mrs Youldon would like to have him back. He kicked one foot against the other. 'Is it until Christmas again?'

'Let's hope not, but I don't know. No-one knows. It's until we win the war and London is safe again.'

'Does Mr Durban know I'm going?'

'Yes he does. He's given me something to give you.' He took a hard envelope from inside his coat and slipped it into Billy's case. 'There. A letter. Something to read when you arrive.'

Kenneth was dancing up and down. So he wasn't under the weather now. 'I'll be with Mummy and Aunty. I'll be like Jill's brother.'

Billy looked into the push-chair at the plump little face pressed into a blanket-wrapped doll. Jill wouldn't like a different boy. Kenneth *wasn't* a brother. How would she get on without him to play with her and mind her when Mother was busy?

Jill lowered her doll and peered both ways along the platform. As her gaze swept back, it reached Kenneth. A sunbeam momentarily blinded her and she grimaced.

'She's smiling at me, see?' said Kenneth.

'She's not.' The words slipped out so quickly they sounded like *snot*. Billy turned his back on them all and walked away up the platform.

Grandad and Nanny would miss him. They'd need to check the carrots. The first two rows were nearly ready to pull. What would happen to Jim and everyone at school? And he hadn't been to Mr Durban's house to see Angela. They were all staying behind and would sit in their Anderson every night. He closed his eyes. He could see the shashka. It would be shimmering in its scabbard. He would never forget it, waiting for him, until he was old enough to use it.

'Billy!' Mother pointed down the platform away from him. A chimney length of steam headed the train rolling in, smoke and grit with it.

He picked up his case and ran to stand ready, as near as he could to Mother so he wasn't put in a different carriage.

The station master strode alongside the slowing train. Crowds of soldiers, grinning, smoking, or slumped in their seats, showed at every window.

Dad stepped forward with the bigger cases as the station master opened a carriage door.

'Here you are, ladies, you can squeeze into the corridor. That's best. Fold that push-chair. You'll have to stow your cases on it. Perhaps the nippers can perch on top.'

Mother clutched Aunty's arm. 'Oh my goodness! We'll suffocate, Doreen.'

Dad hugged Mother. 'Keep calm, Marcia. Just a journey, then into safety.' He slid the cases into a gap while Mother folded the push-chair and Aunty took Jill, then he helped all of them up the steps where they stayed squashed against the door.

'Stay safe, Doreen. You'll all be best off down in the country.'

'And you get away from London, Bert, as soon as you can.'

Billy swallowed. 'Goodbye, Dad.'

'It's not forever, son. I'll get down to see you as soon as it's possible.' He put a hand on Billy's head then on Jill's. If he gave a quotation, Billy didn't hear it.

There was a great press of soldiers and rucksacks in the corridor. They squeezed forward into the train, stepping over the big black toe-caps of the soldiers. Some of them whistled at Aunty, and she blushed. Mother lifted her chin. They were still struggling to find even a foot space when the train started. Aunty lost her balance and nearly landed on a soldier's lap. There was a cheer and a lot of laughing.

Kenneth lowered his lashes at the soldiers and one of them pulled him into a space between them. Two others lifted Jill up high. She opened her mouth to bawl but a soldier put a sweet into it and her mouth turned into a smile.

The train lurched again, and Billy hung onto a door-frame. He peered through the spaces between soldiers' heads and arms towards a window. He caught a last glimpse of Dad's face shaded by his trilby, a blob of grey against the brown carriages, not moving, while the train drew away.

It was a terrible journey squashed up against the soldiers, many of them smoking. Some of the men looked really sad but most of them were loudly joking and shouting to each other.

'Just boys, really,' murmured Aunty to Mother, but she was busy smiling at one with a ginger moustache. The soldier stood up for Mother and she squeezed into the seat with a 'Thank you'. Aunty took Jill from the soldiers, sat her on top of a suitcase and leant against it.

Nothing was easy. They needed to change train twice, struggling with Jill, push-chair and suitcases onto platforms and looking around wildly for information, before finally reaching the small station where Uncle Frank had arranged for the vicar to meet them. Mother had got herself into a state because the station names had been painted out. She almost screamed when she spotted the vicar on the platform. 'It's this one, we're here. Quickly, Billy, cases,' and she hurried them all out.

The vicar stepped towards them, nodding. 'Safe landing, thanks to Our Gracious Lord.' He seemed pleased to see Mother again, and even Jill. 'What a big girl, now. You'll soon be able to come to Sunday school.'

Jill shrank back into Mother's skirt. The vicar wasn't a Daddy sort of person. He greeted Aunty and Kenneth and introduced them to a lady standing nearby. Then he opened his arms slightly, as if he was holding a hymnal and looked around at them all. 'My dears, you got out just in time. There's been a huge convoy of planes coming right down the Thames. In broad daylight! Dreadful bombing. In your prayers tonight, give thanks that you can all come here to safety.'

Billy frowned What about Dad and all the people left behind to face the awful bombing? What could they say in their prayers?

Aunty started chatting straight away, although her curls had started to droop with the stress of the journey. Kenneth stood near to her, brushing train smuts off his camel coat.

'And a matching cap. Fetching,' the lady said as she patted his cheek.

It was only a small station, the late summer sun still shining on its wet surface. Perhaps recent rain had washed it, but there was none of the dust of London or rubbish lying between the rails. There was a sweet smell, a grassy bank and clumps with red blobs. When Billy looked closer, he saw they were wild strawberries. It would be nice to pick them.

Mother took hold of his arm and checked his packages and gas mask. He looked around for the person come to collect him. No-one else was there except the station cat.

Meanwhile, the lady led Aunty and Kenneth away. 'The vicar's car is full. We shall walk. It's not that far.'

'Bye, Billy,' said Kenneth with a toothpaste smile, his hand firmly grasping Aunty's coat sleeve. 'We'll see you when we see you.'

Aunty turned and smiled sadly at Billy. 'Ta-ta for now. Hope to see you soon, dear.' She started to walk off, then suddenly dropped Kenneth's hand and ran back, pushing something into Billy's coat pocket. 'Here, ducky. You won't be that far away. We'll be visiting you, I'm sure.' She blew him a kiss before following their lady down the road.

The vicar turned to his car. 'I think we can squeeze everything else in,' he said, stowing the push-chair into the boot, 'if you have this little one on your lap,' and he held the car door open for Mother and Jill. 'And what about this boy? Who is he?'

Mother said, 'It's my son, Billy. You met him, Vicar, remember.'

'Of course! You have a son, too, Mrs Wilson. I remember now. My goodness. I didn't recognize you, young sir. You look so—different.'

'Yes, well he won't be going to that billet again.' Mother neatened Billy's collar. 'This is where we say Goodbye, Billy. You're not to worry. You've only a few miles further to go.'

He looked anxiously from side to side. It was evening, and now that the train had drawn out of the station the place was quite silent apart from Mother's voice. 'Someone is coming to meet you,' she went on. 'The billeting officer has arranged it. We said you'd wait at the station.'

He looked around for the someone. The vicar might drive off and leave him on his own. 'We didn't say Goodbye to Nanny and Grandad,' he said quickly.

Before Mother could answer, a farm cart clattered to a halt nearby. Mother went up and spoke to the driver, then came back to Billy. 'There, lucky boy. You're going to ride on this cart all the way to your village. Hand your suitcase up to the carter.'

He went to the cart with it.

'That's right. Now, say Goodbye to Jill.'

He saw her chubby face through the car window, damp lips open as she stared at Mother's back. He waved, but she didn't seem to notice.

Mother said in her anxious voice, 'We'll come and see you as soon as we can. Pull those socks up. Keep yourself clean and be good.' She bent towards him and he smelled her Parma Violets talcum powder as she gave him a small hug.

Then he was so busy scrambling up high to sit in the front of the cart that he hardly had time to say Goodbye, and when he turned to wave, the vicar's car was disappearing down the road.

He kept staring at the back of it until five rabbits hopping across the road surprised him, they looked so cheeky and carefree. He pretended they were family. That's us, that is. Mother and Aunty, the big ones; Kenneth, Jill and me, the little ones. Running free in the country, leaving all the bombing behind. I am a lucky boy, riding on a cart.

'Looks like I got you all to myself,' said the carter. His voice was rough, but sounded kind. He jerked the reins and the cart-horse plodded back the way he'd come. 'That your Ma, eh? And your baby sister. Off with the vicar. I know he. Been to one of his sermons. Keeps them short, he do. Very pop'lar.'

Billy took a look at the man. His face was leathery and browny red, not like Uncle and Dad at all. He didn't quite manage a smile but his hand creeping into his pocket found the little bag that Aunty had pushed into it. Pear drops! His favourite. Aunty was nice. He popped a pear drop into his mouth for it seemed the right time to eat one. Then he remembered his manners. He leant forward and held out his bag. 'Would you like a sweet, Mr Carter?'

The man shifted his cap and smiled. 'No, no, you keep your sweeties, young'un. Coming out of that there London, you need all the sweetness you can get. I'm Jed Turnbull, I am, a carter but not Mr Carter, see. You call me Jed, right? I can see as you're going to get on real well with folks round here.'

Billy thought of the way the vicar looked at him that first time. And the teasing from the local children. Suppose the new billet people didn't like him? And he'd be living there till Christmas or even longer. He held onto his suitcase tightly.

Jed looked down, 'Have you got your favourite toy in that case to show me?'

Billy clicked open the latches. He could show Jed the special whizzer. Jed might not ever have seen one, living in the country. Before his hand even got to the whizzer it felt the envelope Dad had given him from Mr Durban. How could he forget? He opened it and pulled out a letter and a photograph. It was the shashka! The shashka had come with him on this new evacuation to keep him strong as strong!

It was ever such a good picture. You could see all the letters along the blade and the decorations on the scabbard, which was lying on the table nearby.

Jed was geeing up the horse. Somehow Billy didn't want to share his shashka with anyone, not even the sight of it. He put it carefully back in the envelope and read the letter. He could see that Mr Durban had especially written it in print to make it easier for him to read. That was the sort of thing he really liked about Mr Durban.

Dear Billy,
I am going to miss your visits to my hut, but you need to be safe and away from London. You will have a jolly time in the country with lots of boys you know from school. Your mother and baby sister won't be far away from you, I hear.
This photo will remind you of our chats and I know you will like looking at it. Keep it covered.
One day you will be back here again, looking at the shashka for real. Until then, I know you'll be a credit to your family and that your foster family will be pleased to have you. Best foot forward, as they say. You are a brave boy.
I send you all good wishes from Mrs Durban and Angela, as well as from me. We shall be thinking of you until we meet again after the war.
Keep safe,

Peter Durban

Billy put the letter in the envelope with his wonderful picture. Both were something special to keep. He felt suddenly proud, and sat up a bit straighter. He put the pear drops in the case and pulled out his whizzer, then clicked the case shut. 'I've got a whizzer to show you, Jed.'

Jed turned towards him, 'A whizzer! I wonder what that be. Come for'ard and sit up by me so I can see it. And lookee— you need to see around proper. Sit up on these sacks so you're like a king, a king coming into his village. Right?'

His village? Billy scrambled over the rolls of firewood until his legs reached the pile of sacks next to Jed. A king might own a shashka; he probably would in far-off countries. He put his hand on his hip where the shashka nobble would fit in his hand. He was nice and high now, like an important person. He looked hard at the road ahead. 'Is that our church tower?'

'Yes it be, tallest thing in the village.'

Now he could see the church as well and that was only a quick run away from Mrs Youldon's. She'd be really pleased to see him. Timmy and Sally would shout out 'Billy!' and jump up and down. 'Jed, I've got friends here from last time.'

'Is that so? And now you'se a be making some more friends, right enough, that's a' sure.'

The cart slowed and turned down a wide lane where there was a field and a brick house beside it with animal noises of all sorts: neighing, clucking, barking.

Jed stopped the horse and grasped hold of Billy's suitcase. 'Here we are, laddie. This'm the place, and the dogs already shouting a welcome, see.'

END OF BOOK ONE

BOOK TWO

INFILTRATION

CHAPTER ONE

September 7th 1940. *The German air force unleashes a wave of heavy bombing raids on London*

The cart came to a halt. The only noise here was from animals. Dogs were barking inside the house, chickens clucked somewhere to the left and the horse harrumphed beside him.

'It's this house,' Jed the carter said. 'Mr and Mrs Pawsey's. You can jump down now.'

Billy clambered down slowly, for the horse was swishing his tail very near his face. He didn't want to hurry. He needed to take in the place that was his billet before he went to meet his new foster parents.

Was it only this morning that he was standing on the station alongside Jill's pushchair while the grown-ups discussed how to squeeze into the packed-full train? Was it only last night he was squashed in the cellar with all the terrifying whistling and crashing above?

He breathed in the country smells and turned to look at what was waiting for him. It was very different from last evacuation. This house was quite big. There was a lot of muddy garden in front and not far from a pig pen there were chicken houses. It might be nice, nicer than the vicarage where Mother was evacuated with baby Jill. He swallowed. He mustn't be sad to be left behind.

'Brave laddie. Chin up,' Jed encouraged him as he looped the reins to keep the horse still and safe. 'I s'pose it's a bit hard to be here on your own, when your cousin and Aunty are billeted right near your ma and sister. But they'm not having animals, like here now.'

Billy nodded. 'Yes and K-Kenneth hasn't ever been evacuated before and I know this village from last time.'

'That's right. You're nearly a local.'

That wasn't really so – the locals had always called him a 'vaccie' – but he'd certainly be very welcome at one place. Perhaps he could soon visit the tiny cottage where he'd been billeted before.

Jed was already at the gate. 'You still standing waiting? Come you on, Billy. I's'll make sure you're all right.'

Billy followed him. The path was thin with flower bushes on either side, quite untidy. A dog barked again somewhere at the back of the building and hens clucked nearby. He peered around for them, ready to step away. Chickens might peck strangers. He didn't know, he wasn't used to them.

Jed pulled a rope with a rusty bell on it. It sounded a single dong.

A man opened the door but peered out as though he was looking beyond them focusing on the far distance. Two black dogs rushed forward, barking. The man shouted 'Basket!' and pushed them back. He had whiskers right down over his ears and coming out of them but not a lot of hair on his head. A few strips covered his topknot but veins showed through and there were great veins on the back of his hand when he held open the door. Billy peeped along the passage. There must be a lady somewhere.

The old man said, 'Jed— where you been about? You brought the London lad?' He smiled but he didn't seem to be looking at Billy. He pointed out a wooden box 'For your boots,' but Billy wasn't wearing boots so he left his shoes on.

The carter seemed to take charge. 'Seth, how be you, then? This chappie here be Billy. His mother'm gone to her billet at the vicarage down over. I reckon as she'll be visiting afore long to see he's settled in o'right.'

'I see, I see,' said the old man.

But he didn't see, for he was fumbling his way to the back room, touching the hall walls. It was dark except for a small lamp with a parchment shade, an open book beside it. Mr Pawsey stood opposite it and opened his hands to the room with its large wooden table and heavy chairs.

'Sit you down, lad, my Missus will brew up once she's done with the hens. She has to shut them up carefully at night against they foxes.'

He pawed around in the air, bending over a little until his hands found the table and book. A pair of glasses were underneath it. He grasped them and put the wire handles over his ears. Now he peered straight at Billy through lenses as thick as the bottoms of bottles. His eyes were big pale blotches behind them. He looked quite different now. 'Ah. So here you are, safe and sound.'

The carter put his hand on Billy's head. 'Nice lad, this'n, Seth. He'll be able to spot your specs when you lose them.' He gave a rumbling laugh and the old man joined in.

'You'm right. That'll be useful. Bane of my life, they glasses. Too heavy to wear all the time and can't see without them.'

Jed gave Billy's shoulder a friendly pat. 'I'd better be off, you folk. My supper'll be on the table. Billy, you'll settle down with Mr and Mrs Pawsey afore you know. You'll see my cart round and about these lanes and I'll give you a wave.' He winked, first at Billy, then at Mr Pawsey and stomped back to the front door.

It was now that Billy had that nasty fluttery feeling like months ago, the first time he'd been away from home. It was when he was walking round the village with the teacher trying to find him a billet, and he was the last child to be taken. Now the sight of friendly Jed going out of the door started the flutters again.

The old man sat down heavily in a chair whose leather was cracked all over, and kneaded the veins in his hands. 'Billy, eh? Hmm.' He peered at Billy. 'You a useful boy?'

'I think so, sir. I'll t-try.'

There was loud cackling outside the window. The old man

laughed. 'One of they hen's got out, and the Missus'll be chasing it. They lead her a dance. Perhaps you'll run fast enough to get 'em in order, they hens.'

Billy said nothing. He wasn't too sure that he wanted to get near the feathery, clucking things with their poky beaks. He sat still, hoping he wouldn't be asked to help right away. He fiddled with his suitcase wondering if Mother had put in a tin of food at the bottom or anything he should hand over.

The back door opened and the lady bustled in, brushing her hands on her muddy apron. She stopped short when she saw Billy, sitting on the edge of his chair.

'Our little lad, is it? I thought I heard the cart. Well, well, well. Now then. Welcome to your new home. That nasty bombing in London, we've got to get you out of that, eh. Got to get you a little nest, here, haven't we. A little nest.'

'Billy, his name is,' said the old man, and spat very accurately into a special bucket with brass straps sitting beside the fireplace.

'Billy, is it?' said Mrs Pawsey. Her sentences seemed to end in questions although she didn't have a questioning sort of face, more like a cushion with lines and dents pressed into it as well as two blackbird eyes. 'We'll soon make you at home, my dear. Stand yourself up, can't you, let's have a look at you.'

Billy sprang to attention, keeping his polished shoes smartly together.

'My goodness, what a fine lad, aren't you? Strong as well, I should think. Shouldn't you think, Seth?'

The old man leant forward and felt Billy's arms. 'We can put a bit more muscle on that, Missus.'

'M-my uncle was trying to t-toughen me up before the bombing started. I had to do lots of r-runs and wrestling.'

Mrs Pawsey shook her head. 'Doesn't look like you enjoyed it, lovey?' She shook her head again. 'No, no.' Dry tresses of grey hair fell across her face. 'Leave him, Seth. We won't be getting you wrestling, don't you worry, my dear. You're quite tough enough for us. We shall be feeding you well and you'll be a help to us old folks, won't you just?'

Billy nodded. 'Yes.'

'So it's all fair and dandy.' She smiled in a dimply way. 'I spoke to your father on the phone. He said you'd been evacuated to this village afore.'

'Yes, I was with Mrs Y-Youldon.'

'Joan Youldon? I know her. Kitchen maid up at the Grange, straight from leaving school right up to having her first little one. She's hardly grown up herself, poor girl.'

'Hardly a woman size, she,' added the old man.

'And scarce enough room in her cott for a vaccie, I'd think.'

'There were two of us. I made friends with him. Alan, he was called.'

'Two vaccies! Well fancy be. Now how did Joan manage that in her place?'

'She was nice, really nice. We p-played with her little children, they're called Timmy and Sally. I made toys for them, and did j-jobs for Mrs Youldon.' If only he could go over right now and see them all. His voice came out rather shakily, 'Is her house far from here, please?'

'Bless you, no house is far from any house here, if you can call some of them houses,' said Mrs Pawsey.

The old man looked at her and chuckled.

She beckoned Billy to the scullery where the two dogs lay. Their noses lifted eagerly, and one gave a rough bark. 'Enough of that, Noah! Here, Billy, you'd better come and introduce yourself or there'll be no peace once the master moves from his chair.'

They were quite big dogs. Billy put a hand towards the head of one. Immediately, they both leapt up, barking. He started back.

'There's no need to worry. It's all noise. Not a nasty streak in either of 'em. Just stand still a minute till they get used to you being here. Here's Noah.'

One dog had a white slash across its right ear and a patch on its back. The other had a white muzzle and chest. 'And this is Japhet.'

'Are they for burglars?'

'Burglars and all sorts of things, you'll see. Working dogs, aren't they.'

She took him through the house, which seemed full of big shabby furniture, and then up the wooden staircase where there was a proper bathroom and three bedrooms just like a London house, except that the landing floorboards weren't straight and creaked dreadfully.

'Now we sleep over the landing just there, and this bedroom's for you.' Mrs Pawsey opened a door and showed Billy inside.

There was a wardrobe for his clothes and he saw toy cars inside it. The bed was plenty big enough for two, if only Alan had been here. It had a dark blue coverlet and looked very comfortable. All he needed was some of his own special things to put in the wardrobe. He placed his suitcase in it.

'Where should I keep my gas mask?'

'On top of that wardrobe, lovey, but doubt if you'll need that here.'

'Have you had bombing?'

'No, bless you. Nothing like that for you to worry about, is there. Now, do you like your room?'

'It's ever so nice, Mrs Pawsey.' He looked at the cars in the wardrobe and then at her.

'Yes, I put those cars there specially for you and there's a pile of comics under the bed, so you'll be all right, you see.'

'Thank you ever so much.'

'Oh, a London toff, you are, no mistake. Shan't we get on fine?'

She took him down into the garden before it got too dark to see everything.

'It's dry now, but we shall have to find you some boots for outside.'

Luckily, she had got the chickens away, safe in their hutch. He'd expected that they would be rushing around inside it, pushing each other for space but they sat in a line pressed against each other in a friendly way, only making the quietest of clucks when Mrs Pawsey opened the door a crack for Billy to peer inside.

'You might like giving them their grain. And there'll be eggs to collect.'

He might, if the chickens weren't looking. Eggs were good for exchange and who knows what they might get in return. He looked at the feathery things doubtfully. Their beaks were poky and their eyes rather mean. The ones with closed eyes looked better.

'Oh you're having a good look, aren't you, love, but now let's go over here.'

There were two pigs in a sty with a small, small yard and a low brick wall round it. They looked a lot bigger than he'd expected pigs to be. They were as big as him only their bodies were sideways on. They walked like ladies on high heels but with two points at the front of the foot instead of one and their bottoms were the size of a fat man's. The taller pig was snuffling up towards Mrs Pawsey.

'Both boy pigs,' Mrs Pawsey said proudly. 'The fattest one's Hardy. Two years old. Look at him, he knows I'm talking about him. He's smart.'

The pig lifted its snout and fixed its tiny pale eyes on Billy. They looked dangerous.

'Tell him I'm eight and he's only two. If he's smart.'

Mrs Pawsey checked the pen's door catch. 'They won't hurt, but they can get nasty if they don't get what they want.'

'Like camels?' He remembered Dad saying that camels could turn nasty, ages ago. That was at the zoo where they'd gone on his fifth birthday.

'My goodness me,' she shook with laughter. 'That'll be the day when I have camels to look after.'

'Don't under-estimate pigs,' Mr Pawsey advised, coming up behind them. 'They can't talk but they can think. It's thinking that counts. Look at old Laurel.'

The pig with the black blob on its back was pulling the peelings dish towards himself with his snout, and away from Hardy.

'See. He's worked out how to get one up on Hardy, although he's smaller.'

Billy watched. Laurel was like Cousin Kenneth, smaller than Billy but smarter at getting his own way. He put his hands on the pigs' wall, but jumped back as Laurel snorted and Hardy put his snout up high. It was time to look somewhere else.

In the field nearby was a dun brown horse with a ring of fluff round its hooves, surely the same size as a camel. Mrs Pawsey followed him as he went over to it.

'Do people ride the horse?'

'Only Mr Sinclair. That's his horse. He just uses our field. We used to have cows when we were younger, you see. Too much for us now.' She sighed and patted a squashy part of her front, which might have been tummy or bosoms, he wasn't sure. The horse looked really strong. He screwed up his eyes, trying to imagine riding it, waving Mr Durban's Cossack sabre. It would be a wondrous way of escaping Hitler, or even turning on him, scaring him to death so he couldn't do anymore bombing.

'Come on. Up this way.' Mrs Pawsey led the way between the field and the side of the house. Behind, there was a small patch of garden with two wooden chairs beside some rose bushes. Then a large patch with green things growing upwards, and some more brown patches with ridges along them.

'They's our vegetables, over there, so you won't go hungry with what we grow. As long as I can keep those slugs off it all, and the rabbits. Wish we could put a wall round it to keep the blighters out.'

'My Granddad grows v-vegetables. I used to help him weed the carrots.'

'Well now you can help with ours.'

Billy felt a bit more cheerful, although the carrots reminded him of that shocking time: Uncle Ted like a scarecrow shuffling towards home after the rescue at Dunkirk. Where was Uncle now? He'd be doing more fighting somewhere foreign and not having baths or dinners or bedtimes. Billy crossed his fingers on both hands that Uncle would get home safely again. He thought of his stripy spinning top Uncle had sent him from France. If only there'd been room in his suitcase for it.

An ominous rumbling in the sky stopped the tour. It was like in London but there hadn't been an air raid warning! He spotted the formation and pointed to the sky. 'They're German, they're German. Where's the shelter?' He looked around but there was no mound with an Anderson underneath. He wanted to pull Mrs Pawsey to the cellar. She didn't seem to know she was in danger. 'We must run, Mrs Pawsey,' and he took her hand, pulling her towards the front door.

Mr Pawsey had come out. He put binoculars up to the sky. 'That's reconnaissance, that is. Wretches. Looking for the lie of the land while it's just light enough.'

He looked down at Billy. 'Not bombers, my lad. Don't you worry. There be nothing to bomb hereabouts. They's getting information, that's all what it is.'

By then the noise was louder. He crouched behind Mr Pawsey, he couldn't help it. It was too like the times at home in the cellar, and any minute the ground would shake and the house fall down.

Mr Pawsey hauled him up to his feet and took him indoors again. As the planes flew over he said, 'You'm not in London now. You'm safe here, that's as why they've sent you. We haven't a shipping port here, no big factories. Those are the sorts of thing they want to bomb, they Jerries, not pigs and chickens.'

Billy took a deep breath. He must believe Mr Pawsey knew right. Dad wouldn't have evacuated him again, if not. He stood in the hall, waiting until the plane sounds had gone.

Mrs Pawsey took her hand back where Billy had been holding it, perhaps a bit too tightly. 'See it's all right now. No bombs. You pop upstairs and unpack your case. Then you'll feel properly at home, lovey, won't you? You wash your hands after, and I'll get the food on the table, won't I?'

He went up to the bathroom and found that Dad had been right. This was a better billet than Mrs Youldon's, for there was a proper towel on the bath specially for Billy, a big bar of carbolic soap and even hot water. For all that, he still wanted to go to see Mrs Youldon and the little ones, the lane where they lived and Big Ronnie next door – even the privy in the back yard. Seeing something he already knew would be so nice.

He went into the bedroom, clicked open the suitcase latches and lifted the lid. He might put his comic by his bed ready for bedtime. But there, on top of everything was the envelope from Mr Durban. Inside, he had something precious, a secret. Although Dad had passed the letter over, he didn't know about the photograph inside, he didn't even know about Cossack sabres or this one's story and its special name, shashka. Only Billy and Mr Durban knew about this.

He had a funny shuddery feeling as he fingered the flap of the envelope, knowing that the shashka had come with him. He pulled the photograph out and laid it on the bed to look at it properly. Mr Durban had taken the sabre out of its scabbard so that both could be seen clearly. Billy could almost feel the pommel in his hand that last time when Angela had let him hold it for a moment. Remembering the fearsome swish of air that rushed past him when Mr Durban demonstrated how the Cossacks used the shashka, cut, thrust, made the little hairs down his arms stand on end. So did the wicked curve of the blade, its super sharp edge clearly picked out by the light from Mr Durban's high study window. It was almost as if Billy was there right now.

Could he ask Mr Pawsey for some see-through stuff to protect it? Then he could stick it on the wall by his bed. Perhaps not. He had only just met him, so he wasn't ready to share his secret. He'd better not put it on the wall where anyone could see it. And it would be nice to be able to hold it whenever he wanted. If aeroplanes zoomed over low or there was an air raid he'd feel brave holding the shashka, even if it was only a picture. If anyone came, when Mother visited, the shashka picture should be safely out of sight. She mustn't know about the time he'd run off to Mr Durban's and heard the wonderfully scary Cossack story. And if she brought Kenneth! It would be awful if he saw it.

For the moment, he'd keep it under his pillow, until he could find a special secret hiding place in his bedroom.

Just knowing he had the photograph made his insides feel warmer as he carried on unpacking, putting away his clothes and washing things.

When he ran downstairs Mrs Pawsey led him into a dining room, where he was very glad to see a heavy table laid up with food.

'You'll be hungry; won't you be hungry? Aren't boys always?' Mrs Pawsey asked and answered herself.

He hadn't actually thought about food since eating his sandwiches, sitting on a suitcase when they changed trains, but actually that was a very very long time ago. Perhaps he was really hungry, like Mrs Pawsey said. He sat down, staring at the brown crumbly cake on the table with currants in it while Mrs Pawsey brought in eggs, tomatoes, grated carrots, margarine or it might even be butter, and a large crusty loaf.

Did she have to queue for ages and ages to get this?

'I see his eyes brightening, Seth,' she smiled across to Mr Pawsey, little dips appearing in her folds of cheek. 'Nothing like having your own, Billy, is there? Own tomatoes, own eggs, own carrots, own cake. We don't go hungry here and we're not going to either unless the Jerries cross the Channel and steal it from us.

'Do you think they will? The seaside, that's where they're going to land. Everyone says so. They could climb over the barbed wire.'

Mr Pawsey wagged a finger. 'Too busy bombing London, aren't they? And there's lots of guns waiting for them all along the coast if they get cheeky enough to try to land, don't you worry. Now you get yourself stuck in and eat right up.' He forked a tomato on to Billy's plate, followed by a hard-boiled egg and Mrs Pawsey cut him a thick slice of squashy bread, not at all like the dry bitter loaf Mother served up.

Then he ate the best tea he'd had since Nanny and Granddad's, which was ages ago, and even those last times hadn't been so good because of the rationing. He delved into the lovely things on his plate until he'd had some of everything.

'More, lovey?'

He shook his head. He had more than he could eat and Mrs Pawsey was asking if he wanted more! It was lovely that he wasn't hungry even though he was evacuated, and that everything was so yummy. The remainder of the brown cake sat on its plate, moist with its bits of date inside. He could have asked for a second piece and saved it, perhaps. Next mealtime, should he save some and get it to Mrs Youldon? Timmy and Sally would love the cake. He'd never seen them have any.

He got up to help clear the dishes. Mrs Pawsey said there weren't any chores for him because it was his very first day with them.

'But you can find my glasses any time I need, can't you?' Mr Pawsey was half joking, but he did actually need someone to do that. 'And a strong lad like you can do lots around the yard, save me bending.'

'Yes, I will. It will be fun to help.'

He wanted to do chores, but whether it was digging or feeding animals, it wasn't like war work. In Wandsworth, he could have been helping Mr Durban in the ARP hut, by running messages, or even picking up bricks after the bombing had stopped. There'd be bombsites, and people needing someone to carry all their indoor things to wherever they were going to live next.

'Where will people live, when they've been bombed out, Mr Pawsey?'

Mr and Mrs Pawsey started up and exchanged glances before Mrs Pawsey said, 'Whatever made you suddenly think of that, Billy?'

'It's this time bombs usually start, the evening, and the nights, sometimes all night. Houses get bombed and the fire engine comes. There's no front to the house and just rubble.'

'You're safe down here in the country, now. You don't want to be worrying yourself. You're going to have a lovely time tomorrow learning all about the pigs and chickens, just concentrate on that, my love.'

He started stacking the plates. Mrs Pawsey was being very kind but she didn't know about bombing, or how Mr Durban might not get his tin hat on in time, or about Nanny and Granddad being uncomfortable in their Anderson shelter. It was a guilty feeling, being safe down in the country.

Mr Pawsey put a veiny hand, as large as Dad's, on Billy's arm. 'Leave the plates, Billy. We men can listen to the wireless before it's your bedtime. My favourite programme's on tonight.'

They went into the first room he'd been taken into where the lamp and the book were. He sat with Mr Pawsey on a squashy chair that had straw poking out at the edges. The great brass bucket in the fireplace had lots of logs piled up in it and nearby was a thick black rug that the dogs were allowed to lie on.

Soon enough, both of them sidled round the door and lay down, their paws outstretched, Noah's on top of Mr Pawsey's slippers.

Billy steeled himself for the ominous boom that announced the news, but Mr Pawsey didn't listen to it. 'All that'll be different soon enough, so as I might as well be up to date', he said. 'And you don't want to hear that war stuff.' After stacking the wood neatly and repairing the fire, he put on Band Wagon. It was such a funny programme, and Billy laughed when he did. Sometimes, Mr Pawsey said the same funny things after the wireless men and then it sounded even funnier. Everything felt very cosy.

Billy was away from everyone he knew, but now he didn't seem to mind. He did cross his fingers that Dad and everyone in London was safe. What were Mother and Jill doing now and did they miss him? Was Jill having a tantrum because everything looked strange? Was it cosy like this for Kenneth in his billet? He might be nervy, or going to be ill, like often he was. But he wouldn't let himself worry because Kenneth had Aunty. And, of course, he didn't have to put up with Kenneth being mean.

Bandwagon ended, and then there was some jolly music. 'Guess what I've got?' Mr Pawsey groaned a bit as he bent down to get something out from under the sofa. It was a shove ha'penny board. 'We can play this while we listen. Bet you can't beat me at this, Billy.' They played two games and Billy won the shiniest of halfpennies. It could go with his Uncle Ted shilling and Mr Durban crown, still in the little wallet ready for a special event. Treasures were good for making you feel safe.

When it was going to be the nine o'clock news Mrs Pawsey came in. 'Come along you.' She took Billy up to bed and tucked him in, which was very nice of her. 'Did you bring any special comfort, my love? A little blanket, a teddy?'

He shook his head, but thought about what was hiding under his pillow. 'I have got a special picture. I might show you one day.'

'That's right. When you're ready. A picture can be very special. Perhaps I've got one too, in a quiet place where it's safe. I might show you it, one day.'

Billy smiled. He understood. She'd want to really know and trust him before she showed him her special picture.

'You going to lie down, then? Any problems, and we're just across the landing, mind.'

Billy snuggled down. It was really comfortable but rather lonely, even with the shashka right under his head, keeping him safe. After he'd been lying down a while, he remembered his pear drops. He slid out of bed and found them safe in his pocket. It felt like the right time to eat another sweet, although Mother would've disapproved. He took one to bed and by the time he'd sucked away the last sticky bit, he was ready to go to sleep.

CHAPTER TWO

September 15th 1940. *A day of heavy bombing, but RAF Fighter Command causes big losses for the enemy.*

Billy opened his eyes to a new morning. He'd slept all night and there hadn't been an air raid to disturb him. It was as if the war was over already but after shooting him from home. It was odd not to hear Jill's babble or whingeing, or Mother's voice from down below.

He sat up. The first thing to do was to find a special place for his precious picture of the shashka. He took it warm from under his pillow and held it to his face. Mr Durban would be thinking of him and willing him to always be brave. The heroes book was in the wardrobe. He remembered the day Mr Durban had given it to him, knowing Billy was going to be evacuated when Billy hadn't known himself. He bent down and found the wooden frame of his bed had a little space between the base and the mattress. No one would know the photograph was there except him, and it was close enough for him to stretch a hand down when he was lying in bed and get it out. Perfect! He'd keep it in the envelope to keep it clean and flat. Mr Durban's letter could slide inside his book and stay with any other letters he got. Dad had his address this time to give to Nanny and Granddad.

There was sun making a warm orange patch on the carpet. He padded to the window and opened the curtains. There was no aeroplane noise, no traffic. Down below the pigs snorted, and above, the sky was empty of everything except clouds. He took a deep shuddering breath. He just had to get downstairs and smell the country.

At the back door, the dogs pressed themselves against him and rushed out alongside him. Billy took another deep breath in and smelled the damp grass, the flowering bushes, even the manure and smiled to himself. *I love it.*

Mr Pawsey came up behind him. 'Hello young Billy. Had a good sleep? Taking in the morning air, are you?'

Billy nodded and turned to go back indoors. He'd never been outside in pyjamas before. Mother would be shocked. He could feel a little smile creeping to his mouth. There were no neighbours here to peep behind net curtains and mind whether someone was outside in their pyjamas.

Mr Pawsey put a hand on Billy's shoulder. 'I suppose it'm be a bit hard, not having your cousin to share all this with; that what you're thinking about?'

'No!' Kenneth! It would be awful to have Kenneth here. Thank goodness for Aunty going with him so that Dad didn't billet both boys together. 'No-o. We're not really friends. It's just that our fathers are brothers so we have to see each other. A lot, actually.'

'Ah. Is that how it is? A bit glad to be an only boy here, are you? Well, up you go and get yourself dressed. Our breakfast'll be ready in two shakes of a bee's knee.'

After they'd eaten, Mrs Pawsey took him to the lean-to at the back door where the messy coats hung. She put on a scabby mac with muddy marks down its front and all round its hem. Then she pulled on black wellies.

She went to a pile of old boots in the corner and turned them over and over. She pulled out a small pair, but gently, looking inside them. 'These will be about right.' She was gazing at the boots sadly, although they looked quite old. Then she passed them to him. 'Here, you'd better put these on, Billy boy,' she said. 'They can be yours now. Pull'em on. Always mud round pigs.'

He followed her round as she fed the animals, collected the eggs, cleaned out hutches and pens, brought in vegetables. It all felt very strange, but rather wonderful. Early morning was very different from mornings in Wandsworth, watching Jill whingeing and Dad striding off in his trilby hat, then running to school down the grey concrete path with a sense of trouble pending.

He couldn't help noticing that Mrs Pawsey had a lot more to do than Mother, even after Mrs Donnington, the home help, left to work on the buses. Mrs Pawsey did all this animal work as well as the washing and cooking, although she was old like Nanny.

Mr Pawsey did outside jobs too. He talked to the pigs, which he said was important, and mended bits of fence and hedge so that the hens wouldn't escape. He couldn't bend easily but he had a leather cushion that he knelt on to trowel around his vegetables and pull carrots and swedes.

Billy went over to watch.

'Here by, young Billy. I'll show you how to do this and I shall be glad of your help from now on.'

Billy bent down and helped pull the carrots. 'I've done this before, with my Granddad.'

That felt rather good until Mrs Pawsey, tramping by in her shabby mac, reminded him of Uncle Ted shuffling up the road after his rescue from Dunkirk. Billy stood up and looked at his black nails. He'd been pulling carrots when he'd seen the scarecrow-like figure in its trailing greatcoat and not known it was Uncle Ted. When the grown-ups let Billy see him, it was three days later and he wasn't Uncle Ted anymore but a wordless stranger with a white lock in his hair.

He screwed up his eyes. 'Is the war still in France, Mr Pawsey?'

'The war's most everywhere, my lad. Too many places. But we're Great Britain. We always win. And look at your work on those there carrots. You're a winner, I can see that.'

Billy bent down to his work again. It was nice being on the winning side. Like in school games, the team with red bands were always beating the blue bands. He always went for the red side, and he was a good runner and good at catching and kicking balls. Perhaps there'd be games here when he started school, though teams would probably be locals against vaccies, which wasn't so nice because then there were fights later. Funny, really, to think of Germany being the same – not being friends if a country didn't want to be invaded. Last evacuation, the locals made fun of the vaccies and put out their tongues. Were the locals in France rude and unfriendly to Jerries because Germany had invaded? Was it their fault, like everyone said? Londoners had invaded this village, and it wasn't their fault because they'd been sent by the government.

'The Jerry soldiers, Mr Pawsey, they've been sent to fight by their government, haven't they, so is it their fault they're in France?'

'Don't know about that, Billy. They didn't have to support Hitler, did they now?'

Hitler. He knew it! The fighting, bombing, war – it was all Hitler's fault, nasty man with his silly moustache and arm sticking right up in the air like a wooden doll. He stamped the earth around the baby carrots, one, two, three, and pretended it was Hitler's face.

~

It was Sunday so after they'd all cleaned themselves up, Mr and Mrs Pawsey took him to church. They set off down the lane and out to the road that led to the places Billy remembered from last year.

It was exciting to see the people he knew when they reached the church. There were no rude faces from local children. This time, all the faces seemed friendly. Some boys actually waved and inside the church, people who'd grunted about vaccies before, now turned round and smiled. It was rather nice sitting between Mr and Mrs Pawsey.

Two women sitting in the same pew asked, 'Is this a new evacuee?'

'Yes. What a nice boy I've been sent by the billeting officer, don't you see?' she answered. 'His father phoned and there was just time to make up the spare room, and the next thing here he was, wasn't he?'

The organ began, and everyone stood to sing. Mr Pawsey pointed to the words in the hymn book, so altogether Billy felt quite easy. Even the organ sounded nicer as they walked out after the service.

'Do you think the people here are used to us now, Mr Pawsey? They weren't very nice to us last year.'

'It's more that they know what you'm suffered in London, that'll be it.'

They moved back into a hedge as a van drove by. It turned into a very large stone house, more like three houses in one. The sign outside read 'Larch Manor.' The van parked just inside its leafy drive. The doors opened, out jumped a group of girls and boys, one of whom had a very familiar freckled face.

'Alan, Alan. I'm here too!' Billy yelled.

'Oh my stars, you varmint,' said Mr Pawsey. 'That's the first time as I've heard any noise out of you. You made me jump, you did.'

'It's my friend. From last time I was here!'

Alan was looking up at the huge ivy-covered house but he turned sharply when he heard Billy shout. His hands went up and his face creased into a grin. He waved, but couldn't run over because a man was shepherding the whole group up the drive to the double door where a lady stood. She was so fat that her crossed arms stuck out far in front of her. If Alan had been near enough, Billy would have whispered that she probably ate all the vaccies' food rations.

'Well, there's a thing,' said Mrs Pawsey. 'The Manor's taking all those vaccies.'

Alan was hesitating by the door.

'You coming to school when it starts?' Billy yelled. After all, Dad was too far away to be angry about shouting across the road. Alan waved and held up his thumb, so Billy knew he'd be looking out for him. There was so much to tell him. He watched until Alan was taken inside.

Mrs Pawsey said, 'Come on, you. We need to show you the right route to school before it starts and then it's dinner-time. Won't you be hungry after your work outside this morning?'

Billy nodded hard. He certainly was very hungry. He was just a bit worried, because the nice tea might have been only for his first day. At Mrs Youldon's there had never been enough and it was usually only bread and a tomato, or soup. He and Alan had always been hungry.

Today, when they got back he found she'd done a great stew for dinner with apple and custard afterwards. He ate lots and it was lovely. It was really true what she'd said, he wasn't ever going to be hungry here. Mrs Pawsey cooked hot meals with huge portions and he was going to tell Alan all about it.

All through dinner time Mr and Mrs Pawsey told him things about the village and the people who lived there. Billy told them about Wandsworth, the shopping, the shelters, the *Run Rabbit Run* games, and Mr Hendrick banging his stick.

Sometimes they laughed at what he said, and they smiled all the time, as if they really liked him. Billy felt quite different, sort of full inside and not just with food.

~

In the morning, Mrs Pawsey gave him a new pencil in case there weren't enough at school and Mr Pawsey gave him three cigarette cards for swaps. 'Just to make sure they're all friends with you. I know what some of they rascals be like.'

Billy set off down the lane and cut through a farm path the Pawseys had shown him. He wasn't frightened. He'd see Miss Johnson and Mr Finlay in church, and goody, goody, Alan would be there too. It wasn't like starting a new school.

Mother would say he was lucky. Kenneth would be starting a school he'd never been to, where he didn't know anyone. That meant he wouldn't be able to give blocked ink-wells to anyone. He wouldn't be the monitor. He was worse off than Billy.

In the school yard there were lots of grubby children he'd never ever seen before. They weren't locals and they certainly weren't from Wandsworth. They'd chalked a hopscotch on the playground and a queue of boys and girls waited a turn. He went forward slowly in case he could join in, but one of the boys looked over and put out his tongue. Another said, 'Who the hell are you?' No one had ever been that rude to him before. Two of the girls nudged each other and giggled nastily. Billy leant against the playground shed until he spotted Alan.

'Alan!' He ran over and clapped him on the back. They jumped up and down together. Billy nodded towards the grubby children. 'Do you know those lot?'

'Some are at the Manor with me. East Enders. Bombed out, a lot of them.'

Billy looked at their torn plimsolls and odd clothes. Their others might have been lost in the bombing. Perhaps he was lucky, he'd only had to shelter in the cellar. He nudged Alan. 'Did you get bombed round you?'

'No, but we heard it every night. All the planes fly over our street because we live between Croydon airport and Big Ben. Bombs dropped not that far off and my mother said she had to get me back here quick as quick because the Jerries might bomb houses anywhere. We got a bus to her office. It's in Piccadilly and all to do with war things. We slept in the basement with all the people who worked there. It's safe, but ever so noisy in the raids. She wanted to get me on the train at Paddington. She found out this lot of children were coming to our village so she joined me up with them on the platform. Alan took a big breath.

'I came here on a cart from the station. I sat up front just behind the horse's head.'

'Smashing. I'd like that. Remember the twins riding around on that hay cart?'

Billy nodded. The twins must still be here. 'Guess what? My cousin's come too. He's billeted with Aunty. They're near my mother and Baby, that same vicarage place but there wasn't room for me.'

'Goody, because now you're here with me.'

Billy grinned. 'And where I am now, there's room for two in my bedroom.'

'And do *you* know what?'

'What?'

'Buckingham Palace was bombed.'

'Blimey, the King and Queen bombed?'

'It's all right. They weren't in. Anyway, the RAF downed loads of

Jerry planes yesterday. There were all these white smoky trails in the sky.'

They started kicking a big pebble between them.

Billy said, 'What's it like at that Manor house?'

'Inside is very smart but we're not supposed to go into the main rooms where the furniture's covered up. We're in the servants' quarters, quite jolly in the dormitory under the roof. Food was alright last night. There's nuns as well as children billeted, so we have to look out when we mess around. And there's two land-girls. You can come round. There's a big garden at the back. Just turn up. It doesn't matter, no one will mind 'cos there's such lots of us there.'

'And you can come to mine. Mr and Mrs Pawsey said so. That's those people you saw me with. I'm with them, up the hill from the shops and down the lane with the big mud ruts. There's dogs and pigs and chickens. They give me lovely dinners. It's nice.'

'You and me can call for each other.'

'And go down and see Mrs Youldon,' Billy said.

'Yes, let's.'

The bell went and they ran to see Mr Finlay who'd grown a moustache. He was busy cutting exercise books in half. 'Hello. Wilson and – Firbank isn't it? Welcome back, you two. You'll have to muck in. Find yourself a place.' He started giving out paper and stubs of pencils.

The classroom was already full. John was back.

Billy leant over his desk. 'Hey, John. Remember coming down on the train with me, last evacuation?'

'Hello, you two.'

Alan slid in beside him while Billy went to see Sonia who was at the front, helping several smaller girls. Her hair was down to her neck.

'You're not at the same woman's are you, Sonia? The one who shaved your head?'

She shook her head. 'I'm with these girls.'

It was quite noisy, the twins at the centre of it. Dick and Mick hadn't gone home at all. They were bigger and redder than ever. They bounced up and down and elbowed each other.

Dick said, 'Yeah, super-duper! It's Billy. Squeeze in here, you. We can copy your sums.'

Mick said, 'Wotcha, Billy. Sit by us.'

Mr Finlay gave them a little cuff over the ear each. 'Just to start the day right, twins, before you ruin my appetite. Now, new children, please be careful not to sharpen your pencils too much. We have to make them last.'

'You get into terrible trouble if you lose yours,' John leant forward and whispered.

Billy showed him the nice long pencil that Mrs Pawsey had given him.

John wrinkled his forehead. 'Look out. I bet that gets nicked. All sorts here now,' and he jerked his head towards the children with dark eyes, dirty knees and fierce expressions.

Mr Finlay settled them all down and pointed to the blackboard with the date and twenty arithmetic problems. Everyone groaned. 'Get going, class,' he said. 'I'll be coming round to see which of you can tackle the difficult problems, that's numbers seventeen to twenty. The others, try the first ones. Just do your best.'

Dick said, 'You do 'em, Billy. Show us.'

'Yeah, we'll copy yours, you're good at sums,' said Mick.

Mr Finlay noticed but didn't hear what they said. 'That's right, Wilson, sit between this pair. Keep them apart and keep them quiet for me.'

'Hey, Billy, do you still do that d-d-d-d stuff?' said Mick, but Mr Finlay wagged his finger before Dick could join in.

The day went by very slowly because the lessons were all the same as last year. Billy started to think how to get up to Mrs Youldon's with some food. He couldn't steal, but he could use his leavings. If he hadn't eaten everything at mealtime, wasn't what was on his plate still his?

~

There was a fruitcake for tea and a plateful of buns. 'Can I eat these later, Mrs Pawsey?' he asked after polishing off two buns, and leaving another bun and his cake on his plate.

'As long as you don't give them to those hens and pigs. Too good for them, mind.'

He skipped down the lane, where it met with the wider one which led to the village.

Alan was waiting at the corner. 'Bet you the little ones will squeal when they see us.'

'Specially when they see what I've got for them.' Billy held up a bag with his bun and piece of cake inside.

They raced down to Mrs Youldon's road together and found Timmy hopping around in front of the terrace. He stopped and stood there with an open mouth as they rushed up.

'Timmy, Tim. We're back.'

Sally's head peeped out of the open front door then ran inside. 'Oh, Mu-um.' Mrs Youldon came out to see, smiling as if they were saviours.

'My big boys! When did you get back? The billeting lady didn't tell me. Come on in, come on.' She made a space for them on the bench. 'I did hope you'd be back, lots of Londoners have come now, but rough ones, not toffs like you two. We heard about being bombed out – such awful times for city people.' She looked them up and down with her nice kind face. 'So you're all right, thank goodness. I really have missed you.'

Alan rubbed one shoe against another.

She looked at his face, and then Billy's. 'You're not coming to live at mine, then?'

Billy spurted out in a rush, 'No, Alan's at the Manor and I'm up the hill with Mr and Mrs Pawsey.' If only Mrs Youldon had proper food, a bathroom and two spare beds they'd beg to be here. He pulled held out the paper bag. 'For you and Sally and Tim. I had too much at tea-time.'

'Oh, Billy! Are you sure you're allowed?'

He nodded.

Mrs Youldon went to the scullery and found a knife. Its handle had broken long ago. The bun divided nicely but the cake had crumbled quite badly on the way. Mrs Youldon gave Sally a handful, and then Tim. She licked a finger to get out the remaining crumbs one by one from the bag.

'You'll be all right there, then, Billy. They're nice and they've got plenty, the Pawseys. They'll perhaps be glad of a boy to …' she broke off.

He was going to ask why but she went on quickly, 'And Alan, how posh you'll be at the Manor! I've never seen inside it, don't think any of us locals have. Even the servants came from far away. All these big houses are offering billets now there's bombing. The Grange's got seven kiddies! Funny to think of those fine rooms all run over with noisy vaccies.'

Billy remembered her Tuesday work at the Grange. 'Do you have to do all the vaccies' ironing?'

'Goodness, they haven't asked me. I just go up and look after the ladies, now the men are away at war. Perhaps they will need more help. It would mean another pound or two for me. Do they have help at the Manor, Alan?'

'No. I think the nuns do housework and things.'

'You won't get too posh to come up here, will you?'

He shook his head, 'Course not, and I'm allowed out after chores and so is Billy.'

Billy nodded. 'We're often going to come down here to see you.' Every day if he could manage it. He couldn't tell her how he'd missed her; Mother wouldn't like that. He looked around at the bench, the stove, the airer with damp clothes. His whole body felt lifted up and settled down. A sort of sigh came out of his mouth. It was good to be in this little room again where Timmy's car still had three wheels, and the pack of cards waited for someone who could really build a good home with them.

CHAPTER THREE

September 27th, 1940. *Pact signed by Germany, Italy and Japan.*

The telephone bell jangled throughout the house. It made Billy jump because he hadn't heard it before and the dogs went wild. Japhet bounded down the hall with a red mouth and tongue hanging out. Noah woofed loud and long from the back door as Mrs Pawsey bustled in from the front.

'Goodness, dogs, anyone would think the calls were all for you. Stop that wretched noise, won't you?' She held the receiver to her ear and soon beckoned Billy over.

It was Dad telephoning to see how things were.

'Have you settled down and are you being a helpful boy?'

'Yes, I am, Dad.' It felt so special to have a phone call specially for him. Dad had never been able to do that at Mrs Youldon's because she didn't have luxuries like telephones and wirelesses, or even a table and chairs to eat at. But Dad was in London being bombed every night.

'Are the air raids still terrible, Dad?'

'I can't pretend they're not, son. But I left London for the

Winchester Court two days ago with the sky full of activity. I was glad to be on a leaving train. Now there are more countries for Great Britain to fight against. As I told you, war is the worst thing. However, *Shame upon the soul, to falter on the road of life while the body still perseveres,* Marcus Aurelius.'

Dad's sayings. That was like being back at home, Dad puffing on his pipe, probably looking at the sky where the sayings seemed to come from. This one sounded churchy. 'Who's Marcus— '

'Aurelius. A good Roman emperor, a philosopher. He was someone who had to drive the Germans away. An intellectual leader, whose first act was to share the leadership with his adopted brother, Verus.'

Billy turned up his nose. *Verus* was a horrid name. He wouldn't have wanted to share leadership, especially if Verus wasn't a real brother.

Dad was going on, 'You'll read Roman history when you're fourteen or so. Perhaps earlier if you show your mettle. I was thinking of asking Uncle Frank if I should introduce Kenneth to it—' His voice trailed away.

That would be flipping terrible if Kenneth started doing sayings as well as Dad. Billy didn't want him learning Roman history and quoting all sorts of people he'd never heard of.

'Well, Kenneth has settled, glad to say. No sign of the nerves now. I rang your mother yesterday. I gather she hasn't arranged to get over to see you yet with Kenneth, but I'm sure she won't be long. You are all right, aren't you?'

'I am, Dad. Really.' Better get that in quickly in case Dad decided to move him. 'Mr and Mrs Pawsey are ever so kind, and I have lots to eat.' He had been going to tell Dad that Alan was here too, and about the pigs and chickens, but Dad's hotel served the meal at a set time and it was nearly that time now, so he didn't get to tell any of his news at all. He just managed to get in, 'I'm glad you're in Winchester, Dad. You don't have to go back to London soon, do you?'

Dad told him not to worry himself and rang off. It was a sad feeling. Although it was good that Dad was away from the bombing, the hotel food wouldn't be nearly as good as Mrs Pawsey's, and poor Dad was living all on his own.

He mooched down the hall to where the dogs were lying. Animals never looked sad. Japhet bounded forward and licked him, so he squatted down to stroke him. 'That was my phone call, see Japhet. Dogs don't get phone calls.'

Mrs Pawsey came out. 'Will you be a bit homesick, lovey? Why don't you pop up to the Manor and get that friend of yours to come here for a bit?'

Billy jumped up. 'Can he? Thank you. He's very nice, you'll like him. He's called Alan and his face is all covered with little brown spots that are called freckles. Actually, his arms are too. And his back, come to think of it. I know because we shared a bed at Mrs Youldon's.'

Mrs Pawsey laughed. 'That's fine, my dear. He can come, and welcome. We might invite him to stop for some tea when we have ours. Off you pop, then, and get him.'

Alan was in the Manor's side garden in a line of children, all with forks. A land-girl was showing them all how to dig trench lines ready to sow vegetables. He didn't go too near, in case he had to join in? He called from the top of the drive, 'Are you allowed to stop, Alan, and come up to my place?'

Alan waved. He gave his fork to the young lady. 'It's all right, we're volunteers and I've done quite a bit. Haven't I?' he added, turning to her. She nodded.

He ran down to where Billy was waiting. 'Is it okay to come, then?'

'Yes. Mrs Pawsey said to bring you up, and you might have tea with us. And I want to show you everything. What were you doing, anyway?'

'I wanted to help her,' Alan followed Billy out into the road. Her name's Rachel. Her father's a Jew and stuck back in Austria. He couldn't get out when she left. She's worried he'll get killed.'

'Is he a soldier? Do they have Jewish soldiers? My father said Austria was against the Jews. I saw a bit about Jews in the newspaper once, the Nazis bullying them.'

'No, he's not a soldier. He was a shop-keeper but the shop was taken. It's horrible.' He linked arms with Billy. 'Rachel says the Jews are being lined up and all their things taken from them, then they're shot or driven away and then murdered.'

He gasped. It wasn't like Alan to make things up. Not like Kenneth. If it was true, what the land girl told him was really scary. It meant there were lots of real thieves and murderers in Austria. 'That's dreadful.'

'I know. It's almost as bad as being bombed.'

'No, worse. Murder's really, really bad. If you're bombed, the planes don't know who they're bombing. If it's you gets bombed, you're just unlucky to be the one that's hit. But being *murdered* is someone means it to be you. They want you to die, because they hate you.'

They kicked the muddy cart ruts until they crumbled away. These thoughts weren't right for running, and for a few moments Alan didn't answer. Then he said, 'You're thinking of that cousin of yours, aren't you?'

Billy hadn't been, but he did now. 'Kenneth wouldn't *kill* me.' He might get near it, but he couldn't imagine Kenneth looking as though he was going to murder someone; that would be the wrong kind of face. Kenneth had more a white, or yellow or green expression. Hate and murder was dark red. He started walking on again. 'Don't know whether Kenneth actually hates me ... he likes being mean and spiteful, and coming off best always – 'Billy took a breath, 'He has really hurt me sometimes, like Chinese burns, or when he smothered me with the gas mask or trapped me in the Lloyd loom basket, but he can be nice. He made me a smashing card last Christmas that he painted himself. Hey, I wish I'd brought it. I could show you.' Then he had the happy feeling in his tummy. 'But I've got something else to show you. Something secret. Come on,' and he pulled Alan's arm until they were trotting down the lane.

They reached the horse's field and saw Mr and Mrs Pawsey near the chicken house. They waved.

'Hello and welcome to you, Alan. You can show'm round everything, Billy.'

The dogs rushed out barking like mad but Alan was used to dogs and wasn't worried. He wasn't so keen on the chickens so

Billy clapped his hands at them to make them run off in their fussy way. 'We won't go into their house if you don't like chickens. I wasn't sure about them either when I first got here, but now I'm all right with them. Still, we'll just look for their eggs under the hedges.'

'We used to do that at Easter before the war, only it was for chocolate eggs. My father used to bring them home from London and they had sugar stars stuck on them.'

'Cor, I bet that was expensive.'

'Cadbury's Dairy Milk!'

'Yes, we used to have that. Yum-ee.'

'People say we won't get it till after the war, now.'

They both held their tummies and bent over groaning with the longing for it.

A patter of rain started, so they ran indoors. Billy showed Alan all the downstairs rooms, then led the way upstairs and let Alan nose around for a bit. Then he stood importantly by the bed. Alan was the right person to share his secret.

'I'm going to show you something ever so ever so special, but you mustn't tell ANYONE, not ever. My parents don't know; it's a secret between me and Mr Durban. Turn your back.' He drew out the photograph and held it up.

'Let's see.'

Alan came nearer but Billy stepped back. It was too much for anyone else to touch it. 'See?'

'What is that— golly! A curved sword.'

'Sabre. A Cossack sabre and it's called a shashka. That's a special name for the extra special sabres. It's Russian and it's Mr Durban's.'

Alan's eyes went very big. 'Is Mr Durban that man who works with your father?'

Billy felt even prouder. 'Yes. Mr Durban sent me the photograph to bring here, because he's shown me the shashka and he knows it's my favourite thing.' He looked at Alan's eyes to make sure he could trust him, but Alan's freckly face looked nice as nice, just as it always did. 'Actually, holding it keeps me safe when everything's scary. I hide it in a secret place that no one knows. You're the only person that's ever seen this!'

'Gosh! You're flipping lucky. Why is Mr Durban giving you it secretly?'

The bedroom door was safely shut. Billy sat down on the bed with the photograph and let Alan sit beside him. Then he told him about running down to Mr Durban's house to escape beastly Kenneth and Mr Durban showing him the shashka and telling him the dreadful story of the beginning of the Great War.

'He was younger than my Uncle Ted and Nanny said *he* was too young to fight a war. Mr Durban was only seventeen. He went to stay with a German school-friend in the summer holidays before going to university… and then war started. He was stuck! The German friends told him it wasn't safe for an English person. He had to escape all by himself— in the night with no luggage!'

'Not even pyjamas?'

'Not even anything. He had coins sewn in his trousers to buy food from farmers. He kept walking through woods and fields until he was across the border into Russia. He saw Germans in the villages behaving quite awfully, so he thought he'd fight with the Russians.'

'Cor! Where did he get a gun?'

'He didn't. The Russians put him at the back of their army where the cannons were. When they got to battles, his job was to pass the shot to the cannon soldiers to feed the barrel for firing. He couldn't speak any Russian so he had no idea what was happening or who was winning. Each day fighting went on for hours. Then the brave Cossacks galloped past them riding into battle, waving their sabres. They were very fine sitting high on wonderful horses, not like the one over in our field. I wish I had a picture of a Cossack I could show you.'

'So do I!'

'Actually, I haven't seen one but Mr Durban says they're handsome with the smartest uniforms.

The trouble was, the Germans had more weapons, but the Russians fought on and on ever so bravely. After one battle, Mr Durban stood on a cart and saw fields full of dead bodies, miles of them. He saw an injured Cossack with some Germans coming near, so he ran over to pull him to safety. That was the Cossack who gave him this shashka. He was dying, and he gave it to Mr Durban saying this strange word *Liko* something, I can't remember it just now. I'd have to ask Mr Durban to say it again because it's a Russian word, but it's a special name for a shashka that has been in many fearsome fights and killed so many enemies.

So that's the shashka in this picture. When he owned it, all the Russian soldiers respected him. They treated Mr Durban really well and helped him back to England.'

'How?'

'When they got to the sea and there were ships. He'd been nearly a year away by then. His family thought he'd been taken by the Germans and kept as a prisoner, so were ever so excited to have him back. He didn't dare tell his mother what had really happened to him or about the battles in case she fainted or something. But,' and Billy straightened his back and put up his chin, 'Mr Durban forgot I was only eight and he told me all of the story, all the scary bits and bloody bits and everything. Then he was worried about Dad not liking me to hear it, and Mother would have been shocked! So *that's why it's a secret*. I wasn't going to tell Dad anyway. But Mr Durban gave me half a crown after Christmas.'

Alan's eyes were still big. 'Gosh. All that happened to you. I wish I'd been there. The story's smashing and that shashka looks a super dangerous sword.'

'Sabre. It is, it's fearfully dangerous. You can't touch the blade. I had to sit right back away when Mr Durban showed me how they,' he put the photograph on the bed and jumped up to demonstrate, 'hack, slash, cut, thrust, probe' with it. All the air whistled, I was scared, AND he said that the Cossacks do it with a sabre in each hand.'

'What *two!* Cor! I wish I could tell all the boys at the Manor about that.'

Billy sat down so hard beside him that the mattress bounced them. 'Secret, deadly secret. You must promise never, ever—'

'No, I won't. I really promise. You know, we're—' and they chanted together while they clenched hands and swung them up and back, *'Best friends, best friends, never, ever break friends.'*

Billy had anxious feelings about sharing his secret, but he had to trust someone. He made Alan turn his back and stand by the wardrobe while he hid the photograph in its special place, then they ran downstairs to see whether Mrs Pawsey had buns or anything nice for tea.

~

The village bus ran twice a week. Soon, it brought Mother. Billy saw her turn into the top of the lane neatly belted into her checked jacket. She was watching her pointed lace-up shoes so carefully, avoiding the ruts and stones, that she didn't notice his waving arms.

There was no Jill with her, no Aunty, but, bother, she had brought Kenneth, who was carrying his notebook and pencils and wearing his cap although it was quite hot. He looked left and right. He'd be judging the lane, the meadow and the house and thinking of something mean to say. His nose seemed to twitch, like the corner of his mouth.

Mother stepped ahead of him and put her arm on Billy's shoulder. 'Here I am, Billy, you see, just as I promised.' She stretched a hand far out towards Mrs Pawsey, who stood with Billy by the gate. 'How nice to meet you, Mrs Pawsey. I hope Billy has been good. I didn't bring his baby sister. It's just too much while she's so young and always wanting something. It's two buses to get here, and you can never be sure of the connection. Quite a feat.' She fanned her face. 'This is my nephew, Kenneth. He and my sister-in-law are billeted very near to us. She does WVS work so I look after Kenneth. He's absolutely no trouble, a really civilized child.'

Billy watched Kenneth smile up at the grown-ups. Mother really seemed to like him now, even though she had to look after him.

'Now, aren't you very welcome, Mrs Wilson?' Mrs Pawsey said in her funny question way. 'Come on in,' and she ushered them forward.

Mother and Kenneth both stepped carefully through the yard, which was untidy with straw from the mucking out. Billy followed them.

Mother had brought a bag of sweeties. 'Some treats for you, Billy.'

Kenneth's eyes were already on the bag.

'Thank you, Mother.' Billy pushed them quickly into Mrs Pawsey's hand. 'Mrs Pawsey will keep them in the larder for me.'

'I hope Billy passed you the corned beef tins when he arrived, Mrs Pawsey? I didn't bring anymore food, knowing you had a sort of farm here. You'll have your own produce. I expect you have a wonderfully peaceful life, your animals and garden, just the faint buzz of the odd aeroplane, nothing threatening.'

Mrs Pawsey didn't smile back. 'We manage to find enough excitement, being wartime, and now we have Billy for light entertainment.'

Mother took off her green hat with the feather. 'Yes. I have my work cut out with my little girl. She's only a baby, really. She's having trouble settling. She misses her familiar things so she cries a lot.'

'Tantrums,' said Billy, but no one heard him except Kenneth, who moved to the sideboard where he could stare across toward Billy.

'My sister-in-law joined the local WVS immediately she got here. She's a knitter amongst other things. She's hardly around, so it's left to me to take Kenneth to different homes on different days for schooling.'

Billy scratched his forehead. And he'd been imagining Kenneth nervous in a strange classroom! 'Aren't you going to a real school, Kenneth?'

Kenneth raised his eyebrows at him. 'Me?'

Mrs Pawsey said, 'Dearie me, a big boy like you needs school, Kenneth.'

Mother went on. 'Well – you know, Kenneth is delicate, frail. The school's too far and anyway, we were told it was full. Kenneth's receiving quite advanced tuition. He's in a group being educated by the old verger who went to University when he was young. Kenneth's a real learner. The verger thinks he could get a place at Friar's Court, the grammar school, when he's old enough. Fancy that! My husband was the same, you know, successful at all his study. So, taking Kenneth to different homes has its benefits, meeting mothers of other successful children.'

Mrs Pawsey had her hands folded across her fat front bits. 'Now isn't that nice for you? But, Billy here has been so—'

Mother hurried on. 'But as well as having a baby girl who still needs just everything doing for her, taking Kenneth for education isn't the end of it. On Sundays he has to be taken to church, as well as on Wednesday evenings. The verger noticed his wonderful singing voice, so now he's a choirboy. If Doreen's tied up, I have to take him.' She sighed and ran her long fingers across her forehead. 'All go. But he has the talent, you see. Such an easy, quiet boy.'

Kenneth leaned on the sideboard and traced a pattern round the woodwork as if it was someone else they were talking about.

Mr Pawsey came in from tying the dogs up at the far end of the yard. Mrs Pawsey gave him a long look and hurried off out to the kitchen, ruffling Billy's hair on the way. Mr Pawsey stamped the worst of the mud off his boots and came forward to shake hands. 'How do, how do. We're very glad to have your young lad with us, Mrs Wilson. I think the Missus has gone to make you a nice pot of tea. This Billy of your'n is doing fine, just fine, so tell us how you're doing yourself, now.'

Mother seemed very keen to speak about her troubles. Billy eyed Kenneth up and down and saw that he was doing the same back. Mother jerked her head, which meant he was to take Kenneth up to his bedroom. Kenneth carefully placed his notebook and pencils on the parlour table, wiped the straw from the sides of his shiny shoes, and followed Billy upstairs.

'Hmm,' he said, surveying the comfy room and the half-open door of the large wardrobe as if he was going to buy them.

Bother! Kenneth would be able to see the cars and paper planes kept there. It wouldn't be long before he hauled them out.

Kenneth plumped down on the bed. His bottom made a hole where the coverlet had been beautifully smooth before.

'Phew! Pigs! You can smell them from here.' He pulled his bony knees up and put his feet on the bed. 'Where we're living, my window looks over flower beds. You can't even see the veg from it.'

Billy didn't care, didn't even answer.

Kenneth went on, 'Pigs for you, flowers for me. That's like us. Like how it's going to be. I'll be at Friar's Court Grammar next year doing Latin and Physics and Art. You'll be pigging it in that tin pot village school, still having your bit of Arithmetic and Spelling, staying ignorant.'

'I'm not ignorant. I know lots of things.'

'What do you know then? Can you name all the countries in the British Empire?'

'No-o. But I know other things.'

'Like what? The names of leeeaves and treeees?'

Actually, Billy had been about to say what he'd learned on the school Nature Walks, but now he wouldn't. If only he had the shashka, he'd show Kenneth. He circled both arms in the air imagining the shashka swishing through Kenneth's sarcasm. 'I know about Russians in the Great War.'

'You don't.'

'I do. They had to fight the Germans. Hundreds and thousands of them died. Their bodies sank into the snow.'

'How do you know that? How can you know?'

Billy tensed his shoulders. This was dangerous. 'A long ago story.'

'You never had a book on it. I know all your books.'

'Well I just know.'

The hole in the bed became a cave as Kenneth knelt up to dominate Billy from a higher position.

'How. You tell me how you know. Go on, go on, you tell me.' His hand grasped the back of Billy's neck. It was just like Mr Finlay did to the naughtiest boys when they were going to have the cane. Billy hunched forward letting his jumper ride up in the hope that Kenneth would let go. He didn't.

'Tell me now. Go on.'

'A m-man told me.'

'What man? I'm going to ask him.'

'You can't, he's not h-here.'

'At home, then? I know all the men you know. I can write to him and ask.'

'Shan't tell you. Get your hands off my neck or I'll shout to Mrs P-Pawsey.'

'Go on then. Guess what I'll tell her! I can get you into trouble, all right.'

Then there were footsteps on the stairs. Mr Pawsey's voice sounded from outside their door. 'Billy's room's just here, Mrs Wilson. I'm sure as you'd like to see it.'

'Yes, I would, thank you. He slept in something like half a cupboard at his last billet,' Mother trilled.

Kenneth quickly put his hand down and moved his feet so that he was sitting neatly by the time she came in.

'I want to make sure you have enough changes of clothes, Billy.' She began talking to him as she checked all his clothes, which left Kenneth free to wander around, examine the toys, conkers and other treasures. He was soon nosing inside the wardrobe.

Meanwhile, Mother chatted. '...and now Jill can be relied on to say Please and Thank you, I can take her about more and Mrs Shawditch says ...'

When Mother stopped telling Billy things about Jill and the vicar's wife, Kenneth asked politely,

'Aunty Marcia? Apart from Daddy and Uncle Bert, what men does Billy know at home?'

'Goodness me, what a strange question. The people I know, of course.'

'Of course.' Kenneth, sat down on the bed, crossed his legs, and waved his shiny shoes, left, right, left, waiting.

Mother said idly, 'Who do we know, Billy?'

His face was hot. He was up against the enemy. He needed a weapon and he hadn't got one. 'Mr H -Hendrick?'

'That's your teacher. And it's not as if we know him socially.'

'H -He knows lots of things, though.'

Kenneth was speaking over him. 'A man who talks to Billy out of school ...'

Mother was looking beyond them out of the window now. She was probably noticing the pig smell and waiting to go downstairs again and be brought a nice cup of tea and something home-made by Mrs Pawsey.

Billy tried jumping up and down like Jill did. It always worked for her.

'Aunty?' Kenneth pressed on.

'Well there's only a few people, Kenneth: the people next door, but they hardly chat, and we certainly don't speak to the noisy people opposite. Uncle doesn't really bring his colleagues home except, well, the only other people we know that Billy knows are the Durbans.'

Billy jumped up and down faster.

Mother flapped her hands. 'Stop it, stop it, noisy thing.'

'Durbans,' said Kenneth deliberately.

Billy whizzed around so fast and close that Mother's collar blew up round her chin.

'Enough! I shall get really cross, Billy.'

'Can I meet Mr Durban, Aunty, when we get back to London? Daddy will like to meet him, too.'

'I'm sure you can, if only we could get back there.'

Kenneth smiled across to Billy, one half of his face looking friendly for Mother, the other leering a threat to Billy.

It would be terrible having Kenneth in Mr Durban's house and doubly terrible having Uncle Frank there too. Uncle Frank might teach Mr Durban how to bully. Like all the other grown-ups, Mr Durban would think Kenneth a dear little boy and he might even show Kenneth the shashka. Then Billy would be left with nothing special for himself. He pushed in front of Kenneth so that Mother could only see one boy, her own boy, bobbing up and down so she'd be sure to notice him.

'Now, Billy,' Mother put her hands on his shoulders. 'I expect you're dying to show me around, but be a dear boy and let me have a nice little sit down with Mrs Pawsey and enjoy my tea. You and Kenneth must have such a lot of news to exchange.'

'Lots,' said Kenneth.

Billy turned round to glare at him then clattered downstairs after Mother, never mind that Kenneth would get his hands on all his bedroom treasures. He kept very close to Mother, almost treading on her heels so that Kenneth couldn't possibly come between them.

'Oh, Bill-y!' Mother was saying, but Mrs Pawsey came into the hall with the tray of tea.

She smiled. 'Isn't he thrilled to have his mother here, bless him? Doesn't he just want to stand beside you as you have your tea?'

Billy nodded his head hard enough for Mother to notice. She sipped her tea and asked him some questions, but when he told her about seeing Alan, the lessons and the naughty twins and nature walks, she looked blank. She hadn't been to his school so she didn't know anyone he talked about. She'd even forgotten all about Alan. He sighed, but none of this really mattered if he could keep Kenneth from learning about the shashka. As he heard Kenneth tripping downstairs, he said quickly, 'There's chickens here, Mother. They sit in a line in their hut, you know. We could go and see if there's eggs.'

'A fresh egg.' She finished her tea and stood up. 'That would be a treat. I swear the vicar gives any we get to the refugees.'

Kenneth came in, holding a pair of cars from the wardrobe.

Mother went on, 'The vicar has to share our food out between so many people. So nice for you to have things all to yourselves, Mrs Pawsey. You are lucky.'

Mrs Pawsey said, 'We meet our quota, of course, but we are blessed in a number of ways, that's true enough. You'd better take your mother and Kenneth to see the chickens then, Billy. They may let you take an egg from them.'

Kenneth followed Mother out towards the chicken house, but turned round and gave Billy a long look, his mouth pursed. Billy knew what that meant. Kenneth wasn't going to forget about Mr Durban.

As soon as Mother took Kenneth home, Billy was going round to see Alan. He was the one person he could tell about Kenneth. They would have to put their heads together and think up a plan. If Alan came round next time Kenneth visited that might fix things. Meantime, Billy had a bad feeling in his tummy.

Mother said she would be coming on her own next time because Aunty was taking Kenneth to help at the WVS centre. So Billy felt a little bit better. When no one was looking he put his tongue out hard at Kenneth, then quickly turned away before Kenneth could tell on him.

CHAPTER FOUR

October 14th 1940. *Bomb penetrates tube station and explodes between the two platforms.*

When he was first billeted, Billy was a bit afraid of Laurel and Hardy. He hadn't seen pigs for real before. He remembered how Hardy had peered at him with tiny blue eyes and he'd been scared. Mrs Pawsey had warned him, 'Just don't let them out, will you, my dear? Be careful to keep the catch on their gate.' He was very careful especially as his morning and evening job was to throw the scraps over Laurel and Hardy's pen wall.

He was about to collect the scraps bucket when Mrs Pawsey made a shocking announcement. 'Leave the bucket, Billy, and get your mac on. Those pigs'll be off this morning and be meat by afternoon, so we better get their ear rings on before you get off to school.'

'Earrings? M-meat?'

She nodded hard enough for her chins to wobble but he still couldn't believe it.

'They'se come to their time, my dear.'

'What time?'

'Off to the butcher, my love. We've done out bit getting 'em fat enough.'

Billy swallowed and then gasped. 'You're going to kill Laurel and Hardy?'

Mr Pawsey was pulling his boots on. He chortled, 'They's pork. That's what they're for.'

'But, Mrs Pawsey, they're your pets.'

She laughed and laughed, holding her stomach and having to sit down with the awful effort of it. 'Bless you, lad. We've all got to eat. No one's got money for pets. It's like Dig for Victory. You do that, you know all about that. It's the same. We have to give the butcher our pigs so there's a bit of meat for folks, just like the farmers who send their cows and lambs.'

He knew about meat, of course he did, but he hadn't thought of animals he *knew* being meat. It felt horribly wrong. Laurel and Hardy were family.

'Isn't it the way of the world, Billy?' Mrs Pawsey said in her questioning way. 'And without our meat lots of people would be without their ration, see.'

He tried to be brave as she was. Sending her pigs off to the butcher must be really awful.

'Come on, Billy,' said Mr Pawsey. 'Here's the staples. You come and help me put them on.' He held out two metal things and picked up a heavy thing which was a stapler. They went out to the pigs together. Billy's feet seemed too heavy to move forward. As they got to the pen, Laurel lifted his snout hopefully, then turned his black spot towards them.

'Can't staple your rear, silly pig, you. Turn around, let's have you.' Mr Pawsey stood with his back against the gate, ready to slide out of it if either pig got nasty. Because they did get nasty, Billy remembered, which is why he took so long to feel happy about feeding them. But now it would be awful not to have to feed them, to see an empty pen.

'Doesn't it hurt?' he asked. After all, it was a metal thing going right through the ear and out the other side. Poor pigs. First this, then being killed and then being eaten. It was worse than being sent to war.

Mr Pawsey gave a sort of humph which might have meant 'No'. He was pressing his backside against the gate and holding the stapler thing ready over Hardy's ear. 'Grab it lad, hold on hard.'

Billy could have said 'No', he could have run off, but he didn't. He held on hard to Hardy's ear and screwed his eyes shut. There was a loud squeal, and a spurt of hot air against his hand as Hardy kicked his way free, but the ring was in. Hardy stomped around the pen while Laurel pointed his little blue eyes towards them.

'Now you, Laurel. Let's have you, my beauty. Oho, you know what's coming, do you? Be brave then, my hearty.' And as Laurel squelched over the mud on his high heels, Mr Pawsey grasped his ear. 'Again, lad, again. Quick sharp.'

Billy held on to the hairy ear, but stroked it with his thumb. Laurel's squeal was much louder and longer than Hardy's. It was really hard to bear it. It must be like that at war, being a soldier and having to hurt an enemy, to hear him scream, even to kill him, because that's what soldiers were for. He didn't want to do that to the pigs, or to let anyone else hurt them. He had helped, just like Mr Durban had helped the Russians put shot in the cannons.

He clasped his hands round the end post of their pen gate, peering at Laurel and Hardy to see if either of them had painful ears, but by now they both had their noses down snuffling about in the mud. They didn't know what was going to happen to them. They were like prisoners who hadn't even joined in with a war. Poor things, it was *we have no choice.*

Mr Pawsey clapped a hand on Billy's shoulder then moved off toward the barn, pitchfork at the ready.

It was nearly time to go to school. Billy spent a long time leaning over the pig pen saying a tearful Goodbye. For a moment he thought about lifting the latch of the gate and letting them escape, but Mr Pawsey would get someone to catch them and it would cause lots of extra work. He would be in dreadful trouble too. He took his hand off the latch and mooched slowly to the barn. 'Do the pigs really have to go, Mr Pawsey?'

The old man spat into the fire bucket by the gates. 'We don't want folks to go hungry, do we, my lad? The pigs have had a fine life, you feeding them so well. Now their time's come. That's what they're for, pigs; eating, and being eaten. What you're for is school, so off you go and don't worry yourself.'

Perhaps Mr Pawsey might change his mind later. After all, he was the one who was going to have to walk them down the road.

Billy turned away and scuffed his feet down the path, casting a last look at the pigs. Then he turned away quickly in case he caught their eye. Laurel had poked his nose upwards as Billy turned into the lane. Perhaps he was praying.

All the way up the lane he could hear their grunts. It was truly dreadful. The sky was dark and he buttoned up his mac. He knew what was coming.

Inside the small, dusty school, Billy forced the loop of his mac on to one of the pegs. They all held five or six already.

Other boys jostled him into the classroom where Miss Johnson had pinned a large chart on the board. He didn't even feel like looking at it.

'What's up?' Alan came alongside.

'The pigs. They're going to the butcher's this morning.'

He couldn't say anymore because his voice was choky, but Alan understood.

'I say, poor things. Rotten luck, Billy.'

'Silence!' Miss Johnson was taking them for History. 'Look at the board and start work.' When the class had their heads down writing out all the kings and queens of England in the right order, Billy thought of Laurel and Hardy being walked up the road. Was it happening right now? Mr Pawsey would lurch behind them with a stick, tapping their pink hairy behinds, not too hard, saying 'Come on, you hairy pig, come on my beauty,' and the pigs would trot onward as long as food was in front of them, not knowing what lay ahead. And that would be the back yard of Mr Churn the butcher with his shiny knives. The pigs would have no choice. He knew what that felt like.

All day at school he felt a sense of doom. It felt worse than a rainy day— more as if the heavens were going to fall in. There was a downpour by playtime, so everyone had to stay in the hall. The school was hot and stuffy, everyone was noisy and bad-tempered and the pelting rain against the windows felt like an attack.

At the end of the day he pulled on his wellingtons and trudged home under the heavy sky. He tried to think of cheery things. It wasn't really raining much now. He hadn't got properly wet. When he got home perhaps there'd be a letter for him, perhaps a postcard. He stamped in a couple of puddles. As Dad had taught him, he didn't count on good fortune.

Mrs Pawsey was standing at the gate, her hand to her eyes, as he sloshed through the muddy ruts in his leaky boots, uncaring. It wasn't worth hoping that she was waiting to tell him the pigs were still there, for there was none of the usual snorting and honking as he approached. Why was she standing there and not in the kitchen?

'Billy, my dear. You come along in straightaway, you come and sit down right here.'

His tummy tightened up. Mrs Pawsey's special welcome was as sinister as the lumpy black clouds had been that morning. Something awful had already happened when Mr Pawsey took the pigs? Or was Jill poorly so that Mother couldn't visit him for a whole month? He sat down in the squashy chair where Mrs Pawsey pointed and gazed at her, ready for disappointment.

'Your mother telephoned, my dear. I'm afraid I've got some very bad news. They've asked me to tell you.'

'She's not coming this month?'

'She is coming. Quite soon, and with Kenneth. Because she and your Aunty need you to cheer him up.'

'*Me* cheer him up?'

'Yes, dear. Isn't it cheerful company he'll need? His father – I'm sorry this is awful news for you. There was a bomb landed on Balham tube station. It killed lots of people, and your Uncle Frank was there. Be brave, now.'

'Killed?'

She bit her lip and nodded.

He looked at the window, the door. They still looked the same as when he'd gone to school that morning. No more Uncle Frank? How could that be, the size of him? So he wouldn't be there ever again? He'd never come and strip Billy's jumper off, ready for a freezing run to the park? He'd never pound Billy's arm muscles and put his fists up to 'make a man' of him? He'd never be there for Kenneth to sidle up to. There'd just be Dad – and was he in Balham? He gasped, 'Dad – was he there too?'

'No, dearie. Your father is fine. He's the one who phoned and told your mother the dreadful news. Now your poor Aunty has to go to London in all that bombing for the funeral and your mother's going too. They don't think Kenneth should go. I've said I'll have him here for a day or so.

'Oh! But their billet's only down the road from that vicarage. He could go to the vicar's.'

'Yes, perhaps, but perhaps the vicar's wife can't manage him as well as the caring for your little sister. And your mother thought Kenneth would want to be with you. You'll be a good support to your cousin, that's for sure. Now you stay sitting there and I'll get you a mug of sweet tea for the shock. I've got a bit of extra sugar this week. Stay put there, won't you.'

Billy did stay put for his legs wouldn't seem to move. Bombs were awful, and he remembered that bomb site where he'd played and all the furniture showing with the front of the house blown away. And the people had been blown apart, and Uncle Frank was at the tube station when the bomb came and now he was in bits. It was the worst kind of scary. And it was surely terribly sad. He should be crying or something. He looked at his knees, which were quivering. It was a shocking thing that had happened...but he wasn't sad. He felt a sort of lightness, then he felt bad, really bad because he hadn't felt sad when he heard there was no Uncle Frank, and he still didn't. Kenneth would. He thought about Kenneth and how Uncle Frank had always fussed over him, made sure he had the best of things. Now Kenneth's Daddy had gone. He would mind dreadfully.

Mrs Pawsey brought his tea and a special biscuit. He shouldn't have eaten it, but it was terribly nice. Afterwards, he went upstairs and sat on his bed. Not having Uncle Frank was all right for him, but not for Kenneth, and not for Aunty. She liked her husband a lot. It would be very awful when he had to see her now. And Kenneth – he'd really punish Billy if he knew he wasn't sad.

He wasn't sure what to do. He knelt down by his bed and tried to think of a prayer. That seemed to be the right thing. But the only one he knew by heart was what he'd learned at school – Our Father – and he didn't know if there was any bit about people dying. Trespassing wasn't dying, was it? He said it all the way through in case. Then he told God that he was sorry Aunty didn't have a husband anymore and Kenneth didn't have a father anymore. That was true. If he'd said he was sorry Uncle had gone, it would have been a lie. The Sunday school teacher once said that whatever words they used, God would hear them if they prayed. That was much better than God hearing them when they weren't praying.

He stood up and leant on his windowsill. There were the empty pens. He remembered with a lurch to his stomach that the pigs were gone, dead, cut in bits by Mr Churn's cleaver. Then he began crying. Soon Mrs Pawsey came in and put an arm round him. She smelled like the inside of a musty wardrobe, quite comforting. She said it was very, very sad to lose an uncle. Then he cried harder, for no one was thinking about the pigs.

CHAPTER FIVE

October 19th 1940. *Very heavy night bombing in London, Bristol, Liverpool, Manchester and Coventry*

Mr Pawsey was quiet at breakfast and just put a large hairy hand over Billy's before pouring the Sunny Jim flakes into his bowl.

It wasn't easy to swallow the food but Mrs Pawsey just took his half-finished plates without a murmur. It felt like a special time but not in a nice way.

After breakfast, she came up with him and took him into her bedroom. He hadn't really been in there before, except to just put his head round the door. She sat him on the green silky quilt with its puffed up squares and said, 'I think now's the right time to show you that special picture I told you about. Do you remember, on your first night here?'

He did, and he remembered thinking he'd show her the shashka one day. Not now. They couldn't look at weapons on such a day.

She was moving to her window-sill to bring a silver-framed photograph across. She sat down by him and held it between them.

The picture showed a nice boy or man, he was between the two, with a crisp shirt and dark tie. His eyes were kind.

'That's my son, Gordon, a very special person. I keep this picture where I can see him every day.'

Billy swallowed. 'Is he lost?'

'Yes, lovey, lost is right. He was going for his first job, an important interview, but before he could get there, a thunderstorm started. He ran for cover, probably thinking he shouldn't spoil his new jacket. His father bought it special for the interview, see. He didn't think about traffic and the bus couldn't stop. I'm afraid that's how he was lost.'

'That same bus Mother comes on?'

'The very one. But it wasn't the driver's fault. That was gone into, and it was found he wasn't to blame.'

Now it was sadder than ever. His secret picture was a dangerous weapon: Mrs Pawsey's was of a good son that she'd lost. He couldn't show her his picture, he'd be ashamed to act as if it was even, his secret with hers.

'Was Gordon your only son?'

'He was.' She sighed in a gulpy way. 'And that's why we told the billeting officer we'd take a bigger boy for evacuation, while Gordon's ways were still fresh in our minds, so we'd know how to look after a boy properly.'

'You look after boys very well.'

She hugged him. 'You came as though you were a gift, different from dear Gordon of course, but lovely in your way. Now you've seen my special picture, Mr Pawsey's special picture too. It seemed the right time to show you, after you'd lost someone in your family.'

'It's very sad,' he muttered. It was another sad thing. People he cared about, Aunty, Dad, even Kenneth, losing someone they loved and now the Pawseys too.

'We look on the bright side. Our Gordon never got to that first interview, or any interview, but he was saved from going to war. War started the September after he died, so he'd have been called up as one of the first. We may well have lost him by now and in a more dreadful way, see.'

She put the photograph back and sent him to his bedroom to get ready for what was to come.

The black car rolled into the front yard.

The vicar came to the doorway as Mrs Pawsey hurried forward, bringing Billy by the hand.

'Ah, Mrs Pawsey. I've come to be a support to Kenneth, and to Billy at this tragic time.' He looked at Billy with a solemn face.

Billy coughed. Should he say 'Thank you?' What did 'support' really mean? Anyway he didn't know the vicar, apart from being looked at by him, twice. He just said, 'Hallo' because he didn't know what he should do.

'Your Mother has gone with your Aunty, Billy. That's some comfort for her, God willing. And she'll be needed by your father who has sadly lost his brother.'

Yes! Dad was Uncle Frank's brother. Now Dad didn't have one, just like Billy didn't have a brother.

Mrs Pawsey took Kenneth's hand and led both boys into the sitting room, saying 'Vicar, so good of you to bring Kenneth. You must need a nice cup of tea and my husband's bringing you one right in a moment.'

Kenneth sat in his camel coat and cap on the hardest chair without speaking. He looked at the carpet and didn't bother speaking.

'Just about the arrangements, Vicar,' Mrs Pawsey started. 'You put me in the picture and I shall do what's best, so no one needs to worry.'

When Mr Pawsey brought in the vicar's tea it was just a cup for him because it wasn't like a proper visit.

'Do you want orange squash, Kenneth?' He put his hand on Kenneth's shoulder.

Kenneth shook his head.

'You boys pop upstairs, then, while we folk work out the comings and goings.'

Upstairs, Kenneth sat on the bed not looking anywhere.

Billy brought out his cigarette cards and put them in Kenneth's lap. 'You can play with these, if you like.'

Kenneth shook his head and left them lying there. It was very quiet. Billy looked around for ideas of what to give Kenneth to do. The window was shut, and none of the normal sounds were there to make Billy feel easier. Without the pigs snorting or the dogs barking, things didn't seem right. The dogs had been tied up at the end of the yard before the vicar arrived, the hens were at their feed behind their henhouse. Even the wardrobe door stayed shut, the toy cars inside.

Billy walked round to the side of his bed where Mr Pawsey had put up a camp bed for Kenneth. He was going to point to it, but Kenneth wasn't looking. It was very very difficult to know what was best to do.

Eventually Kenneth spoke. 'We're not going home anymore. Mummy doesn't want to be there without Daddy.'

'Not go home to Balham? Where will you go?'

He shrugged. 'Don't know. Don't care.'

'Is Aunty – all right?'

'No. Daddy should have been evacuated, like us. She says there's no end to this war.'

'But it will have to end one day. It can't just go on and on. Even the Great War ended.'

Kenneth gave a little snort. 'That was then.' He sounded like Dad.

A plane flew overhead, quite low. Billy could tell it was German.

They heard the door latch click. The vicar had gone. Mrs Pawsey came upstairs 'Wouldn't it be nice for Kenneth to walk round with me as I feed the animals?'

Kenneth didn't answer, so she took his hand and started down the stairs.

Billy didn't tell her what Kenneth thought of animals as he trudged after them and out of the back door.

Kenneth wouldn't be able to say anything about the pig smell now that the pen was horribly empty. He didn't even seem to notice. Mrs Pawsey gave him a basket to collect the eggs in. Billy trailed behind, while she chatted all the time to Kenneth, one arm around him. He found an egg in the hedge and put it in Kenneth's basket.

Mrs Pawsey started bending down, but Kenneth stayed where he was, not looking at anything.

They went towards the horse, who had his head over the fence. Mrs Pawsey stroked him, but Kenneth didn't bother. He didn't like horses either, even when things were normal.

'Shall we see if the carrots are ready?' Billy tried.

But a black cloud had come over just like yesterday's and they hurried inside quickly before the rain came down.

'My goodness, aren't we lucky we escaped that?' Mrs Pawsey said cheerily. 'Best if you play cards in the sitting room, boys.'

The rain came down and down as if each splash was chasing the next, hundreds and thousands of splashes making great puddles where the dogs had dug for bones and where the pigs had once stood with their noses up, waiting for their swill. The heavy rain was like crying and crying from the sky.

The cards were already in a pile on the table. 'Shall I deal?' Billy tried again.

Kenneth told him to play Patience and he'd watch. But he didn't.

That night, as he'd dreaded, they were both to sleep in his room. Mrs Pawsey made up the camp bed with sheets and cosy blankets. She ran Kenneth a nice, warm bath which she said would help settle him in a strange house.

Billy got into bed, put his head in his book and read about knights in armour. Kenneth came back from his bath without talking. Mrs Pawsey came in to say Goodnight. Then they listened to her footsteps all the way downstairs and into the parlour. The door shut.

Perhaps Kenneth would read a long time to take his mind off. Billy had put his comic and annual by his bed.

'Kenneth, you can put the light out whenever you like. I won't mind.'

Kenneth turned it off straight away.

The knights had been riding to battle, protected by their armour. Billy had been right in the middle of a sentence.

Everything but the rain was quiet.

Billy lay still, trying to sleep but was horribly uneasy. The rain slashed against the window. He didn't like someone else in the room who'd had something terrible happen. There was just him and

Kenneth. It felt as if he'd been left in charge and he didn't feel old enough. He ought not to be silent. Kenneth had his back turned. What words should he say? He tried to remember words he'd heard grown-ups say. He practised a few.

Sleepiness was slow coming and just after he had managed to nod off, or perhaps much later, Billy was kept awake by an awful sobbing and muffled moaning from Kenneth's bed. He kept quiet because what should he do? He waited for Mrs Pawsey to come and see to the trouble. But it wasn't loud enough for her to hear and it was too late at night for him to go and fetch her. All he could think of was getting his precious shashka photo to help. He pulled it out of its hiding place and waved it to and fro opposite the hunched lump that was Kenneth. 'Be brave, be brave,' he mouthed silently.

Eventually the crying died down and stopped. Only the rain spattering the windows kept on and on.

In the morning, Billy came back from the bathroom with his words ready but Kenneth didn't sit up. Mrs Pawsey put her head round the door and said it was time to get up, so then Kenneth did. His eyes were sore-looking and dark. She put an arm round him and pushed him towards the bathroom.

'Nice egg for you when you're dressed and downstairs, my dear.'

Billy had to wait until they were at the breakfast table before he could say the words he'd rehearsed. 'Kenneth, you'll feel better soon about – Uncle.'

'You don't know what happened.' Kenneth pulled viciously at the table cloth so that the dishes jerked. That was shocking.

'Don't!' whispered Billy. 'I know it was a bomb at the tube.' He didn't want Kenneth to talk about Uncle being blown to bits.

'Daddy wasn't down the tube.'

'Wasn't he?'

Kenneth pushed his head towards Billy, his eyes glittering like a madman. 'He was on a bus, going to visit Uncle Bert. The bus fell down into a great hole where the bomb hit.'

Billy swallowed. That did seem better than being blown up. 'Fell down? A whole bus?'

'Yes. And Daddy shouldn't have been on it, visiting. Why couldn't Uncle have come to Balham? It's always us visiting you.'

Mrs Pawsey bustled in with the teapot and the eggs.

Mr Pawsey followed her. 'A good breakfast, you boys. That's as what you need.'

There was a steely silence. Mrs Pawsey shook her head slightly at him and continued passing dishes and serving things out. She took the top off Kenneth's egg. 'Try to eat that up, dear. From our chickens. Do you good.'

Billy struggled with his breakfast, toast crumbs sticking in his throat. It hadn't been his idea for Kenneth to always visit, or usually. He'd have been happy if they didn't visit at all, or perhaps just Aunty. But he couldn't say that. He shouldn't. It was hard to imagine a hole by Balham tube and a whole bus fallen into it; harder even than hundreds and thousands of dead and dying Russian soldiers.

He'd have to say something soon. He was the one with a father still alive. All he could think of was the same words he'd rehearsed upstairs. 'Aunty will come quite soon, Kenneth. Then you'll feel better. And you don't have to go to school when I do.'

Kenneth looked at him bleakly across the table. 'She's going to come after the funeral's over.'

Mrs Pawsey said that Kenneth would probably feel happier going with Billy to school than staying behind on his own.

'No. I don't think he'd like that. He doesn't know anyone. He could feed the chickens,' Billy suggested. It would be awful taking Kenneth to school.

'I'd thought he might like to be with your friends. I've written a note for your teacher.'

The sky was still grey after the day of drenching rain before.

'I'll stay here,' said Kenneth. 'I want to sit and draw, please. I've got my pencils and book. I always have them.'

'Yes. He's ever such a good drawer,' Billy said to Mrs Pawsey. 'You should see his drawings.'

She looked at both of them and nodded. 'All right, dear. You draw us a lovely big picture.'

'Can't do big. Paper shortage,' Kenneth muttered.

'That's all right, just so happens I can find some big paper. And when Billy's back from school and Mr Pawsey from the market, perhaps there'll be something come here to cheer you up.'

He didn't answer, and Billy didn't know what to say next to make things better. It was a relief when Mrs Pawsey came back with some huge sheets of paper which had wrapped up some documents long ago. They weren't very grubby. Kenneth was dusting them off as Billy left for school.

~

When he got home, expecting the parlour to be decorated with drawings like at Uncle Frank's house, Kenneth was just putting the rubber band round his pencils.

'I'm not showing you, so don't ask,' he said. He used the largest piece of paper to wrap up a sheaf of drawings.

Mrs Pawsey called them to the front garden and told them to look out for Mr Pawsey, who was expected back any minute.

Soon enough, he came ambling along, his trouser bottoms tied up over his boots because some of the lanes were very muddy after the heavy rain. He was drawing a cart behind him and as he got close there were unmistakable sounds coming from it. Billy rushed into the road.

'Mr Pawsey, Mr Pawsey. I know what you've got in there. I know.'

Mr Pawsey grinned. 'And I knew as you'd be pleased. You come and help, then. What about your cousin? Something to cheer him up. Kenneth, laddie, come and see.'

Kenneth moved forward slowly. Billy ran to the pig pen and opened its gate, then ran to the back of the cart as Mr Pawsey leaned inside and carried out a piglet like a baby in his arms.

'Shut the pen gate, lad. I'll lift each one over, that's easiest.'

There were four: one pink, one pink with black blobs, one black with pink blobs and one pink with a black bottom. They were really smashing.

Kenneth stayed at the front of the cart, watching. It was best not to tell Mr Pawsey that Kenneth didn't like pigs. Or any animals, really. He didn't even draw them.

Billy hung over the pen for ages watching the piglets. They were such fun, all wriggly and squeaky that he almost forgot what had happened, until he thought about Aunty coming to collect Kenneth.

Perhaps when he saw the car, Billy would be too busy helping with the animals to come indoors. The vicar would hurry Kenneth and Aunty back to the Vicarage. That would be best.

He ran into the kitchen to tell Mrs Pawsey about the piglets, to tell the dogs. He sat stroking Noah, because Kenneth wouldn't come near dogs. It was tea-time. Mrs Pawsey would sort Kenneth out. She had nice biscuits in her red *East West Home's Best* biscuit tin. It had a jolly picture of houses with red roofs, a neat circle of front garden in front that just made you ache to open it and see whether there were custard creams or pink wafers inside. His first day there, a chocolate digestive had been on top of the wafers. If Kenneth had one of those, he could sit and nibble it until he felt better.

It was all a great worry. However much he hated having Kenneth here, so sad and odd, it would even worse when the grown-ups returned with their misery. It would be truly dreadful if they cried. Aunty would likely cry and that would be really embarrassing. Perhaps she'd get it over with before they got here. When people died, did the grown-ups feel all right again once the funeral was over? It was four 'o'clock now. It must be long over. They'd have to hurry to catch the train before the night-time bombing started.

He saw Kenneth trailing indoors with Mr Pawsey, so Billy pulled Noah into the back lobby and filled his water bowl. There were some large jam jars on the shelf above the sink. That gave him an idea. He hurried into the garden to find something cheery. In October there weren't many flowers. He checked round the bushes for ideas, until he saw some lavender. It wasn't very blue now, but it smelled nice. The grown-ups would all like that. He picked a big bunch and took it inside. He half-filled the jam jar with water and separated the lavender stalks so that they looked good. Best to put it in the front room where grown-ups would go.

At tea-time everyone was quiet, and there were buns left over. It wouldn't be right to take left-overs down to Mrs Youldon's today, so he just watched as they were cleared away. It would be toasted buns tomorrow, because grownups wouldn't eat buns after a funeral.

It was growing dark when, kneeling by the front window, he saw the vicar's car draw up in the front yard. Mrs Pawsey had said it was best if Billy didn't work outside after tea.

The car shuddered and stopped. In the back, Aunty's head and Mother's showed clearly. The back car door opened and Mother started to get out. He could see that they were both in black and Aunty's hat had a little net veil which was rolled upwards. He ran to the parlour before he saw anymore, his insides fluttering and panicky. 'Mrs Pawsey, Mrs Pawsey. They're here!'

She went to the door, bringing Kenneth by the hand. Lingering in the background, Billy started, as he saw that Dad was with them! He hadn't expected that. Dad was holding Aunty firmly round her upper arm, while Mother carried both their handbags.

Dad said 'Good evening, Mrs Pawsey.' then murmured more things. Billy only caught the end '. . . compassionate leave.'

She said in a low voice, 'So I should think, Mr Wilson. We're very, very sorry to hear of your loss.'

Billy tried to remember those words because other people he knew might die soon. Dad wouldn't cry of course, but he would be thinking about Uncle Frank and his being in a bus crashing right down into a hole, and being his brother, so it was best not to look at him. Dad nodded to Mr Pawsey, then greyly to Billy, hardly seeming to notice things.

Aunty threw her arms round Kenneth and stroked his face, her eyes watering already. 'Poor little fatherless boy.' Kenneth hung into her, his knees weak and bendy.

Mrs Pawsey supported them both into the front room where the chair cushions had been plumped up, ready.

Mother stepped forward, putting the handbags on the hall dresser. 'Hello, Billy,' she said very quietly and he said, 'Hello, Mother.' Then he stood to one side, out of the way, but Mother put a hand at his back pressing him forward into the front room, and the vicar followed with Dad.

Mrs Pawsey said, 'So good of you to collect them from the station, Vicar.'

The vicar's face looked long and sad, although he didn't even know Uncle Frank. He waited while the grown-ups thanked Mrs Pawsey for looking after Kenneth who was hanging limply on Aunty's arm. Then he leaned forward and shook Billy's hand. 'You must be a strength to everyone.' He turned to shake Kenneth's hand and clapped one shoulder very firmly as if he was holding him together, 'My boy.'

Mother turned to Mrs Pawsey, 'I hope they've been no trouble to you. Well, Billy, really.'

Mrs Pawsey said in a low voice, 'No, no. He was so upset when I had to break the news.'

No one else was listening, hunched into their coats, but Mother put her head on one side and raised her eyebrows at Billy. He looked down quickly.

Mrs Pawsey told them all to sit down. 'I shall get you a nice tray of tea.'

Billy started forward, 'I can help.'

'No dear, best to stay with your family.'

Billy sat on the extra chair behind the vicar's.

Mother perched on a high chair, crossing her legs at the ankle. Aunty tucked a piece of curl under her hat and sat on the sofa. There were lines round her mouth and her skirt was badly creased. Kenneth sat beside her, leaning against her. He looked ill. Dad hitched up his trousers and sat heavily in the wide low chair, clearing his throat. He'd be making one of his sayings soon.

Billy kept his eyes on the jam jar where he'd put the lavender and breathed in the smell. It was too difficult to look at anyone's face.

The vicar said, 'I will lead you all in a little prayer for this very sad time.' He started off with the groaning words, *Ohs* and *Los* and *Dear Father* and *Beseech*. It seemed a very long prayer.

Billy had his eyes screwed tight but he could squint at bits of people while they had their heads down and eyes shut, praying with the vicar. He kept taking huge breaths of lavender smell, he couldn't help it, although he was scared the breaths would sound throughout the room once the praying stopped and then everyone would look at him.

They didn't, because just then Kenneth threw up all over Mrs Pawsey's best rug. There just wasn't time to get a bucket. And now Billy couldn't smell the lavender at all. In the fuss, he was able to run to the kitchen to get rags and water and Mrs Pawsey. She had to do the cleaning up because Aunty was seeing to Kenneth, and Mother had good clothes on. A bit had splashed on to her skirt and shoe, so she went outside to get it off. Billy left the cleaning things and quickly disappeared into the parlour where Mr Pawsey was just reaching a hand around for his glasses, a long way wide of the mark.

'I've got them, Mr Pawsey, I've got them.' He put them into Mr Pawsey's groping paw. 'Kenneth's been sick and it smells awful. Don't go into the front room.'

'I won't, Boy. And you stay here and keep me company. They've got my good lady and the vicar to help. I was just going to do my crossword and couldn't find those glasses for the life of me. If only Billy was here, I thought, he'd find 'em for me, and here you are.'

Billy sat on the arm of his chair. 'You'll need me to fill in your crossword letters, won't you?'

'I will.' He scratched his forehead with the end of his pencil. 'Now two across, seven letters. How about 'thunder'? Do you reckon that fits in?'

Billy counted across carefully, then nodded.

'So put in just the T and the R, till we're sure. Now then, eight down. Will that start with a T? Trouble, that's what I think it is.'

'I think it is, too,' said Billy.

It was some time before the tray of tea got to everyone. Now that the front room was spoiled, it was put in the dining room and everyone moved in there. Kenneth was lying down upstairs for a little while, a bucket beside him just in case. It would be awful if he was sick again and made Billy's room smell.

From his vantage point beside Mr Pawsey and his crossword, Billy heard the vicar say they would drink the tea Mrs Pawsey had kindly provided and then have their little prayer again. He sat tight, hoping he wouldn't be called in. After all, the table wasn't laid for his supper. He always had his supper there with Mr and Mrs Pawsey, and because they hadn't eaten much tea, it was going to be ham and tomatoes and chutney and chunks of bread and dark fruit loaf.

After a while, he heard Kenneth come downstairs, saying he felt better, he just wanted to go back to his own bed. Billy hoped he only meant his billet bed. If Aunty had decided never to go back to Balham again, Kenneth would never have his own bed. Aunty fussed round him and then said he should join in their prayer before they got his coat on.

If they were going, Billy thought he'd better come to the front door. He'd wait until he heard them saying their Goodbyes. He left the crossword and hovered at the doorway, then looked back at Mr Pawsey whose glasses were off again, his head slightly bowed.

He waited to hear the prayer begin in the dining room, and soon the rhythmic, sighing words came. He frowned. It would make no difference the vicar doing all that. Uncle would still be dead.

There was a little silence, shuffling, then a chorus of muttering from everyone together. They were all murmuring the same prayer words. Then it ended. Phew. Billy felt his breath shoot upwards over his nose. A chair grated as the vicar said he would take a brief turn around the garden before driving them home.

Mr Pawsey stood up. 'Go and join your family now, Billy. I'll be needed to show the vicar round.' He went to the front door and ushered the vicar out.

Billy followed slowly and slid into the spare seat by the dining room door. The women were softly talking with Mrs Pawsey who was tutting and sympathising '... we did worry whether you'd get a train before any air raid.'

'Yes, it was an added worry. And do you know,' Aunty was saying in a shaky voice, 'the very worst thing, when we got on to the train to go to the funeral, there was a notice right in front of us, *Is your journey really necessary?* It was the last straw, I can tell you.'

Mrs Pawsey patted her arm, 'There, it's a terrible time, that's for sure. You're taking it all so bravely. Now, you sit awhile, sort yourselves out, no hurry, before Vicar takes you all off backalong. I'll just see to the dishes if you'll excuse me,' and she bustled back to the kitchen.

Dad stood up and came towards Kenneth who was leaning against Aunty's arm. 'You look a bit better, Kenneth. Are you?'

'I'm all right now.'

Dad beckoned to Billy to stand by him. Was this a father's prayer? Billy obeyed. The vicar came back in, but only as far as the doorway. Dad cleared his throat, then looked at Mother and Aunty as if to see that they were paying attention. He put a hand on Kenneth's shoulder and another on Billy's. 'Frank and I had an arrangement,' he said to everyone. 'We promised each other when war was declared that if anything happened to the one of us, the other would look after his boy.'

Mother's eyes widened, but she didn't say anything. She held one of her prettiest hankies between clenched hands. There was a long pause. The piglets were squealing their loudest. Mr Pawsey was doing the feed without Billy.

Dad went on, 'My brother Frank did a wonderful job as a father. Now he's gone, I will try my level best to do the same. So now I've got two sons. Billy and Kenneth.'

The room went black for a while. Then Billy realised his gaze was fixed on the vicar's coat on the chair in front of him and he wasn't looking beyond it. What was it Dad had said? He couldn't really have said *two sons*. He only had one son.

Aunty said with a sniffle, 'Thank you, thank you, Herbert. That is a comfort, I must say.'

Kenneth looked up at Dad, his face still whitish, one curl smeared across his forehead. 'What do I call you, then? Aren't you Uncle anymore?'

Dad put his large hand on Kenneth's shoulder and softly closed it round. 'I am uncle and now I'm father too. If you'd like to, you can call me Dad.'

Billy stared hard at the vicar's black coat. Kenneth couldn't call him *Dad*. Could he? They couldn't *both* have him as Dad, surely. He looked up at Dad, confused.

'So, sh- should I call you *Uncle*?' he asked.

Dad answered with a cuff round his ear. 'None of that. Especially at such a time. Be a bit Christian.'

The cuff didn't hurt much but something did, low down in his throat and lower still. Billy ran out to the sanctuary of the parlour. It had been jolly bad having Uncle Frank but it was even worse not having him. Mr Pawsey's glasses were glinting on the side table. Billy plucked them up and shoved them on his face. Now he couldn't see anything but pale splodges. He staggered round the room knocking into things, his hands in front of him, blinded to all that was happening. He heard them come in after him, the women exclaiming, his father saying his name in an irritated voice. It didn't matter, he'd be a pale foggy splodge to them, not Billy anymore.

His father began speaking angrily, the black patches of his trousers coming dangerously near, but then the more fanned-out black of the vicar's robe swam near the doorway.

'A confusing time, a very confusing time for a young boy away from his home.'

Dad went quiet, and the wide black shape came near and a pale pink one grasped Billy's arm, firmly but kindly. It was a safe hold but Billy's own hand shot up protectively to his glasses. It seemed important to keep them on his nose, the only thing between him and all of them.

The vicar spoke softly to him. 'Time to take those off now, my son.'

So was the vicar going to be Billy's father, now? He cowered backward. No! He just wanted to stay here, with Mr and Mrs Pawsey, without Kenneth, feeding the piglets and collecting the swill from the village and being talked to at teatimes.

Mother's voice came from a distance. 'Billy! Take the glasses off. This is no time to be clowning around.'

Aunty said, sniffing, 'Oh, Billy, stop messing around. Isn't it bad enough? Let's get back and settled down as best we can, the few days your father is with us.'

The vicar's hand swam forwards and gently removed the glasses. 'I think Mr Pawsey will be looking for these in a minute.'

'You should come to the Vicarage for a few days, Billy,' said Mother.

'If you can avoid making things worse for poor Kenneth than they already are,' Dad added.

'Vicarage' sounded like *viçar Cage*. He didn't want to be trapped in it.

Mrs Pawsey came from the kitchen to see them off. She didn't know Billy had done anything wrong. She hadn't known Uncle Frank so she couldn't be sad about him. All the dark figures in front of him, the whole blackness of it made Billy suddenly turn and hide his head in Mrs Pawsey's bulges. She smelled of flour and disinfectant.

Mother tutted and said, 'Stand straight, child. We're going now. Last chance to join us if you're going to stop being silly.'

Stop being Billy, he thought she'd said at first, because his ears were well into Mrs Pawsey's Aron.

Aunty said, 'It's all a bit much, Billy, isn't it? Perhaps you'd rather come to see us a bit later on?'

Kind Aunty. He kept his face hidden so he couldn't hear or see what the adults said or did. Perhaps Aunty had saved him. Mrs Pawsey gently turned him around.

'I have to get Kenneth's things, dear. See your family off nicely, now.'

Dad looked down at Billy. 'Disappointed in you, Billy. Buck your ideas up and do better when I see you next.' He ushered everyone towards the vicar's car.

When their backs were safely turned and disappearing through the front door, Billy rushed into the front room stepping over the newspaper where the sick had been and grabbed the lavender out of the jam jar. He ran to the car just as they were getting in. He thrust the lavender at Aunty.

'This is for you. Because ...I like you.'

Aunty started. She blushed and her eyes watered as she took the lavender gently from him and held it close. She looked really pleased. Mother didn't.

Kenneth glanced at the lavender at Aunt's chest, then unfolded the large paper with all the drawings he'd done while Billy had been at school.

He put the top one on his mother's lap.

There was a choked gasp, then Aunt's wail began. It was a really detailed likeness of Uncle Frank.

CHAPTER SIX

October 20th 1940. *Long range bombers in Belgium ready for operations against England.*

Billy couldn't get to sleep that night for thinking of the terrible day just passed. He kept remembering the round, black bottom of the vicar's car crunching slowly away down the lane with Mother's small white handkerchief waving from the window, the sounds of Aunt's light wailing and the perfume of lavender masking the rancid smell in the front room. However hard he screwed his eyes shut, he still saw Kenneth's drawing of Uncle Frank and his pile of sick on Mrs Pawsey's nice rug.

'Look at those dark rings round your eyes!' Mrs Pawsey remarked in the morning. 'We shall keep you home from school. What you need is a quiet, ordinary day.'

He mooched around for a while and overheard them discussing the terrible incident that had killed Uncle Frank and so many others. He didn't want to hear anything about it, yet found himself creeping below the kitchen window to hear more. Something about water gushing and no chance of escape and a bus driver who couldn't stop in time. And if only Uncle hadn't decided to visit Dad. It was just like Gordon. If only he hadn't gone for the interview, or if only the thunderstorm hadn't started.

Then he heard Mrs Pawsey say, 'That little lad's face, I'll never forget. Tragic, bless him. Beautiful features. Wasn't that face like one of those porcelain ornaments in the county museum?'

'Tragedy for him, yes. I should watch him, though,' said Mr Pawsey. 'Bain't porcelain right the way through.'

Billy crept away miserably. Porcelain or not, whatever that was, Kenneth was bound to come again. This was Billy's billet, but now *his* Mr and Mrs Pawsey would be looking at Kenneth. Like an ornament.

Later they called him to help with the chores.

'Nothing like work to show you that life goes on,' said Mr Pawsey.

After they'd seen to the chickens, the piglets, the fences and the yard, they had a dinner of Mrs Pawsey's vegetable soup with hunks of fresh warm bread.

Mr Pawsey put his jacket on afterwards and said they'd take the dogs for a walk. There was a lot of barking and rushing around and panting and wet tongues. Mrs Pawsey almost pushed them out of the door, saying she needed an empty house to do a good clean-up.

Mr Pawsey winked at Billy, his eyes all little and wrinkly without his glasses, and they set off down the lane, the dogs setting a fast pace. Mr Pawsey could keep up with them better than Billy, much better than Granddad would. Mr Pawsey didn't seem so very old to Billy now. He could do all sorts of strong things. He might even be able to swing a shashka if someone taught him right.

'Are you along-a-me, Billy, or what? Do you want to try taking a dog?'

Billy ran up alongside him. Japhet came up to his waist. He was the slightly larger dog so he tried holding Noah's lead but his arm was pulled straight and his body nearly followed.

Mr Pawsey put a bear-like paw on top of Billy's grasp. 'You've got to be firm, you know. Show who's master. If a dog thinks he can rule the day, he will. Same with people, you know.' He demonstrated how to jerk the lead so that Noah had to stop. Japhet was padding along in a superior way as if he never barked or rushed away. 'Look at this one. He's only behaving because he knows I'm top dog. We'll do the same with Noah.'

Noah looked top dog, lips pulled back, eyes bulging, raring to go, but Mr Pawsey with his screwed up eyes and shuffling feet, he was the one in charge.

They got to the village outskirts and the lanes were fairly dry so the dogs were let off their leads. Billy let out a little laugh as they whizzed off so fast that little hairs from their necks blew up into the air.

'How will we ever get them back?'

'One whistle. They know. You have to have a sign, you know. A noise for an animal. For a person it can be a look on the face.'

'I know that! Mother has a 'No' face sometimes and I stop doing whatever it is.'

'There you are, you see. Your mother's top dog with you.'

'Dad's top dog of everyone, though, isn't he?' and suddenly he remembered with a thump in his tummy that Dad was top dog of more people now. Kenneth. Would he stop being nasty if there was a look on Dad's face? Would Aunty?

'Mr Pawsey?'

'Mmm.'

'If a man can have two sons, can he have two wives?'

'Oho, no. Not at the same time. Not in our country. Only one after the other, sometimes.'

At that moment there was loud barking and when they rounded the corner, a small lady was stroking the dogs.

'Mrs Youldon!' He rushed up to her.

'Down!' Mr Pawsey said, some way behind him, but it was the dogs he was shouting to. They were jumping up and that wasn't allowed.

Mrs Youldon was in a blue dress with a dark blue cardigan. She might be going to a party except for her shoes, same as before, brown, baggy and lace-up. He'd never seen her prettied up before. Nice, stroky. Like Angela.

'I like your dress and everything. It's pretty.'

Mrs Youldon twizzled round, then smiled bashfully. 'Nice? It's from The Grange. They gave me these when they were turning stuff out for the war effort and I only had to alter it a bit. Guess what I've got it on for?'

Billy shook his head.

Mr Pawsey came up to them. 'Good morning, Joan. How are you managing these days?'

'Oh not so bad, Mr Pawsey. I think there's some more work coming up for me. They need women at the tinning factory, and they're going to collect everyone by van in the morning and bring them back at the end of the day. The church have started a nursery and that's where my little ones are now. So I'm feeling quite excited.'

'And you're looking very smart.'

'Thank you.' She blushed. 'I thought I'd try it on to show Billy, really. I was just on my way to your house to see him.'

'Me?'

'I haven't forgotten. Your birthday.'

He looked up at Mr Pawsey with a gasp. The last days had been so terrible that he'd actually forgotten. 'I'm nine!'

'My goodness me. A birthday. We didn't know that, the wife and I.'

Mrs Youldon smiled. 'And last year I didn't know and all we could do was sing the birthday song, but this year is different. Here's a little present from all of us.' She handed over a parcel wrapped up in brown paper. It was a good shape, all knobbly and interesting.

'Thank you.' He opened the parcel and found a set of aeroplane cards and three large pine cones painted mainly red.

'They're topping! I wanted these ever so! I'll know all the planes now.' He looked at the cones.

'The little ones did those at the nursery,' she said. 'They wanted to give you something too.' She looked up at Mr Pawsey. 'They think the world of Billy, my little ones', she said. 'I'll get back to them now I've bumped into you, Billy. Saved me a walk. I'll go and show them my dress. Make sure you come up ours, soon.' She turned back down the lane with a wave.

Billy hugged the things to him. He would go again soon, and he'd have to tell her about Uncle Frank, but he'd never take Kenneth there.

They walked on and on, the dogs speeding away and then back again.

'We're going far!'

'We are that.' Mr Pawsey's face had folds around his mouth, and just now they looked longer. 'Haven't done this route since we—' He stopped.

And suddenly Billy guessed that Mr Pawsey was thinking about Gordon. He probably walked the dogs with Gordon, and now he couldn't. He'd gone forever, like Uncle Frank. It was horrible that one person dying made everyone think of other people they'd known dying, so the sadness spread across all sorts of people. He put his hand into Mr Pawsey's hairy one. It was like having another Granddad. You *could* have two Granddads. It was only Mother who had a father alive. Would Dad mind that Billy had Mr and Mrs Pawsey instead? That they weren't just a billet?

Mr Pawsey was saying, 'It's a day for a good long walk, especially now as it's your birthday. Exercise. Do you good.'

The dogs ran ahead with cheerfully wagging tails until they came to a stream.

Billy ran to see. 'Cor. Super!'

Japhet barked once, and both dogs went to charge down the bank, but Mr Pawsey was too quick. He'd already grasped their collars, one in each hand.

'Now we put their leads on,' he said.

'But they want to swim.'

'They do. Oh, they do that. But look here. The bank's high and straight up so once they're in they can't get out, and the water's deep because the river's near. Look how it's swirling around. Water going two ways. Dangerous for them. And if you're ever here, don't ever try to swim or even paddle. There's a much better place a bit further on where it makes a pool.'

He yanked the leads as the dogs strained to get near the water and led the way through a dark woody path until they came out into the sun again. They clambered over the stile and down a slope until a flat, grassy patch was in front of them and a stony-edged pool at one side of the main flow. The dogs were let off their leads and rushed in, making crystal drops fly in all directions.

Billy laughed. 'Can I paddle?'

'Now why do you think I've walked this far?'

Billy tore off his shoes and socks. He paddled out to the dogs and splashed around them. There were a few flat stones in the middle of the pool. He looked around for more and placed them down so that he'd made crude stepping stones. 'Look– a path, Mr Pawsey. You'll be able to walk across.'

'I'd better not risk it. I used to. You'll not be the first one who's thought of making one of those, young Billy. Do you like this place then?'

'It's top-hole. Did you really know it was my birthday? Is this a birthday treat? Did my mother tell you it was?'

Then he fell silent, there certainly hadn't been any cards or packages left for him. It was like last year. They'd forgotten.

'No. But if you think about it, your family have been tied up with other things, haven't they?'

Other things. The misery came back like a huge thump. He kicked at the water a few times, but the sun of the day had gone. Mr Pawsey was putting the leads back on the dogs.

'Come on now. It's nearly four. Must get back before it's dark. I shall need you to find my glasses back home, and we left that crossword at eleven across, remember? L- it began with.'

Billy was stamping the water off his feet on the longer grass.

When they got back, Mrs Pawsey already had the tea on the table, so Billy ran upstairs to get washed. He could hear Mr Pawsey muttering to her but he stopped when Billy ran down again.

It was not until they'd finished their tea that Mrs Pawsey said, 'We didn't know it was your birthday, Billy, but we're going to celebrate it properly. We shall take you to the pictures on Saturday.'

He leapt up. 'The pictures! Really, truly? I haven't been for ages and ages.'

'Yes. *Pinocchio*'s on, all about a naughty puppet boy. Isn't that just right for making boys laugh?'

Mr Pawsey was holding a brown cardboard box. 'And this. Open this 'un. The Missus gave it to me around twelve years ago, but my eyesight's not good enough to use it now. I think I can teach you to use it properly.'

Billy opened the box and a huge gasp escaped. Inside was a camera, a real one. He took it out and held it tightly. He could feel the metal under its soft black covering. It folded up, click, and you could put it in your pocket.

'It's a Kodak,' said Mrs Pawsey proudly.

Mr Pawsey took the camera from Billy and removed the entire back. 'This is how you load your film, but you must do it somewhere dark. Never, never outside in the daylight.'

He took Billy by the arm and they went in the cupboard under the stairs. It was pretty dark there. Billy giggled, it seemed such a funny thing to do. Mr Pawsey took a film out of his pocket, unwrapped it and slid the edges into a slot on the metal winder.

'See that? Think you can do it?'

He took it off and gave it to Billy who could do it easily. Then they shut the back of the camera and came out of the cupboard again. It was fun; mysterious and important, like a secret.

'That was a bit like hiding in an air raid,' Billy said.

Mrs Pawsey pressed her lips into her teeth. 'We're very lucky we don't have all that,' she said. 'I try not to forget it.'

It was nearly reminding Billy of the bomb at Balham so he pressed the camera into his chest until it hurt. Then he could think about the camera and how wonderful it was. He jumped up and down a few times then asked,

'Can I take a photo right away please?'

'A bit of a lesson, first, I think. Each snap you take uses up some film and when it's finished, we have to go and have it developed and printed, which costs money.'

'I've got a shilling, Uncle Ted gave me last year. It was for something special, and this is.'

'I think it's going to cost more than that. But I'll teach you how to take 'em tomorrow.'

~

Early the next day, before Billy had to set off for school, Mr Pawsey showed him the adjustable range finder. 'It'm worked by this small thumb screw, see, on the right side.'

He put his hands up as if they were a picture frame. 'That's how you choose your shot. You must hold the camera very steady. Best to rest it on a post or sommat.'

Billy listened very hard as Mr Pawsey explained about the light, the composition, and the shutter speed. Kenneth didn't know anything about these things.

The camera was so exciting Billy could ignore his heavy inside places where memories of Uncle Frank and the after-funeral visit were fluttering about like horse-flies.

They all flew back into his mind once he got to school. Alan was waiting for him on the lane leading to the school. 'I heard. Rotten luck, but it was the bully uncle died not your special one, wasn't it?'

'Mm. Uncle Frank, Kenneth's father, and Kenneth had to come to stay with me. It was awful.' That was as far as he got for once they got to the playground, everyone crowded round him, shoving Alan out of the way. They'd all heard about the Balham bombing and wanted to know the details.

Mick said, 'Cor, Billy. Your uncle got blitzed in that bus outside United Dairies. Our Mum shops there.'

Dick said, 'United Dairies has got a great socking hole outside it and the bus tipped right in. Everyone dead.'

'Lumme,' one of the East Enders joined in. 'Wish I'd seen it. Did your uncle die straight away?'

'Was your uncle burned up?'

'Was he drowned when the water gushed up?'

'Burned or drowned or blown up?'

Billy whirled his shashka arm round and round, saying 'I dunno, dunno, dunno.' He ran the length of the playground whirling and chanting, the others following with their 'Tell us, then. Tell us'.

Alan pushed forward, 'Shut up, you lot. Leave him alone.'

But they didn't. It was like a swarm after Billy and around him, buzzing and fussing until the bell went.

The teachers had been telephoned with the news, probably by the vicar. They were extra kind to Billy and let him off his spellings, but he just wanted things to be ordinary. At home time, the buzzing around him started again but he folded his arms and said loudly, 'I've got a camera. It was for my birthday.'

'Yaw. I bet!'

'Well, I have.'

'All right. What make is it?'

'It's a Kodak.' That stopped the sneering.

'I say!'; 'Real truth, Billy?' ; 'Bring it to show.' ; 'Photograph all of us?'; 'What's it do?'

Then he stood still and told them about his present, the shutter speed, putting in the film in the dark and everyone stopped asking about Uncle Frank.

Alan walked home with him. 'You will let me have a go with it when I come round, won't you?'

'The film's very expensive and I'm not to waste snaps.'

'Swap you, then.'

'What for?'

He knew what. If only Alan could go to Mother's vicarage instead of having to go himself. But that was no good. Alan ran into the Manor and Billy mooched off down the lane alone.

All days end. That was one of Dad's sayings, usually when Mother complained of a bad day. Billy thought of this as the red roof of the Pawseys' house showed behind the trees. This normally gave him a cheery feeling. The curving front path looked like a smile and he was sure the dogs were grinning at him as they rushed to him with their tongues hanging out. There was a bit of barking, but it was only to welcome him, or perhaps to tell Mrs Pawsey he was home. He would ask Mrs Pawsey if Alan could come over on Saturday for the whole day. Then they could do exploring and forget all about horrible things.

As he came to the back door, Mrs Pawsey put an arm round him and pulled him into her bulgy middle.

'Was it all right at school today?'

'No, it was rotten. They all kept asking horrible questions.'

'Never you mind, lovey. Let's go and have some tea then why not go and show Mrs Youldon your camera? I've put some of my fairy cakes in a bag for you to take.'

His mouth stopped feeling so tight. He did want to show the Youldons his camera and it was nice to have the cakes to take them.

After tea, he put the camera round his neck and ran off down the lane. He'd take three photos: one of Mrs Youldon, Tim and Sally together, one of just the children, and if big Ronnie next door and the usual crowd were playing on the street, he'd photograph them too. He was around the corner and into the main village before Mrs Pawsey had had a chance to tell him what time to be home.

He saw Mrs Youldon before she saw him. She wasn't in her nice blue dress now. She was back to the baggy thing with threads at the hem and a great apron round her. She was at the doorway looking hassled, for there were no big children in the street to mind the little ones.

Timmy and Sally jumped up and down when they saw who was coming. 'Billy! Billy!'

He ran up to them. 'Thank you for the fir cones. You painted them jolly well. Look at what I've got! It's all mine, my camera!' He turned round, 'Mrs Youldon, look what I've got. Mr Pawsey gave it to me and I'm going to take photos of you.'

'Well I never. It's a proper one, too.' She felt the top reverently as he let it concertina open. 'My little ones have never had their photo took.'

'I'm going to take it.' He put Timmy and Sally side by side outside the front of the cottage. They nudged each other and started to giggle. There was no gatepost to balance his camera on, but he held it very still while he examined them through his viewfinder. 'Keep still now.' He pressed the shutter as soon as they'd stopped fidgeting. It would be a picture of them giggling together. That'd be nice. 'Can I take one of you, Mrs Youldon?'

'Ooh dear, I don't know. I'm in the middle of some extra washing for the Grange.' But she took her apron off, and stood stiffly.

'Smile.' He took one of her on her own, and another one of her standing shyly behind her children. 'Finished.'

Sally ran to peer into the camera. 'Where are we, where are we, Billy?'

He laughed. 'Not inside the camera! I have to finish the film and then take it to get prints. Then I'll show you them, and you'll see yourselves in a picture.'

Mrs Youldon put her apron back on again. 'It'll be lovely to have photos of the little ones so I'll always know what they looked like, young. It'll be nice for them, too. I don't know how I looked as a child. Just no idea.'

'Didn't your parents get you photographed?'

She smiled in a way that showed him it was a silly question. She was poor. She hadn't lived the sort of life where you went to a town and got photographed.

Billy knew exactly how he looked when he was young, flat-haired, clean and ordinary in new clothes. There was a photo on the mantelpiece in the lounge at home: he stood on a stool wearing a pale blue buster suit, Mother on one side and Dad on the other, all very serious.

He clipped the camera shut, the little ones watching closely as the inside concertina'd flat again.

Mrs Youldon looked at him proudly. 'You do look grown-up with your camera, Billy. I hope you're very careful with it.'

'I am,' he said as he followed all of them indoors. Steam from the copper at the back belched into the small room. 'I'm not going to let Kenneth even touch it.' He swallowed. He knew he must tell her what had happened. 'I ought to let him, because his father died, my Uncle Frank.'

She gasped. 'What – just died?'

'A bomb in London.'

She gave him a hug. 'That's dreadful, really, really dreadful.'

He thought he wouldn't tell her the whole story. Like Mr Durban protecting his mother when he got back from Russia, Billy didn't want bad stuff going into Mrs Youldon's head; she was only a small mother.

'Your cousin, poor young boy with no father now. And you, losing your uncle, Billy. You must be very sad.'

Billy remembered that he should be, and hung his head. Then he said, 'It was Aunty's sad loss. I picked her some lavender.'

'Lavender? That was nice. You are a good boy.' Mrs Youldon picked up the damp clothes ready to iron. It was a huge pile. So was the dirty pile waiting for the copper. She must be taking in extra work because she had no evacuee money.

He picked up a pair of sheets that had fallen off the load of dirty washing and took the whole pile towards the copper.

'Thank you, Billy, such a help. I wish you'd come over more often, you and Alan. You could earn tuppence an afternoon if you'd look after Tim and Sally safely so that I can go to work. When you're not at school, of course.'

He nodded. 'Righto, I will. I like looking after them. Not for the money. You can buy more food to put on your shelves instead.' He smiled down at them as Sally tugged at his jumper and Tim measured his height against him. His insides already felt better. He did so like being here. He pointed to his paper bag. 'Guess what I've got in here? It's fairy cakes for all of you.'

CHAPTER SEVEN

October 21st 1940. *New Zealand cruiser drives Italian destroyers away in Red Sea.*

When he got home, Mrs Pawsey was in the kitchen peeling a huge pile of carrots. He opened his mouth to ask if Alan could come over on Saturday but Mrs Pawsey was already speaking.

'Here, Billy. Can you cut these heads off and sit them in this tray of water? Then they'll be ready for you to plant out in a couple of days?'

He rolled up his jumper sleeves and took up the knife.

'Your father telephoned.'

He put the knife down. What now? His chest thudded and he crossed his arms over it, hard.

'He wants you over there for two days, before he has to go back to London. Jed'll take you and the vicar'll bring you back the following evening.'

'Then I'll have to stay the night! Can't I come back with Jed? Couldn't he wait for me and have his dinner there?'

'Oh no, no. It's what's been arranged, dear, and it's for your parents to decide. At such a time as this, you'll want to be with your father.'

He wouldn't, not with this happening. It would be awful. They'd all still be cross with him as well as being sad as sad. He wouldn't know what to say. Two whole days! What would they do all that time? There'd be grown-ups with funeral faces, and they'd make him be with Kenneth, who was all quiet and strange.

Mrs Pawsey broke into his thoughts, 'Your little sister will be glad to see you. It's been several weeks since you were together.'

Jill. It was ages ago since that night at the station when he'd last seen her. She might still have that little bear he'd put into her baby hand. She would be glad to see him. She hadn't had him to play with her and perhaps she'd cried when Mother came here, leaving her behind. He brightened. 'I bet she'll jump up and down and say her words over and over again. That's what she does. And she'll want me to read to her.'

'That's right, my love. Won't that be nice?'

Yes. He could play with Jill, and not look at the others much at all. He might ask Mr Pawsey if he could take his camera. He could snap Jill, then he could show Mr and Mrs Pawsey what she looked like.

At the sound of Jed's horse next morning, Billy leant out of his bedroom window. It would be good to have a photo of Jed on his cart with the nice brown horse, bright red on his harness. He put his hands up like a frame. He called down.

'Jed! Stay there, please. I got a camera for my birthday. I'm going to take your picture.'

He rested his elbows on the windowsill and adjusted the distance. The photo would look smashing.

Jed sat like a statue. 'Well, I'll be blowed. No one's never taken my picture afore.'

Then Billy ran down to clamber aboard, the camera around his neck.

'You'se be very, very careful with it, Billy. There'm be no chance you'se'll get another camera if you break that, or let anyone else break it.' He knew Mr Pawsey had only let him take it with him because of how it was going to be for him at the vicarage.

'I know. I'm not going to let anyone else TOUCH it.' If anyone tried, he'd make the 'Don't' face. Anything else they could take or make him give to poor Kenneth, but not the camera.

The jogging journey was quite nice, all through the red and gold trees, the horses kicking up the thick layer of fallen leaves. Soon the branches would be bare.

Jed dropped him off by the vicarage. He stood where the cart had left him and watched Jed disappear over a browny-green bank and down into the distance.

What would the vicarage be like? He'd never been in one before. He held his overnight case in one hand, the camera still strung round his neck. He wasn't going to put it down if he could help it.

The vicarage was a grey stone house with a tiled roof. It was near to the church, which was very like the one in his village. The gate was green like Nanny's and there were flowers at the sides of a path running to the front door where a pale woman stood, a duster bunched in her hand.

'Are you Billy? I'm Mrs Shawditch.'

She wasn't as smart as Mother and Aunty. He'd have expected her to be smarter – a vicar's wife – but her cardigan bagged around her waist, there was no little white collar on her blouse and her shoes were clumpy. He wouldn't have been looking at clothes, only her face had nothing on it, no smile, no expression, as if that sort of thing had all been worn off.

'Come in. I'm sure it will cheer everyone up to have your visit.' He saw that she had green eyes and pale hair, but she didn't look cheered up herself. She turned to call his mother. 'Billy's here!'

Billy held out his hand, ready to shake hers. She started, as if she'd been dreaming and now had to return to work. Her hand was moist, limp. 'Well. Your father's busy for a while with the vicar but I think your mother's still in the kitchen. She's helping me prepare the vegetables. Quite a lot of us for dinner today.'

He stepped inside. There was no dog to bark. He could smell soap and old clothes. A box of them waited in the hall for giving away.

They looked faded and very old. Who was going to want any of those?

A set of wooden picture frames all along the hall wall frowned down on him with different texts: *Behold, I waited for thy words, I listened for thy wise sayings*. That one had a pretty border round the words in green. *Lo. My Redeemer cometh* had sun rays around it. And *He forgave them their Sins* was on plain grey. *Jesus Loves You* was in thick coloured block capitals. The coir mat said *Wipe Your Feet*, so he did.

'Marcia! Your son!' the vicar's wife called again, running a hand through slightly messy fine hair. 'She won't be a moment, Billy. I just have to see to a – a gentleman who needs a set of new clothes and something to eat.'

He peered down the hall after her as she opened a back room door. He caught a glimpse of a long-haired tramp standing in rumpled grey trousers, everything else bare. Mother was just passing him, whisking aside her skirt as she did so. She wouldn't have wanted to accidentally touch him. She closed the door behind her. Clip. Her eyes lighted upon Billy.

'Hello. You get bigger each time I see you, I do declare. It's all that football I suppose, that and your farm food.'

'Hello Mother.' It had only been a few days since she'd seen him. Could he have grown in that time? He looked down at his legs. It must be his trousers, which had got so short lately. His boots were a long way from the trouser hems. He stood behind the hallstand where only his top half showed, his big legs hidden by the bottom of several coats hanging from the curly hooks.

Mother didn't seem to be sad. Perhaps it was all right about Uncle Frank now. He wasn't her brother, after all.

'Now. Your father's only got two more days with us. So you will be a good boy, won't you?'

He nodded. 'I didn't m-mean not to be the other day.'

'No, perhaps not. Very well, we'll pass over it.' She took a couple of steps towards him, her arm outstretched. Perhaps she was going to pat his face.

'What's that round your neck?'

'My c-camera.' He stepped back. 'Mr and Mrs Pawsey gave it to me.'

'Really!'

'Now that I'm n-nine.' He would have looked straight into her eyes if it hadn't been for the other day, his behaviour, and Uncle Frank dying. When someone died you didn't look at people, at least, not at their faces. He looked at her waist where a checked apron was tied round her tweed skirt.

Mother twitched and her hand shot up to her mouth. 'Nine? Oh, my goodness! We've missed your birthday, haven't we? And I think that happened last year. It's too bad.'

He felt guilty, as though he always made his birthday come at the wrong time. 'It's all right, Mother. Mr and Mrs Pawsey are taking me to the pictures on Saturday.'

'How kind. Well, you do know we would have sent you cards. I mean, you've even had a party in the past. With a clown, games and everything. That was before the War, of course.'

She looked back at the door she'd just closed and bustled him back out of the front door. 'We'll go this way, and I can show you round the garden at the same time. I've been busy in the kitchen, peeling vegetables. There are— people here. The vicarage helps them with food and clothes. I feel I must help out in some way, not that I'm any cook. I sorted out a whole cupboard of old clothes for the WVS. Aunty's busy down there now, packing food parcels. She says it takes her mind off her tragedy. Some other women there have lost their menfolk, too.'

Outside the front door they turned right and through a gate into a large but shabby garden where Mother spread her arms wide as if she might be taken in flight. 'Here we are!'

It was not as if there were swings and slides or anything. He could see it was farmers' fields beyond the garden and when he hopped up on a pile of wood he could see a horse dragging a plough in the distance, neat rows churned up behind. A flurry of birds surrounded the plough as if to help it move along. 'So free, away from the noise and everything. This is the best place.'

She moved on. They passed a vegetable patch and a border of flowers with dead blooms flopping forward. 'So much to do,' said Mother. 'Anyway, we must make you a cake. Oh dear. I hardly like to trouble Aunty, and Mrs Shawditch has all these extra people to worry about.'

'It doesn't matter. I don't mind.' Mrs Pawsey's cakes were super anyway.

They moved down the garden, Mother turned her head from side to side as if troublesome people were about to come at her or even the Jerries. 'Well, hmm. Good boy.' Her eyes moved back to the door. She must be thinking about the man with a bare top, or all the things she had to do.

After a minute, Billy said, 'Is Jill looking forward to seeing me? It's been ages.'

'Jill? She's at nursery. Better for her to be occupied. But Kenneth's here. We'll go and find him.'

'It doesn't matter.'

'I think we should.' She pushed a tall gate open and pointed. 'That's the church. See the tower? Quite high, isn't it? And look through the hedge. Those are grouse padding around.'

He bent down to watch them. 'Grouse. Funny name. All hunched backs and spotty. They look like their name.'

Mother wasn't listening. She led him back towards the house and round to the far side. They stood on a knobbly path where the borders were filled with weeds. 'Not sure where he'll be. Probably drawing somewhere. It's not good for him to be on his own for too long.'

She looked at an upstairs window with a metal bar across it and lifted her chin so that her hair fell backwards towards her waist. 'Ken-neth?'

A pale face appeared at the window. A pale hand followed, just the one, and it had a pencil in it.

'Yes, he's in his bedroom.' Mother beckoned him down.

Billy frowned. '*His* bedroom? I thought K- Kenneth and Aunty were living with that other lady, d-down the road?'

'Yes, but because of what's happened, Mrs Shawditch thought it best for them to be with us, not fretting on their own up there. We've popped Kenneth into Jill's little room for comfort.'

'Oh.' It hadn't been much comfort when they'd popped him into Billy's room at the Pawseys.

While they were waiting for Kenneth to come down she said, 'I think a bit of fresh air will be good. You two can go for a walk while Mrs Shawditch and I finish the dinner. Kenneth can show you the village.' She took his overnight bag and led him back to the front gate. 'Do you want to leave your camera with me?'

'No thank you.'

She looked at him, so he tried a *No* face for her to see.

'Oh, all right then. Snapping the countryside, are you?'

He didn't need to answer because by then Kenneth had appeared, long socks and polished shoes as if he hadn't been evacuated. Or perhaps he had to go to church all over again because of Uncle Frank.

Mother looked relieved to see Kenneth carrying a jacket. 'All ready to go for a walk, Kenneth, dear? You must have read our minds,' and her laugh trailed amongst the faded flower heads and grass stumps. 'I'll leave you boys to have fun together.' She pulled the front door open, then sidled past the box of old clothes and Jesus texts.

Billy looked at the weeds peeping between the flagstones at his feet. Fun? What was he supposed to do? What sort of things?

Kenneth shrugged into his jacket although it wasn't cold. He looked at Billy as if he was the tramp in the back room. 'They thought you'd cheer me up.'

'Oh.' Billy hesitated, looking around. It would be better to be near the house than out on a walk alone with Kenneth.

Kenneth said, 'No good waiting. Dad's in the study with the vicar.'

Billy jerked around. Could dead people come alive?

Kenneth saw the jerk and snorted. 'I said *Dad,* not Daddy. We all know where *he* is – dead and buried under the ground. Gone. All that's left is your Dad. But now it's our dad, isn't it?'

His voice was horrible, mean and bitter like a witch. That awful night-time crying had been better than that. Even the sick. Billy stood still. Should he say, 'I'm sorry for your loss' right now?

But Kenneth was pointing at him and saying, 'And what's that supposed to be?'

Billy stepped further away. 'My c-camera. No one's supposed to touch it. Mr P-pawsey gave it to me.'

'All right. Why would *I* want to take photos? I can draw. You can't draw. You have to use a camera to get pictures. It's like cheating, really.'

Kenneth stomped off, heaving his arm up into a beckon as if it weighed a ton. Billy followed slowly.

They went out of the gate and down the lane, the opposite direction from the one Jed had gone in. Billy didn't rush to keep up. If he was behind, he wouldn't have to speak or even to listen. They went downhill, one behind the other, between two high hedges and round a corner. Now the vicarage was out of sight. It was rather scary with no one else there. He kept his eyes on the church tower. He'd be able to follow that if Kenneth meant to run ahead and lose him.

He followed Kenneth down lanes where the houses were set well back with green patches in front of them, then along an avenue of large trees whose few golden leaves allowed the day's sun to glint between the branches. They went past a little pond where some small children were fishing. One of them smiled. He smiled back. It would have been nice to join in, filling jars with minnows. Kenneth had already passed by without looking.

Eventually Billy said, 'Are we going to the p-place where you're staying?'

Kenneth said, 'No,' and didn't turn round.

'The village?'

Kenneth didn't answer.

'Where are we going?'

'Just don't talk, Right?' He kept on, three paces ahead, kicking a little pebble before him.

They passed the village school, squat and stony. The playground wasn't concrete. It had grass and two trees. A teacher with a big smile was helping a few children who were digging up some potatoes. It looked fun. He searched for words. If he was supposed to cheer Kenneth up, he ought to say kind things.

'Are you sorry the school was too full for you, Kenneth?'

Kenneth stopped, looked over to the school and then to Billy. 'Huh. Place for peasants. Sums and spellings. I think I'm a bit beyond that now. Mr Robyns-Curtis is doing Shakespeare with us older ones.'

'Shakespeare! I know. Angela does that!'

Kenneth whipped round, pushing his face forward. 'Who's Angela?'

Billy took a step back. 'A-a girl.'

'Where? Not here?'

'Mmm, not really.'

'At home, then? I don't know her. Does Aunty Marcia know her?'

'Y-yes.'

'Where? Where is this Angela who does Shakespeare?'

Billy turned round and started running. 'I'm going back now. I'm going to see Dad.'

Kenneth caught him up. 'Stop. You'll be in trouble if I say you ran off without me.'

Billy stopped.

Kenneth drew a breath. He didn't usually run fast. 'There's no Angela in our school back home. There's no Shakespeare.'

'No. Somewhere else.'

'Where?'

'Just people we know. You don't know them.'

'So now I will. When we go back, I'll be going where you're going. I'll see this Angela. We'll talk Shakespeare to each other. But you won't understand it.'

Billy stared. When they went home Kenneth would be there, being petted, into everything. Going where they went, coming with them. Even when they went to the Durbans.

Kenneth stared back making goggle eyes. 'Bluh! Look at you, stare cat. Soppy and stupid.' Then he turned away as if he felt sick again.

'I want to go back,' Billy said, and moved off, but not running.

Kenneth said nothing but walked the same way, this time behind Billy. Now it was uphill so it took much longer. A dark cloud was following them. Billy didn't want it to catch them.

He said, 'Let's run.'

'No.'

Billy compromised with a fast walk, just the occasional hop run. He could hear Kenneth's stomping feet behind him.

Dad was standing at the vicarage gate as they came near.

'Billy! Why don't you wait for Kenneth? Don't walk ahead like that, walk together. What did I tell you about being a bit Christian?'

Billy tried to remember the texts in the vicarage hall so that he could sound a bit Christian, '*Lo . . .* something', '*Jesus ...* something,' but all he could remember clearly was '*Wipe your feet.*'

'*Lo ...*' he began.

'Hello? Is that all you can say to me? I've only got today and tomorrow, then I have to be back. Your behaviour the other day meant you've lost several days with me.'

'Sorry.' Billy looked down at the knobbly stones at his feet. Wartime could be ever so sad.

Kenneth passed Billy and stood beside Dad, his eyes alive now. He leant against Dad, who looked down and put a hand very softly on his head.

'Are you all right, Kenneth? Take it easy, now. Go indoors and see if Mrs Shawditch can find you a glass of milk to go with your malt and cod liver oil. Build your strength up.'

Kenneth flicked a curly lock from his eyebrow and looked up at Dad with a Christian face. And Dad smiled sadly through his beard.

When Kenneth reached the door, Dad walked back down the path with Billy.

'It is good we could get you brought here. He'll need you, your strength, as he adapts to the changes. If only I could be here more often. Travelling through London is a nightmare at the moment. Raids every day, hopping between shelters, transport chaotic. He looked at the sky. *If we don't end war, war will end us,* as H.G. Wells says.

Uncle Frank had been travelling through London when the war had ended him. He wanted to ask if there would be bombs when Dad would be travelling back, but it was best not to say 'Bomb'. It was a *No* word, now, like Bum.

Instead, he said, 'Will you get back home before dark?'

'I'll be sure to, don't worry.' He put his large hand on Billy's shoulder. 'It's a bad thing, war. Boys play at it, spotting the aeroplanes, cheering the flames when an enemy one's hit. It seems exciting. But it's not.'

Dad was thinking about the games Billy played with his friends. Or perhaps about Uncle Frank. It hadn't been exciting to be blown up. It was a bad thing, even if it was good that the bomb had ended

Uncle Frank and not Uncle Ted or Dad. 'Dad, do you have to go on buses in London?'

But Dad was going on without listening, 'As you grow up, you must do your best to keep the peace.'

'I shall,' said Billy fervently.

'At home, as well as in the wider world. Keeping the peace means not being selfish.'

He looked hard at Billy. He must mean something.

At home. Billy thought back. There were Jill's tantrums, but he didn't shout back at her. He'd played with her to stop her tantrums, so he did help keep the peace. But Kenneth's visits, every Saturday. It was Kenneth who was selfish. Would he be able to keep that peace? Is that what Dad meant?

Dad took his hand off Billy's shoulder and stretched his arms out wide as if to relieve a load on his back. He put his hand in his pocket for his pipe and lit it. He leant on the vicarage gate, looking outward down the little lane towards the church. And then he said it.

'Things will be different when we get home, Billy. They have to be. I'm responsible for two boys now, and Aunty won't have much money. It doesn't make sense for there to be two houses. She doesn't want to go back to Balham. And she needs us for company.'

There was silence in the lane. The autumn light fell dark red on the hedge tops and the clouds hovered lower, threatening to cover the last of the day's sun. Next week it was going to be November, all grey outside and readying for winter.

Dad took another breath, 'So . . . we shall all live together. We don't use the front room much. We've decided that it will be Aunty's room. She'll need some of her own things round her as well as somewhere to sleep.'

Billy didn't have to tilt his head upwards to look at the sky for it seemed to be getting lower and lower. Soon it would land on his head.

Somewhere for Aunty to sleep. His back teeth hurt as he clamped them harder and harder together. He didn't need to ask.

'As for Kenneth, well, your room's quite big enough for another bed. You can share a room, boys much the same age. You can be best pals. Kenneth will like that.'

Best pals! 'No! I w-won't.'

'You *will* share. Now that's what I mean when I say don't be selfish.'

'No, I meant, I w-won't be – being b-best pals. I can't.'

'Billy! Of course you can. You are.'

It was too much to bear. He wanted to shout out into the silence, tell the whole ruddy world, *I don't like Kenneth. He's mean and hurts me and takes my things and pretends everything's my fault.* But he didn't. He just looked down at his boots. The lace of one was untied and it trailed over his foot like a line of snot.

'Now then,' said Dad. 'I know these are difficult days, being away from family on your own, and the shock of – poor Uncle Frank passing away. But think. How would you feel if that had happened to me and you had no father? Wouldn't it help if Kenneth was a real pal to you?'

And Uncle Frank had been his new father! 'No! It would make it worse!'

'Take that back!'

Billy didn't answer. He kept his eyes on his bootlace. Dad just didn't know. He didn't even know Billy as well as Mrs Donnington, or as Mrs Youldon and Mr and Mrs Pawsey did. He really didn't know Kenneth, what he was like. He never heard what went on upstairs. It wasn't Dad's fault. He had to work away from home lots of the time. And now his brother had died. It was only Billy that Uncle Frank had been nasty to. Everyone else probably liked him. Kenneth did. Aunty did and Dad did. He was sad. So Billy ought to say something kind right now.

'Sorry.' It caught a bit in his throat because he wasn't sorry for what he'd said about Kenneth. He swallowed and lifted his camera. 'If I t-take your photograph with Mother, you'll be able to l-look at it when you're away at work.'

'Yes, that would be nice. Mother told me you'd been given a camera. Lucky chap, aren't you? I expect Kenneth must think you get all the luck.'

Billy paused. 'I've g-got two p-pictures left on the film. I saved them for you, Dad.'

'That's nice of you, Billy. Yes, take a picture, one of us all. I'd like to have a family photo on my desk at Chambers.' He tapped his pipe out on the top of the gate and moved down the path. 'Come on, let's go in. Jill will be back in a moment from nursery.'

They wiped their feet, then passed the other messages. Billy looked up at the *Jesus Loves You* text. The children in the picture didn't look at all like Billy. He looked away. Not worth looking at Him.

Mrs Shawditch came out of the back room in her white girls' socks and her men's lace up shoes. 'Billy!'

He lifted up his eyes. 'Yes, Mrs Shawditch.'

'You haven't seen around yet. We must see to that later. You'll need to wash your hands before lunch. Up the stairs, second door on the right, and then you can go and see Kenneth in Jill's room.'

Billy plodded upstairs and used the bathroom as ordered. He came out but didn't know where to go next. Jill's room? There were three more doors and then the stairs went up again. It was a big house.

One door was slightly open. He stepped towards it. Kenneth was sitting on a pink bed, postcards of fat children with dimpled knees on the wall behind him. He had his feet on a camp bed covered by a travel rug. He was like an invalid but busy drawing. He looked up.

'It's squashed in here. No room for you. They're putting you in a niche on the upstairs landing.' He went on drawing.

'A niche? What's that?'

Kenneth tutted and lifted his eyes to heaven. 'You just don't know anything. It's a bit where the wall goes in, room enough for a shelf or chest of drawers. Or a camp bed.'

The front door opened and closed below them and Jill's jabber started immediately. Billy hurried to the stairs. Jill would be excited to see him.

'Ji-ill. Ji-ill!'

The curly head lifted up towards him. The same plump cheeks and a bit of a dimple. Her knees were a bit like those in the post-cards. She stared at him as she struggled to her feet.

Mother, folding the pushchair, said, 'It's Billy, pet. Billy.'

Jill went on staring.

There was a footstep behind him. Kenneth squeezed past and

padded down the stairs. Jill toddled towards him and hugged his legs.

Mother hesitated, then said to Billy, 'Kenneth's been teaching her to draw. She loves it. You could try doing that with her. Both of you, perhaps.' She hurried towards the kitchen.

Jill looked after her with a little scowl.

Kenneth's face had no expression. He placed delicate fingers on her head and moved past towards the nearest door. 'I'll lay the table for Mrs Shawditch first,' he called after Mother.

'Thank you, dear,' Mother's voice wafted from the kitchen with the boiled meat smell.

'Draw,' Jill moaned as she trailed after Kenneth into the dining room, making a large detour around Billy.

Billy stayed where he was, in the hall, alone. Aunty came in shortly afterwards. She looked tired. She patted Billy on the cheek. 'Billy. Hello dear. Nice ride over on the cart?'

But her eyes were dull and her stockings wrinkly. 'Time for dinner now, isn't it, and I'm too late to help. We've been so busy today, packing food parcels for the prisoners of war. Does your school collect?'

He nodded, not sure what to say. Their collection was for people who'd been bombed out in London. She'd cry about Uncle Frank if he told her.

Mother saved him for once, scuttling into the hall. 'There you are, Doreen. Good. I think you need something to eat. Come and sit down, Billy. It's dinner time.'

As Aunty went upstairs to wash, Billy moved into the big room where Kenneth had gone to lay the table. Jill was on a throne of cushions beside him at the far end of the room. An old but muscly man was coming through another door from outside. He didn't look at anyone; he didn't say anything.

Mother and Mrs Shawditch brought plates of gristly stew to sit on a large table with no tablecloth. Several men were already sitting round. They looked the right age to be soldiers. One was the tramp, now in a clean checked shirt, his hand hovering over a plate of bread. People nodded to each other and took their seats, plates steaming in front of them. There was a big dish of potatoes and another one of carrots.

Kenneth leaned over and whispered in Billy's ear. 'They're prisoners-of-war but we're not supposed to know. They don't even speak English.'

Everyone just sat there until suddenly the vicar came in like an actor on to the stage. He lifted one hand and said his prayer so that everyone could mutter 'Our Men'. Billy always thought of Uncle Ted when he had to say this. Today he should think of Uncle Frank too. Did *Our Men* mean dead ones too? He couldn't ask now. Or at all really. He might ask Mr Pawsey later.

The vicar sat and lifted his knife and fork. Everyone began. The tramp's chewing sounded above any clinking or muttering from the others.

After dinner, the other people went out of the side door behind the table nodding thanks to Mrs Shawditch. The vicar explained that they were land workers and people who couldn't manage by themselves. Kenneth looked over at Billy and twisted his mouth. So wasn't the vicar telling the truth? The vicar!

It was a very odd sight to see Dad start to pack the dishes. Mrs Shawditch told him that he was just to enjoy his family while he could, so Mother, Billy and Jill all went outside under the lowering sky. Dad turned towards Aunty and Kenneth, bringing them out too. Jill started jumping up and down, seeing how loudly she could make her shoes sound on the tiled porch floor.

Kenneth raised his eyebrows at Mother and said, 'I'll take her off, shall I?'

'Thank you, dear. You are such a help.'

Billy watched the two figures disappear past *Wipe your Feet* and *Jesus Loves You,* hand in hand.

Jill didn't look back.

'Such friends,' said Mother.

Aunty walked beside the flower beds filled with weeds and rusty rose petals. 'I told Mrs Shawditch I'd help in the garden. This all needs attention. So much to do.'

Dad said, 'Doreen, you do enough, especially now you've put your name down for war work. No point wearing yourself out.' He turned to Mother, shaking his head as Aunty moved off down the path.

Mother said, 'Are you hinting that I should help? What do I know about gardening? Anyway I am the one taking Kenneth to and fro, as well as Jill, and helping in the kitchen. None of it exactly my forte.'

'Rich gifts wax poor when givers prove unkind,' Dad said softly, staring into space. 'Shakespeare.'

'Shakespeare!' Billy said. 'Angela . . .' Then he stopped and checked behind him, but it was all right. Kenneth was upstairs with Jill.

'Oh you've heard of Shakespeare, have you?' Dad asked.

It was risky to put the Durbans into Dad's head, so he said, 'Kenneth's doing it with his teacher.'

'Is he indeed? Good. Glad to see you're talking to each other about such things. You'll be able to learn about Shakespeare from Kenneth, then.'

'From Angela,' Billy muttered softly to himself. 'Shall I take your photo now, Dad? While it's still light enough?'

'Ooh, you are sounding professional,' said Mother coming up behind him. 'I'll just run and comb my hair. My bag's still in the hall.'

She came back looking brighter. He rested his camera on the gatepost. Just as Dad put an arm on to Mother's shoulder, Billy pressed the shutter before she had time to set her mouth. The sun was low behind him so that his parents were framed in a backdrop of shaded trees. It should look good.

Dad said, 'That was quick, Billy.' He removed his arm from Mother's shoulder where it had looked so friendly. He was putting the hand into his pocket. He pulled out some coins and put them into Billy's hand. 'This is to help with developing and printing. It can be an expensive hobby, photography.'

It was three half-crowns! Billy paused, making sure they were for him. 'Thank you, Dad. Thank you very much.'

'It was your birthday. Your mother and I are sorry we missed it.'

'It doesn't matter. I can get my photos done now.'

'How many photos have you got left on that film?'

'Only one, now. I want to take Jill, if she'll let me.'

'You go and take one of Kenneth,' said Dad. 'If Jill's around she can sit with him.'

Billy twiddled the cord loop on his camera, but he knew it was no good. He turned and went back into the house. He plodded upstairs. Only one photo left and now he must waste it on Kenneth. Even if Jill was there, he wouldn't want a photo of her with Kenneth. He'd just take one of Kenneth alone. When the prints were done he'd give it to him. He jolly well wouldn't want it himself.

In the bedroom there were pieces of recent art pressed on to the far wall with parcel tape, a parrot, two aeroplanes in a dogfight, a castle, really smashing pictures. Kenneth was ever so clever. He had his head bent over a drawing of something. He didn't hear Billy. Jill was lying on the floor on her front doing her scribbles with a fat red crayon.

Billy slid in, his back to the wide-open window and lifted his camera. Just as he put his finger on the shutter, Kenneth noticed him and put up both hands saying, 'Don't snap me. I don't want a picture of me now.' But it was too late, the shutter clicked.

'Kenneth! You've spoiled it! Your hands were in the way. Now you've wasted my very last photo.'

'I didn't ask you to take it, Dimwit.'

Billy flung himself through the door and stomped on to the landing. If only he hadn't snapped quickly he could've told Dad that Kenneth didn't want a picture, and then taken a nice one of Jill. He'd have let her stand on the porch ledge.

He went downstairs slowly. He'd finished his whole film. What was he supposed to do now? There were no toys in sight, no football. They all thought Kenneth wanted to play with him, but he didn't. And Jill wouldn't even look at him. He reached the hall again.

'Not playing with the others?' Mrs Shaw ditch asked softly, bringing a pile of clean cutlery back into the dining room.

'They don't want to.'

Aunty was lying down, but Mother and Dad were in the front room. Mrs Shawditch took Billy to join them. She suggested they all play a nice card game. She picked up a pack of Happy Families from the sideboard. She called up to Kenneth, but he said he was busy drawing.

'A real artist,' said Dad. 'We'll leave him to it.'

Dad, Mother, Mrs Shawditch and Billy sat on the hard chairs round a card table. There was no room for anyone's elbows.

'Let's enjoy this.' Mother said very firmly. 'It's going to be a very long time before we have the chance to play games again.'

Again? Billy couldn't remember Mother ever playing games with him.

Dad looked over at Billy. 'I've said, haven't I, that it's really not easy to travel these days. And now I've got Aunty's house to sell. It may be some time before I can visit everyone again. So we must make the best of these times as a family.' His face was grey, and he didn't look as if he was having the best time at all.

The vicar's wife dealt the cards. 'We must trust in the Lord.'

Billy looked at her dull eyes. She had to, married to the vicar. But all that Billy trusted was that he could collect all of the Bun the baker family because they looked the jolliest.

He concentrated on their fat red faces with the deep dimples and adopted them as his own. He was Master Billy Bun. He would spend his life running in and out of the bakery while Mr Bun in his white apron shouted 'Oh Ho Ho' and dusted flour on to cake trays. Billy would be giving Mrs Bun a hand, stirring things, licking the bowls she passed to him and eating the tasty bits which crumbled off her sugary cakes and the fresh crusty loaves.

CHAPTER EIGHT

October 25th 1940. *French leader Petain meets Hitler.*

It wasn't late, but the sun had long gone down when the vicar's car stopped outside the Pawseys' house. The tiled roof was outlined by a sliver of moon and Billy could just make out the two trees near the pig pen. The dogs barked in anticipation. They'd be all round his feet when he got in. The house was in darkness, of course, but inside the fire would be crackling and Mr Pawsey would be feeling around for his glasses.

If he hadn't known, if he could pretend he didn't know, then everything could be just the same as it was before the horrible times with Kenneth staying and the adults coming for him. The funeral had sickened all the days following, and now it was hardly worth wishing to go home again, or for the war to be over, with how things in Wandsworth were going to be.

The vicar cleared his throat. 'Well, here we are, young man. Please give my regards to your foster parents. I won't stop.'

'Thank you for the lift, sir.'

'Possibly the last one, I fear. Petrol's getting more and more expensive, over three shillings a gallon now. Rationing is going to get worse too. So I may not be able ...' His voice trailed off as he turned to lift a set of Red Cross parcels on to the passenger seat, hovering them in the air ready to put them where Billy had been sitting. 'I've slipped a prayer book into each of these packages,' he said. 'I like to think of our boys having an hour of quiet reflection before they go into— conflict.'

'Does that help, sir?'

'I like to think so, my boy. Yes, of course it must help. And here's a prayer book for you.'

Billy looked at the scratchy red cover. 'Thank you. Is it a birthday present?'

'Ah... for reflection.'

Billy slid out of the vicar's car and shut the door carefully. An hour for reflection? Uncle Ted had three days and nights for that, standing in the sea while his boots went green. A prayer book wouldn't have helped.

He bent to the window and thanked the vicar for letting him stay, then ran quickly indoors, putting the prayer book on the hall table. He might meet a soldier who'd want it.

The dogs rushed to meet him and he bent his head over them as they barked and licked alternately. Mr and Mrs Pawsey gave him a quick look. They didn't ask him if he'd had a nice time but set him to work straight away. Mr Pawsey said he had terrible difficulty with the crossword. Billy could help him just as soon as he'd fed the piglets. Mrs Pawsey put a torch and the slop bucket into his hands.

Out by the pig pen, he ran the torch over the piglets. They lifted up their snouts and came running. They must have missed him. Billy hadn't been away quite three days but they seemed to be bigger already. He hoped they'd take their time becoming pork.

Mrs Pawsey had nearly finished making a cake when he came back indoors. She needed him to scrape the bowl because she couldn't bear anything to go to waste and somehow she couldn't seem to scrape as cleanly as she used to. He would be like Sonia, whose mother allowed her to scrape the bowl.

Once he'd washed the pig mash off his hands, Billy was able to help Mrs Pawsey very well and she reckoned he had more mixture round his mouth than she'd left in the bowl. She found that very funny and laughed just as if she'd been Mrs Bun the Baker's wife.

He put his hand in his pocket and pulled out his half crowns. He ran to find Mr Pawsey. 'Look! My father gave me all this for getting my photos done. I've finished my film. Now I can take it to get photos, can't I? When we go into town to the pictures?'

He looked at him quickly. He wouldn't have forgotten, would he?

'Yes, Billy boy. We'll see to all that on Saturday,' Mr Pawsey said, holding up a page of newspaper. 'Now. My crossword ...'

Billy ran out of the door on Saturday, a wonderful Saturday, the Pawseys both behind him. He wanted to be the one who put out a STOP arm at the bus stop.

The village bus trundled up around eleven. It was quite full but they got seats together up at the back. He sat down with a big bounce.

'You excited, Billy?'

'Rath-er. I've only been to town once before, Mrs Pawsey, except for the very first day we got here, all of us from my school who were being evacuated. That time we got straight off the train on to the coach and then to the village, so we didn't see town. Then when it was winter-time, the Grange lady got a coach and took all the vaccies to see the Christmas tree and we all got two sweeties, a balloon and sang songs. There was a piano and …'

'Oh my goodness me, haven't you a lot of chatter? I reckon as you are excited. Yes, I do.'

It was lovely travelling through tree-lined roads and past grassy mounds instead of the dirty high buildings and brick walls of London. There were winding lanes through trees with golden and brown leaves. They reminded Billy of Dad leaving home in Wandsworth for a month's work at Court, Mother saying crossly the trees would be bare before he got home. And they were.

Now the trees looked lovely to him with hills behind them. They passed a field with a land girl pushing a plough. An old man in a torn jacket walked slowly behind her, and a crowd of black birds followed. 'Look!'

Mr Pawsey knew him. 'That be Mr Jackson, still hard at it. Four good sons, he has, all soldiers doing their bit, God rest 'em. Reckon it'll be a while till that young lady gets her furrows straight.'

As the bus passed the first houses of the town, a lot of people pressed their faces to the window. A row of ladies was lined up outside a big building. They were in their ordinary clothes, jackets, headscarves, pleated skirts, but each held a long pole pretending they were guns. A man in uniform was shouting at them so that they stood straight, shouldered their poles, then pointed them at the enemy, all keeping together in line. He giggled, and some grown-ups laughed too. It was quite funny, but Mrs Pawsey said it was important for women to join in the Home Guard so that there weren't just old men looking after the country. Billy looked at the floor. He should be in the Home Guard, at least when he was twelve. Would the war last that long, three whole years more?

The bus reached the market place, where there was a little tower with a big clock at the top under a pointy pink roof. Shops surrounded it on three sides, and another road went uphill. Most people stood up and Mr Pawsey moved to the gangway. 'We get off here, Billy. Come along, you.'

It had been a long time since Billy had been in a town, and he'd only been in this one once before, when all the vaccies were taken there to see the Christmas tree. It was a very different town from Wandsworth, much cosier and not so crowded.

Mr Pawsey was helping Mrs Pawsey up saying, 'You going to shop, Missus?'

'I am that. I'll see if they've got any biscuits or currants.'

'Then I'll take the boy, while you queue.'

Mr Pawsey led the way up the hilly road to the chemist's but Billy soon overtook him. They passed the blacksmith's, an exciting place that he'd always wanted to see. In London, he hadn't even known that horses had shoes or a man to put them on. He peeped inside but there was no horse inside being shoed. He made a disappointed face at Mr Pawsey.

'The blacksmith has gone to war, leaving his old father to work on small jobs.'

Gaps showed all over the black wall where big tools had hung. Billy pointed to the spaces. 'The walls are all empty,' Mr Pawsey.

'All the metal's been taken away for weapons, lad. Not much for a blacksmith to work on.'

There was a new poster on the outside wall. Billy stopped to read *If you can't go to the factory, help someone who can.* There was a little boy and girl going into a kind lady's house while their mother, holding a little suitcase, waved Goodbye. 'That's like what Mother's doing, isn't it, Mr Pawsey? Looking after Kenneth while Aunty works at WVS?'

'I suppose so, laddie.' Billy looked at the picture again. Aunty was too sad to look like the happy lady waving Goodbye, and Mother wasn't a smiley lady bending down to a little child. She definitely would not want to look after other children, but Kenneth was older and did his drawing all the time, so was never a nuisance to her.

The hill was quite steep. Mr Pawsey was panting a bit with the effort so Billy slowed down. They passed a shop with knitting wools and cotton reels in a small window and then came the chemist's.

'Here we are, see the sign.'

The shop was painted black with Mr E. Winthrop, Chemist, Druggist, painted in curly white letters over the door. As Mr Pawsey opened it, a wonderful smell filtered towards them. Billy recognised lavender and the stuff you sniffed when you had a heavy cold. The shelves had row after row of old-fashioned bottles with funny words on them. The chemist was smarter than Dad in his three-piece suit with a fob watch showing on his middle. He stopped arranging the bottles of cough medicine and came to serve them.

Billy handed over his film to be developed and watched the five pale fingers close over it. When it was placed in its envelope and the order form filled in, Billy used some of Dad's birthday money to pay. There was some over. He looked at the handful of change. 'Sir, please may I buy another film?'

'Just about. I've only got two 120s left,' the chemist said, passing one over.

'Tight is it?' Mr Pawsey asked.

'Like anything and everything. The supplier's just told me I'm not getting anymore. All film's needed for aerial reconnaissance, now. They're going to let us have that Tint rubbish to sell. We must warn your young man. It'll be no good for his camera.'

'No? We shan't risk it then. Thank'm kindly for the warning.'

As they made their way out of the shop, Mr Pawsey put one hand on Billy's shoulder and the other on the precious film. 'You be careful not to waste any snaps, now. Probably no more films for us folks until the war's over, not unless you have friends in high places.'

Billy looked at the sky, but no one up there would give him any special favours. He started counting in his head the photos he really must take before the new film ran out.

The hilly street led out into the country soon after the chemist's. Mr Pawsey said his 'How do's' to two old men who were sitting outside their small houses on hard chairs. Then they turned downhill again towards the picture palace.

Billy started skipping. 'Mr Pawsey, I've been to the pictures before but not for ages. I went to the pictures in Wandsworth. It's the Gaumont, and I saw Robin Hood. Some of my friends go to Saturday pictures, but I'm not allowed because of the bad behaviour. Some of the locals come here on Saturdays but none of my friends have seen Pinocchio yet, I'm the first one.'

'That'll keep the varmints wanting to friend you then, won't it?'

The picture palace was quite grubby down its front wall and paint was crumbling off. Billy looked up high to see where it said *Pinocchio*. Above that it said ABC not Gaumont. They went to join the queue where Mrs Pawsey was saving them places. Two girls in front of them were jumping up and down, so he couldn't see the poster of Pinocchio properly. A bigger boy was showing off with his yo-yo, making it whizz round in a circle as well as up and down. There were a lot of grown-ups too, and some grizzling small children.

When the usherette opened the heavy black door there was a squeal from the girls. The first people pushed in to pay, the queue pressed forward and Billy felt worried. 'Will we get in before the picture palace is full?'

'Don't fuss yourself, we will.'

Billy started counting the people in front. How many seats did a picture house have?

He'd counted to thirty-four before they reached the front.

'Here we are, Billy. All in nice time, see.' Mrs Pawsey showed the tickets, and the usherette beamed her torch in front of them to three seats right near the aisle.

Mr Pawsey turned to help Mrs Pawsey who had to tuck her shopping under the seat.

The velvety seats tipped up so that small people could perch high. They'd only just sat down on them when the lights went down. The news came first. It was quite scary and thunderous, lots of grey tanks rolling through dust, soldiers mostly with dirty faces, but smiling widely at the camera while a horrible serious voice told what was happening. He searched for Uncle Ted's face amongst the ranks of soldiers marching and in trucks.

Afterwards there was a film about sparrows which was boring. Then it was the interval with a crowd at the toilets, and the worry about finding the right seat again afterwards. All the children there seemed to be chatting or squealing or jumping up and down. It was very noisy and exciting. The usherettes took their torches away; the lights went down. When it went dark, everyone was quiet straight away.

The moment soft music began and a picture of a big old brown book with its fancy lettering came on to the screen, Billy sit still as sill. The spotlight fell on this tiny, weeny figure and you saw it was Jiminy Cricket starting the wonderful tale in his big book. A lovely song about wishing on a star helped things come true. A nice old man, a bit like Granddad, had a coloured wooden puppet and it was Pinocchio. He so wanted a boy and then a fairy came and made Pinocchio live, but not a real boy until he deserved it. Was it like that for Mr Durban, wanting a boy of his own and then meeting Billy – although really Billy belonged to Dad. But then, so did Kenneth now.

Pinocchio had little red shorts with straps and the sun shone round him. He made a lot of mistakes and got into all sorts of trouble. He told whopping lies so that his nose grew and grew. All sorts of funny and scary people led him into bad things. There was even a smarmy one cheating at the billiards table who was quite like

Kenneth. Pinocchio was a bit bad, but he got better, and at the very end he was a real boy. Gepetto was sort of his father and was so happy. It would be wonderful to be a boy that made a Dad laugh with joy.

When the lights went up, Billy could hardly bring himself to leave the picture house. The super songs that the characters had sung went round and round in his head. All the children were chattering and begging to see the film all over again. It would be smashing to just sit back on the velvet seat and see the whole thing right through as if it was new.

Mr and Mrs Pawsey were smiling because Billy was so happy. 'Reckon as you'm enjoyed that thorough,' said Mr Pawsey.

'I did, I did. I wanted it all again!'

As they got on to the dark and chilly street outside, Billy started hopping and skipping, 'Hi Diddle de dee,' he sang, 'an actor's life for me.' He would forget the dreadful things that had happened and were going to happen. He skipped all the way to the bus stop singing. Perhaps this would be a magic song that would come true for him, like wishing on a star, even though he had no blue fairy to wave her wand.

That night, he lay in bed late going through the whole story in his mind and humming the tunes.

In the morning, after breakfast and chores, he ran off to the Manor to tell Alan all about Pinocchio. Two boys were working on their own in the vegetable patch.

'Where's the lady – the land girl?'

'They're all up at Barfell Farm, digging the potatoes.'

Alan was inside, which meant going past all the nuns at their prayers in the hall, to get to the dormitories upstairs. This made him tread so quietly that Alan didn't even hear him coming. He was deep in a book but when he saw Billy's head round the door, he grinned in welcome.

'I've come to tell you all about Pinocchio.'

They sat on his bed for ages being all the characters and trying out some of the songs.

'The best part was when he told lies. His nose kept growing with each one, until it was as long as a sausage.'

'Wait.' Alan went to his box. All the Manor children had a box for keeping their own things and some treasures, like letters or comics or a sweet. He rummaged around for a moment and brought out a piece of brown plasticine. 'This was stuck to my shoe after Craft at school, so I kept it.' He rolled it into a sausage and pressed it on to the end of his nose – 'Pinocchio, see!'

Billy's giggling sent Alan to the mirror on the back of the door to see how he looked. They took it in turns to put it on their noses and make up whopping lies, just like Pinocchio.

'I can jump twenty feet high.'

'I can spell all the words in the dictionary.'

'I've got a gun and they're sending me to war.'

'I've got a shashka that is the most powerful weapon on earth and can kill a hundred Hitlers.'

They were laughing and rolling about on the floor making a noise loud enough for a nun to come in and shoo them away downstairs. She was on house-cleaning duties so they'd be in her way even if they were quiet.

They ran into the rough ground at the back of the Manor where before the vaccies came it had been lawn and flower beds. It was quiet there, because there were no trees for people to climb up or anything else to do.

Alan said, 'Was it all right when you went to the vicarage, and all that?'

Billy's stomach went thump as if all the potatoes the land girl was digging had fallen out of his insides. He sat down on the grass and told Alan all the serious news about Kenneth.

'And now Dad is going to be his dad too. It's silly, because he's Kenneth's uncle. You can't have two dads even if one is dead.'

'If he's Kenneth's dad, that makes him your brother.'

'No! He's never going to be my brother. They can't make me.'

'Bet they'll say he is. If you live in the same house with the same father, people will think he's your brother, anyway.'

Billy thumped the grass beside him. 'No. No. No. It's flipping awful.'

Alan was quiet for a bit. 'It is rather rotten, but at least you aren't sharing your mother.'

There was no point answering. Alan didn't understand. Having Kenneth as a cousin *was* like sharing his mother. Although Kenneth had his own mother who thought he was perfect, Mother was always nicer to Kenneth too, because Kenneth was quiet and pretended to be good. And now he would always be a boy whose father had died, so everyone had to be nice to him.

Alan stood up and whirled around a couple of times. 'Come on,' he said. 'Cheer up. Tell me about your camera. Have you taken any snaps yet?'

CHAPTER NINE

November 14th 1940. *German bombers devastate Coventry and its cathedral.*

It seemed like weeks and weeks waiting for Mr Pawsey to take him to the town again. Would his photographs come out? How good would they be? He knew that going to town wasn't something that happened at all often, but eventually a slight accident caused another visit.

'I've gone and sat on these wretched glasses, all while I was looking for 'em too! You'se 'll be glad about it, Billy, for I shall have to be off to town again to get 'em mended. So we can collect your photographs, see.'

The glasses had broken where the metal bit sat over Mr Pawsey's nose. He hadn't been able to fix them himself, for he had to do that with them off his face. When he was wearing them, he couldn't see anything.

'You'll have to find the bus stop, I reckon, Billy, or I s'll land up in the next village, the amount I can't see without my glasses.'

Billy held Mr Pawsey's arm all the way to the bus stop.

'At least I can see the bus,' Mr Pawsey joked as it pulled up beside them.

The bus was crowded and when they got to the town, the queue outside the grocer's was very long.

'I suppose as we'll have to join it, lad. Not that I've a ha'porth of an idea what they're queuing for.'

It was a long wait and when they got to the front it was only suet. Mrs Pawsey would be pleased, but it wasn't a very exciting buy, like chocolate biscuits would have been.

After they'd dealt with Mr Pawsey's glasses, which took a long time, they went up to the chemist's. Billy started hopping and skipping, chanting, *I've got no strings to hold me down.'*

'Let's see what sort of job you've done on those photos, young Billy my lad, before you get too chirpy.'

'Chirpy! That's what I am, just like Jiminy Cricket.' Billy reached the black shop front first and pulled the handle down. He opened the door for Mr Pawsey, just as Dad would have liked.

'Good morning, and to you, young man.' The chemist found the folder of photos and checked the contents.

'Did you take some of these, then, Mr Pawsey?'

'No, no. The lad did the lot.'

The chemist put his hand on the packet. 'Well. Some of them are remarkable. Beginner's luck?' He slid them over to Mr Pawsey, who left them for Billy to pick up.

Billy pulled them out one by one. How amazing to see things exactly as he'd seen them weeks before! Everyone was held just in that moment for ever. He gazed down at Jed sitting on his cart looking up at the bedroom window, the horse's mane lifted and his nostrils slightly flared.

Mr Pawsey looked over his shoulder. 'Goodness me, you've as done a grand old job with that, young Billy. Looks just like something out of the picture papers.'

Billy pressed his lips together, almost holding his breath.

He looked carefully at each snap before passing it on for Mr Pawsey's judgement, all except one.

'Ha, the little Youldons. Well done, well done. Now this of the chickens, should have waited a bit for better light. This one – you needed to put your parents more in the foreground, but still a good job.'

'And that one's rather something, isn't it?' said the chemist.

He pointed to the one Billy was putting quickly to the back of the pile. It was Kenneth, his glaring eyes just showing over the top of his hands. 'Indoor snap, sideways light. Daring. And he's captured that as neatly as a professional, hasn't he?'

'Hmm. Seems as Billy doesn't like'm much,' Mr Pawsey said watching Billy put the photo back in the envelope. 'Thank you very much, Mr Winthrop. I suppose it'll be a while before we're back with the next film. Billy's making it last, aren't you, lad?'

'Yes, I am. But when the war ends, I can have another film, can't I?'

He saw the men grimace at each other as though they'd forgotten Great Britain always won wars.

'Can I have an extra print of these three?' Billy passed the chemist the negatives of Mrs Youldon and the children. He turned to Mr Pawsey. 'Mrs Youldon will want them, and I want copies. I've still got lots of Dad's birthday money left.'

'Aha. You're angling for another visit to town, I see.'

They left the chemist's and made their way down the hill. 'Reckon as you've got a special talent for photography. Fancy that, being as a coincidence that you had the camera as a birthday present. It's a good thing to have a skill outside of book learning. Something to develop for your future.'

'If I don't have to be a soldier, you mean?'

Mr Pawsey sighed and put a hand on Billy's shoulder. 'Even at its worst, the war shouldn't last that long,' he said.

A thundering of aeroplanes in the sky suggested he was wrong. Billy hunched his shoulders. When he became a man, he must serve his country. If only he wouldn't be cannon fodder, which had been what Uncle Frank had told him.

When they got home, Billy showed his photos to Mrs Pawsey. She held up her hands in amazement. 'You've taken your first photos and they're like a – I don't rightly know – a studio's. I reckon we've chanced on a real talent in you.'

'Can I take them to show Mrs Youldon?'

'In the morning.'

He was up early and after breakfast and chores, he cantered down Mrs Youldon's lane. She was outside cleaning the front windows. He waved the envelope at her. 'They've come!' and they went indoors to look at the photos.

She took each one carefully by the top two corners and peered closely each time. 'Coo, Billy! They're clear as daylight. Look at my youngsters, bless them. And look at me.' She giggled. She looked at each one and then at Billy. 'They're all ever so good. You are a clever stick.'

He held out the three photos of her and the children. 'These are for you to keep. I'm having extra prints done for me.'

'Really? Ooh, Billy, I've never had true pictures of anything, let alone my own face. And it's a wonder to have them of my little ones, and all. You wait till I show them to Mary! She won't be able to stop talking about it.'

Her face was so happy it made Billy's insides tickle and a strong and important feeling spread through him.

Mrs Youldon called the little ones in. 'Look what Billy's got, look what he's done!'

They ran up to him and he held each photo up for them to see. Their eyes went huge.

'It's Mummy! Look, in that picture!' Sally squealed.

'Is that us? Is that what we look like?' said Timmy.

What a funny thing to ask! Billy wrinkled his eyebrows. Then he remembered that the only mirror in the cottage was the little broken bit Mrs Youldon used to comb her hair, and that was too high for the children to see in. They hadn't really seen themselves before. Both of them peered a long time at each photo.

'Your Mummy's going to keep those photos. You can look at them every day now.'

Mrs Youldon glowed. 'I'm ever so proud of them, Billy. Of you. Really'.

Mrs Youldon was smiling and nodding. Her face looked really pleased. But she wasn't as pleased as Billy was. He'd done something right. He was good at something.

CHAPTER TEN

March 24th 1941. *Hitler says there will be war with the United States.*

Billy put his toes on the underside of the ball and lobbed it high into the air. It was his last kick before he had to go back to the Pawseys' for Mother's visit.

Now that Mr Finlay was organising football games two afternoons a week, all the boys were practising everywhere, up and down the lanes, in the field by the school and at home there was enough space beyond the chicken coops for practising goals. There was even more in the back field of the Manor and, like most days, Billy went there after school.

Alan, at the other end of the field, lobbed it back, straight as a die.

'Super. You're quite a good player,' he said as Alan ran up with the ball.

'Okay, we all know you're the star.'

Billy turned his mouth down at him. At this very moment, he had to leave the others to play without him. 'Got to go. Tell me what happens later.' He pulled his socks up, then turned the tops of them down. His knees were filthy.

Alan turned towards the group of boys a little way off, waiting to go on with the game. 'Shame, but it'll look bad to be late when your mother's come on the bus to see you.'

'I know. It won't be just Mother, though. And football's my favourite thing. Kenneth coming is my worst. He's always trying to make me look stupid. I wish you were my cousin and not Kenneth.'

Alan screwed his face up. He'd played round at the Pawseys' a couple of times when Kenneth had been there. 'He's all right, I suppose. You just like doing different things, and he gets at you because you're stronger although he's older.'

'He's nastier! You haven't been up against it. He's always nice when you're there, when anyone else is there.'

'Well I won't be this time. I'll be goalie for once. Go on, shove off, you.' Alan was only joking. It was his way of showing Billy he was on his side.

Billy jogged down the lane, in time to wash his knees and change his socks before Mother's bus arrived. Mrs Pawsey was putting cups and saucers on the dining room table. 'I thought we'd have a nice sit-down tea this time, not just a cup of tea on a tray. I've made scones and ginger cake, something to put a bit of brightness in your poor cousin's cheeks, isn't that so? I hear he's been poorly again.'

Billy nodded. It hadn't been serious, just a chesty cold. He went to the gate to wait for Mother. Perhaps she'd bring Jill. Perhaps she wouldn't bring Kenneth if he was recovering. But as she came into sight around the horse's field fence, he saw that she had brought both of them. The sun was bright behind the three of them and shone right in Billy's eyes. It made him squint to keep his eyes on them. A strong light shone on Kenneth's forehead and knees as he moved between the brief shadows of trees, and then he became just a silhouette, the brilliant sun rays making him a golden child from another world. Close to the fence, Jill trotted beside Mother as they came up the lane. Billy waved, but she didn't.

Mrs Pawsey came to the door to welcome them. 'Come along in, Mrs Wilson, Kenneth, and the little one too. Isn't it a treat for us to meet Billy's sister at last? Isn't that nice?'

Then they were in the hall and Mother was giving a long account of happenings at the vicarage that went on right until she had her hat off and they'd all gone into the sitting room. He glanced at Kenneth, who was unsmiling as ever these last months, but not too terribly sad, and then at Jill, who put her head in Mother's skirt. It wasn't worth saying anything. None of them wanted to know about the goals Billy had scored, or the time the pigs escaped and he'd had to chase them all the way to the Blackstop milestone.

Mother's account ended with Kenneth's news. 'He's studied so well with the verger, that he's been given a place at the Friar's Court Grammar, although his age group don't normally start until September.'

Mrs Pawsey nodded at Kenneth. 'Well, my dear. Isn't it good that you're going to be at a proper school at last? That's what you need; other boys, the noisy playground and sitting in a classroom.'

The left side of Kenneth's mouth lifted in a small smile or something like it.

Mother wasn't listening. 'Such an honour to be taken. It's not just his written work, it's more about his art. The Senior Master was so impressed. He told Kenneth to prepare a portfolio. A portfolio! And he's scarcely eleven, mind you! Think of that. He started there a fortnight ago. He loves it.'

Kenneth lounged against Mrs Pawsey's dresser fingering the worn runner.

Billy said, 'Does it feel funny to be back at school, Kenneth? Do you like it better there than our old school?'

Kenneth flicked his hair off his eyes. It had grown long at the front. 'The Friars Court boys are very civilised.'

'What does "civilised" mean?'

Kenneth gave a soft laugh and exchanged glances with Mother as though he was an adult with her, rather than a boy with Billy. 'We don't spend our time kicking muddy balls around to amuse ourselves.'

Mother was pulling Jill's hair into neater bunches where the ribbons had slipped. 'He comes home as clean as when he leaves! When I rang my husband about Friar's Court, Mrs Pawsey, he was over the moon. They have a superb art room and even though it's wartime, they haven't run out of paints or brushes. Kenneth will have ideal opportunities. Herbert was always pleased to have an artist in the family and the good thing is, Jill's getting so much from drawing with Kenneth.'

'Will you do me a drawing, Jill?' Billy scrabbled in the drawer for paper and a pencil with a good point.

She hung her head.

'She's shy,' Kenneth said. 'Only used to me, nowadays, old thing.'

Billy was just about to shout, 'She's *my* sister, remember,' even with Mother there, when he did remember. Now, she was Kenneth's sister too. He bit his lip hard. And he didn't like being Kenneth's old thing at all.

Mrs Pawsey set the paper and pencil on the table for Jill. 'There, dearie.'

She put an arm round Billy. 'I'm going to take your cousin into the kitchen. I've got some malt extract to help top up his vitamins.'

Mother made herself comfortable in the pink damask armchair. 'Thank you, Mrs Pawsey. So kind. Kenneth needs all the boosts he can get.' She put her elbows on the padded scroll arms and said, 'Now, Billy, I'm all ears.'

Once Mrs Pawsey had taken Kenneth out, Billy said, 'I miss Aunty, Mother. Why can't she come with all of you?'

Jill hadn't even touched the pencil. She stepped in front of Mother, one step, two steps.

Mother leant round her. 'Aunty Doreen's always busy nowadays. We hardly see her. In the evenings they're up the road, where they're living. She devotes herself to Kenneth. They read together and listen to the wireless. She works all day every day at the WVS while I'm left to fetch and carry, collect and deliver. That's my lot, Billy!'

'I could help you, Mother, if I was there with you.'

'I've explained already, haven't I? You've seen for yourself. The vicarage is full.'

Jill started jumping up and down as Mother spoke, blocking Billy's view.

'She's probably bored, Mother. Jill, Jill, let's play with your little ball.'

She stopped jumping and hid her face in Mother's skirt.

Mother called out, 'Kenneth – can you take Jill upstairs to play, please. Let's have your bits of news, Billy, then I'll have a chat with Mrs Pawsey.'

What would hold Mother's attention? He knew not to mention the Youldons. He gave her his latest school marks, then started talking about Alan at the Manor, the many rooms, the land girls and the nuns but, with his mind on the game being played right this moment at the Manor, he soon got on to football. Because Mother wasn't interested in that, his news didn't last long. She was ready for her women's chat. Football was something Billy was really good at and if only he could tell Uncle Ted, because he'd be pleased. Dad wasn't interested in games, neither was Mother and even if he'd been alive, Uncle Frank, who was really, really good at games, wouldn't have liked for Billy to be good at them too.

As she moved to the kitchen, Billy started up the stairs to join the others. He heard a slight scuffle, a giggle from Jill, a whisper from Kenneth:

'Quick, Billy's coming, he might be nasty to you. Hold on to me, I'll save you.'

'What did you say?' Billy challenged, as he reached the top of the stairs.

'Nothing,' said Kenneth, eyes large and precious, like barley sugar. 'Did I?' he added, turning to Jill.

Her little plump face peeped out from behind his corduroy shorts. She shook her head.

Billy clenched his fists. He could feel how very cross he was all over, and sad inside. It was like when they'd been told about war at school and why countries got into it. Jill was Kenneth's *collaborator*. That was the word. Letting him do nasty things and helping him, really.

Billy used the bathroom while he listened to Kenneth helping Jill to explore all around his home. *His* billet, he reminded himself. He was the one who should be showing Jill around it all. His eyes traced the pea-green paint of the dado rail and imagined the shashka hanging there. He saw himself lifting it down, turning and standing proud at the bathroom door holding it aloft at Kenneth. That would make him shake and stand away from Jill. Then Jill would admire

Billy again and she'd know she was much safer with him. He would be the one in power.

He moved to the landing and called, 'Let's go outside and play all together.'

'No thanks, old thing. We're happy as we are, aren't we, Jill?'

Billy plodded downstairs to Mother, who was trying to avoid the snuffling and lickings from Noah and Japhet. They didn't know she wasn't keen on animals.

'Mother, I used to play with Jill all the time when we were in Wandsworth. Now she doesn't even speak to me. You said that teacher that Mrs Shawditch gave a room to has gone to her new job, so why aren't I at the vicarage with you?'

Mother moved her head from side to side so that her hair swung over one eye and then the other. She was a bit like a film star, the one on the newsreel that came on before *Pinocchio* started. He'd be so proud if she came to his school, if the other children could see her and say breathily, 'Is that your mum?' But she never visited him on a school day.

She spoke in a sensible voice. 'It's the responsibility, Billy. There's only so much I can manage. You know I have to help Mrs Shawditch with the housework and cooking. I might as well be Mrs Donnington! Wartime, all these changes, it's very difficult. Nothing's as it should be, and then . . .' she dropped her voice to a shadow, '. . . with what happened to Uncle Frank. You know. We told Jill that Kenneth would be very sad and she must be nice to him. She follows him everywhere. I think she's a comfort, dear little thing, keeping him company. Whereas you would be – more of a challenge. Boys can't comfort, can they?'

Billy thought back to the awful death day last October, Kenneth's white face in the bedroom, the playing cards loose in his lap. The not speaking, the not playing with anything. But Billy had helped find the drawing paper, and saved Kenneth from having to go to school. At bedtime, he'd said Kenneth could turn the light off whenever he wanted. His shoulders hunched as he remembered the terrible crying in the middle of the night. 'I did try.'

'His art,' Mother went on, talking over him. 'He's so talented and makes so little mess. Either a pencil or a tiny box of water colours, that's all. He only uses a spot of each. Now he's helping Jill along that path too. Aunty thinks all of it's helping Kenneth to get over everything. The new school will help too. Dad's so glad.'

'Dad said I should go to the village school. But Kenneth's going to a grammar school.'

'He's eleven, you're not yet ten. You're fine where you are. Your father was so pleased with your marks. All ten out of tens.'

'But that's b-because I keep doing the same work over and over. Each time we get new children from London, we have to go over the old things all over again. And some of them c-can't even do hundreds, tens and thousands and I have to help them.'

Mother sighed and swung her scarf over her shoulders. 'I'm sure I don't know what to do about it. And now your father can't. I came to tell you today. He's being called up.'

Billy's breath came out in a whoosh. 'He s-said he wouldn't be! He's in a – a reserved occupation. He's *exempt*.' That word immediately whisked his thoughts back to the day he'd first heard it and thought it was *X-M-ed*. Uncle Ted had laughed. He was his proper self then, making jokes. He'd explained what 'exempt' meant, saying Billy might be exempt from dinner. That lovely roast that they ate nearly every Sunday at Nanny and Granddad's.

Nanny! Grandad! It was so long since he'd seen them! He scarcely knew what they looked like now. And Uncle Ted; his favourite person, he missed him so. Would he get home safely, in the end? Billy sighed. It was no good pretending that white lock at the front of his hair would have gone back to black, even if he wasn't fighting in the trenches.

He put a clenched fist into each of his pockets. 'Will D-dad have to go in the t-trenches?'

'I really don't know, dear. I thought you'd lost that stutter at last. Hands out of pockets, please.'

'It's not fair. He was exempt.'

Mother looked down at her shoes, the brown ones with the pattern of dots. She looked sad. Perhaps it was because she hadn't got enough rations to buy new ones. 'The war needs men his age now, even in his job.'

'But Mr Durban's not going to war and he works at Dad's Chambers. He's still in the Home Guard. I know, because Angela's been writing to me.'

'He's training others in the ARP. Otherwise he might be called up. We need all the fighting men we can get.'

Billy swallowed. 'Has England run out of soldiers?' Were they nearly all lost? In the Great War, Mr Durban had seen snowy fields with hundreds and thousands of dead bodies in Russia, and that was just the first year of the war. He screwed his eyes up. If Great Britain had run out of soldiers, was there field upon field of them dead? They'd be lying on top of the earth because there was no snow for them to melt into. He put a hand up to his face. If only Uncle Ted wasn't one of them.

Mother gave a hard smile. 'Of course there are more soldiers in England. Just no more young ones.'

'Couldn't they send Scottish ones, and – um – vicars?'

'Oh they have, don't worry. My vicar has a murmur on his heart, so he can't serve.'

'Would Uncle Frank have been ...' his voice tailed off as he looked around to check that Kenneth was still far enough away not to overhear the upsetting name.

'Called up? Yes, perhaps he would. But what happened to him was surely worse than being a soldier. Poor Aunty. Now your father's going away. We women have to manage without the men – we just have to get on with it. We all have to. That's war for you.' She tip-tapped hurriedly away, saying she must help Mrs Pawsey with the tea things.

It was 'We have no choice' again. Billy mooched off towards the chicken houses. Dad was far too old to fight. He'd never even seen Dad run. How would he escape the guns? It wasn't right. Look at the state Uncle Ted had come back in, and he was quite young. Now he wasn't a jolly uncle who did handstands, but a scarecrow with a white streak in his hair. If he was there at all.

CHAPTER ELEVEN

March 31st 1941. *Germans draw up plans for the invasion of Yugoslavia.*

In the morning, when they had done all the outside chores, Billy and Mr Pawsey tackled the pile of paper bags in the scullery. They all had to be folded into neat squares for re-use.

Billy slid another square onto the enamel table. 'You know my father's been called up?'

'I know, lad. It's hard.'

'He doesn't know where he'll have to serve. We're sending more and more soldiers. Mother says we haven't run out of them yet but Des Seabright is only five foot two and he's gone to war, and big Ronnie says sixteen-year-olds will have to go next. He'll be sixteen in 1943. Do you think the war will last that long?'

'If that's what it needs to win it.'

'Suppose we lose? Will all our soldiers be left in foreign lands?'

'They's'll be brought back. Let's not have those worries or that long face, Billy my lad,' said Mr Pawsey. 'We shall win this war, just like we did the last. Look what Mr Churchill is doing. He's not going to let Hitler get away with all this evil, you'll see.'

Mrs Pawsey called out that their dinner was on the table. 'It's only Homity Pie, I'm afraid. We've used our meat ration up until Monday.'

Mr Pawsey groaned as he led Billy into the dining room. He loved his meat. 'Tell you what, Billy. We'll delve into those tins of corned beef you brought when you came. The Missus has had them at the back of the larder all this time. I reckon as now we need 'em to cheer ourselves up.'

Mrs Pawsey nodded. 'Well perhaps as we should. Tomorrow. But instead of fretting about the rabbits getting our lettuces, it's about time you lay in wait for the blighters and get me some customers for rabbit pie.'

Billy shuddered. He loved leaning out of his bedroom window, watching the fluffy tails bouncing around the fields.

She cut into the pastry and served out a large slice on to Mr Pawsey's plate, and another on to Billy's. The leeks and potatoes slid out of their pastry case but they looked pale.

'Sorry there wasn't cheese to put in the pie but I've made bubble and squeak to go on the side, so we'll have something tasty.' She took the lid off the vegetable dish. 'At least we'll never be short of cabbage or carrots. Come to think of it, why don't you run down to the Youldons, Billy, and take a couple of carrot lollipops for those kiddies. I've scrubbed a couple of nice straight ones ready. That'll put the smile back on your face. And look, sun's coming out.'

He did feel more cheerful when he saw the carrots stuck on to sticks ready for Timmy and Sally. He put them into a paper bag and went to the back door. There was a glimmer of sun, although it wasn't really nice spring weather yet. He had a plan.

'Can I be out until tea, if Mrs Youldon lets me stay?' He searched around for some jam jars. 'These are for tiddlers, in case I find any.'

Mrs Pawsey smiled. 'You be back well before dark, then.'

As he cantered down Mrs Youldon's lane, he saw her outside cleaning the front window. He waved the bag at her and they went indoors to the children.

Sally and Timmy peeped in the paper bag and started sucking their carrots straight away.

'Look at my youngsters, bless them. Nice of Mrs Pawsey. You thank her from me.'

It was a good time to ask if they could go to that stream where he'd walked with Mr Pawsey and the pool where he'd paddled. 'Can I take them?'

Sally and Timmy stopped their sucking immediately. 'Yes, yes, yes!'

Mrs Youldon hesitated, but he saw she couldn't bring herself to say 'No' with both of them dancing up and down in front of her.

'All right then, it'll be a treat for them. Don't lose sight of them, Billy. Right?' She wrapped a pack of sandwiches in greaseproof paper. 'There's their dinner. You had yours? Go careful now, it'll be muddy on the banks. No mischief, mind, you two. You're in charge, Billy. It's half past one now, and you be back at five at the very latest.'

His jam jars bounced around his middle on some string Mr Pawsey had given him as he went off, one little one on either side. Sally danced down the road in front of Billy. Tim trotted beside him trying to make his footsteps the same length.

When they got to the big road beyond the shops, the boundary of Tim and Sally's everyday world, they saw the signpost was damaged. The village names had been scraped off, especially the capital letters. Now no one could read them. Someone had painted an arrow and 'To Hell' and underneath in brackets 'France'. He thought of Uncle Ted there, the green boots and dirty hairiness when he came down the street back from Dunkirk. Was he any better off in the trenches?

The baker trundled up in his van, interrupting the thought. 'Off down to the stream, are you, kiddies? I might be down later myself for bit of fishing while there's a touch of sun to see. We must have some fun, even in war.'

They moved off the road and on to the lanes, last year's leaves flying up around the kicking feet of the children. Tim was in high spirits, whooping and turning while Sally ran in front. Billy had been worried the walk would be too far for her and he'd end up having to give her a piggy back all the way back, but so far she was just as fast as Timmy. He looked at her little body in a rough green dress cut from something Mrs

Youldon had brought back from the church's bring-and-buy. Mrs Youldon wasn't very clever with her needle, not like Aunty Doreen.

Tim was racing Sally now and they were squealing loudly as one touched the other. He steered them past a muddy section of track and then they were into the snatch of trees and the grassy track up to the small hill. Tim lay sideways and rolled down, laughing. Sally watched, hesitating.

'I'll show you, how. I'll show you,' Timmy called.

But she was dancing on, daring him to catch her. 'Don't go too far!' Billy found a fallen tree and was just climbing it to call down to them when he spotted a bike juddering along the track between tree stumps.

'Alan! Yippee!'

The freckled face looked around bewildered until Billy leaped down beside him. 'Hello!' They'd only seen each other two days ago, but there was so much to say.

'Wait on. I've Tim and Sally.' They'd run out of sight so he started after them. 'C'mon Alan, we're going down to this nice place with stepping stones.'

He ran down the path, calling the children, Alan followed on his bike as best he could.

There were little squeals ahead as Billy rounded the bank where the overhanging trees began. He could see Sally getting ready to roll downhill with Tim instructing. They were on the steep bank leading down to the deep water.

'Stop!'

Tim started and obediently stood still, looking round for Billy, but Sally had already begun her roll forward. Her breathy giggles punctuated the air as Billy dashed forward. 'Look out!' He made panicky leaps over clods and tufts but they were no match for a little body gathering momentum on a steep slope. He had no breath to yell as the other little body raced downhill to catch his sister and both boys hurtled forward on to a bush at the water's edge just as Sally plopped into the water and disappeared.

Tim clung on to the bush wailing as Billy waded straight in and found himself up to his stomach yelling with cold and shock. He flailed around among stones and weeds, lost his footing and went under. He came up again yanking Sally's arm, and yelled to someone, anyone, 'I can't swim.'

Even in the urgency and terror of the moment, he registered a movement high above him on the bank as Alan. He bent again to get hold of Sally's face, went under again but came up holding her by her chin and her arm. She was lifeless. He looked wildly up at the bank but only Timmy was there, gasping and hanging on to a branch, looking very tiny and in danger of falling in too.

Amazingly, Tim bent down, picked up a decent-sized branch, and threw it forward into the water. Billy looped both of Sally's arms over it and pushed her towards the bank. There was no good purchase for his feet, which were slopping about in slime. He'd lost both shoes and he could only just manage to keep Sally's face above water while he coughed and spluttered out all the water he'd swallowed. Timmy hovered on the bank, one arm vainly held out towards Billy who was still waist deep. It was a struggle to stay upright and hang on to the icy little body swathed in weeds.

Billy was too cold to feel any part of himself. He could almost hear himself think, 'I mustn't fall,' even while the water was pulling at him to lie down. He pressed his feet down and apart to keep his balance, while two eddies swirled around him. His arms were locked around Sally but he couldn't get her upright. This was going to last forever and he'd never get Sally on to land.

At last shouts approached the bank and there was Alan with two men. They almost slid down to the water's edge carrying a rope between them. One of them waded in and put Sally over his shoulder, while Billy grasped the rope. His hands were so frozen they kept slipping as the other man pulled them into the bank. He just saw it was the baker, then he doubled up coughing and coughing out all the water he'd swallowed. The baker got hold of his shirt collar and pulled him the last stretch up on to dry land. He ripped off all the clothes on his top half, put his big jumper on Billy and wrapped his coat round Sally where she lay, a wet slimy bundle, under the large hands of the first man, who was pressing her chest getting the water out of her.

Alan took hold of Timmy and pulled him to a safer position but Tim kept trying to kneel by Sally, wailing loudly.

'Is she dead, is she dead?' was all Billy could whisper in a shuddering voice to the men. They didn't answer, their hands both at work on her tiny back.

Finally they got a breath from her, Sally was turned over to make her cough everything up. Billy's knees buckled under him. The first man stood up and wrapped his clothes round Billy.

He said they must all get back to the village as quickly as possible.

'Here's my jumper,' Alan said, pulling it over his head, and the baker put it on Sally with his own jacket on top. The he lifted her up to his shoulder, where she hung, completely limp.

Billy felt himself put on Alan's bicycle and pushed along by the first man. He couldn't talk for the huge shudders that kept racking his body and he kept his eyes on Sally the whole time to make sure she was still breathing. Her face was a horrible colour like cabbage water. Alan's wasn't a whole lot better under his freckles. He only had a shirt on now, and he was shivering. He kept a tight hold of the whimpering Timmy and kept looking at Billy in a frightened way, his eyes goggling.

Timmy's wailing got louder as he lost sight of Sally's face, hidden in the baker's shoulder. The baker looked down at him. 'Come on, laddie, your sister's going to be all right. We just have to hurry along to get you all dry and warm.'

Billy's feet were freezing, the sodden socks hanging off his toes as he was pushed along on Alan's bike. His bottom half was soaking, water dripping over the bike wheels and great shudders kept rushing through his body. All the time he was thinking, *Sally might die. Timmy needs carrying. I was in charge of them. It was my fault.*

He was going to get into the most awful trouble, the worst, worst Billy had ever been in. He'd have to tell Mother he'd lost his shoes, and when she saw Sally, Mrs Youldon would hate him and no one would ever trust him again.

When they got out of the leafy paths, the bike ran more smoothly. He heard the baker tell the other man to call at Fern Cottage where the midwife lived so that she could see what was best for Sally.

'I'll take Timmy home and fetch his mother,' Alan said.

Billy shut his eyes again and only opened them again when he felt strong arms deliver his drenched body to the waiting Mr Pawsey. 'Oh, lawks. Come quickly, Missus. Here he is, but in a state.'

Mrs Pawsey came straight out and led them to the settee in the sitting room. The baker said what had happened. 'I'd better not put him down, look.'

'Oh, Billy, our lad! You're like ice, and dripping wet. Heavens above, I better run a hot bath.' Mrs Pawsey sounded as if she was almost crying.

Mr Pawsey peeled off the rest of Billy's clothes and wrapped him in blankets straight away. 'Must get you'm warmed up. Time for a bath later. The Missus'll do you hot food and tea. That's what you need.'

'Tea. Right and I must find some sugar for it.' Mrs Pawsey hurried down the passage to the kitchen.

Mr Pawsey kept hold of Billy so tight that the blanket roughened his skin.

Billy squeezed his eyes shut while Mr Pawsey dried him and laid him bundled on the settee. 'You rest there now, till your tea comes, stay still.'

Mrs Pawsey brought hot sweet tea and held it while he drank and then he lay back again.

There were sounds of the baker being taken to the kitchen, the telephone, grown-ups talking, whispering, then exclaiming. Perhaps he dropped off to sleep, but it felt like a long, long worrying, a shivering and aching all over his body.

When he realised that Mr Pawsey was sitting beside him, he jerked upright. 'Mr Pawsey? Sally– is she still nearly dead?'

'Now, now. Not so. She's been taken up the cottage hospital just to get warmed through. She'll probably be up and about in a day or so, don't you fret.'

A cold wind blew in as the front door was shoved open. A man's voice called, 'It's Denson, *Sirius* reporter, Mr Pawsey. Can you give us the situation with the lad?'

Mr Pawsey shooed him off. 'He's resting. He's doing all right.'

'We need the story.'

'It's too soon.'

'I want it in the next edition, Mr Pawsey. I've just been up to the cottage hospital. The lassie is doing fine, considering. Not in danger.'

'We know that, thanks. We're in touch.'

'Rightie ho. So, see you in the morning.' The front door slammed shut.

'Huh. Local reporter thinks he can butt in everywhere.' Mr Pawsey lay Billy back on the baggy settee and tucked him in. 'You stay comfy here, my lad, and I'll see you're not disturbed again.'

Billy snuggled lower under his blanket. He felt easier now a stranger said Sally was doing fine. His eyes felt heavy. It was so good to be warm, even if there was going to be trouble later.

'You'll be in all the papers, Billy,' Mrs Pawsey said as she brought him a hot meal.

He struggled up a short way. Everyone would know it was his fault! 'Will I get t-told off?'

'Goodness no, my dear. People will say you're a hero. Here, eat this up.'

He looked at the plateful. It wasn't long since he'd been sicking up green water. 'Not sure I'm hungry.'

The Pawseys were always on his side, but they couldn't stop what other people would say. Worst of all, what would Mrs Youldon say? She'd trusted him to keep her little ones safe.

'It was my f-fault. I was in charge.'

'You pulled the little lass out. You were very brave, and now she's getting better with nice nurses to look after her. So eat this up, will you.'

'Is she really all right?'

'She really is, and it's thanks to you. She just needs a day or two to get to rights.'

He sat up and took hold of the dinner plate. It was stew and tasted super.

Even though he'd been told and even seen the newspaper saying that Sally was fully recovered, Billy was scared to go back to school. He'd been away for a whole week.

'We shall come too, and it'll be a special day.' Mrs Pawsey put out his best clothes as if it was a Sunday, but she insisted he get dressed in them.

She and Mr Pawsey followed him out of the house. 'Are you coming all the way with me?'

'We are. You'll see why.' She looked smart in her tweedy jacket that she'd worn to the pictures, and Mr Pawsey was in a proper suit with shoes. Would the teachers mind Mr and Mrs Pawsey coming to school?

At the end of the lane, they turned a corner and up ahead there seemed to be a line of people at the square, and not in a queue. 'What's all that?'

'You'll see soon enough, lad.'

As they walked nearer, Billy saw there was a platform in the square. On it stood the newspaper man, the Mayor with his big chain on his chest, and the head teacher. In front sat all the school children in rows. Everyone watched the Pawseys bring Billy near.

A cheer went up.

Mr Pawsey pushed him forward. 'Go on, our Billy. That's for you.'

What they'd said was true! It was a special gathering. Alan was already there with his mother, standing near the platform and he was in his best clothes too. He grinned at Billy and put his thumb up.

Mr Pawsey helped Billy up on to a big wooden box at the front of the platform. Alan followed. There were so many people looking at them! Was the whole village there? Mrs Youldon was at the front of the crowd. He didn't look at her face in case she was angry with him. Further back he saw Mother waving and smiling. Mother had come, and she looked pleased! When a lady in front of her moved Billy saw that Aunty and Kenneth were beside her. That was worrying. Kenneth would be bound to sneer or say something to get him into trouble.

It felt wrong to be standing up high in front of everyone. His face was hot and his hands were sweaty. Alan nudged him and told him to stand straight. 'It's for you all this, Billy.'

He looked down at Mr and Mrs Pawsey. They were nodding to everyone around them.

'They're proud because you're their evacuee,' Alan said.

The Mayor rang his hand bell and everything went quiet. He talked about the local soldiers at war, about how there could be bravery at home as well as abroad. He told everyone what had happened down at the stream, the whole story. All the people in the audience clapped hard, nodding and smiling, 'Good for you, son.'

The Mayor bent to put a shiny medal round Billy's neck. The reporter passed him two whole boxes of sweets, one for Billy and another for Alan, because he was part of the rescue, fetching help.

The medal felt heavy against his chest as Billy's hands gripped the box of sweets. A whole box! That was so unbelievable it was difficult to get a thank you out. He and Alan looked at each other making big eyes while the three cheers sounded. The children in the front leapt up and down and shouted out, 'Give us a sweet, give us one,' but Mr Finlay waved them to stop.

'Sweeties are for the heroes, children. The school is proud of you, Wilson and Firbank. Responsibility and prompt action to help others in trouble, facing danger for the common good, putting urgent need before your own comfort. That's what Great Britain is all about. So you two take your sweets home and don't open them yet.'

Mrs Youldon came forward at the end of the speeches but could hardly speak, patting herself on her front.

He tried to mutter, 'I'm ever so sorry,' but she squeezed him round the shoulders lots of times.

'My Sally, you saved her. If she'd drowned ... oh—' She shuddered. 'You're a good, good boy. If I had any treasure, I'd give it to you, Billy. And you, Alan.'

It was happy and it was embarrassing. He wanted it all to stop, but to be there too. He felt like running away. He felt like leaping high, high in the air. But he had to stay, standing straight.

After it was all over and the local head teacher had sent everyone back to school, Billy muttered to Alan. 'You should have a medal. It wasn't just me. You went for help and everything.'

'The thing is, I can swim, Billy. You can't. And it was you went in and saved her.'

The two mothers were walking over to collect them, Kenneth jogging in front. As he came up to them Billy whispered, 'Look out, Alan. *Kenneth.*' He waited for a sneer, or worse. But Kenneth only leant forward to finger the medal. 'I'm going to show people this when you come to the Vicarage.'

For once, Kenneth looked ordinary, nice, as if he even liked Billy. 'It was brave to go in after the girl when you can't swim.' He nodded twice, looking rather like Dad. 'That was brave.' He turned to the people nearby. 'He's my cousin.'

Alan muttered, 'Kenneth seems all right, Billy.'

The shock of Kenneth being nice made him wonder if everything had changed. He had a moment of imagining the three of them, Kenneth, Alan, himself, running through the grass beside the horse's field, playing chase. But no, that couldn't happen.

Aunty came up and hugged him. 'So proud of you, dearie.'

Mother stood beside her with a pleased smile, 'Well done, Billy. Your father will be proud.'

It was nice, of course it was really nice, but all of everyone's praise didn't take the guilty feeling away. Going into the water to rescue Sally didn't count. He should have been at the little ones' sides the whole time, not talking to Alan or climbing a tree.

He knew what he could do. He had something special to give Mrs Youldon on Christmas Day, a real treat, a real surprise. He tucked his box of sweets under his arm. When they all got home, he'd put it on Mrs Pawsey's high larder shelf until Christmas, wrapped up with a sheet of her draught paper. That hadn't been brought out since Uncle Frank's funeral.

CHAPTER TWELVE

December 8th 1941. *Japan makes massive attack upon United States*

They were all in the kitchen when the news announcer told about the bombing at Pearl Harbour. Mrs Pawsey gasped and let a dish slip back into the washing up water.

A section of Mr Churchill's speech followed the announcement. Mr Pawsey gave a sort of groan. 'They must have done that bombing even before they properly declared war. Now this situation is bigger than anything we've had before.'

Billy's stomach lurched. 'Will it be hundreds and thousands dead in that harbour?'

'Dreadful, dreadful. More like thousands and thousands.' Mrs Pawsey wrapped her dishcloth round her hand like a bandage. They were all quiet for some minutes.

'So we'll be at war with Japan now,' said Mr Pawsey at last.

Japan. Japanese people had slit eyes and bobble feet. He remembered that doll Angela had on her bedroom shelf. They'd probably be meaner than Kenneth ever was. Suppose they came over here! Angela had better throw that doll on to the fire.

Mr Pawsey got to his feet. 'Now there'll be action. The Yanks'll have to jump in with us at last.' He put his hand on Billy's shoulder. 'This could be a good thing. They'll be backing us up like they should have done in the beginning.'

The kitchen looked just the same, the blue and white striped dishes stacked up for Mrs Pawsey to wash, the tea towel ready in Billy's hand, the tin bucket with the scrapings waiting to be taken to the pigs. Mr and Mrs Pawsey were there. Things must still be all right. And if they weren't, the Americans would have to help.

Everyone had been saying for so long that the war couldn't be won until the Americans came, that now they were coming it felt as if war should stop immediately. Christmas was over and there had been a party at the Manor with jelly and iced biscuits. Now there were GIs to look forward to.

The biggest boys stood in the playground with their arms folded across their chests, looking important, while everyone else huddled around to listen. 'See – now that they've been attacked themselves, the States are sending soldiers over here to be trained.'

'—and some of them are at a camp right near.'

'Two miles,'

'Very near.'

Billy knew something about America. It was where film stars came from. He'd seen some at the Picture Palace, and in old magazines of Mother's. The women had fur coats, and wore bright red lipstick and the men drove big black cars. America was a huge place. The nine- and ten-year-olds had had a lesson with Mr Finlay's globe. America's proper name was The United States and it was an ally.

It wasn't a brave thing to say, but Billy couldn't help thinking that such a huge country would be full of men for the government to use as soldiers, so they wouldn't need to enlist English boys.

He was at the shop with the ration books queuing for sugar when he first saw some of the G.Is pass. They jerked their heads toward the queue with wide grins saying 'Hi there' or 'Howdy, folks.' Everything stopped and everyone stared. There was even a chink of blue in the thick white sky. The American soldiers were sort of glowing, their faces smooth and cheerful, really cheerful. Their uniforms were different, crisp and smart. Best of all, one of them threw sweets into the queue saying, 'Have some candy, buddies.'

Billy wasn't near enough to catch a sweetie, but he took home the shopping at a run. 'It's true about the Americans, Mrs Pawsey. American soldiers! I saw them. They threw sweets called candy.'

He went over to the pigsties to tell Mr Pawsey, the dogs running beside him as if they knew of the excitement.

Mr Pawsey rubbed his hands. 'So they'm at their training camp now? Let's hope it's a good thing, having 'em here.'

'I'm just going up to the Manor to see if Alan knows and we can tell Mrs Youldon. She needs to look out for Americans. They throw candy, and the little ones might get some.'

'Right you are, young-un, but pick all they titchy turnips from the side patch first.'

He worked as quickly as he could. Mr Pawsey gave him some turnips to take to the Youldons, a string bag full.

He called for Alan who said, 'Yes, saw them, saw them. They paraded past here, and we all lined up to watch.' He acted it out, the way the GIs marched and Billy tried to copy. Then they both ran down the lanes. They found Mrs Youldon had her sister indoors. They were nattering together and giggling.

'Hello my big boys,' she said, hardly looking at them.

'I brought these turnips for you, Mrs Youldon,' Billy said. He held the string bag near to her to make her see. 'Mr Pawsey said I could bring you the small ones. It's to make soups, you know.'

'You're a kind boy. Thank you,' she said, smiling quickly at him before returning to her very, very interesting chat with her sister. 'I don't know, Mary. I shouldn't, really. And what'll I wear?'

'You've got that pretty blue dress if you're going anywhere special,' Billy interrupted. He wasn't having Mary take over his place in Mrs Youldon's life. 'Is there a fête on?'

Mary burst out into a peal of giggles. 'A fête! Ooh, I want to be fêted, Joan. Don't know about you.' She did a twiddle in the middle of the floor, holding the edge of her skirt. 'Nylons, the Yanks have got. No kidding.'

Mrs Youldon's face was a little pink. 'All right for you, Mary. I've got the nippers.'

'Get them sat for, go on.' Her sister turned her back on the children. 'Their bus will come at seven by the congregational church, Joan. See you there, we will. So get a minder.'

'Oh, Mary. I don't know ...' Mrs Youldon scurried into the scullery without looking at Billy. He knelt down and brought out his knuckle stones to play with Alan and Timmy. Sitting beside them, Sally had her tongue at one side of her mouth while she struggled to put a needle in and out of a piece of cloth without losing the thread. There was banging from the scullery as the pans were hung up and a lot more chatter.

Alan made a face at Billy. 'Yanks'll be arranging socials with the locals.' He pulled some conkers from his pocket to add to Tim's collection and they started sorting them in size. Sally leant on Billy's knee with her sewing square. They played with the little ones for quite a while without Mrs Youldon coming into the main room.

Alan said, 'She's no time for us with Mary here.' He stood up and stretched. 'Anyway, teatime. Got to go now.' He put his head round the scullery door, and the chattering stopped. 'Goodbye Mrs Youldon.' He gave Billy a nudge and went out of the door.

Billy played on for longer, helping Sally make a row of conkers from smallest to biggest. His tummy reminded him it was teatime. He stood and put his head round the scullery door. 'Should I go back now, Mrs Youldon?'

She turned to him looking rather shy. 'Oh– you could have some tea with us. I was wondering– do you think Mrs Pawsey would let you mind the children tonight while I go out?

'But I've brought my dominoes and Happy Families. I thought we could all play together. I've been waiting till you're ready.'

'Another time, Billy. I'd really like to go to that dance. Can't remember when the village last had one. You could bunk down by the hearth and go back in the morning.'

'A dance? You mean dance with men?' He and Alan had never asked about Mr Youldon, but they'd always assumed he was away at war like all the other men. She surely couldn't dance with anyone else.

He watched her cheeks go red but her eyes sparkled. 'Why not? I'd be going with Mary.'

'But she's not married. You're a mother!'

Her chin went up. 'Mothers can dance too.'

He stopped himself answering. He remembered. Mother could dance. She'd done one at Uncle Frank's that time he'd decided they would do an 'entertainment'. He'd forced Billy to recite a rhyme, then was cruel about the stutter. And, yes, when he was really little, Mother used to go to dances with lady friends who came to tea and had fancy cakes. In those days he'd thought of them all dancing together in a ring, like he did in infant school. How silly. Now he was older he knew what dances were for. They were where men met women and then took them out.

He said sternly, as perhaps Dad might, 'Dances. That's for young people.'

Mrs Youldon bent towards him. 'How old do you think I am, Billy?'

'I – hadn't thought. Just, a mother, really. A young one.'

'I'm twenty-one. Twenty-one. And I haven't been out since Sally was born. Think of that.'

Twenty-one. That was when you got the key of the door. Mrs Youldon had two children. He looked at Timmy catching the knuckle stones. He was nearly six. So she'd only been a girl when Timmy was born. The same as Angela, almost. Angela certainly wouldn't get married when she finished school, years before she'd had the key of the door.

When Mother went to dances, the lady next door used to look in on him every hour or so, she didn't really babysit. Those evenings hadn't been very nice. He muttered, 'I do want to look after the little ones but Mrs Pawsey wouldn't like it if I stayed out all night. I could go next door and ask big Ronnie's mother to sit for you.'

'It's all right Billy. I was going to go and ask her anyway before you turned up. I just thought – well, the kiddies would like it better if it was you. But you could ask at the Pawseys' if it would be all right for another time.'

He twisted one foot round the other. 'Another time?'

He felt very cross inside. Cross that he hadn't thought about how old – how young she was, and cross that she wanted to go out and dance with men instead of staying in with him and the little ones playing dominoes or even Happy Families. If she'd asked him over for the evening he'd have let her collect the Bun family even though they were his favourite.

He looked at Sally and Tim. He didn't want them to be on their own, just having Ronnie's mother popping in to check on them. It would be far better if Mrs Youldon didn't go out. He didn't want her to, even though it was a shame for her never going out and being only just grown up. What could be done about it? He couldn't do dancing, or be a man for her. He frowned and shuffled his feet. Should Mrs Youldon go out? It was rotten, being only ten. You couldn't just do what you thought was best, even if you knew.

He slouched off home. She'd be popping next door and arranging things with big Ronnie's mother. He thought all evening about it. If Angela was sixteen, Mr and Mrs Durban would never give her permission to marry. She hadn't finished doing Shakespeare yet.

At breakfast, he took the risk of asking Mr and Mrs Pawsey. 'If I was sixteen and wanted to get married, you wouldn't give permission, would you?'

Mr Pawsey grinned. 'And have to find my own glasses and get stuck on my crosswords? Not likely.'

Mrs Pawsey said quietly. 'It wouldn't be for us to give permission, dear, would it? It would be your parents.'

'Oh! Oh, yes,' said Billy. 'Course.' He'd only ever thought of asking the Pawseys, the people he lived with. When he thought about being at home, he couldn't imagine asking Mother and Dad such a thing. He said quickly, 'Anyway, it'll be years and years before I want to be married'.

'That's good,' said Mr Pawsey. 'Then let's go up the back field and fix that fence afore you do.'

When they got outside and found the wire, he left lots of time for Mr Pawsey to forget his earlier question, before he said as casually as he could, 'I wonder when Mr Youldon will be home from the war. Leave, you know. He hasn't had any.'

Mr Pawsey put down his pliers and looked at Billy. 'You's a doing some guessing, young fella-me-lad. Aren't you?'

Billy hung his head and nodded.

'Well now, no one's seen that Mr Youldon since the little'un was born. Before that even, if I remember rightly. So those kiddies haven't ever known their father. That's her tragedy, poor young woman, struggling on her own. There's those knew her as a girlie, they feel for her.'

'I do too.' Billy worked on twisting wire for the fence while Mr Pawsey talked about the news in Europe, but Mrs Youldon's age, the whereabouts of Mr Youldon and whether she should be going to dances seemed much more important than the progress of the war.

CHAPTER THIRTEEN

February 15th 1942. *Our stronghold, Singapore, surrenders to the Japanese.*

It was an awful day. All the grown-ups Billy saw from home to school and the village square had very long faces. Mr and Mrs Pawsey said that Great Britain had suffered a terrible blow. He couldn't imagine it. Surely, going to war was the worst?

He went to collect wood with the little ones at the end of their lane.

Timmy whispered, 'My aunty's walking out with a G.I. She gets nylons, chocolate.'

That was only Mary. It didn't mean Mrs Youldon would follow. He thought of Jiminy Cricket and whistled, *Always let your conscience be your guide* as he thrashed the bushes with a stick.

Timmy tugged his hand, 'Mummy says it'll be the end of Aunty's problems.'

He didn't answer, but took the children home, holding Sally's hand very tightly. Inside their home, he looked up on the shelf to see if there were goodies, presents from some GI, but everything looked normal.

Mrs Youldon was folding the sheets from the Grange. She looked the same as usual.

'Did you go to your dance the other week, Mrs Youldon?'

She chucked him under the chin. 'My little guardian, aren't you? Yes, I went to the dance and had the best time of my life. And I'm going again, if I can get a sitter. No good asking you, then, Mr Straight-and-Narrow?'

He shrugged, and thought about what Mr Pawsey had told him. He looked at Timmy and Sally, playing quietly in the corner with the conkers. He knew in a way what it was like not to have a father, Dad being at work so much when he was little and now being away altogether, and the shock of Kenneth not having a father anymore. But he and Kenneth were big and knew what their fathers looked like. Timmy and Sally didn't.

'I'll have to ask Mrs Pawsey about staying over,' he said.

'That'd be so nice, Billy. If you can.'

When he got back home, he saw to the pigs and spent a few moments looking at their clever faces with those know-all eyes. Then he went indoors.

'Mrs Pawsey?'

She was knitting, not like Aunty knitted with a neat, quick clicky-click, slim needles darting, lengths of smooth fabric, green, pink, grey appearing – but on thick wooden needles with a shove, a poke and her tongue stuck to one side of her mouth. Her knitting was all colours, left-overs and unravelled jumpers from the last village jumble sale. She saw him watching.

'It's a blanket. We've all got to do what we can for our poor soldiers out in the field, even if we're no good at it, like me.' She chuckled. 'I got in trouble for it in school. The teacher said I wasn't trying, but I was! I was just no good at that sort of thing. And now look at me.'

'Mother says she's no good at it either. She doesn't do any.' He thought of Kenneth unravelling the old jumpers for Aunty's knitting. Billy supposed he should that too, but perhaps he was no good at that sort of thing 'Mrs Pawsey?'

'You're still muddy, off and wash now.'

'I will.'

'But?'

'If Mrs Youldon was going to a dance, would it be right for me to stay over and look after the little ones?'

She put her needles down, criss-cross on her lap and sighed.

'Lots of our girls are walking out with strangers now there are dances. Americans.'

'Yes. Mrs Youldon's sister is. She wants Mrs Youldon to.'

'It goes to their heads. The excitement. The money those American boys have got! And when our poor boys get back from the trenches, worn out and ready for fun, all the best girls will be gone.'

All the best girls! Would it be like that for Uncle Ted, none of the best girls left for him? He was already worn out two years ago after Dunkirk. If he was fighting in the trenches his hair might be *all* white by the end of the war, and then who would marry him? 'So should the ladies here go out to those dances?'

'Well. I don't know. With all these hardships young people do need some fun. Joan Youldon, she deserves some sunshine in her life.' She picked up her green and pink and purple knitting mess. 'You can sit for her, Billy. Stay over, as long as you call next door if anything goes wrong.'

~

It was the third time he'd stopped over and now Billy was meeting a real American face-to-face.

'This is G.I Joe, Billy,' Mrs Youldon said.

'Howdy,' Joe said. His legs were as long as tent poles and Billy had to tip his head right back to look at his face. It was a nice one, freckled like Alan's, with a great wide smile. 'I hear you're a football player. Good goalie, eh?'

'I'm quite good, but I'd be better if I had boots and studs.'

Joe laughed. 'What do you play in?'

'Just wellies or shoes.'

'Our game's different in the States, but I'll kick-around with you and your mates, some time.' He squeezed further into the room together with his friend Dwaine, who was much older and had a black moustache and eyes as dark as the gypsies'. They'd brought their own mugs and a tin of condensed milk for their tea and some candy bars. Timmy and Sally couldn't take their eyes off those, and it wasn't long before they had some in their mouths.

'You're older, Billy. You try this,' and Joe pushed some fat sweets wrapped in twisted yellow and blue paper. 'Bubble gum. You chew it, then blow bubbles. Look!' and out of Joe's mouth came a bright pink bubble as high as his nose.

The little ones giggled until their faces went red. Billy thought he might need to practise doing that so he put them in his pocket for later. 'Thank you very much, Joe.'

The Americans laughed and looked at each other. 'Neat! Get that real English voice.' They leant forward on the bench, arms on their thighs. Joe was next to Mrs Youldon, his trunk arms by her sticks. Her legs in socks and canvas shoes would probably go three times into one of those shiny black boots. 'Y' know, it's great to be in an English home, lady.'

Probably this was very different from what Americans had. Did Joe and Dwaine have a proper bathroom and were they shocked when they found the privy outside, just as Billy had been when he was first evacuated?

The two men totally filled the little room but sat respectfully as Mrs Youldon chatted to them in a high voice.

Timmy and Sally were squatting on the floor. They nudged each other while they listened, their faces lifted to the visitors. Billy stood beside them like a guard. It was exciting to hear the funny way the Yanks spoke, but he felt anxious too. The men didn't belong here.

But after they'd gone, the small room was suddenly lighter and bleaker.

Mrs Youldon went back to her work with quick steps, chatting over her shoulder to Billy. 'That Joe's a young regular soldier, but Dwaine only wanted to join up when the Jerries started bombing the supply ships. He thinks it's awful, all our food being wasted in the sea and all of us going without decent food. He joined up then, but because he was older, he was put on administration jobs. He's the one who helps organise the dances so he's very popular.' She laughed. 'We girls had the time of our lives at the dance, the best way of cheering us all up in these dreary old times.'

Billy thought of Aunty. She badly needed cheering up. She worked all hours at the WVS to take her mind off losing Uncle Frank, and never had any fun. She could do with some dances.

In the kitchen, the range fire was spitting out sparks because the wood had got wet. He and Mr Pawsey hadn't managed to fix the leak in the wood store. He moved the tea towels off the rail in case a spark caught them.

'That's right, Billy, thank you.'

'Mrs Pawsey?' he started. 'When you telephone Mother next, please can you ask if my Aunty can get free to visit on Saturday?'

'Yes, dearie, I will. You miss her?'

'Mm. Aunty's nice, and does kind things. When Baby was new she taught me about babies having different cries, and how to hold her. She put the pear drops in my pocket when they were all leaving me alone to go to their billet.'

He looked at the floor remembering the awful funeral day, and how she'd saved him from having to go back right then with all the misery and crossness about his behaviour. He wanted to be kind back. 'Mrs Pawsey?'

She was packing up Red Cross parcels for soldiers, and he was cutting the string.

'You know last Sunday, when the sermon was about families taking G.Is into their homes for Sunday lunch?'

'Ye-es ...'

He could act out the vicar, he often did it with Alan. The vicar here was very, very old, and sometimes his voice was quavery. Often he wagged a finger at the congregation. He acted the vicar for Mrs Pawsey: 'You may think Americans are different, but these are home-sick boys. Giving hospitality to them is next to having your own Tommies at your tables.'

She laughed. 'You're a case, Billy. What are you asking?'

'Can we give hospitality to Dwaine and Joe, please? They visited Mrs Youldon but she hasn't got a table for them to sit at.'

'I'm sure as we can squeeze in two more round ours.'

He grinned and as soon as the lengths of string were laid out beside the parcels, he ran off. Time to tell Alan. GIs were bound to go to the Manor where there were huge tables and it would be super if he, Billy, was the first one who invited Americans.

On the Sunday, the two men marched into the front yard smiling. After they'd shaken hands all round, they hitched up their sleeves. Joe said, 'We're gonna make ourselves real useful before we eat.'

Mr Pawsey looked glad, and took them down to the field. Joe picked the apples from the high branches. When he climbed up the ladder, his long arms reached to the top of the furthest fruit.

Dwaine helped with fixing the barn door and the broken wall behind the pig pen. It was embarrassing that these were things Billy hadn't been able to do. He was Mr Pawsey's proper helper. He watched carefully so that he could have a stab at the jobs next time. The leak in the wood store roof would take much longer to fix. Perhaps Dwaine would come again.

Indoors, Dwaine opened a haversack and pulled out goodies. He and Joe half-filled Mrs Pawsey's store shelf with tins of meat and tinned fruit. They finished with two brown oblong packets. 'Heath bars, you folks. They're everyone's favourite. Chocolate in them.'

Billy twirled in a circle. 'Mm. Mm. Love chocolate! We'll have to make these last, won't we, Mrs Pawsey?'

'We? Are you thinking Mr Pawsey and I would share something like that with you, Billy?' she teased him. 'Thank you from the bottom of our hearts, boys. These'll certainly boost our spirits.'

'You guys got nothing in good ol' England,' Joe said. 'Now we're here an' we gonna win you back your world.'

'Good Lor',' muttered Mr Pawsey, fiddling with his glasses. 'So mebbe you'll give me back full sight and be done with it.'

Mrs Pawsey got the food out of the oven, and everyone helped get it to the table. It was a jolly meal, having the GIs around the table.

They said they'd never had rabbit pie before, or mashed carrots so nice.

Billy hardly said a word, because of listening to all they said about America. Their stories of Iowa and Minnesota showed how foreign they were. They seemed to have a lot of parties and picnics and fancy times out. They didn't even call pavements 'pavements' but 'sidewalks' and said their trousers were 'pants', which seemed very, very funny.

Joe was nice, but Dwaine was quieter and safer. His hair gleamed and his trousers – or pants – had creases. What's more, he drove a jeep. Aunty would like that.

Billy went in the yard with him when it was time to go. He stood by Dwaine, watching Joe jog down to Mrs Youldon's.

'Can you come over next Saturday, Dwaine? My family are coming for their visit, my mother and my aunty.' Kenneth would be coming too, but he wasn't going to announce that.

'Say, that'd be darn good. It'll be swell to meet your folks, buddy.'

'Good.' He took a breath. Better let Dwaine know who was married. 'My father's a soldier now. Mother doesn't like that and I don't, because he was in a retained occupation and I think he's too old to fight. My uncle didn't get to be a soldier because he got killed first. He was on a bus that went down a hole when the underground station was bombed.'

'Shucks. That's too bad. Real hard on your aunty.'

'Yes, she does war work to take her mind off her loss.'

'Say, I guess that's all anyone can do,' said Dwaine.

'She doesn't have any fun, really,' Billy added, in case Dwaine didn't think about the dances himself.

'You don't say? You people sure have it tough.'

After the GIs had both gone, Billy had a run round the garden to think things out. When Mrs Pawsey came out with the pig swill he took the bucket off her. 'Dwaine is going to come over on Saturday so I can introduce him to my family.'

'That's nice, Billy. I see as you've taken a special liking to him.'

He hadn't particularly thought of that. It was what Aunty might like about Dwaine that mattered. Aunty would surely like Dwaine. He was big like Uncle, but jolly, and he didn't say nasty things or make people arm wrestle. It was exciting to think of having a grown-up to introduce when Mother visited. Annoyingly, Kenneth would be there too. Billy needed a proper plan so that neither Mother nor Kenneth got in the way of Dwaine meeting Aunty.

On Saturday, Billy did all his chores extra fast, then he went to where Mrs Pawsey was bringing in the washing. He collected the pegs and started putting them in the peg bag, which meant he didn't have to look at her.

'Mrs Pawsey?'

'Mm ...'

'Could you specially chat to Aunty today when they all come, because the last time she visited here was the awful funeral time, and anyway if Mother's there when Dwaine comes, she'll do all the talking.'

'The things you think of, Billy boy! But I'll be glad to see your aunty and enjoy a chat with her if you're taking your mother off on your own.'

As soon as footsteps sounded on the gravel outside, Billy ran out to take charge. The weather was cold and breezy so it didn't seem odd to be hurrying the women inside. He handed Jill and Kenneth the kite Mr Pawsey had recently made him, so that they'd go in the field, then took Aunty to the sitting room. Mrs Pawsey took Aunty's arm and started asking her how she was.

'I've got some shabby clothes up here, Mother.' Billy pulled her upstairs to check all his clothes for mending and outgrowing. He'd worry her with tales of sagging socks and buttonless shirts to keep her busy in his bedroom. Aunty was safely drinking tea and chatting to Mrs Pawsey when Dwaine arrived.

As Billy heard Mrs Pawsey doing the introductions, he ran downstairs, shutting the door quietly on Mother and her folding-up of clothes.

'Delighted, ma'am,' Dwaine was saying, and he bowed his head. Aunty blushed. Billy remembered her praising Dad's manners but Dad had never bowed.

Dwaine passed four tins of Spam and some fruit juice across the side table between them. 'I thought you'd like these, ma'am, back in your billet. I've got more for you, Mrs Pawsey.' He nodded to where he'd placed them ready. Dad had never brought things, even for Mother, so it wasn't likely that Uncle Frank had. Aunty should be impressed.

Billy worked quietly at the back of the room piling up the logs ready for banking up the fire. Things were working well. He knew his arrangements were exactly right. It was all in a love story book *Time and Together* he'd found in the vicarage charity box a month ago. The next thing, after a man had been introduced to the lady, was to leave them alone to talk.

It was time. He arranged the last log on the pile and stood up. 'Mrs Pawsey, can I help you take those tins to the kitchen?'

She let him pick up the tins and followed him out there. She put her hands on his shoulders, looking deep into his eyes. 'Not yet eleven, and you're acting the man of the world, Billy.'

He didn't answer. So she knew what he was up to. He didn't care.

Mother soon came downstairs but because Mrs Pawsey was already in the kitchen and there were new tins to put away, she spent some time exclaiming and discussing all the benefits that Americans brought with them. By the time she got to the sitting room to meet the visitor, Dwaine and Aunty were well into their conversation. Mother was the newcomer and had to join in as best she could. Billy followed her in, absorbing his pleased feeling. He was able to look useful, feeding the fire with firewood.

The front door opened, bringing a draught of freezing wind. Kenneth came in to dump the kite. Billy went to the hall to divert him.

'Did it fly well?'

'It was okay. I've finished with this. Jill got fed up with holding the string. She's still out there making a wood house so I'll get my paint box.'

Bother. That was in the sitting-room. He couldn't stop Kenneth going in for it and the roll of lining paper that Mr Pawsey had given him. He stood against the door. 'We've got a visitor.'

Kenneth raised his eyebrows and pushed Billy to one side.

'This is my son,' Aunty said as he walked in, 'Kenneth.'

Billy stayed at the door watching in case he stayed too long. Kenneth hesitated looking Dwaine up and down, then leant forward to shake hands with the tips of his fingers.

'Good to meet you, sonny.' Dwaine smiled at him, then went on talking to Aunty. Kenneth would hate the 'Sonny'.

Billy moved to the sideboard and picked up the paint box. 'Here you are, Kenneth.'

Kenneth took it without looking, watching his mother chatting for a moment or two. Then he collected his roll of paper and went out to paint in the kitchen, his bottom lip pushed forward.

Billy followed him out and shut the door behind them both. He should have realized that Kenneth wouldn't be pleased.

'And who's that supposed to be?'

'It's a G.I. We had two for Sunday dinner. It was fun.'

Kenneth closed his eyes, briefly, as though it would have been terrible to be there. He took a jam jar from the draining board and filled it with water. He took it to the table and dipped in his paint-brush, twisting the end over and over to make a fine point.

Mother was helping Mrs Pawsey bring plates from the kitchen to the dining room. 'You're able to put a lovely tea on the table with the extra stores you've been given.'

Mrs Pawsey nodded, as though she didn't realise Mother wanted her to put some in her going home bag. 'We are lucky, aren't we? It's so cheering to have these little treats. Billy deserves some.'

'Billy! I hope your mouth isn't full of chewing gum. I don't want you to spoil your tea.'

He shook his head. Mother thought chewing gum was common, so he and Kenneth would be the only boys for miles around that weren't allowed it. His bubble gum was still in his other trousers, ready for trying out the bubble blowing when no one was watching.

At teatime, the grown-ups were very jolly but Kenneth was quiet all through the bread and butter, Spam, carrot cake and even the tinned peaches.

'So tasty this Spam, Dwaine. More evap, Kenneth? It'll fill out those cheeks,' Mrs Pawsey encouraged him.

'No thank you.' Kenneth sat with his hands folded on his lap.

When Billy finished his last peach slice, nibbling as slowly as he could to make the taste last, Aunty turned to Kenneth and said. 'Go and spend some time with Billy, dear. You've almost been ignoring him.'

Billy stood. 'Coming, Kenneth?' Horrible though it was to spend time with him, it would keep Kenneth out of the way.

Kenneth picked up his paper, paints and brushes and elbowed Billy upstairs to his room, kicking the door shut behind him. 'Damned Eyetie,' he said. 'Don't even like Spam.'

'He's not an Eyetie! He's a G.I.'

'An Eyetie G.I then. Look at that greasy black hair and gypsy face.'

'Shut up. Brylcreem keeps his hair all neat. G.Is and Eyeties are nice. I like them. I like Dwaine, and Mr and Mrs Pawsey like him – and Aunty likes him.'

'She's just being polite. You don't know a thing, you're just a football twerp.' Kenneth picked up his paintbrush with a flick of his head, then turned his back. Billy so badly wanted to hit him, but as Kenneth bent to his painting, the back of his stringy neck looked weak, like something that shouldn't be hit.

'If I'm a football twerp then you won't want my company,' Billy said and stomped downstairs. He scooted out of the back door and made for the field. 'Huh, meanie!' he said now that no one could hear. It was cold enough for his breath to come out in little clouds, which was very satisfying, like being a fearful dragon. All the fence posts had sparkly white tips and spiders webs laced across the long grass. Beyond the horse's field he could see Aunty and Dwaine walking in deep conversation. Apart from Kenneth, it was all going very satisfactorily.

He leant on the pigs' wall, keeping out of the way. He hadn't given them names, because Mrs Pawsey said that way he wouldn't feel so upset when they had to go to market. He did so like them, though, especially the tubby little one they called the runt.

'Well, I say!' said Mother, coming up behind him holding Mrs Pawsey's egg basket. 'A bit of company is certainly doing your aunty some good. I gather Dwaine's invited her to a dance. Perhaps he'll bring some friends next time I visit you, then I can go.'

Billy swung round fiercely. 'You can't. Dad's away somewhere being a soldier. He can't go to dances.'

Mother looked almost alarmed. 'You're going to be– eleven, soon. Growing up, and I hadn't been noticing. I must ask about the secondary school. Mrs Pawsey might know if it's any good. You can't stay where you are until you're fourteen, given there's no sign of this infernal war ending.'

Billy stood upright, firmly. Surely, Mother would see he was as good as Kenneth, worth the same?

She went on, 'Or fifteen, it's said the school leaving age is going to be. I wonder if there's a technical school. Your father would want to know the reputation, the discipline. So important. Kenneth's school makes them into little gentlemen. Too far away for you to go, unfortunately, even if you were accepted.'

Billy was going to say, 'Unless you got me a billet near you,' and then thought of how truly awful it would be to leave this place, to leave Mr and Mrs Pawsey. He walked beside her, silent until they reached the chickens.

'Oh. There's no eggs,' she said, looking at an empty pile of straw.

'Wait.' He scrabbled in the hedge and in a patch of tangled dandelions. 'Here's two, Mother. And there's another one under Sparky, that gingery hen.'

She looked at him rather sadly. 'I can see you're going to be rather a useful boy to have around.' Then with a strange switch of subject, which Billy fully understood, 'Anyway, not much football at Kenneth's school. They don't pride themselves on their sports. It's all literature, Latin and algorithms.'

'And Art,' said Aunty coming up behind them, 'if you're talking about Kenneth's grammar school. I was just telling Dwaine about it.'

'Quite an artist, I hear, ma'am, that young man. I guess we don't go in for culture stuff too great in the States. Some say we should. No opportunity to partake in culture at the present time, of course.' He laughed, but not bitterly.

'But you do have time for football,' Billy put in. He wasn't sure whether that counted as culture.

Dwaine winked at him. 'Too right, buddy.'

Aunty's eyes were bright as she said, 'Well if you're short of culture, and if your – unit – will let you, you could come to Kenneth's art exhibition. It's before the end of the summer. You'll come, Billy dear, won't you?'

'At Kenneth's school?' he said. He'd like to see the place, what it was all about. 'Yes. If someone can take me over, I'll come and see Kenneth's paintings.' (And if he went, surely Dwaine would want to go with Aunty?)

CHAPTER FOURTEEN

May 1942. *Rommel readies for a new offensive.*

Billy was the biggest boy amongst the evacuees now. Even the twins and all the farm food they had every day hadn't made them grow as tall. His muscles were the sort that Uncle Frank couldn't have scoffed about. But you needed more than muscles and speed to play football really well, you needed proper football boots with studs.

Alan's mother had managed to get Alan some. Billy stared at the studs as Alan ran. They made a smashing pattern of holes in the mud. 'Flipping heck, you're so lucky, Alan.'

'I know. It's that job she has in Piccadilly. There always seems to be a visiting officer that can put his hand on something special. Or even stuff from abroad. There's people working there who go secretly to other countries and no one's supposed to know. But these are English boots.'

'I don't think you can get them anywhere near here, can you?'

'Ask your mother for some. She gets to the town. Say it's for an early birthday present.'

'Five months early? Bet she won't.'

Jill had come with Mother, looking smart in a little skirt cut-down from a woman's tweed one, and with shiny strap shoes. Kenneth held her hand. He always looked smart, like a boy on a knitting pattern or a Persil advertisement.

As soon as he could choose the right moment, Billy said, 'Mother, my shoes pinch my toes. If I could have new boots, they'd last longer than shoes. And if you don't mind it being so early, they could be my birthday present if they had studs on.'

'Studs!'

Mrs Pawsey looked the other way and took some cups and saucers from the dresser, putting them quietly on a tray.

Mother sighed, a loud sigh. She looked at Billy, then Kenneth, then Jill and then back at Mrs Pawsey and rolled her eyes.

'Just when the rationing's got even worse. Always something more to get for children, isn't there, Mrs Pawsey?'

Kenneth had hold of Jill's hand. 'Looks as if you'll have to wait a bit longer for your coat, Jilly. There won't be enough rations. You won't cry now, will you?'

Mrs Pawsey stood in front of Kenneth. 'I'll get Billy's ration book.' She came back into the room and showed how many rations were left. 'Here you are, Mrs Wilson. You should be able to get him some boots. We've not used many for him, not really.' Then she took the tray out to get tea.

Mother squeezed the toes at the end of Billy's shoes and counted the points left in his ration book again. Billy waited, watching her face. Did this mean she would be getting boots or not?

Kenneth sat on the low padded chair, his legs stretched out before him. It looked as if he was showing off his shoes. They looked newly polished and shiny. 'Do you polish all the shoes, Kenneth?' Billy asked.

Kenneth didn't answer, and Mother, with her back to him, mouthed to Billy, 'Prisoners of war.'

There were buns for tea and some butter too. It was a proud moment. Mrs Pawsey had swapped her extra eggs for it. Billy helped look after the hens, so if they laid more than the quota for collection, it was partly thanks to him. And he'd done the swap deal with the twins' farm.

'You have such treats, Billy,' Mother said as she spread a sliver of butter reverently on the half of her bun which didn't have currants. 'I wish things weren't so hard for Jill. And Kenneth, of course. But at the Vicarage, we're aware of how much we need to help others.'

'We get by, don't we, Jill?' said Kenneth, smiling at Mrs Pawsey with his sad head on one side.

Mother leant towards her, 'Kenneth draws pictures that his mother puts in the Red Cross parcels, and he unravels the old jumpers people give in to the Vicarage. Then Doreen knits scarves and socks with the wool.'

'And it's all wriggly, not nearly as good as new wool, Mummy says.'

Everyone started as Jill spoke. She spoke so rarely that Billy had hardly taken in that she could talk properly now. She probably had done for ages when he wasn't around.

Mother went on, directing her conversation at Mrs Pawsey. 'I don't knit, of course. Doreen's tried to teach me, but it's not my sort of thing. I was taught deportment and elocution at school, not much help to the war effort.'

Mrs Pawsey bent her head to her tea cup. 'No, it wouldn't be, that.'

'I help in other ways, don't I, children?'

Kenneth said, 'Yes, Aunty. You're a tower of strength.' He looked at Mrs Pawsey so that she could encourage Mother.

Mrs Pawsey said, 'You mustn't grow old before your time, Kenneth. How about popping into the yard for a game of football with Billy?'

'I think I'll say *No* to that, thank you very much, Mrs Pawsey. Falling about in the mud is more Billy's thing than mine. I can clear the table for you.'

'Such a help,' said Mother.

'No thank you, Kenneth. I'll see to it,' said Mrs Pawsey. 'But you should try to play football, even if Billy's a much stronger player. He does so well, even without boots.'

Mother leant forward to take the half-bun off Kenneth's plate. 'Can't waste this, if you're leaving it, dear. Such a treat, Mrs Pawsey.'

It was hopeless. Even with Mrs Pawsey mentioning football, Mother wasn't remembering about the boots.

Mrs Pawsey handed Billy his freshly ironed best clothes; a cream shirt, a green v-neck, and his jacket that he only wore on Sundays. 'I's'll want you to look just as good as all those grammar boys, won't I?' she said, as she walked down the lane with him to meet Dwaine. He couldn't help skipping along. Even if visiting Kenneth's school turned out to be boring, it would be topping to turn up in a jeep.

At the road, you could hear immediately it was coming. It was going at a slow pace because of boys running alongside.

Billy put his thumbs up to them. 'I'm going to ride in that!'

He sat in the front all the way to the Vicarage, where Mother and Aunty were waiting in the front garden. They'd both done their hair in waves and had curls with Kirby grips. Aunty's plum-coloured dress made him look twice, and then he remembered her wearing it that Christmas Day they'd spent at her house, when Uncle Frank dressed up like Father Christmas. Dad had asked Aunty if her arms were cold because they were bare. But today was quite hot, and Mother was wearing the blue spotted dress she liked best.

He hopped out and into the back seat, still high above the ground and the ladies slid gracefully into the front as if they always travelled that way.

'Marvellous you can get the fuel, Dwaine.'

'For reconnaissance,' he said, grinning.

Billy didn't know quite what he'd expected of a grammar school. Probably a great brick building like his Wandsworth school, doubled or trebled in size. But Friary Court was more like the Grange, a great drive up to the front and an archway to one side. As they got near, they could see through the arch that there were vehicles of all kinds parked, including some army trucks. Kenneth had told him that upstairs there were dormitories and because of the war, some boys were boarding.

'Boy, this is quite something,' said Dwaine, as they walked to the huge open doors. 'A lot different to my high school, I'll say.'

'It is impressive,' said Mother, adjusting the feather in her little hat.

Aunty grabbed hold of Billy's hand. He held it limp, so that she would realise he was too old for her to do that. She dropped it, and held his elbow instead.

'This is exciting, isn't it, Billy? Kenneth's going to be quite a star. His paintings were chosen although he's one of the youngest in the school.'

Billy was interested to see the many people, especially servicemen on leave. All were rather quiet, rather like a crowd going into church. Yes, it was exciting. Mother led the way, Dwaine held Aunty's arm and she was still holding Billy's elbow. Once inside, they were ushered into the great hall. Lots of screens on feet surrounded the walls and people had to step between them and look at drawings, written work and designs pinned on each one.

Dwaine gave a running commentary as they admired each display until finally they passed the last screen to face the back wall of the best paintings. Beside it stood Kenneth.

Aunty breathed out. 'Kenneth, dear, here we are!'

'Well, I say,' said Mother.

Billy looked up at a scene of soldiers parading past the local church. It looked as if he could see them for real through a window. Then there was a smaller drawing of a man working at a desk. There was one of a huge vase of flowers and another of a pile of vegetables, a painting of the church and children coming out of it, and two which were just like patterns, all sorts of colours and shapes swirling about. Kenneth smoothed his hair and grinned as they gazed at the colourful paintings. Billy had never seen him look like that.

'These really yours, Buddy?' Dwaine was saying. Kenneth nodded but didn't reply.

'Cor, Kenneth, they're ever so, ever so good,' Billy said.

Kenneth looked surprised. 'Do you like them?'

Billy nodded very hard. He didn't like Kenneth, but his paintings were super. 'They're like a real artist's.' It was true what Uncle Frank had said back in Wandsworth. Kenneth was going to be famous.

'Herbert would so love to see these,' Mother said to Aunty who stood, glowing and silent. 'He'd be so proud – he always wanted to paint himself.'

Aunty's face tightened. 'And don't you think Frank would've loved to have seen his son's work? If I was lucky enough to still have a husband like you?'

Mother fluttered her hands. 'Sorry, Doreen. Of course. I suppose I rather forgot, what with Herbert taking Kenneth on as another son and you now having . . .'

Dwaine interrupted Aunty's gasp. 'Ladies! I gotta thank you for showing me this fine school. It's time to admire some scientific work now.' He took the arm of Aunty and marched her off to look at the science laboratories. Mother gazed after them, nodding to herself. One of her eyebrows twitched. She wandered to the nearest table to look at some sketch books.

Kenneth leant down towards Billy and muttered, 'Let that be the last time we have to set eyes on him! You won't invite Yanks round anymore, will you? Don't you hate them?'

Billy shook his head. He really liked them and the more Dwaine came round, the better he liked it. Of course, Kenneth wouldn't know how often that was, or that he played football with Joe and Dwaine and other GIs at the Manor whenever they could get free.

He gazed at each of the paintings again and again. It was amazing that a cousin of his had done them. There were other super drawings and paintings around, but they were by much older boys.

The hall was enormous. Two large corridors led off it, as well as a square area with several doors. He'd never find his way around if he had to go to school here. 'Can we go to where those big maps are and then to the biology labs?' He knew there'd be animals in jars from what Kenneth had talked about before.

'In a bit. There's tea and cakes.'

'That will be welcome, Kenneth.' Mother followed him to the dining hall at the end of the first corridor.

They sat with their tea and rock cakes until Aunty and Dwaine re-joined them. It was good hearing other people around commenting on the paintings, and saying admiring things about Kenneth's. Aunty got pink and breathy. Billy saw Dwaine take her hand. Perhaps he was going to love her.

A bearded teacher with a caved-in chest stepped beside them. Kenneth stood up. 'Sir, my mother, my aunt, my cousin and a – an American.'

'Delighted. I'm Kenneth's art teacher, so naturally feeling very proud. And are you another budding artist, Kenneth's cousin?' the teacher asked Billy, hope in his eyes.

'No, sir. I'm rotten at drawing.'

'Shame,' said the teacher, turning away. Then he took the adults off to see round the rest of the school. Billy was left with Kenneth.

'Brilliant teacher, Mr Woodhead. Did you see his chest? Some boys say he had consumption, all his lungs eaten away. Don't know if it's true, but it's good that he doesn't have to go to war and can stay teaching us, isn't it?' He stood up, away from the crumbs on the table. 'Come on. There's lots of subjects on display. We'll go and see the interesting bits. Bit different from your little school, isn't it?'

Billy nodded. He'd never imagined a school like this. The inside was larger than the Manor. He grew quieter and quieter as they went from the maps to the gymnasium with its leather horse and wooden bars all up one side, then the science laboratories full of instruments that he'd never seen before, and lastly the art room. That was only to look at the materials because all the decent work was on display.

They ended up in a cloakroom area that looked on to a playing field. It was the sports area. There were changing rooms with basins for washing, and a small office by the rear doors. Kenneth knocked on the door and went in. Billy could see shelves of clothes and shoes inside.

'Look!' said Kenneth, coming out again. 'Lost property.' He led Billy out of the sports area. 'Here you are, right size.' He passed over a pair of nearly perfect football boots. And they had studs.

'I thought there wasn't football here.'

'Well, there is for some. We're not forced to do it. I don't, of course. Here you are.' Kenneth pushed the boots into his middle.

Billy felt as if his eyes were falling out of his head.

'Take them, then.'

Billy hadn't even put his hands out, not daring to think they were for him.

'I can't – they're not mine.'

'They are now. The teacher in there will think they're for me, but I'm not going to use them, am I? I do extra art when it's footer. Go on. They're what you wanted, aren't they?'

Billy looked hard at Kenneth's expression in case this was some cruel trick, but Kenneth's face didn't look mean.

'I-I do want them. They're smashing,' he said, stroking the leather, 'Thank you. Thanks ever so much.' He hugged them to his middle, hard, in case they disappeared into thin air.

Kenneth found a piece of newspaper on the changing bench. 'Here, you'd better wrap them up. Let's go and find the grown-ups. I've had enough touring now.'

Billy followed, clutching the boots. They were better than any birthday or Christmas present he'd ever had and it was *Kenneth* who'd given him them. It was almost too difficult to speak. Now he couldn't wait to get back to the Pawseys to put them on and try them out.

Dwaine and Aunty were deep in conversation so didn't notice him holding anything as they walked back down the drive, but Mother did.

'What's that messy bundle, Billy?'

'Football boots,' his voice was jerky. 'A present from Kenneth.'

Aunty turned round. 'You found boots for him.'

'They were in Lost Property. No one wanted them.'

She looked across at Mother. 'Heart of gold.'

Mother was looking into the distance and muttering, 'Of course, I do remember you once saying something about wanting boots, Billy. Well, now you have some. Lucky boy. Make sure you thank Kenneth.'

Dwaine had a little smile round his mouth. 'How you goin' to make that up to him, Billy?'

Kenneth marched ahead as if not hearing.

Billy started. 'I – d-don't know.' He grabbed the boots tighter to him. Whatever was coming, he wasn't going to part with them now.

CHAPTER FIFTEEN

June 25th 1942. *British RAF make 1,000 bomb raid on Bremen.*

The second-hand boots were actually quite worn at the heels, but it didn't matter. They had studs. They were proper football boots and they were his. He'd already put his name inside by the ankle, using a laundry pencil of Mrs Pawsey's. She understood how important football boots were for someone like Billy.

'See? You thought Kenneth all bad and he's seen to it that you've got exactly what you need.'

At the first opportunity he raced down to the Manor. There was the whole story of the grammar school visit to tell Alan, but most importantly about how he'd got the boots.

Alan was impressed. 'That was really decent of Kenneth.'

'Yes! I thought he was sneering and not at all on my side when I was asking Mother for boots, but all the time he must have been thinking how much I wanted them, and then how he could get me some from his school.'

He and Alan compared boots and studs and played an even longer game than usual, so that Alan was called away for yard sweeping duty before Billy was due home.

Now he just had to tell the Youldons about the boots. They felt deliciously heavy on his feet as he ran down to their lane.

When he reached their open doorway, Timmy met him with big eyes. 'She's crying.'

Sally was hanging on to her mother's skirt while Mrs Youldon tried to mangle some sheets. The airer was low enough for her to spread them on but she was making heavy weather of the mangling. Billy stepped forward and took the handle. 'Hello'. He saw her red eyes, but it wouldn't be polite to mention it.

She sent the children to play out.

'But Mu-ummy ...'

'No, Sally. Play out. Go with Timmy.'

Timmy looked at Billy trustingly as he took Sally's hand and slipped through the doorway. Sometimes, Billy felt like a dad here.

Mrs Youldon took the handle from him. 'We'll take turns,' she said in a wavering voice.

He breathed out. 'What's wrong, Mrs Youldon?' But he wasn't sure he wanted to know. He looked at the chipped enamel bucket with its steamy soda smell. Would she have to tell him? He didn't want to say, 'I'm sorry for your loss' again.

'It's Mary.' She began to sniff and her eyes dripped more wet on to the sheets as they pulled the next one flat between them. 'I should be happy for her. She's going to marry him, that Chuck. And that means going to America with him after the war.' She smothered a sob as she lifted another heavy sheet. 'She'll have a machine for doing all this. A washing machine. Imagine! Joe showed me a picture in a magazine. It's like a small train carriage with a lid. You put the clothes in, then a hose for the water, add the soap stuff and press the electric switch. It swills round and round does all the wash for you, even getting the water out! That's what they have in America.'

'It's a long way to go to do washing.'

'Oh, you!' She nudged him in the ribs. 'What'll I do without her? Why can't I have someone to look after me?'

'You've got me and Alan.'

She started crying again. 'I mean a man. It's so far away. If she goes, I'll never see her. Grrr, this sheet just won't go through the mangle.'

Billy grasped one end of the sheet and twisted. He knew the drill. Mrs Youldon grasped the other and they held the middle over the wooden sink. His hands stung as he struggled with the steamy linen. Her hands didn't seem much bigger than his, although they were bright red with doing this so often.

'Why do the Grange people need such thick sheets?' he said when they'd flattened sufficiently for the mangle.

'They lie more, I suppose.' She cried and laughed a bitter laugh at the same time. 'I know one of them that does. Not that Timmy'll ever know him.'

Billy carried on turning the handle. He supposed it was because she was upset she was saying nonsense things. Wasn't Mr Youldon ever going to come back?

She pulled out the sheet. 'I shouldn't be saying those things. Especially not to a child. You forget what I said, mind.'

'About Mary going to America?'

'No, not that, she's telling everyone. Anyway, she'll have to wait for the war to be over before she goes with him. What I said about the Grange people. Don't repeat that.' She passed Billy one end of the wet sheet. 'Can you fold? Joe's off soon, he thinks. It might be to Africa. Fancy that, fighting the war over there in jungles and that!'

Africa, America. It was all very far away.

'Then, when it's all over, Chuck will send for her and they'll get married out there so his folks can give them a proper do.' Her voice crumpled into a choke.

'I'm sorry she's going. But Joe hasn't told you to go has he? I don't want you to go to America. Or the little ones.'

She laughed. 'No, Billy. He's a lovely boy and a good dancer, but still a boy. I do worry about how he'll cope with Africa, boiling sun and natives.'

Billy had a sudden thought. 'What about Dwaine? Is he going too?'

'I suppose so. Same regiment.'

He dumped his end of the screwed up sheet in the second bucket, the dry one. Now Aunty would be sad again.

It was time to fold the mangled sheets ready for hanging out. He said in jerks between turning them, 'Please stop crying. Cheer up. Mary hasn't gone yet. Perhaps Chuck will like Africa so much he'll find a black lady to marry.' He felt in his satchel. 'Look, I've got biscuits. I saved them for you and the little ones. So don't cry anymore.'

He hadn't had much time to talk about his boots with Timmy and Sally before it was time to run home. There was a worried feeling in his stomach about Dwaine.

He rushed indoors to ask Mrs Pawsey if he could telephone the Vicarage. She looked at him closely.

'Something up, Billy?'

'No. I just wanted Aunty to come on Saturday. Mr Pawsey's going to invite Joe and Dwaine again. Aunty had fun last time and I think Dwaine's called for her, down at the WVS centre.'

'Ho, ho. Aren't you doing a bit of match-making?' She chuckled.

'I think the GIs are having to go away, that's the thing.' He picked up the egg basket to start his evening chores.

She nodded several times so that her under-chin shook, 'All right, my dear. We need to give them a good send-off, if that's the case.'

~

'No Kenneth?' Mrs Pawsey asked as Billy's family arrived on the Saturday.

'No. He made some excuse – and after all he's mature enough now to have his own friends and pastimes.' Mother sounded more than happy about that. 'Although I was a bit surprised. He's normally so keen to be round you, Billy. You haven't fallen out, have you?'

He shook his head.

Aunty said, 'Of course they haven't fallen out. Kenneth's just so busy with his art assignments. He's even sent him a note. Here you are, Billy.'

The envelope was closely sealed with a blob of pink sealing wax on the V.

Billy went upstairs with it, sensing trouble. He took out the folded sheet. It had skulls and crossbones all over the bottom of it but even the underlining looked threatening.

Billy

You're a measly rat. I told you at my show I didn't want that Eyetie around again. You said No, and so I got you the boots. I heard Aunty Marcia on the phone to Mrs Pawsey so I know it was all your idea to have the Eyetie round and get Mummy to visit you. You better watch out.

Kenneth

Billy put his hands on his middle, which suddenly felt very cold. He remembered shaking his head when Kenneth said didn't he hate Eyeties, and wouldn't he stop inviting them over, but he'd meant, No, he didn't hate them. Explaining wouldn't help. It would make it worse if Kenneth knew he'd planned for Aunty to go out with Dwaine.

How could he keep the boots safe? Suppose Kenneth pretended he needed them himself for school? Mother and Aunty would insist Kenneth had them back.

Loud barking below announced the GIs' arrival so he ran downstairs. Noah and Japhet wound themselves in and out of his legs as he waited for Dwaine to come up the path.

Dwaine had brought sugar, which made Mrs Pawsey throw up her hands and hug him. He also had cookies and two Heath bars. Without Kenneth, there was more to go round, but Billy couldn't enjoy his share. He put them in the cutlery drawer until he could take it to the Youldons.

While Mr Pawsey was talking shipping routes and war strategies with Joe, Aunty and Dwaine sat down together. Billy hovered near. They soon started chatting with smiles on their faces. They were getting on ever so well. Kenneth would hate it if he could see.

It was only after tea, when the men were lolling back smoking, that Dwaine told everyone they were being sent off to war, the two regiments together.

Everyone clucked and sighed. Billy's sigh was long – sad, but relieved too. He didn't want Dwaine to go and Aunty to lose her new friend, but if they weren't to be together, the problem of Kenneth doing something awful to the football boots was gone. He tried not to look at Aunty's doleful expression.

Dwaine's was rather serious too.

Joe said, 'I'm all for it. Shucks, we didn't come all this way to see no action. And how else would someone like us see North Africa, huh?'

'Had to happen, Dwaine,' Mr Pawsey said. 'You'se trained up now, ready for action, baint that so?'

'You bet,' said Dwaine, 'although we sure were having a darned good time here.'

'Super-duper,' said Joe.

'Do you know what you'll be doing?' Mrs Pawsey asked.

Joe laughed. 'Making it darned hot for the enemy, in a place where it's already darned hot.'

Billy thought of his Tarzan pictures. 'Is it jungle?'

Dwaine said, 'North Africa's more desert, so the nobs say. He tapped his nose. 'Seems I'll be driving a jeep for some colonel across those distant sands.' Then he looked at Aunty. 'But I'll be hoping to get back to jolly old England for someone more important, once we've won the war.'

Auntie blushed, and Billy rubbed his hands under the table. It was lucky Kenneth wasn't around to see that blush. Would he change his mind about Dwaine by the time the war was over? How could everyone stop Aunty being sad until then?

When Joe went down to the pigs with Mr Pawsey, Billy said, 'Can you stand by the gate, Dwaine? I'm going to take a photo of you. I've been saving my film for special things.'

'You want a snap of me! Gee, I'm bucked to think there'll be a record of me in Ol' England. Let me fasten my jacket and put my cap on for this.'

Billy collected his camera from the sideboard. Even though Aunty couldn't have Dwaine nearby for a few years, she'd feel a bit happier with a photograph of him.

'Reckon you'se a hit with our Billy, Dwaine, if he's using one of his precious snaps on you,' said Mr Pawsey.

'It's for his Aunty he wants it,' Mrs Pawsey whispered. It was embarrassing that she knew what he was thinking.

Billy got Dwaine to go outside the garden gate and into exactly the right position for the light.

'Well darn it, you're like a pro, Billy. Guess I'm like a film star now!'

They both were, great tall Joe and handsome Dwaine, with their wide smiles, corn cob smell and neat collars. They were like the green and red Sunny Jim pictures on the corn flake boxes, promising something much more special than plain, unsugared flakes.

He decided to put his camera away in the dark of the wardrobe until another special occasion. That might be Mr Finlay getting the football team together, or new piglets arriving or, if the war did ever end, Uncle Ted doing handstands on the garden path.

In any case, this was going to be a good photo of Dwaine in his cap, the summer sky blue behind him. He could fold a piece of cardboard to fit round it, like real photographers did. That way Aunty could hide it in her bag and then Kenneth wouldn't see it.

Mr Pawsey winked at him. 'Yes, my laddo. It might be a long time these Yanks are away. It be as well your Aunty has a photo.'

It was just a photo, but Billy had a very guilty feeling about the whole Dwaine thing. He was the one who had made it happen. He'd only wanted Aunty to be happy and go to dances like the other ladies, but he'd sort of cheated Kenneth. And he still had the boots.

CHAPTER SIXTEEN

November 1942. *Oran, Algeria falls to US troops*

He was with Alan standing behind the chicken coops ready to play, but the ball was still under Alan's arm. Billy looked down at his boots, so perfect for tipping the ball right to the edge of the lane. Alan stayed where he was.

'Come on.' Billy dropped on to one foot then the other. He rocked on his feet to and fro so that he could feel the studs under them. He and the boots were ready for action. 'Alan, come on. We haven't got long before my mother gets here.'

He peered at Alan's face. Working in the fields had made his freckles so close together he'd soon have a brown face instead of a pink one, and he was frowning. He grumbled, 'It's not the same without any of the GIs.'

'They gave us a smashing party, though, didn't they? All that singing, the grub and the hokey-cokey. I had two coca-colas. I *love* that drink.'

'So do I, but it's months since we had one.' Alan scuffed one foot into the dried dust of the chicken run. 'And I haven't had a letter from my father since September the second, and my mother hasn't either. She thinks he's in Asia.'

Billy thought of something cheery to say. 'Asia's the desert. He might meet our GIs there because it's very empty. I've got a picture of the desert in my *Best Boys' Stories*. I got it at the party. It's the first book I've had since I was eight and it's got airmen in it, too.'

'Has it?'

'Yes. You got *Marvel* with Captain America, didn't you? We can swap if you've finished it.'

'Okay.' His hair needed cutting and a lock trailed miserably over one eye.

'Listen, Alan.' He linked arms. Alan was his best friend. They told each other everything, like having to eat tripe, or being bullied, or worrying about whether their fathers were being shot. Even Alan's mother was right in the thick of it, because of her secret work in the Piccadilly office and Alan hadn't had a visit for ages. Billy jerked at his arm. 'You're coming to my place. There's sponge for tea with red jam. It's because Dwaine left a big bag of sugar for us so Mrs Pawsey could bake stuff. We'll play football a bit later, won't we?' He took the ball from Alan and toed it to and fro.

Voices sounded from down the lane.

'Hey, the bus must have been early. That's Jill's voice.'

Mother's sounded soon after. He pulled Alan to go and meet them. Aunty wasn't with them this time, but Kenneth was. He wore a pale blue shirt with short sleeves and it was too large for him, mostly round the chest, so that it bagged and flapped as he sauntered along, holding a notebook under one arm. Mrs Shawditch must have had another pile of jumble to share out.

Alan stood smartly, feet together, pushing his hair into better order while Billy ran forward.

Mother bent down to look at his knees. 'Not too bad.'

He opened his mouth to tell her all his latest news but she held up a hand. 'I'll tell you our news in a bit, Billy. I must get indoors and take the weight off my feet first. Hello, Alan. What a nice, smart boy you always look. Thank goodness Billy has one decent contact in this place.'

Kenneth passed Billy then nodded to Alan. He followed Mother past the front gate and into the front yard but not through the front door. Once Mother was out of hearing range, he turned to Billy and Alan, putting a finger under his nose and cocking his chin up, 'I note, you two, few nasty smells here today. The company in this environment has improved.' His eyebrows raised a touch. 'Civilised without Yanks and especially Eyeties, isn't it?'

Alan scowled and clenched his fists. Billy nudged him to walk away a few steps. 'Typical.'

'He's talking about Dwaine.'

'I know. It's because of Aunty. I feel like bashing him.'

Alan nodded. 'Swine. But aren't you scared about him taking back your boots? Anyway, it wouldn't be right to bash him. Let's just ignore him.'

Alan always knew the right thing to do. Billy sighed. 'All right.' He pulled him towards the front door.

The dogs barked and ran around in circles claiming attention but Mother was striding down the hall with flushed cheeks, pulling Jill almost fiercely behind. Jill was getting a little bold these days and she rolled her eyes at Billy as Mother pressed forward into the kitchen.

'Mrs Pawsey, good afternoon. Listen to the latest government demand. Would you believe it! I've been sent to work at the garage to take calls and fill petrol tanks. It's two miles walk each way, too. As if what I do at the vicarage isn't work enough! I'm sure you're glad you're not a woman under fifty so that you can remain here at leisure with your dogs and chickens.'

'I dare say I shall keep busy enough,' said Mrs Pawsey. She'd been cooking since early that morning for a fundraising tea. Billy had done all the washing up. All the tea money was going to prisoners of war. And she had all her ordinary work on top.

Mother was an embarrassment. She turned to Billy. 'I have to warn you that I won't be able to visit so often, Billy. The weekends will be my only chance to do things for myself.'

'And I'm having to stay at school all day,' said Jill in a happy voice. Now that she was mixing with other children, Jill had stopped clinging to Mother and Kenneth. She smiled up at Billy and Alan. 'Shall we go in the room where the dogs are?'

Billy had a quick check around. Kenneth hadn't come inside yet. He was still outside sketching the doorway in his notebook.

Billy led Jill and Alan into the parlour. Japhet slid off the leather chair with a guilty expression. 'Naughty boy!' said Jill, then stroking and hugging him. When they'd played with the dogs for a while, Billy said, 'Let's play cards. Beggar your Neighbour?' He took out a pack of cards from the sideboard drawer and dealt.

They were playing a slow game for Jill's benefit when Kenneth came indoors to see what they were doing. Alan played a card, Jill followed.

'You have to pay me two for that, Jill.'

Kenneth butted in, 'For goodness' sake, teach her the suits first. She's a novice, remember.'

Jill put down two cards. Billy played on, remembering to ignore Kenneth, and his last move made him the winner. He put a thumb up at Alan.

Kenneth flicked the jokers across the table. 'Don't you aspire to something more than games of chance at your age?'

Kenneth's fancy words made Billy feel stupid. It would be jolly nice to kick his sarcasm away and leave a stud pattern on his skinny legs.

Alan stood up and stretched. He wouldn't like being told what to do. 'I've decided to go back to the Manor, Billy. We'll play later, right?'

'But there's jam sponge.'

'Still.' Alan jerked his head at the cards to show what he meant, and made off down the path.

Now Alan was out of the way, Kenneth turned mean and grouchy. He lifted the cards and tipped them all over the table.

'Hey! What's that for?'

'Mummy's getting airmail from that greasy Yank. Your fault.' He dug a finger into Billy's chest. 'Interfering dummy!' He stomped around the room, wagging his finger.

Jill tidied up the cards, watching carefully. Perhaps Kenneth was sometimes like this back in the Vicarage, perhaps even with Aunty. There wasn't anything Billy could say.

Kenneth did another round of the room, his stupid head wagging as if he was an old teacher telling the class off. 'Mummy needn't think *Doo Wayne*'s coming back from war to walk out with her again. When the war ends, they'll send the Yanks straight home to *Tha Stades*. I'll be an adult by then and then she'll have to listen to my advice.'

Billy pushed his chin forward. 'It's five years till you're sixteen. The war's never going to last that long.'

'Fat lot you know, twerp.'

'The U.S troops won Algeria.'

'Won! Huh! They just happened to be there when the Algerians gave up. We brought the newspaper so Mr Pawsey could read about *Britain* in the war, allies who've been there from the beginning fighting in the *difficult* places.'

'Like my Uncle Ted.'

'Probably a prisoner of war by now.'

'Rotter.'

Teatime interrupted Kenneth's rant and Jill ran into the dining room ahead of him. It was because of Dwaine that Kenneth was being so mean. Billy played safe and moved his football boots from their usual place. He hid them with the cleaning cloths in the scullery. Kenneth wouldn't look for them there.

Mother dominated the conversation over the tea table. 'Wonderful to wash my hands in your bathroom. I never thought I'd appreciate something so simple as Lifebuoy soap. Oof! That petrol pump makes my hands so dirty and smelly that I can't wash them clean enough. There is *no* soap at the garage, although I've asked and asked, and we're reduced to a sliver of Sunlight at the vicarage. Dwaine gave Doreen a lovely bar of soap, lucky thing, so she and Kenneth have that luxury at their billet all to themselves. All my headscarves positively stink of petrol now and by the time Friday comes, my poor hair is just desperate for its wash.'

Kenneth ate his bread and marge grimly, refusing the fish paste and only pushing it towards Billy after he'd been asked twice. The cake was jolly nice, but when everyone else said so, Kenneth just continued chewing silently.

As soon as tea finished, Billy made himself busy with his outside chores. That way he couldn't get into an argument.

~

After the family had gone home, his own words seemed to hang in the air. *The war won't last that long.* To say it might be like a jinx and make more war last even longer. It was like boasting you'd be best at something, and then finding you weren't. It was a very scary thought.

If the war did last until Kenneth was sixteen, think of all the soldiers who wouldn't be coming home, the children at school crying and crying because it had been their father who'd bought it. Uncle Frank had bought it although he wasn't fighting, Dad had to fight although he didn't believe in war, and Uncle Ted had fought right from the beginning and must, must, must be safe.

In the parlour, Mr Pawsey was settled into his old leather chair with the newspaper. He didn't normally bother with one, now that wartime newspapers were so skinny. After reading Billy the headlines, he just grunted every now and then and didn't chat. Mrs Pawsey said he'd seen the names of men he knew among the dead.

Were people Billy knew from Wandsworth among the dead? Could Uncle Ted really be a prisoner of war? He fetched his old heroes book from the top of the settle. Although he'd read it umpteen times already, he liked holding an old book, a book that came from Mr Durban's home, the home that held the shashka. Dad might be in danger, the G.Is definitely were, Uncle might be lost in Belgium or Holland or France. They were all heroes. He hadn't thought he could ever be a hero himself, until that time Mrs Youldon said he was one. But being nearly drowned was as much as he could bear. He really didn't think he could manage being a British soldier under constant fire, like Mr Durban had been in Russia, like the soldiers were in Europe. He turned a page. Joan of Arc died in an actual fire, and there was a picture of her standing in it.

The only way to calm the wonky feeling inside of him was to imagine the shashka in his hands. It was what he always did when things were scary. He hurried up to his bedroom to pull it from its special place. He slid his hand under the mattress and into the gap of the wooden frame, but it wasn't there!

He sat down low, level with the mattress and peered all along the gap. He put his knee under the mattress edge to make sure there was no way the envelope could have dropped out. He felt around until his legs had cramp, squatting by his bed, one hand under the mattress. His shashka picture really had gone.

His chest hurt and he felt sick. No one knew this hiding place so it meant someone had been snooping around. The only people who ever came in were Alan, Mr and Mrs Pawsey, Kenneth and Mother. Kenneth was the obvious person to snoop, of course, but then he'd have taunted Billy with it, waved it around and sneered at Billy's keepsake. In fact, he'd gone off home quite politely, even praising Billy when Mrs Pawsey mentioned his latest football triumphs.

Alan was his best friend; he wasn't the sort of person who took things that didn't belong to him and he'd never, never take Billy's most special possession, even for fun.

Mother might take the photo, thinking a sabre wasn't the sort of thing he should look at, but then surely she would have said something critical like, 'It's disappointing that you want to spend your time looking at weapons.'

Mr Pawsey – if he'd been moving the bed or taking the mattress off – might not have realised the picture was special, might even have thrown it away! That would be dreadful, for then it would never come back. It would be truly lost.

Mrs Pawsey might have accidentally shifted something when she changed his sheets. But then why wouldn't she have given it to him? He thought back to the first time he'd hidden it there. It was after his first night at the Pawseys. Mrs Pawsey had asked if he had a comforter, a teddy or a blanket. He'd told her that he had something special and he might show her one day. But he never had! She'd shown him her special picture after Uncle Frank had died, she'd trusted him and shown him it in her bedroom, the picture of Gordon. He'd never shown her his picture in return although he had always trusted her really tremendously. There just hadn't been a time when the subject of sabres came up. Was Mrs Pawsey so disappointed that he hadn't shown her his secret that she'd taken it away to teach him a lesson?

Without the shashka to hold, he was alone against all enemies. He put his arms around his middle. His insides fluttered horribly.

Everything felt very shaky, especially not knowing who had taken the picture away. He sidled downstairs. How best to ask?

In the parlour Mr Pawsey was fixing the shove-ha'penny board where the markers had come loose.

'Please, did you ever have to fix my bed, or move it?'

Mr Pawsey looked mystified. 'Your bed? Move it? No, my lad. Far as I'm concerned that bed's as fixed as my own. There for good, see.'

'I just wondered if anything had fallen out, any time?'

'Fallen out? What you on about, lad? Have you been jumping on the mattress and broken sommat on it?'

'No.' This was going wrong and it was obvious that Mr Pawsey knew nothing about any picture. It would be even more difficult asking Mrs Pawsey, especially as it was more likely her. He moved slowly into the sitting room where she was struggling with her knitting again.

'What's up, lovey?'

'I've lost something. I wondered if you'd found it? It was in a secret place in my room.'

'What sort of thing would that be?'

'A picture. A photo, in an envelope. I did mean to show you, but it isn't of a person, you see, and . . .'

'No, dear. I haven't seen any picture. Tuesday I cleaned your room and I haven't been in there since. When did you last see it?'

He hung his head. 'I look at it most days.'

The sick feeling was worse. He didn't want to think about what was obvious. Kenneth, so angry about Dwaine. Billy had stayed out in the garden after tea, and Kenneth had stayed in. He must have spent the time up here, searching for something to take or spoil. A photo of a sabre would be far more interesting to him then boots. He'd have lots of questions about it. Would he tear it up out of spite? Would he ever give it back? What could Billy do to persuade him?

Mrs Pawsey clicked her teeth. 'That's a shame your picture's missing, Billy. Perhaps it will turn up.'

'Was Kenneth in my room when I was feeding the chickens and collecting the pig swill?'

She kept on knitting. 'I reckon as he was. He wasn't down here with your mother.'

Billy didn't need to say anymore. He knew it was Kenneth's punishment for bringing Dwaine into Aunty's life. He went to the scullery and sat by the dogs. Noah licked his knees and Japhet put his head against Billy's side.

He couldn't tell Mrs Pawsey how important the shashka was. A boy of eleven holding a photo to make himself feel safe! It would seem dreadfully silly. The only person he could complain to was Alan who knew the whole story and what the shashka meant. But how had Kenneth known that he had anything special or where to search for it? It couldn't just be luck. He'd never ever taken out the shashka when Kenneth was even in the house, had he?

Billy sat on the stairs, his head in his hands, thinking back through all the visits. Then he sat up with a jerk. There had been one time. The night Kenneth stayed, the night after Uncle Frank died. The time when there had been the terrible crying, Billy had pulled out the shashka and waved it to and fro, lending its power to Kenneth. Surely, Kenneth hadn't been watching him even then?

That night, Billy didn't find it easy to sleep. It was the first time that he'd had to sleep without his shashka on guard under his mattress. He'd had it from the very first day he arrived at the Pawseys'. Thank goodness he'd taken Mr Durban's letter out of the envelope when he'd found the hiding place to keep with other letters. At least Kenneth wouldn't have any hint about where he'd got the photograph, or who had given it to him.

~

When he got to school, he told Alan straight away. Alan was quite clear what had to be done. 'You must face him with it.'

'They're not even coming over much now because of Mother's job. It might be six weeks before their next visit, and even then he might decide not to come. He's got good reason not to! By now he could have binned it, or torn it up.'

'You could phone him. Phone your mother and get your Aunty to go through his things.'

'She wouldn't. Even if she did, how can I explain what I've lost? I'd have to say where I got it, and then Kenneth will know about Mr

Durban and the whole thing. It'll be awful. As it is, when we're back in Wandsworth he's going to want to go where I go, and know who I know.'

Alan made a fist and crossed it over Billy's fist. 'Rotten business. I'll help if I can.'

Billy hunched his shoulders and followed Alan into school. There was no way round the problem. He'd have to wait until he saw Kenneth next. He'd get him away from the house and have the whole thing out. If only Kenneth was a German, he could kill him and no one would mind.

Meanwhile, he'd be like a soldier without armour, a Cossack without his horse, Kenneth without his art.

CHAPTER SEVENTEEN

April 11th 1943. *Cheese ration to be cut to 3oz per week.*

Alan and Billy had both learned to knit now and a hated job was easier if they did it together. They were as fast as Mrs Pawsey. They all sat in the parlour with the wireless on. There was pretty miserable stuff on the news. Just as the allies were getting some successes abroad, the rationing was getting worse.

Mr Pawsey seemed to mind it the most. 'This'll be the third cut this year. Goodness me, we thought as we were badly off in January when it was ten ounces, and worse in February when it was seven! Three ounces! Ha — one bite, an' it'll be gone!'

Mrs Pawsey always took things in her stride. 'They've let us have another pint of milk instead, so that'll be for making butter and cheese.'

'Curds and whey at the Manor, I bet,' Alan groaned. 'We already get it at school dinners and I hate it.'

'Now, now. We have to think - it's better than our boys are getting in the trenches.'

Billy started knitting faster at the thought. Soldiers needed socks more than anything.

Alan's father was an officer working in communications, but that didn't seem to help Alan. He hadn't had a letter for months. 'My father might be a prisoner of war and not get *anything* to eat.'

Mrs Pawsey put a comforting hand on his. 'No, Alan. You'd have heard if he was a POW. They're allowed to write letters home as long as they don't say where they are. Ronnie's brother is a POW and I know his mother gets letters.'

'An' even them as has become prisoners, there's that Geneva Convention. It's the rule - prisoners of war have to be treated right, see.' Mr Pawsey nodded at Alan.

Billy couldn't imagine Dad as a prisoner of war. It was easier to think of him in a Nissan hut, probably teaching the others what to do. 'My father doesn't write much and then he usually quotes things. *Best foot forward,* and that. He always quotes sayings by famous people, like dead writers or even Romans. I don't know what he means half the time. When I think I do, I get it wrong.'

Kenneth accompanied Mother to the Pawseys next visit. This time he came up the lane with a long decorated jacket and no sleeves that fitted over his ordinary clothes. It was very foreign-looking, and when Kenneth got near, the decorations turned out to be sewn flowers and leaves. He looked flipping stupid.

'Like my artist's jacket? Mrs Shawditch found it at the church fête and thought it would be just right for me.'

Billy didn't answer. Did Kenneth really think he'd forgotten about the missing picture?

'Shame about that American ship going down with all hands, isn't it? Full of GIs, it was.'

Kenneth was trying to rattle him. Dwaine's regiment had all been flown out, so they wouldn't be on any ship.

Mother breezed indoors with a case full of woollens and cast off clothes. 'Some woollies to unravel and some of these men's clothes will fit Billy, or can be altered, Mrs Pawsey. The rest will find good homes, I'm sure. I must say our vicarage is quite rich in clothing materials.'

She was flushed and cheerful, full of stories about her garage job.

'It seems to be suiting you well,' Mrs Pawsey remarked.

'Oh yes. Now that Kenneth can take himself to school and choir, and Jill is settled in nursery school, I'm much freer. Freer to work, don't you know?' and her laugh trilled down the hall.

Billy tried to get Mother to one side, but Kenneth kept picking up something for her, or sorting her piles of clothes so that his head was always between Billy's and Mother's. Billy's clenched fists itched to grasp hold of Kenneth and get some answers about his shaska picture. 'We'll go down to the field, Kenneth. There's something I need to show you.'

Kenneth looked pleased at first, as if Billy had made him a present, but then as Billy marched smartly down past the pig sty, the chicken house, the coops and towards the horse's field, his expression became wary.

It didn't matter. Billy wanted him to be uneasy, to wonder what was coming, a football challenge, a beautiful plant to paint or some baby animals.

There was a shed with old farming tools not far from the horse and this was the spot Billy had chosen in all the weeks he had been waiting for this moment. He leant against the door and crossed his arms, partly to stop himself hitting out.

'Is there something you need to tell me, Kenneth?'

Kenneth hesitated. There was nowhere for him to sit or lean without standing right close to Billy. His expression became sly. 'Are you sure you want me to tell you, old thing?'

Billy's muscles tensed from the top of him to his feet. Had the blighter torn his photo up? 'You'd better come out with it,' he said through his teeth.

Kenneth swept one foot over the other and rested it on its toe, his foreign jacket billowing out behind him in the wind. He put one hand over his chin as if he had a beard to stroke.

Billy leant forward and grasped Kenneth's shirt collar. 'You have something of mine, haven't you? Something that you took, stole, from my bedroom after snooping around last time you were over here.'

Kenneth raised an eyebrow and tried to shake his neck free of Billy's hold. 'Have I? And what might that be, pray?'

'Stop talking in that soppy voice with stupid choirboy words.'

'Then I can't answer your query if I'm not allowed to talk.' He tried again to wrest himself free.

Billy held on more firmly. 'I had a secret place in my bedroom, it's not secret now and I shan't use it again, but I had something hidden there and after your visit, it was gone.'

'Oh dear. Tragic. What was it now — a colouring page, a set of pretty scraps?'

'You know jolly well,' Billy gave a shake to each word.

'Remind me.'

'A photograph.'

'Ah yes. Let go and we'll discuss it.'

Billy let go, and strode a few paces to and fro in front of Kenneth, breathing heavily. Would the rotten beast have torn it up?

'Let's see, now. If I did have a little snap safely amongst my treasures, what might it be worth if you wanted it back? You do want it back, do you, or should I bin it with the other rubbish?'

'Why are you doing this, Kenneth? Why are you so beastly all the time? What's *wrong* with you?'

Kenneth's face lost its superior smirk and his eyes hardened. 'I think you know. People who interfere in other people's lives deserve to be punished.' He turned swiftly, pushing his face into Billy's, 'Don't they?'

Billy pushed first Kenneth's chest to move his face from his, then his back, just hard enough to unbalance his pose. Kenneth wobbled and couldn't prevent a couple of running steps. 'Oh, it's going to be fisticuffs, now, is it? All about a silly little sword. Shall we call Jill to be referee?'

Billy gave him another push and started striding back to the house. Firstly he needed to check with Mother about Uncle Ted and *mental problems*. Secondly, now that Kenneth had admitted stealing the photo, it should be possible to shame him into returning it.

Kenneth walked behind him. 'You could get it back by telling me where you got it and why it's important.'

Billy slowed his stride. Of course Kenneth would want to know that, and anything else he could get out of Billy. But if he told Kenneth, if he even told Mother what Kenneth had taken, he'd have to go on to explain why he had it. At the moment, Kenneth didn't know. That was obvious because he'd called it a *sword*. He gritted his teeth. Best to keep things that way. He strode on and left Kenneth to guess what he would do next.

Indoors, Kenneth took out his sketch book and began drawing the three Toby jugs on the dining room mantlepiece. Mother would still be in hearing distance.

Billy said loudly, 'So you admit stealing my picture, Kenneth?'

Kenneth outlined the handle of the fat coachman jug. 'Sorry?'

Billy said it again, more loudly.

'I've no idea what you're talking about. You've lost something, have you?'

'What is it you've lost, Billy?' Mother called.

Billy leant against the wall, outside the open dining room door. He'd looked forward to saying, *It's all right, Kenneth's admitted stealing my picture*, and then everyone exclaiming so that Kenneth had to hand it back, looking sheepish and guilty. But if he had to explain what the picture was, and whose it was, and why he'd been given it, that was too high a price to pay.

The tomato-coloured jacket with its fancy stitching lay across the chair next to Kenneth. How would he like losing that? Suppose it went missing, stuffed behind the straw in the pig pen, given to the clothes collection at the church hall? But then he'd be as bad as Kenneth, a liar, a thief, or even worse, if he damaged it. And sure and sure, Kenneth would still have the photograph, ready to wave in Billy's face on the right occasion. He might even have the cheek to pretend he was just keeping it safe. He always kept himself looking as if he was in the right.

All in all, better to let Kenneth keep the photograph, not knowing what it truly was, until he forgot all about it.

Billy had been without his picture for so long, managed without it so long, that if he could just wait till the war ended, he could see the real shashka, and not just its picture. He strode on down to stroke the dogs, and then to the kitchen where he was due to peel potatoes.

If he was at home, he could at least go to Boots library to find pictures of sabres in one of the encyclopaedias. Here there was no library apart for the small private one in the town. The school had only a few battered books on the headmaster's bookcase, apart from the small pile of Beacon readers.

Billy found Alan in the lane next day struggling along pushing a pram overloaded with bags of paper for re-cycling.

'I'll help you with that.'

'Thanks. It'd help if this pram had four wheels!' It was Alan's turn to take all the scrap paper to the tin shed on Broad Street.

Billy took the corner of the pram hood, holding in the paper and keeping the pram from tipping to one side. It was a good chance to offload all he had to tell Alan about Kenneth's latest.

'I did confront him. I could've bashed him, but I didn't. He admitted it, you know, but indoors when Mother was listening, he pretended he didn't know what I was talking about.'

Alan nodded, listening sympathetically as Billy explained why he couldn't go further. 'Listen, I've found something super for you. It'll cheer you up. Come up to the Manor when we've finished this.'

Billy began to feel better. It was good having someone to tell who knew the whole story and understood. Perhaps Alan had some goodies to share out of a parcel from his mother.

They dumped the pram load in the shed and turned the high wooden catch so that little kids couldn't get inside.

'Race you to the Manor,' and Alan took off at speed.

They slowed down and caught their breath as they got to the Manor's side entrance.

'We have to wash our hands first, and then I'll show you why.'

Upstairs, but only on the first floor, the arched area that led to the huge mahogany door was empty of nuns and everyone else. 'I am allowed, don't worry.'

Alan led him through the door and up to another. When he pushed that open, Billy couldn't help gasping. It was full of books, up to the ceiling and around all four walls. A little staircase with a post stood beneath a pair of glass doors that someone had left open. For a few moments, they both walked round each wall in turning, looking up and down the millions of books.

Alan was proud. 'This is the Manor library, and only two of the nuns and the land girl are allowed in here, and that's because they look after it.'

'But who lets you?'

'It's only recent. Remember Rachel? She wasn't much good at the farming work, but Mr Partington senior who owns the Manor and lives in this private wing, heard that she had a degree in history. He said she could look after the books and just do the packing of fruit and veg.'

'So she lets you come in and read all the books? Whee. Why just you?'

'Rachel's specially nice to me. It's because my mother's office did something that helped her father. It was to do with hiding him or getting him away from one place and off to do war work. I don't know, I'm not allowed to know. I just know he's alive and she didn't expect him to be. When Kenneth took your sabre picture, I asked her to see if there was one in here so I could show you.'

Billy grasped Alan's arm. 'Really, truly? Did she find one?'

'No, but she kept on looking and last week she did find this.' He pointed to his right. 'Now you see why we had to have clean hands. This is valuable.' A book with faded maroon covers lay closed on one of the padded seats that surrounded the room beneath the bookcases. 'Look at this! *Classic stories from the Russian Empire.* Shame there aren't any pictures.' He picked up the book and carefully opened it where a cardboard strip marked the place.

Billy saw small print on yellowing paper, a line drawing halfway down the page. He started reading, and perched with Alan on the seat, the book placed between them.

The new Cossack, strong and dark, mounted his horse, ready to embark on a raid in a distant land. Beneath him, the kazachii ybraynii sedlo, a saddle decorated with the booty of Grandfather's previous raids and pillages. Now his old life of idle freedom was behind him together with his adolescence and he must accept his responsibilities as a member of the group. Thus he would be identified as a man.

Last night, the songs round the campfire had described the possibilities of death and glorified the brutality of war. Death would be an honour! He threw out his chest. He was young, death just could not happen. A sword that managed to kill him would be honoured with the name Shashka lixodaika, the name which identified it as legendary for downing an invincible Cossack warrior.

He already had a shashka himself. He put one hand on its hilt as the sun hinted a presence on the horizon. He sniffed the air, fresh with the scent of feral cat, ripe for the hunt.

If he was the grandson of a rabble-rouser, one of the motley escapees of the political and penal systems of Polish Ukraine seeking the freer frontier, he was, above all, a Cossack. His grandfather's generation had developed military prowess to defend themselves against raids, and thus his father had been raised. Like other Cossacks, Father had learned a nomadic lifestyle to avoid enemies. He lived in a constant readiness to fight. So impossible was it to settle, farm and feed themselves this way, they depended on fishing, hunting but mostly pillage. The spoils displayed on Grandfather's saddle symbolized the honour of a Cossack warrior.

He had only known his father part-time, for Cossacks must leave their wives and children the moment duty called to embark on raids. But during those times at home before his honourable death, Father was memorable. He starred in all aspects of Cossack culture – the haunting folk songs, wild athletic dancing and dramatic, aggressive horse-riding.

Eventually the Tsar employed the fearless Cossacks to defend Russia's borderlands and it was in such a way that Father died. His compatriots brought him to the family for his final hours, enough time for him to croak his wish to his only son.

'Take this shashka, son of mine, and let it only leave your hands in those of your son, or in death, of a noble warrior as brave as you must

become. Mind its path, protect it well. It will inflict the most terrible wounds.'

After his father's death, he put it to one side, had wild times, passionate times, ruined his mother's hopes of his heroism then sped back to renew them.

And now, the camp fires dead and his comrades mounted beside him, it was time to ride forth. Ahead of him, twenty years and many skirmishes on, would be the Great War. But for the Shashka, a much longer history awaited its terrible potential.

When he reached the last words, Billy's eyes stretched wide as he looked at Alan. 'Whoa!

'See. The story's like Mr Durban's, except it wasn't his father who gave him the shaska.'

'Isn't there any more to the story? I want to know what happens next.'

'Rachel says these are extracts.'

'Oh. Can I borrow the book?'

'Course not. We can only look at it here. No-one's allowed to take anything out of the library. They trust me to come in and not touch anything behind glass. I think it's only because of Rachel, and Mr Partington being at the ceremony when we got rewarded for saving Sally.'

'But I saved Sally, so I'd be allowed in.'

'You're not a Manor vaccie, though.'

It was a difficult book to read, and Billy hadn't understood all the words, couldn't even read one or two of them. 'But I need to read it again. Well, lots of times.'

'When I'm with you, it's probably all right. Anyway, does it make up, a bit, for losing your photograph?'

'Rather. It was spiffing of you to find it. Well, of Rachel too. And I'm glad about her father, if that was really true about Jews.' He sat further back on the seat and read right the way through again. He didn't need a picture of a shaska so much now. He could just think over this story as many times as he liked.

'Look here. *On into the Great War,* Alan. Hey, that means this story's before the time of the Cossack who gave it to Mr Durban! Suppose it was the same shashka!'

Alan gave a little shudder. 'If it was ... it says it has a longer terrible history after that.'

CHAPTER EIGHTEEN

June 12th 1944. *U.S troops liberate Rome*

It was jolly hot! Billy plodded beside Alan as they made their three-mile walk home from the secondary school. He pulled his satchel off his shoulder. 'Phew. I'm flipping well going to rest in a minute.'

At the grassy hill-top leading down to the village, they flopped down and chucked their heavy satchels to one side. They lay on their backs in the sunshine watching the buzzards wheel. The four fields around and below them shone blue, baby blue, Mother would call it.

'You see all that flax? It's the same colour as an awful buster suit I had to wear when I was small. It made me itch all over.'

'Flax? I wondered what it was. Those fields weren't all blue last year.' He pulled a dandelion out of the ground beside him and chewed the end.

'Mr Pawsey says the farmers will be glad when they're allowed to change crops, flax needs so many workers. They haven't got enough land girls. They need us boys. You don't even go up to the farm although you're *sinewy and spry.*' He laughed and poked Alan in the ribs. That's what Mr Finlay called you, and it's about right.'

'You're a head taller. I'm better delivering the groceries. It's hard enough work.' Alan blew dandelion seeds to the wind. He said, 'We won't be doing any of that stuff when we get home. How long've we been here now?'

Billy thought a moment. 'We got here August '40 the second time, wasn't it? Or was it before?'

'End of July, I think. No, I'd just started junior school, so it was early September. That makes it - nearly four years. And if we add the first time, 1939, when we were at Mrs Youldon's, we've spent a good third of our lives here.'

'You reckon? It feels like half of it.'

'It was my father pointed it out when he wrote. Now he's safely back in his regiment, he says he really resents how much the war has cost him in time, let alone anything else. I bet he can't wait to get home.'

'I can't imagine living in London now; here feels like home.'

'Not for me. I can't wait for the war to end. It's more like a boarding school, lined up in camp beds in that attic room. I'll be flipping glad to get my own room back and all to myself.'

'Yeah, lucky blighter.' Billy sighed. 'Think of me sharing mine with Kenneth.'

'It's only fair. You've been lucky these years up at the Pawseys, a room to yourself.'

Billy lay back and looked at the plain blue sky. He had been lucky. Now that the allies had some successes, war might end. There'd be no bombing, no killings, no sending soldiers to foreign lands — but without war, he'd lose this life. There'd be no farmhouse, no dogs, no pigs, no Pawseys. No Alan.

He sat up, slowly. 'When this lot's all over, you and me'll still be able to get together, won't we? It's not that far from Wandsworth to Thornton Heath.'

'You can bus it. I remember going to Wandsworth when the new council building opened. It's a 109 isn't it?'

A couple of terrier dogs appeared, barking and leaping at each other. Billy whipped out his camera from his satchel. He lay down and snapped upwards. 'I'm going to need an album soon, I've got so many photos now — thanks to your mother getting those 120s.'

'Thanks to those Belgians working with her. Can't you ask for an album for your birthday?'

'I didn't get far with her over the boots, did I? If Kenneth hadn't got me some, Mother would never have got round to the idea.'

'You're going to grow out of those boots soon.'

'Already have. Mr Pawsey split the backs for me so I can still wear them. They do hurt a bit, but not as much as playing in plimsolls.'

Alan grinned, 'So a hard choice, chum, new boots or album.'

'Won't get either. Mother won't see the need for a photograph album. She thinks photos are for the mantelpiece in silver frames.' Screwing up his eyes, he could visualise the ones at home in Wandsworth. They were on the bookcase in the garden room; himself as a toddler, two of Jill in frills, and the wedding photo. Both Mother and Dad looked stern, almost as if they knew a war would start a few years later.

'Those aren't the sort of photographs I'm interested in taking. I want real life action, people doing things, not just standing and looking. If I can just get photos of exciting or interesting things like ...'

Alan was lying full length, his head on his satchel. '...like one of yourself pulling Sally from the water that time!'

Billy grinned. 'Yes, you bet.' That would be good, just so that people always know he'd really done that, so that he'd know himself.

A droning in the distance made them both jump up.

Alan shouted upwards, 'Hey - yippee! A heck of a lot of 'em.' A lead plane came into view through a sliver of cloud and then the whole formation. 'There must be a hundred, two hundred!'

They whooped and leapt up, waving, watching the vast bank of planes come over then fade into the distance.

'What about that!'

Alan peered at the white trails. 'Some German town is going to cop it tonight.'

Billy shivered. 'Suppose all the people there want revenge? They'd put iron helmets on and pour over the Channel, all up the beaches and along the lanes, coming for us.'

'Daft! You know what happens to people when there's bombing. No chance of them going anywhere.'

Billy gave him a push. 'So! Just saying, *suppose* ...'

They watched till sound of the planes had faded to a murmur. Billy said, 'Your mother'll come for you one day soon, and then we'll know war's nearly over.'

Alan punched the air. 'We'll have toys and sweets and lights in the street at night and meat and ice-cream and no queuing.'

Billy shrugged, blinking hard. That seemed far away. 'Can't think what it'll be like now in Wandsworth. Angela said loads of it's bombed.' He kicked a pile of pebbles into a straight line.

Alan leant over and lined them all up into the formation all the planes had just made. There was no sight of them now. He jumped to his feet and shouldered his satchel. 'Come on, forward to the downward path!'

This was their usual game. Billy took the hill at a run and they reached the bottom, and the edge of the village side by side. 'Come to mine, then we'll go to the Youldons after tea, okay?'

When they got as far as the horse's field, they saw Mr and Mrs Pawsey pulling rhubarb. Billy shouted, 'Did you see all those planes? Alan'n me saw them, hundreds of them.'

'No missing'em, was there?' Mr Pawsey said slowly. 'We're on the offensive, no doubt about that. We's'll have to wait and see what happens now.'

They were eating bread and dripping and Mrs Pawsey was topping up the tea-pot when the telephone rang. She wasn't in the hall long.

'There's news for you, Billy. Your mother's had a telegram from your Nanny. Your Uncle Ted has been invalided home. He's in a military hospital, recuperating.'

All the crumbs fell off Billy's lap as he leapt up. 'Uncle Ted! He's my favourite person. Recuperating? That means getting better, doesn't it?' He whooped and whistled around the room.

'It's wonderful news to know he's safe, dear, even though he's injured. The receiver's still off. Do you want to talk to Kenneth? It's him who's phoned.'

Kenneth. All these weeks since the business of the shaska and Kenneth had only come that once, probably to avoid trouble. Now something wonderful was happening it was Kenneth giving the news. *Billy's* news. He rushed into the hall. His hand felt damp on the telephone receiver as he squeezed it tight. 'Kenneth?'

'Yes, it's moi. Long time, eh, Billy? Aunty Marcia though't you'd be pleased to hear this, so I said I'd phone. Your Uncle's back - in a hospital, in Sussex.'

Was it true? Kenneth wouldn't dare make that up. That very thing he'd been aching for, Uncle Ted safe in England. *Hospital.* What sort of injured? He jolly well wasn't going to ask Kenneth. It was too bad how he always knew everything first.

And there was the secret matter of the shaska between them. Did Kenneth really think that a gap in visits could make Billy forget?

'Pass me over to Mother, Kenneth,' he said, trying not to let the quiver in his voice sound.

'But ...'

'I need to speak to her.' He couldn't let Kenneth be top dog.

Mother came to the phone. 'Hello dear. Yes, good news. Nanny was informed yesterday. She says that Uncle Ted is quite safe and in a military hospital.'

'But what's his injuries? Will he be better soon?'

'I don't have much information, Billy. We'll see. The main thing is, he's home.'

Alan stood up and clapped him on the shoulder. 'See, chums stick together. News from my father last month, from your Uncle Ted today.'

~

Sickeningly, just when Billy wanted Mother to himself to find out all possible details about Uncle Ted, Kenneth decided to visit with her. This time, he had his science exercises under his arm. Each page held a different topic, diagrams and notes in tiny neat writing.

'Science, old thing. Even if they get you to a secondary school, I doubt if you'll do much of that. It won't be for proper studying, more for teaching you how to hold a block of wood or metal, I expect. That place probably doesn't even own a bunsen burner!'

Billy put one hand in the centre of Kenneth's bony chest and pushed him firmly backwards into the yard. 'Stay there with your rotten pieces of science notes. I'm going to talk to Mother.'

Kenneth stepped forward again. 'I shouldn't.'

'Why?' Billy crossed his arms over his chest.

'Well, you see,' Kenneth leant forward as if he was explaining something basic to Jill, 'Aunty Marcia hasn't told you, Billy, but your uncle's got mental problems and he'll be in hospital for some time.'

Billy's arms uncrossed and fell down to his sides.

Kenneth had his superior expression, although he hadn't even GOT a second uncle and if Dad was really now 'Dad' to him, Kenneth hadn't even got *one* uncle. 'Sad, isn't it? Mental problems. I wonder if it will run in the family.'

Billy took the four steps that separated him from Kenneth. From here, he could actually look down on him, and he did. 'I shall check with Mother.'

'Do. Although, that's less than kind. Madness of her brother? An embarrassment to her, probably.'

Billy's need for his precious support surged back. *Take this shaska son of mine, never let it leave your hands.* 'Never mind that. If *you* had an Uncle Ted, you'd be proud of his army service.' It wasn't a kind thing to say, reminding Kenneth that his father hadn't served, and Billy's father had, as well as Uncle Ted. It stopped Kenneth saying anymore so Billy strode to the parlour and asked Mother straight for news of Uncle Ted.

She swallowed. 'Yes, dear, that is true. Uncle Ted needs treatment for his nerves.'

'What nerves, if he's not in the war? Why can't he go home to Nanny's and be looked after there?'

'It takes time and doctors' help.'

Kenneth had followed behind, close enough for his breath to stream warm on the back of Billy's neck. 'You can't rush these things, Billy,' he said in a kind voice, as though he was a nurse and Billy was small and ignorant.

'No. But we don't need to worry. Ted only had minor injuries otherwise. He might be to rights in time for the end of the war. Who knows.'

Billy left Kenneth in the parlour and dragged along the hall, sliding his fingers along the dado rail. There never seemed to be any good news that didn't have bad behind it. He took refuge in the kitchen.

'Let's not have that long face, Billy lad. Be thankful your Uncle is in one piece,' comforted Mrs Pawsey. 'Many aren't.'

Billy nodded. It was far better to have Uncle Ted with mental problems than in many pieces, like soldiers who were blown up by cannons and bombs.

'Be proud of your Uncle Ted. He'm just a wounded soldier. Minor injuries.' Mr Pawsey said.

It was time to feed the pigs. Billy went to the back lobby, picked up the swill bucket and started off across the yard. He wouldn't let Kenneth's sneers get to him. He started marching, just as Uncle Ted had taught him before the war even started. He hummed to the marching rhythm, *Pack up your troubles in your old kit bag and smile, smile, smile.* He imagined Uncle Ted, smiling, his kit bag holding his few minor injuries.

There would be lots of football matches during the next months and when Uncle Ted got out of hospital, he'd tell him about all of them, and with Uncle Ted around, no-one would be listening or caring about Kenneth.

CHAPTER NINETEEN

May 7th 1945. *Germany surrenders to the Russians*

Billy was lying on his stomach trying to get a good picture of the pigs feeding through a hole in their wall. He'd learned a lot about photography since having his first film. As well as talking with Mr Pawsey about photographs in some books which sat on the shelves upstairs, the science teacher had offered to help him on Tuesdays after detentions. He knew how photographs were developed and how different degrees of light changed your snaps. He'd given Billy a fat book full of information. The Pawseys made a special place on their bookshelf to keep it safe until Billy went back to London.

And that was near, not just a hope like in the hymns they'd been singing in school. All the victories and the wild events, like Mussolini's capture had made everyone very jolly. They'd had a wonderful May Day with a full maypole, and the very next day just as Big Ben sounded on the wireless, the church bells rang out nearly drowning the announcer's voice, 'London calling. Here is a news flash. The German radio has just announced that Hitler is dead. I repeat that. Hitler is dead.' It was a moment Billy couldn't ever forget. Mrs

Pawsey whooped, Mr Pawsey whooped and they grabbed each other round the waist and danced around.

Billy almost couldn't move with shock. Dead! He'd wished for it, and even German officers had wished for it. They'd tried to assassinate him but failed, so it seemed as if Hitler could never die and now he was really, really gone for ever. He'd looked at Mr and Mrs Pawseys' beaming faces and said, 'We haven't got an enemy now, have we?'

On the street everyone was cheering, but then he heard jeers too. Not far behind him was Des on his crutches, both feet blown off in Belgium, his mother and two old men next to him in a small crowd.

'Yeah, who believes the German report "Died fighting bravely to the last", what? Not me, for one.'

The huddle around him shouted agreement. 'Too right. Wish I'd been the one to stick a rifle down his throat.'

Billy turned round to stare. Those people looked horrible, their noses turned nostrils upwards, all the lines deepening round their mouths, their worst teeth showing. Everyone hated Hitler. Billy did too. Hitler was the one who'd started all the fighting but when people wanted to punish, they were very ugly. This was the face you would wear when you felt like killing someone.

He hurried across the square to the group who were cheering. A lady gave him a little union jack on a stick and he jogged with it to the Manor. The side garden was full of bobbing heads where all the children were outside jumping and leaping around. Billy saw Alan and joined in. They clapped each other on the back, yelling, 'Told you, told you.' No one did much work for they had to get ready for a victory day.

Mother had been too busy to visit for a month, so another of Kenneth's phone calls updated Billy. His voice sounded grating.

'We're having a splendid do here for V.E day.'

'So are we.' Billy was going on thirteen. He'd dealt with elementary school toughs, he'd starred on the football field. He could talk back to Kenneth. 'The Grange will do something super and we lot are going to go up there soon to get everything ready. You can stay at the Vicarage and say prayers with the vicar.'

'I'll tell them you said that.'

'I bet there's something about *sneaking* in the Bible, so you'll cop it if you do.' Billy put the telephone down and swaggered down the hall. It was good to have the last word.

He put the camera back around his neck and scuffed his shoes down the path towards the chickens. One of them was about to transfer from being fed to being food. He wanted to give it a good last meal.

'Reckon as it's a one-time event.' MrPawsey commented. It would be criminal to be had up for it. Roast chicken, tomorrow night, Missus if you please.'

'I'm glad I'm here for VE Day.'

Mr Pawsey took the pipe from his mouth. 'So are we. So are we. Got to be truthful, our Billy, we're dreading the day when you have to go back home.'

'Now, now, what a silly thing to say,' Mrs Pawsey corrected him. 'Aren't we very happy the country's safe enough for Billy and all the evacuees to go back home. His family should be together again, you dotty old man. Billy, it's only right you should be at home where you belong.'

He didn't answer. Gordon couldn't be here, where he belonged. Billy was here now, had been here for ages. Didn't he belong here now? It was something he didn't like thinking about.

When he went to Mrs Youldon's, she said the same sort of thing as Mr Pawsey had. 'I know I've got to be glad about the end of war, but, you know, Mary going to America, you going to London, me staying here without either of you.' She looked very small, as if the piles of extra laundry would swallow her up.

Billy looked at the children. How would Timmy feel? He'd been following everything Billy did for the last four years, and Sally had been his shadow since her rescue. He felt the pull of her wherever he went. He felt the pull of his wish to stay, whichever of the Youldons or Pawseys he thought of.

He had to be glad. It wasn't just *Keep your sunny side up, up*. 'It's the party tomorrow, Mrs Youldon. The Manor's got jellies and iced biscuits and all the nuns are making hundreds of sandwiches. You'll have lots to eat. Alan and I have got to help putting out all the tables and chairs and the land girls are putting up streamers.'

If war was over, people wouldn't be killed, Dad would come home and help with Uncle Ted. They'd be able to eat proper meat, sweets and get things like pencils and 120 film. The end of war would be a jolly good thing.

There was dog barking from the back of the house. 'Best shut 'em in with all this excitement,' Mrs Pawsey said.

'Come on, Billy! Time to go.' Alan was calling up from the yard.

Billy ran to the front door. Mrs Pawsey, dressed all in red, white and blue, almost pushed him out of the door. 'Go on ahead. We're coming after you.'

Alan raced him up to the main street where everyone was gathering. A horde of boys pulled them towards the line of trestle tables Billy had earlier helped to lay. They were covered with white sheets and red and blue streamers with Union Jacks fastened to the table legs at each corner.

After a lot of shouting and laughing and cheering, everyone was in their chosen seats. John sat on one side of him, Alan the other and the noisy twins opposite. There were some speeches and a lot more cheering, then the feast began.

'Sandwiches first, you lot,' ordered a large woman presiding over the food. 'Cakes and jellies after. Hold out your cups and I'll pour your drink.'

A hundred hands wavered over the pile of food and like the rest, Billy filled his mouth. Someone put a silly paper hat on his head, someone else waved a rattle in his face. A young woman filled his beaker with weak orange squash.

For this moment all that mattered was the thrill of knowing the war really was over and sharing that wonderful fact with all the village.

The twins had their mouths full, but open as usual. John passed the biscuits and said, 'No more war! You realise we're now witnessing the end to all that beastliness.'

Billy stared at John, who looked almost old enough to be called up. He was talking rather like Kenneth.

The noise of the celebrations went on long after dark. Everyone had shouted and sung themselves so hoarse that, despite himself, Billy fell into bed, too tired to dwell on what was going to happen next.

~

In the next weeks Billy ran round the village snapping everything he thought might change, taking people in their daily tasks as though they might disappear in a cloud of smoke.

He took the camera to school and photographed, from underneath, all the closed desks with their Union Jacks poking up. The helpful science teacher let him photograph in peace. He was marking test papers. They were on eighth-of-a-page slips written both sides (bad luck if your handwriting was large). He had the sort of cough that echoes like a church organ before the tune comes. He was an old man, far too old to be a soldier and probably too old to be a teacher.

'You'll be off to London soon, Wilson. You and your talent. Shame. I warn you, you may not get much attention there – schools'll be so crowded, I predict. Now, I'll find you some photo corners. Place all your best photos in your album carefully. Keep old envelopes for the other snaps – you never know if they're important. Then, when you're ready to leave school, you can take them to show important people what you can do. It's like your evidence, you see. People might book you to photograph their weddings, christenings, family celebrations, that sort of thing. You'll be able to make a living, I'm sure. Better than being a teacher anyway.' He gave a wry smile.

He was too old to keep proper discipline in class. But the boys had some respect for his knowledge.

Billy said, 'It would be good if to get respect for my photographs.'

'Indeed, you should, Wilson.'

He could almost see a life ahead. That made a difference. When he ached at the thought of leaving the Pawseys and the Youldons, it helped to look far into the future, beyond life in Wandsworth, which would now be shared with Kenneth and which would be for good. It was very scary. He was needed here, everyone liked him here and they wouldn't have a proper football team in the village without him.

It wasn't even as if he would be going back to his Wandsworth school with Miss Johnson and Mr Finlay. Thirteen was too old, so he'd have to go to some secondary or technical school.

His time was going to end here. Name plates were going up on roads, signs were already back on the signposts. He could see how many miles he was from Brighton, from Salisbury, even from London.

Billy went back to his bedroom and sat on the bed, thrusting his hands deep into his quilt. In Wandsworth there would be no dogs to greet him every time he got home from school. There wouldn't be any pigs or hens or fields to hear outside the windows, and he'd be too far away to ever visit Mrs Youldon and the children. His parents just thought of the Pawseys as elderly fosterers and the Youldons as poor folk to avoid. They wouldn't understand that he needed to come back to visit. They wouldn't bring him. When he left here, it would be so very long before he was twenty-one and could decide to catch trains by himself without permission.

When they saw his long face, Mr and Mrs Pawsey told him to think about seeing Nanny and Granddad again. He had to think back four years. He hadn't seen them since the very first night of bombing. He could just remember helping Granddad in the garden and shed, stomping around in his wellies after him, trying to make things with little bits of wood and a tiny hammer that Granddad had given him. He could almost smell the lovely roasts Nanny had made, and nearly remembered her hugs.

'And your Uncle Ted. I expect he'll be out of hospital soon, Billy. Think of that.'

He whistled a few of his cheery tunes, but they didn't seem to work as well as when he was younger. He tried to imagine the hospital helping Uncle so that he could do handstands again and go home to Nanny's and Granddad's. Then they'd all be laughing around their dining table like long ago. Now he was big, Billy might be more nearly one of the men, and let into their conversations. Then of course there was Angela and Mr Durban to see. They'd be pleased he was back, and at last he could hold the shashka once more. Kenneth could keep the photograph, still not knowing what it was.

Billy could take his own photographs of the shashka and everything else.

It was best to think of all these things directly the sad feelings came on. It was going to have to happen, this going away. He went to his bedroom. He was going to have to deal with it. It was going to happen tomorrow. His suitcase was packed and stood beside the wardrobe, all ready.

He looked all around. When he was gone and the sheets were taken off his bed, he needed something of himself to stay behind. So he made a guilty cross with his penknife under the mat. He put presents on his bedside table: his first photo of Mr and Mrs Pawsey, his best essay and a bar of chocolate from Dwaine that he'd been saving.

In the morning, Mr and Mrs Pawsey were rather quiet, although determinedly cheerful. Billy could hardly look at them at breakfast. He knew they didn't want him to go. It was best not to say anything because he might start crying. There were three more hours before he was collected for the journey.

He went to the scullery and hid his head in the dogs' backs, pretending to find clumps in their fur. He walked them all around the village for a last look at the familiar lanes and cottages.

A crowd of the lads from the village school were kicking a ball in the middle of the road.

'Billy! C'mon, be goalie.'

But for once he didn't want to. It wasn't worth getting into a game he couldn't continue.

'I'm off back to London soon. Got to get ready,' he said, practising for more difficult goodbyes.

'Yaw, we'll lose our best player. Not fair. Can't you ask your folks if you can stay put?'

He shook his head.

It was time to go down to the Youldons for the very last time. He'd spent his half-crown that Granddad had given him at the very beginning of war. He bought frames for the three prints of his photos for Mrs Youldon, so now she could put them properly on the shelf. He'd bought a skipping rope for Sally, a toy tank for Tim.

He saw them in the distance, talking to Big Ronnie's mother, Sally on one side of Mrs Youldon, Timmy on the other. Suddenly he couldn't face the goodbyes. He could hardly manage his own sadness, the children's would be awful. He went back round the corner to the newsagents and asked for a pen and paper. He wrote his note and left it there with the presents for Mrs Youldon to collect, then he went round to Alan's.

'I've already been down there,' Alan said, smart in a new shirt and slipover with damp, combed hair. 'You can't not go. She's always on about you saving Sally. It's all right for me, Mum's said she'll bring me down here sometimes if I want. But if your mother won't, you've got to say a proper goodbye. Mrs Y. will be sad and she'll think you can't be bothered.' He walked Billy back down the lane. 'Go on.'

Billy walked as slowly as he could. He would just say goodbye and then go. As he went inside the familiar cramped space, he saw with relief that the little ones were out playing with friends. Their mother was piling the ironing up like a wall, while the two side irons heated on the stove. Billy sat hunched on the bench as Mrs Youldon twisted her apron.

'Billy, you're really off then. Oh my, this is awful. I knew it would be.'

'I've left stuff for you at the newsagents.'

She came and gave him a hug. 'You're such a dear.'

He held on to her until he could trust his voice. 'Will you go to America if they ask you?'

She shook her head. 'I'm staying right here until Sally and Timmy are grown, husband or no husband.'

He looked at her. 'But Joe, or someone, might come and ask you.'

'No, Billy. Listen. When the G.Is were here I wanted to go out, have some fun, but I'll tell you a secret. I keep thinking Mr Youldon will come back for me. Now the war's over, he'll find out that things he thought he knew – the fine gent up at the Grange – wasn't anything to me. That gent just used to pester me and I couldn't do a thing because I was only an under-maid. I couldn't complain. But Mr Youldon thought I wanted to be with him and waltzed right off before our Sally was born, never even clapped eyes on her. So Timmy lost his Daddy 'n all. Mr Youldon had it wrong. He's had time now to find that out. So I'm going to wait right here, like I always have, and hope he'll come back.'

Billy leant towards her. 'I hope he does too. Really soon.' He tried to take in her story, but Mr Youldon had never seemed very real. *He* was Mrs Youldon's support. 'When I'm a photographer I'll earn money. Then I'll come down here on the train. I will see you all again, I have to.'

She hugged him again. Her head only came to his shoulder now, although he was the child. Her voice was really, really sad. 'It's such a long time.'

He didn't ask whether she meant that he had been in her life a long time, or would be away a long time. Both were true.

'You'll be too fine to come back. Up there in London.'

He shook his head, wordless, and looked straight at her for the last time. 'Never.' Then he forced himself out of the tiny room into the cloudy light of his last day of evacuation.

Slowly, he meandered back to the Pawseys', now no longer 'home'. Mother had arranged to collect him early afternoon. That was not far off now.

Instead of faces full of gloom, Mr and Mrs Pawsey met him with what seemed genuine smiles.

'Billy! You're not going on the train now. Your aunty has gone on it with Kenneth to see his relatives. You'll never guess who's going to come to collect you! Your uncle.'

At first Billy felt a sick thump inside, and then shook his stupid thoughts away. People couldn't come back from the dead. When Mrs Pawsey said 'Uncle', he'd had a sudden image of Uncle Frank rising up in the middle of the front room, showing his arm muscles.

'Your Uncle Ted! Isn't that lovely? He's got a car, don't ask me how, and collected your mother and sister and after their dinner they're coming over for you.'

'He's out of hospital?'

'Yes, all ready to go home and soon he'll be here.'

'Really? Wheeee.' He whizzed round several times, all his sadness mixed with relief.

'You are packed and ready, Billy, aren't you?'

He nodded, then went upstairs to look at his already packed suitcase. Last time he'd used it was when he arrived here on Jed's cart. He slung his precious camera round his neck. Uncle Ted. After all this time and all that longing to see him and then hospital and now he really would see him. He'd see Uncle Ted just as he had to leave the Pawseys. It was like leaping into a pool of marshmallow and ice, sweet and thrilling but chilling and shocking. He so wanted to see Uncle Ted. He so wanted to stay here. Silly fantasies came to his mind like Uncle Ted moving into the Pawseys' home and telling everyone that Billy had to stay there too.

Mrs Pawsey looked at him dithering on the stairs. 'Well, our Billy, no good us being sad. You have to think of all the people, all the things you've missed in Wandsworth, so you'll set off from here looking forward, not looking back.'

He nodded and tried to stop thinking how much he wanted to stay. He'd be seeing Mr Durban. Angela. The shashka would be there in its scabbard just waiting to be drawn out, shining. If it could be magic, waved in the air, brandished, he could make everything, everyone just as he wanted. He'd stay right here and all of them could visit.

'Now, we've a while till your family get here. We'll have some dinner first.'

'I ... couldn't.'

But when Mrs Pawsey pushed him gently into dinner, he saw that she'd somehow found some of his favourite foods to put on the table: sausage pancakes, cauliflower cheese, apple pie. So he had to eat.

'Had these saved in the back of the larder, specially for you, Billy.'

'But your rations, Mrs Pawsey!'

Mr Pawsey waved a paw. 'You'll be queasy in the car if you don't fill that stomach of yours. Now I've left my specs in the other room so pass me the right things so I don't end up eating the salt and pepper instead of my dinner.'

Billy almost laughed. Then the very last meal, those dreaded last moments with the Pawseys, were filled by Mrs Pawsey talking about Uncle Ted and how the military hospital had put him almost to rights. A soldier friend had lent him a car and someone on the staff had found him some petrol from their own ration. Now he was coming hot foot to take up with all his family where he'd left off.

Hot foot? He must be better.

Billy said, 'Nanny and Granddad will be ever so glad.'

'Reckon they'll be over the moon,' said Mr Pawsey. 'Their only son. Lots haven't been so lucky.'

It was a terrible thought. Mr and Mrs Pawsey hadn't been so lucky. They had lost Gordon and now they were losing Billy, at least until he was grown up.

He thought of his grandparents standing at the door, their welcoming arms out saying, 'Ted!' And then 'Billy!' But would they recognise him now he was the size of a man?

If there was more talk, Bill didn't take it in. It seemed only seconds between his last wonderful mouthful of Mrs Pawsey's food and the barking of the dogs announcing that his family were at the door.

Jill, newly bold, led Uncle Ted in by the hand, a grey-clad Uncle Ted, unsmiling, blinking.

Mother busily talked and greeted, while she organised Billy's belongings.

He tried to take in the reality of Uncle Ted. It was as if he was back from the dead. He was nodding to the Pawseys, standing in the hall with loose trousers and bony wrists. He stared at Billy, the white block of hair highlighting his forehead. He was thin, pale, serious.

Billy stared back, longing for the grin. 'Hello Uncle Ted.'

Mother stepped forward. 'Told you Billy was huge, Ted. Look at him, how am I supposed to look after a boy like him?'

'I'm sure you'll manage a lot better than old folks like us,' Mrs Pawsey bit in, 'and we loved every minute.' She turned away quickly.

Mr Pawsey's glasses were firmly on his nose as he strode forward to Ted with a large outstretched hand. 'So this is one of our heroes? Welcome back, soldier. Here's as hoping you'll settle back home, happy to be with your folks.'

Ted's handshake was listless. 'Hello. Thank you. Hello.' He nodded to left, right and straight ahead, as though trying to take in everyone. He kept blinking as if the lights were too strong, but they weren't even on.

Billy risked an approach. 'You sent me a top that first Christmas of the war, Uncle Ted. It was super. Thanks ever so much.'

Uncle Ted frowned. 'A long time ago. I – yes – I did send that. You're a bit big for tops now?' His voice sounded funny, sort of strangled and perhaps something had happened to his teeth. 'I am trying to get used to everyone, but you all look so different. Baby's a little girl, and you're growing into a man.'

There was a silence while everyone thought what to say.

Uncle Ted was trying hard. 'Do you still like football?'

Billy nodded hard. Would Uncle Ted ever kick a ball to him again or was he too weak? He looked it.

Mrs Pawsey said, 'Oh, he's a wonderful football player. Quite the star of the team here. Have you packed your bravery medal and your newspaper picture, Billy? You must show them to your Uncle Ted. He will be proud.'

Uncle Ted looked confused.

Mrs Pawsey explained. 'He saved a little girl from drowning three years ago. Very brave.'

'You're a hero, then, Billy. More than I am.' Uncle Ted's forehead puckered.

Mother stepped in hurriedly, 'Right everyone, we must be off. Billy – have you said thank you? And of course I must thank you both, Mr and Mrs Pawsey, for having my son. We none of us knew it would be for so long.'

'Not long enough,' Mr Pawsey muttered, but Billy heard.

He nodded to show Mother he had said his thanks. The adults' to-and-fro of thanks and goodbyes, reminders and checks washed over his head as he concentrated on getting his suitcase into the boot of the car. This couldn't be happening, he couldn't be going.

He spotted the bin for the pig swill. 'Just a minute.' He ran to the pig sty for a last look, ignoring Mother's aggrieved call, the 'Billy!' fading as he ran further from the house. The dogs were loose and ran after him, pushing their bodies against his, nosing at his hands for a stroke.

'Look I've got to go,' he whispered. 'Noah, Japhet, I've just got to. I don't want to. Just don't forget me, right?'

He turned to the piglets. 'You'll be pork before long anyway. It's we-have-no-choice for you, too.'

He walked back towards the house treading his boots hard into the mud, so as to leave a set of clear imprints, the dogs at his heels. Mother's complaints filled the silence in his head as she prodded him forwards to the car. 'What are you doing? You've had oodles of time for all that.'

He could hardly look at the Pawseys now the leave-taking was upon him.

'Don't lose your glasses,' he said to one, and 'Your dinners are super,' to the other. He wanted to say how much he'd miss them but no more words would come out and he found himself hustled into the back seat with Jill who was bouncing happily on the folded blankets.

'You've been the best young lad we could have wished for, and I hope you find your way back here just as soon as you're old enough,' said Mrs Pawsey in a wobbly voice as she pushed a basket of goodies into his hands.

Mr Pawsey said something too, but it was drowned in the noise of Uncle Ted cranking the starter handle. The engine coughed into life. Uncle Ted slid into the driving seat and slammed the car door. He raised a hand to the waving Pawseys. The car rolled forward and away. A belch of petrol vapour was all Billy saw and smelled as he knelt on the seat to hold the Pawseys and their home in his vision for as long as he possibly could.

The car turned left out of the lane and all sight of the homestead had gone.

'Phew!' said Mother. 'The wretched evacuation is finally over. Can you believe it?'

'Ov-er, ov-er. Off to London town,' Jill sang. She bounced up and down on the seat jogging Billy's knees. Each bounce caused a miserable squelch of his skin against the leatherette car seat.

'I know how it feels, not trusting that a terrible time has really come to an end.' Uncle Ted said, fingers twitching through his white forelock. He turned round to Billy. 'Now you can put your evacuation right behind you.'

'Running wild amongst pigs and chickens. It certainly wasn't good for him, Ted.'

'No, and on your own there. Can't have been good for you, Billy. Rotten war, rotten for all of us.'

As they passed the road with the congregational church, Billy saw a group of little girls. They turned to see the car. There was Sally. She started running wildly after the car, waving and waving, her little arms high above her head. 'Bill-eeeee.' It seemed as if she was drowning and he wasn't staying to save her this time. He pressed his face to the window until she was a tiny spot in the distance.

'Don't kneel up like that, Billy,' said Mother. 'It's not good for you.'

The windows were steamed up already. Billy wrote where they couldn't see, 'I will come back. It *was* good for me.'

END OF BOOK TWO

BOOK THREE

IMPACT

PREFACE

"We are responsible for what we are, and whatever we wish ourselves to be, we have the power to make ourselves. If what we are now has been the result of our own past actions, it certainly follows that whatever we wish to be in future can be produced by our present actions; so we have to know how to act."

Swami Vivekananda

CHAPTER 1

July 1945

Inside the car, the seat felt rough and hot. A tuft of stuffing was poking out of the covering beside him. Billy fingered it. It felt like the fur of Noah and Japhet, Mr and Mrs Pawseys' farm dogs, when they greeted him every morning. In Wandsworth there would be no dogs. No pigs, no chickens either. He stroked the stuffing over and over to calm himself as the car moved forward and away from his sanctuary.

Uncle Ted drove, not very well. Billy had so longed to see him, but not strange like this. He searched the lean face in the driving mirror and met its staring eyes. Uncle spat out three questions. 'Billy – been living there all this time? Twelve now, are you? And your sister, seven?'

Billy nodded. Even Uncle's voice sounded odd.

Mother took over. 'I told you that already, Ted. We've all been evacuated since the Blitz. The vicarage could only take me and Jill, so Billy was billeted here. We have sent you our news regularly.' She turned to look at him. 'But perhaps you've been in no state to take it in.'

'No state,' Ted laughed, if that croak could be a laugh. 'Bet you're glad to go home,' he directed at Billy.

'We certainly are,' Mother said. 'I'll say!'

Billy didn't answer and slumped back into his seat. He'd dreaded leaving the Pawseys even more than Hitler invading. Ever since VE Day he'd felt sick at the thought, but hadn't been able to picture it actually happening. It was truly terrible to leave the people who'd loved him and given him a safe home; but it was wonderful to see Uncle Ted at the door, back safe from war. That excitement had muddled his dreadfully sad feelings, and then how different he looked! The Uncle Ted he remembered from before the war had made jokes, played magic tricks, done handstands.

Billy had stood at the door with his suitcase, confused, and made the shortest of goodbyes to Mr and Mrs Pawsey when there were so many words in his heart. His misery about leaving, excitement and bewilderment just couldn't sit together inside of him. It was a wonder he wasn't sick all over the place before even getting into the car.

A car! Billy hadn't been in one since the vicar had delivered him back here four years ago. He wriggled uncomfortably. He'd expected to make his goodbyes to the Pawseys privately, when he was on his own, with Jed the carter collecting him. The arrangement had been for him to meet Mother and Jill at the railway station, where he'd go in the horse and cart. But an officer at the hospital had lent Uncle this car to take the family home, so they'd all come to the Pawseys' to collect him.

It turned a corner rather sharply just then, so that Jill slid across Billy's lap. 'Whoops,' she giggled.

'Mind the eggs.' He clasped the basket Mrs Pawsey had given him close to his middle.

The car jerked into the lane that led to the main road. 'I bet Uncle hasn't driven before,' Jill whispered.

He frowned at her.

'Thank goodness,' said Mother. 'Evacuation's finally over. It's been so long since VE Day, waiting to get away. Such an imposition, expecting me to work another six weeks at that wretched garage.

Home! I can't wait to get my shoes onto proper pavements. Just look at those muddy ruts.'

Jill nudged Billy and rolled her eyes. She didn't seem at all in awe of Mother. Then she whispered, 'Who's that little girl crying and waving at you?'

He pushed his face to the window. Sally! Her little figure pushed away from the girls around her as she ran forward, waving wildly and calling. He couldn't say anything; his throat was chcked. His hand didn't feel it belonged to him as it lifted and waved. The car passed and left her behind, crying alone.

'Billy?' Jill nudged again. 'Who is it?'

He swallowed hard. 'Sally Youldon, from where I used to live, the first time I was evacuated.'

'Oh, I know. That little girl you saved from drowning? The peasant family?'

'They weren't peasants!'

'Mummy said they were. She didn't like you minding them. Anyway, Sally's all sad you're coming away.'

He swallowed harder. 'Yes.'

Mother called over her shoulder, 'Open the window wider, Billy, please. It's still so hot. I never have liked high summer.'

He wound the handle a few more times. The wind blasted his face as it whistled past the window. It felt as if his heart was sucked out too. He imagined it whisking away to Mr and Mrs Pawsey, then flying past bushes to Mrs Youldon, Sally and Tim. How would they manage without him? He pressed the hard bit of his chest where it hurt. Something vital had surely gone and left his stomach churning up and down with every rut in the road.

'Awfully bumpy, Ted,' Mother complained.

Uncle grunted. 'Better than queuing for a coach for hours, or squashed up on the train, standing all the way.'

'That's true. I had that awful experience in 1940, coming down here with Doreen and the children. Never again!'

The car juddered to a stop. 'Oh, for heaven's sake!' Mother sounded cross already. The farm's herd of cows had begun to cross the top lane, back from milking.

Uncle Ted put on the brake and groaned. 'Just my luck.' The engine spluttered.

'Better not let it stop, Ted. You don't want to crank the handle again.'

As the cows lumbered past, one of them lowered its head, peering straight into the car. Mother and Jill squealed. Its huge eyes penetrated to the back seat to look at Billy's misery. Did cows feel sorry for people, like dogs could?

It mooed, its breath smearing the windscreen. Mother screwed back into her seat. 'Oh make it go away, Ted, do. Great, horrible thing.'

It lurched off as if it had heard. The car engine spluttered again as the line of cows ambled past and into the field. Uncle Ted drummed his fingers on the wheel. Mother sighed.

The wicker basket on his lap scratched Bill's legs below the edges of his trousers. The basket held eggs laid by the chickens he'd fed every day. Tucked underneath to save them from cracking was a green checked napkin from the set Mrs Pawsey used every meal-time. Now she'd have one missing. The paper bags beside the eggs were filled with cakes made with the last of their rations. They'd gone without to send Billy off with all the best of what they had. He'd known he was special to them, just as they had become to him. When Mother unpacked the basket in Wandsworth he'd save the napkin, secretly. Then he'd always have something of the Pawseys'.

'Come on, cows. We want to go home to London!' Jill chirped, making the words into a little song. 'Lon-don, Lon-don, we're off to London town.'

The last cow flicked its tail before stepping leisurely into the mud lake by the open gate, and Uncle Ted bent to the controls again with shaky hands. He didn't look very sure about which knob did what.

Jill's dark curls brushed Billy's neck as she leant close to whisper, 'Uncle Ted's a bit loopy, isn't he?'

'Of course not!' he muttered back. 'He's just out of hospital, recovering, that's all.'

'Kenneth said—'

He pressed a hand across her mouth to shut her up.

There was a new noise from the engine and the car lurched

forward. The farmer lifted a hand in a wave and the gate shut behind the black and white backsides of the cows.

'We're off!' Jill bounced a few more times, Billy protecting the precious eggs by holding the basket in the air.

Mother gave a triumphant sigh. 'And now back to a civilized normality, I trust. Foot down please, Ted. Let's get away from this' – she waved a hand towards the field – 'smell of cows and pigs. Billy's billet.'

Billy scowled at his lap. There weren't ever cows at the Pawseys' and this farm was two lanes away from their smallholding. He kept his eyes on the eggs. Mother should see how unfair she was.

The car turned left at the main road. Billy turned, trying to see out of the back window, but it was set too high on Austin Eights. Outside, all sight of the village would soon be gone, even the church spire.

'Now you can put it right behind you –' Uncle Ted's fingers were twitching through his white forelock. '– your evacuation. They told me to do that about my service, now that war's over.' He leant forward over the wheel as if his ribs needed propping up. 'Easily said when you're a doc in a white coat, safely away from sh—'

'Ted!' Mother put a hand on his arm. 'It *is* all over.'

A growl came from his throat, 'Over? Rotten war, rotting—'

Mother put a hand over his mouth. 'Shh.'

'Will we get home before dinner time?'

Mother turned to Jill, still bouncing happily up and down on the back seat. 'No. And pull your bow up. It's slipped right down to your ear.'

Jill took the side lock of hair and shoved the ribbon a little higher. 'Will we have to eat in a restaurant? I've nev-er e-ver ea-ten in a re-stau-rant.' She bounced in time to her words.

'For heaven's sake, child. Can't you sit still?'

Uncle Ted had the car under control now. It began to speed up once on the main road. There were fields outside the car window, and then arches of trees blocking sight of anything else. The trees became skimpier and further apart revealing a set of huts in a clearing. A wooden signpost near the road read 'NAAFI' and someone had scribbled 'Not known here'.

Billy's legs were sticking to the cracked leather seat. It would take hours and hours to get back to Wandsworth, his insides were screwed into a ball, everything was awful. The car sides and roof were a shell around him, like being in an Anderson shelter, but sheltered from where he wanted to be, instead of from bombs. He hadn't felt worse, not even in the cellar with the noise of bombing, Kenneth shaking beside him, and that scary whining squeal of the air raid warning.

Gradually he became aware of Mother's one-way conversation in the front, and Jill's excited chatter beside him in the back. He stopped pulling at the stuffing. It wasn't their car and he was making the slit worse. He put his hands in his pockets and gazed at the back of Uncle Ted's head where the hair was still black. Nanny and Grandad would be so happy to have him and all of them back again. Mrs Pawsey had urged Billy to think of all these good cheery things. He shook himself sensible and let himself hear the end of Jill's chatterings, realising they were intended for him.

'...And I said to him, "it will be such a squash and you and Billy will quarrel and I don't want to sit in the middle of you two," and he said, "Anyway, Mummy's taking me to visit some of our relatives. They haven't seen me since I was four".'

Billy jerked to attention. 'Who?'

'Kenneth of course!'

'I thought they were going to London by train.'

'They are, but that's what I've just said. *Not yet.* They're going to Northampton first. That's where they live, Kenneth's grandad and grandma. It'll be two whole weeks before he and Aunty come to settle in.'

Billy sat back, imagining two grandparents fussing and adoring Kenneth, just as Aunty did. Two weeks. That was something. At least he could get used to 'home' before Kenneth invaded the place.

Jill nudged him. 'Won't it seem funny, all of us there? I'm used to having Mummy to myself, and funny people coming in and out to see the vicar. But I shan't miss them.' She giggled. 'Or the tellings-off and sermons at dinner. I saw Kenneth and Aunty every day because their billet was down the road, but I can't imagine all of us in the one house every day!'

'No.' He felt for a hanky and wiped the back of his sweating neck. It was flipping hot in the back, even with the wind blowing in. Jill's chatter wasn't helping. It was so rotten to leave this place, and doubly rotten to think of Kenneth living with them.

'I can't even remember our house, can you?'

'Yes,' he said, thinking about it. 'I can. But it will seem strange now.'

Mother came to the end of her conversation and overheard. 'We shall all find everything strange, children. You'll both have to buckle to.' She turned back to the front.

Jill leant towards Billy. 'And, I will have my very own bedroom, instead of sharing with Mummy.' Her voice dropped to a whisper. 'I'm going to have secret things in it. There'll be treasure. And if I make a friend at my new school, I'll bring her home to play in it. It will be ever so private. You won't be able to join in.'

He managed a smile. 'Don't worry. I won't.'

Jill nudged him in the side. 'But *you* won't have your own bedroom now.' She chuckled. 'We're opposites. I'm getting my own room at last; you've had your own bedroom all this time, and now you'll be sharing.'

'Yes.' The last time he'd shared a room with Kenneth had been the dreadful night after Uncle Frank had died, while the grown-ups were at the funeral. That was definitely the worst night of his life.

He kept quiet while Mother and Jill went on chatting. Uncle Ted was silent too. Outside the window, fields of blue spread like ball gowns across to the gentle hills beyond. Flax. Mr Pawsey had told him flax was important during the war. The blue might change to some other colour now, just like men's trousers would change from army khaki to business black. Billy couldn't imagine Dad's legs in khaki, but he wouldn't see them until Dad was demobbed.

Billy started as Uncle suddenly spoke. 'You'll be *Bill*, I suppose, now that you're big.'

Immediately, he decided he must change. 'Yes,' he said out loud, and turned to Jill. 'You must call me Bill from now on.'

'Jill, Bill. It rhymes,' she squealed.

'I know,' he said grimly. 'I told Mother that when I was your age. Can't be helped.'

Uncle went on as if no-one had spoken, '—and you can call me Ted.' After that he said nothing. He didn't answer Mother, just nodded to her chat.

It had been a long while of her talk and his silence before she turned round to them, 'Uncle Ted has to concentrate on driving, so don't talk to him.'

'*She* has been,' Jill whispered, thumbing towards Mother below the seat level.

Bill frowned at her. She was getting quite cheeky.

The next sound was Jill again. 'Are we halfway yet, Mummy? This is a proper town.'

The fields had given way to streets of houses. Mother peered out of her window, looking ahead. The houses became closer together and there was a church. 'Is this halfway, Ted? Shall we stop for something to eat? We'd better, I suppose.'

'Goody,' said Jill. 'I'm ever so, ever so hungry.'

Ted pulled into the kerbside beside some public toilets. The engine spluttered twice and then stopped. He opened his door and the full heat of the day swept in.

Jill was pushing Bill forward. 'Go on.'

'Wait for Uncle to open the door on the pavement side. It's dangerous to get out onto the road.' He looked out at the row of houses and the shops ahead. Everything looked big and brick and not like places you could just run past, whooping and calling out as he'd been used to for the last four years.

Ted opened the door for Mother. She swung her legs as one towards the pavement, just like the lady film stars in the newsreels. 'Oh what a relief to stretch my legs. Proper pavements! Wonderful. I'll ask a local if there's a restaurant. Surely there'll be something.' She tip-tapped away down the road.

Uncle wrestled with the front seat until it swung forward and they could clamber out. He went into the Gents.

Jill spotted a chalked hopscotch game on the paving outside. 'I used to play this at the village hall, in the yard at the back where they kept the fire engine. My friend Iris and me got ever so good at hopscotch. Can you do it, Billy-Bill?' She lifted one foot and started hopping.

'I can, but Mother wouldn't approve of hopping in the street.' He remembered his shock when Mrs Youldon first told him to 'play out' and Mother's horror when she found out that he played in the street.

Jill carried on hopping and jumping, as if he hadn't spoken. 'And Iris lives in Wandsworth, too.'

Mother reappeared as Ted came out of the Gents. 'I asked at the post office. Two streets away up there, the WVS run a British restaurant at the Workers' Institute. It's the only place.' Her face spoke about how she felt about that.

Ted said, 'I'll eat there, whatever it's like.'

'We'll go and wash our hands first. You, too, Bill.' Mother grasped Jill's shoulder, stopping her mid-hop, and ushered her to the toilets.

Afterwards, Ted led off down the street, forgetting to take Mother's arm as he should have done. Jill nudged Bill. 'Look. He does look loopy, whatever you say.'

Ted was flicking his head as if he had a long lock of hair over his eyes, but he hadn't. His hair was army short. His walk did look odd, fast and jerky. Mother wasn't hurrying to walk beside him. They followed Ted past the few shops and across the road at the Belisha beacon. On Mother's far side, Jill leapt from each metal stud to the next all the way across the road. 'Oh, for heaven's sake!' but Mother didn't stop her.

A short way on, a dirty brick and stone building with a pointed roof had its doors open and a WVS lady standing at the entrance. Jill spotted her. 'Look, a lady like Aunty, green uniform, see?'

'That'll be it,' said Mother.

They joined the string of people paying and collecting their tokens, one for each course.

'Can I keep them afterwards, Mummy, they're so nice?' Jill held up the bright blue counter and then the yellow one. 'I could use them as Ludo counters.'

But the tokens were taken as they paid. At a counter, more WVS ladies handed out their plates of mince, mash and peas and dishes of spotted dick and runny custard. 'Is there rice pudding?' Mother asked, but the WVS helper said it was *off*.

Mother only tutted, but Uncle Ted turned his mouth down. 'Rice pud's off. Doesn't matter where you go, this is off, that's off. All set out to make you feel miserable.'

'Yeah, so much worse than eating rats in the trenches, isn't it, mate?' A large man wearing part of a check shirt, a flat sleeve where his lower arm should have been, leaned over Ted's shoulder. 'Demobbed early, like me, eh? But without a good reason. Like this.' He jerked his head at his flat arm sleeve and then at his foot, which was in some kind of box with a metal strip under it. 'Where did you serve, then?'

'Belgium,' Ted muttered trying to squeeze past Mother to take his tray to one of the four long trestle tables.

'Oh, yeah. Until it was occupied by Kraut thugs, 1940. It's been a long time since then.'

'Better help my family get to a table.' Ted followed Mother and slid quickly along the bench beside Jill. Bill closed the gap behind Ted, who looked very uncomfortable. How could he help Ted out?

Lumbering awkwardly, the man followed Ted. The metal bar clanged on the floor like a bell tolling. 'What regiment, mate?'

'East Surreys.'

'Royal Hampshire, me.'

Mother sat down opposite Jill so Bill hurried forward to flank Ted's other side.

The man put his tray beside Mother's as best he could, one-handed, and sidled along the bench. 'Good-day, Missus. All right if I take this space beside you?'

Mother nodded briefly, then turned her face away.

Ted now had to face the man over the plates of dinner. He picked up his knife and fork and began to eat hurriedly.

The man shoved his plate along the table, gravy slopping onto the table. 'Yeah. We had all the worst. France, Belgium, Algiers, Salerno, Egypt, back to Italy and that's when I copped it. Lucky to be alive.'

Ted's face looked hard as a brick.

Bill turned his face sideways so that Ted could seem totally involved in a separate conversation. 'It's quite nice this mince, Ted, isn't it?'

The man hadn't shaved very well. His stubbly face and way of speaking wasn't what Mother was used to. She was ignoring the man, looking across to Jill, as if checking what she ate.

He didn't care. 'Good to have hubby back home so soon, Missus?'

'This is not my husband. He is still serving.'

'Oops. Sorry. Didn't mean to embarrass you. Enough said!'

Mother drew herself up until her back was as straight as a soldier on drill, and raised her eyebrows alarmingly. She didn't look at the man. 'I am eating with my brother and my children, thank you.'

'Yeah. Course you are.' He pushed his chin forward towards Ted and gave a huge wink to Bill since Ted was looking down at his plate. He took his fork in his one good hand and lifted a large dollop of mash and gravy to his mouth. Several drops of gravy dripped onto the table. Mother flinched slightly. He leant towards her. 'I was just asking your *brother* where he served after Belgium. Escaped to Dunkirk and rescued, I expect.'

Ted nodded.

'Then?'

Bill needed to rescue Ted again. What could he say? He knew Jill would be staring but with Ted between them he couldn't nudge her. She hadn't met many younger men before, especially not one with only one hand. He bent forward to his plate and tried to catch her eye. Sure enough, she was watching the man, fascinated. The man noticed.

'Do you have lots of uncles, Missy?'

She smiled back at him. She was too little to know that 'uncle' could mean something else. 'No. We did have one other one but he got killed by a bomb.'

'Jill.' Mother threw a stern warning glance across at her.

The man sat up. 'In Belgium?'

'No. In Balham.'

'What, on leave there?'

'No. He wasn't a soldier because he was a tax inspector, wasn't he, Mummy?'

She frowned at Jill. 'Just eat up.'

The man snorted. 'Love them! Exempt, weren't they!'

Mother bridled. 'That's quite enough about our personal business, if you please.'

The man turned his attention back to Ted.

'You serve in first battalion?'

'Various.' Ted was busy with his plateful. He'd found hard lumps of potato in the mash and was pushing them to one side.

'Were you in the BEF?'

'No.'

'I knew a bloke in the East Surreys. Harry Thorpe. Know him?'

Ted shook his head.

'Not much to say for yourself, have you?'

Mother still didn't look at the man but put her knife and fork neatly crossed on her plate. She would have touched her mouth with a napkin if the place had such a thing. 'It's best not to worry my brother with too many questions. He is only just out of hospital.'

'Ah. Right. Where's the injuries?'

'Internal,' said Mother crossly and picked up her knife and fork again.

Ted was eating bit by bit as if swallowing poison. Actually, the food wasn't too bad although the mince was very runny. Bill had nearly finished his plateful and so had the man, even though he only had one hand.

'Anyway, Harry Thorpe was off to Africa when I last saw him, so I guess that's one place where you were.'

Bill jerked his head up. *Africa?*

Jill squealed, 'Were you in Africa, Uncle?' Several nearby diners looked up as her voice echoed around the hall.

Ted stood up and flung his knife and fork on the plate. 'Enough flaming questions.' He swung one leg over the back of the bench, and then the other. He moved back away from the tables. 'See you back at the car in fifteen. I'm going for a walk.'

'Go for a walk. Lucky you,' the man called after him. 'Wouldn't I like to! Only I never can again.' The man moved onto his spotted dick and custard. 'My word, this is tasty.' He raised his voice. 'You've left yours, mate. Waste not, want not.'

Ted was already at the door ignoring the WVS lady who was saying, 'We all clear our own dirty plates, dear.'

Bill looked at Mother for guidance. Her face was tight and red. 'I did say that was enough, Jill. Now see what's happened. Eat up. The custard is good for you. Then we must go.'

Bill finished his own pudding and then started on Ted's.

The man leant over to him. 'Better appetite than Uncle, eh? You looking forward to soldiering then, now you see how smashing it is?'

'Please leave my son alone. He isn't even thirteen yet.'

'Flipping heck. He's the size of a sixteen-year-old.'

Mother ignored him. 'If you've finished, children, let's clear the plates and get going.' She stood up and waited for the man to stand so that she could side step to the end of the bench. When he raised himself, taking his time, she moved her skirt aside as if she didn't want it to touch him. Bill held the packed-up plates and signalled a *Hurry up* to Jill with his eyes. She rolled hers back, but followed behind him.

Outside, Mother walked them very briskly along the road, as if worried that the man would follow them. A little way ahead she said, 'You must be careful of talking to strange men, Jill.'

'But he had no arm! When we had the collection for wounded soldiers, you gave me sixpence to put in the tin.'

'Even so. Men you don't know. Just – don't talk to them, and certainly don't discuss our private business.' She strode on.

Jill lagged behind, sulking.

Mother turned her attention to Bill. 'I know that was very awkward and the man was obnoxious, but he's bitter because he's been badly wounded. He'll have difficulty getting any sort of work again, and that means his useful life is over. It was surely dreadful enough being in trenches under fire.'

That would have been awful for Ted too. Bill's heart didn't have room for the man's problems. 'I knew Uncle Ted was in France first. No-one said where he was afterwards.'

Jill caught up. 'Was Uncle Ted really in Africa, Mummy?'

'Yes, and other countries. He really doesn't want to talk about the war, so please, both of you, no questions.'

'Oh,' Jill whined. 'But Africa is where black people are and piccaninnies, and great big fruits grow on the trees and it's baking hot all the time. I want to hear all about it.'

'You'll have to learn about it in school, then. Not from Uncle Ted. Mind, I shall be very cross if you disobey, Jill.'

Jill tossed her head and skipped ahead. Did that mean she would or wouldn't obey? He'd have a quiet word with her. Ted had been in Africa. The GIs had been sent there in '43. Supposing they'd met!

Ted was leaning against the car, waiting for them. He wasn't wearing army trousers like the man in the restaurant. Where was his uniform and what had happened that Ted didn't want to talk about? Bill remembered how he'd been in a dreadful state after Dunkirk, but he did talk about that. This time he was like a shop with the 'Closed' sign.

Ted stood up as he saw them. 'Ready, then? Let's get going.'

Jill sprang forward. 'Can I just press the horn?' It was attached to the front of the car, its rubber ball just asking to be squeezed.

Ted shrugged and Jill sprang to squeeze it before Mother could say *No*. It gave out a satisfying honk. Bill wanted a go himself but Mother was waiting at the passenger door with the seat tipped forward for them.

Bill squeezed in, changing seats so that Jill could be on the pavement side for seeing London. Ted leant down to crank the engine and it started obediently. He got into his seat and placed his hands on the wheel firmly enough.

As the car moved forward Jill's voice rang out. 'Lon-don, Lon-don, off to London town.'

Ted looked moody and Mother didn't chat either. Jill filled the silence with chirpy singing until Mother said, 'Enough, dear. We've heard enough songs.'

'Will it be long before we get to London? I want to see all the famous buildings.'

'What's left of them,' muttered Ted.

Bill sat back and closed his eyes. Best to pretend he was sleepy to avoid saying the wrong thing.

Jill nudged him, but when he didn't move, she pulled a comic from her little bag and turned the pages slowly. She couldn't read much yet. He'd read to her, now they were going back to live together, like a proper brother and sister again.

CHAPTER 2

It surely wasn't long since he'd closed his eyes but he must have slept, for now they were passing the ruins of buildings. Piles of rubble and wooden work huts sat alongside blackened brick walls. Factories, pubs, banks or homes had once stood there. It was difficult to believe it.

Jill shrieked. 'Look at that house! Its insides are all showing. I can see a bath upstairs.' She giggled. 'Look, Bill, you can see the stairs and everything.'

The dingy houses and blocks of flats were so close together and had no gardens. There were holes in the pavement where railings had been, dirt on the walls, cigarette stubs all over the pavements. The streets of houses had cleared spaces surrounded by brick rubble. London was different from what he remembered, lighter, yet blacker. The buildings looked filthy, an edging of black fluff on every surface. Even with blue skies and strong sunlight, it wasn't a cheerful outlook. Bill stared hard another ruin of a home. Supposing they'd stayed home in Primley Road instead of escaping to the country!

'Oh my goodness,' said Mother. 'What a mess! We've lost the London we knew.'

'Look! Red buses, buses with upstairses!' Jill squealed as one thundered past.

'Double-deckers,' Bill muttered. They looked huge after the village bus. He peered at the next one passing. He'd almost forgotten what they were like. 'Upstairs, Jill, at the very front, you can see all around, and you're right close to the buildings.'

Mother turned around. 'We're coming into the centre of London, now.' She turned back to Ted. 'Do a little tour, Ted, can you? Goodness, how long since I've been here!'

Another squeak from Jill. 'Look at those ladies in high heels.' The people in the streets did look different from the country folk.

Ted drove grimly on. Mother had gone quiet.

Bill saw that, to Jill, this was all new and exciting. She'd grown up with no knowledge of London.

'Ooh, look at that great big church thing.'

'St Paul's Cathedral. It's famous.'

'All over the world? Did Hitler know about it?'

'Yes,' Ted suddenly joined in. 'He'd have bombed it if he could. Look how it's bombed all around.'

Last time Bill was here, tall buildings had blocked the sight of St Paul's apart from its dome. Now they could now see the whole of it, flanked by the blackened bases of ruined buildings and a great cleared patch in front. But it still looked magnificent, a king amongst paupers.

'St Paul's Cathedral,' Jill murmured. 'And what's that, Bill?'

It was rather nice having a little sister wanting him to point out everything. Jill had been Kenneth's shadow for the past four years. Bill pointed out the Houses of Parliament, not that she'd understand what 'government' meant. He stared himself, everything so close together, so big. So damaged. It was a strange thrill to be back after so long, but shocking too.

Ted drove over Westminster Bridge.

'Let me see the river. Is it big, is it blue?' Jill was as near to standing as she could manage, her face pressed to the window. Bill eyed the muddy banks full of debris, slightly green on top of its satiny surface.

'Oh it's nearly black and all the bank is mud. Ugh.' But the boats pleased her and she stayed excited as they drove past the dinginess of Stockwell, Oval, Elephant and Castle.

When he saw the crush around Clapham Junction and heard Mother breathe, 'Arding and Hobbs,' Bill knew they would soon be home.

They passed the common. Even the stretches of green were soiled. It was blighted by corrugated iron huts, piles of iron, bricks, unkempt grass and overgrown bushes. They drove down roads with gaps where a house had been the unlucky hit. All this had been happening while lucky people were safe away in evacuation.

Jill laughed at another sliced open house, a stray bath lying in the garden and the upstairs rooms displaying the sad broken furniture. 'How funny! It looks as if someone's just gone out.'

'Just gone,' Ted said bitterly.

Bill felt queasy. Would Primley Road look this bad?

Mother looked out of the window, holding her handkerchief in front of her mouth. Bill had known, of course he'd known, that loads of buildings had been hit, but while he was living with the Pawseys he'd been so safe that the news was like a wireless play; scary but not real.

Mother said, 'We're not far from Wandsworth now.'

The buildings did look more familiar, and he looked keenly in case he recognised something. 'Isn't this the road we used to walk to Mr Durban's, Mother?'

'Yes, that's right.'

'Who's Mr Durban?' Jill piped up.

'He's Dad's friend, he works with him.' A bright orange feeling joined all Bill's black ones. He couldn't wait to see Mr Durban and the precious sabre. Once his secret photo of it had been stolen, he hadn't had its magic protection. Now he'd be seeing it for real.

The car turned a corner into a road where nothing was bombed. Primley Road looked the same as the day he'd left, carrying his suitcase and a bag of food, with his parents pushing Jill's pushchair ahead of him. He screwed up his eyes and tried to remember the scene through the smeared glass of the car window.

Mother got out of the car while Ted collected the luggage from the boot. He set it all in a line, military style.

Jill had already pushed the front seat forward to scramble out. Bill waited. If he placed his feet on this pavement it was like accepting that he belonged here. He looked up at the front of the house. It was strange, recognizing it so well yet feeling so apart from it. He stayed sitting until Mother waved him to get out.

'Help, then, Bill!'

'Is this our house or that one?' said Jill, pulling a case onto the pavement with one hand and waving a finger with the other.

Bill pointed to their black gate. He wasn't sure the house had a friendly look. A flickery feeling swirled inside his tummy.

Ted stretched. 'Long drive. I won't come in, Sis.' He put their suitcases at the front door. 'I've got to take the car to the station for Lieutenant Trent's brother to collect. But I'll do that in the morning. First, it's time to settle back home with the parents.'

Mother held him at his elbow and her voice was kind. 'You must be so relieved to be back with them at last.'

He shrugged, his face stiff. 'It'll all be changed there. You'll see.' He drove away with a brief wave of a white hand.

Bill looked around, trying to remember this road. When he was six and seven, he used to run down to school that way. Turning left led to Reg's house, and a few streets on, to Andrew's. Would he see any of them? Not when it was time to go back to school. They were all too old for junior school now. He turned back. Jill was standing still, large-eyed, until Mother put a bag in her hands and ushered her through the front gate. Then she gave Bill the keys. He opened the front door, quite slowly.

A damp and musty smell met him. He and Mother dumped the suitcases in the hall. He picked up a large pile of post and put it on the hall stand.

She sniffed. 'You can tell how long it is since your father was here. I can positively smell abandonment.'

The cream gloss wallpaper under the dado rail was far dingier than Bill remembered, and the patterned tiles on the floor needed a good clean. He glanced out at the road again before shutting the door. How close together the houses were, pressed in, like people on a crowded train. He shook his head. No fields between houses here. There wouldn't be any smell of country. Perhaps he'd never smell it again. *But when I'm grown up, getting there will be down to me.* Only, it was such a long time until he was twenty-one.

'Phew,' said Mother. 'Home at last. I can't believe it! My own home again after all this time.' She opened the front room door and started pulling dust sheets off the chairs.

Jill was silent, standing with the bag Mother had passed to her, like a party guest who was waiting to be welcomed.

He said, 'Shall I go round and open some windows?'

'Yes, do that, Billy.'

'*Bill*, now.'

'All right, all right. And collect the dust sheets. Tea. I need some tea. Surely there'll still be a packet of tea in the caddy. There won't be any milk. We'll have to open a tin of condensed, but at least we'll have a fresh pot of tea for a nice change. Pray your father didn't use it all before he left.'

He heard her footsteps down the passage and then a cry of glee. 'My old kitchen. All to myself! I shall have to remind myself where everything is.'

'I don't know where anything is,' Jill piped up. 'Can you show me, Bill?'

He pointed to the front room and she put her head round the door.

'Front room, we don't use it much. You mustn't touch the ornaments in it. Anyway, it's to be Aunty's room now. The next door's the cloakroom. I'll show you the rest of the house later. I'm going to help Mother, so why don't you go upstairs and find your old bedroom.'

'Where is it? I'm going to put all my secret things there.'

He smiled. 'Your room's the furthest one. Go on. You might find your old toys in the cupboard.'

He felt better for the sound of Jill's voice counting the stairs while she hopped up them. He went back slowly into each room, pulling the sheets off the chairs, turning the pictures to face the right way, removing the blackout and opening each window. It felt slightly shocking to do these things without asking permission first.

Each room brought a memory: galloping horsey out of the front room, helping Mrs Donnington polish the spoons in the dining room, watching Dad smoke his pipe in the parlour where the wireless voice doomed misery, the pack of unopened colouring pencils on the garden room bookcase and Dad's disappointed voice, 'He has no interest in drawing, whatsoever', Uncle Frank measuring Kenneth and himself back-to-back against the hall wall; the wrestling, the exercises, Uncle Frank's death. He shuddered. It was uncomfortable, those past times flitting into his mind, one fragment after another.

It must be ages since Dad was here, and even more years since Mrs Donnington had been in to clean. Would she come back now war had ended? Everywhere was terribly dusty, cobwebs were hanging from all the corners of the ceilings. He took the dust sheets into the hall. The dust would have to be washed out now.

Mother called out, 'Bring down some sheets from the airing cupboard, Bill. We'll peg them on the line to freshen while there's still sun. They haven't seen the light of day for years, so I hope there's no moth.

He bounded upstairs. His room hadn't been touched since 1940. Before Dad was called up in '43, he probably only came for the post and a night's rest, and to keep the house from being requisitioned. He was mostly wherever Court was sitting.

Horsey was propped in one corner. Bill remembered putting him there after returning from the first evacuation, because a seven-year-old was too old to play with hobby-horses.

He closed his door and leant back against it. He'd enjoyed his own space here, way back before he'd known there was a man called Hitler, before he heard bombs or saw dogfights. He stretched his arms out trying to occupy the whole space. Horribly soon he'd be sharing it.

Along the passage he could hear Jill squeaking in her bedroom, then her footsteps as she peeped into Mother's room, the bathroom, the spare room, and finally his. 'It's big this house, like the vicarage, but there's only one upstairs.'

'There's the loft, but you need a ladder to get up there.'

'Golly, I can't remember anything,' she said. 'I'm like someone who's never been here.'

'But you were. I remember the day you were born and a nurse was with Mother in her bedroom. When you were a toddler, I read you stories up here, sometimes. Once I found you a little bear. It fitted just snugly into your hand.'

She looked at her empty hand as if he was making it up. 'Can't remember. Do you like being back in your old bedroom?'

'Yes, quite.'

'Where's Kenneth going to sleep?'

He took a big breath pressing what felt like a metal band round his chest. 'There'll be bunk beds. This one will have to go.' He looked around, imagining the changed room.

'You've never shared before.'

'Actually I have. My first evacuation. Alan and I shared: and not just a room – it was more like a cupboard – but the bed, a little camp bed.'

'Goodness! That must have been a squash.'

'It was, but we got used to it.' If only it was Alan he had to share with, not Kenneth.

Jill used her grown-up's voice. 'You can get used to anything if it goes on long enough. The vicar said that once when I wanted jam on my bread and there wasn't any. Come on. You said you'd show me the downstairs rooms and I want my tea.'

He collected the sheets from the airing cupboard and led Jill downstairs. He found Mother laying tea in the kitchen instead of the dining room. The mound of dust sheets now filled the scullery doorway.

'Take a cloth from the scullery,' she said to Bill, 'before you hang the clean sheets outside. You'll need to clean the washing line first.'

He went outside and ran the cloth along the line of rope that stretched from the scullery to the shed, the ugly part of the garden. Mother was right, when he got to the end of the rope the cloth was filthy. He looked up and remembered the searchlights, the flak and planes overhead. The cloth was thick with dirt from the war in the skies as much as the smoke from London chimneys. The top of a factory chimney in the distance had a steady plume to join the rest. How it spoiled the blue sky! He spread out the sheets for their first night home.

He washed the cloth and his hands in the scullery sink. Through the doorway, he saw Mother putting the teapot on the kitchen table.

'Come on, Bill. We'll eat here for now. I've got everything to do now we're back, and I've only the one pair of hands.'

'You'd look funny with more.' Jill giggled.

'Don't be smart.' Mother looked at them both as if they might suddenly multiply into several children. 'I expect you're both hungry. I'm not sure what I can find you to eat.'

Bill picked up the basket from Mrs Pawsey. He slid it forwards. Inside were eggs, fruit cake, butter, crusty bread and tomatoes.

'Bless her!' She unpacked it. She cut the bread, then three very thin slices from the fruit cake.

While she was busy, Bill managed to put the napkin in his pocket.

Mother rescued a raisin that had fallen onto the table and put it with the fruit cake. 'We're certainly glad of this today. We're used to rationing, but it will be much worse here in London, so you children will have to get used to it.'

Bill spread a scrape of butter carefully onto his bread. Mother had found some Bovril in the larder. The thick, sticky paste at the bottom of the jar was still worth scraping up. He looked at the padlock hanging from its metal loop on the larder door. Mother and Mrs Donnington had piled the stock there when war was expected. 'Do you remember Mrs Donnington, Jill?'

'Who?'

'Our Home Help,' Mother said. 'We shan't be seeing her again. No-one can get any help now. Everyone's told me that.'

Jill wasn't listening. She finished her tea quickly and got up without asking, but Mother didn't say anything until Jill started opening cupboards. 'Enough!' Mother shooed them both out of the kitchen. 'I want to clear up and find what tins are left. Then I must write the shopping list and a note for the milkman so he knows to start delivering again.'

'Show me round, Bill. You said!' Jill ran in and out of the downstairs rooms. 'Isn't it funny that I was here, sitting in my highchair.'

'And hiding,' Bill said. 'Come here.' He opened the cellar door and peered under the stairs. There was no light and Dad hadn't left the torch hanging on its hook. He pushed Jill's head down in the right direction so that she could make out the outline of the camp bed where they'd sat those scary nights. 'Do you remember being down here in the middle of the night sheltering from the bombs?'

Jill shook her head.

'Not the noise?' He pointed. 'That's where we had to sit. Next to the coal hole.'

'Ugh. Bet there are spiders down there.'

'Probably. They have to live somewhere. Can you see the round iron flap up at the end of the cellar? That's where the coal comes shooting down when the coalman comes. Mother let me stand here sometimes and watch. I thought that was very exciting.' He smiled. 'You can stand there, next time he's due.'

'Not likely! Why would I want to put my head in a horrid, dark stairway and see coal coming through!' She wriggled back out of the doorway, brushing cobwebs off her hands. 'Ugh.'

He wasn't used to having girls around. It was odd, the things they liked and didn't like. He took her back to the kitchen where Mother was opening the post. 'There's one for you, Bill, somewhere.' She rifled through the pile. Could Dad have written one just for him? It surely couldn't be from Mr and Mrs Pawsey already. Mother pulled out a postcard. 'Here.'

The card showed a picture of a large building with pillars in front and a green hat-like thing on its tower. He turned it over. He recognised the neat print immediately. His excitement dashed down to the floor. It was from Kenneth.

Billy,

I am having a lovely time with my granny and grandpa. They have given me loads of things. They took me to the pictures and I saw Anchors Aweigh with Gene Kelly and Fred Astaire. It was funny and excellent.

Yesterday, Mummy heard that I have been awarded a place at Dulwich College. It's the best school in the whole of South London. Have you been told which school you are going to yet?

Are you getting your bedroom ready for me? We will be coming soon.

Kenneth

Bill swallowed twice, then held out the postcard to Mother to read. Her head was bent over one letter after the other. 'Yes, dear, I've read it. Kenneth seems to be cock-a-hoop.'

'Come on, Jill, I'll show you the garden.' He took her outside. He wouldn't have her attention for many days more. Kenneth would take it over.

Mother had so much to do that it was late when they went to bed. The thin slice of fruit cake and two slices of bread felt like a long time ago and there was nothing more. He was hungry. Mrs Pawsey had always given him a good supper in the evening.

He sat on his bed with a thump. It was only this morning he'd been at home with the Pawseys, with the Youldons' cottage just a short run away. He was almost a son to the Pawseys, he'd been with them so long, and because they'd lost their only son, Graham. As for Mrs Youldon, whose little cottage he'd been billeted in on the first evacuation, she was the first person to make him feel special. She said he was her big boy. She depended on him for looking after her little ones. Now he'd gone from all of them forever. His eyes smarted. Mother wouldn't ever take him for a visit, that was for sure. He screwed up his eyes, trying to see them from memory. Were they all missing him? He pulled the green and white napkin from his pocket, hugging it to his chest. It was his little bit of the Pawsey home that he was going to keep always.

By his bed there was a certain crack in the wall which before evacuation, he'd always peered at as he dropped off to sleep, making it into a spider, a thin man, a steeple with bricks hanging below it. He could still do it. He pulled the blanket further towards his chin. The smell of his blanket, the iron base of his bed and the rail above it took his thoughts way back beyond the wail of the air raid siren to a time of soft toys, pyjamas with stars on them, hot milk in a blue chunky cup, and a faraway da-dit-dit-da of cross voices below the floorboards.

CHAPTER 3

Bill's eyelids felt too heavy to open but unfamiliar sounds around him stopped him from curling up into oblivion again. He thrust out his hand to feel for the damp nose of Macbeth or the thick ruff of Othello. Air blew through his searching fingers. They remained empty. He turned over and faced the crack in the wall. He heard gates opening, an exchange of *Good Mornings*. Primley Road people were off to work. He was not at the Pawseys' any more.

He pulled the sheet above his head, lying still to recapture the morning sense of restless dogs, the huff and puff of Mr Pawsey on the stairs, the whiff of honeysuckle and parsley, the snorting and clucking of piglets and chickens awaiting their feed. He wanted to remember all of it forever. One day, when he had his own money and was allowed to go away on his own, he would buy a train ticket and go back for real. His throat hurt. It hurt badly. He put his fingers on it in case there was a great lump Mother or Jill would see. No, only he would know it was there.

After another few moments of shutting his eyes to the new day, he sat up. The napkin fell off his front. He held it to his nose. He could smell the Pawseys' dining room, the home-baked bread. He wanted the napkin with him all the time. It was too big to keep on him without someone noticing, but he had scissors in his soap-bag.

He got out of bed and found them. He cut the best piece, the middle, into a neat size. He could put that inside a full handkerchief every day, and no-one would ever know. He hid the rest of the napkin under his handkerchiefs and socks in his top drawer, and held the cut piece close. Mrs Pawsey had told him to think about cheerful things, like the people he'd be seeing again. She'd want him to do that.

Think of seeing the sabre again; Mr Durban, and Angela, a person who told him what was going on when no-one else did. She'd be pleased he was back. Nanny and Grandad's faces would glow when they set eyes on him. It was nearly five years since they'd seen him and Jill, who was still in a pram back then. They'd hold out their arms and their hugs would go on and on. They'd be amazed at how grown up he was. Uncle Ted would be absolutely fine now that he was safe at home. Everything would be back to how it used to be when he was small. Nanny would make a lovely dinner — well, the best meal she could on rations. Visiting them had always been the best day of the week.

He slid out of bed and was the first washed and dressed. He put the piece of napkin inside a clean handkerchief and then in his trouser pocket.

After laying the table for breakfast in the kitchen, he went into the garden in case there were some flowers he could pick for Nanny. She'd like that. The garden was quite a mess, everything overgrown. He went to the shed but couldn't open the door. Swollen wood at its bottom pressed into the mud. The lowest two overlapping planks needed replacing where they had rotted. Perhaps there was a saw in the cellar. He had better see to this.

Apart from a patch of rotting rhubarb, there didn't seem to be any vegetables, and the flowers had been sabotaged by weeds. He kicked at a patch of soil. It was light brown, thin and stony, not like the rich ginger of the Pawseys' garden.

Mother always used to want something pretty to look at from her chair in the garden room. She'd never liked to garden, and hadn't wanted a vegetable plot, but with rationing, how would they manage without? Until Dad was demobbed, he'd better take the garden over. He'd learned so much from Mr Pawsey, so he could do it. He picked the largest stones from the patch where he would grow the carrots and things and threw them as far down the garden as he could.

When he went back indoors, Mother was in the kitchen holding the packet of cornflakes. 'This is only half full and it's probably stale.' She put round three dishes. 'You'll have to be the main food shopper, Bill, because people go early to queue. Even without this horrendous pile of washing, by the time I've seen to Jill and breakfast, everything will have been snapped up.' Her voice rose higher. 'And I don't know how I'm going to get this house clean and straight and feed everyone. Without Mrs Donnington, I have everything to do.'

He wasn't sure how best to help. He picked the ration books up from the table to see which shops they were registered at. Mother commented from the larder, 'Not even any oats. Goodness me, your father must have eaten loads of porridge. And all these shelves are so dirty! Pass me the Vim, will you?'

He found the cylinder of Vim under the sink, its cardboard soggy where the tap had leaked into the cupboard. He spoke towards the larder. 'We could keep chickens, so we'd get eggs. There's plenty of room in the garden.'

Mother squeaked. 'Ooh, I couldn't cope with feathery things. Suppose they got indoors? I wouldn't have a clue how to deal with them.'

'I would. I could look after them.'

Mother emerged from the larder holding the dishcloth and Vim. 'You did that at the Pawseys' of course. How out of touch I am with what you can do.' She put her dishcloth under the tap and wrung it out.

Jill came down in her dressing gown. Aunty had knitted it, but there hadn't been enough wool to make it all one colour. The top part was mustard yellow, the middle, grey and the bottom quarter was army green. 'Can I have my cornflakes before getting dressed, Mummy? I couldn't find any clothes.'

Mother pushed her hands through her hair. 'None? Not in the brown suitcase?'

'They were dirty when they were packed, remember?'

'Oh my goodness. All this washing on my very first morning home.' She fluttered her hands towards the largest suitcase, not yet unpacked. 'Who'd be me? There must be something you can wear, Jill.'

'Only these, if you mean in the chest of drawers.' She opened her dressing gown to show a tiny frilly skirt hanging off one hip and a blouse that must have fitted her when she was in her pram. Bill gave a shout of laughter and she burst into peals of giggles and rolled on the floor.

Mother wasn't amused. 'Get up, get up. You were far less trouble when you were that size, I'll have you know. Sit up for your breakfast, please.'

Jill didn't rush to get up or to finish giggling. Mother sighed and turned her back. She poured some milk into each cornflake dish.

When he was seven like Jill, the kitchen had been a place where he feared trouble. Jill, twisting round to make Bill laugh and in full view of Mother, obviously didn't have such a problem. She looked totally confident. Had Mother changed? He sneaked a glance as she placed a dish neatly into Jill's place, and another more randomly into his. No, she just preferred girls. He pulled his dish towards him and began eating the flakes, stale as old cardboard. No napkins for kitchen meals! How things had changed, post-war.

Jill munched away happily. 'My friend Iris lives right near here. She's the one I played hopscotch with and I want to go and see her.'

Mother didn't appear to be listening. She was eking out the last of the condensed milk into her pale beige tea, the pot 'hotted up' from last evening.

It would probably help Mother to have Jill out of the way. He said, 'What street does Iris live in?'

'Look. Her mummy wrote it down.' She passed over an old birthday card with an address written on the inside.

'That's near St Ann's Hill. I know it. Perhaps I can walk you there when I go for the shopping – if Mother says.'

Mother looked up, her mind probably on other things, and nodded. 'When you're dressed.' Then as an afterthought she added, 'If people are right about the length of queues, it will probably be dinner-time by the time Bill finishes, so he can collect you as well.'

'All right,' he said. If she wasn't in a hurry for him to get back, he could scout around a bit after delivering Jill. He might come across Reg or Andrew, or take a look at his old junior school.

'There are quite a lot of chores to finish before you can go,' Mother interrupted his thoughts.

He swept the larder and kitchen, pulling the bag of dirty washing from the large suitcase and piling it beside the dust sheets against the scullery sink. He checked the mangle. He remembered that if you left it unused for too long, the rubber rollers stuck together and left tiny flecks on the wet washing. Their last holiday, he calculated quickly, six years ago, they'd had a smashing two weeks at Cooden Beach. When they'd got back it was a baking hot day. Mrs Donnington had been sweating over the washing while she minded him. The mangle roller was soggy. He'd been sitting on a bucket in the scullery picking the rubber bits out of his knitted swimming costume when Dad came in to tell her the fearful news that war was almost certainly coming.

He wound the mangle handle a couple of times and grubby grey streaks showed on the roller. There was a stockinette dishcloth on the draining board. He was going to clean the rollers with it, but it had dried into such hard folds that it stayed stuck on the draining board, and when he yanked on it a splinter of wood went into the side of his hand. He didn't like wooden draining boards. Mrs Pawsey had an enamel sink and drainer. It was chipped and badly stained, but you didn't get splinters.

'Why are you sucking your hand?' Jill was now dressed in the things she'd worn yesterday.

'Here, can you pull this splinter out? I can't do it with my left hand.'

Her fingers were small enough, half the width of his. She leant over him and pulled it out. 'You see, I am a useful girl.'

'Thanks. Are you ready to go?'

Mother was sorting the remainder of the suitcase into piles on the kitchen chairs. She nodded at the table. 'There are the ration books and the form to show we're back. I've written you a list. Standard loaf, cheese, marmalade, two tins of beans, cornflakes, half a pound of biscuits – broken will do, they taste just the same – the meat ration, three pounds of potatoes, onions, carrots and a cabbage. Take two baskets to even the weight.' She passed them over. 'Here's three florins. That should be plenty. You can buy a comic each with the change.'

'Thank you!' That was a whopping surprise. He hadn't had a comic for ages.

Jill started saying, 'Don't get me *Sunny Stories*. I want a comic with more pictures.'

He nudged her to the front door. She was chancing their luck by sounding ungrateful. 'Tell me outside, silly,' he muttered. They left the house to its dank, neglected smell. Sunshine beamed onto the front path.

'It's hot!' Jill hopped towards the gate swinging what had once been a very smart lady's bag. Its gold coloured clasp hung open, revealing a number of small dolls and a Knitting Nancy.

'Where did you get that bag, Jill?'

'Aunty gave it to me because the clasp's broken. Look—.' She let it fall open wider and stroked the inside. 'This is satin.'

'If you take that, you won't be able to help me carry the shopping home.'

'No. I can carry the comics, though, under my arm.' She skipped ahead, her dark curls bouncing on her shoulders as cheekily as her words.

'I hope it'll be all right with Iris's mother, you coming without any notice. If not, you'll have to come with me.'

Iris's place had a low brick wall topped by a hedge. The double-fronted house with its bay windows looked inviting, and when Iris's mother opened the door to them, she smiled widely. 'Hello, Jill! Iris has been saying you'd be back home by now. It is a nice surprise to see you so soon. Come along in.' She pointed to the handbag. 'I can see you've brought things to play with. And you are Billy, the brother?'

'Bill, Mrs Nokes. I'm just dropping Jill, if that's all right. I've got to go and queue for the food. We only got back yesterday evening.'

'Your mother must be up to her ears. Tell me where you live and I'll drop Jill back after dinner. She can stay and eat with us.'

'Hooray!' Jill stood peering down the hall for her friend without a backward glance at Bill. 'We live in Primley Road and I know the way!'

'Thank you very much, Mrs Nokes.' Bill shut the gate behind him. Even better. Now he had time to scoot around for a recce.

The nearby roads still had their trees but many of the front gardens looked neglected, no fathers, no husbands to work in them on Sundays.

Around the common, the iron railings had been ripped out for the war effort. The regular gaps along the grass looked like a mouth with pulled teeth. The white S for Shelter was still clear over the entrance, but Mr Durban's ARP hut had been removed. That's where Bill had rushed for information and comfort when Ted returned from Dunkirk in boots that had gone green, a greatcoat and nothing else. Kenneth had scoffed that he'd been defeated but Mr Durban said Dunkirk was a miraculous success and asked for Bill's help in eating a bar of chocolate. Bill smiled. He realised, now he was older, that Mr Durban was just being kind. And it was probably his last bar. When sweets came off the ration, he'd buy Mr Durban loads of chocolate.

He walked to the top of St John's Hill overlooking the mess of London. Fulham was where Mr Durban's Cossack sabre lived in a cupboard, the scarlet top of its pommel just showing above its scabbard. How thrilling it had been, that first Christmas Eve of the war when Mr Durban told him its terrible tale and its special name - *shashka*. And now he had his own sabre story to tell Mr Durban, the one Alan had found in the Manor library last year.

Mother should hurry up and telephone Mrs Durban to say they were back. They must visit soon, before Kenneth got back. He mustn't hear about the sabre; it was Bill's secret that he had seen it, dreamed up its power, and Mr Durban's secret that he had told Bill its story.

He ran down towards the station. That's where there were a lot of bombed houses. One had bits of chairs, an exposed staircase, and a tree continuing to grow right through the rubble. Next door, a pram stood outside an undamaged house and a woman was scrubbing the step, as if nothing had ever gone wrong. Nearby, a house was sliced open from front to back. A small gang of rough children scrambled up to the first floor. Others were rummaging through rubble for war treasure: shrapnel, pennies, ornaments and crockery under heaps of brick dust. A group of girls played house in a back room that still had three of its walls and a mantle-piece. Two were 'cooking' in a battered saucepan with a long spoon, and a bigger girl was sweeping dust from under a horse chestnut tree. Another sat on a backless chair, pretending to be The Mistress. Several boys were playing tight-rope along one of the remaining joists on the first floor. It did look fun, but he didn't know any of them.

He stepped back onto the pavement. Joining in would be much better when he'd found one of his old friends. They'd do a whole tour of bomb sites. That would be spiffing. He turned away. He was supposed to be shopping. It would be awful if everything had been sold because he had been off exploring instead of queuing. He ran back towards Garrett Lane.

The line of women stared at him when he joined the baker's queue. He was a newcomer, just the same as when he was first evacuated. He wanted to shout out, 'I live here. I'm from Wandsworth.' After about ten minutes he got to the front. He handed over the ration books and took hold of the greyish National loaf. It had no smell. Mrs Pawsey had always baked her own, swapping her eggs for flour. He put the hard oblong into the basket. When would he enjoy a baking bread smell again?

It took longer to get served at the grocer's and after that, the greengrocer's had the longest queue of all. There was a whisper about a new delivery and when he reached the front he saw a carton of small oranges with a large notice, 'Children Only'. He passed the ration books over but the greengrocer only let him have one. 'You're too big to count as a child.'

Bill pointed to his ration book, but the greengrocer shrugged. 'Sorry.'

Bill hesitated. Should he argue?

The lady behind Bill said, 'Hurry up, ducky. We all want to get served, you know.'

He asked for the potatoes. When the greengrocer threw them on the scales, they were so thick with dirt that he didn't get much for the money. He wouldn't look forward to coming to this shop again, but you had to go where you were registered.

He got Jill's comic from the newsagents and although it had *The Wizard*, he bought stamps with his share of the change so he could write to the Pawseys and Youldons.

The baskets were too heavy to walk over to his old school. That would have to wait for another day.

Arms aching, he walked on until Primley Road stretched in front of him, unharmed and only slightly shabby, as if it had been unaware of the war. The gate was swinging loose as he came back up the path. He could mend that sort of thing now. He went to find Mother. She had emptied the large suitcase which was now propped against the door, while beside her on the floor, a tin bucket held the dreaded washing.

'Here's the shopping, Mother. I'm going to mend the gate later; the hinge is off. I know where the tools are.'

'Good. If you can, Bill. I've made a huge list of things that need doing.' She looked up as he started to unpack the baskets, holding out each item like a trophy.

'Loaf.'

'If that's today's bread, I'm a film star.'

'Cabbage. Potatoes.'

'They look as if they've brought half the garden with them.' Then she saw the orange. 'Ooh, an orange. What luck! Where is Jill?'

'Mrs Nokes is bringing her back after her dinner.' He hung the empty baskets on their hooks in the larder. 'Are we going to Nanny and Grandad's afterwards?'

Mother looked at the tin bath full of washing and sighed. 'Tomorrow. I have to wash a second load now and get it hung out.'

'Can't we go after that?'

'I shall be all in. Anyway, it's probably best to let Ted settle in properly before we go round there. They have to adapt to having him home. Find me some more pegs, will you? Then we'll have our dinner and afterwards, I can start dusting everywhere. It will take an age to get the living room clean, but we must have somewhere to sit besides the kitchen. We can't live as though we're paupers.'

The doorbell rang, and Mother went to thank Mrs Nokes for having Jill. Jill's voice trilled down the hallway in a sing-song.

'Thank-you-ver-y-much; can-I-come-again?' She skipped on towards the kitchen.

Mother followed. 'Jill, you are in luck. Bill got an orange from the greengrocers.' She passed it over. 'Give him a couple of pieces, will you?'

Jill took up the orange, sniffing it and closing her eyes. 'Aaahhh! We had one of these at the vicarage Christmas party.' The skin was very tough and the white stuff wouldn't come away from the fruit for ages. 'Here you are.' She handed Bill two segments.

'Thanks, Jill. Smashing.'

She sucked at one herself. 'It's not very juicy. How do I eat it? It's hiding under a white blanket.'

Bill couldn't help laughing, but Mother tutted and took a knife to the orange. 'Be grateful, child. Fruit's a rare enough treat. It's only you who got one.'

'You can have this boat, Mummy,' said Jill.

Mother slipped the segment into her mouth and chewed it slowly. 'Not very good, I agree.' She sighed. 'I remember real oranges. Before you were born, Jill.'

It was at the Manor party, with Alan and all the other vaccies, that he'd last had an orange. This one was a very poor substitute, but he kept the last mouthful of orange in his mouth for as long as he could as a way of bringing back the memory. He had a long drink of water to savour the taste.

Jill looked impressed. 'What a big drink, Bill! I saw your throat wobbling up and down. Isn't it lucky that water's not on ration?'

'Perish the thought, child,' said Mother. 'That's all we need!'

Bill hid his smile. Jill's funny comments were the only cheer in Wandsworth. 'Is it all right if I go back out for a bit, Mother? I'll fix the gate when I get back.'

'Yes, you go, Bill. I'll teach this young lady how to dust and tidy her bedroom, now that she has one.'

CHAPTER 4

Bill shut the front door behind him and started up the street. The air smelled full of bus fumes and coal dust. A grey mist spoiled the blue sky behind it. He turned away. He belonged in the country, not here.

A shout came from across the road. A rough lad on a bicycle with an overloaded basket on the front shouted, 'Hey! It's you, isn't it? Billy? Billy Wilson, eh?'

He saw a bony face, red from the sun, under unruly greasy hair. The lad wore a man's jacket that hung very loose. Something registered, but not the deep rasping voice. The lad swung his leg over the bike, making the pile of vegetables in the basket wobble dangerously. Bill lifted a hand halfway, not to seem unfriendly.

'You back then, Billy? Look at you, you're not half tall! Ages since we sat together in Mr Hendrick's class, i'nt it?'

It was Jim, the chunky boy he'd once played football with! He was so changed; skinny and rather grubby-looking. 'Goodness. Hallo, Jim. I'm just back – yesterday. Call me Bill now, will you?'

'Okay. What's it like, the country? You gone and went the first, di'n' you? I remember you lot all filing out for the station that day. It went flipping quiet in school after. I thought Ma would send me away, but she never. Bet you had all the fun.'

'Mm, it was good. I liked it. Did you stay here all through everything?'

Jim nodded. 'Yep. Dog fights. Bombing. V1s, V2s, seen it all.'

He was like an old soldier. All the stuff on the newsreels Bill had seen, Jim had been in it.

'What happened to the rest of our lot? Andrew, Reg and everyone? They didn't end up with us. Did they stay behind too?'

Jim's face lengthened. 'Andrew did. He bought it, him and his mum.'

'What – not…?'

'Yeah, on the way to the shelter. Both together, in '41.'

'*No*.' That was something Bill had been scared to think of, his own friends caught by bombs. It was shocking enough to lose an uncle, even a nasty one; far worse to lose a friend. He leant back against a low wall. He'd been looking forward to exploring bomb sites with Andrew, and now his house was one of them. No Andrew. He could almost see his back view, a rumpled shirt and pullover, the only boy with brown plimsolls, running after the tennis ball, the only thing they had to play football with at that time. It was Andrew who told him to stand up to Kenneth after a bad spat in the playground. Now he wouldn't say anything anymore. Bill wouldn't bump into Andrew around the shops or see him climbing on anything. He was gone. Just gone. He looked back at Jim. Who else might be lost? He managed, 'You've been okay, your mother and everyone?'

'Suppose.' Jim shrugged. 'Except she's been working nights; sleeping when I get up, getting ready for work when I get home. My dad's going to be demobbed, though. September, he says, 'cos he was one of the first went. Lucky he didn't cop it, over in the thick of it all.'

'Rath-er. I'm glad he's okay. Mine is, too. I'm waiting for him to be demobbed.' He hesitated. 'Sonia was in my village. She's staying on for a while, and the awful twins. Do you know about the others, Reg? Fred? Mavis? Danny? June?'

'I've seen June around, and been on the bombsites with Fred. Reg is okay but doesn't hang around with me any more now he's at the posh grammar. Danny got sent to Wales and he isn't back yet, doesn't want to come back but probably he will. He sent me a postcard with all these hills on it. He has to go up one to school every day, right beside the sheep and all. Which school will you go to, then? I'm at the Sec. Mod. Failed my eleven-plus. Mr Hendrick said I would.'

'Don't know. No-one's said yet. Anyway, another three weeks of holiday, isn't it? I only got back yesterday. I was going to take a look at the old school. I was hoping to spot one of you.' His voice faltered at the thought of the one missing.

'We can go up the bomb sites; there's loads. It's smashing fun. I'll call for you. I've got to go now or I'll get it in the neck. Have to deliver this lot to the prefabs up Spencer Park.'

'I'd like to see prefabs. I saw about them in a newsreel.'

'Yeah,' Jim was already back on his bike, 'they have refrigerators!'

'No. What like Americans?'

'Yeah, and I know how to squeeze into that secret park up Spencer. I can show you. Cheery bye.'

Bill watched the lean legs cycling off, the backs of Jim's heels showing above his sock tops. The socks must be three sizes too small. A bony Jim working with no mother at home; Reg up hills in Wales; Andrew dead, not even time to hide in a shelter. Meanwhile, the worst he'd had to suffer was leaving the Pawseys and the Youldons. He felt miserable enough about that, but now he felt guilty too, which was worse.

He pulled his socks up and went back home. Jill was sitting at the table with her comic in front of her. 'You got me *Chicks' Own*, Bill. That's for babies.' She was flicking the pages over, nevertheless.

'Sorry. You didn't want *Sunny Stories* and there wasn't anything else for girls.'

'Where's your comic, Bill?' Mother put another pile of socks to soak in the bucket.

'I used the money to buy stamps.'

'Goodness, I can give you stamps. But what for?'

He hadn't wanted to tell her. 'Writing to people back at the village,' he muttered.

'Oh, a thank you letter to your billet. That's polite, dear. You can take a sheet of the small notepad from my writing desk in the garden room.'

'Thank you.' Too awkward to explain that he needed large sheets, and several of them, to write all he had to say to the Pawseys and Mrs Youldon, as well as a drawing for Sally and Tim because they couldn't read much. Tonight he'd write to Mr and Mrs Pawsey in his bedroom privately, taking as long as he needed, without Mother looking over his shoulder.

He should tell Mother about Andrew, but Jill would hear. He would tell Alan, when he was allowed to telephone.

CHAPTER 5

Bill folded all the sheets ready for ironing after rolling them one way and then the other so that the damp was evened out. He smoothed the vests, blouses and shirts over the clothes horse, one by one, to air around the boiler.

'Good boy, that's helpful.'

While Mother was pleased with him it might be a good moment to ask if he could phone Alan. He waited until she had the iron running smoothly to and fro and then asked.

'Yes, you can phone him this evening after we get back from Nanny and Grandad's.' She clanged the iron onto the boiler to heat up again and turned to Jill. 'Going there will be exciting, won't it?'

Jill didn't answer. She fiddled inside her lady's handbag, arranging her small dolls.

Mother sprinkled water on the last sheet and the iron hissed as she pressed it along the top edge. She looked at the pile of folded linen. 'I'm going to put this first load away and then get ready. Come along, Jill, let's tidy you up as well.'

Bill locked the back door and tightened the handle on the boiler door. He was ready enough; he was longing to see Nanny and Grandad again.

Mother came downstairs red-lipped, Jill lagging behind. 'Here, take this, Bill.' She picked up a basket from the chair and passed it to him. 'It's important to take some food wherever you go these days.'

There wasn't much in the basket. Bill went to the larder. 'Can we take some of those eggs? They won't have any as good as these.'

'All right, take three, one for each of them.' Better not say that would only leave one egg for themselves.

Mother checked her appearance in the hall-stand mirror. 'Come along both of you. You won't need that cardigan, Jill.'

'Do we have to go?' Jill muttered to Bill.

'Yes!' He took her hand because he knew she didn't want to go.

'Mummy, can I stay here? I really want to play with my dolls and put things into my bedroom cupboards.'

'Not now. Nanny and Grandad will be longing to see all of us, probably especially you. You were a baby last time we saw them. They don't know you as a girl.'

'And I don't know them. I won't know what to say.'

'Then keep quiet for once. That will be a nice change.' Mother skewered her hat on. 'Let's go, and if Nanny's not up to making tea, we can be back for a supper here with whatever we can scrape together.'

Bill took pity on Jill's pouty face. As they walked together behind Mother, he said quietly, 'You don't have to say much, just answer their questions. And you can play in their garden. It's quite big and it has an Anderson shed with a bed and books inside, and there's vegetable patches.' He saw in his mind's eye the row of carrot tops he'd been pulling when Ted shuffled home from Dunkirk, filthy, his boots green from standing in the sea for three days.

Mother turned. 'And do try to be civilized for once, Jill.'

'Yes, Mummy.' She skipped along in front of them, a bow on her wavy bob that always matched whatever she was wearing. Passers-by smiled at her. Bill was glad. Jill would make Nanny and Grandad happy.

The walk there had always seemed very long while he struggled to keep up with Dad and Mother. Now he had to slow down for Mother and it seemed hardly any time before they were walking up the leafy street. A flutter in his chest matched the movement of the trees. He took Jill's hand. 'That's Nanny and Grandad's house. See the green gate? When you get up the path, there are two garden gnomes.'

He waited for the door to be flung open and dear Grandad and Nanny to be standing there with open arms, the smell of roast meat circling him as warmly as their hugs. But the door stayed closed until they had rung the bell twice and waited for achingly long seconds afterwards.

'Give Nanny time to answer,' Mother said as Bill paced from foot to foot.

Slowly a shadow grew into a shape on the coloured glass section in the middle of the door. Then there was the clink of a chain and a key turning. At last the door opened and an old lady with a chiffon scarf over her almost hairless head stood breathlessly saying, 'Oh, here you are, dears. Wonderful.'

Jill took two steps backwards. Then she gave Bill a small shove in the back so that he was jerked forward in front of her.

Mother suddenly seeming tall, bent over the old lady as she kissed her. 'At last we're home. Hasn't it been simply ages! It's all been so hard for you but we're back now.'

Nanny finished hugging Mother and looked up at Bill, blinking. 'Billy. My goodness me. Billy!' It was he who had to outstretch his arms to hug her, though gently, for he felt bones more than the flesh of her body. He scanned the folds of skin hanging from her cheeks, searching for the Nanny he'd known. She wasn't as he remembered and he stepped back, feeling uncomfortable.

She turned to Jill and hugged her stiff figure. 'Just a little mite, you were, dear, not even speaking when we last saw you. Now a big girl of six isn't it?'

'Seven.'

'Yes, a proper schoolgirl, dearie me.'

Mother put a hand on Jill's head and looked over it to Nanny. 'How are you both, really?'

'We're managing, Marcia.' Nanny turned away, motioning them down the hall.

'Are you managing Ted, or is he managing you?'

'He's settling down,' Nanny muttered, then she smiled at Jill. 'Come along in. Poor Grandad's stuck there in his chair. He can't wait to see you all.' She walked on carefully, her lace-up shoes bagging around her feet swaying outwards from her swollen ankles. Her shoe heels were worn down at the outer edges. Bill kept his eyes on them. If he could get Phillips soles he could build those up so that she could walk better.

They all followed her into the back room where a fire glowed, despite the warmth of the day. Grandad was in his old smoking chair, two sticks beside him. He was pressing hard on them, trying to stand.

'Sit down, Daddy, do,' said Mother moving forwards to him and kissing the top of his head. 'Here we all are at last. Here's Jill,' and she motioned Jill forward. Grandad held out a hand, smiling gently at her and nodded lots of times. 'What a lovely little lassie.'

She looked embarrassed, twisting one foot round the other. Grandad let his eyes travel upwards to Bill.

He stood awkwardly beside Mother. Was this the Grandad he'd sorted tools with in the shed? Should he bend forward to Grandad or stay upright?

'Our Billy! What do you know,' he said in a croaky voice, looking over at Nanny. He met Bill's eyes. 'I'm stuck here most of the time nowadays. No more gardening, not like we used to, you and me. Useless old'un I am now. And you're a man, nearly. Fancy that. All those dreadful years, keeping us apart.' He put a hand out towards Bill's, and nodded to himself.

Bill swallowed. The beastly war had changed them. There was no smell of roast. What smell there was seemed damp, almost unpleasant. The walls were dingy and the skirting boards needed cleaning.

'Where's Ted, then?' Mother asked them.

'In the garden, tidying up for us. I'm hoping he'll find some beetroot or something to dig up. I wanted to give you all something nice to eat but…' Nanny's voice tailed off, and Bill saw her eyes watering.

'Don't you worry, we haven't come for a meal,' Mother said quickly.

Bill held the basket up. 'We've brought you food. There's an egg each from the chickens where I was living.' He tilted the basket forward, showing them off.

'My oh my. That's a treat. Look at the size of them!' said Grandad turning to Nanny.

'Wonderful. We'll have those boiled tomorrow. What a kind boy you are, to think of us.'

Bill smiled. He'd cheered them up already. 'Nanny, I can help in the garden so you get enough vegetables.'

'Thank you, Billy. Grandad will be pleased.'

Grandad banged his stick on the floor in time with his words, 'Just too old for it all, Billy, that's the thing.'

'Never mind, Grandad. I'll go out to the garden now,' said Bill, hurriedly. He'd leave it to Mother to tell them not to call him Billy any more. 'I'll see whether Ted needs a hand.' He went out to where the vegetable patch had been. It was terribly overgrown. Ted was standing with one hand limply on the spade handle, gazing into space.

'Hallo Ted. We've all come over.'

Ted looked over at the house vaguely and did that tossing of his head again before pushing the edge of the spade into the soil.

'Shall I do that?' Bill reached forward to take the spade.

Ted reacted slowly as if his time was running at a different pace from Bill's. By the time he wrenched his gaze from space to consider Bill, the spade was turning the soil. Ignoring Ted's silence, Bill worked away to make a fair start at preparing a vegetable bed, but no beetroot or anything else showed itself.

'Found any vegetables here, then, Ted?'

'The old man hasn't been able to get out for months.'

'Time to get something sown, then. Are there seeds in the shed?'

Ted wandered a few steps towards it, and then came back. He watched the spade turning the earth.

'Ted, are you glad to be home? Is everything all right now?' Bill asked with a hopeful heart as he dug and dumped, dug and dumped.

'Everything all right.' It wasn't a question, more like the beginning of a thought. 'It can't ever be, though I thought of home long enough.' Ted took a couple of uncertain steps and then retraced them. His eyes moved vaguely in Bill's direction. 'The old man hasn't been out in the garden for months. His legs were damaged when that V2 nearly got them.'

'What V2?'

Just minutes after they'd left Woolworths at New Cross, a V2 hit it. They'd only gone there because it had saucepans for sale - not been able to get any for years. The explosion knocked them both off their feet. All the passengers on a passing bus were killed in their seats. That's why the old man still can't walk more than a step or two. But it's what they saw on the bus, all those bodies, they can't get over.'

Bill stood very still. His insides felt the same as when Mr Durban told him about the Great War in Russia; the fields and fields of dead bodies, stained with their blood.

'When it's your turn, Bill, the next time there's a war, don't get talked into it. Just say No.'

'Be a conchie?' Wandsworth prison with its grey brick and tiny barred windows was where Dad had said conchies were put as punishment. How scary! Dad was a pacifist, but he'd said he'd do his duty whatever his views.

'But you did your duty, Ted. Soldiers are heroes. Shouldn't I do my duty? If there's another war...'

'Another war. There will be. There's always wars. People wanting more than they've got, hating people who've got more, wanting other countries as well as their own. You stay out of it. It's evil. War makes you do things you know are wrong. It lets other people do awful things to you.' His voice trailed off.

Had the enemy done awful things to Ted? What had happened, in Africa or any of the other faraway places the army had taken him? In the newsreels soldiers filed onto trucks with big smiles on their faces, giving the thumbs up and V-sign. Why wasn't Ted like that? What could he say, to help Ted be happy again? It was as difficult as finding the right words for Kenneth had been, when Uncle Frank was blown up. He tried his best at a comforting voice, 'It's all over now.'

'All over for lots of people. Most of my mates, for starters,' and Ted wandered off along one row of the bare vegetable patch and down the next. He must have forgotten what he was there for.

It was all over for Uncle Frank and for Andrew and hundreds of servicemen, perhaps thousands. Best not to think about it. Bill shoved the spade hard into the earth and carried on digging until at last he saw leaves. He pulled out some limp beetroot and seven potatoes. 'A fork-over will soon bring this lot to rights, Ted,' he said encouragingly, just like Mr Pawsey would have done. 'Just needs a bit of attention. But we need seeds, or potato and carrot tops to start the rows off.'

'Yes.' Ted walked closer to Bill. 'You're right. I'll be able to have a go at that. Plenty of time now.' His vacant tone suddenly changed and he said, 'I've got to learn to cook. They can't really manage.'

Bill's heart thumped. This was awful. 'Isn't it just Grandad's legs?'

'No. He's got diabetes, lungs bunged up, hip joints gone. Mother's got a dicky heart.' He spoke in short sharp bursts, as if he was giving a report to his commanding officer.

Bill didn't want to believe it. Nanny had a lovely heart. Ted's head wasn't quite right, he knew that. 'I can come over to help nearly every day while I'm on school holiday.' He put his vegetable findings into a woven basket. It had many sections missing. 'I'd better take these into Nanny.' He moved towards the back door.

Ted moved slowly forward. 'I suppose Sis is here? I'll come in.'

Indoors, Bill put the few poor beetroot and potatoes into the kitchen sink, washed them clean and then his hands. He followed Ted in to find Mother and Jill sitting with Grandad, Jill at the furthest point of the room. Mother nudged Ted towards a chair. She had made a large pot of tea and Nanny had found a packet of rich tea biscuits.

There were little red threads in Nanny's cheeks. Her hands shook when she took her cup so that it rattled in its saucer. 'You must have such news to tell us, Billy, dear. This is so lovely, having you all back home. And safe. We must count our blessings.' She ran out of breath and her cup rattled again.

'We do count our blessings,' said Grandad. 'Ted home in one piece, all of you back from evacuation, your father unharmed and this dreadful war over. So now, fire on, young man. Fill us in with your last five years.'

Everyone's eyes turned to Bill. He felt a heavy weight of responsibility. Jill was sitting awkwardly with her milky tea, toes not quite reaching the floor, not looking at anyone. Grandad was stuck in his chair, not able to go into the garden he loved. Nanny was shaky and couldn't really cook. They desperately needed cheering up.

He put on a smile although his face hurt around it. Talking of the last five years meant thinking about the people and places he missed so much. The pain around the bottom of his ribs was there all the time. He couldn't tell that to anyone here. He must think of the war effort and talk about that.

Grandad leaned forward. Nanny said, 'Well, dear? We're longing to hear all about it.'

His mouth opened and he began to talk.

CHAPTER 6

He'd gone to help Nanny and Grandad but when he got back home, it was difficult to answer Mother's 'How were they?' Ted had burned the food dreadfully and Nanny had told him it was best if he just did the clearing up, not the cooking.

Bill said, 'Ted's doing his best to help,' and then changed the subject. 'Grandad got stuck on a difficult crossword clue.'

Mother nodded. 'Poor Grandad. He'd love to be doing more than a crossword.' She pushed a knife into a lump of swede simmering on the stove. 'Let's see whether this economy recipe is something Madam Jill will eat.'

Jill was perched on a stool, pinching her nose. 'Your dinners are much worse than the vicarage ones, Mummy. That smells horrible.'

It did, but Jill said the same whether it was porridge, mince or boiled fish.

Mother snapped, 'You can be horrible yourself, Jill. Just wait until you're a mother!' She pulled out the newspaper Aunty had bought that morning and jabbed a finger at the first page. *There is a world shortage of food. In this country there is enough bread for everyone. Don't waste a crumb!* The Ministry of Food is talking to people like you, Jill.'

'I don't mind bread. It's your dinners!'

'It doesn't mean just bread, child. It means there are people starving so we should be glad of every crumb of food we get. We're the lucky ones.'

Jill hitched herself up onto tiptoe so that she could see inside the saucepan. 'Ugh. I don't feel lucky.'

Bill heard the second post land on the doormat. 'Come and collect the post, Jill.' He'd probably saved her from a sharp slap. She ran to the hall with him and picked them up. Two government envelopes, and one from Dad. That would cheer Mother up.

'Post, Mother.'

She read out Dad's news. 'More dismantling and reorganising, he says. No date for his demob yet. Jill – Daddy says to be good. Bill – he suggests you join a Scout pack.' She opened the other letters. 'Oh. You've got to re-sit the exam for Wandsworth Grammar school next week. The LCC don't recognise that test you took at your elementary. We must make sure you have two pencils with sharp points.'

Exam. He didn't mind. It would be interesting to see inside the school, and he wanted to see whether anyone he knew would be taking the exam there.

He reached for his jacket. 'Can I get off to Alan's now, Mother?'

'Yes, you deserve some free time. Here's a shilling. That should be enough for bus fare, sweets and emergencies.'

'Thank you!' How super that Mother let him go out now.

He ran first to the hall in Wiseton Road to see when the Scout pack met. Jim had said he'd fallen foul of Boss Wright, the Scoutmaster – a little matter of missing sixpences – so Jim wouldn't be at Scouts, but some of the others might be, and anyway it would be fun.

There weren't many people catching the Thornton Heath bus so he was able to get the front seat up top. It was super looking down on everything and exciting to be meeting Alan. There was so much news to exchange. Alan had said he'd wait at the clock tower stop. Bill had to watch out for a church, a crossroads and then the road with the clock tower. They were going to walk round the pond and get some sweets before walking up to his home for dinner.

Alan was standing right near the clock tower looking like the Macleans advert, all smiles and good health. Bill leapt off as soon as the bus stopped. 'Like your blazer!'

'It's for my new school!' Alan was in very good spirits. 'I had to re-sit the exam but I've got a place at the school I wanted.'

'I've got to re-sit next week, Wandsworth Grammar.'

'I know it. They play rugby there, like at mine.'

'Rugby! I don't want to go there if they play rugby!'

Alan shrugged. 'Doesn't matter. As long as there's a decent field and sports master, it'll be fun.'

Bill didn't answer. Football was far too important to be just fun. Was it worth bothering with an exam for a school that didn't have football?

Alan led the way to the pond and they jogged around it as he chatted on about everything he'd been doing since they'd last seen each other – two whole months ago.

'Have you been bored?'

'No time. Shopping in the mornings. My Uncle Ted's back. He's not – very well; my grandparents aren't either. A V2 just missed them. I'm going up there to help, gardening and that. What about you?'

'I've been working on our allotment, and I ride around on my bike while Mum's at work.'

'Hasn't she given it up now war's over?'

'No. Civil servant, she's always done it.'

When they reached the sweet shop its jars were mostly empty. Alan pulled out his coupons. They could only buy boiled sweets and wood chews. 'See who can keep chewing the longest!'

'Yes, even when all the taste's gone and there's just wood.'

Alan's father had just been home on two weeks' leave. 'It was spiffing. We played cricket and went to the Geology museum and a race track and swimming, but now he's away again. Diplomatic work, like I told you before.' Alan turned his mouth down.

Bill said, 'I can't imagine my dad doing any of that stuff with me.'

'What will you do when he's demobbed?'

'Don't know. I would like to go to his Court, see the villains, if he'd take me.'

'That would be spiffing.'

'Specially as Mr Durban works there too.'

'Mr Durban of the Cossack sabre?'

'Yes. The shashka,' he breathed.

'Did you tell him about the Russian book in the Manor library?'

'No. We haven't been round there yet, and I can't risk showing him the story you wrote out for me until I can get up there on my own. I've hidden it somewhere no-one will ever see it – in my dad's law volume, one on the highest shelf.'

'Why?'

'Because when Kenneth moves in, he'll suck up to everyone. If he finds out about the shashka he might try to get it for himself.'

'Why should he?'

'Just because he wants to take over everything I have. He used to take my toys. He took all my friends that first evacuation when we were away and he stayed behind. You remember how he was with Jill and Mother when they were billeted at the vicarage – like he was their boy, and I was just someone they visited?'

Alan scratched the back of his neck. 'But this time, he'll be far too busy settling in. Look. Don't show too much interest in the Durbans when they're mentioned, then he won't know it's important.'

Alan always said sensible things. Bill picked up a thick twig and poked at a broken boat some child had abandoned. 'It'll be awful sharing my room with him and putting up with his sarky remarks.'

'He's not so bad.'

'You don't know. He was always trying to be nice when you were around.'

'Just don't rise to it when he riles you. I mean, you're big enough.' He put a hand on top of Bill's head and laughed. 'Anyway, Kenneth might be painting all the time, too busy to follow you around.'

'I'll suggest it!' Bill managed a grin.

'Come on, let's see what Mum's made for dinner.'

Alan's house in Norwood didn't have any others joined on either side, and the garden went right round it. The straight path to the front door had a line of oval pebbles keeping clumps of flowers in their beds. 'I did those,' Alan said proudly as they went to the front door.

Indoors, Mrs Routledge was making a special pie. 'In your honour, Billy. We're so pleased to have you visit. I'm only sorry my husband's not still here to meet you. We've often talked about you.'

'Really?' How super, the Routledges actually talking about him!

She had put some cheerful music on the gramophone. It stood in the lounge but could be heard all round the downstairs. Alan lifted the lid to show him the record twizzling round and the little dish for used needles. There were cupboards with doors underneath for storing the records.

'This is super, Alan. My dad would love one like this!'

'Go along into the dining room, if you're ready,' Mrs Routledge called.

They went in and sat down at the table. It didn't have a tablecloth, but mats on its shiny surface. A photograph on the sideboard showed Mr and Mrs Routledge with their arms around a young Alan, who was holding a large ball. It looked as if they'd just come back from a happy time in the park.

Bill pointed to it. 'How long ago was that?'

'Before our second evacuation. Must've been early that summer, 1940, before the bombing started.' They grimaced at each other, remembering the air raid warnings.

Mrs Routledge brought in the pie, smiling. She didn't seem bothered about having another boy to feed. Her face was calm as she spooned out some carrots, beans and mashed potato onto each plate from the flowered serving dishes. Why was she different from Mother? Dad would say they were both the same class. They both wore pretty jumpers and skirts and no hair rollers under a scarf like many ladies had. And Mrs Routledge had an even bigger house to keep clean without a home help. She smiled across at him. 'You must be glad to be home at last, Bill! Such a long wait. I brought Alan back the day after VE Day.'

'Mother had to finish war work. She was really cross about it.'

'Oh dear.'

'She says a woman's place is in the home.'

Mrs Routledge nodded. 'So many people think that; mostly men.'

Perhaps he shouldn't have spoken out, since Mrs Routledge had stayed working.

She held the vegetable dish. 'Have some more beans. Since he got home, Alan's been quite a gardener. I doubt if they're as good as you had in the village; the soil is poorer.'

Bill felt his throat tighten as he thought of doing the vegetables at the Pawseys. 'I'm doing some digging for my grandparents, but Mother doesn't have an allotment. It's not her sort of thing.' Bill forked up another mouthful of mash, all smooth with no lumps. 'This potato is lovely.'

'It would be lovelier for some butter in it. I do miss that.'

Alan said, 'I've been to see my new school. There's science with laboratories. There's a gym with wall bars and a horse, and proper playing fields. We didn't get any of that at the elementary, did we?'

Bill thought of visiting Kenneth's exhibition. 'No, but I saw it at the Priory Grammar – you know, that school Kenneth went to. Now he's got a place at Dulwich College.'

Mrs Routledge's eyebrows went up. 'Goodness, he's a very lucky boy. How special!'

'Is it?'

Alan put in, 'Bill's got to re-sit for the grammar next week.'

'Ah. No problem, then.' Mrs Routledge piled another helping of pie onto Bill's plate. 'I'm sure you'll do well.' There wasn't any pudding but Mrs Routledge gave them an apple each to take into the garden.

'Let's go.' Alan took him round. There was a slope for rolling down; around a corner there were circles with rose bushes in them, and some way down a path, an old swing. They each climbed up one side of it then tried to touch hands when they stretched forward. Afterwards, they clambered into the swing, Alan sitting on it and Bill standing, with his feet either side. 'We're nearly too big for it!' They swung to and fro, looking out over the hedge and commenting on any aircraft coming out of Croydon airport. He was the happiest he'd been since being torn away from the Pawseys. It was ages since he'd played like this.

They went inside again and up to Alan's bedroom, where there was a huge bookcase filled with books.

'You lucky thing! Bet you won't read them all.'

'You can borrow some if you like.'

'Gosh, thanks! Let's see what you've got. Any Biggles? I love those.'

When it was time to go back. Alan put a couple of Biggles books under Bill's arm and some comics.

'You're a sport, Alan.'

Downstairs, Mrs Routledge held out a large volume. 'Bill, I remembered how keen you were on photography. This is a professional manual my husband needed once, but no more. You'll make good use of it, I'm sure.'

It was full of pictures and diagrams. She was so kind! 'Thank you ever so much.' He took it carefully. 'Without that film you got me last year I wouldn't have been able to take photos of our last days.'

'I'm glad you did. You'll have to bring your album to show us when you come next.'

'I will!'

'You can be studying this manual before school starts and you get loads of homework,' she smiled as she showed him to the door.

On the bus home Bill looked at his manual instead of out of the window. It had lots of chapters with small writing, as well as diagrams. He'd really need to work at understanding it if he was going to be a proper photographer.

CHAPTER 7

There was still a tin of corned beef from before the war. The last one. It was rusty but the little key worked, the lid rolled off and the smell of meat hit them deliciously. Mother boiled some potatoes and Bill got the knife and chopping board and gave the cabbage a salty rinse.

The large saucepan had pock marks and thin patches. It made him think of Nanny and Grandad buying their new saucepan and only just escaping being blown up. The hateful smell of cabbage boiling made the image worse.

'Ted told me what happened to Nanny and Grandad. Why didn't you say? Why didn't you warn me that they're different?'

'You needn't take that tone with me. I do what's best for everyone, I'm sure. I thought you were too young to hear about it.'

'It's not as bad as what happened to Uncle Frank and you told me that.' Then he stopped. She hadn't told him. 'Sorry, Mother. It was Kenneth told me he was blown up on the Balham bus when the bomb dropped on the station.'

'Ah. I wondered if you knew as you never asked any questions at the time.' Mother's tight face hardened further when she mixed the egg powder into milk for custard. 'We'd better save half this milk for breakfast, so please don't complain if the custard is watery.'

Even the cruet was the Bakelite one, the proper one was still in the dining room, probably with the same pepper as it held in 1940. They ought to be settled in at home by now, but they were still eating in the kitchen as if proper meals wouldn't happen until Dad got home.

They'd just finished eating when the doorbell rang. Mother came back with Jim behind her, and Bill could see she didn't approve. Jim's creased shoes were bent out of shape like old dinghies and had a crust of mud around each heel.

'Perhaps you'd leave your shoes on the mat if you're going upstairs, Jim,' Mother said, her tone making it clear that this wasn't just a suggestion.

'All right, Ma'am, Mrs Wilson.' As a delivery boy, Jim was used to dealing with customers. His voice sounded like the shop-keepers'. 'Fact is, I've got things to show Bill, here, he being away all wartime. We'll probably play in the park.' He winked at Bill behind Mother's back.

'We'll go now, Mother?' Bill hurried Jim out.

Outside, Jim grinned at him. 'Bit posh, your place. I remember it from that party you had when we were nippers; games, clown, presents, big cake!' He punched the air. 'Now I'll show you what's what. C'm on.'

He gave Jim a wary glance. 'Where to, then?' He shouldn't get up to mischief, with everyone relying on him.

'There's this really smashing bomb site. It was a church, empty inside now where the bomb fell, but there's a hole you can climb down to the secret part below. Fred 'n me found where the priest kept his robes and that. There was a kettle and cups all broken in bits. There's bits of statues, and I found a little pile of sixpences. Afterwards, we bought a football second-hand with it, and two liquorice sticks. Do you want to see? There's long slabs of stone and we reckon there's bodies buried under. Super fun.'

The thought of Andrew stopped him wanting to go there, and surely they'd get caught? He said, 'No. Let's go up to Spencer, those prefabs and the secret garden.'

'Right'o. Follow me.'

The prefabs looked quite ugly outside, low and made with some white stuff, no bricks. Some people had started gardens outside their doors and not just vegetables.

'Old Ma Fenchurch'll let us look round hers. Her old man's in the hospital and she's got a soppy boy who's in an institution mostly.' Jim took Bill round to the back door. A cat with tousled fur slid out as he opened it. 'Mrs Fen-church! It's Ji-im.' There was a pile of coins on a saucer on the windowsill. Jim took two and put them in his pocket.

Bill gasped. 'Don't!'

'It's all right. She often gives me stuff. She won't mind.'

A croaky voice called out. 'Jim? Come in here, then.'

Jim pushed open an inner door with a double bed and an old lady standing beside it. 'You can give me a hand. I want to put this blanket on the high shelf.' She saw Bill. 'Oho, who's this?'

'My friend come to see your prefab. He's never seen one.' Jim went to the bedside and took the folded blanket from Mrs Fenchurch. He nipped up onto the chair and put it on a shelf behind double doors. 'Look, Bill, see? The wardrobe's already fitted in.'

Mrs Fenchurch smiled at Bill. 'Yes, isn't it lovely? The prefab came with cupboards and shelves all ready to put our things in. Not that we've got much, thanks to the bombing. You wait till you see the kitchen. All cupboards there, and the refrigerator. Keeps the food fresh for ages.'

Bill followed them into the kitchen where there was a line of cupboards under a shiny surface.

Mrs Fenchurch pulled a cloth along it. 'See! Cleans just like that, no scrubbing.' She turned and pointed to a white metal cupboard. 'My refrigerator.' She pulled its silver handle to open the door and a shock of cold air blew over them. There was a bottle of milk on its door rack, a shelf for the meat and another with lard, a bowl of dripping and a plate of jelly on it.

'Goodness,' he said. Mother would think it was smashing.

They saw into a bright bathroom and then the sitting room with its fitted gas fire. 'Everything's very neat and convenient,' Mrs Fenchurch said proudly. 'We hardly know ourselves. Much better than what we lost.' She went to a sideboard where there was a large screw-topped jar. 'I expect you're both after sweeties.' She pulled out a few wrapped boiled sweets and passed them over.

'Thank you very much.' They weren't Bill's favourites, but it was very kind of her.

'Thanks, Missus,' Jim said. 'Can I take anything for helping you with the blanket?'

'There's tuppence in my purse. I might find you more when you bring my shopping. The list's in my bag, too.' She pointed to her bag on the easy chair.

Jim opened it and took out a piece of paper and the purse. Bill watched in case, and sure enough Jim took a sixpence as well as the tuppence and the shopping list. 'Thanks, Missus. We're off to the park, now, but I'll see you tomorrow. I've got your list. I'll sneak you an orange, if I get a chance.'

'Thank you, dear. You're a good boy.'

Jim grinned.

Bill nudged him, hoping he'd put the sixpence back, but he didn't.

'We have to go now.' And Jim yanked Bill's arm so hard that they were both at the door.

'Thank you for showing me around, Mrs Fenchurch,' Bill got out as Jim pushed him through the door. 'It's a lovely home.' Outside he said, 'That's awful, Jim. You took an extra sixpence as well as money from the saucer. That's wrong. And all you did was put a blanket on a shelf.'

'People like her, old, rely on me to help; there's bits and pieces I get back. That's fair.'

'I don't think it is.'

'Yah.'

Bill knew it wasn't fair but he wasn't going to get Jim to understand that.

Jim handed him another sweet. 'Come on. We're going across to the garden now. Quick, while no-one's about.'

The secret garden was exciting. It meant squeezing through a section of wire fence on one side of Spencer Park, and running like fugitives until they reached the part that had little walks, hedges and a stream. It was private, only for the rich people who lived in the nearby big houses, but now it was overgrown and neglected. It didn't seem so very wicked to play in it because it was being wasted. Most people didn't even know it existed.

As they were scrambling out again they heard footsteps, and Bill was on the wrong side! 'Get down,' Jim whispered, and Bill crouched beneath a bush while Jim pretended to do up his shoelace. The footsteps passed and Jim's arm came through the gap to pull Bill out. Half of him was out when the footsteps stopped, and a voice called, 'What are you up to, boy?'

'Nothing, Missus. My friend's just getting his...'

The voice came from a lady bus conductor with untidy black hair and Bill knew her straight away as Mrs Donnington. It was very embarrassing. Luckily, she was turning away with a shake of the head and hadn't seen Bill.

'Cor, that was close!' Jim grinned at him.

'Yes, not half. We could've been for it.' There was no way he wanted to go on a bomb site now. 'I'm going back now.'

'D'you have to? We haven't done the bomb sites.'

'Later. See you another time.' It wasn't comfortable playing with Jim. He wasn't going to again.

Running fast, it was easy enough to catch up with Mrs Donnington. He walked a little way behind her until she turned down a narrow road and into a doorway. She was getting out a key. It must be where she lived. He stopped, then as she opened the door, ran forward. 'Mrs Donnington?'

'Yes?'

'I'm Bill Wilson, remember? You used to help in our house.'

'Billy! Well, I never. The size of you! Look at you, away all of the war and now you're back, eh?'

He nodded, smiling with hot cheeks.

'It's a long time since you were helping me polish the fire brass, isn't it?'

He nodded. 'I just thought...' How could he ask about coming back as their home help?

'Come on in, Billy. Have a cup of tea with me.' She led him into a small hall past a row of hooks smothered with coats, cardigans and jackets. Boots and shoes were paired neatly in the corner left by the stairs. Another front door was at one side on the second stair. How funny. There must be a separate flat upstairs.

Mrs Donnington led the way into a room where the settee was jammed under the window and the easy chairs almost touched the cooker and sink. 'It's a real treat to see you after all this time. How's that baby of yours, although I suppose she must be a little schoolgirl by now?' She took the clippie's uniform jacket off and hung it on the back of a hard chair, then filled a kettle. Her piled up hair on the back of her head wobbled just as it always used to.

'Move those blankets off the settee and sit yourself down.'

By the time he'd answered her questions she had a cup of tea in front of him and popped in a lump of sugar. 'There. I was saving that for Colin, but he's gone over to Croydon to try for a job with his uncle. I don't expect he'll get it. No experience, see.'

'Colin?' He only just remembered Mrs Donnington's son. 'Is he demobbed?'

'Class A, conscripted first, demobbed first, only fair. It's lovely he's home safe, only we're a bit crowded,' she gestured to the settee. 'He has to bunk down on that. I'm so proud of him, our hero.' She pointed to his photograph on the sideboard, smart in his uniform. 'Such a tough war, they had, North Africa, Sicily, Italy. They weren't allowed to say at the time, but he's told me bits now.'

'Africa? My uncle served there.'

'East Surreys, Colin was in.'

His heart leapt. 'Yes, Ted was too.'

'Was he? Then I'll tell Col when he gets back. They'll want to go for a drink together.'

Bill sipped at his tea. Perhaps it would be better not to mention hospital. Ted wouldn't like that and Mrs Donnington might ask what his injuries were. He said, 'Ted's back with Nanny and Grandad. He won't talk about the war.'

'No. They want to forget all about it and protect us from knowing what they suffered. Best let them concentrate on knowing we won the war, ducky.' She drank from her chipped cup. 'Your mother must be glad to be home after all this time.'

'Yes, but she finds it ever so difficult to manage the house all by herself and she has to get it ready for my aunty and cousin to move in.' He explained about Uncle Frank's death.

'Poor souls. It was a terrible disaster, that Balham bomb. I knew the driver, poor chap, though he survived. Mind, we had bombs all the time then. Day, night, we just had to put up with it.'

'Are you going to do Home Helping again?'

'No, ducky, no-one's doing home help these days. We've all been doing war work and mine's the best paid for a woman. We get the same wage as the men! Our worry is the men taking back their jobs when they come home.'

'I suppose Mother will have to make do with me helping.' He drank the last of his tea.

'Your aunty will help in the house, don't you think? And you'll have another boy for company. Just what you need.'

He smothered his sigh and looked back at Colin's photograph. 'Mrs Donnington, I could pop in to run your messages if you like.'

She smiled. 'Maybe. I have got Colin to help, but you drop round when you're passing. You're a fine lad, tell your mother, and give her my best.'

He made for home, without the good news for Mother he'd hoped for, but if he saw Colin next time, they might talk about Africa.

CHAPTER 8

The post lay fresh on the kitchen table, Aunty's familiar handwriting on the top envelope. Mother tore it open. She no longer used the paper knife with its ivory handle, but then she no longer sat at her desk in the garden room to open her post. She kept to the smallest area so she had less housework. He watched her read the letter, knowing what it would say.

'Aunty says they'll arrive back Thursday, early afternoon.'

Bill nodded, ignoring Jill's squeaks of delight. He put his chin on his hand letting his fingers slide up to cover his miserable mouth. Kenneth was coming.

'I think the front room's all ready for her, but goodness, you'll have to get your bed out of your room. The bunk beds must go up there today!'

'Yes.' He must hide his misery from Mother. He wouldn't be able to cope with her hostility too.

'They're coming straight here, taking a taxi from Clapham Junction. Doreen can't face going to her house, understandably. It would bring home Uncle Frank's absence all too strongly. The new owners are having most of the furniture, but she's arranged with Quilters and Co. to bring her favourites here. Those should arrive this afternoon, so make sure you're around to help move it in.'

Bill cleared his porridge dish away. 'I'll go and find some tools for taking my bed apart.' At the open cellar door, he pulled a hammer, screwdriver and wrench from the hanging post Dad had made. They were all covered in dust, showing how long since they'd been used. He couldn't go down the steps for a rag; the light bulb had gone. They needed a new bulb and a large torch so that he could see to fit one. He ought to make a list of these jobs. He gave a shake of each tool to send the dust into the gloom of below. That would have to serve.

Jill followed him when he went upstairs looking excited. She was so stuck on Kenneth after five years of living right near him. He'd seemed like her brother, not Bill whom she only saw on visits. How Kenneth had enjoyed taunting Bill by encouraging Jill to avoid him!

Jill danced around Bill's feet. 'I can't wait to see how you'll both fit into your room. Will you quarrel? I'm going to listen outside your door and tell Iris if you do.'

So it was more that she was curious! He turned away from her. 'We shall be all right.'

'But I bet you will quarrel. Mummy won't hear. I shall. I'll hear all the cross words.' She puffed and crossed her arms across her chest importantly. 'Iris wants to see Kenneth.'

'Well she can. Take him down to her house for tea. Grown-ups always like Kenneth, I'm sure he'll get invited.'

Jill wouldn't notice, but Bill heard his sharp tone clearly enough. *I'm getting to sound like Mother. Perhaps I am like her. Is that why people like Kenneth better?*

Jill elbowed him in the ribs, squeezing into his bedroom beside him. 'Iris wants to see his paintings. He'll probably pin them up on the bedroom walls. They'll be all over your bedroom.' She waved expansively to the bare walls.

A grunt escaped through his gritted teeth. That was a new thought. He liked the walls as they were now, plain, so that his hanging aeroplanes were what you saw immediately you opened the door. He pushed Jill gently onto the landing saying, 'I've got to get my bed to bits and clear wardrobe space for Kenneth now,' and shut the door behind him.

He spread out his arms, bi-plane style and twizzled around,

feeling the private space. There was just a chest of drawers and the toy drawer under the bed. If Aunty sent a chest of drawers for Kenneth, there wouldn't be much room beside the bed. They couldn't have one side of the room each, only a section of floor and half the windowsill.

He hoisted the mattress off the bed and leant it up against the window, then bent down to see how the bed might come apart. He tried the screwdriver and then the wrench but the nuts under each bed corner were as tight and closely fitted as Kenneth was in Aunty's heart. He'd have to go next door to ask Mr Bentham for help. He went downstairs again, not in the best mood.

Mr Bentham was quite happy to follow Bill up to his bedroom, leaving his wife trying to find seaside accommodation. 'We just want a week by the sea now the barbed wire's off. But all the rooms are still taken by servicemen, Americans a lot of them, waiting to be transported home. I'm fed up with hearing "No vacancies" everywhere. The Missus is telephoning, non-stop.'

After some puffing and blowing over the bed frame, he said, 'There's no way of taking this apart, Bill. We'll have to man-handle it down the stairs in one piece. Put the mattress back on top.'

It wasn't easy, but once they'd negotiated the sideways turn for getting through the front door, they took one end each and walked it from Primley Road to the second-hand store, resting every few yards.

'Suppose they won't buy it? We'll have to lug it all the way back.'

'No worry of that, son. There's plenty will snap up a good solid bed like this.'

They struggled on to the shop and sure enough, a woman asked to buy it before they'd even got fully inside. Mr Bentham did the talking and then handed the money to Bill. 'Right. Let's get back.'

Bill took a last look at the blue bed knobs, the stripy mattress, hating the idea of some other boy lying on it. It was another part of him being given away. He was having to keep leaving things behind, and face things he didn't want to happen. He sighed. In October, he'd be thirteen so he must have more grown up thoughts.

He brought Mr Bentham indoors for a cup of tea. 'The bed's sold, Mother,' he called out.

She tripped into the parlour. 'That's good. Mr Bentham, you're a tower of strength. Let me pour you some tea. I'm sorry it's a topping-up of the pot, so it might be rather watery.'

'Never mind, Mrs Wilson. Hot and sweet, if you've got any condensed milk, have you?'

'I have, and I think I can find you a biscuit.' She went to the forbidden tin embossed with Father Christmas of 1936. The biscuits for very special occasions were kept there. She brought out a wrapped chocolate wafer. Luckily Jill was out at Iris's or her eyes might have popped out of her head, and who knows what words from her mouth.

Bill sipped his tea. 'The bed's gone, and here's the money for it, Mother.' He pulled it out from his pocket.

'Hooray. That's a help. I don't know what may need buying when Aunty and Kenneth arrive.' She passed the plate with the chocolate wafer. 'Please. My widowed sister-in-law is moving in, Mr Bentham, and her son of thirteen. Artistic and quiet, you won't need to worry about noise. You must remember Bill and his football? How I didn't go mad with the sound of it bouncing against the wall! No more of that; he'll be playing football down at the common now he's a big chap.'

'Boys will be boys, Mrs Wilson.'

'Luckily, Kenneth is different. How is Mrs Bentham?'

She listened to the Benthams' difficulties with gaining seaside accommodation. 'Nothing's easy, is it?' She took his empty cup and saucer. 'The bunk beds are waiting in the sideway, if we could prevail on your kind help again, Mr Bentham.'

CHAPTER 9

Bill drove the last screw into the gate hinge and went indoors to put the tools away.

'There you are, Bill,' Mother called from the garden room. 'I thought you were still at Nanny's.'

He went in to her. 'No, I got back a while ago. I've been mending the gate.'

Watching her tidying the bookcase, he said carefully, 'I could borrow some books for Grandad from Mr Durban if this is a good time to go over.'

She straightened up. 'Perhaps it is. I'm certainly missing adult conversation. I'll ring.'

He waited in the doorway while she phoned. Mother was smiling as the receiver tinged on its rest. 'Mrs Durban was delighted to hear from us and she's invited us down this afternoon. How nice!' She went to the stairs. 'I'll just go and tell Jill.'

He waited for an argument. Jill wouldn't want to join them. She'd want to go to Iris's, or Dawn's, a girl only four doors up whose mother had already invited her in for orange squash and biscuits.

Mother came back downstairs wearing a smart outfit, one she'd had before the war. 'She's begging to go to Dawn's instead. Should I make her come with us, do you think?'

'No, Mother, let her go. She won't remember the Durbans and she's excited about having other girls to play with at last.' He felt like Dad or a teacher, telling Mother about how things were for Jill.

'True. She has been a bit starved of other children's company. There were so few opportunities for her while we were marooned in the depths of the country. You and I will go alone, then.' She was probably relieved not to drag a moaning Jill along. That hadn't gone well at Nanny's. Also, he knew how Mother liked spending time with other women, and without children.

Jill lingered halfway down the stairs, ready to pout if Mother made her come with them.

'Very well, Jill. Come down and we'll see if Dawn's mother will have you for the afternoon.'

Jill's face changed from cloudy to sunny and she let Mother tidy her curls without a fuss.

'You'll have to behave well or you won't get asked again. Dawn's a private school child, remember. Make sure you're polite and not too noisy. We'll collect you when we get home.' She stood at the hall mirror to pin on a jaunty hat that matched her suit.

Jill gathered her two dolls and skipped out of the gate, Mother in tow. Bill waited until the front door conversation with Dawn's mother ended and Jill was taken inside. He pulled his jacket on and shut the gate. This was going to be a good afternoon.

He and Mother set off down Primley Road. Last time they'd gone to the Durbans, he'd walked behind his parents watching Jill's pram wheels. He hardly came up to Mother's shoulder then. Now they walked side by side, and he strode along feeling like the man with Mother, until she asked him to slow down. She had her high heels on. He took her arm saying, 'I'm as tall as you, now.'

She half smiled, half grimaced. 'Yes. You certainly are. Do you know, we could have taken the bus. We always had the pram before, so had no choice.'

'Actually, it's nice walking. I like going over the bridge.'

They paused a moment when they got to it, watching some children poking around the river edge with their sticks. She laughed. 'I remember seeing children doing that when I was a girl. I doubt if I was allowed to, but I believe there was one time I did.'

So she had once been disobedient, like Jill! They walked on, chatting almost like friends. It had never been like this with Mother before. He let go her arm as they got to the Durbans' road. His heart thumped rapidly at the sight of the familiar line of houses. He let Mother ring the ding-dong bell.

'That used to be your joy when you were little, Bill.'

It must be Mrs Durban opening the door but her face was not as smooth and lipsticky as he remembered.

'So lovely to see you, Letty.' Mother stepped forward.

'Marcia! Welcome back. My goodness, is this really Billy…?'

'Bill, Mrs Durban,' he nodded, as Mr Durban came forward to shake hands.

His eyes went straight to Bill who felt his cheeks tighten around a wide grin. Mr Durban, his own grown-up friend, his ally. 'Bill now, is it? My word!' His warm and firm hand thrust forward. 'Hello, a larger Bill. All grown up, I see.'

He turned to Mother. 'Well, Marcia, very glad to see you again. How well you look. And it won't be too long before Bert's demobbed and back with us, I'm sure. Category B.'

'Mopping up operations, he calls it. It surely can't last long.'

'Definitely not, or Judge Ware-Simpkins will be writing to his commandant, demanding Bert's presence. We struggle to manage, without him.' He led the way down to the lounge where everything seemed untouched by the war. The chairs were flowered and comfortable, the pictures were the right way on the wall, not turned backwards against windows to black out any light.

Bill was so busy reminding himself of the time Mr Durban had told him the shashka story that he missed the initial to-and-fro of the catch-up conversation. He latched on at the point where Mrs Durban was saying, 'You'll be out of practice, Marcia, feeding a grown son.'

Mr Durban turned to give Bill a grin.

'Not that easy,' Mother put in worriedly, 'a boy his size. It's true I'm not used to it. And Jill's got so fussy. The food problem is so much worse in London.'

While the adults discussed the shortages, Bill surveyed the hallway and landing. He was waiting for a door to open, for Angela with her blonde curls and neat white socks to trip in.

Mrs Durban went to the kitchen. 'Do you drink tea, these days, Billy?' she called out. 'Or do you still have orange squash?'

He tried not to scowl. 'Tea, please, Mrs Durban.'

'I expect you're waiting to swap all your news with Angela,' she said as she brought in the tea tray. 'It's so long since you've been here. You've had a great chunk of your lifetime away. What a lot you'll have to say to each other. She'll be home from work soon,' she said.

'Work!' He accepted one of the biscuits, which were disappointingly plain.

Mr Durban said, 'Yes. She's finished School Certificate and will start evening classes at college in September. She's landed a good job at the bank.'

The women looked at each other with a little nod and Mrs Durban poured the tea.

Mother said, 'Good prospects.'

Mrs Durban said, 'It gives her time. A while in business does no harm before she starts walking out with someone. Early days yet, I think.'

Mother nodded, sipping at her tea. 'I wouldn't want a girl of mine walking out when she was only sixteen.'

Walking out! The last time Bill had seen her, Angela still had dolls on her bed. By the time he was biting his next biscuit, the grown-ups were discussing the run-up to the next election.

'Herbert will hate not being here to vote, but he'll tell me how I should. The newspaper says. *Vote for Him,* and they mean our husbands, stuck overseas and not able to put their cross where it counts. Still, there's surely no question of the result after what Mr Churchill has achieved for us. It's inevitable he'll get in.'

'Don't be too sure,' Mr Durban lifted a warning hand. 'Churchill's as popular as ever, as a person. As a politician, putting this country to rights – I don't know. Most people will vote with the need for housing and jobs in mind, I think.'

Jobs. Jim had one, Angela had one. Ted didn't have one, couldn't have one yet. As Bill finished the last of his tea and took another biscuit, the front door slammed and a cheerful voice called out 'Hello!'

'Here she is,' Mrs Durban beamed. 'Come and see the Wilsons, Angela, back home again. Isn't that nice?'

A strange woman in a tweed skirt and shoes with heels stepped into the room. She walked over and shook hands with Mother. Her hair was fastened into some kind of knob at the back of her head with a big wave at the front, and it looked as if she had lipstick on.

Bill was sitting on the pouffe with his mouth full of biscuit. She stared at him, then gave a small smile.

'Hello, you. Back from your adventures? You've changed more than I'd expected.'

She was the one who'd changed more! It took him a few moments to finish his mouthful, and to take in that this was still Angela.

'Yes.' He should have stood up. Too late now, and the low pouffe didn't make it easy.

Angela smoothed her wave from her forehead as she answered Mother's questions about her job, perching herself on the sofa beside her father. 'Yes, I am enjoying it really. Sometimes it's a bit scary. The Manager is quite old and can be crotchety if any of us make mistakes. But the other girls are nice and we help each other out.'

'And with your wage you can buy yourself little things,' Mother said.

'Yes! Clothes, if Mum and Dad share rations with me. I'll go without butter and bacon to get another pair of stockings. I'm fed up with painting a brown line down the back of my legs. But I got this blouse last week from Allders.' She moved her shoulders from side to side. 'If only there was more choice.'

The women grimaced to each other. 'Or even the right size!'

Angela turned to Bill. 'Well, Billy, are you going to tell us all your adventures?'

'Yes, have you been running wild in the country whilst we've all been hiding in air-raid shelters?' Mrs Durban asked.

'Running wild. Some get all the luck, isn't that so?' said Mother.

Mr Durban looked carefully at Bill. 'I expect he's glad to be home. It must be difficult for returning youngsters to know where to start – telling five years of news.'

'He wrote little letters to people,' said Mother.

'Yes but it's not the same. I want to hear all about it,' Angela said. 'Bet you had fun, Billy.'

'He's *Bill* now, Angela. See how grown-up he looks?' Mr Durban said to her.

'Yes. He'll have lots to tell us.'

Mother leant back in her chair. She crossed her legs and gave a tiny yawn. 'Of course I've heard it all, so are you going to take him off for a natter, Angela, while we adults chat, or are you too grown up for him now?'

Angela didn't look at Mother. She stood up with a flounce and said to Bill, 'Come along, then.'

He heaved himself out of the pouffe, feeling clumsy, and followed her out of the room, his eyes on her legs which did have lines up the back, painted on like she'd said.

He hovered near the closed door of the study. Did she know he was waiting, was she deliberately making him wait?

'Come on, we'll go to my room.' She tripped upstairs and opened her door. Her room looked different now, no sign of toys. There was a pink gauzy thing hanging up, a film star poster from a girls' magazine and on the dressing table, a little mirror behind a tray full of bottles and sticks.

She saw his glance. 'Mother says I may use cosmetics if I apply them lightly. Pond's powder cream and lipstick.'

'Oh. Are you wearing them now?' Her lips did look pinker than he remembered.

'Yes. Do you like it?'

He shrugged and looked away.

'It's a new lipstick. I bought it on payday. I wish I could have my room that colour, like the ones American girls have; pink and green and pale blue.'

They both glanced at the utility paint on the skirting board, shiny brown, like everyone's everywhere in Great Britain. He waited. Angela plumped up a cushion on her bed. She sat down. 'Have you missed me?'

He said, 'I've been longing to come over again.'

'I know.'

'So…' he said, still standing, waiting for her to lead the way back to the study.

'So,' she said holding out her arms to him. 'I said you'd grow into a handsome man. Another year or two, and then…'

He gawped at her.

Angela put her head on one side, smiling. 'You said you'd been waiting.'

'For the sabre. To see the sabre.'

She sat still. At first he wondered if she'd understood him. Then his heart lurched in case there was no shashka any more. She gave a slight flick of the head. Then she stood up. 'That sabre. Huh, stupid. You just want to see the sabre? Come on then, let's see the wretched thing.' She stomped off and left Bill to follow, bewildered. *She* was the one who'd shown him it back before the war, the most special thing she could think of. She led him down to the study, not even glancing to see if the grown-ups noticed, and opened the cupboard. There it was, still in the same place. He bit his lower lip. Would it really be the same as he'd remembered it or just a rusty old blade in a torn scabbard? But even at first sight he could see the hilt was as handsome as his memory of it. Angela drew it from its shelf and laid it on the table, not across her hands. She didn't look at him, but put her hands on her hips.

'One Cossack sabre. Okay?'

Now it seemed more a punishment than a treat. And it wasn't even secret. She left the study door open and called out, 'I'm showing him that sabre, Daddy, all right?'

'Be careful, then.' Mr Durban didn't seem to mind.

Angela took the shashka from its scabbard, not particularly slowly. He followed the movement, his eyes searching for detail. The blade was tarnished, the letters too difficult to distinguish their shape properly. The studs had been polished, though. As his eyes followed their design, he could see flecks of colour reflected in them from the curtains. He thought of the next war and imagined Kenneth ogling the blade, then trying to get it from him. He saw himself slashing his way through the fields with his shining blade, holding it aloft and Mr Durban saying, *I'm too old for war. This shashka needs a younger man, someone who has proved his bravery and can draw it clean from its scabbard. I have no son, so, Bill…*

'I suppose it's all right if you hold it, now you're older.' Angela picked it up and put the hilt in his hands. 'As long as you don't muck about with it.'

He picked it up reverently. This shashka had been given to Mr Durban at the point of its owner's death. It could kill many men. He held it against his right hip, feeling its weight. He paused a long time, then placed it slowly into its scabbard. In Mr Durban's story, the cannons had stopped its success. This war had been all bombs. The next war would have even bigger explosions, not swords or sabres for this soldier or that. He held the shashka out to Angela.

She took hold of it as if it was a pan handle. 'Satisfied?' she said, her mouth a purse of pique, '*Bill*.'

He watched her shut it away again. Mr Durban would be so interested in the Cossack story Bill had waiting for him.

When they returned to the lounge, Mrs Durban was talking about cutting some old curtains up to make skirts. 'The material's too good to waste and there's certainly enough to make three. Angela, you and Mrs Wilson are more or less the same size, so we can cut out a pattern twice more. Come on, we're going to decide on patterns. I've got a Vogue and two Simplicity.'

'I prefer Vogue, but I've never risked making anything alone. It's my sister-in-law who sews,' Mother said as they disappeared through the door.

Now there were just the two of them. Bill turned to Mr Durban who smiled in a *Men Only* way. 'Well, Bill. It's been a long hard time. We have missed you. How does it feel to be back in Wandsworth?'

'Funny, sir. And it's all different.'

'Different, yes.' He turned his mouth down. 'So much damage. It's strange for me, too. Time on my hands instead of rushing off for fire patrol or lookout after work.'

'It must've been bad during the bombing. I've been round looking at the bomb sites.'

'Well, don't go on them. There's always the chance of an unexploded bomb. We were lucky. No hits in this road.' He pointed to his ARP helmet hanging on the wall. 'Just decoration now, thank the

Lord. Tell you what, though. I'm going to make that snug,' he pointed to the small adjoining room which had a desk and chair in it, 'into a war mementoes room. I'll have the helmet and operational maps on the wall, albums of photographs on the table. My items from the Great War as well.'

'So the shashka will be there?'

'Yes, the shashka will be there.' He nodded, his expression showed that he knew how important it was to Bill. 'And things from this war, too.' He lit a cigarette and bent forwards to search Bill's face. 'So, changes around here and even more changes for you. Your father wrote me about Kenneth coming to live with you all.'

'Like another son.'

'That must be difficult for you.'

Admitting to *Yes* would be disloyal, but *No* would be a lie. He swallowed and said nothing. Mr Durban would probably understand.

That was more than Bill did about Angela, he was thinking, as the women's footsteps sounded on the stairs. Why had she been so friendly, and then moody about nothing?

Mr Durban stood up. 'Sounds like you're going to be taken off home.' He led Bill into the hall where Mother was putting her hat back on. 'Come again, Marcia, before my leave ends.'

'Thank you, and you must meet my sister-in-law and Kenneth, my artist nephew, once they've moved in.'

Mrs Durban said that would be charming, and Angela was nodding. He felt cross with Mother for mentioning it.

He was cross with Angela too, but he still couldn't wait until he saw her again.

Jill was hot and excited when they called to collect her. From the sideway of the house they could see the girls climbing over discarded boxes in Dawn's back garden and jumping off the top ones. Dawn's mother brought Jill out, laughing. 'Here's your pickle, Mrs Wilson. She's been great fun.'

'It looks as if she's been rather a bother. Thank you so much for having her. Very kind. We'll be glad to see Dawn at our house, too.' Mother turned away, her glare at Jill hidden from Dawn and her mother.

'What a mess you are,' she said as soon as they were out of

earshot. 'Come along home for a good wash and a quieten down. Why is it that unless I watch you the whole time you behave like some wild peasant? If only I could get you to a private school like Dawn!'

Jill made googly eyes behind Mother's back as Bill pulled her along.

Mother's perky hat and matching jacket seemed to signal to him, *best be quiet,* so he didn't stick up for Jill.

CHAPTER 10

Thursday arrived far too quickly. Bill lay in bed savouring his last moments of being the only boy in the house. It wouldn't be long before he was showing Kenneth where to put all his things. Would the top bunk would be better than the bottom: Kenneth clambering over him, or having to clamber over Kenneth? How he'd hate feeling Kenneth's movements above him, but was it worse knowing that Kenneth could feel his below? Whichever bunk he chose, Kenneth would want that one. So he'd choose the top bunk. Kenneth would demand it, Bill could give in and end up with the bottom bunk. He'd see less of Kenneth on that one, for he could slide out of bed first.

He got up, smoothing the sheet and tucking the whole lot in tightly, so that no-one could see which bed he'd occupied. He left his room with a long glance. He'd never have a bedroom to himself again until he left home.

He kicked himself on the back of each calf because he'd had over four years to face this. Dad had announced directly after Uncle Frank's funeral that he now had two sons, that they'd all live together. Yet away in the country, with the war going on and on and London so far away, this had seemed unreal. Happy at the Pawseys', he'd so wanted it to be.

He nearly slammed the bathroom door. By the time he'd washed,

Mother was down in the kitchen. From the smell as he sidled in, it was clear that she'd burnt the porridge. It wouldn't be Jill's dish the black bits landed in. He wouldn't say anything, for how could this morning be worse?

He'd swallowed his last mouthful when he heard Aunty's *Cooee* through the letter box. He couldn't face going to open the front door because it wouldn't just be Aunty standing there but Kenneth too. The doorbell rang and he let Mother go.

He stood up. The time had come to face that Kenneth would be part of his family every single day, and in his bedroom every single night. Soon he'd go upstairs and help Kenneth fill his side of the wardrobe with his neat clothes, his side of the windowsill with his books, his under-bed box with his art materials.

Aunty caught sight of him hovering near the hallstand. 'Billy! Come and give me a hug.'

She deserved a welcome. He didn't want her to be sad about not having her house or Uncle Frank any more. He came forward for the hug, nodding to Kenneth as best he could.

'You're so huge,' she giggled. 'Surely it's only two months since I've seen you, and you're even taller than before.'

'Yes I think I am, Aunty. And I'm *Bill* now, you know.'

Aunty made big eyes at Mother. 'Fancy that! We shall have to watch our step with two new men to rule us. Bill absolutely towers over us.'

Kenneth slid one shiny shoe to stand on its toe across his supporting foot, like a film star. He raised an eyebrow and turned down one side of his pinkish mouth, showing what he thought of an extra-large twelve-year-old.

Bill tried not to scowl.

Mother was already in the front room directing operations. 'Bring everything in here, boys.'

Kenneth began to push the smaller of Aunty's two suitcases into the front room. 'Here you are, Mama.'

Mama! How stupid that sounded! When had Kenneth stopped calling her *Mummy*? It must be something he'd started at his grand-parents in Northampton. It might be French or something foreign. Mother had an old, old doll she sometimes let Jill touch. If you swung it forward and back, it said *Mama*. He'd like to say 'Dolly voice' to Kenneth but he shouldn't when he'd only just arrived.

Kenneth placed a small bag into the room and flicked his head at the large suitcases. 'Big boys carry big suitcases, Bill.'

This wasn't the time to take Kenneth on. He took the suitcases in and undid their straps.

Mother directed. 'Over there with that, Kenneth. Bill, put those down. Aunty can unpack later when she's had a cup of tea. You'll have to put up with our curtains, Doreen. They're probably not what you'd choose but at least they're not—'

'Not blackout.' Aunty joined in. They laughed. It was an easy sound, at least on Mother's part. So Mother didn't mind Aunty sharing her house as he did about Kenneth? Aunty was smiling, but she usually was brave.

What about Kenneth? Dad had sold their house because Aunty needed the money to live, so Kenneth had lost his whole home, not just his bedroom. Bill stole a glance at him. Mother and Aunty were chatting as they put things away, paying the boys no attention. Kenneth was lolling against Uncle Frank's mahogany tallboy which now stood where the armchairs had been. He was looking at furniture from his old home squeezed now into Bill's. His mouth was set. Then he caught Bill's glance and his expression became smooth.

He took a little breath and spoke in a snide, sing-song voice, 'Come on then, Bill-y. Up to th-the aewoplanes, just like old t-t-times.'

Immediately Bill was furious with himself for not taking the aeroplanes down, even the best one that had always hung from his ceiling.

'You can c-cut that out.' He stopped himself. There was a lot more he wanted to say but he'd only stutter more if he went on. It was a flipping nuisance; he'd hardly been troubled by the stutter for ages.

He led the way upstairs, letting Kenneth carry his own cases. He gestured to Kenneth's side of the wardrobe, 'That's your half.' He'd wait a few moments before tackling the bunk bed confrontation. 'Why don't you unpack? Your chest of drawers came, see. Make yourself at home.' He tried not to sound sarcastic. 'I've left you this half of the windowsill.'

Kenneth ran his finger along Bill's treasures on the right-hand half, as if planning how to use his own half. He took off his jacket and hung it up.

Bill said, trying to sound nice, 'Which bunk do you want, then?'

Kenneth clicked open the catches to his suitcase and drew out two beautifully folded shirts. He looked up. 'Which do you prefer, Billy boy?'

'Top, really. That's best.'

'Is it really? I'd better have it then, if that's best.' He pulled out another hanger from the wardrobe. 'Shall I keep these folded or hung up?'

'Either.' Bill bit back his moment of satisfaction and climbed on the chair to remove his aeroplanes. 'I was just about to do this when you arrived.' He held them carefully as he stepped down. 'Be back in a minute.' He took his aeroplanes down to the cellar where they'd be safe. He'd sorted the light problem yesterday, so now he could see where things were stored. He found an empty box and placed the aeroplanes carefully in it. There was a roll of string hanging from a hook and scissors on the bench. Dad was well organised. He made his aeroplanes safe, tying the string round the box using double knots. Nearby, another box had a newspaper neatly folded on top. He saw the word *Disaster*. It made him pull the paper out. It was a report of the Balham bombing. The picture showed the bus that Uncle Frank had been on, its front stuck down a hole with its back end poking up. He shuddered. Even though Uncle Frank was a bully, no-one deserved to die that way.

He read on. It got worse. The bomb had crashed through the gas and water pipes, both cascading onto the poor people on the platform. They hadn't a chance of surviving. But the story described how the bus driver escaped with minor injuries. He had been alone on the bus. There hadn't been any passengers! So Uncle Frank must have been on the platform. Dad must have lied about what happened. He swallowed. Dad lying? He squatted down, trying not to get dust on his clothes, folding the newspaper up carefully. He'd better put it where Kenneth would never see it. Dad would have had a reason for lying – like wanting to save Kenneth, even Aunty, from knowing the worst. Dying on a bus above ground didn't sound as bad as being trapped way below it with tons of gas, water and rubble smothering you.

He stood up. For once, there was something he knew that Kenneth didn't, but he wasn't glad.

He sniffed the dank air in the cellar remembering those nights when they'd huddled together, scared stiff. They were lucky they hadn't been bombed. He climbed back up to the daylight. He was lucky. He hadn't lost his father. He'd lived happily with the Pawseys while Kenneth and Aunty were stuck in the home of some spinster relative of the vicar's. He'd never visited their billet, but if it was like the vicarage, it probably had texts on the wall telling you about *Sin, God's love* and government reminders about *Doing Without*.

He plucked a couple of custard creams from the kitchen table as he passed through. Kenneth liked those biscuits. He'd take them upstairs for him.

CHAPTER 11

'I must say it's a shock,' Aunty said. 'All that hero-worship, and now we've let Churchill go.'

Mother raised her arms helplessly. 'It's so difficult without Herbert here to guide me, but I'd have thought it inconceivable Churchill would lose.'

'Remember, Aunty Marcia,' Kenneth broke in, 'the paper says that a hero's all very well for war, but no good for peace.'

Bill said nothing. He'd always wanted to be a hero. Now he'd have to think again. Peace was important.

He'd endured twelve days of having a cousin living with him. Things hadn't been too bad. Kenneth generally came up to bed after Bill and got up later so they weren't in the bedroom together much of the time. Kenneth could also slide into Aunty's room for privacy. The trouble was, he had nowhere to be free of Kenneth.

Luckily, Jill took a lot of Kenneth's attention. She'd brought Iris round to admire him. 'He's a painter, just like I told you, Iris. Look!' and they huddled round Kenneth, one either side while he painted. He pretended to take little notice of them, but his smirk showed that he liked their attention. This was a help. He wouldn't risk losing their admiration by being nasty to Bill.

Because Mother relied on him to fix things and for shopping, Bill could avoid Kenneth most daytimes. But when he and Mother took Jill to see Nanny and Grandad, Aunty and Kenneth went along too. When they got there, Kenneth didn't hang back like Jill. He was more than happy to be centre stage.

Bill squatted beside Grandad as Mother began, 'You remember my sister-in-law, Doreen, don't you? You may only just remember Kenneth.'

Nanny came forward and held Kenneth's hands. 'Oh I do. It was so lovely seeing the little boys together when Kenneth first moved to live near. Billy always wanted a brother.'

Bill watched Mother's face tighten. She wasn't pleased at the reminder. 'All right, all right. I did have a second child to please you all, remember.' She turned to Jill. 'And here she is.'

Jill cringed back behind Kenneth. Nanny went on, 'And here you are again, Kenneth, so Billy has a playmate now he's home at last.'

'Yes. I was able to keep him company when we were evacuated, too.'

'Good lad.' Grandad leant forward to shake Kenneth's hand.

Kenneth smiled, pulled chairs out, passed cups around, picked up papers that had fallen beside Grandad's chair, and all the things grown-ups think make a lovely person.

When Bill went round to help the following day, Nanny stopped pushing the carpet beater over the mat to praise his cousin: how bravely Kenneth was dealing with losing his father, how thoughtful, what a support to his mother, how sweet with Jill. Bill took the carpet beater from her hands and took it apart, emptying the dirt. Grandad and Nanny didn't know what Kenneth was like!

Worse waited for him when he got home. Aunty had found a part-time job in an accountants'. The firm had known Uncle Frank. 'Bill, you'll keep Kenneth company, won't you? You can show him where to shop, how to queue. He hasn't done shopping before, but he can help you.'

Kenneth moved his shoulders slightly and widened his eyes with his head on one side. Bill knew what that meant: he'd only make a gesture of doing it to keep Aunty happy.

Sure enough, when Bill showed him the shops the next morning, Kenneth looked at the queues of women with their prams and shopping baskets and said, 'That's women's work, or for little boys.'

Bill ignored that. 'Come on, Aunty told me to show you about the shopping. Here's the list. Look. First the baker's, then the grocer's. See, that's the longest queue today, which means they might run out of things if we leave it too late.'

Kenneth stood alongside Bill, leaning on one foot, then the other, like people do when they're really bored.

'You need to look out for sudden queues, Kenneth. That'll mean there's been a new delivery of something useful. Last time it was tin openers at the hardware store, and I had to be pretty quick to get the last but one.'

'Exciting for you.'

'All right, sarky, but think how hungry you'd feel if you couldn't open any tins.'

After the baker's and grocer's queues, the butcher's one stretched so far along the road that Bill sent Kenneth to do the greengrocer's. 'I'll wait for the meat. You take the list and this basket. Go on.'

Kenneth slouched off with a bad grace.

With the mince and liver resting on top of the second basket, Bill got to the greengrocer's just as Kenneth came out. He peered in the basket. 'Where's the cabbage?'

Kenneth said, 'Horrible stuff. I forgot it.'

'Flipping heck. Now we'll have to queue all over again. We need it for dinner.'

Kenneth sighed. 'The sun's too hot on my head to be standing out here. You don't want me to faint, do you?'

'You look all right to me.' But it would be awful if Kenneth fainted. What would he do?

'Go on, Bill. You're much better at this sort of thing. It's more sensible if you do the shopping.'

'So what will you do? I do the jobs around the house and I have to help at Nanny and Grandad's. You have to do *something*.'

'I can look after Jill. Keep the mothers happy, that sort of thing.'

Kenneth wandered over to stand at the Spread Eagle pub, because of its shady archway.

It was flipping annoying, but Kenneth was pretty useless. Bill queued for the cabbage in a bad mood. Worse still, when they were walking home, Bill with the heavier basket, Kenneth started asking awkward questions.

'Why do you need to help your grandparents?'

'They're old and not well.'

'So! They've got Ted.'

He didn't answer.

Kenneth nudged him hard in the ribs.

'Ow.'

'Jill said Ted's loopy. Too loopy to help his parents, is he?'

Bill turned on him, scowling. 'Jill's a naughty girl. That's an awful thing to say. He's not loopy, just convalescing.' That mightn't be true, but it sounded good. He'd heard the word in the shopping queue. 'We unpack now.' He pushed Kenneth into the kitchen, their baskets scratching against each other.

'Big day for you, Thursday,' Mother was polishing the silver.

'What, Aunty Marcia?'

'Not you, dear. Bill. His resit exam at the grammar.'

Kenneth gave Bill a pitying look that suggested *Fat chance you've got*.

Bill had more or less forgotten about it; it was still holidays. 'Veg goes in the basket in the larder, Kenneth.'

Kenneth took the cabbage in loose hands while Bill unpacked everything in his basket.

Mother said, 'I wonder how difficult the test will be. Education is so different, now these secondary school changes have come in. When I went to Larchmere Girls' High we had Literature, Arithmetic and Nature Study, Elocution, Needlework, Deportment.' She turned to examine Bill, as if he'd suddenly been switched from grey to coloured. 'You're a practical sort of boy, aren't you, Bill? Good at fixing things, not intellectual like your father or Kenneth.'

He caught sight of Kenneth pressing his lips together and inward, as if he must be modest about being more able, more everything than Bill.

Kenneth said, 'Would you really like to study Latin and calculus and physics, like me?'

'How can I know? I've never tried any of them. What is Latin for, anyway?'

A smug smile spread over Kenneth's face.

'Your father needed it for getting his position in the Court,' Mother said, 'but I can't see you going in that direction.'

'I was going to ask Dad if I could go and see the Court with him.'

Kenneth's left hand came up and touched his nose. His upper lip lifted. Bill longed to thump him.

'I mean, what you think you'll do when you leave school?' said Mother. 'That's the point.'

'But I'm not thirteen yet. I don't know what there *is* to do.' This was making him cross. How could he decide things like this? Kenneth hadn't had to; the Priory school had arranged everything for him. But of course, *he* did know. He was going to be a painter, an artist.

Mother held up a just-ironed shirt. It already had its name tape on the inside of the collar. *Kenneth Wilson.* 'And there'll be the problem of uniform.' She picked up Jill's skirt and sprinkled it with water. The iron hissed as it tackled the creases.

'Your father won't want you with the hoi polloi. If you don't pass to the grammar, it'll have to be St Werberg's. Those boys have nice manners, I remember.'

Bill was relieved when the subject was interrupted by Aunty coming in, smiling broadly. 'What do you think I've got?'

Kenneth shrugged. 'New socks?'

'No, it's something to open.'

'A mammoth box of chocolates, oh ha ha ha.'

Aunty smiled in a knowing way. 'Yes dear, chocolates would be completely impossible. But wait there.' She stepped out into the hall and brought back a large box with American stamps on the top and the red capitals C A R E.

Mother squealed, 'Doreen! You dark horse. Treasure. When did this come?'

'First thing. That's the advantage of sleeping in the front room, I get to see the postman first.' Aunty put the parcel on the table. It seemed heavy. 'Look, boys, a food parcel!'

Bill cheered. 'American food. How spiffing!' The box was big enough for everyone to have a good share of whatever it was, ham, biscuits, and surely there would be chocolate too!

Mother passed Aunty the scissors. 'Is this from Dwaine, bless his heart?'

She nodded, and started to open it. 'Isn't it exciting, Kenneth? Who knows what you'll find.'

It was *terribly* exciting waiting to see inside the package, but Bill just longed to watch how Kenneth would manage to resist its treats.

Kenneth cast a superior glance at the package. 'Are you suggesting that the Yank has sent me something?'

'Don't call Dwaine that! How disrespectful.' Aunty's hands hovered over the top of the box. 'You're going to be very glad of this, I promise you.' She tore open the box and pulled out some tins exclaiming at each one's label: 'One pound of steak and kidney! One pound of beef and gravy!' She pushed a tin over to Bill, and one to Kenneth, who left it where it was. 'Corned beef loaf!' she went on. 'Bacon, apricots, raisins!'

'Tinned peaches!' Bill put the large tin to his lips.

Mother's hands groped inside the box. 'Tea! Bless the man. Evaporated milk.'

'And sugar and rice,' Aunty started to put things on a large tray.

'And a very large bar of chocolate.' Bill looked across at Kenneth whose eyes were fixed on the treats, despite himself.

CHAPTER 12

It wasn't the first time that the doorbell had rung and Kenneth had got to it first. Bill could hear his beastly polite-boy voice chirping away before the voices came into the hall.

Kenneth put his head round the parlour door. 'There you are, Bill. This gentleman's come to speak to *you*.' The emphasis was meant to show how unusual this was.

Bill came out. 'Hello.'

The man held out his hand. 'Colin Donnington. My mother told me about you.'

Kenneth was still in the hall.

Bill led Colin quickly back into the parlour. 'Glad to know you. Would you like to sit down?' He turned to shut the door, but Kenneth was already through it.

'I'm Kenneth Wilson, Bill's cousin, brother really.' He sat down opposite.

Colin turned to him with a smile. 'I didn't realise.'

Bill scowled at Kenneth. How could he find a way of getting him out? 'How about making Colin a cup of tea, Kenneth?'

'I would, but I think we're out of tea. I saw Mama cleaning out the caddy.'

Colin raised one hand. 'Look, don't worry for me. I'm not a great tea-drinker.' He turned to Bill. 'Ma told me Ted's back. Smashing to hear there's someone else from the regiment nearby. Where can I get to see him?'

'He's back living at my grandparents. I'll take you round.' Bill stood up and opened the door. 'It's not very far.'

'Smashing.' Colin followed him out. 'He got demob way before me. He wasn't in the same battalion, but my mate was. He knew Ted.'

Kenneth's voice came from behind them, butting in. 'Ted was invalided out. Got sent to a military hospital.'

'But he's been out of hospital a couple of months now,' Bill put in quickly.

'There were loads of injured in our battalion all the way up to Italy.' Colin was setting a smart one-two pace down the road.

Bill met his pace and turned to Kenneth. 'We're going to Nanny's. No point in you following us.'

'I might as well come too. I'm not doing anything special.'

'I go to do their chores. Are you offering to help?'

Kenneth didn't answer but came to Colin's far side. 'Italy?'

Bill strode faster, catching hold of Colin's sleeve. 'Ted hasn't wanted to talk about the war. I only know he served in Africa.'

'Right. We moved on from there to the Med. Sicily, then Italy. Got harder then.'

'We'd love to hear about it, Colin.' Kenneth was almost running to stay in the conversation.

Bill said, 'Better to wait till we get to Ted. We turn right at the bottom of the road.'

'Okay.' Colin's fast pace, left-right, swinging arms, reminded Bill of Ted, still yet to go to war, demonstrating his marching in Nanny and Grandad's garden. He strode alongside Colin hoping Kenneth wouldn't keep up. 'Do you know why Ted was sent back to England?' he asked in a low voice.

'Bullet in his back, removed at field hospital first.'

'In the back! You mean – he was running away?' Kenneth squeaked breathlessly.

Bill swallowed a gasp. This was terrible. Was this why Ted wouldn't talk? Bill looked ahead where the shire horses plodded along to deliver the barrels of beer. 'Look at those horses, Kenneth. You could paint them.'

He nudged Colin's arm. 'That wasn't why Ted was sent to hospital over here. It was his nerves.'

'Oh right. Yeah, some of the blokes got hysterical when the enemy were at close quarters. That sort of thing couldn't be handled, not in action.'

Kenneth was like an irritating puppet. 'Hysterical?'

'Shut up, Kenneth.'

Colin stopped walking. 'Listen, lads. You've no idea what it was like. Anzio, Salerno and Monte Cassino. We'd done well in North Africa; left Tunisia, defeated the Huns in Sicily. We were ready for a break. But no, we landed in a flipping storm. So there we are, marching through the mud, days and weeks struggling uphill to gain each position, shell fire around all the time. The regulars knew how to handle it, not the ordinary squaddie. One battle, two. Weeks of it, low rations, streaming rain, no change of clothes, delayed mail, shell fire or grenades landing every which way. It doesn't take much more to break the spirit.' Colin started walking again.

'Ted's spirit was broken?' Kenneth's bony knees poked forward as he loped along, his mean face alight with eagerness to suck up the worst news. He had probably never enjoyed exercise so much.

'He'll have done his best,' Bill growled. 'Isn't that so, Colin?'

Colin nodded. 'Surely. In most platoons it's only a few men do the real fighting. Most follow the fighters, if things go well. Some run away. They're kept in line by the older chaps, but when the captain's killed, the next in line isn't usually trained to lead. He dithers. There can be panic. I wasn't in the same platoon but probably when he was hit, Ted thought he was done for. The bullet was in his backside, that was easy for the doctors to fix, but say he lost his bottle, seeing his mates killed around him – well! Some blokes went plumb crazy under heavy fire, especially when it was coming from close by.'

'Crazy?' Kenneth's lips were pulled back like a weasel's.

Colin pressed on. 'It's one possibility. If he didn't let up, the doc would've passed him unfit to fight. Mentally.'

'Mentally,' parroted Kenneth, still puffing.

How he'd love to pummel Kenneth until he was as flat as a

pancake! He touched Colin's arm. 'We'd better be getting on.' He shoved his hands in his pockets, his eyes on the ground. What was Kenneth going to do with all this secret information? Loudly, so that Colin didn't miss it, he said, 'Kenneth. You'd better not tell any of this to Mother or Aunty, right?'

Kenneth's face became full of concern. 'No, mustn't upset the women, of course.' But there was something in his tone that suggested he had plans to broadcast it.

'Or anyone at all, mind.'

Finally, Kenneth dropped behind, unable to jog any further. He began to wheeze and for once, Bill was glad.

Once they were ahead he asked, 'Will he get better, Colin?'

'There's supposed to be help with whatever problems you have. There was a film about it for returning servicemen.' He waited for the panting Kenneth to catch up. 'You'll have to do more PT, mate, get fit.'

They were silent until they reached Nanny and Grandad's road. 'It's just up there,' Bill pointed. 'We won't knock. Ted's not expecting to see anyone from his battalion. I'll go round the sideway and tell him, then bring him out.'

'Righto. We can go down to the High Street for a pie and pint, a good old natter will cheer him up.'

Bill blocked Kenneth from following him. 'You stay here, Kenneth. Once Ted's come out we can go in and do Nanny's chores.' That'd stop him! He ran down the sideway. Making a brief turn back, he saw Colin leaning on the gate, and Kenneth, like a long-term mate, leaning on it beside him.

Ted was having a cup of tea in the kitchen. He looked alarmed when Bill told him about Colin Donnington waiting outside. 'I don't know anyone of that name.'

'Colin's our Home Help's son, just demobbed. He was in another platoon but he's keen to meet up with you. Come on. He wants to go for a pie and a pint.'

'That all?' Ted looked relieved. 'Right.' He found a jacket on a hook by the back door and followed Bill round the sideway.

It was lucky that Ted seemed fairly okay. Bill watched as the two men shook hands and went down the road together. Kenneth had already turned to go into the house.

Bill called after him, 'All ready to get on with some chores, Kenneth?'

Of course, that didn't work out. Kenneth was already in the sitting room with Grandad when Bill went through the back door.

'It's nice to see you again so soon, Kenneth,' he heard Nanny's voice. It sounded warm.

'And nice for me to see you.' Kenneth's voice rang out down the passage. 'Ted's found a soldier pal. They've gone down to the café and Bill's just about to do some chores.'

'We both are,' Bill growled, but no-one paid any attention.

'So frustrating for you, Grandad, to be stuck in here,' trilled Kenneth. 'Perhaps I can entertain you.'

"Grandad?" Kenneth had his own grandad. What a cheek!

'I was wondering if you'd like me to sing for you?'

'My, my, that'd be a rare treat.' Grandad had perked up.

'Your aunty Marcia has told us about your lovely voice,' Nanny added.

Bill stood in front of Kenneth. 'Shall we do the dishes first, Nanny?'

'Thank you, Bill,' was all she managed as she sat back to listen to Kenneth, standing with his back against the fireplace. The sun shining from the left-hand window highlighted his curls, his cheek-bones. He loosely folded his hands and lifted them to his middle. He cleared his throat. 'I'll start with something cheery, "Widecombe Fair".'

Bill went straight to the kitchen and started on the dishes. Last night's tea hadn't been cleared away. Ted had obviously started, but the cheese was still on the table, not that there was much, and the plates were only half stacked. Potato peelings were blocking the sink. By the time he'd tidied up and washed the last dish, Kenneth was on to his fifth song.

'Really lovely, dear,' Nanny was saying as Bill came back to ask where he'd find a clean tea towel. 'In the third drawer down, Bill. You are such a help.' Then she turned to the shining face of Kenneth.

'Oh Danny Boy,' his voice rang out. Bill felt slightly sick at the sight of Kenneth's scrawny neck, his lips curved to gain exactly the right sound. But the plaintive tune and the soaring notes were so super that he left the door open to listen. He jolly well wouldn't let Kenneth know he liked it. He found a clean tea towel for the last dishes.

Clearing up had taken too long to do anything else. It was time to get back home. He saw a load of dry clean washing thrown into the basket any old how, and bent to fold each item. Suppose Colin was wrong about Ted? It was only what his mate had told him. Bill badly needed to discuss it with someone he could trust, like Mr Durban.

Kenneth came in. 'Should we get back, if you've finished this clearing up? Can you get me a drink, orange squash preferably? My throat's parched after all that singing.'

Too cross to answer, Bill pointed to a glass then to the larder door. After a distinct pause, Kenneth found the squash and poured himself a drink. Bill watched his beastly throat move as he glugged it. 'And remember – no mention of Ted's war to anyone, mind.'

Kenneth shrugged. 'Who's interested? Not me.'

They went home, not speaking. However hard Bill tried to listen to the bicycle bells and distant rumble of trains, the wretched 'Danny Boy' kept playing in his head in Kenneth's trilling voice. He imagined himself grown up still having 'Danny Boy' ringing in his ears and the sight of Kenneth's pulsating throat always in his head.

CHAPTER 13

It was Aunty's turn to cook and serve dinner. She was putting food on everyone's plates with jerky words and movements. 'Bit more? Gravy? No greens? You must.' She seemed agitated.

Mother didn't notice. She was intent on finishing the meal quickly because she needed to buy new shoes. 'I'm off, wish me luck!'

'Can I come?' Jill whined.

Kenneth offered to take her to the park. Bill scowled and started packing up the plates. Kenneth wouldn't want to do the dishes.

'Bless you, Kenneth!' Mother said as she disappeared through the door.

With the house empty of any sound but washing-up, Aunty confided, 'Bill, I have to tell someone. You'll be the first to know.' Her hands came out of the washing-up water and waved around, drops splashing on the lino. 'This morning's airmail—' her breath came in a rush, 'Dwaine's sure he'll be demobbed in the next few weeks, and afterwards, he says he'll be securing his income so that he can marry me. Imagine!'

That would cause some ructions. He said, 'That's super, Aunty. When – I mean, how?'

'He'll come over here for a few weeks. If we still get on, then we'll get married. I'm hoping it won't be too long. All I've had since he went is that photo you took of him, Bill. To think of a time when I'll see him every day!'

'We can show him London; he'll like that.'

'Yes. I'm so excited, I'm all in a tizz. And scared, because I have to prepare Kenneth for Dwaine coming, and he's going to be f—'

'Fed up, yes.' *Furious* was what they were both thinking.

'So if you can do anything,' she plunged her hands back into the hot water, 'anything to talk him round, I'd be so grateful. I mean, with everything being so different for Dwaine, all our English ways, we don't want an atmosphere at meal-times and that sort of thing.'

'No. But, Kenneth won't listen to me of all people!'

'Oh he respects you so much, Bill.'

He smothered a bitter smile.

'You're so steady, so reliable. I'm so hoping he'll listen to your reasonings, boy things, whatever you discuss up there in your bedroom.'

Poor Aunty, she hadn't a clue! She wasn't there in the silences while he and Kenneth avoided each other.

'Shouldn't I take over the washing up for a bit, Aunty? Your hands are all red with the washing soda.' Anything to change the subject.

Dwaine would want to take Aunty off to America. That's what had happened to Mary, Mrs Youldon's sister. She'd gone to America to get married, and was still there. Aunty would never leave Kenneth. He'd have to go too. Yippee! But it would be very sad to lose Aunty.

She passed him the last dish to wipe. 'You'll chat about it, you two boys, won't you? And you'll be in support.'

'I should think Dad will pronounce on this, Aunty, when the time comes. He's top dog.'

'Yes, when he comes. I mean, clearly Dwaine can't arrive first.' Aunty dabbed her red hands on the roller towel, looking embarrassed. 'It's difficult, Herbert not having met Dwaine yet – and Frank being his brother. . .' Her voice tailed off.

Bill put an arm round her waist. When Jill was born, Aunty had been a comfort to him and now he was the bigger, stronger one, even if he was still in short trousers. 'Dwaine promised he'd come for you, and now he's keeping his word. I like Dwaine a lot, and I'll tell Dad that when I write. But you'll have to break the news to Kenneth. Otherwise, if I say anything tonight he'll think I've read your letters!' He moved away quickly as Kenneth came into the kitchen.

'Five minutes on the swings, and Jill wants to come home again. The real reason she asked to go out was that she could see Dawn. She's gone in there for an hour. Will you collect her?'

'You can, Kenneth, can't you?'

'No, I will.' Bill gave Aunty a look that was meant to convey *Tell him now* and he made a point of going out noisily so that Aunty would know that she could speak to Kenneth privately for as long as she needed.

He took a long run, keeping to the park instead of the common. He needed to think and didn't want to bump into Jim. Being with him was a risk. They were too different these days. It was exciting about Dwaine coming. For him it would be a treat, and Alan would be cock-a-hoop. But for Kenneth – he couldn't pretend that it was just a pen friendship now. Aunty would have to come right out with it. She wanted to marry Dwaine.

His stomach leapt. Then Kenneth would have a new father! Surely, he wouldn't need Bill's any more? Dad would get so cross if Bill asked him, but at some point, he could ask Aunty about that. Dwaine visiting – how would Dad react? He'd never had Aunty and Kenneth sharing the house before, let alone a man he'd never met. And would he mind Aunty being sweet on a man that wasn't Uncle Frank?

Mother was already home and in high spirits when he jogged back for tea, and there was no sign of Kenneth. Mother had actually found three pairs of shoes in her size to choose from! She described each in detail to Aunty, who had to admire the pair Mother had bought, so he couldn't tell whether the conversation with Kenneth had gone more or less all right. Aunty was obviously avoiding telling Mother about Dwaine until they could speak in private. He'd better go for Jill now.

She said, 'Kenneth's gone for Jill, so you don't need to after all, dear.'

He soon came in with Jill, whom he'd struggled to get out of Dawn's, and she chattered all through toasting the bread so that no-one could get a word in edgeways. Usually, she wanted a turn at holding the toasting fork, which meant someone holding her arm to make sure she didn't burn herself. This time, she was too busy saying what her dolls had done, how she and Dawn had made them clothes out of leaves and plasticine.

'You've got half of it under your nails!' Mother complained. 'And it's not your bath night.'

Bill sneaked a look at Kenneth as he bit into his toast and dripping, but his expression didn't give anything away. Had Aunty actually told him?

It wasn't until bedtime that he faced the problem. Aunty gave him a long look as he said Goodnight, a look that probably meant *Please say something to help*.

Kenneth had already gone up, saying he was deep in a book about Henry III he'd got from the library.

When Bill came in from the bathroom, Kenneth was up in his bunk, his nose in his book, but he must have been waiting for Bill, because as Bill climbed into bed, he began to talk – a very rare event in the bedroom. He obviously didn't guess that Bill knew about Dwaine because he spoke with an announcer's voice. 'Bill. I must inform you that Mama's friend, the Eyetye, is proposing to come to this country. To this house, if you please.'

Bill allowed a pause to suggest surprise. 'Well, that'll be good. He might bring American things to show us.' Best to help Kenneth look on the bright side.

'He could bring the Statue of Liberty and I wouldn't be interested. I shall be tremendously busy with my school by the time it happens. If it happens.'

'What do you mean – if?'

'Don't you think Dad will forbid it? The Yank in his house? No, Duh-waaaine will have to stay somewhere else, and hopefully it'll be too expensive. I doubt he's a man of means, or a man of much at all, once out of his uniform.'

'We don't know what his work is. I remember Mrs Youldon saying he only joined up after becoming a widower.'

Kenneth snorted. 'Wife probably died of boredom.'

Bill persisted, 'Aunty will enjoy some company. I mean Mother's got Dad, and she…'

'…hasn't got my father. You needn't rub it in.'

Oh dear, this wasn't the kind of conversation Aunty had hoped Bill would have. He was meant to get Kenneth to accept the idea of Dwaine so that everything ran smoothly when he arrived. 'He'll know lots of things we don't. He could be a good friend for us, for you.'

'More likely we'll have to teach him civilized English ways. And if I want to know anything, I'd hardly ask him! I shall have an excellent school to inform me. As for friendship I have you, don't I?'

Bill stiffened. Lying below Kenneth, he couldn't see from his face whether he was being sarcastic. He must be, surely! Bill made a last attempt. 'If Aunty's happy, it will be nicer for you than if she's unhappy.'

There was a long pause. Bill wondered momentarily if Kenneth had dropped off to sleep.

Then in an anguished, grating tone Kenneth said, 'I shall call on help from Dad. We'll see how happy he is about his brother being replaced by some ignorant GI.'

CHAPTER 14

The weather had turned dull in tune with Bill's spirits. The clouds seemed low enough for him to punch in their sides. He'd have to be off to Nanny's in a minute. She needed extra help because Ted was in bed with an ear infection. He pressed his lips together. The chances were that when he got there, she and Grandad would be swooning over Kenneth's lovely singing.

In the scullery, he finished sorting the good wooden pegs from the ones whose ends had broken. 'You need about a dozen new pegs, Mother. I've thrown away more than that.'

'Mend any of them where it's just the metal bent out of shape, will you?' Mother let the clothes airer down and started hanging the wet clothes over the wooden slats. 'For all I know, the hardware shop will be out of them. Just find the clothes horse, Bill. I think there are two, in fact. There's far too much washing to fit on the airer. I wish I'd left the sheets on the beds for another week if it's going to rain.'

'It is,' Kenneth's voice informed them from the kitchen. He had his paint box open on the table. He unrolled a length of the old wallpaper that Bill had just brought him from the cellar. 'I'm going to try to paint the rain.' He cut off a large piece of wallpaper and pinioned it down with four breakfast cups. The surface wasn't really smooth and he stroked it, tutting to himself. 'While you're in the scullery, Bill, get me a jar of water, will you?'

It wasn't much more to ask, but still jolly irritating. Why could Kenneth sit amusing himself with his paints while Bill had to do boring household chores? He brought the jar of water and banged it down in protest as he went to find the clothes horse. He knew his mood was not about the weather and the chores, but about Kenneth.

He found one clothes horse in Mother's bedroom. He took it downstairs and saw through the window that it was now raining hard. The smell of wet clothes filtered from the scullery into the kitchen. Kenneth had moved off and left his work unfinished. He often painted one part and let it dry before adding another wash or some details. His paintbrush, washed and dried, lay beside the wall-paper and paint box. It would be so satisfying to smother the picture of the rainy garden with black paint and gash huge crosses across the delicate work. His hand prickled, but of course he didn't do such a dreadful thing. He put the clothes horse beside the remaining wet washing.

Mother nodded towards the dry washing that Aunty had just ironed. 'Thank you. Take your clean sheets from the ironing pile, please, and Kenneth's too.'

He took the sheets upstairs. As he opened the bedroom door there was a quick movement. Kenneth stood up and turned. Bill held out the sheets and looked hard at him.

'All right. I was just – you know, finding a safe place for my special things. Somewhere you won't poke into.'

'I wouldn't.'

Their eyes met and their gaze held.

And suddenly there it was between them, the knowledge that Kenneth had stolen Bill's precious photograph of the sabre, that time, years ago, when it was hidden in Bill's special place in the base of his bed frame. He said, 'Whereas *you*...'

Kenneth's chin went up. 'That was ages ago. And you still remember. So you see why I mustn't risk you getting your own back.'

'I'd have done it by now. I don't pry into people's private stuff, or steal. What would you have that I would want, anyway? A special paintbrush?' Bill could hear his voice hard and sarcastic. He didn't like sounding this way, but Kenneth was making him into a nastier person.

Kenneth opened the folds of his sheet and started making up his bunk. 'You're not worth bothering with, not worth listening to.'

Bill dumped his own sheet onto his bunk and left the bedroom. He'd do it later when Kenneth wasn't there. Let Kenneth hide whatever stupid thing he had in some secret place. Bill truly didn't care. He ran downstairs where Jill and Dawn were dithering by the back door with their dolls' prams. 'Is it going to stop raining soon, Bill?'

'Don't know, girls, but doesn't look like it. Sorry. Tell Mother I'm off to Nanny's.'

The clouds were clearing, although not enough for the sun to shine warmly. Bill could have taken the girls to play in Nanny's garden. That way Nanny and Grandad could get to know Jill better. There was much more space there for throwing a ball or pushing their prams. He had thought several times about taking Jill. He was her real brother, after all, although he'd be in terrible trouble if he said that.

It wasn't the rain, but Ted that stopped him taking Jill round there. He came out with things that little girls shouldn't hear: *Darn it; Damned if I will* and even *Shitloads of shit*. The worst of this was that he wasn't saying it to anyone you could see, and you couldn't tell what he was saying it about. That was scary. Jill had already called him 'loony' before they'd even got back to Wandsworth, so it was too risky to bring her without Mother. He ran down the sideway and pushed the back door open. 'Nanny?'

She came through from the parlour, a duster in her hand. 'Hello, Bill, dear. Ted's up and about but he's left some digging unfinished in the garden, tools lying around. He's a bit down. His ear's better but they've said he's not fit for any work yet.'

'That's rotten luck. You were hoping he'd get a little job nearby. Until he's ready for his proper one.'

'Yes, we were.' She sighed. 'His old job, that's out of the window. I can't see Ted getting back to anything responsible for quite a time. And at nineteen, he was onto such a good thing at his office. Grandad says Ted's chances of getting back in that sort of position are poor. While he's been away serving his country, his place has been taken by a man who's over fifty. So many men are wanting work and there's many more to come. What the government can do, I really don't see. We thought if Ted came back alive he'd get a big welcome, not left here to wash dishes and manage a bit of garden.'

He'd better not show Nanny how glum he felt about Ted too. He said, 'I thought seeing Colin might cheer Ted up.'

'I'm not sure it did. We were glad Colin looked him up, but Ted was very quiet when he came home afterwards. Just sat in the lounge, smoking. He doesn't even seem to read anything. Grandad keeps trying to get a conversation going.' She sighed again. 'But the rehab office have got Ted got a new appointment. I think it's only to do with jobs, not for someone who helps with... Ted's sort of illness.' She didn't say what the illness was. Did she know it was mental?

'Where is it best to start helping?'

'Dig us another trench, dear, will you? I asked Ted to start one but he hasn't finished. It'll be quicker if you do it. We need to plant as much as possible. Next door kindly gave us all these starters – there's beetroot, lettuce, onions, radishes.'

Bill took the bowl with its promise of autumn and winter vegetables and went into the garden. It wasn't raining and Ted was standing at the bottom hedge, smoking.

Bill waved. 'Coo-ee. Shall I go on with that trench, Ted?'

The spade was lying half in and half out of a two-foot hole. Ted picked it up and started digging. Bill thought it best to leave him while he was actually getting on with something, but after a few spadefuls Ted ambled forward. 'Digging trenches. Just what I came home for!' His voice was raw.

Best to change the subject. 'Did you like having Colin to talk to, Ted? Did you spend a nice long time together?'

'Nice bloke. We had the same rotten time, though he seems chipper enough now he's back. Probably because he's got a spanking new job in Streatham. Nearly as good as the one I had before they sent me off to war.'

Bill started digging. What was best to say? *Keep your sunny side up. There'll be bluebirds over, the white cliffs of Dover.* He said, 'I bet you learned a lot of new things. Colin said you had months of training. It'll come in useful, won't it? When you get back to work, I mean.'

Ted laughed an awful laugh. It was like a choke in a black tunnel. 'Oh yes. Learned a lot, I did. This is what I was taught, Bill. See if it'll come in useful. Watch.' He picked up the garden fork and ran down to the bottom of the garden. Sheets and an eiderdown were hanging on the washing line. Ted bent low and thrust the fork towards them threateningly, then turned, and rushed screaming and yelling towards Bill who backed rapidly up the steps and into the flower bed at one side.

Ted turned round and made another dash to the washing line. 'Yaaaaah.' He thrust the fork with huge force to each sheet and, then bending low with the fork held full length before him, rushed at the eiderdown and ran it through. 'Yaaaaah, yah, yah, yah.' It hung limply, four great gashes open to the wind. Small white feathers escaped wispily to the sky.

Ted's yelling was enough to bring the whole street running, but no-one came. He walked forward, unsteady, his hips and legs so skinny. 'That's what I learned, see. With a bayonet. Come in useful, will it? I killed one Jerry and left another twitching. Enemy shooting down on us from all around, four of my mates wiped out. We had to retreat – bodies lying all around us, men we'd ate with and run beside.' His face was pasty, glistening.

Bill stayed backed up behind the steps, his feet pressed into the flower bed. He was very scared, but he needed to protect Nanny and Grandad. He put out his arms to either side, but Ted wasn't trying to get past him.

Ted threw down the fork. 'Don't you fight, Bill. Don't go to war. It's barmy.'

Bill held one hand up as if pressing the idea away. 'No. I won't.' He risked taking a few steps forward. Ted didn't move, so he rescued the fork and poked it deep into an innocent pile of soil.

Ted straightened up but his eyes were glazed and his eyelids twitched. 'Now I've shown you the sort of things you'll be expected to do, perhaps you won't sign up. They mustn't recruit you.'

'No.' He needed to calm Ted down. 'The war's nearly over, Ted. Soldiers are coming home now, not being recruited.'

Ted wasn't listening. He went on, 'No more signing up, see. Bert understands. He's a pacifist at heart.'

'I know.' But Dad had said he would do his duty, even so.

There were several silent minutes before Bill thought it safe enough to pick up the bowl and show it to Ted. 'Look, we've got to put these in, beetroot, onions and things. You need these growing. There's not enough food, without.'

Ted's hands didn't move towards the bowl.

'Will you do a bit more digging while I start putting these in, then?' Was it safe to turn his back on Ted and bend down or would he be a target?

Ted nodded. 'Okay, if I must,' and picked up the spade, but gently.

Starting at the finished end of the trench, Bill started planting the carrot tops. He felt shaky from Ted's outburst. What on earth would Nanny say about the eiderdown? Did she have another?

Thank goodness she hadn't seemed to hear, for everything was normal when he got back indoors after planting out the vegetables. He should say what had happened, but it would upset her and Grandad. He hesitated at the front door, but couldn't find the words. He shouted *Goodbye* and ran down the road. He might be able to talk to Mr Durban about Ted. He wasn't going to tell Mother. You didn't worry women with men's troubles.

CHAPTER 15

The really heavy rain saved itself for August 1st, the day of the exam. Mother fished his raincoat out of the under stairs cupboard. 'It doesn't look as if you've worn this for a year.'

'I haven't.' He put his arms in it. 'It doesn't cover my knees now. I'll look silly.'

'Well we haven't anything else so you'll have to wear it.'

'It's all right,' Jill said, pulling at the hem. 'It covers your top half.'

Mother took her umbrella from the elephant's foot stand. 'Jill, you're to stay indoors with Kenneth until I get back. All right, Kenneth?'

'Yes, Aunty.' He turned to Bill and said quietly, 'Good luck. Remember that WRITE has a W in it.'

Bill glared at him.

Jill said, 'Does it? It doesn't sound like it has.'

Bill saved his worst expression until he was at the front door behind Mother. He turned and stuck out his tongue as far as it would go and turned again to meet the drenching rain.

Once they had sloshed along the pavements to the school, Mother got him signed in and then hurried off, almost hidden under Dad's black umbrella. 'Come straight home once the exam is over.'

It was jolly uncomfortable sitting with wet legs in wet socks and looking out of the large dusty windows until all the exam papers had been handed out. The school building was impressive but he could see that the field had no football posts. Mother thought he wasn't brainy like Dad or Kenneth, so why struggle to answer loads of exam questions?

On each desk there were three white leaflets. When they were told to start, Bill saw there were loads of questions. The first leaflet was English, then next one was Arithmetic and the other paper was called Verbal Reasoning, but it was just puzzles. Surely those weren't important? He pushed it to one side. He did some arithmetic problems and part of the English while the points on his two pencils were sharp, but when his pencils got blunter it was more difficult to ignore his wet socks and the idea of having no school football ever.

After the set papers, there was a break when they had a glass of weak orange squash and were allowed to talk to each other. Most boys were saying how nervous they'd been, so it wasn't a very jolly chat.

Afterwards, he was interviewed by a senior teacher and invited to ask questions. He asked if the school had photography lessons, and the teacher looked surprised and said there were not.

So when the letter came a few days later saying he hadn't got a place, Bill didn't mind.

'Oh dear,' Mother said, holding the letter. 'Your father will be disappointed.'

He folded his arms across his chest. 'Surely it doesn't matter. You said I was more practical!'

'Yes. Well, it'll have to be St Werberg's. Only a short walk. It's even on the way to Nanny and Grandad's.'

That was useful, but the main thing was that St Werberg's played football. Bill went to sit in the parlour until dinner-time. He would study his photography manual. No-one had said how much homework you got at St Werberg's but he wouldn't chance it. With his luck, there could be loads.

After a while, he heard the phone bell, then Mother talking, then a pause. 'Yes, Letty, that would be lovely.'

He was alone, so no-one could hear his groan. It would be an invitation to bring Kenneth to the Durbans, Mother's fault for saying he was moving in. Angela and Mrs Durban would definitely make a fuss of him, because he'd lost his father. How rotten it was going to be, seeing Kenneth suck up to all of them. He slammed his manual onto the wireless top and came out to see if dinner was ready.

There was no Jill to lighten the conversation over the dinner table. She was at Iris's for the day. Aunty came in a little late. She'd finished work at twelve thirty. 'Sorry, Marcia. I did hurry.'

'Mama, you look flustered.'

She patted Kenneth's hand. 'Home now, dear.'

Over the spotted dick, Mother said, 'We're invited to Fulham tomorrow, Doreen. The Durbans. I said you didn't work Fridays. Peter Durban works at Chambers with Herbert. Letty's very nice, you'll like her. They're keen to meet you, and Kenneth of course.'

'That'll be nice.'

'I'll leave Jill at Dawn's again. She'll only be a nuisance – the journey, and then no toys or children there.'

Kenneth's spoon was in the air, his chin raised. 'Mr – D – who did you say, Aunty Marcia?'

'Mr Durban. It will be nice for you. Their daughter, Angela, has just left school. Such a pleasant girl. She plays the piano.'

Kenneth's face was tight, alert, like the dogs used to look when Mrs Pawsey was scraping a bone for them.

'Durban,' said Kenneth almost dreamily. 'I've heard that name.'

Surely he couldn't remember? It was years ago that Bill had almost let out where his secret power came from, when he boasted that he knew about soldiers in the Great War in Russia. Kenneth had pressed him and pressed him to say who'd told him, and when Bill wouldn't, Kenneth had asked Mother the names of any men Bill knew. That was ages ago, around the time Uncle Frank died.

Bill kept his face stiff and tried to look as if Kenneth's words were unimportant, just as Alan had advised.

But that night, when Bill had his face to the wall ready for sleep, a quiet voice came from the bunk above. 'Mr Durban. That's the man that told you about the dead bodies in the snow, isn't it? I'm looking forward to meeting him.'

Bill didn't answer.

'And Angela. She's the one who likes Shakespeare.' Kenneth's memory was amazing. Why were Bill's secrets so super important to Kenneth?

He attempted a little snore, hoping Kenneth wouldn't know he'd even heard his words.

But Kenneth went on in a whisper. 'Of course, I doubt if you'll study Shakespeare when you get to your local school. But Angela and I will have that and the piano playing to talk about.'

Bill gritted his teeth silently. How on earth was he going to stop Kenneth smarming his way into the Durban family?

CHAPTER 16

'It's best we catch a bus,' Bill said. Otherwise the mothers would walk together and leave him to walk with Kenneth.

Aunty was glad. 'Yes, let's. I have enough of a walk on work days, and I'm never sure how far Kenneth can get without tiring.'

Kenneth had slicked back his hair and was wearing his best jersey, the one Aunty said the vicar had admired. A long walk would do him a lot of good, but he spread his pained expression around so that everyone felt sorry for him. Luckily, the bus was empty enough for them to sit separately. Bill pointed things out to Aunty on the way to avoid having to talk to Kenneth.

Once they'd alighted in Fulham Broadway, Bill strode ahead towards the Durbans' road. It felt important to be the one to ring the doorbell. He was their real friend.

As the front door opened Kenneth tried to link arms with Bill, to look like a dear brother. How *odious*, but Bill couldn't wriggle away without putting himself immediately in the wrong.

Mother stepped forward. 'Here we are, Letty. Can I introduce Doreen?'

While the three ladies were making introductory remarks, Bill tried to sidle past them to talk to Mr Durban but he was shaking hands with Aunty and asking a few polite questions about settling in.

She introduced Kenneth who was at his most charming. They'd hardly got as far as the lounge when, holding open the door for the ladies, Kenneth found an opportunity to shine. He set his eyes on the piano. 'What a lovely piano.'

'Thank you, Kenneth. It's for Angela.' Mrs Durban smiled proudly. 'She's just passed her Grade Six, even though she didn't quite manage a merit.'

Bill had never discussed piano playing with Angela although they were such friends.

'Such a benefit to a girl to have something to offer in marriage, when the time comes,' said Aunty. 'Music is something wonderful to share. Kenneth sings, you know.'

Kenneth turned his best smile onto Mrs Durban, a dimple showing on his left cheek.

'Yes, beautifully,' Mother added.

Bill frowned at the floor. Did she really need to join in?

Mrs Durban was delighted. 'Really? He'll have to join a choir here.'

'I should so like that, Mrs Durban,' he said.

She went to her desk to look for a list of music societies and wrote down information about a choir in Wandsworth.

Aunty took it. 'Oh, that is kind. We'll be glad of this, won't we Kenneth?'

Angela came in just then, and attention turned to her. She was so taken up by the grown-ups talking to her and about her, she hardly looked at Bill.

Kenneth went to the piano and looked at her music. He knew the right questions to ask, talking about Bait Hoaven and other strange foreign names Bill hadn't heard of. The talk was all about music, singing and societies. Soon Bill was mooching in their garden on his own while Angela was playing the piano and Kenneth's treble soared over the remains of the Anderson shelter. His voice should flipping well have broken by now. Bill's was husky already and Kenneth was nearly fourteen. It would be smashing to say 'There's something wrong with you', but he couldn't risk it. Kenneth was so often poorly, suppose there really was something wrong with him?

At tea-time, he went indoors with half a hope of cakes, but Mrs

Durban hadn't any flour left to make any, so there were only buns. 'I'm so sorry. I never seem to keep within our ration. I'm always running out of everything. It makes me realise how very much we had before rationing came in.'

Mr Durban said, 'We can't grumble. Going without our luxuries is nothing in comparison with the thousands starving in Europe.' There was a silence while everyone nodded. Recently, newspapers had shown wafer-thin children in Germany and Poland.

Aunty passed a half packet of tea to Mrs Durban. 'Almost as precious as gold,' she laughed.

'Are you sure you can spare it? I can't deny it's so welcome.'

'I got it in Northampton where my parents live. It's not so hard to get things there.'

'Well, thank you.' Mrs Durban gave it to Angela. 'Pop this to the kitchen, dear, and put it in the caddy.' She turned to the teapot and began to pour out while Bill handed round the plate of buns.

After tea, the talk was about Japan and how long it was holding out, delaying the real end of the war. This was the point at which Bill and Angela should disappear to play Ludo, but she was tidying the sheets of music on the piano.

Kenneth was leaning forward, his full attention on Mr Durban and the newspaper he was holding up.

Aunty said, 'We keep hearing about Allied attacks, but the Japs don't accept they've lost, it seems.'

Mr Durban folded the newspaper onto the side table. 'Well, ladies, I think we have to be patient for another three or four months. The blighters will have to give in eventually.' He pulled out his packet of Craven A.

'Their stubbornness is causing so many unnecessary deaths,' said Mrs Durban.

'Yes, but as we step up the attacks, hopefully we really will see the end of the war before Christmas.' He clicked his lighter and the flame punished the cigarette end. Bill kept his eyes on its glow.

'I read in *The Times*—' said Kenneth.

Bill frowned. 'We don't take *The Times*.'

'I use the library. Don't you?' That surprised tone was a wretched sham, and if they'd been alone together it would have deserved a shove in the stomach. It was all right for Kenneth, taking it easy. Bill was too busy with chores at home and at Nanny's to sit in the library.

Kenneth turned to Mr Durban. '—that it was a mistake to put Labour in power before the Far East is conquered.'

'The US won't let up, and neither will we, you'll see. But, it's good that you keep yourself informed, Kenneth.'

'Until Dad gets home, one of us has to stay informed at home.' Kenneth spread his hands as if he was managing all the information Mother and Aunty had available. He leaned forward a short way so that a long piece of hair fell over his forehead. This meant he could push it back with one delicate hand. Bill saw Angela watching the small movement. Ladies liked that sort of thing but it made Bill want to spit. Kenneth sat back. 'So I always read the main feature and Letters to the Editor.'

Mr Durban nodded approvingly. 'Angela, you should take a leaf from Kenneth's book.'

She gave a pat to her pile of music. 'Far too busy with work, Daddy. The newspaper's so big and you get cross if I crumple the pages. Anyway, what do I know about Japan? It all sounds horrid and I just want the war to be over, over, over.'

Mrs Durban put a hand over Angela's. 'We all do, dear.'

Aunty sighed and nodded. 'We're all sick of it. It will be so marvellous to get things back in the shops: proper food, clothes, everything. Once the war's really over.'

Kenneth nodded, as if he was her teacher or something. 'Patience, Mama.'

Mr Durban didn't seem to notice how sickening Kenneth was. 'Good lad. That's the way.' Anyone would think Mr Durban had forgotten it was Bill who was the boy he knew and liked.

When the time came for them all to go, both Mr and Mrs Durban said how much they'd enjoyed meeting Aunty and Kenneth. Even Angela smiled at Kenneth and said she'd liked playing the duet, before she said goodbye to Bill. He and Angela hadn't had a moment to themselves but she didn't mention that.

'Well, wasn't that nice,' said Mother as they went home.

'A lovely visit,' said Aunty.

Bill stuffed his hands in his pockets and Mother didn't even notice. Altogether, it wouldn't be surprising if they were all invited again before Bill had a chance to pop down on his own. When would he get a chance to talk about important things, like his own shashka story? Suppose Mr Durban stopped liking to see him and wanted to hear Kenneth sing instead?

CHAPTER 17

Saturday morning pictures had been super. Roy Rogers was fighting a great mass of Red Indians lined up on the dusty rock. They looked so scary, dipping their arrows in poison. Then they pulled their bows, and all the arrows went flying through the air! But Roy Rogers escaped and later, he won. Everyone cheered.

Aunty had given him the sixpence to go. 'You deserve it, dear.'

Kenneth said, 'I'm not interested in sitting with a lot of rowdy kids.' He hadn't done any chores, so he didn't deserve it anyway. He'd not said a word during dinner.

Now Aunty was writing to Dwaine. Bill could guessed that from Kenneth's black expression as he strode out of the front room and straight out of the house, slamming the front door behind him. Bill peeped out of the small hall window to check that Kenneth was actually going up the road.

Mother was also out, visiting her dancing friends and had taken Jill with her.

The feeling of freedom was wonderful. But was Aunty upset about Kenneth's temper? Because Bill had been the one who'd introduced Dwaine to Aunty, there'd always been a special feeling between them. Now it was even greater, with Kenneth so furious at the idea of Aunty having any man friend.

Bill slipped into the kitchen and poured her a cup of tea. He took it in to her, to show he was still on her side. As far as Kenneth was concerned, 'Daddy', Uncle Frank, was supposed to last all of Aunty's life even though dead. It wasn't fair. Kenneth had a new father – Dad – so why shouldn't Aunty have a new husband?

Afterwards he went up to his bedroom, a rare chance to have it to himself. He pushed the window open wide to let the essence of Kenneth blow away in the light breeze. The extra chest of drawers made it too squashed now to hold his arms out wide and pretend to be a Spitfire, or twirl around to see how fast and long he could do it without being dizzy. He couldn't do that anyway with Kenneth around to sneer and make superior comments to the mothers. He could shut his eyes to the pile of Kenneth's books and painting things on the windowsill, and to the sight of his clothes hanging in the wardrobe. But he couldn't escape the smell of the medicines Aunty gave Kenneth: Vick if he had a cold, bitter drops for Vitamin D, cod liver oil for health, Virol for strength, and sickly liquorice stuff to be regular.

Bill leant out of the window and breathed the outside air. No sign of Kenneth either left or right along Primley Road. This was his chance. Leaving the window latched open a little, he bounded downstairs, two at a time, another thing he couldn't do with either Mother or Kenneth around. Now, most importantly, they wouldn't see him go to his special hiding place: the largest, highest law book in Dad's study, too boring for anyone to want to read, even Dad, otherwise he wouldn't have it on a shelf too high to reach.

He put the Windsor chair before the fitted bookshelves, and stood on it, then pulled out the tome. Inside were the letters he'd had from Mrs Pawsey, and Mrs Youldon's postcards. Behind them were those handwritten sheets from a Manor notebook: Alan's careful copy of the shashka story. Although he was keen to go out, he couldn't stop himself reading the story again, pushing his head into the pages that still held the slight chestnut smell of the Manor library. One day he would go back there and beg to see that book again. He knew the first sentence by heart. 'The new Cossack, strong and dark, mounted his horse, ready to embark on a raid in a distant land.'

He put the chair back, ready to leave. At last he could tell Mr

Durban about the Russian book and perhaps slip in a question about Africa or soldiers escaping battles without Mr Durban realising he had Ted in mind. He slipped on his jacket, too short in the arms these days, but it covered his shirt, which wasn't clean on.

He set off towards Putney Bridge, and soon found he was panting although he wasn't running. His chest was thumping too. He was anxious about Ted, and about Kenneth pushing himself into the Durbans' home.

How long would it be before Ted got back to normal, and what could anyone do about it? Mother was worried about food, clothes, and housework she wasn't used to. Aunty had just started her part-time job and had her mind on Dwaine. Anyway, Ted wasn't her brother. Nanny and Grandad were old and ill and didn't seem to know what to do about Ted. Until Dad came home there was no-one who could help and meanwhile beastly Kenneth might tell everyone about Ted in a sneering way.

When he got to Fulham, Mrs Durban came to the door, allowing a wisp of stewed lamb smell to escape. 'Ah Bill, we've just finished dinner. We've all been out today so we're late eating. If you're hungry, I think there's just a little mutton left and two dumplings.'

He saw Mr Durban approaching, his newspaper under one arm. The smell was wonderful but he couldn't eat yet. 'No thank you, I'll be having my tea...' He left his voice in the air hoping she'd realise he was here for a chat with her husband.

'I'm afraid Angela's out at Guides. She heads the pack these days, very important,' Mrs Durban smiled.

'Yes. I'm joining Scouts. Dad said to.'

'I can entertain our Bill,' said Mr Durban in a rescuing voice and Bill followed him swiftly into the lounge.

'Anything special today?' It was like an invitation, suggesting that this would be one of many private visits Bill might make. Mr Durban put his newspaper on the table and tapped it. 'You know what's happening, of course? Japan.'

'About them holding out?' He didn't really know much more but he didn't want to sound ignorant. 'I remember the Japs bombing Pearl Harbor and then the Yanks coming into the war.' He smiled at the memory of the GIs in the village, what fun they were, the sweets and gum, the dances for ladies.

Mr Durban slid a cigarette out of its packet and flicked his lighter. 'The Japanese onslaughts have been lethal. And now it's payback time.' He drew a breath and the end of the cigarette glowed a bright red. 'I believe there's going to be a huge reprisal.'

'Reprisal?'

'Reprisal means getting back at the enemy with a vengeance.'

Bill nodded. He sometimes wanted to get back at Kenneth with a vengeance. 'But the war is finishing, isn't it?'

'Japan has to fall before war's really over. But it will. Their last day of action is coming. Then the many servicemen they're holding prisoner can be released. We want them home just as much as our men in Europe.'

'Yes. I want Dad back. Things won't be right until he is. There's all sorts of things to be sorted out.' His voice trailed away.

Mr Durban nodded slowly several times.

'Aunty's having a romance with a Yankee soldier and he'll come one day to collect her. It was me who introduced them.'

'You sound proud of that!'

'Well, Dwaine's really nice and other ladies were having fun and Aunty was sad after Uncle Frank died.'

'Yes. A very tragic affair. So you wanted her to have some fun too?'

'Mm. And not be lonely.' He thought *and to have a nice new husband, not like bullying Uncle Frank.* But that would have been an awful thing to say. Bill looked down. 'But Kenneth isn't glad.'

'Understandable. Imagine how you'd feel if your father had died.'

Bill blushed and hurried on, 'Anyway, I thought when you and I were alone I could tell you what I found out when I was evacuated, a bit about the shashka. It's sort of a secret that we discuss it, isn't it? I haven't told anyone I've seen it, except my best friend, Alan. And Angela, of course. But she doesn't know the shashka story, does she? Because it's not a story for women.'

Mr Durban's face might have had a smile or that could have been his lips gripping the cigarette. 'So what did you find out down in the country?'

'Read, actually. Alan wanted to cheer me up when—' he stopped. He mustn't let Mr Durban know that the precious photograph of the shashka had gone missing, '—when I was a bit miserable,' he finished. 'At the big Manor where Alan was billeted there was a library; a whole room of books on shiny shelves from down low to right up high. Alan got help to find something old about Russia, and there was *Russian Classic Folk Tales. Extracts*. It was on this yellowy paper with crinkly edges; only a few pictures, black line ones, small. *And:*' he took a breath, 'there was a story about the Cossacks. Alan and I read it over and over, lots of times. It said the sabre that killed in a specially brave fight was called a *shashka lixodaika*. There,' his words had been coming so fast, 'I've practised saying that so many times especially so that I could tell you.'

'I'm impressed, Bill. Spoken almost like a Russian.'

'Actually, Alan wrote it down, and we both practised it. *Shashka* is like a reward name that other sabres didn't have.'

'Ah, interesting. A special name, as if it's a person. They do that with the bravest bulls in Spain. Spanish bullfights, you know.'

He didn't know. They could discuss that another time. 'Therefore,' a grown-up word to make Mr Durban attend, 'because – your sabre (he nearly said "our") is a shashka, it must have killed someone after a fierce brave battle. You kept seeing huge battles, didn't you? And in that last one, the Cossack who gave it to you owned it, so he will have been very brave.'

'He was.' Mr Durban waved a flat hand downwards.

Bill slowed down and caught his breath. 'But at the end of the story, it said that the shashka would have a terrible future. What did that mean, sir?'

Mr Durban took another pull at his cigarette and blew the smoke out towards the open window. The smoke joined the clouds lowering over the garden. It was going to rain. 'Let's think about that a moment.'

Bill watched the cloud of smoke disappear, but its smell remained. It was a different smell from Dad's tobacco smoke, and different again from Mr Pawsey's Old Holborn. He said, 'I wonder if I'll ever find out why the shashka had a terrible future.'

Mr Durban finished his cigarette and stubbed it out on the Bakelite ashtray, grinding it hard as if it had done something wrong. 'All weapons are dangerous, and some are so dangerous that we shouldn't touch them without supervision. Just think. A rifle and most guns have safety catches. A sabre, now, that's dangerous every moment it's out of its scabbard.'

Bill looked at the floor. Angela had let him have it out of the scabbard. Mr Durban might tell her off if he knew. 'That story we found. I read it loads of times. It was about the olden days, way before the Great War. Your story was at the beginning of it, wasn't it?'

'It was. 1914. Cossacks, horse-back forays, hand-to-hand fighting. I think we've seen the end of that.'

'Yes. It's all bombs, now, isn't it? Hundreds and hundreds of thousands.' Bill thought of the hundreds and thousands on Nanny's iced cakes before the war; how they'd melted like the bloodied bodies sinking into the Russian snow that Mr Durban had talked of.

'Mass killings, yes. Governments want to save their country from being invaded, but in the fields and trenches and mountains, who knows if the poor servicemen really understand what they're fighting about.' He gave a sour laugh.

'Yes. War's so very bad when you're in it that it wouldn't be terrible for a soldier to turn away to escape it, would it?'

'Run away from enemy fire? If soldiers really ran away, they were deserters. Punishment by death, often.'

Bill felt a pain the back of his eye sockets. 'Death!'

It is a fearful thing facing the enemy under fire, but that's what we come into war to do. To save our country, not run away.'

'Even if a soldier had been in lots of battles already, and the next was just too awful?' Bill's throat seemed to be in his mouth and his stomach in his shoes.

'The regiment stands together, you see. They don't turn and flee, unless the order's given – RETREAT!' His voice rang out making Bill's head turn sharply to the window in case Mrs Durban was obediently rushing into the garden. 'Otherwise, the regiment stays put. That's what training is all about, Bill. You learn to obey orders, support your mates, stay with your regiment.'

'What if a soldier is ill?'

'A trained man has a duty to do his best. That's why soldiers are heroes.'

Bill kept his eyes on the ashtray. The ground-out cigarette was a crumpled black mess that needed clearing away. He must quickly change the subject; Mr Durban had begun to look at him too closely.

'The Cossack always fought on to the death, didn't he? I remember you telling me that. This book we found was more than a hundred years old. It had leather covers with ridges outside and coloured wavy lines inside. I can even remember some of the words, I read it so often.'

'Fascinating. I'd like to have seen it myself. I wonder whether I can get hold of a copy, or something like it.'

Bill pulled his prize piece from his pocket. 'Look, Mr Durban. I saved it to show you. Alan copied it all out for me on Manor note-book pages. Smell! It's his best writing and it took him ages.' He held out the pages proudly.

Mr Durban took it. 'What a good friend! Let me see,' and he began to read closely.

The new Cossack, strong and dark, mounted his horse, ready to embark on a raid in a distant land. Beneath him, the kazachii ybraynii sedlo, *a saddle decorated with the booty of Grandfather's previous raids and pillages. Now his old life of idle freedom was behind him together with his adolescence and he must accept his responsibilities as a member of the group. Thus he would be identified as a man.*

Last night, the songs round the campfire had described the possibilities of death and glorified the brutality of war. Death would be an honour! He threw out his chest. He was young, death just could not happen. A sword that managed to kill him would be honoured with the name Shashka lixodaika, *the name which identified it as legendary for downing an invincible Cossack warrior.*

He already had a shashka *himself. He put one hand on its hilt as the sun hinted a presence on the horizon. He sniffed the air, fresh with the scent of feral cat, ripe for the hunt.*

If he was the grandson of a rabble-rouser, one of the motley escapees of the political and penal systems of Polish Ukraine seeking the freer frontier, he was, above all, a Cossack. His grandfather's generation had developed military prowess to defend themselves against raids, and thus his father had been raised. Like other Cossacks, Father had learned a nomadic lifestyle to avoid enemies. He lived in a constant readiness to fight. So impossible was it to settle, farm and feed themselves this way, they depended on fishing, hunting but mostly pillage. The spoils displayed on Grandfather's saddle symbolized the honour of a Cossack warrior.

He had only known his father part-time, for Cossacks must leave their wives and children the moment duty called to embark on raids. But during those times at home before his honourable death, Father was memorable. He starred in all aspects of Cossack culture – the haunting folk songs, wild athletic dancing and dramatic, aggressive horse-riding.

Eventually the Tsar employed the fearless Cossacks to defend Russia's borderlands and it was in such a way that Father died. His compatriots brought him to the family for his final hours, enough time for him to croak his wish to his only son.

'Take this shashka, son of mine, and let it only leave your hands in those of your son, or in death, of a noble warrior as brave as you must become. Mind its path, protect it well. It will inflict the most terrible wounds.'

After his father's death, he put it to one side, had wild times, passionate times, ruined his mother's hopes of his heroism then sped back to renew them.

And now, the camp fires dead and his comrades mounted beside him, it was time to ride forth. Ahead of him, twenty years and many skirmishes on, would be the Great War. But for the shashka, a much longer history awaited its terrible potential.

Bill let him read uninterrupted, his mind on the dreadful words *punishable by death*. Would many other soldiers know that Uncle Ted had tried to run away? Wasn't getting a bullet in his backside enough punishment?

Mr Durban reached the last page, shaking his head slightly. 'Well, I never, Bill! How wonderful to have found this.'

'Yes. It's my secret treasure.'

'Then keep it somewhere safe. I'd dearly like to have my shashka's full history. The shashka is the most valuable thing I own, not only its antique value, but—'

'—your own story; when you were just a school leaver!'

'Yes, indeed. What an adventure! How can I ever forget the shashka's owner and having him give it to me!'

'Well, you deserved it for trying to rescue him.'

Mr Durban smiled. 'I'm no kind of hero, but like your father, just turned to the job when needed. Now that I have more time, I might seek out a military expert in Russian weapons to fill in more information, once everyone's demobbed. The best chaps from the universities are still in service. Life's been difficult at home with our finest brains unavailable.' He began to talk about how difficult it was to find someone to fill in for Dad while he was away, someone who had the right knowledge.

Mrs Durban came in with a tray of tea. 'It's a fresh pot. You'd like a cup of tea, Bill?' and as she poured out, added, 'We were pleased to meet your cousin. So nice that he's musical. Someone for Angela to play duets with. Here's your cup, dear. I'm sorry there's no sugar.'

He nodded, trying not to look too glum, and slid the story sheets back into his pocket.

CHAPTER 18

As he got close to home, the sky was hanging in a threatening manner over Primley Road. He took the rest of the road at a fast run. He joined Aunty and Mother in the parlour with relief that he'd got there before the rain.

The front door opened before he'd hardly said *Hello*. That would be Kenneth. He came in with library books and the loaf, which he put on the table with a noble expression. He'd shopped!

'You're just in time, Kenneth, dear. And you, Bill. Just escaped the downpour.' And she was right. The sky seemed to split apart as she spoke, and a loud bang made them all jump. Rain hit the window at an angle, sounding angry and aggressive.

'Goodness,' said Mother. 'More like March than August.'

There was a bright flash, and after a few moments, another boom. 'Lightning.'

Jill ran in and put her arms round Mother. 'I'm frightened, Mummy. Put your hands over my eyes!'

Fierce raindrops bounced off the surface of the concrete yard, hard and high, with a regular drumming sound.

'Ooooh,' Jill kept her head buried in Mother's front, and Aunty patted her hand.

'It can't hurt us, ducky.'

Kenneth had picked up his paintbrush and was trying to paint the bouncing drops, each with a little overhang and a speck of light at its top. 'It's too dark!' And it did look like night-time rather than early evening. Beyond the window, the sky lit again, this time brilliantly.

'Cor! I'm going to watch it properly from the garden room,' Bill said. 'It's not often we get a really big storm.'

Kenneth followed him, holding a tray of his painting things. There wasn't a table in the garden room so he put it on the bookcase. Bill went to the French windows where he could look up and sideways, left and right. The flashes came one after another, then dramatic zig-zags slashing through the navy blue sky, lighting it up more colourfully than ever the searchlights had done. The garden became vivid, yellow one minute, orange and scarlet another and a backdrop of a deep mystic purple. Boom. It was as though the thunder was announcing the light show.

'If only I had some film in my camera,' he couldn't help himself saying, even though it was Kenneth standing with him. 'This might never happen again.'

'If only I had indigo and carmine red. I can't paint this without the right colours.'

Bill found his head nodding in sympathy.

They carried on watching, the storm continuing and even intensifying, one or other of them letting out a 'Phew' or a 'Golly' as a shard of orange hit the ground or slashed the sky. It must have been an hour before Mother called them for tea. Until then neither of them had moved.

It was odd, he and Kenneth had never felt so close. Yet, as they went towards the parlour for bread and dripping and a currant bun, the fury of the sky and the deadened thuds of thunder seemed to signal that something dreadful and dramatic was going to happen.

CHAPTER 19

Mother came into the kitchen looking serious. 'Where's your mother, Kenneth?'

'Reading a wretched airmail in her room.' Kenneth was examining both his shirts on the ironing pile. 'Mama will need to turn my collars. Look how worn they are.'

Bill snorted. The comment wasn't meant for him, but Mother had a faraway expression and didn't answer. Instead she said, 'I think the end of war may come earlier than we'd expected.'

'Why?' For once Kenneth didn't insert his superior knowledge.

'I've been listening to the news.'

'What's happened?' Kenneth pushed his face towards her as though she had wilfully kept him from information.

'The Americans have dropped a bomb on Japan. A huge one, apparently.'

'Many killed?' It sounded as if Kenneth was keeping a tally.

'I couldn't take it in. The newscaster said a great dust storm was covering the city where the bomb was dropped. A town called Haro or Hiro – something. Bill, run next door and see if the Benthams have a newspaper.'

When he came back with it, Aunty had finished her private time with her airmail and was just coming into the parlour.

Kenneth held out both his shirts toward her. 'Look at these collars, Mama. You really need to mend them or something. By the way, the USA has dropped some great bomb on Japan, but you probably know that from your Yank friend.'

Mother said quickly, 'I think it's that atomic bomb.'

'Oh my goodness,' Aunty sighed. 'This Japan business!' She took out her small scissors and started removing the stitches from around Kenneth's blue and white shirt collar. 'Is it too much to hope that the Japanese have given in?'

Bill spread the newspaper over the parlour table and Mother leaned over it. The front page announced, 'The Bomb that Changed the World' and showed an enormous cloud in the shape of a mushroom standing in an almost blank landscape. He couldn't stop a huge breath whistling out.

'Look at that, Mama!' Kenneth sounded impressed. He read out 'Japs told to quit.'

'Just like the wireless announced,' said Mother in a small voice.

'Horrific,' said Aunty. 'Much as I hate the Japs, I hope the women and children got inside their homes fast enough. That dust in their lungs – it could be a killer.'

'That'll put paid to Japan,' said Kenneth. 'I'd like to hear their fighting talk now!'

Mother was trying to read the detail. 'They don't know the casualty level or the damage. The dust is covering everything.'

Bill said, 'How will people be rescued?' but the phone rang and Mother hurried to answer it.

'I don't understand. I thought we were holding off from invading to avoid civilian casualties. Now they'll be huge' Aunty put her scissors down and stretched forward to turn the page, Kenneth's shirt still in her hand. She started to read silently, Kenneth and Bill looking over her shoulder. Most of the article was about how enormous, how much bigger than anything before this bomb had been.

Mother came back. 'That was Nanny, Bill. Ted's not too well and they need you to sleep over. Did you know he was ill?'

Bill swallowed. Nanny must have found the eiderdown. He'd counted on Ted clearing up the feathers and getting rid of it. Or had the neighbours told her about the yelling in the garden? What was best to say? 'He wasn't that well, Mother, but I don't know what's wrong.' That was true enough.

'You'd better go upstairs and pack overnight things. Is there anything we can spare them to cheer them up, Doreen? My mother shouldn't be having this extra worry on her hands.'

'How about some Jenner's Soyacream? It's supposed to be good for health and energy. Vitamin B, I think. I've got a packet in the back of the larder.'

'Thank you. You know, I *said* Ted was run-down. Didn't I say that?'

Aunty nodded. Her expression showed that she'd guessed something different was wrong with Ted. She made room for Mother beside the open newspaper. 'What a world this is coming to, Marcia.'

Bill didn't think extra vitamins would help Ted but Aunty was being kind. He went to find the Soyacream. Horrible stuff. At least he didn't have to eat it. Then he hurried upstairs and put a change of clothes and his toothbrush in a carrier bag.

'Good riddance,' Kenneth muttered as Bill left, the mothers still bent over the table.

Was he talking about the Japanese victims or Bill? Probably both. Bill slammed the door behind him and hoped Kenneth would know that was for him.

CHAPTER 20

The doctor had already visited Ted when Bill arrived, but it hadn't changed anything. Ted was mooching around in a shirt and pyjama trousers, trying to help and not finishing the jobs he started.

It was hard, trying to talk to Grandad cheerily with Ted in that state and the worrying news on the wireless. Nanny was too upset to speak about the eiderdown, but Bill saw the remains in the dustbin, and the bulgy canvas bag in the parlour where she was saving its feathers.

At night, Bill slept on the spare bed, which was in Ted's room. This meant he heard and saw Ted's dreadful nightmares. He sat bolt upright and flailed around with his arms, shouting out, swearing and even making crying sounds. The first night Bill rushed out to get Nanny, but she told him, 'Just wake Ted up and tell him he was only dreaming. It often happens, dear. He can't help it.'

Bill woke him and tried to calm him down, but Ted didn't seem to hear anything he said. By the morning, Bill felt tired through, then it was the same the following night.

Nanny used his help to get Grandad down the stairs. Leaning on Bill's arm, Grandad whispered, 'It's perhaps a bit safer to have you alongside rather than Ted, at the moment.'

'How did you manage before he came home?'

'Slept on a camp bed downstairs for months. I don't want to be forced back to that. It's not like my own bed.'

'What's going to happen to Ted, now?' Bill asked, once Grandad was safely settled in his easy chair. Until today, the sticks, the medicine bottles and being stuck in the chair had turned Grandad into a remote figure. Now he was more like an equal.

'The doctor said there's a place Ted can go to during the day, some days, not all. He'll be taught things to make, probably. He has to wait until there's a vacancy.'

'Will that make him better?'

Grandad moved his lips to and fro as if he was chewing a toffee. 'It's always better to be occupied. He can still help us out at home when he's at his best.'

Bill really didn't want to mention the eiderdown incident, but someone ought to know how wild Ted had been with the fork. 'Did the doctor think Ted should be digging the garden?'

Grandad nodded. 'It's all right if he does a bit, even if little comes of it.' He stretched his top half. 'Lordy, I'm stiff.'

'Grandad, have the Japanese given in yet?'

'No, they haven't, stubborn fools. Wouldn't you have thought that great bomb would have done it? They've only themselves to blame when they get truly clobbered.'

Nanny came in with a cup of tea for Grandad at that point and Bill went to start peeling vegetables.

Next day, the sun was bright but not beating down too strongly. Nanny wanted the lawn mown. He pulled off his V-neck and shirt so that he could feel the warmth directly on his back. It was comforting, and bare-chested, he felt like a proper workman. The smell of cut grass made everything feel fresh. He couldn't believe in atomic bombs with this smell and this blue sky.

Ted wandered out.

Bill called, 'Can you pull the deckchairs out of the shed, and help me get Grandad outside? It would be nice for him to sit in the sun for a change.'

'They're a bit done for. Not been used for ages.'

'Can you fix them?'

Ted went to the shed.

Bill enjoyed making the stripes on the lawn with the mower. They weren't as neat as the farmer's ploughing back in the village but it started to get the garden into some order. He stopped to pull lumps of grass from the blades and surreptitiously check on Ted.

Ted opened one deckchair out and twisted a screw, then sat in it. 'Just testing. This one's all right now.' He moved the wooden notch to its next position and lay back. 'It's nice.'

'You will do the other one for Grandad, though, won't you?'

Nanny came down towards them, walking carefully on the uneven stone path.

'You should go home, now, Bill. You've been such a help, but your mother will want you back and we're all right now for a bit. Aren't we, Ted?'

'I've fixed one of these deckchairs, and I'll do the other in a bit.'

'I thought we could get Grandad to sit out here, Nanny.'

'Ted can do that. I'll see that he does. You come inside, Bill.'

He followed her indoors. Nanny found three shortbreads from a tin on the high shelf in her larder and wrapped them in greaseproof paper. Goodness knows how old they were. 'One for you, one for Jill and one for Kenneth. There you are, dear. And there's your overnight bag.'

Bill called *Goodbye* and started off down the road with relief. When he was little it had been a great treat to be going to Nanny and Grandad's, and really thrilling if Uncle Ted was there. Nowadays it was rather awful.

When he reached Primley Road, the postman was just ahead of him. He was quite old and the heavy bag on his shoulder bent him forward. Bill ran to take their post before he got to their gate.

'That's saved me a few steps, young'un. Here you are,' and he held out a few envelopes. One was from Dad. Bill rushed indoors with it. Dad wrote as often as he could but they hadn't had a letter for a couple of weeks.

'Ah you're back, Bill.' Mother was in the hall, dusting, and Kenneth was on a step-ladder dusting the high part, the top of the dado rail. 'Nanny rang me. She said things are calmer.'

Kenneth looked down. 'Calmer? Who isn't calm?'

Quickly, Bill held the post up between Mother's face and

Kenneth's. 'Letter from Dad! Perhaps he's coming home?' He almost pushed the letter into Mother's hand.

Kenneth stayed where he was up the step-ladder. Bill saw that by peering down, he'd be able to read the letter over Mother's head.

Mother was reading quickly through, peering at tiny writing up the margins where Dad had saved paper. At the end, she turned back to the beginning. 'Get down, Kenneth. I'm to discuss this with you both.'

They all went into the parlour, where Aunty was sewing.

'Herbert's written, Doreen. You're to hear this too. He says,

---

...I want you all to know. The bomb dropped on Hiroshima was mammoth and I cannot imagine the extent of death and injury. Any published figures are unlikely to be accurate. I want the boys to think seriously about the wrong of hitting back with ever more powerful weapons. Retaliatory force – where will it end?

We've been told the explosion spread far and wide. Those within its reach will have been most horribly burned. The fumes will be noxious. Therefore, there must be dreadful consequences even for those who survive and deaths will surely continue for years as result of this atrocity. Needless to say, it's the civilians who suffer, the families, babies, innocent of any part of their mad masters' machinations. I am not in tune with the edict "Kill them all, for God will know his own". In fact, since God accepts ALL as his own, the comment – translated from the Latin – is nonsense in religious terms also.

I would not be able to write this letter such if the war in Europe had not ended, for the censors would destroy it, and probably my good service record too. In any case, I am no longer 'serving' as being a soldier is so horribly described (serving to kill, which is not, of course, God's purpose). I am now temporarily helping the Education section prior to my demobilisation. We are told this demob will happen on a certain date, and it does not. We wait upon another date. Some go, some stay, and while this inefficient mess is being sorted out, I make myself useful to the many who need the education they have lost for the war.

Meanwhile, my words to the boys will not wait. I wish them to

consider the dreadful massacre that has occurred before newspapers and schools encourage them to rejoice when the Japanese military sign a peace treaty, as of course they must. We all desperately want an end to world war, but this way cannot be right. I do not want my sons to believe in mass destruction or to applaud it. So I trust you to read this to them while you have their full attention, Marcia.

My love to Doreen, whom I trust is well settled in our front room, to dear little Jill, and to the two growing boys who will shortly be considered ready to hold a gun. Let their minds reign supreme! And my true love to you, Marcia, "holding the fort".

Herbert. X

'Dear Herbert,' said Aunty. 'Such a pacifist! What a dreadful day it was for him when he was forced to take arms. Especially after being assured that both he and Frank were in reserved occupations.'

Mother was still gazing at the letter. 'Yes. If poor Frank had been spared, it would have been far easier for him to be called up. He was all for fighting the enemy from the beginning.'

Kenneth came down the step-ladder. 'Aunty Marcia! How can you suggest Daddy should have been called up when he's dead?'

Mother put an arm around his shoulders. 'I am sorry, Kenneth, dear. It is so hard for you. I only meant that your father wasn't a pacifist like Dad.'

And neither is Kenneth, Bill thought.

'True.' Kenneth shook his head slightly from side to side as if acknowledging each father in turn. No-one had ever spelled out the difference between the two fathers before. Kenneth's chin went up. 'It is such a well written letter, one I'd be proud to show my future masters if it didn't criticise war.'

Bill stepped in front of the step-ladder. 'Dad wants us to be thinking about all the people who died and whether such a bombing is right.'

Aunty said, 'Let's see what the effect has been on the Japanese military, and whether they'll sign the treaty now. It's nearly news time.' She opened the parlour door and the crackle of the wireless began. 'Come and tune this, one of you, will you? I never seem to get it right.'

Bill turned the knobs until the voice became clearer. The pips sounded.

Mother was re-reading Dad's letter. Perhaps there were private bits she hadn't read out loud.

Then the news began with a shock announcement. A second atomic bomb had been dropped on another Japanese city.

'Another!' Mother exchanged an anguished glance with Aunty.

As the size and extent of it was being spelled out, Kenneth screeched, 'Serve them right! Now they know what it's like to be smattered into bits. The Japs are done for!'

Aunty put a hand over his mouth. Her eyes were screwed up. She and Kenneth would be thinking of what happened to Uncle Frank.

Mother gasped at the wireless's words. She bent to the wireless, trying to hear more clearly. 'Twenty thousand times greater,' she muttered.

Greater than what? What on earth would Dad say about a second A-bomb? Bill stayed in the parlour doorway, one arm pressed on either side, as if holding it up. Dad had said the first must be killing thousands. Now it would be thousands of thousands.

Kenneth pushed Aunty's hand from his mouth and leant back against the table with one foot across the other in his film star manner. His chin was lifted, almost as if he didn't need to hear the news because he had found the solutions to everything.

Bill had to get out. He needed fresh air. He needed a long time outside. As soon as Mother turned off the wireless, he strode down the hall to the front door. 'Won't be too long,' he called, shutting the door before anyone stopped him.

He'd run. He'd run anywhere to breathe easily and not look at Kenneth or hear all the war words. He didn't want to think about people being blown up, burnt or what happened to them if they survived. It was horrible to think that Andrew would never walk down the road, that a bomb had fallen on him and his mother; that one had nearly got Nanny and Grandad, changed them and made their lives miserable; that thousands of Japanese survivors would be full of – what did Dad say? – nocksous fumes. Then, think about Ted!

Even without injuries that you could actually see, war could make a man ill and batty and not able to work. Even without joining the army or helping it in any way, even being a baby, you could be killed in war. He'd always known that, of course, but this Japan stuff was forcing him to think of it all, and his chest heaved, as though each breath was desperate.

The street was too crowded for him to run and as he passed a dustbin, he saw yesterday's *News Chronicle* on top. He took it, turning back to find the front page. It was more detail about the first A-bomb. The colonel who'd dropped the bomb on Hiroshima said it went down like a clap of thunder. 'Hiroshima disappeared in cloud, boiling smoke and flame.' That colonel must have known what he was doing to the people underneath! But that wasn't mentioned, only his award, which he got immediately afterwards. The article went on to report some other colonel who saw the bombing from a distance saying it was 'awe-inspiring and magnificent'. His tummy churned at the words. Those colonels were so disgusting. If only Dad could have spoken to them before they dropped the bomb. He stuffed the paper down inside the dustbin and jogged on until he reached the common, then he ran fast. He ran along the main path, dodging around prams and slow walkers. He ran through the trees until he reached a deserted path, and there he ran his hardest until his breath came fast and loud. He ran as far as the lake. That felt better. He stopped under a group of trees and bent double.

The smell of the grass was fresh and good. He stayed bent over, but looked upwards through the tree tops and between their leaves where the sky showed bright blue. He was so lucky not to be in Japan, and he was glad he had a father who hated the bombing.

CHAPTER 21

It had been a long run and the overgrown grass had made it harder. He straightened up once he'd got his breath back.

A couple of kids dodged around the trees near him. 'Watcha. Got any chewing gum?'

'No, sorry.'

'Aw.' They ran off, disappointed.

Being at Nanny's the last three days had stopped him from going to Mr Durban's. Now he simply must, to discuss what Dad had written. If he'd heard Kenneth's last hateful words, Mr Durban wouldn't be so keen to advise Angela to 'take a leaf out of his book'.

Alan would say it wasn't Kenneth's fault. Awful things had happened to Kenneth's father, and when you got hurt you always felt like hurting back. He knew that; he and Kenneth used to do hitting back when they were small. Only it always felt like him, Bill, getting hurt the worst and no-one sticking up for him.

He left the common and crossed Gants Hill between the buses. The water under Putney Bridge was smutty and grey, the blue sky showing in fits and starts between clouds. Would Mr Durban be in?

By the time he arrived, after his long run and the walk from the common, he was very thirsty. Mrs Durban opened the door to him and took him in the kitchen. 'Bill, you look over-heated and dusty. Come in here and have a drink.'

He drank the glass of squash gratefully and so quickly, that she poured him another.

'You have got a thirst! What have you been up to?'

He had so much to say, but they weren't things you really talked to ladies about. War, bombing, being blown up, Kenneth getting round people, Ted being batty. 'Nothing. Just running on the common. I've been away a couple of days. To help my grandparents, you know.'

She screwed the top on the squash bottle. 'Good for you. I'm sure you are a help, especially with their trouble over Ted.'

His head snapped upwards in a query. Then he put his glass down carefully. What did she know? 'Did Mother telephone you?'

'No, dear. Your cousin came round the other day to bring something for Peter.'

Kenneth had come round on his own! Brought something for Mr Durban!

'He was chatting to me and Angela afterwards. So sad that your uncle buckled under the strain of battle. I'm sure he's not the only one.'

Kenneth had come round here on his own, and then told about Ted! Bill could feel his teeth grinding in an effort not to spit and snarl. No-one should know! He hated Kenneth. It wasn't his information to spurt.

'I can see it's really upsetting for you. Kenneth said that Ted was a favourite with you before the war. But cheer up, dear, I'm sure there will be help for him.'

She found two ginger nut biscuits but he couldn't eat them. He had to sip the last drops of orange to stop his lips wobbling. He could throttle Kenneth. Nothing would get his words back. Thank goodness no-one knew about the eiderdown. He wasn't ever going to tell anyone.

As her mother left the room, Angela came in. She looked pretty. 'Hallo, Bill.' She put a hand on his shoulder. 'Oof, you're hot. I can feel you burning through your shirt. What've you been doing?'

She was sounding like her mother. He said again, 'Running.' It was embarrassing talking to her, now that she'd heard about Ted.

'Do you like my outfit? Do you recognise it?'

He blinked hot eyes and looked at her properly. She was wearing a silky blouse and a cotton skirt. 'Should I?'

'Your mother's skirt. We cut it up to make me and Jill blouses. Don't you remember her wearing it?'

He shook his head.

'Boys! These little green flowers are pretty, aren't they? Has Jill got hers yet?'

He had seen Aunty sewing. Perhaps that was what it was. 'I think Aunty's working on it.'

He heard Mr Durban's cough, but he hadn't come in.

Angela twirled around. 'This skirt's not very full, but I'm saving up for one that makes a balloon shape when you twizzle round. It takes lots of material.'

Didn't she know what had happened to Japan? Or did Mrs Durban hide news that was too horrible for her to know? At least she wasn't saying anything about Ted. Perhaps she'd been too busy thinking about skirts and twizzling to pay attention to what Kenneth was saying.

But she went on more seriously, 'I'm going to start evening classes in September. There was a notice up in the library. English Literature. I always loved English at school. Kenneth and I were talking about it, and all the famous authors. He knows a lot, although he's younger than me.'

Bill stood up. It was just like Kenneth had threatened. He and Angela had lots they could talk about. But she wouldn't like Kenneth if she really knew him. Didn't she remember back before evacuation when he'd told her some beastly things Kenneth had done? She'd said then that he sounded mean. And he was, he really, stinking well, was.

Now, standing beside Angela, his eyes were level with the roll of hair over her forehead. He could smell a sweet soapy smell. Shampoo. She was too nice to be friends with Kenneth. He bit his lip and looked towards the hall. 'Is your father busy?'

'No. Just reading the paper, I think. Go, then, if you're bored with me.' She stepped away.

He always seemed to be saying the wrong thing, but he went

anyway, and put his head around the door of the lounge. 'Mr Durban?'

Mr Durban lowered his newspaper slightly, 'I heard your voice, Bill. Had some squash, have you?' and then he went back to reading.

Bill sat himself on the sofa at right-angles to him, ready to get an idea of what Mr Durban thought about Japan. He waited.

Mr Durban went on reading, almost as if he'd forgotten Bill had come in. Was it because of what Kenneth had told him about Ted?

While he waited for Mr Durban to finish his article and turn his attention towards him, Bill looked around the room. The snug door was open and he could see some books, an album, a couple of framed pictures in a pile on the mahogany side table. The plan for a memorabilia room was underway. His glance swept over the newspaper Mr Durban was reading to the side table beside him. He couldn't prevent a gasp. On top of a book about tanks, there lay a photograph of a Cossack sabre, the sabre, the *shashka*. It was the same as the precious photo he'd lost. 'You've got another photograph, the same!' He hadn't meant to interrupt but the words were out before he knew it.

The newspaper lowered. Mr Durban glanced down at the photograph and turned his head to Bill, his smile – was it a smile – just a flat line with a quirk on one edge? 'No. It's the one I sent you, if you remember, and which you apparently didn't want any more.'

Bill shook his head as if to shake the puzzle out of it.

'Young Kenneth kindly brought this round for me. He noticed my name on the back and thought I might want it. He found it in your waste paper basket.'

No! So Kenneth had kept it all these years and then brought it round here! How dared he do such a thing! And to make Mr Durban think Bill had thrown the photo away! 'I didn't. I kept it safe for ages, it was precious and—' It was too embarrassing to explain how he'd hidden the photograph where he could reach it in the night, so that he could wave it like magic when things were miserable to make himself brave. '—then it … went.'

Kenneth stole it. That's what he wanted to say, but was it right to tell on someone, even if they'd done something wrong? He'd never been a tell-tale-tit, people hated tell-tales. The furious feelings in his heart and his tummy were so enormous that he couldn't go on. He needed to explain how he wouldn't *ever* have thrown the precious photo away. He licked his lips, trying to find the words.

Mr Durban had turned back to his newspaper. 'It can add to the display in the snug,' he said, almost to himself. He turned the page.

For a while Bill sat on, wanting so much to speak about what had really happened, but too afraid now of tears coming, because he couldn't shout out that Kenneth was a thief and a traitor. It was difficult to say anything, especially as he'd have to interrupt Mr Durban when he was concentrating on reading.

It felt as if half an hour had passed, but it might only have been minutes, before Angela came in. 'Would you like to come to the pet shop with me, Bill? I have to get some Macleans paste and a bar of carbolic soap for Mummy, and the pet shop's next door. They have some new rabbits, so sweet.'

She was still at the door, and with Mr Durban's face still slanted down to the newspaper, it was easiest to go with her.

He got up, slowly, hoping Mr Durban would look up and say he must stay longer for a chat, but he didn't.

'Goodbye, Mr Durban,' he said in a choked voice, and then, 'I didn't throw it away,' but the words seemed to land in the cushions of the sofa and he could hardly hear them himself.

'Coming?' Angela said, cheerily. And then, as their front door closed, she said, 'Daddy's deep into the world situation. Dreadfully serious.' She almost skipped out of the gate but her heeled shoes slowed her. 'Do you realise? After today, everything will change. The war's really, truly going to be over.'

His war wasn't. He tried to keep calm but the fury kept rising from his tummy to his chest and through the top of his arms, his shoulders and into his mouth. He wanted to shout and punch – almost drop a bomb. Everyone in the road looked normal, but he wasn't. Things were not all right.

Angela was chatting happily about how it would be now the war was bound to end. I'm so looking forward to the end of queuing and having things – like bananas. I can just about remember them. I don't suppose you can?'

Bananas? How could he think about anything but what had

happened to thousands of people, and what Kenneth had done to him? He must have answered for Angela went on,

'No. You would have been too young to remember the last ones.'

At first he thought she was talking about the last people dying but then caught the rest of her sentence.

'...didn't like that little tiny bit on the end, but I would definitely be eating every morsel if I got one now.'

After a pause she said, 'You don't seem happy about war ending. Don't you believe it? It really will be at an end now, you know. Daddy said so, after this morning's news, and he's always right.'

He kept his silence, and Angela bent down to stroke a little dog that was passing. 'I'd love a pet, wouldn't you? Perhaps I can have one now. Perhaps Mummy will let me have a kitten. You can help me choose one. Then we'll go back and tell her about it, and beg. The shops are only a bit further.' She stood still a moment, and turned to him. 'Why aren't you talking?'

He ground the heel of his shoe into a hole in the pavement, this way and that. Angela had been a good friend all these years. Could he trust her with what had happened? He tried, 'What would you do if someone had done something really bad to you, like lying about you, or being a traitor?'

'Like Germans spreading propaganda? All lies. That's horrible, I know. Daddy said both sides did that sort of thing, it was necessary.'

'Great Britain did? No!'

'Yes. It was like a weapon. But Mummy doesn't agree that *All's fair in love or war*.'

'He didn't like that thought. Nothing was fair in war. But what about a traitor...?'

'Horrible again. We had them. Lord Haw-Haw, for one, and he's in Court now. Soon he'll be in prison, I bet. Come on, the pet shop's here.'

He turned away. It was no good, he wasn't going to get a useful answer about dealing with a liar at home; his roundabout questions were no good. He would talk to Alan.

Meanwhile, he'd have to look at rabbits and kittens and pretend he was all right.

CHAPTER 22

Scuffing his shoes as he made for home, Bill saw that the soles were loose and his toes were curled up. He needed a new pair of shoes, or even boots. His toes were trapped by the toe caps, trapped like the whole of him. He looked at the bombsite beside him. He was like that blade of grass under a pile of fallen bricks and debris, one small green tip trying to become tall and straight. He wanted to be Mother's right-hand man, he tried to be the best help to Ted, Grandad and Nanny, and to prove himself a hero to Mr Durban but he had a traitor in his home and what could he do about it without being a tell-tale, and causing more problems?

Angela would be back at her home begging for the white and brown kitten she'd fallen in love with. Mr Durban would be putting the shashka photo in the snug, believing that Bill had thrown it away. Kenneth would be warbling his songs, head in the air, top dog with Aunty and now with Mr Durban too. How he'd be crowing to himself, beastly Kenneth. How spiffing it would be to push his stupid head into a dustbin. He kicked every fag end he saw into the gutter and pretended it was Kenneth.

When he got home, Aunty was getting the tea. It was beans on toast, one of his favourites, but that didn't change the way he was feeling.

Jill didn't notice his mood of course. 'Beans on toast, Bill. Mummy's out. Gone to her friends and they're going dancing. She was wearing a pretty dress.'

'Pretty old,' Aunty smiled.

Kenneth sat at the table, fingering his knife and fork while humming a melody. Its trilling notes were like a taunt.

Bill sat down with a thud.

'You're late,' Kenneth said.

Bill couldn't trust himself to look at him.

'Not answering?'

Bill glared, his eyes feeling like glowing embers.

'What's wrong?'

'You know.' The words spread slowly over the space between them like a poisonous stain.

Kenneth's face showed some alarm. 'What?'

Jill giggled. 'You're going to quarrel. I can tell.'

Bill couldn't say he'd been down to the Durbans, revealing that he went there alone. Even Mother didn't know. He drummed his fingers on the table while Aunty was out in the kitchen. He wanted the drumming to sound like Africans in the jungle before they did their war dance.

'Am I supposed to have done something?' Kenneth brushed the stupid lock of hair from his forehead.

'You know what you've done.'

Kenneth raised an eyebrow, but he was looking uneasy. Even Jill had gone quiet.

Aunty came back and served out the beans. 'At least the juice from the beans means we don't notice there's no marg on the toast. I've done a nice big plateful for all of you.'

At first, Bill thought he wouldn't be able to swallow but as he saw Kenneth's tension, his fury began to die down. Kenneth knew Bill had found out something, but he didn't know what, or which. There were lots of nasty things he could have done. That would make him nervous. He'd worry about how much Bill knew, and what Bill might do back.

He put his fork into his beans and lifted his knife just above the toast, then cut it very deliberately as if causing it the maximum hurt. Kenneth would be watching. Hopefully, Kenneth was afraid.

The beans were good. Aunty didn't overcook them like Mother who had the juice bubbling until it tasted stewed and the beans went to mush. He took another mouthful, aware that Jill was peeping at him and then Kenneth.

Aunty leaned over the table. 'Have your glass of milk, Kenneth. You know how important it is for your health. I don't want you back in bed with a bad chest, now.'

Kenneth drank and didn't argue. Was he getting worried?

Bill ate a few more mouthfuls. 'The beans are nice, Aunty.' He sat up straighter and smiled across at Jill, an idea coming to him. Of course – if Kenneth thought Bill had told Mr Durban about the stealing, then he jolly well would be worried. He'd done the deed while Bill was away and relied on not being found out.

He allowed himself a slight smile as he cut the next mouthful. Kenneth would be noticing.

Kenneth would worry that Mr Durban would tell Aunty. How awful for the perfect Kenneth to be in trouble! And Mr Durban worked with Dad. Kenneth would be scared of Mr Durban telling him. Dad would certainly see stealing the photo and pretending to return it as very, very wrong. Not behaviour he'd want in his new son.

The beans were going down very nicely. Looking across the table, he saw that Kenneth's plate was still quite full.

Kenneth always told tales so he'd assume that Bill would tell on him too, like he'd assumed Bill would nose into Kenneth's secret stuff. Ah! He took a sudden breath and nearly choked on the next bean. *That* was what Kenneth was hiding when Bill burst into the bedroom; the photo was one of his secret things! No wonder he hadn't wanted Bill there. He felt his chest swell and his shoulder blades against the chair back. It felt so powerful knowing things, and working out things, that he didn't have to stifle fury any more. He polished off his remaining beans. 'Thank you, Aunty.' He took his cup of tea and his share of the broken biscuits. He passed one with cream on it to Jill. 'Did you go to Iris's today? Can you skip with both feet yet?'

'Silly. You can't do skipping with one foot. Boys are rubbish at skipping.' She nibbled the last of her biscuit and nudged Kenneth. 'Slow coach. You're still on your beans. I'll eat your biscuit if you don't hurry.'

Kenneth forked up another small mouthful and didn't answer.

After tea, and the clearing up, Bill didn't go outside as he usually did, but hung around looking at the books Alan had given him. He knew that Kenneth wanted to borrow them but now couldn't risk asking.

Kenneth went into the dining room. Bill followed, putting his books on the sideboard, closing the curtains, by which time Kenneth had slid out and Jill had come in to play with the line of china dogs on the windowsill.

Bill then left for the parlour, walking softly. Behind the door, Kenneth was turning the pages of a years old *Readers' Digest*. Bill called out, 'Jill come in the parlour, your snap cards are here.'

Kenneth put the magazine down quickly, pretending to tidy it into the pile of papers before going out. He went towards the front room for sanctuary, but Aunty stopped him as she walked in there herself.

'Don't come in just now, Kenneth. Let me have a bit of a lie down, my headache's come on again.'

Kenneth heaved a sigh and went into the kitchen.

After a moment, Bill followed.

Aunty noticed. 'While you're in the kitchen, Bill, could you fetch me the aspirins, please?'

It was quite fun, in a dark way, finding an excuse to be in each room in turn.

Eventually, when Aunty was safely in her room, and Jill upstairs, he went to corner Kenneth properly without interruption.

These moments had made him feel much stronger, less trapped. He couldn't take away what Kenneth had done, but he could deal with the wrong.

He strode into the garden room where Kenneth was standing at the far end, studying some sheet music. He'd joined the choir that Mrs Durban had told them about, and these were the songs he had to practise.

Bill stood by the reclining chair, watching. Kenneth couldn't pretend he was just leaving the room when he had the music in his hands. He kept his eyes on it as if he hadn't heard Bill come in. He traced the notes with one lily-white finger, mouthing 'semi-breve, diminuendo'. Dim something he'd be, if Bill really got going on him. But words would be enough. Bill stepped back to the door and shut it, very firmly. It made a loud enough click. He stood against it, straight and upright, feeling his shoulders and the muscles of his calves hard against the door.

Kenneth raised his eyebrows at the interruption and moved his finger to the next block of black wiggly notes.

Bill let his voice carry across the room. 'So what will everyone think of you now, Kenneth?'

Kenneth didn't look up, but his finger stayed pinioned to a big note with an empty middle. '*What?*' he said in the kind of voice he'd use to a small child or imbecile.

Normally, that would feel intimidating to Bill but it didn't today. He just hmmed, as if considering his words.

Kenneth was sounding rattled now. 'What? What do you mean?'

'Does Aunty want a thief and a traitor for a son? Will Dad be proud of you when he gets back?'

Kenneth looked up, and his face paled. Now he'd know what Bill had found out, but he wouldn't know how. Bill would leave him guessing. That felt good. He folded his arms over his chest and stayed with his back against the door. It would look as if he was preventing Kenneth from escaping. Kenneth might be expecting a thumping. He certainly deserved it. Bill let the seconds pass, and enjoyed the tick of the mantle-piece clock. Tick, tock, tick. How threatening it sounded.

Kenneth turned a page, avoiding Bill's gaze. 'I've no idea what you're on about. I'm trying to practise.'

Bill waited.

Kenneth put the music down. His hands were clenching. 'So, um, what—'

Are you going to do, was he thinking? Bill let him wait a moment longer before saying, 'So you won't want to be visiting the Durbans on your own, will you? In case stealing is mentioned. Better to have Aunty there to protect you, and Mother chatting away, so that the subject doesn't come up— if you want to go to Fulham at all, that is.' He turned and opened the door, walking out very deliberately, leaving it open.

How satisfying! Kenneth had done something really dreadful, thinking he wouldn't be found out. Bill had shown him up and paid him back without thumping him, without even telling a lie about how he'd found out. He'd left him scared that Bill would tell the grown-ups. AND, he'd scotched Kenneth's attempt to sidle into Bill's own special place. The rat wouldn't want to risk going to the Durbans on his own now. Tonight, at bedtime, it would be Kenneth in bed first, pretending to be asleep.

He told Alan all about it next day, phoning when everyone else was out. He was glad to hear Alan shocked.

'Golly! That's dreadful. I wouldn't have thought Kenneth would be so slimy.'

'Yes. Think! Hiding it all through evacuation and bringing it with him – waiting four years for the opportunity.'

'Bad enough stealing it in the first place. He is a rotter, after all.'

Bill told how he'd dealt with Kenneth. 'He's got the wind up now.'

'You did well. But what he did was so odd. Was he paying you back for something he was upset about?'

Bill hadn't thought of that. 'Upset? He's only upset about Dwaine coming over. And that's more to do with Aunty.'

'Dwaine! Is he really coming? That'll be smashing.'

'Yes, super. I'm going to let the Pawseys and Mrs Youldon know. They'll love to know Dwaine's coming.'

'But Kenneth won't.' Alan put in.

'No...' Suddenly, Bill realised the connection, 'Yes!' He punched one fist forward. 'Of course! *That's* what Kenneth is punishing me for. He was always furious about me arranging for Aunty and Dwaine to meet in the first place. So! And now he's counting on Dad scotching Aunty's plans to have Dwaine here.'

'Your dad's going to have a lot on his plate when he gets back! Shame it's not now. We're getting ready to celebrate VJ Day, are you?'

'What? Have they signed, the Japs?'

'Mum says they have no choice. Wait till the news. Then there'll be another great party on the common.'

'That'll be spiffing. Do you think there'll be a funfair?'

'Probably. And after that, new school the following week, Bill. Are you excited?'

He wasn't. It was embarrassing to let on that he'd deliberately failed to get a grammar school place. He'd leave Mother to tell Mrs Routledge about St Werberg's. He shrugged. 'I'll let you know after I've tried it.'

CHAPTER 23

Summer was over, together with the excitement of the real end of the war. Bill had been in the crowd cheering the King and Queen. Aunty had enjoyed the VJ Day holiday so they'd all gone to the festival on Clapham Common. Now it was Autumn, the news had got miserable again.

Kenneth crowed when he read that the Japanese war minister had killed himself. 'That's what they do, the Japs. Either win or do yourself in.'

Mother and Aunty shushed him. They were worried about the Lend-Lease being ended by America. 'Herbert says Britain will be bankrupt. That will mean even less food and goods. No wonder the government gave us all a holiday and let us celebrate.'

'Party then Poverty,' Aunty said.

Kenneth raised his chin. 'Ending the lease without notice. Now you know what sort of country America is, Mama.'

'You'll feel differently when the next food parcel arrives, Kenneth.'

Bill privately wondered if Dwaine might arrive first, his suitcase full of goodies.

Mother waved towards the near-empty larder. 'Goodness knows how we'll survive if the shortages get worse.'

Bill shut his eyes and tried to remember a plate full of roast dinner. Poor Jill was too young to know what a decent meal tasted like. Now she'd have to suffer school dinners for the first time! She'd find out that there were far worse meals than Mother's. She was already full of misery because she'd never gone to school before. At her village the vaccies had to be taught in people's houses. The thought of real school must be scary for her.

Kenneth was the most cheerful of them all, still uppity because he had Dulwich College to look forward to.

Bill had no idea what St Werberg's would be like. He'd never known anyone who went there. Somehow, he didn't care. It would be all right, and he'd have football at last.

At the start of term, he filled his satchel with a pencil box, a handkerchief and a new notebook. St Werberg's wasn't far to walk so he wasn't hurrying.

Upstairs, Mother was struggling with Jill who was determined not to start school.

'I won't know what to do. I don't know anyone. I've never been to school before, I won't go-o-o! She was scared to bits.

Behind him, Aunty was in a fuss. She couldn't take Kenneth for his first day because of work. Kenneth smoothed his collar for the third time and did up all the buttons on his striped blazer. He had long trousers, lucky devil, with sharp front creases down them. 'The firm could have given you the day off, Mama, for something this important.'

'So sorry, dear but you do know which bus to take to Dulwich, don't you? Make sure you drink your milk at break. Have you got all your things?'

What a fuss! Kenneth would be fourteen in November!

The front door opened wide, Jill's sobs floating out. Kenneth left in one direction in a flurry of Aunty's fussing, and Bill left in the other, swinging his satchel. Just ahead was a boy in the same uniform. He vaguely remembered him from junior school. He fell in step with him and they went on together.

St Werberg's looked rather grim, with cement flaking off its arches and danger notices where the surfaces needed mending, but at least it had a decent football pitch. It was also part of the way to

Nanny's, which would cut down the time it took to get there after school.

A teacher in a black gown came out and gathered people into groups. Most of the boys had been there a year or two, but some were back from evacuation like Bill. He was directed to an upstairs classroom, its windows set too high to see outside. 'No-one enjoys lessons but we put up with them,' the boy sharing his desk told him. 'It's boring but not beastly.' And Bill soon found he was right.

The dinner was almost the worst he'd ever had, so it was good to hear moans all around. The other boys were friendly enough and he soon found that, like him, they just longed to be outside playing. He'd definitely be all right when they found out he was a whizz at football.

That night, when Alan phoned to exchange news he seemed sad that Bill wasn't at a grammar.

~

But school was all right. He did his lessons and they weren't difficult, and made sure he played lots of football. Only History was actually interesting. It was taught by an old man who told them stories about kings, abbots and cardinals instead of making them read from the boring textbook.

For football, there was one actual lesson a week, two practices and a chance of being picked for the school team. That was one thing Bill felt he could be sure of.

At home, there was less nastiness. He saw less of Kenneth, whose journey from Dulwich took some time, while Bill went to Nanny and Grandad's to help out after school. In the evenings, Kenneth was too full of the wonderful things he was doing at Dulwich College to bother about Bill. Altogether, it was easier to avoid each other now. Bill was too busy to get down to the Durbans hardly at all, so it was a relief to know that Kenneth couldn't, even if he'd dared to, for he had choir and travel and after-school *societies*.

Bill only had Scouts, though that was pretty good. It was quite fun working towards badges as well as playing a bit more football after Scouts had finished. He had a school-friend to go to Saturday morning pictures with, and Alan to meet on some Sundays.

He was worried that he wasn't at Nanny and Grandad's for long enough to be really useful. Meanwhile, nothing had happened with the Rehab Office for Ted, so he was more fed up than ever.

One afternoon after school, Bill bumped into Colin. He was wearing a jacket that was quite smart, brown but scratchy.

'Colin!'

'Watcha, young'un,' he said, pointing to Bill's uniform. 'St Werberg's is it? Right near our place, but you haven't dropped in.'

'Sorry. I will, but I go to my grandparents after school, and one evening I have Scouts, and there's homework and chores at home.'

'Phew, you're busier than me, a working man. I've just been picking up a fridge part for my boss. Normally, I get home quite late.'

'Are you busy in the evenings? Is there any chance you can get round to see Ted again? Nothing's happened and it's a bit of a problem.'

'If I can help, I will, mate.' Colin fell in beside him. 'Shall I walk up to Primley Road with you while you tell me what's what?'

'Righto.' They walked in step while he explained how Ted was. He ended, 'You might help with that rehab thing. Nothing's been done for Ted.'

Colin nodded. 'Typical. It's not right. I'm going to get into politics now we've got Labour in power.'

'How do you do that?'

'Go to meetings, complain, stand up for the lads. There was supposed to be help on hand when we got demobbed.'

'Will there be help for Ted? He's a super chap, really. He did handstands and card tricks before he went to war. And he was always joking. I want him back like that. Everyone does.'

Colin laid an arm across Bill's shoulders. 'It's tough. He's not the only serviceman come back a different person.'

'But will you go up to see them sometimes, after you finish work? Ted may cheer up, seeing you,' His voice tailed off, 'sooner or later.'

Colin's lips were pushed forward, like someone solving problems. 'There is a way this could work for all of us.'

'How?'

'You've seen how cramped Ma's place is. I have to sleep on the settee and it's a small living room anyway. Apart from her bedroom, the scullery and privy, it's all we've got. When Dad died, Ma had to let out the upstairs and my old bedroom with it. So now I'm back home, it's made life difficult for her, though she's glad to have me.'

'Yes.' It was true that Mrs Donnington's home was hardly big enough for one.

'So,' Colin took a breath, 'if you could persuade your grandad to let me do out their box room, I could rent it off them. It would be a bit of money for them and I'd be around to help with Ted after work.'

Bill nearly jumped in the air. 'That'd be spiffing! Sorting the stuff in the box room would give Ted something to do. I'll ask them tomorrow. I go up almost every day.' He stopped.

'What?'

'But if you find out more stuff about Ted and what happened in the war, will you tell me but NOT Kenneth? He sneers about my uncle, and I don't want Mother to know what happened, or Nanny.'

'I see. You're a real old protector, aren't you? Big for your age and grown-up with it.'

He felt his cheeks flush.

'So. If you're going to your nan's tomorrow, I'll wait to hear what she and your grandad say, eh?'

'Right you are.' Bill turned into the gate of forty-three, smiling.

Colin hitched his jacket further onto his shoulders and raised a goodbye hand. 'See you in a day or two, then.'

At last there was some sort of solution. Colin would help Grandad move about, keep an eye on Ted, find out what rehab help there was.

He went inside to get Mother's help to persuade Nanny and Grandad that it was a brilliant idea.

CHAPTER 24

Dad had missed Bill's birthday and Kenneth's, and now it was December. His last letter said that he would be properly demobbed before the end of 1945, but hadn't given a date for arrival, so no-one was expecting him this Tuesday evening. Bill was on the stairs fixing one of the stair rods when the doorbell sounded twice. Kenneth's warbling paused. 'Who's that at the door?'

Bill had been trying not to listen, let alone admire Kenneth's choir practice, so he concentrated fixing the stair rods. They kept getting loose. 'I can't get the door, Mother, I'm holding this rod in place.'

'Coming,' Mother called as she came out of the parlour, irritated that her wireless programme was being interrupted. 'Another wretch doing his ring-and-run-away, no doubt.'

Round the Horne boomed down the hall together with her sigh, while Kenneth shouted out, 'Is that him? Is it Dad?'

Did he have a sixth sense? For at that moment, the front door opened with a key. And it was him.

'A bell to announce, a key to open. You didn't expect me so soon, Marcia?' Dad stepped inside, a raincoat over one arm, his swollen kitbag preventing the door from shutting at first.

'No,' Mother squeaked. 'No! But it's wonderful.' Mother's hug and kiss only stopped when Aunty rushed to hug Dad too.

'Oh, Herbert! Home at last! Lovely!' Then she ran back into the kitchen to put the kettle on. She must have held Jill back because Jill's squeaks of excitement didn't get further than the door.

Bill put his head through the banisters and took a long look. It was very odd to see Dad in khaki uniform wearing ugly black boots that turned up a bit by the toes. He was like an actor stepping off a newsreel; only newsreels always showed soldiers with a wide smile making the victory sign. Those were missing on Dad.

Kenneth had glided rapidly to the landing but Bill made the rampant stair rod a barrier. He pressed his face to the banisters, blocking Kenneth's way. He wasn't going to let Kenneth be first this time. Anyway, they shouldn't interrupt Mother and Dad just yet.

After they had kissed and hugged again, Mother held Dad at arm's length. 'I'll have to learn to know you all over again.'

'I know, dearest, I know.'

Bill knelt still, ignoring Kenneth's pushes from behind. It was exciting, Dad arriving, but he hadn't lived with Dad since he was seven, or even been with him more than the odd two days at a time. Things were going to be different at home now. It felt like a loss as well as a gain. He was the one who'd been Mother's handyman, the person she looked to when things went wrong. He wouldn't be important now, with Dad in charge.

Mother's smile made her whole face glow. She looked Dad up and down as if to make sure he was there. 'Thank goodness you're home at last. Thank goodness you're in one piece.'

She shouldn't have said that because Uncle Frank was in lots of pieces. Had Kenneth heard? Luckily Aunty was still in the kitchen.

'Indeed I'm fortunate to be so. And how well you look, Marcia.' He smiled and held her by the tops of the arms. He turned to the boys coming down the stairs, one behind the other. Somehow, Kenneth was now in front.

'Hello, boys!' Dad stepped forward to shake Kenneth's hand hard and long. 'Are you settled in here, Kenneth?' He put his hand on Kenneth's bony shoulder. 'I hope you feel fully at home? Yes? *All things must change, to something new, to something strange* – Longfellow. Studied him yet? There's a copy of his work on the garden room bookshelf, I recall. Ah, we shall be all right, shan't we, son?'

'Hello, Dad.' Bill came forward as Dad turned to him. Now their eyes were at the same level, which was a shock. Dad's were hazel coloured. Bill hadn't noticed that before. He must get his own green eyes from – not Mother, hers were dark, dark brown. A tiny shudder went through him. It was Uncle Frank who'd had green eyes.

Dad was looking Bill up and down as he shook hands. 'So here I am, back again to family life. It's been a long time since you galloped up the hall on that wooden horse, isn't it?'

A giggle sounded behind. Kenneth was paying close attention and would rag Bill about that for sure.

'Made yourself useful since you've been home, Bill?'

He nodded, not sure what to say.

'Good, good. *Choose the life which is most useful and habit will make it the most agreeable,* Sir Francis Bacon.'

One saying for each of them. Bill grimaced at the habit of living with Kenneth. It wasn't agreeable. 'Change to something strange' was nearer the mark.

Now Jill pelted down the hall. 'Daddy, it's me. Here I am.' And Dad had to catch the flying leap she made towards him.

He held Jill up high. 'So my little lady, not so little nowadays, isn't that so?' He placed her down gently to stand beside him. 'And heavier than my kitbag, which is certainly saying something. What has your mother been feeding you on? Roast lion?'

She giggled and held hard onto his arm. How strange for Dad to joke. So, Jill wasn't going to have the sayings to puzzle over; no quotations for girls.

Kenneth was smiling but silent. Bill looked at him out of the corner of his eye. What was he planning about Dad's presence? Oh heck. He'd be thinking how to get Dad to prevent Dwaine from coming.

The kettle boiled and when they crowded into the kitchen, Aunty had already roughly laid a table for speed. Bill's lips felt dry and he couldn't stop his hands fidgeting. Jill was at Dad's knee fiddling with his badges, then one part of his uniform, then another. The two mothers gabbled away with all the news until Dad held up both hands. 'Tea first, say? The cup that cheers.'

Mother inclined her head. 'Of course. So much to say, so much to hear about, Herbert.'

'We're all energized by the arrival of our hero,' Aunty turned to the boys, 'aren't we, boys?'

But Bill was as silent as Kenneth, who was probably thinking about his mother's hero in the USA.

After two cups of tea and a Bath bun with a scrape of marg, and the shortest reference to the fact that he had been serving in a major war, Dad stood up and stretched. 'I must unpack my kitbag. It's stuffed full of washing (Mother groaned) and a couple of souvenirs.'

'Oooh,' Jill pulled at its strap.

'Wait, young lady. Most of it is very dull indeed.' He began to pull out the contents. After the clothes for laundering and his soap bag, Dad pulled out a large fat rolled package, wrapped in brown paper. He turned down his mouth as he looked at Mother. 'Now, dearest, you will hardly recognise me if I wear this ill-fitting suit. We were offered the following: a flat hat or flat cap. A clear choice there! A double-breasted pinstripe three-piece suit, or trousers and jacket. The suit sounded good but they failed to warn us of the limited choice of size. You can tell what I think of it from the fact that I chose to return home in uniform.' He threw back his head and laughed, not sounding like himself. 'And guess what, round every corner some spiv offering good money for the suits. They'll sell them on the black market, of course. Nice profit.'

'That's dreadful, Herbert! The government are trying to fit servicemen out properly.'

'And what's a chippie or decorator going to do with a three-piece pin-striped suit? Go to a funeral, that's about it.'

The women shook their heads at each other, tutting.

'I'm also the owner of two new shirts with matching collar studs, the least awful tie I could find, a pair of shoes that almost fit, and that raincoat,' he jerked his head towards it, lying across an old *Sunday Chronicle*. 'And I get to keep the kitbag and anything of my own I managed to salvage. Lucky me.'

Kenneth actually swapped a glance with Bill, one that recognised the sour tone of Dad's cheery words.

Mother said in a housewifely voice, 'Well, Herbert, someone will be glad of the pinstripe. Obviously someone in your position couldn't sell it to a spiv. You don't have to wear it. Luckily your own suits are still hanging in the wardrobe with fresh mothballs inserted in the pockets. You'll soon be looking your old self.'

'And old is how I feel, let me tell you.'

He delved into the depths of the kitbag and handed over two pairs of gloves. 'One pair each.'

Mother and Aunty took them, looking impressed. 'Thank you so much. They're very fine.'

'Strangely, good shops in France don't seem to be suffering the shortages you have been talking of, and clothes are not on rations there, either.'

'Well!' said Aunty, stroking her gloves. 'The French caved in and let us fight without them, and now they're better off than we are! A fine state of affairs.'

Dad pressed bloodless lips together and nodded. He pulled a knobbly parcel loosely wrapped in brown paper. 'Here, Marcia. Booty.'

Jill crept near as Mother unwrapped it, but then sank to her knees disappointed.

'I don't quite know what we'll do with these,' said Mother doubtfully, turning over the carved wooden bottle stoppers in one hand. 'It's not as if we were drinkers.'

'At least they haven't been taken off some poor dead soldier,' said Dad. 'I found them in an abandoned inn. I thought they were rather decent. And here's some food.' He placed some army tins on the dining room table. 'Bully beef plus some unmarked surprises. Not caviar, but still welcome in these harsh days of rationing, isn't that so?'

'Definitely, Herbert.'

Bill waited for the quote, but Dad was now pulling out a lengthy piece of white material. 'You'll be able to make good use of this, Doreen.'

Aunty squealed. 'You've managed to save your parachute!'

'Yes. Although everyone was told to turn them in, I reckoned I'd earned this. We were dropped a trifle short so we came down in a forest. I narrowly missed being the fairy at the top of a tree.'

Kenneth laughed, his voice trilling up and down. It was certainly rare for Dad to crack a joke.

Aunty was running the white stuff through both hands. 'The silk is wonderful for ladies' clothes, Herbert. Clever you. The things we can do with this, Marcia!' She probably meant *I*. After all, Aunty was the one who cut and sewed. The material went on and on unfolding itself from the kitbag as she pulled.

'Wonderful. It's so smooth. There'll be enough for gowns, nighties, petticoats for both of us,' said Mother holding a section up to her face.

'I like that stuff, Aunty. Let me feel.' Jill scrunched up the material in one hand.

'We shall get you a pretty blouse out of this, dear,' Aunty nodded to her, 'as well as our ladies' things. What riches!'

Jill held onto Dad's arm until he pulled out some ribbons and some elaborately decorated postcards. 'I got these somewhere in Holland. You see, little missie. I didn't forget you.' He straightened up, bringing the almost empty kitbag onto his knees.

'Now boys, under these socks, for which you will be very grateful this winter, there's something else for you.' He placed several pairs of khaki wool socks on top of Aunty's mending basket. She would darn the toes to make sure they lasted longer. 'I managed to get you a book each. Not easy, I can tell you. There's a German grammar and a Dutch history. Who would like which?' He held up both volumes.

It was so disappointing. Other boys' fathers had brought back all sorts of goodies. 'Thank you, Dad.' Bill was in no rush to take either book. Kenneth could choose. There was little chance Bill would be learning German or Dutch at school.

Kenneth put a hand on each cover and stroked them. 'Lovely leather. May we look inside?'

Dad held them forward with a satisfied smile. 'I guessed these would please someone scholarly.'

Kenneth opened each book part way. 'Look, Bill. Such soft paper and it's lovely print. Which do you like best?'

Bill shrugged. Why play Kenneth's beastly game? He jolly well knew Bill wouldn't be interested in foreign language books, whatever their pages were like.

Dad still had both large hands opened flat, supporting the books.
'Very nice, Dad,' Bill said, to be safe.

Kenneth turned to him with a sweet smile. 'Then, Bill, do you mind if I take the German? I can start learning the grammar before the others at school. They offer German in the fourth form, Dad.' Kenneth took the grammar text in one hand and passed the smaller book to Bill.

He took it, closed. 'This will be useful if I'm parachuted into Holland during the next war.'

Aunty squeaked, 'Ooh, Bill. Don't say that, dear. Another war!'

Dad was looking at Bill closely. Was it a surprise to him that his son was using sarcasm? 'Hmm. We're going to take many years to get over this one.'

'Otherwise, Daddy would have given you the parachute,' Jill said brightly.

Bill suppressed a chuckle.

Kenneth put his heel on Bill's toe, pressing down hard, while at the same time turning the pages of his grammar religiously. Bill extracted his foot but said nothing. Now was not the time for a good kick on the back of Kenneth's calf, nor for highlighting Kenneth's sneaky attacks.

Dad asked, 'How's Ted, dear?'

Mother's mouth turned down a trifle. 'Things were dire when we got back and I didn't know how my parents would manage once Bill had school again, but now they've got a lodger, Mrs Doddington's son, and that's made all the difference. Colin was in the same regiment.

'The Doddington boy. He must be, what, in his twenties now?'

'Yes. My parents like him. It's worked out well.'

'Before that, Bill has been round almost every day helping out. Quite a godsend,' said Aunty.

'Well done, Bill. *We do not so much need the help of our friends as the confidence of their help in need.* Epicurus.' He turned to Mother before Bill had worked out the meaning. 'I shall go round, see what I can do for Ted. I'm well aware of having had a light burden during my service and even then, would like to forget what I've seen. Ted had a hard innings. 'These boys,' he waved a hand at them. 'Young men to be. Thank the Lord they were too young to serve. Now that I'm home I must involve myself in their schooling.'

He looked round the kitchen as if he'd never seen it before, and then at him and Kenneth as at items in a museum or a library. 'So Kenneth has a place at Dulwich College. Fortunate, very fortunate.'

'Yes, we're so lucky,' Aunty smiled. 'I did nothing! After VE Day, the head of Friary Grammar contacted the headmaster of Dulwich College on Kenneth's behalf, anxious that he continued with the same advantages he'd been enjoying there.'

'No entrance exam?'

She shook her head. 'Although that is normally essential, it seems that admitting "a student with exceptional artistic talent" was possible. That's as I heard it. I think it was Kenneth's work in the Priory's exhibition that did it. His paintings did seem to be the star attraction. But it's so lucky to get a scholarship when Dulwich College needs restoring. After the big fire there, the parents have to pay increased fees! £18 a term now!'

'Good heavens!' Dad's eyebrows jerked upwards.

'So we're feeling so proud of Kenneth!'

Kenneth was leaning against the wall, one bent leg crossed over his supporting leg, in the way he often did. It looked neutral and superior. Bill hated the pose as much as Kenneth's smirk, a half smile, with one side higher than the other.

'What an excellent opportunity for you, Kenneth. Are you enjoying it there?'

'Wonderful, Dad. The masters are top-hole. The science is so exciting, I adore Latin, and the Art is absolutely fine, which is the main thing for me.'

Dad nodded, and his pleased expression stayed put some moments.

Bill waited for the inevitable.

'And Bill?' Dad turned towards Mother. 'How has school worked out for you?'

'It's all right, Dad, I mean, good.'

Dad continued looking at Mother. 'So – St Werberg's.'

'Yes. I didn't want him with the rough children at – you know where.'

'I assumed Bill would go to Wandsworth Grammar.'

'The school only came back from Surrey this summer, and now they're amalgamating with the Central School. I thought that might bring the tone down. Anyway, he sat an exam and didn't do well enough, I don't know why.'

Keeping his eyes on the floor Bill justified the poor exam attempts to himself. He'd lost everything else by coming back to Wandsworth, so he needed to keep football even if he went to a school that wasn't as good as a grammar.

'St Werberg's boys are always so polite. We used to share lessons with the top year when I was at Larchmere Girls, and ballroom dancing.'

Dad didn't look impressed at the thought. 'But academically?'

'Bill seems to me a practical boy, all the things he's fixed in the house and garden. I did write to you all this.'

'You did, Marcia, yes. And it's a great pity I wasn't home in time to sort this out. But I dare say you're settled, Bill? What do you think about the school?'

'It's all right, Dad. Football's super. I play left wing and I score lots of times.'

'Well enough. But the work, the actual reason you attend school?'

'I enjoy not having to write essays all the time,' Bill said, trying a bit of cheek since Dad had been making jokes earlier.

Dad's eyebrows beetled up towards the ceiling. Another saying was coming. '*Whoever neglects learning in his youth loses the Past, and is dead to the Future* – Euripides. And it would be too much to hope that you know who that is, so I will tell you he was—'

'A Greek playwright,' put in Kenneth. 'Our English teacher adores him.'

Bill saw Dad's eyes brighten.

He shrugged before he could stop himself. His own English teacher had enough difficulty getting the boys to stay in their seats during the lesson. Bill struggled to think – had he heard of any playwright? Only Shakespeare – and that was through Angela.

'It would have been lovely for the boys to be together,' said Aunty. 'Bill is clever as well as practical.'

Dad corrected her. 'No. You just heard him. He doesn't like

writing any more than drawing. So he's different from Kenneth, and academic work might be wasted on him.'

'Never mind, old chap,' said Kenneth, placing a hand on Bill's shoulder.

He heaved it off vigorously.

'So protective,' said Aunty. 'Don't shrug Kenneth off, dear.' She gave Bill a mildly resentful glance. It was a beastly shame, Aunty deserved a nicer son than Kenneth.

Bill waited to hear Dad's plans for him, but Jill clamoured for Dad's attention, clambering onto his lap, full of chatter. 'Daddy, Daddy. I am one of the best readers in my class and I only have to share a book with two others.'

'I'm more worried about Jill,' Mother said. 'Forty-one in her class and she cried every day for her first two weeks.'

'Thank goodness she's not a boy,' said Dad.

Bill went to the hall to take his jacket off the hallstand. He could call on Colin, or someone from school, but his hand stopped halfway to the pegs. It was Dad's first night home. He shouldn't go out. He left his jacket hanging beside Aunty's mac, Mother's shopping coat and Kenneth's blazer. They needed more hooks now Dad was home. Would it be him who banged some up? He mooched back to the kitchen.

Mother was saying, 'If we'd known the date of your demob, Herbert, we'd have had a special meal ready.'

Aunty flapped her hands. 'Go and sit in comfort, all of you. I will find something. We saved the peaches and evap. from Dwaine's parcel, and I think there's jam for our bread.'

'Ah, Dwaine. We must have a talk about him, Doreen.'

Aunty blushed, and as Mother pulled Dad into the garden room, Kenneth added, 'Yes, Dad, that's important.'

Kenneth had now dropped his film star pose and sidled nearer to Dad. 'They play cricket at Dulwich, but I haven't any whites.'

'We must get you some. You haven't had a sport before, Kenneth. That's important. Frank would have wanted that.'

Everyone's eyes turned downwards.

Bill's did too, so that he was looking at his shoes. If Kenneth needed cricket whites, gosh, Bill badly needed football boots. How would he ever get to play like Stanley Matthews in ordinary boots? He blurted out, 'Uncle Frank liked football. He might have wanted me to have proper football boots.'

'Like the ones I gave you,' Kenneth put in quickly. He wouldn't let anyone forget the one nice thing he had done for Bill.

'They were super, but my feet have grown so much since then. It was two years ago.' His voice trailed off. 'May I have football boots, Dad?'

'Succeed in your studies first, Bill. Play comes later.'

Kenneth nodded as though he was one of the masters. 'Yes, Bill. Like how I have to learn my declensions before I go to choir on Wednesdays.'

Bill gritted his teeth. Moving well away from Kenneth, he said, 'You never got to see my bravery medal, Dad. I'll just go upstairs and get it.'

Once in his room with the door shut, he gave way to his fury. He felt like kicking the wall, and ripping the wretched Dutch book in half. He put it on his bookshelf to be safe from his feelings and went to his secret place to get his medal out. He wasn't innocent any more, like at the Pawseys' where he'd relied on his bed base as a hidey hole for the precious shashka photo. Kenneth's theft demonstrated that Bill needed to be more cunning.

He went to the wall. Aunty had put one of Kenneth's paintings in an old wooden frame for Kenneth to hang up. The back had several layers of card behind the painting because of the thickness of the wood. Kenneth would never think to search for Bill's treasures among things of his own. He slid the cardboard aside and took out the medal, its stripy ribbon band a little faded now. The medal wasn't secret, but it mustn't go missing like the photograph.

Perhaps Dad would tell everyone about it, boast about it, even. Kenneth had excellent paintings and would be bought cricket whites, but he hadn't won a medal and he wasn't even brave at all.

CHAPTER 25

Sunday. No school, no football. Kenneth warbling some kind of chant in the bedroom. The cellar door open. A draught along the hall. The weather was cold.

He peered down into the cellar. Dad was removing all signs of their wartime shelter and checking the level of their coal. Bill moved off to find Mother.

Well out of Dad's earshot, Jill was whining, 'When can I go to Iris's again? We'll be good. Please, please. I like her better than any of the girls at school.'

Mother made a face at Bill as if she expected him to help out. 'I'll phone Iris's mother, Jill. Perhaps she'll be able to come over here. So shh now. Run and play outside.'

'It's co-o-old!'

'Upstairs, then.'

'That's cold, too.'

'Just put on a second cardigan, then, and stop making a fuss.'

Christmas was coming soon and there was no sign it would be jolly. He thought he'd better get his own request in quickly before Dad came up from the cellar and asked to see his homework. 'Can I go to Alan's?'

'*May*, not 'can'. Go on, then. But get back before dark.'

He pulled his new school mac on, and slipped out before Dad emerged from the cellar.

When the bus slowed to a halt, he could see Alan waiting.

'My dad's back,' Bill shouted as he leapt off the running board. 'Got home last Tuesday.'

'Super. Bet you're glad.'

They trotted side by side alongside a row of trees whose colour had turned to a brittle brown. All the other trees were already bare.

'Is he okay about Dwaine coming?'

'I think so. Kenneth kept making pointed remarks, hoping Dad would scotch the idea. When he didn't, Kenneth whinged about it being inconvenient for Mother. Dad's discussed what's appropriate with Aunty. Dwaine isn't to stay at our house, but nearby, so Aunty is reading accommodation adverts all the time now.'

'That'll be tough with everyone who's trying to get a room. Mum says the *Share Your Home* drive is a nightmare. There isn't enough accommodation.'

'Kenneth will be flipping thrilled if they can't get anywhere. I'm looking at all the cards in the shop windows. Someone left a newspaper on the bus and I tore this advert out in case it will do. *Well-furnished, every convenience, suit person out during day, use of bath (geyser).* Sounds okay? And Dad said he'd talk to likely people. He has contacts.'

'And he's on leave with nothing much to do. Where did he serve?'

'Holland. France. He didn't say much but I don't think he killed anyone. He wouldn't.'

'Any souvenirs?'

'Bottle top things, carved wooden figures with cork underneath. Mother wasn't very pleased because she and Dad don't have alcohol, except at Christmas.'

'I was meaning for you.'

Bill almost growled. He stopped by a bench. 'Ha. I'll show you if we sit down a minute.' He sat and opened his satchel. 'Jill got ribbons, our mothers got posh gloves from France as well as the parachute silk for making petticoats. Kenneth and I got boring books. We were supposed to choose which one of two. Kenneth was pleased, of course. He had the grammar because he's starting

German, so that left this for me.' He almost threw it onto Alan's lap. 'Not Russian history, but Dutch. Double Dutch to me,' his laugh was hollow. He hated himself for saying it but the words spat out. 'Other boys at school got sweets and toys and all sorts of things their fathers brought back for them. And Dad was so interested in Kenneth's new school he hardly bothered with me.'

Alan was opening the book and examining it, page by page.

Bill went on. 'And look at the stuff your father brings back! Foreign comics, that spicy sausage, the wind-up boy that walks, and I bet that's not all.'

Alan looked embarrassed and hunched his shoulders. 'I know it doesn't seem fair, but perhaps this book is valuable. Look, it's signed and it's by a professor. Do you know what I think?'

'No, what?' Bill could hear his voice sounding sulky, like Jill when Mother said she had something nice for dinner. Jill never agreed that it was.

'You know knights?'

'Uh?'

'Knights. To be a knight you have to have three things, and I reckon you've got two now. The first is the sword of a brave man. The second is a book written by a learned man.'

'Is it? Interesting.' Bill stopped huffing and complaining. A sabre was a sword and its owner had been brave. But it would take some miracle for Mr Durban give it to him. *Bestow* it. If ever. He did have the wretched learned book. 'And what's the third thing?'

'A flower from a faithful lover.'

Bill pushed him in the ribs, laughing. 'Oh yeah! I don't know any girls, except Jill and her kid friends. We don't even have girls at school.'

'You'll have to wait until there's dancing in the top year. If it's like our school, you do it with the top class of the girls' school.'

They shoved each other, laughing and rolling over the frosty grass together.

Knights! Bill remembered how often he'd got *Tales of King Arthur* from the library before he was evacuated. 'I used to imagine being Lancelot, handsome and gallant, the bravest knight of all.'

'Not a good choice! Lancelot went on to steal Guinevere's love.'

'Really? That's awfully rotten. Then I should be Arthur himself, the only one who could pull the sword from the stone. I used to dream about it, only it was never the sword that came aloft in my hand but the shashka.'

Alan shoved him in the side as they both burst out laughing, and Bill shoved him back.

'Do you think I'm daft, thinking about the shashka so much?'

Alan knelt up, brushing the grass from his smart blazer. 'I hadn't thought.' He paused, obviously thinking now. 'It's just part of you, same as Biggles was part of that boy, Marley, remember him?'

Bill frowned. Marley was a dolt who ran about wearing old sunglasses, mounting the fence, pretending to climb up into the cockpit of his plane. 'I don't want to be a kid just pretending,' he said.

Alan clapped him on the shoulder. 'We found some real history, remember. You can find some more now, at school or at the library. You can become an expert about Cossacks and their sabres.'

Bill felt a grin start at the sides of his mouth. That was more like it. If he became expert, all the more reason for people (Mr Durban) to realise that he, Sir William of Wilson, was the rightful owner of the shashka in the future.

CHAPTER 26

There was a New Year's Day postcard from Mrs Youldon on the mat. It was the first with a 1946 postmark. He hid it in the pages of an old *Boy's Own* so that he could read it over and no-one know. He knew it annoyed Mother that he kept in contact. He turned a page of the comic as he perched on the edge of a chair to be nearer the small fire in the parlour.

A bitter wind whooshed in as the front door opened and shut. Kenneth came in from the library wrapped in about six scarves. He stood rubbing his hands by Bill's chair so close that it was obvious Bill was supposed to move from in front of the fire. Since it was only a few days since Kenneth had been in bed with laryngitis and a high temperature, Bill thought he'd better move. He put his *Boy's Own* under one arm and stood nearby. It was jolly cold.

Aunty hurried in with a mug of hot cocoa. 'Here you are, Kenneth. Sit and drink this slowly, and not too close to the fire or you'll get chilblains.'

Kenneth huddled himself into the chair, grasping the hot mug, while Aunty took his scarves into the hall.

Bill snapped, 'You could at least have hung those up!'

'I've brought you a library book, so stop complaining. *Robinson*

Crusoe. About time you read something more challenging than a comic.'

Bill took it and slipped his comic inside the front cover. The story did look interesting, not that it reduced his anger at Kenneth's jibe, though he should be used to that by now.

Before they could get into an argument, Dad came in, also rubbing his hands. 'Make the most of the fire, boys, there's not much coal left or even Coalite and we've reached the limit of our ration.'

'How bad?' There'd been ice on the inside of the bedroom windows for over a week.

Dad jabbed at the newspaper notice.

'"*You may not obtain more than 8 cwt coal including Coalite between January and February*." Ha! and your total can't be more than thirty-four hundredweight over the twelve months!'

Kenneth looked up with a pained expression. 'We'll just have to pray that the weather thaws, then.'

It would be nice to retort, 'You can always return to your sick bed if the house is too cold,' but Dad was standing too near, rifling through the library books Kenneth had brought in.

'*Life of Byron*, Kenneth. We must compare notes. And for Bill? *Robinson Crusoe*. Good choice. Now, Bill – did you know that Daniel Defoe (Foe was his real name) was virtually the first novelist?'

Bill shook his head. He'd never heard of Defoe, *Foe* would have interested him more.

Kenneth's body blocked the warmth from reaching Bill. Better to go for a run and leave Kenneth to hog the only fire in the house. Or should he go up to Nanny's – unless Dad had just been. 'Have you been visiting Ted, Dad?'

'I have. I do what little I can.'

'He's in a bad way, isn't he?' said Kenneth in an old man's gossipy voice.

'Not good, I'll allow. When Colin's at work, I think the grandparents struggle.'

Kenneth leant towards Dad. 'Poor things. I shall go one Saturday and give them a little concert. They enjoy my singing.'

'They do.' Dad nodded, one hand stroking his chin.

'I feel a bit sorry for Bill,' said Kenneth, as though Bill were not immediately behind his chair.

Dad raised his eyebrows questioningly.

'I mean, we have no madness,' he coughed to indicate he must find a better word, '*mental* problems in our side of the family, do we, Dad?'

Dad turned, and now he wasn't pleased. He sat down on the worn leather armchair opposite Kenneth. 'A few years older, Kenneth, and you could have been up a mountain or hunkered down in a trench, hungry, muddy, wet, suffering what Ted suffered, facing the constant bombing around you, seeing death, day after day. Don't be surprised if that's had an effect on decent men, probably many hundreds of decent men. We don't know. But combat stress is not madness.'

Kenneth's face tightened and he readjusted it to look sympathetic. 'No. It's tremendously tragic, of course.'

Bill hid his grin. At last Dad had seen how mean Kenneth was and had corrected him! He wanted Kenneth to know he'd heard. 'Dad, I'm just off for a run if you've been to Nanny's.' How Kenneth would hate him witnessing Dad's put down.

Dad softened it immediately. 'The Odeon National Cinema club have a nationwide painting and drawing competition for children up to the age of fifteen, Kenneth. There's a good prize.'

Kenneth swung his body around. 'Should I enter?'

'You should. *Draw or paint anything relating to the sea or the Merchant Navy.*'

Bill went for his coat and balaclava. 'I'm going now. I've got football practice later, Dad.' How would Kenneth know about the Merchant Navy? But, then, he really could paint just about anything.

~

It was four o-clock when he got back from football practice. Kenneth emerged from the dining room. 'Try to clean yourself up, dear chap. I am having school friends to tea any minute and I would prefer not to introduce some ruffian as my cousin.'

Bill clenched his fist deciding what he could say and what he couldn't. *This is my house. This was always my home before you got here.* It was like having constipation, being the boy who hadn't taken his Syrup of Figs: so much to come out, and so much held back.

Mother came in with a cake that must have been baked with the precious American sugar and the week's egg, as well as a lace cloth for the dining table. She said, 'Run along and get washed, Bill. Isn't it nice that Kenneth has Dulwich College friends that will come to an ordinary home?'

Did she really think it nice? To be safely neutral he answered, 'You're doing them a fancy tea. They should be glad.'

Mother smiled, a smile with lips as hard and smooth as old marg. 'That's not the way the world works, Bill.'

In fact, Kenneth's friends turned out to be perfectly decent, polite to Mother and Aunty and quite friendly to Bill. After tea they even helped clear the table before going into the garden room to play Monopoly with a set that Dad had borrowed specially from someone at his work. No-one had done anything like that for Bill when Alan visited.

Then, as January took hold, Bill had no time to think about niggles over Kenneth. When the snow fell and stayed on the ground, crisping up with worsening temperatures, the boys at school were thrilled. The prefects allowed snowball fights within reason. Then the snow was so high that it came over the tops of wellington boots and stopped the fun. There was a lot of shovelling in the freezing roads and paths; he was often called on to do it.

As the cold went relentlessly on and on, the difficulty of getting food supplies meant dinners were even worse than before, so that people were bad-tempered with hunger.

At home, there were not enough clothes to keep warm, not enough blankets for the bitter nights. Dad didn't dare use up the last of the Coalite, but eked out the supply with coal dust from the far reaches of the cellar. It was only enough for the boiler, so only the kitchen had any heat. This made every day totally wretched, and ice coated the inside of the bedroom windows.

Worse, Mother caught 'flu and then Kenneth fell ill. Even Bill felt anxious about Kenneth's hacking cough and the doctor could not call; he was too tied up with emergencies and heavily pregnant mothers. Aunty, and then Dad, had very heavy colds. Bill ventured out in wellington boots and all three of his jumpers under his coat to shop for what he could find, and then to take hot drinks to everyone as well as fragments of food. If only he could cook! Soup was what people needed and he didn't know how to make it.

Kenneth had grey dents in his cheeks and was coughing too much to hold the mug of Bovril Bill had brought him. Bill pulled the blanket from his bed and wrapped it round Kenneth's shoulders. 'What medicine do you need? I don't want to worry Aunty. She's asleep.'

Kenneth shook his head. 'Best not bother. It's too hard on my stomach.'

Each day, Bill scraped out a hole from the ice on their window and peered out, desperate for signs of a thaw. Each day the cold remained, or got worse.

The wireless told of extreme weather country-wide. The sea froze over in Minehead! Bill remembered that was a long way south.

The electricity cuts for five hours every day continued even now, as if the government didn't know that everyone was freezing. It was almost a relief to be out of the house, so despite everything, he did get to school.

On the long-awaited day of the thaw, he got home to find Mother on her feet again and Dad huddled in a blanket in his study. Bill went into the parlour still in his coat and balaclava to start his homework, and found Kenneth there, up and dressed.

'I've made you something,' he said. 'Sorry it won't warm you up much.'

It was a still life drawing of a red mug, steam coming from its top. Bill did actually feel warmer from looking at it, and not just because it looked so life-like.

CHAPTER 27

'If this last winter was the worst I've ever known, I think spring 1947 will be the best!' Aunty was looking pretty in a lemon coloured blouse she'd found in the church Bring and Buy sale.

She delved into her pocket and waved an airmail over the kitchen table. She'd obviously waited to tell her news until Dad had left for work and Kenneth to the library. 'Ten days and Dwaine will be here! It's been such a long wait.'

Mother said, 'Goodness! Will he? Let's have all the details.'

'He's arriving on the *Queen Mary*, leaving New York.'

Bill asked, 'Is that near where he lives?'

'No, it takes a whole day on the bus to get there. Imagine that! The bus goes through four states!'

Bill thought of the bumpy coach that had taken him and the other children from the evacuation train to the country village hall. How terrible to be stuck on a bus all day.

Mother obviously thought the same. 'What a journey, Doreen! And think, that's what you'd have to do if you went there.'

'He'll stay a night or two there before embarking, so he can do some shopping.'

'And then a week or so on the sea passage?'

'Yes. I'll go to Southampton on the train to meet him. Even that's an excitement for me.'

'Will you come straight back, I mean he'll be tired and perhaps travel sick?'

'No,' she blushed. 'We will stay at a hotel for two nights before coming home.'

It was lovely for Aunty to have all this to look forward to. Before he'd even thought about whether they would be sharing a bedroom, Mother giggled and gasped. 'Staying over, Doreen! What shall I say to Herbert? Won't he think it risqué?'

Mother's face had an expression he'd not seen before. It was a mixture of envy, embarrassment and shock.

Aunty tossed her head. 'It will be totally decent. Dwaine is a gentleman. She leant forward. 'Marcia, I'll be able to wear my new dress. It was worth every one of the minutes I queued for it, or was it hours! If only I could travel first class so that it won't get grubby in the train!'

Bill knew the dress was pale blue. It would be a risk to wear it. Every time Dad went on a train he needed a clean shirt the next day. His collar and cuffs had black stains by the time he got home. London was so dirty, and it was worst around the rail stations. Aunty needed to look her best for Dwaine's arrival.

'Oh Doreen. Take your old mac to cover it until you get there. I wish I could get to wear a new dress and stay in a hotel! Count your fortunes.'

Aunty laughed, a trill like Kenneth's soprano. 'I do, but I must warn Herbert and then—' she sighed '—Kenneth. Even though he's still so pleased about his painting competition, I'll have to choose my words carefully.'

Kenneth had won second prize for his Merchant Navy painting. Disappointingly, the money went into National Savings Certificates for him. It could have bought a cake or something that they could all share. About food, yesterday morning's news headline had made them all feel worse, *'Austerity Must Continue'*.

Kenneth should jolly well accept the Dwaine situation. He'd tried his best to poison Dad against him and had gone into the study with Dad several times. He must have lost the argument, for Dad had arranged Dwaine's accommodation with the Benthams next door. He'd told Mother and Aunty, 'The *Share Your Home* scheme means people like the Benthams with a good house and no dependants would have some stranger billeted on them, so they're jolly glad to have a lodger that you two know.'

Bill rubbed his hands. It would be super-duper having Dwaine. There'd be an excuse to go to the West End. He'd get Alan over and they'd take Dwaine to play football up at Garretts' Green, perhaps even to watch a match at Chelsea!

He came to from these thoughts to hear Mother and Aunty exchanging excited comments about clothes, and places to show Dwaine. The chat went on and on, until the front door opened, and they all fell silent. It didn't take long for someone to go to the library.

Mother stood quickly, saying, 'He's back. I'll leave you to it, Doreen. Best if I'm out. I was going to do the shopping now, anyway.'

Bill slipped upstairs. Poor Aunty, it wasn't going to be easy. He sat on his bunk. Aunty's voice sounded from downstairs, calling Kenneth into the parlour. Safe from interruption for a while, Bill bent down and got his camera from under the bed. Last time he'd used it was when he'd run round the village snapping his memories. That was months and months ago and he still hadn't had that film developed. He had no new film, of course, and no money to get one. Perhaps he could get a paper round or errand boy's job. He was thirteen, after all, although in the bread queue, women were complaining that the demobbed soldiers were taking anything that was on offer, even boys' jobs.

He opened the camera, cleaned the lens with his breath, dusted the concertina bits with his hanky, and closed it again before putting it back beneath his bunk.

His album sat tied into its own box on his side of the bookcase. Because Kenneth sneered at pictures that were photographed, rather than painted, the album was fairly safe from his prying fingers. Bill opened the cover. His photos were stuck with the black photo corners his village science teacher had given him. Some had lost their glue so that photos wobbled between perhaps two corners instead of four.

On the first page were the pigs, Laurel and Hardy. They'd been so important in his first months of evacuation. He missed them even now and the memory hurt; the awfulness of seeing Hardy's nose, lifted up towards him as if in prayer before they were driven towards the butchers that dreadful day, their very last. It had been even worse when it ended with the empty pen and the shocking news of Uncle Frank's death. Worse still when Kenneth had to stay with him while the mothers went to the funeral. He shuddered. And the scene after the funeral! That had been a truly terrible few days.

He turned a page. Sally and Timmy. Mrs Youldon had been so thrilled with the photo. He smiled at the little ones' faces. When he'd shown them, how amazed they were to be in a photograph! It was the first time they'd actually seen their own faces, for their cottage didn't have the luxury of a mirror.

The next page held photos of dear Mr and Mrs Pawsey, so comfortable and safe. He sighed, longing to be with all of them right now.

He turned a page. Not all his important people were in the album. He needed photos of Ted, Nanny and Grandad and the Durbans, and, if he could get it, a new one of the shashka. There were a lot of blank pages waiting to be filled. He closed his album carefully, before Kenneth came upstairs.

He hadn't thrown away his one photo of Kenneth. It wasn't in the album. He hated the thing, and kept it separate. He'd only taken it because Dad insisted he take one of Kenneth. He could throw it away, of course, but when it was developed, the chemist had said how good it was. Kenneth hadn't wanted to be photographed while he was feeling so sad after Uncle Frank's death. When Bill lifted the camera, Kenneth threw his hands over his face and the window light made them shine.

Now that he'd learned so much from the photography manual Mrs Routledge had given him, he could look at it with new eyes. The photograph was like a – Bill couldn't think of a word. It was like a piece of art itself. You could even see all the paintings Kenneth had done, pasted behind him on the wall. Bill looked at the photo as if he didn't know the pale boy, his curls falling forward on his brow, whose white hands, the sunlight streaming through them, were like angel birds spread in front of his face. Bill had hidden this photo at the back of the pack but now he felt a thrill to have taken a photo that told a story. Anyone looking at it would ask questions. This was the sort of thing they put in *Picture Post*. He would keep it safely, and if he met a proper photographer, he'd show him; but it wasn't a photo to be put in his album with all the people he loved.

He put the Kenneth photo in an envelope under the album at the bottom of its box, which he secured with a length of hemming tape, making a double bow.

Aunty must surely have done her telling by now. He put his head round his bedroom door in case there was any shouting. There wasn't. Kenneth had known Dwaine was coming. Just like Bill had known that Kenneth was moving in last year. Kenneth would have to face it, and get used to having Dwaine around.

Bill rubbed his hands. There was so much he wanted to show Dwaine. He could take him to see Ted. They might even talk about Africa. But what would happen when Dwaine's stay ended? A sad postcard at Christmas told him Mrs Youldon's sister, Mary, had been whisked away across the Atlantic by her GI, and Tim had added little pictures of the steak, ice cream and washing machine she'd be enjoying.

Bill stepped back rapidly as Kenneth stamped up the stairs and into the bedroom. 'Oh you're here.' He flopped onto Bill's bunk without asking. 'Did you know the Yank is already on his way here? Dad's just too lenient. Anyway, the US of A won't let him be away for long, and Great Britain won't let him stay here for more than a short visit.'

'Perhaps he'll invite you both to America. Dad said he wasn't short of a penny – dollars, I suppose.'

'If Mama lets him talk her into going to America, she needn't think I'm going too. I shall stay here with you lot. Dad'll speak up for me, I know it.'

It was an awful thought: Kenneth but no Aunty. Bill took a moment to think of the right comment. 'You know, Dwaine could be a really good friend for you. Remember how he praised your paintings when you had your school exhibition at the Priory? He might get his rich friends to buy your work.'

Kenneth snorted. 'Rich friends! He works in some kind of factory. Probably left school without any qualifications.'

The sound of the front door opening with a key announced Dad's return home. Bill stifled a sigh. *Thank goodness.* 'Let's go down and see Dad.'

'Yes, let's,' Kenneth added menacingly. 'We'll see what he has to say to Mama staying with the Yank in a hotel, even if they do have separate rooms like she says.'

CHAPTER 28

It was such an excitement, the day Dwaine came to Wandsworth. Aunty had been nervous about Kenneth causing an atmosphere. No-one wanted the visit spoiled. He wouldn't dare to be rude or sarcastic when Dad was around, but there would be many other opportunities.

Luckily, Kenneth was in bed ill again before they arrived.

The whole of that first week, Kenneth was tucked up with the curtains drawn keeping his suffering to himself, while downstairs the house almost shook with the thrill of Dwaine. They didn't usually have visitors, and never one from overseas!

Dad was quietly welcoming. If he minded about another man taking Uncle Frank's place, he didn't show it. It helped that Dwaine was very respectful.

The parlour felt too small to contain Dwaine and his fine suitcase and carry bag. They all helped carry everything into the garden room where Dwaine pleased Mother straight away with his, 'Say, Ma'am! This room is grand; real stylish!'

Jill was soon perched on Dwaine's lap. He opened his suitcase and shared out all sorts of goodies; tins of meat, a little dress for Jill, candies, art pencils for Kenneth. Best of all, six rolls of film for his camera! Six!

Aunty hung on Dwaine's arm, beaming. She must have told him the make of his camera, nice Aunty.

Mother had made cakes, specially, and the extravagance didn't matter, because there'd been sugar in Dwaine's suitcase too.

After tea, Dwaine brought out postcards of his home town, Savannah. Everyone hung over them, amazed at its beautiful gardens, fine squares, everything looking so clean.

'Have you got seaside?' Jill wanted to check all the possibilities of the place.

'Yep. Sea, and river. Savannah's got most things.'

'I'd like to go there.'

'Guess you'll have to wait till you grow up, little lady.'

Bill smiled to himself as he turned over Dwaine's pictures, one by one. There wasn't going to be much here that Kenneth could sneer at. Dwaine didn't "work in a factory". He had been a supervisor in a tool-making business before he signed up for military service. He was a skilled engineer and wouldn't be out of a job. It was the law in Georgia that servicemen returning must be allowed their old job back.

'That's the trouble, here,' Mother said. 'The men are coming back to nothing.'

Bill said, 'Ted can't get his job back.'

'Poor Ted. He wouldn't be able to cope with it, anyway,' Mother turned to Dad.

Dad leant forward to Dwaine. 'Ted's Marcia's brother, East Surrey regiment. He served in much the same places as you, but he had a very bad experience in Dunkirk first. He hadn't got over it when he had to serve again, even though it was some months before they got sent to Africa.'

'And now in no state to work. His nerves, you know,' Mother was going on.

'Gee, that's too bad.'

'Yes. He's lost his chance of a good income. I hope you're in a stronger position, Dwaine.'

Dwaine stretched his shoulders into an expansive shrug. 'We-ell, I've been away four years, not getting the promotion I would've done if I'd stayed home. And war's made me grow some, if you get me. So I reckon it's the neat thing to set up on my own now.'

Dad was interested. 'Is that what you've been arranging before coming over?'

'Dead right, Bert: a business loan from the government to set up my own workshop and employ twelve men – ex-servicemen, preferably. Folk'll always need tools and I'm the guy to design them. I'm the guy to train the men, 'n all. I got the building, got the equipment, all fine and dandy. It'll be swell. So it's anchors away when I get back to Georgia.'

Dad leaned forward, blocking Bill's view of Aunty's sparkling eyes. 'This is a fine project. So many men need just that chance. It's clearly a very sound venture with your experience behind it. What was it Einstein said? *Try not to become a man of success but a man of value.* I think you're emulating that.'

'Say, that's real decent of you.'

Aunty was all puffed up with pride. So 'emulating' must be a praising sort of word.

~

By the time Kenneth was over the flu, or bronchitis, or whatever it was this time, Dwaine was part of the home as if he'd always lived here, and it was Kenneth who was more like the visitor.

Aunty didn't know who to fuss over first when Kenneth was well enough to come downstairs. Dwaine was at his nicest, and Kenneth's sore throat stopped him from saying much. If he rolled his eyes when Dwaine was speaking, it could be put down to his feeling poorly, and anyway, it was Dwaine who was the centre of attention. Kenneth didn't like that, but even he was glad of the treats: in his case, the art pencils Dwaine had brought.

Every time Dwaine spoke, Jill hung onto his words, wanting to hear him say things in 'his funny voice' over and over.

'Say, maybe funny for you, little lady, but all folks talk like that where I come from,' he told her.

Bill loved the sound of the place he came from, as well as having him around. It was impossible to have 'an atmosphere' with someone who was always cheerful, never critical, always ready to help.

Mother had been at her nicest since Dwaine's arrival, only worrying about the poor fare every meal-time once his tins had been used up. 'It must be awful for you, putting up with our meals. The newspaper tells us we get only half the food that Americans are used to, but the Ministry of Food say we're lucky.'

Bill could see that meal-times were a shock to Dwaine, although he was polite about it. 'You Brits are certainly suffering but don't fret. I got my brother Ernie to send another of those food parcels. I guess it'll arrive before we all starve.'

'The Benthams are dreading the day they lose you. They say it's taken the rough edge off their days.'

'Gee. That's nice. It's sure nice for this Yankee to be made welcome in a true British home.'

Dwaine was a blessing to Nanny and Grandad, too. He'd only been in Wandsworth a few days before he caught up with Bill halfway down the road. 'Guess I'm a-comin' with you, buddy. Doreen told me what you're doing for your old folks, and I guess they could do with another man's heave-ho.'

'That'll be super. They'll love to meet you. They might not have met an American ever before.'

When Bill took Dwaine inside he could see it was certainly an excitement for them. Dwaine had some Hershey bars that he put on the table near enough for Grandad to reach.

It wasn't the only visit Dwaine made. Ted was brighter having Dwaine's company, and much more gardening got done. But if they chatted about the war, they didn't do it where Bill could hear.

Alan came over to Wandsworth as often as he could. He'd always loved to be with Dwaine. The three of them went down to the common, with Aunty watching on a bench as they played ball and compared British and American rules.

It was like a competition with Aunty, who could collar Dwaine's company first and longest. Kenneth couldn't have liked this, but he didn't act up. How could he be the only dreary face in the house? Altogether, it felt as if a golden ball had descended on Primley Road, lightening and brightening everyone around.

One evening when Dwaine had gone next door for the night and Kenneth was still not back from choir, Dad settled back in his chair. 'Well, Doreen, I think you're sensible to give your friendship time, rather than rush into anything.'

'Yes, Bert. It's lovely to have a man friend after being alone these last years. We get on so well, but I am taking things slowly, as you say.'

'That's good. You didn't know him for very long in the village; it wasn't in your normal home circumstances and there's been such a long gap since then.'

Aunty took up her knitting, this time a V-neck for Dwaine, although he surely didn't need any more clothes. 'I'm a widow. I recognise that some people would feel I should stay that way. My parents are of that mind. Of course I still miss Frank and the tragedy of it doesn't go away, especially poor Kenneth losing his father but…'

She stopped there, so no-one learned what might come after the *but*.

Bill risked Dad noticing that he was still there, hearing all this grown-ups' talk. 'Actually, Aunty, how did Dwaine lose his wife? Was it an accident?'

'No, dear. A heart complaint, poor thing. She was ill in hospital for some weeks before she died. Very tragic.'

'There's a commonality in that, of course,' said Dad. 'It helps the relationship that you've both been through a similar tragedy.'

Aunty nodded sadly.

'It will be a huge adaptation for Kenneth to make if you do go, although a wonderful opportunity. However, he's not fifteen for another six months and what about his Higher School Certificate?'

Aunty said, 'Dwaine's made several enquiries about his education. There's even a fine university in Savannah.'

Dad nodded. He gave a lot more advice, almost as if he was Aunty's father. It was strange for Bill to be present. Fancy Dad having such a conversation in front of him! In the past, voices had dropped or stopped when he was near. Serious conversations happened when children were in bed. Now they were often happening in front of him.

Dad didn't talk like this in front of Kenneth, even though he was older than Bill. Yet he often took Kenneth into the study, somewhere that had always been Dad's private place. They talked about books together, like a twosome.

When Aunty went to get the cocoa, Bill went with her. She was always the safest person to discuss things with. 'Dad never used to say important things in front of me. Is it because he forgets I'm there?

'Oh, Bill,' she put an arm round him. 'You're steady, dear, like a big bear, nearly adult. I think your father trusts that you'll never say a word out of turn, so he speaks freely in front of you.'

He didn't feel like an adult but didn't want to admit it.

Kenneth got home before the cocoa had cooled.

'How was choir, dear?'

'Quite taxing, Mama.' He held out a sheaf of music. 'All this to learn,' but his face was shining. He loved his singing. They must have choirs in Savannah, though.

'Herbert thought he'd seen you coming out of the Evening Institute.'

Kenneth flicked his hair back, and said airily. 'Maybe. I have friends who take evening classes. It's worth finding out the classes they have on offer.'

Friends, choir, Dulwich College, Art lessons: so much Kenneth loved. It must be awful for him, dreading the moment Aunty said 'I've decided that we're going to leave on the next ship.'

By the time of high summer, Dwaine had gone. He had to travel back to start his new business. He comforted Aunty with 'Just a few months, and I'm coming back to collect you, honey.'

Jill cried for a whole day when he left, Bill and Alan were down in the dumps, but it was worse for Aunty.

'It'll be dreadful waiting until the moment is right,' she confided to Bill.

'Dwaine won't let you down,' he said. 'America is waiting for you.' Was he a rotten person at heart because the thought of Kenneth's departure made him glow with sheer joy?

CHAPTER 29

Jill was pouting. She had grown out of the pretty dress Dwaine had brought over from America. 'It will be ages and ages before we see him again.'

'If we ever do,' Kenneth added.

'And I haven't got another one. And it's too hot to wear this skirt.' Her bottom lip stuck out. Tears were coming.

'I shall have to sew a flounce on the bottom of the dress, Jill. You know that Dwaine had to travel back to start his new business, but he'll be back.' comforted Aunty. 'You heard him say so.'

Kenneth gave a rotten imitation, 'Say, honey, just a liddle why-le, and guess I'm comin' right back ter collec' yer.'

Bill butted in to save Aunty's feelings. 'We're all missing him. I've got some paper you can write to him on, Jill, and some transfers and glue to decorate the page. Come on.'

'Goody.' Jill followed him out of the room.

Despite his sarky remarks, Kenneth had seemed to be accepting Dwaine by the time he left. Or it could have been the food parcels and treats that made the difference. Then, because Aunty hadn't gone with Dwaine – "too soon" – Kenneth had been more relaxed, and he hadn't been ill for weeks.

Bill hadn't relaxed, for Kenneth kept his sarcasm anointed like the Red Indians' poisoned arrows: aimed to hit the vulnerable spot.

Recently, this was about girls. Bill did like girls, but didn't really meet any. The one time girls from the neighbouring school joined St Werberg's boys for a geography film and lecture, they just giggled. No-one managed to talk properly with them.

Kenneth, however, was smoothing his hair with water these days, and boasting about girls he knew from choir 'and other places' but he wouldn't say where these were. Sometimes he even got into trouble for being late home in the evening. Afterwards he'd wink at Bill. 'Worth a wigging for the time I've had!' leaving Bill to wonder what sort of thing he'd been doing.

'You must be green with envy, Billy-boy.'

'You're fourteen and a half. I expect I'll have girl-friends when I am.'

'Ha! It's going to be years before any of us (annoyingly, he meant himself and the parents) can civilize you sufficiently to approach a girl. Look at those great knees and bulging pockets!'

'It's not my fault we don't have long trousers at school. And you could jolly well stick up for me when I ask for them for out of school.'

Kenneth snorted and turned away, as if Bill's words, let alone his wishes and feelings, were way beneath him.

Bill could have hit back by referring to America but he didn't. It would be hard enough for Kenneth when he was forced to go. It was only a matter of time.

~

Time passed, months, in fact, and Aunty still hadn't mentioned going to America. Somehow, Bill had expected that she would announce a departure on Kenneth's fifteenth birthday: she would give him the bad news softened by balloons and brown paper parcels. He was wrong. Aunty just took Kenneth for a trip to the National Gallery, with tea in a Fullers' tea-shop afterwards. Kenneth painted a picture of it for his Art homework and it got an A+.

Now it was near the end of autumn term when days were shortest and tempers with them. Bill was so often hearing about Kenneth's achievements that he hadn't thought much of his own, although he had been thrilled to captain the football team. It was a tremendous shock, although of the nicest kind, when the headmaster called him into his study and told him he and the staff had selected him to be a senior prefect, and if he did well, he would be Head Boy next year when many of the fifteen-year-olds would leave.

He left the study in a glow. It was simply spiffing to know he had the teachers' good opinion. Prefect!

And it was a wonderful feeling, having that news to announce at home. It would even things up a little. Kenneth always had art competitions he'd won, or school studies to tell Dad – History, Biology, Latin and World Affairs. Bill just seemed to have *lessons*. They weren't particularly difficult but not very interesting, so it was always Kenneth and Dad in conversation and Bill left with household jobs. But now Kenneth wouldn't be able to sneer at him. He was at the posh school, but he wasn't a prefect.

First off, Bill stopped at the nearest telephone box to ring Alan. He'd be really pleased. He broke the news and sure enough, Alan's whoops and whistles sounded down the earpiece. 'Hooray. Three cheers, Bill. My mother will be pleased. Everyone will look up to you now. Even Kenneth will sit up to hear this!'

That would be good! As Bill stepped out of the kiosk, a sliver of sun hit the glass windows as if it was waiting for him. Football Captain wasn't the kind of honour to excite his parents but surely senior prefect and Head Boy would? He let the sun warm his neck for a moment before he ran home with his news. Tonight he'd phone Mr Durban with it.

Instead of using the sideway, he rang the bell at the front door like a visitor. Mother opened it and before she could complain, he stood high on the step and announced, 'Good afternoon. This is the future Head Boy of St Warburg's arriving!'

'Really, Bill? *Really?*'

'Well, Senior Prefect for now, but Head Boy next year if I do well at it.'

'That's wonderful! Doreen, Jill, come out here!'

Aunty hugged him when he repeated his news and Jill leapt up and down. He couldn't wait for Dad to get home. He'd surely be very proud. Appointments were what he really valued.

But it was Kenneth who got home next. He came into the parlour weighed down with a satchel full of homework.

'Guess what, Kenneth. Bill's been made senior prefect and will be Head Boy next year!' Mother said.

'We're so proud,' Aunty added.

Kenneth's face tightened, his eyes flickered but with only the smallest pause he directed a small smile at Mother. 'Isn't that excellent, Aunty Marcia. Something to cheer you up.' He opened his satchel, busily, and brought out some sheet music. 'I'm going to be busy tonight preparing for the school concert. Since I'm the soloist for the Purcell, I have the responsibility of learning the music before all the others.'

'The soloist, Kenneth?' Aunty squealed. 'What I secretly longed for. The music concert, Herbert will love that. We'll all go, won't we, Bill?'

'Of course,' he said, making his way out of the room and upstairs.

He sat in his bedroom on his own while Kenneth warbled snatches of Purcell downstairs, timing it to catch Dad's ear immediately he arrived home. Bill's own news could be discussed over the tea table, perhaps.

He waited until he heard Dad come in and the snatches of music stop. He ran downstairs for tea and sat himself opposite Dad's chair.

Laying the table, Aunty was saying brightly, 'What have you got there, Kenneth?'

'Birthday cards.' He pulled a pile of them out of his satchel and put them on the sideboard where there was already an envelope for him, probably from his grandparents. The pile must be from boys at school. Strangely, they liked him there, all right.

Dad was hitching his trousers ready to sit down. 'Fifteen coming up soon, eh?'

Was Dad going to talk about school leaving age, and going to America?

Kenneth smiled. 'Quite a nice haul of cards, don't you think? I'll open them on my birthday itself.'

'I like balloons better than cards,' Jill said. 'Can we have some on Kenneth's birthday?'

Kenneth stretched. 'It's the present that matters.' He cast a quick glance at a wrapped package on the sideboard.

Bill knew that Aunty's present was a hardback book of special Art paper. Bill had found a shop in Clapham that had some tubes of paint from before the war. He'd bought the two colours, indigo and red carmine, that ones Kenneth had wanted the night of the storm. When he saw them, perhaps Kenneth would turn into a nicer person.

As if he'd read Bill's thoughts, Kenneth turned to Dad. 'Do you know, Dad? Bill was made a prefect today.'

CHAPTER 30

June was Bill's favourite month. He liked hot weather, and there was swimming twice a week at school, plus a camp at Scouts some weekends. The winter had been so vicious he thought he'd never take sunshine for granted ever again. It had been grim, and Kenneth's constant illness as result of the extreme cold worried Aunty to death. It was probably the reason she still hadn't taken the huge step of telling Dwaine she was ready for America.

On several occasions, Bill had been the only member of the family fit to do anything, 'flu and head colds worsening the suffering of a scarcely heated house and a snow-bound environment. He hadn't felt really well himself until April, and it was a helpless feeling seeing the rest of the family ill.

After a late spring, just as the headmaster had promised last autumn, he was made Head Boy. Striding into school, he sensed some importance, even if this was a shabby building with struggling staff. He was allowed to use the school library whenever he liked. This meant he could do his homework there in peace, instead of sharing table space with Kenneth and suffering his sneers about the simplicity of Bill's studies.

Aunty and Mother had just left to take Jill to see a dancing festival so Bill was enjoying some peace alone in the parlour. He wrote June,

1947, at the top of a fresh page. He was compiling scores for Arsenal's last hundred matches. There'd be some badge at Scouts he could put the information towards.

Kenneth pushed the door open. 'I'm going to do this weekend's homework in here, so don't interrupt me.'

'I was here first.' Should he take his scores upstairs, or would Kenneth follow? He bent his head over the notebook and hoped it would look like some maths.

Kenneth collapsed onto the sofa and put his feet up. That wasn't allowed, but Dad was at the Conservative club. Bill wrote down a few more scores and pretended not to notice. It was getting near the end of school year, Kenneth was taking School Certificate this month and Aunty needed to make her decision. Kenneth had been increasingly tetchy lately, as if it was all Bill's fault.

Sure enough, Kenneth started to bate him. 'Maths is it? Probably what I covered in my first year. It's not like a grammar school, yours,' he said, pulling out his copy of Victor Hugo and his Latin declensions from his satchel. 'No fine traditions. I suppose I've benefited from those in both the establishments I've studied in.'

Bill let a moment pass and closed his notebook, ready for the off. 'You'll have left school soon.' He didn't say, 'left the country', but that's what he meant, and Kenneth would know. (*Haha, Kenneth in America, earning his own living starting at the bottom; and no Kenneth here; Dad with only one son. Me.*)

Kenneth curled his lip. 'No I won't have left school. Sixth form at Dulwich College for me. I discussed it with Dad last night. He says he's glad to support me until I graduate from university.'

Kenneth often lied. 'University! I thought you'd go out to work this summer hols (*go to America*). You'll be sixteen in November. You could've worked last year. I've had to.'

'Go out to work? What, like a coalman or bank clerk? No, that's what you'll do when the time comes, unless you want to hang on as a paper-boy with your seven and sixpences. You're not destined for university, are you?'

But you're destined for America. Bill stopped himself from saying it.

'That's why they've made you Head Boy, sort of compensation.'

Bill stood up and turned his back to stop himself putting a fist in

Kenneth's face. It was time to get down to the newsagents, both for bundling up the day's stock and to manage his temper. Strange how he worked six days a week at the crack of dawn, whereas Kenneth earned his pocket money just by collecting golf balls on a Sunday afternoon, yet they ended up with the same money. It really wasn't fair! Kenneth snaffled lots of his Art stuff from school so that he had cash left for luxuries, whereas films and processing ate up nearly all Bill's money.

He shoved his notebook into his jacket pocket and looped his camera strap around his neck. 'I'm off. Keep your mean comments for your school friends – if you have any left.'

He loped down the road swallowing his anger. At the corner of the road, he hesitated. Did he have enough time to drop in on the Durbans between bundling newspapers and tea? It was always a tricky decision: if he stayed to eat with them, he would have to announce to the family where he was; if he kept quiet about it, he had to be back in time for tea. He might just photograph people piling off the bus instead.

His camera spent most of its time around Bill's neck. He was up to Chapter Eleven of the manual, and trying different photograph techniques. He photographed buildings, animals, too, if they appeared in the street. Although he found it a bit awkward, he'd also started to photograph people.

One of his new excuses for popping in on the Durbans, these days, was to get Angela's help with this. He needed to experiment with the light and shade of a face, he said, and no-one else would have the patience to sit for him. Even if Angela didn't believe that, she did enjoy being his model. He could see that, by the way she arched her back and turned her face up, or to the right, or just as he asked.

It was true that he needed to improve his portrait pictures. One day he would be a real photographer and Mr Durban said it was portraits that people came to a photographer for. People wanted mementoes. But the main reason for taking photographs of Angela, and he was embarrassed to admit it, was the thrill of getting close to her.

Although he was three years younger, Angela had always been

quite huggy with him. At first he'd found that very embarrassing. It still was, but he liked it more each time, looked forward to it – even longed for it; the smell of Pears soap, the close-up of Pond's lipstick, the soft curl of her hair. Angela was the only person who made a fuss of him, although occasionally Aunty gave him a hug. He'd always had hugs from Mrs Pawsey. Now all he had were her letters. And Angela was a young lady, someone who might go on dates. He decided to go up there later. An extra hour sorting newspapers at the shop meant extra money, and by the time he got back, Kenneth might have gone out.

Even though Kenneth had sneered at what the paper-round earned, putting the shillings in his cashbox was one of Bill's greatest satisfactions. Even the sight of the black oblong tin with its narrow red stripe could cheer him up on a dark day. He'd been saving for two things: more film and processing money, and a present for Angela. Dwaine's six films had been used up long ago, and he couldn't very well ask for more. Dwaine would need so much money. A passage to America was about £100, and if Dwaine came here to collect Aunty, three tickets would cost a fortune!

How often did Kenneth think about all this? Was he telling the truth about Dad keeping him here to take his Higher School Certificate? Bill wasn't going to risk asking Dad in case he'd expect *him* to study for it, too! That would be awful, for he'd set his heart on being a photographer. Mother said to keep that to himself until Dad decided on Bill's future. 'He might well have firm ideas for someone who's a Head Boy.'

CHAPTER 31

Bill folded the newspapers for 15th August 1947, ready for delivery. They were so light, now that they could only be four pages long. Rationing was a flipping nuisance. Milk allowances had been cut and he hated drinking tea with only a splash of milk. Kenneth, of course, had the usual amount because he needed it for his health.

But nothing could stop Bill feeling cheery. He loved the hot weather and he had enough money to go swimming. Everything felt rather exciting. Princess Elizabeth was getting married. India had its independence. He knew what wanting independence felt like. A country must feel it a thousand times more. The newsagent's wife couldn't stop talking about the royal wedding, how it would be a grand affair, golden carriages, beautiful dresses, processions. It would certainly brighten up November. Even Dad had agreed that they would all go, and camp overnight in the street, if necessary.

Aunty wouldn't see that great day. She had just given in her notice at work because, at last, Dwaine was on his way to collect her. She'd whispered to Bill 'If I dare go,' and he'd put an arm round her and said, 'You should, even though I really don't want to lose you.' She'd already given her clothing coupons to Mother, saying she'd be able to buy better in New York and without needing coupons.

Would this mean the back of Kenneth at last? No-one was saying anything about him going, although he was past school leaving age now. He'd gained excellent School Certificate results, surely good enough to get into a college, or whatever they had in Savannah? The new school year would begin at Dulwich College next week. He asked Mother if Kenneth was enrolled on a course in Savannah. She just answered, 'Don't tempt Providence, Bill.'

He wouldn't trust what Kenneth said about staying, and he couldn't tell from the way he behaved. He'd been wearing a supercilious expression and smarmed-back hair, and had whisked out after breakfast, most of the holiday. Was he going to go to America with Aunty or not?

Bill would take School Certificate himself next year, then he'd leave school and somehow train to be a photographer, whatever Dad's plans. But today he had something special to do.

Everyone was out: Dad at the Conservative club, Jill at Iris's, Kenneth at cricket, Mother and Aunty at a Bring and Buy sale. He ran upstairs to put on his first pair of long trousers, the best thing that had happened for simply ages. Thank goodness Dad hadn't made him wait until he was sixteen like many boys! It was a sort of reward for becoming Head Boy.

Bill looked in the long mirror on the landing, at the satisfying spread of grey covering his knees and shins. Surprising how different long trousers made you feel. Outside, the August sun was blazing a fierce invitation to do something out of the ordinary, and he would!

Today was the day he'd take Angela her present. He could pass it off as a thank you for posing for all his photographs. He'd thought hard about what to buy. She was always longing for something new. Her tastes were a bit above him. She was a proper working woman, after all. She wore nylons, lipstick and the New Look. She wasn't keen to play Ludo or Backgammon any more, or even Draughts. Even though they didn't share interests, she was the most important thing for him outside of football and his camera. He so wanted to be the one to provide the latest thing she yearned for.

Her most recent desire was for a pin-up photo, a big one, of Gregory Peck, and she wanted it framed. You could get them signed from this fan club. A boy at school had told him about it, but it was ever so expensive, and then there was the frame to buy.

It had taken him weeks to save enough for it. Every time he put his shillings and pennies in the right-hand side of the cashbox he thought of Angela's face brightening when she saw it and perhaps her arm around his shoulders. She'd be so pleased, that she'd probably kiss him. Sometimes he thought of that in bed at night, and it made him quiver. He rehearsed the scene. After he'd given her the photo and she'd put it on her wall, he was going to ask her to the pictures. He actually only liked cowboy films, but whatever was on at the Odeon, it would be super sitting beside her, walking in with her, just the two of them.

Kenneth had taunted him that Bill couldn't approach any girl, but he knew Angela liked him and she always had. Even though he'd be going out with a family friend, it would still be a date.

He'd collected the precious poster from his school-friend yesterday and hidden it in the study to join his shashka story behind Dad's Annals of Law.

He went to the kitchen for a Bovril sandwich before getting ready to take the poster over to the Durbans. Angela didn't work on Saturdays and he wanted to catch her in before one of her girlfriends called. He ate his sandwich, making himself chew slowly so that he didn't get hiccups. Then he checked that he looked his smartest before stepping out into the sun. If they hadn't given in over the long trousers, he wouldn't have the confidence to start on this now. You can't go dating in short trousers.

The sun shone down so brightly on him that he had to remove his jacket. His shirt was clean on that morning and was the greeny one that Angela had said matched his eyes. She'd noticed his eyes!

The poster safely under his arm, he swung his jacket chirpily as he walked up the Durbans' path. He rapped on the door and Mr Durban opened it.

'Hello there, Bill. Come on in. I've just been organising some old snaps you can advise me on.' He led the way to the living room where magazines and knitting suggested that Angela and her mother were not far from home. He continued into the snug where the photographs were spread out over the desk.

'You can see I've made progress. Now these, photographs from the Great War are irreplaceable. I'll put most of them in the red album, but which shall I get enlarged? I want two or three framed for over here.' He pointed to the bare patch on the wall where his wartime duty rota had hung before.

Bill's eyes were on the other wall. The shashka now hung there, resting on two brass hooks. The curved mirror opposite magnified and framed it; the bright sun outside caught the silvered hilt and reflected a spot of light onto the desk.

'I know what you're looking at. The shashka looks good in its new place, right?' He turned to a sheaf of large photographs. 'Here's a photograph of the Middlesex marching back home. Here's the ARP wardens at the hut, remember them? This one's a photograph of the King and Queen when they visited the Balham bomb site.' He drew breath sharply. 'Sorry, Bill. I was forgetting your uncle Frank was in that number.'

'Yes,' said Bill thoughtfully, his eyes still on the shashka. 'It does look really good there. Better than some tommy gun with only one round of ammunition.'

Mr Durban laughed. 'Right. You can remember the 1940s Home Guard then?' He spread out the photographs to cover the whole width of the table. Which of these then?'

Bill picked two. 'These are sharp enough. I'd enlarge these two.' He rocked on his heels, ready to stroke his chin like his father did, waiting.

'If you're waiting to ask where Angela is, she's out shopping with her mother, but she's coming back first on her own. She'll be home soon. She said she was expecting someone.'

He drew a sharp breath. 'Did she really?'

'Yes. I thought it was someone from her evening class but I should have guessed it was you.'

So she more than half expected him, and he hadn't even brought his camera with him!

'Thing is, I've got to be off and out now. Home Guard Social Club, a special meeting. But you make yourself comfortable while you're waiting for Angela. Why don't you have a look at my albums?' He nodded to the albums on a shelf. 'You needn't think you've seen all of them. There's even a photo I got from my father. He served in the Boer Wars.'

'Gosh. I'd like to see that.'

'Black album, fourth page, I think.' Mr Durban went back to the lounge, put his jacket on and straightened his tie in the mirror. 'Toodle-pip. I shall leave you in charge of the house. Angela won't be long.' He swept out, clipping the front door behind him.'

Bill watched him fondly. No fire patrol, no doodlebugs to dodge, no ARP hut, just memorabilia and photos. It was good that war was over.

He pulled out the oldest looking album and took it into the lounge. He arranged himself on the sofa, giving a twitch to his trouser legs before he sat, just like David Niven. He'd practised that a lot of times since he'd had them. He stretched out his legs, proud of the trousers, and the length of them. He propped the poster against the sofa and looked at his watch, his last birthday present, more for style than to check how long Angela would be. If she was expecting him, she couldn't be long. He arranged his position so that he would be facing the door when she swept in with her little bags and strappy shoes.

The doorbell rang. Not Angela – she surely had a key. Bother – it might be one of her friends. Should he wait until they went away? It rang again, loudly; ding dong. He'd loved that sound when he was a little boy; it was darned annoying now. It came again. He was the only person in the house so he'd better answer it. It was nice to be trusted with the responsibility of the Durban house. Just like a son, an in-law or something. He got up and strode to the door, opening it confidently, ready with his advice to call back another time.

The door opened onto brilliant sunlight which momentarily blinded him. He blinked. Kenneth stood there, immaculate in cricket whites.

'What are you doing here?' Bill said, filling the doorway. It surely must be an emergency for Kenneth to risk coming here. 'Do they need me at home?'

'I haven't come to see you, stupid. I've come for Angela.' He peered around the side of Bill's bulk.

'Angela!' Something leaden thumped in his chest. 'What on earth for?' He must get rid of Kenneth now. He said, 'They're all out.'

'That's all right,' said Kenneth blithely. He put two tapered fingers on Bill's chest and pushed him aside. 'Angela said she might be a bit delayed. She told me to come in and wait. So I will.'

She told him? It couldn't be true. Was *this* the person Angela was expecting! Surely he'd scotched Kenneth's keenness to come down here ages ago? He paced down the hall after Kenneth. All the jauntiness and sunshine in Bill's heart sank to his boots, or rather the same old school shoes, earthier and clumsier than Kenneth's trim white lace-ups.

'No-one here, Billy boy? Left you to, what, wash the dishes? That's what people have you to visit for, isn't it? I shall wait in the lounge.'

Kenneth deserved a thrashing. If only he dared! He looked at Kenneth's back. Aunty had spent hours knitting that white cable-stitch V-neck. It certainly looked good over Kenneth's perfectly white shirt. He couldn't have made many runs.

Kenneth turned a smooth face to Bill. 'Twenty-four not out,' he said almost companionably, as if reading Bill's mind.

As they went into the lounge, neck and neck, Bill noticed that Kenneth was carrying a cardboard tube.

'What's that?'

'None of your business, matey. But I don't mind telling you. It's a pin-up Angela's been wanting for ages.'

'How do you know?'

'It was mentioned in evening classes,' he said airily.

So that's where Kenneth had been, those evenings when he was late home. Had Angela really told Kenneth the things she longed for? 'Gregory Peck?'

'Yes, as a matter of fact. Gregory Peck. Her heart-throb. So far. But perhaps that'll change after what I've got in mind for her today.' He gurgled in the back of his throat.

'But Angela's *my* friend, the family are my friends. You can't muscle in like that.'

'Oh no?' Kenneth snorted delicately. 'What's to say that they don't want me as a friend, a musical person, a Dulwich College student?' He looked around the lounge as if choosing the best place to drape himself. Then he spotted the opened snug door.

'What's in there, then? Haven't seen that. The old man's study?'

So he couldn't have been here much before. 'No, it's Mr Durban's private room. You shouldn't go in there!'

But Kenneth was already inside the snug. 'Not here to see, is he?'

Bill followed anxiously. 'Don't touch any of that. It's his memorabilia.'

'Displayed for people to see and admire, surely.'

'Not without permission.' Bill grabbed his arm, but Kenneth shook him off and left him to watch as he moved around softly, picking up one item, peering at another, sliding aside the albums to look at the photographs on the table and finally, dreadfully, looking up at the wall and the shashka.

'Hmmm. That looks brutal.' He placed his long fingers delicately under its curve and lifted it down.

'DON'T you dare!'

Kenneth placed it on top of the spread-out photographs. 'There. A nice little trophy of the—? Well it won't be our war, will it? Which war did this killing object come from, I wonder?'

'Stop it! It's very dangerous. You mustn't touch.'

'And you'd know, of course. From the person who told you all about the Great War, the bodies in the snow?'

Everything he had, everything he did, everything he wanted, Kenneth pushed himself into. And now he'd bought the special poster for Angela. He certainly wasn't going to get the shashka. Suppose Kenneth persuaded Mr Durban that, as Angela's boyfriend, he should take possession of it, hang it over his bed even!

Kenneth rolled back on his heels. His laugh was like slop water down the drain. 'Your face!'

He walked in a circle around the table, pulling out a photograph here and there, looking at it sneeringly and putting it down again. The shashka lay on the photographs, its hilt glinting as the sun streaked through the window beside them. Kenneth stroked the pattern, silver reflected on his fingertips.

Suddenly the small room seemed stifling in the heat, overfull with people. They should get out, get out quickly. Bill gestured with a wild arm to the lounge.

'That's enough. Come out. We shouldn't be in here.'

Kenneth folded his arms, staying put. 'You go then. Angela will be showing me everything in a minute, when you've gone to whatever you do on your miserable Saturdays.'

Bill moved nearer to the table, his eyes on the shashka. Angela wouldn't be showing Kenneth that, she couldn't. 'I'm in charge of the whole house in Mr Durban's absence. Mr Durban said that. Go out.' He must keep everything safe.

Kenneth wasn't moving. He hummed a little tune very quietly with a mocking tone, *Run rabbit, run, rabbit, run, run, run,* the song they'd had to sing at junior school to practise hiding from the bombs. At the same time, Kenneth drew out the shashka from its scabbard almost blinding Bill with its reflected sunlight.

'STOP!' Bill gasped, grabbing the hilt from Kenneth who at the same time bent forward in order to hold onto it, using his left hand to wrench it away from Bill. The shashka leapt upwards in Bill's hand meeting something hard. Kenneth screeched and Bill crashed it back down rapidly using his full force to bring it to the table and safety, but Kenneth's right hand was there, clenched around the scabbard.

Whether the shriek came first or the blood, Bill didn't know, but before he'd registered that it was Kenneth the shashka had hit, a fountaining spurt of blood was before his eyes and it took several seconds for him to realise the shashka's blade was now pinning Kenneth's hand to the table, and had almost severed it below the wrist. The shrieking was so terrible that he didn't hear the front door open and Angela's frantic footsteps running towards them. He stood in the same spot, terrified to move for fear the shashka would do worse work, seeing nothing except the brilliance of blood.

He saw Angela take in the sight of him holding the shashka and start to scream.

'Billy! Let it go!'

He looked at his hand on the hilt, a foreign thing, then at Angela as her bulging eyes swivelled to Kenneth, his left hand stuffed in his mouth, blood covering his face and his hand pinioned to the table.

He saw the little heels of her shoes as she pelted straight out of the open front door, screaming for help.

Bill let the shashka fall where it would and Kenneth fell in synchrony, his cricket whites merely a canvas for the crimson display. The knitted V-neck was smothered in blood. Aunty would never forgive him; she'd never get it white again. There were specks, a spotted line, a little lake and the main feature – an arm ending in blood, the hand hanging from it with its long, helpless fingers.

And then there was airiness in the little room, silent inside except for a light gasping from Kenneth's mouth.

Blood was ruining Mr Durban's Afghan rug. Kenneth was unconscious. He should do something, mop up, tourniquet or – he hadn't done war wounds in Scouts. This was more than bloody, like when bodies littered the earth. His feet wouldn't move. His hands stayed halfway in the air, useless. He tossed his head from side to side. He must do something.

Rushing feet into the room took responsibility from him. A man, neighbour, passer-by, knelt down by Kenneth. Another man was running to the kitchen, bringing tea towels. A tablecloth was bound round Kenneth's arm, a cushion under his head. Bill couldn't look directly, he might be sick. A minute, an hour? Then, Angela, still screaming under her breath, came leading men with armbands, who took over. They leaned over the slumped figure, clicked open their first-aid boxes, lifted Kenneth, his legs dangling, one man's strong arms under the damaged arm.

He had a glimpse of shocked, intent faces as they carried Kenneth away, ignoring Bill. But Angela, leaving with them, turned at the door. Her stunned gaze penetrated him like the tip of the shashka.

He was left alone, and the space was terrible. He crouched down, covering his whole head with his arms.

Suddenly the man, the neighbour, was back beside him, pulling at his arms until he unfolded them, pulling him up from his crouch. 'I know you, don't I? Often round here, I've seen you. An accident, wasn't it? Surely an accident. You, a boy like you, you wouldn't have done that on purpose?'

Bill's mouth was dry and his throat closed up. No words would come. His head was hung so far down he could hardly shake it. The floor seemed the safest place to be. He wasn't here. He couldn't be here.

The man pulled him to his feet, still grasping him by the arm. 'You're in a state. We'll go into my house, wait for someone to take you home.'

But as they moved away from the Durban's front door, a police car drew up and its occupants ushered them both indoors again.

CHAPTER 32

SOUTH LONDON COURIER

September 7th 1947

LATEST: Wandsworth Boy Assaults Cousin with Cossack sabre!

William Wilson, fourteen, swiped his orphaned cousin, fifteen-year-old Kenneth Wilson, with a fearsome sabre snatched from the wall of a family friend's room, severely damaging the victim's eye and right hand. Doctors say that Kenneth, a talented artist, has no hope of regaining the use of either eye or hand.

At the South Western Juvenile Court, the accused youth pleaded Not Guilty, claiming it was an accident. The victim, too ill and traumatised to attend Court, also told his mother and investigating officers that it was an accident.

The magistrate heard evidence from

family members and friends and considered the medical reports. Police evidence about the scene of the assault, and interviews with Wilson, formed the major part of the hearing.

It was clear from the scene at the house of Mr P. Durban, that a tussle had occurred. The weapon, an ancient sabre, had been taken from its place on the wall. Evidence showed that only two people had been present in the small room. William Wilson had suffered no injuries himself. He had been a poor interviewee with little to say for himself except that it was an accident.

The victim gained a scholarship to famous Dulwich College just after VE Day. His Headmaster, Mr P.E. Cambridge, described Kenneth Wilson as a very artistic, sensitive boy with delicate health. He was fully expected to make his name in Fine Arts having shown unusual talent from an early age. Mr Cambridge expressed extreme shock and dismay at what had happened to Kenneth.

Mr Herbert Wilson, coincidentally employed as Chief Clerk to the County Court for the last nine years, gave evidence as the father of William, and uncle and acting father of Kenneth. Tragically, Kenneth's own father, Mr Francis Wilson, tax inspector, died in the Balham bombing of 1940, Mr Herbert Wilson then taking on Kenneth as a second son.

When questioned, Mr Herbert Wilson admitted awareness of some past tension between the boys. However, there was no recent sign of discord in the home. The boys had different interests, were at different schools and kept themselves rather separate from each other. His son had never been involved in a previous incident of violence.

William Wilson's Headmaster, Mr A. F. Rundle of St Werberg's School, said that Wilson was a good student, never in trouble. Other boys looked up to him. He had been appointed Head Boy, chosen by the staff for his reliability and common sense. In 1941 during his evacuation, Wilson had shown bravery in saving a small child from drowning. He was a large, strong lad who excelled at football.

Asked whether Wilson had ever needed correction for his behaviour, Mr Rundle said he had not. At his school, bullying or assault is severely punished. Mr Rundle stated, 'I hate saying this, but what this boy has done requires a birching.'

Evidence from Miss Angela Durban, who came upon the sorry scene shortly after the assault, revealed that the two boys were rivals for her attention. After the assault she discovered two identical pin-up posters that both boys had brought her that day.

Mr Peter Durban told the court that the weapon hung in his study. Leaving for a meeting, he had left the house temporarily in the charge of William Wilson, a very frequent visitor there. He expressed the view that William was very unlikely to have initiated a fight.

There was no witness to the attack.

Was the frailer Kenneth in fear of his cousin in whose home he now lived? Mr Herbert Wilson was unable to confirm or deny the possibility of intimidation of Kenneth by William.

When examined, William Wilson admitted he had not been happy when Kenneth became part of his immediate family. He admitted to discomfort with Kenneth's presence in the Durbans' home that fateful day. He remained unable to describe the tussle during which the sabre caused Kenneth's severe injuries. He agreed that he was holding the sabre when he saw the blood spurt out.

On balance, the magistrate felt reluctant to accept either boy's claim that the wounds were accidental: the injuries were too severe. The motive of jealousy suggested itself. William Wilson, though the younger boy, was larger and much stronger and may have seen Kenneth as an invader in his home.

William Wilson was convicted of assault causing grievous bodily harm. The background information and context of the incident suggested that this was an assault made in temper.

Despite William Wilson's former good conduct, the magistrate concluded that a sentence was required.

For such a serious assault with its devastating consequences a penal term was appropriate. Wilson should be sent to a

Juvenile Detention Centre or Approved School where he could receive education and moral guidance. There he could reflect fully upon his offence and consider how best he could redeem himself in the future.

He should spend a minimum of six months at such a Centre, with a review of his behaviour and progress before release.

CHAPTER 33

'You'll have to wait until an Approved School place becomes available. Autumn's always a busy time.' The man was a policeman, taking him in a van away from the Juvenile Court.

He'd arrived in the dark and so had no idea of the size or the shape of the place, but he was at a remand centre, kept separate from whoever else was imprisoned there. Spasmodically, there were loud shouts, words he'd never heard before but obviously swear words, and there were bars. Briefly, he imagined he'd been left in the zoo.

When things were not happening to him, when he was not being told what to do, Bill sat on his bunk, its thin grey blanket reminding him of the time he was first evacuated, the first time he'd felt abandoned by his family. The humilities and discomforts that so shocked him then, were nothing in comparison with now. He knew he could survive discomforts and hardship. It was his thoughts he struggled to survive.

From that one moment when the sun shone viciously on the shashka, he could only think in fragments; each sharp and painful. He thought of them as scenes. That's how they came in the night. Then in the morning he'd know they were not scenes from a nightmare, but from real life.

There was nothing in his life now that wasn't awful, unless it was terrible. He couldn't *not* think however hard he tried, so he switched scenes, going from one to another before any could become too vivid and hurt him so much that he doubled over.

Sometimes the officers would ask if he had stomach-ache. He nodded. He had everything-ache.

How long was it between the accident and seeing his parents? He didn't know. It felt like a week but it might have been next day. He held his head. The first scene was coming:

Scene A – Afterwards. The scene has Mother in a doorway holding Jill's hand, pushing Jill behind her, saving her from contamination. His mother looks at him with horror in her face as if she's never seen him before, not known him, not belonged to him. She says something, some things, but he doesn't hear: her expression shrieks louder than any words. Then Dad comes into the scene. He's coming into the room, in his work suit, the best one with stripes, but his shoes aren't shined. Where was it, that room? It wasn't in a police station but it was bare, with hard chairs and a table where other bad people like Bill had sat and carved signs and letters.

He's sitting, his eyes level with the table's edge where all the carvings are. He can only see one through his blurry eyes, a Chad with the bubble, *Wot No Sympathy*. Then through a grey sound-mist of cleared throats and scraped chairs, there's Dad saying his words. He may have given one of his quotations. Bill hasn't taken it in.

Dad doesn't make Bill look at him or sit any nearer. 'You realise why you can't come home? Even if it wasn't for Jill's safety' – he swallows the word and changes it to – 'well-being, it's Kenneth. We have to be there, visiting him. Later, when he comes out of hospital, however long that takes, everything must be right for him. He mustn't have any fears or anxieties. Home must feel safe. He needs the right atmosphere, no stress, no sound of raised voices, no arguments, nothing like that, given all he'll have to adapt to, with what's happened to him.' His voice tails off, pauses, then lurches into a shout of pain. 'Unforgivable!'

Bill's body jumps, his knee bashes against the table edge.

'My brother's boy, the pride of his life! I promised to look after him as my own and it's my own that has nearly killed him,' the voice subsides to a whisper, 'and killed what was best in him.'

Bill's shivering. The room's empty but for the chair and table. A person entering, takes his shoulder, pushes him towards the door, away, somewhere. The voices behind him fade to agonised whispers.

Another scene, was it the same room? If not, it's closely similar. Police talking. Bill's retained nothing else of the scene, only the sense of internal horror.

Bedtime is the most desirable part of his day but then there's the tossing and refusal of sleep to come. When it does, in his dreams, the cold, damp forehead signals Scene H.

Scene H is Hospital, Dad marching him down towards a glass-topped door. Jill is sitting with a *Girl's Own* open on her lap on a hard wooden chair in the corridor, looks up, eyes widening. She mouths 'Bill!' almost to herself.

Now he's in the ward. White curtains surround several beds but there are none around Kenneth's. Bandages, tubes, bottle and enamel pan sit on the bedside cabinet. Mother, Aunty are on either side of the bed.

Dad pushes him forwards towards the lump in the lower part of the bed. Bill can't make himself look at any higher part where the tubes and bandages are.

Dad's hand hard in the small of Bill's back, his voice soft, 'Kenneth, my boy. Bill's come to say how – dreadfully sorry he is. Are you willing to hear him?'

No sound from the bed, except a slight rustle of bedclothes.

The hard hand pushes. A choke's got Bill's throat, his cheeks are red hot but his whole body freezing cold. He can't look, he won't. Another choke, another push, then he manages, 'I'm d-dreadfully sorry. It was – you know it was – an accident.' And in a tiny voice, '...Kenneth.'

Silence from the bed.

Aunty breaking down, running outside.

Dad shoving him in the back, getting him out of the ward, into the corridor. Jill running away.

Aunty pulling at his jumper, her whisper becoming a scream, 'His beautiful face. And his hand, his drawing hand, Bill.'

A windowsill, hands over his ears, his face, forehead pressed to the windowpane. The cold damp of it.

He wakes, stifling his own scream.

Scene B is Blood. This can start at any time. He has to screw up his eyes to make everything blur so that he can't see things clearly. Blood trickles down the windowpanes when it rains, onto his porridge instead of milk. At night, blood from Kenneth's hand mixes with the bodies around Ted in the sea at Dunkirk, with the soldiers bombed into the mud of Italy, the fields of Russian dead where Mr Durban is given the shashka. It slashes at mounted Germans whose arms or ears fall off gushing blood, the same scarlet hue as the fountain from Kenneth's wrist, pooling around those whitening fingers.

P is the Police scene. A large policeman stares at him over a table. He's been talking. Saying something, then, 'There's a social worker coming for you, because your father thinks it would be better.'

Bill stands up, of course he does, when she's shown into the room but he keeps his eyes on her clothes. It's dangerous to look at anyone's face. The dark-haired woman is plump, wearing clothes that Mother would never have worn even for war work in the garage. Her jacket doesn't do up and the hem of her skirt is wavy. Aunty would say that she hadn't turned it up well. Dad would say she wasn't turned out well.

'William Wilson, is it?' She is speaking to the policeman who opened the door for her, as if Bill isn't reliable enough to answer to his own name. Probably criminals pretend their names are something different. Criminals lie.

The policeman nods. 'The dad's on his way. The mum's at the hospital with the victim's mother. The kids are cousins. *Dad,*' his voice gains a heavily sarcastic note, 'is Clerk to the Court.'

'No! A pretty pickle!' She nods, and the policeman leaves her to it, to Bill.

'William. I'm Mrs–' (*Lunt, Lamb, Lowe - does it matter?*) 'You can tell me anything that troubles you. I come here for young people who don't have a parent with them. Feel free to talk to me.' (*She might be smiling. Smiling!*) 'It'll be me who takes you to your placement.'

He stares at the table. Someone's carved a cross on it with a dagger.

He can't remember the rest.

Scene R. Road. There must have been something which happened between the remand centre or police cell, he doesn't know which, and the dormitory, but all he remembers is the Road. It's long. Driving along it is the dingy woman who sat in the empty interview rooms with him, talking, expecting him to talk. Bill doesn't look out of the windows to watch the dirt of London become seductive countryside, but focusses on her pudgy hands controlling the car, in charge of what must happen.

An hour, or maybe a month, passes.

She speaks, a man's voice in a stocky woman's body: 'We're here, William, Brigville School. Stiff upper lip. It'll be all right. It's not as tough as a Borstal. Luckily, you're too young for that. The Approved School has football, you know.'

He didn't know, doesn't know anything. He'd never heard of Borstal before it was mentioned in Court. It could have been a pig pen for all he knew.

The long roadway, the large fine building, reminds him at first of the Priory Grammar School where Kenneth had his Art displayed. His first and last display. A shudder goes through Bill. It loosens his shoulders.

The car stops. The woman opens his car door. It had been locked. 'Come along.'

He climbs out stiffly. Outside it's bright sun, but cold, very cold. When had it stopped being summer? Blue sky surrounds stark trees, their vicious arms pointing to the sky. They sway in a keen wind, sigh to him, *Look what you've done. You know who's looking down on you. God. Jesus. My son died for you, suffered on the cross. He bore the wounds for you.* He shudders. *My son, my son.* Uncle Frank in bits, knowing what Bill's done to his son, waiting to mete out the punishment.

He comes to. This is real, he's not in a nightmare. S is something ahead of him, unknown. S for school, *Approved School*, approved for boys as bad as he is. This is not a scene, it's a sentence. His.

Attend! He told himself to pay attention. Unlike his school, this building was surrounded by high walls. A wide path led towards the arch and through to the large front door with a glass porch the size of a greenhouse but with a desk and hatch instead of plants.

The social work woman marched him on, the gravel crunching under her feet like discarded bones. 'Up these steps, now.'

He looked at the brick arch. Behind it, well set back, a wall of windows and a huge front door. Far to the right a cemented area surrounded by fencing. Wire stretched high towards a mean sky, whose blue was smeared with grey, like Kenneth's rough paper where he cleaned his paintbrush.

Right now at St Werberg's, boys would be sitting at their desks learning French verbs. Bill's name would be scrubbed from the register in thick black ink. In the playground, they'd whisper about their ex-Head Boy, ex-football captain.

'Any questions, before we go in?' Unlike his school, this building was surrounded by high walls.

'When will I be going home?'

'That will be discussed in the next few months.'

'Months! Are my parents going to visit me here?'

'You will have visits. Don't expect any the first week or so, though.'

They walked up the flight of stone steps between pillars and towards doors. Inside were men, hatches, shiny wooden tables, papers for the woman to sign, corridors. The woman stopped at a windowed counter, spoke to someone, showed documents.

She stayed beside him as he was taken to Reception.

Another man inside spoke quite a lot, but Bill didn't take in anything until he said, 'So what have you brought with you, Bill?'

He'd been too overwhelmed to think about what might have come with him. For a dreadful moment he thought there might be a bloodied shirt, like evidence of his crime. Somewhere, he had been provided with a small case (was it from home?) that he hadn't packed himself. When it was unpacked at the desk, he was amazed to see his Dutch history book in it. His hand shot out towards something he knew, a hand that surely didn't belong to him.

'No, we'll keep all this for the moment.'

Apart from a sponge bag, his possessions were labelled and taken away.

'You'll get them back.' The man turned to the social worker and they spoke to each other, or was it to him? He felt in his pocket. At least he had his bit of green and white napkin.

The wavy hem moved nearer to him. 'William, I'm going to leave you now. Mr – the name sounded and immediately disappeared from his mind – will get you sorted out. I'm sure you'll want to do well here. You must do your best. Make things up to your poor family. Perhaps I'll see you when you finish your term.'

She put a hand on his shoulder. It felt kindly enough, but meaningless.

Then she went, her footsteps sounding rhythmically down the length of the corridor. A door slammed behind her, keys jangled. The day was shut out.

'We'll get you installed, then.' The man opened the door and led him down the corridor and to a wooden staircase. There was now an upstairs part. He had to undress, shower, put on their clothes, the school clothes, muddy brown Brigville School clothes. And they didn't fit.

'Can I keep my handkerchief?'

'Yes, we won't want that.'

With relief, Bill squeezed his handkerchief tight, knowing the napkin piece was safe inside it.

The man took him to another room, furnished, this one: a desk, easy chairs, framed photographs on the wall, a shield. The man said, 'William Wilson, sir,' and went away.

Bill stood at the desk. Behind it, a teacher, head teacher, social work man, he didn't take in who he was, spoke to him about reforming boys' ways; turning from the bad towards good, education, training, discipline, rules, sanctions. It was probably wise and important stuff, but it didn't make sense to him because everything was like a dreadful headache that stopped you attending to anything else.

There was something about bullying, but since he hadn't been a bully or even been bullied much, it wasn't relevant to him, was it? Other boys something or other. Yes, he had heard their voices down the corridor.

The man ordered him to think hard about what he had done, how he must knuckle down, change. He rang a buzzer on his desk.

Back came the other man to take him down another corridor. There was a dormitory, empty of boys. 'They're at supper.'

His bed was next to the door. Beside it, there was a box for his things, empty. 'Now you know where you'll be. But tonight you sleep in here.'

Down the corridor was a small room with a small table, a hard chair, a towel hung over its back. He put his sponge bag down.

'We'll keep you apart for the moment. Just stay in here tonight, get used to being here. We'll put you with the other boys tomorrow. There'll be lessons. You'll learn to fit in.' The man left him.

Later, he was given a meal, a comic. The day ended, eventually, and the dark night began.

CHAPTER 34

In the morning he was taken to the shower area, then a dormitory where eleven other boys were making their beds. 'This is Bill Wilson. Help him settle in.'

The boys were being supervised so they said nothing, but their eyes said everything. He saw curiosity, dislike, aggression and challenge in their expressions. Settle in? How was he going to ask the way when he got lost in this place, or if they could pass the salt in the dining room? What would they be like, once there was no supervision?

He soon found that there was always supervision. He didn't have to ask for what he needed. The tin dishes held what they must eat. He didn't have to ask any questions. They were told exactly what to do. It wasn't a dining room, but a room for eating, with a hatchway to the kitchen. Boys talked, but didn't laugh. An officer walked around the benches.

Afterwards, there was lining up. They filed outside. The order came to spread out. Each boy stretched out his arms, making sure he couldn't touch the next. A whistle blew. Exercises began, a teacher demonstrating in front. Feet apart, feet together. Arms up, arms down. Apart, together. Apart, together. Up, down. Up, down, faster, faster, faster. Exercises stopped at two blasts of the whistle for lining up again. The line marched indoors, along a corridor with whitish walls and sick green paintwork.

'Morning lessons,' the boy next to him whispered.

'New boy?' the supervising officer came alongside. 'Spell *lesson.*' He waited. 'Correct! What is elevenpence ha'penny plus threepence?' He raised an eyebrow. 'Correct. You're in here, then, top class,' and he opened the end door of three.

'Posh, ain't yer,' whispered the boy again, turning into the first door.

Sheets of printed sums were on the desks inside the room Bill had been assigned. A teacher pointed to the desks, said, 'Sit' and told them to work in silence, but most boys disobeyed. The work was easy and he finished quickly, putting his hands on his lap.

'Don't do that, stupid!' the boy next to him muttered. 'You'll only get given more.'

Before he could pick up his pencil again, the teacher handed him another sheet of sums.

Later, the teacher put a map on the board and talked about it. Bill thought about the boys at St Werberg's and how far away they were now.

He began to revisit the Court scene in his head, what the magistrate said and perhaps that social work woman had repeated, something about his 'term'. A boy at breakfast had asked how long Bill was in for. For the first time he focussed on that idea, *term*. It was six months. When would six months end? He didn't know the date now, so couldn't work it out. Looking around at the bare beige walls, glossy with layers of bad paint, he could see that calendars were not the sort of thing that would be pinned up. There wasn't even a picture, only the times tables on a piece of cardboard and a list of the English counties. He struggled to think of the last time he had known the date. He couldn't remember when summer holidays had ended. Had he started the Autumn term at school? Who was Head Boy now?

The teacher was asking questions. He didn't know any answers.

'Have you been listening?'

'Yes, sir.' A lie. He was a liar now. But he needed to know when he would be leaving here. He needed to have a date in his mind. It was very important. He put his hand in his pocket, to feel the piece of napkin.

'And where is Egypt?'

Bill pointed to the map.

'Next to—?'

He couldn't say which country sat next to it, but none of the other boys could either.

'I've just been telling you all these countries, boys. Sit up! Listen!'

The lesson went on, and Bill still hadn't managed to calculate what date he'd leave here.

After a lunch slopped into those tin dishes that would have appalled Mother, they were allowed in an outside area with wire on top of the walls, where a ball could be kicked around. He joined in, but the game was just an opportunity for boys to thump each other under cover. Old scores were being settled and new ones set up. Larger boys eyed him before kicking out at his shins. It was to see what he would do back. He was glad when the whistle went.

Back in the classroom, there was an officer in charge instead of the teacher. He pointed to their chairs and said they could write their letters.

Bill began to write eagerly, *Dear Nanny and Grandad,* but then dropped his pencil as if it had cut him. Mother's hushed tones came into in his head, 'I shan't tell my parents, Herbert. I can't. It would kill them.' Where did she say that? The hospital, the court, the interview room?

His hand pushed his pencil away. The news might kill the Pawseys too. And Mrs Youldon wouldn't want Sally and Timmy to know about such a thing. Who would understand how *that* could happen by accident? How could he write to anyone without telling them where he was, and why?

Mr Durban was the only one who knew, but he'd never want to even think about Bill again. The awful thing had happened at his house. The rug! It had been ruined; blood staining the precious photographs on the table; the memorabilia room left in chaos. At the Juvenile Court, Mr Durban was criticised for leaving his sabre on display. He'd had to admit under oath that Bill had been 'very taken' with it. The magistrate had changed that to 'obsessed' and made Mr

Durban agree. The Durbans would all hate him. Bill couldn't possibly write to them.

He looked at the empty sheet of lined paper.

'Jeez, I can't spell neither,' said the freckled boy next to him. 'Just write what it sounds like. A lot of the boys here are illiterate. We're the bright set. Anyway, the officers censor everything you write, so you can't say what you really mean.'

Bill twiddled his fingers under the desk. Who could he write to, and what could he say? 'What sort of thing are you writing then?' he asked the boy.

'I'll write slogans, and some of them will get through. I'll write my news in between them, and my mum'll work out what's happening. Like she writes bits between silly sentences to let me know the latest about the uprisings.'

'Uprisings?'

'Sure – I'm only here to stop me taking part in them. I'm Irish, can't you tell?'

He did have a funny accent that was a lot nicer than Cockney. His face was jollier, too.

'So I'm a political prisoner, not a criminal like you lot.'

Criminal! That's what he was now. 'Is everyone here criminal?' Some of the boys were small and didn't look evil.

'Some are just absconders but there's thieves and murderers, too! Him at the back with the black hair and eyebrows.' He gave a cheery wink. 'Done his Ma in with a brick. And I got wind that you done near that with a sword.'

'No!'

'That's enough. No talk of your offences. You know the rules.' The officer walked slowly between each of them with the measured step of a policeman on his beat, his footsteps keeping time with the thump of Bill's heart.

Bill shook his head, the only gesture he could make to show the boy he wasn't a murderer.

The officer's tread, one, two, one, two, stopped beside him. 'You not writing, lad? I heard you were one of those who could.'

Bill picked up his pencil again and twiddled it until it became hot and damp in his hand.

'I don't know who to write to,' he muttered to his neighbour.

'Just anyone, or it's a cert you won't get any letters back.'

The only person he could risk writing to was Alan. He might tear the letter up; he might never reply. He could hear Mother in his head again: 'Everyone we've ever met will read those newspaper reports'. Alan's mother would have seen the newspaper. She'd be horrified. Alan would never, never be in this kind of trouble. But if Bill said it was an accident, Alan would know that it was. He scribbled away at length pretending he and Alan were together. At the bottom he wrote, *Please, please, answer. Tell Mrs Youldon I'm away at school and ask her to tell Mrs Pawsey that.* (That was best and true-ish.) Else they'd wonder why his letters had stopped. They'd think he'd forgotten them. He kicked the heel of one boot into the front of his foot several times. It hurt quite a lot and he deserved it.

Somehow, a week passed, or maybe two. He was now a Brigville School boy. On a pouring wet Tuesday, normally when fierce Mr Sandson (nicknamed Samson) led vigorous PT lessons outside, they couldn't go out into the paved yard and the letters were handed out. One came for Bill, his first. Alan had replied! The letter was short. It had already been opened and one sentence blotted out with a thick blue line.

Alan wrote that he was still Bill's friend, but wasn't allowed to write again until Bill had completed his sentence. At first Bill thought Alan was joking about missing a full stop, but then he remembered that 'sentence' was the thing he was 'serving'. That meant being shut away with other bad boys, where no-one could see him. Alan said he missed him. It was the only bright spot since all this terrible stuff started. Alan said he hoped Brigville was 'not too bad' and that there were decent history books in the library. 'Remember knights.'

He almost smiled. It was a coded message. It reminded of a good, laughing time when Alan told him a good knight needed the three things: the brave man's weapon, the wise man's book, the flower from the faithful lover. That Dutch history book was in the case Brigville had shut away, too wise for an Approved School boy. He wouldn't touch any kind of weapon now, however brave its owner, and he'd never have the flower, for who would love someone like him?

He kept the letter in his pocket with the piece of green and white napkin. Even though it was short, just knowing that Alan was still friendly made the following days bearable, and the idea of reading up about knights gave him something new to think about.

Many boys were hardly able to read or manage anything as difficult as long division and so most daily lessons were of little use to Bill. After many lessons sitting blankly with his finished work, he was provided with a stack of books and left to get on with things himself. Eventually he plucked up courage and asked for a text book on photography.

'When you've earned enough privileges.' Several books were put in front of him. 'You can have these textbooks to study.'

Bill read through the books as if they were set lessons. He actually missed those hours of studying at St Werberg's. These books had been donated, their previous owners sometimes named on the inside cover. They were a strange mix, none of them books for children. *My Travels through Kurdistan*; *Handicraft for Beginners*; *Business Administration*; *Poems to Comfort the Bereaved*; *A History of England, Book II, Tudors and Stuarts*; *Cats and their Care*; *Steelwork in Sheffield.* There was nothing about knights.

In the evening free hour, before supper, he read a library book, *Missing Chums* or *Dick Tracy* and pretended he was at home in the parlour. But the click-click of table tennis and the raised voices of boys waiting their turn to play as well as the frequent tussles and fights made that difficult.

As well as lessons, meal-times, exercises, the rota of tasks, there was football. After the first joyous moment of his foot touching the ball, the roughness of the game and the need for constant intervention of the supervising officer meant he couldn't pretend he was back playing with his friends at St Werberg's. After a few more evening games, the officer tapped him on the shoulder and told him to 'give the others a chance'. After the game ended, he said to 'forget being a star'.

So now football was something else where Bill might do the wrong thing. Until then, he'd always gone full out to play his best.

Visits were allowed after the initial month. It was another trauma; to have to face Mother and Dad for the first time since Juvenile Court.

The room that visitors saw was the neatest and cleanest in the school. There were some easy chairs as well as several small tables with hard chairs around them. He had made himself as smart as he could in the dreary brown uniform and paced in behind the other boys who had visitors.

Dad had chosen one of the tables to sit at. He was looking straight ahead. Mother sat close beside him, holding onto his arm and it was some moments before their wary glance at the boys entering the room latched onto his face.

He came forward and sat opposite them in the third chair.

'Are you well?' Dad said.

Bill nodded. 'Yes, thank you.'

Dad, perhaps *Father* now. *Dad* was surely far too friendly for a boy like Bill to use? Dad sat with his feet firmly planted either side of the table's metal legs. Was he assessing how far Bill had reformed?

'You're doing lessons.'

Nod. What point was there talking about Business *Administration* or *Steelwork in Sheffield,* books that now formed his education?

'Do they talk to you – about what you did? The wrongs you have to think about during your time here?'

Swallow. 'Yes.' There was Mr Jones on a Wednesday who saw him on his own, and the religious assemblies covered most sins.

Bill had rehearsed a list of worthwhile tasks he had performed to convince his parents he was reforming, but now the words wouldn't come out.

'You look well enough,' said Mother in a tone that suggested that he shouldn't. 'There's enough to eat, then?'

'Yes, thank you.'

'You realise the whole thing has been in the newspapers, especially after the Hearing. There have been Letters to the Editor, even articles about it.'

Bill hung his head, imagining everyone reading about it, everyone he knew, his parents knew. How they would have hated it.

'It's been the most dreadful time of our lives.'

'Yes,' he choked out. 'Dreadfully sorry.'

There was a long pause, an expectant one. Before this visit he'd worried about what questions he might risk asking. He longed not to ask any, it would be best not to know the answers, but then they'd say he didn't care about the consequences of the accident, that was called an 'offence' here. The real question: *How is Kenneth?* was obviously ridiculous to ask. Such an everyday question was probably denied to him forever, for the answer would never be *Very Well.* But he must ask something. He opened his mouth. Before he could get the first words out, Mother leaned forward over the ink-stained table top.

'You realise that people blame us?' Her eyes were watering.

It was terrible to see that. She was properly upset, not just being upset like when Uncle Frank had died. He tried to take in what she had just said. Blame. But that was what he had. Blame was his.

Dad put one hand over his beard as if to protect it. He was going to say something, quote something. But no, he gave his own words. 'The theory, for what it's worth, is that when children go wrong it's because of faulty parenting.' He looked around the room as if it was the Court, with benches of people waiting to hear the words of the judge. 'What a travesty of understanding! However, this view is what your mother and I are faced with. Despite my position as a senior officer of the County Court, I am derided behind my back, looked down upon by those much lower in social class.'

Bill stared hard at a point somewhere below Dad's beard, glazing his eyes deliberately, willing them not to fill with tears, his ribs pushing at his chest.

Dad's finger jabbed towards him and wagged once, twice. 'You should be made aware of this theory. You may wish to contradict it – at least in your own case.'

He must answer. With the right words. He choked out, 'I'll say it's not your fault.'

Mother's voice was clear enough for other parental heads to turn, 'No, indeed.' She turned to Dad, as if it was he who needed the explanation. 'He was evacuated for years, that's what I explain to people. I had no influence.'

A tea trolley rattled along the corridor. Teachers would be given tea and a slice of dry fruit cake. Soon afterwards, boys would file to the dining room for bread, margarine, a hard-boiled egg and an apple. Brigville School was careful to provide for the boys' health.

'No influence.' Bill tried to absorb what was being said and not being said. Mother was blaming Mrs Pawsey for influencing him?

'Indulged. That's what you were at that place.' Mother spat confirmation of his thoughts.

Dad's beard was being stroked into place by his large hand. It had become a character in its own right, like a crown on a king, or a cap on a dunce. Dad's voice emerged above it. 'That ruined your character, apparently. Under the surface. We'd never have known. The school thought you reliable, made you a prefect even! Head Boy!' He snorted. 'They never knew either, never noticed a thing. No sign of this – canker.'

Canker had been mentioned in the cat book, but Bill couldn't remember quite what it was. He pulled his earlobe, which was flaming hot. Weren't earlobes the things that police looked at to see if you were a criminal? They could get hot, red, give you away.

'And we didn't notice, Herbert. Did we? We even though him reliable, Doreen did too. She trusted him even more than I did.'

Was he supposed to hear this conversation? Was he part of it? He shifted his feet. Size ten now. Shoes had been provided when he'd arrived, so Mother needn't know just yet. His size had always upset her.

'I ask myself, would I walk down the street with you now? No, I wouldn't!' Mother moved her hand from Dad's arm and folded both hands on top of the table. She was wearing gloves. 'And what have you got to say? Sitting there silent! Don't you want to ask our forgiveness?'

He'd wanted to ask if he'd be coming home soon. But now he saw they wouldn't want people seeing him in Primley Road, the reminder that Mr and Mrs Wilson had a son with a bad character.

He stuttered a start, 'If I w-walk along on m-my own …,' then managed, 'When I'm finished here, am I coming home?'

Dad coughed and fumbled for his handkerchief. He blew his nose.

On the easy chair nearest to them a woman was saying, 'Yes,

Robbie's had his party, but you'll be having yours when you come home, lovey. Promise.'

It was a sudden reminder. His birthday was in October. Wasn't it October now?

Mother twitched. 'At home, it's a matter of Kenneth needing one of us all the time, being there.'

The beard shifted a little. The voice came through it. 'Decisions must come later. In the light of events.'

A bell sounded as if to emphasise his non-words. Dong, dong, dong.

Chairs scraped on the floor. Visitors were preparing for their sad goodbyes, choking back their tears, or in Bill's case, their release.

Dad stood up, placing his chair back under the table with precision. Mother was occupied in handbag rearrangement and negotiation of the fifteen steps to the door.

Bill couldn't manage to come out with the, *Will you come again?*

Mother said, 'Goodbye, Bill.'

Other mothers, fussing, 'Be brave, dear. We miss you so much.' One wiping her eyes. 'I'll write often, lovey pet.'

Other boys were saying, 'Don't go yet.'

A son, mother, their hands clasping, 'Be a good boy. It won't be long.'

Dad lowered his head towards Bill, allowing him a shared breath of tobacco smell, '*Ordinary people merely think how they should spend time; a man of talent tries to use it*. Schopenhauer. I have always tried to guide you with moral thinkers.'

'Yes, Dad, I know.' He had, he always had.

'So spend your time well, and thoughtfully.'

Spend? Surely it was *serve* your time. The door closed behind Dad, the last parent to leave.

CHAPTER 35

They never knew the date for there were no calendars but Bill realised it was his birthday when the post was given out. Dad had forwarded two birthday cards to him with his one of his own, a photograph of Wandsworth that stated *Greetings*. Even Dad couldn't imply that today would be a happy birthday. The second card was from the Youldons and the third from the Pawseys. They didn't know what he'd done, of course. There wasn't one from Nanny and Grandad. At tea-time, his tin tray had a slice of cake with jam in it. The nearest bully nabbed it off him as the warden turned to the table behind. Somehow, he didn't care.

October ended, the weeks after it rolled by, then the winter began. Because of the electricity cuts and the vicious winter of the year past, a dread of its repetition prevented the whole school from thinking of anything else. Christmas Day jollities were minimal and Boxing Day was the coldest day of all.

When February brought snow, the early thrill of being allowed out to build snowmen soon waned when they came indoors to the failed heating. Shivering in classrooms was like a new punishment that the grown-ups had to share.

The teachers, wrapped in scarves and blanket wraps, peering through balaclavas, were in the worst of moods. They said they could hardly face 1948, for they'd remember winter 1947 for the rest of their lives.

'So will we!' murmured the boys who'd been there the longest, 'and not just for the cold.'

For Bill, the Brigville routine kept things manageable. Everything was thought out and Bill just had to do it all; obey.

When he sat on his hard bed at night facing the door, he went through all the awful things in Brigville life: the bullying, the punishments, discomforts, friendlessness, isolation from all he'd known, it was the lack of any personal possessions that felt worst. He'd been lonely and sad before, but not guilty and without absolutely everything he owned except the scrap of napkin he kept hidden inside the day's handkerchief.

In evacuation, he'd comforted himself with a photograph of the shashka. Then it had been stolen from him. Next it was used to try to turn Mr Durban against him. Then the shashka itself had turned against Bill. It had fulfilled the dreadful prophecy written in the ancient book.

What could comfort him now? Only his camera, with its one promise of a future beyond dread and shame. Photographs were in black and white; something you could understand. How long a wait before he saw it again? Or would Dad throw it away as a punishment?

~

After his second review, Bill was interviewed by the governor about his future. All the boys were encouraged to think of an occupation they could work towards once they were released. The Brigville School concern was that they shouldn't continue a life of crime. 'When you're released, we don't want you back here, and you don't want prison as a future.'

The Governor, as the boys liked to call him, had Bill brought into his study. He discussed the wounding, the damaging of Kenneth, the effect on his life, on his parents' lives, on Aunty. Bill kept his hands clasped behind his back, his eyes on the floor where he pressed his heavy regulation shoes down as hard as possible to prevent him swaying to and fro. He nodded from time to time, to show the Governor his understanding, his agreement. He stood as he'd learned a guilty man should.

'Right. Now, before your offence, Wilson, I gather you were studying successfully at school, expected to get leaving exams, then move on to some sort of professional life like your father. When you leave here you will still be fifteen. Many boys leave school on their birthday but technically you're not too old for the end of that last school year, School Certificate year. However, it might be difficult to get a school to take you. Your reputation will go before you.'

Bill had never considered returning to school as a possibility. All his focus had been on surviving the experience of Brigville. He hadn't dared to look ahead. He almost laughed at the idea of returning to St Werberg's – a preposterous notion. He could go to work. He'd shown himself to be useful but what employer would take him, and where? 'Sir, am I to go home?'

The Governor placed his hands on his desk, about two foot apart from each other. His nails were square and beautifully kept. 'When you've finished your term? I assume so. What do you mean?'

'My parents may not want me. I mean, they have Kenneth living with them.'

'Ah.' The skin above his eyebrows was loose enough for folds to come and go. They did so now. 'Well. There are hostels for boys like you. Have you thought about your future?'

'No, sir.' Since he'd been here, Bill had only thought about leaving each day behind.

'I want you to think now. You will have to earn your living as soon as possible. What do you see yourself as doing?'

Relief. That question was easy. 'Before this happened, sir, I was hoping to be a photographer. I need to practise. I have a camera and manuals, but they're at home.'

'I'll contact your father. You realise that you cannot use a camera here, but I'll allow you to have the manuals. When they are brought, you can study them after classes each day.'

His parents were due to visit in a few days' time. Would they agree to bring the manuals? The visits were something to dread. By now, the shame of what had happened, the suffering Bill had caused to each member of his family had been so thoroughly rehearsed with him that he knew it better than times tables or French verbs. And yet he didn't know it at all. Words such as guilt, pain, suffering, anguish, embarrassment, endurance, shame, responsibility, were said over and over, but never an incident or example that would make these real to him. He was expected to know, without being told, what those words meant was happening. Were people shouting at Mother in the street, bullying Dad in the Court? What dreadful things were being done by doctors to Kenneth? He didn't know any incidents, yet he felt he was perspiring his family's pain and shame through every one of his pores. Aunty was never ever mentioned. She must hate Bill so much, her fury too intense for even Dad to risk telling him about it.

Although he'd been told that Approved School was his punishment, the visits were actually far worse. As excitement rose among the boys, even a 'Yippee!' when the announcement came: 'Visiting Time', Bill lined up with dread, envying the boys with no visits who sat on their beds with morose expressions.

Yet, on the day of the next visit Bill saw immediately that Dad had brought the manuals. He placed them on the desk.

'Thank you. Thank you very much.'

Bill knew they meant nothing to Dad, no more than if they had been *Robinson Crusoe* or *Biggles Flies Again*.

'I gather you're allowed to study these after lessons?'

'Yes. It's like an earned privilege.'

Mother said, 'Just as well to keep your head in a book. You can't risk making friends with these boys. Such a dreadful influence.' She'd never understood loneliness. He'd been lonely at home when he was very little and wasn't allowed friends home. He'd felt lonely that first evacuation when she didn't find where he'd been billeted, and the second time when she let him be billeted away from the rest of them. He missed his friends, especially Alan. Even if the boys here were rough and dishonest, he needed to be friends with at least some of them.

'I dread to think what you'll be like when you get out.'

Dad added, 'I trust you're reflecting on those matters that you need to change in yourself?'

'Yes. We get told that sort of thing most days.'

'Because you have to think of that time when you're no longer at Approved School.'

'I do. The Governor is allowing me to study my photography because that's what I'm going to do when I get out – be a photographer.'

Mother looked stunned. 'That seems a long way ahead.'

Dad said, 'You can't just begin a career as though nothing has happened. You'll need to be accepted by some sort of employer, and that won't be easy. The first thing is your base. After your sentence has been worked you'll need a base.'

'To live?'

'Yes. Somewhere.'

That meant, not home.

He didn't take in the rest of the halting conversation. He tried to remember the chapter he'd reached in the photography manual. Something to do with arranging the light.

When the bell went he was sure he heard a joint sigh of relief pass between Dad and Mother. It was time for them to line up with the other parents, none of them acknowledging the others, shuffling out like refugees from the normal world.

'I shall study about light and shade,' he said to their retreating backs.

'We must be willing to let go of the life we planned so as to have the life that is waiting for us,' E. M. Forester,' said Dad.

They said their goodbyes and left Bill to consider each of their few words and all of their meanings.

CHAPTER 36

The officer turned the key and the first door opened. They walked together down the corridor, out of step. This man wasn't one of the teachers, those who set exercises, talked about how to do better, how to make changes, but one of the supervisors who checked boys were in the right place, or broke up fights, chased after anyone stupid enough to run away and held a boy down if he had to be caned. Bill had always avoided this man, for he looked as if he really didn't like boys at all.

The man paused before the second door, clicking his keys in his hand. 'This is it for you, then, Wilson. An out.'

Bill shuffled his feet. The shoes were too shabby for the miracle that had happened to him, too shabby for words. Surely, when he saw him, his rescuer would change his mind.

'You're a lucky blighter. Not just because someone's willing to take you on, but because of your age. A few months older and you'd probably have had a birching for your offence. Birching is *real* character building. That would have cooled your temper. I reckon the magistrate up your part of London has gone soft. We've never had an offence in here like it! Next time...' His voice trailed off with almost a snarl. 'Reckon you'll do it again?'

Bill took a step back. 'Of course not! It was an accident.'

A snort. 'Yeah! I was told. With a sabre. Just appeared in your hand like magic, a sabre. Did for the kid's eye and hand. Your cousin, wasn't it? Accident? Yeah! Marvellous.'

The man turned the key. It was twice forwards, once back. Then the door opened, all the great thickness of it, cranking to the outside. Sunlight, of a sort, fell in. There was glass in the porch window where it said, *Reception* and lower down, *Please show identity document*. Bill could just about remember arriving here. The calendar looked the same, plain, white, the top sewn onto a cardboard backing, but it wasn't. It now said, March 1948, the first time he'd seen a date since – when? He looked around, as if the woman who'd brought him might materialise. She'd stopped at this porch, that came before the corridors, the taking away of things, the undressing, the school clothes.

Now he was wearing his own clothes. The small case and all its contents had been brought to him before he left the dormitory and the bed near the door for another boy. A boy coming to an Approved school for boys who were not approved of.

His clothes felt tight, formal. He had once worn these things, and when wearing them, he'd done a terrible thing, made a terrible accident happen to Kenneth. He looked down at the blue-green jersey which Angela had liked him in. Now she wouldn't. It would always remind her of what he'd done. His grey trousers, his first and only long ones, ended above his ankles. He could see marks where he'd knelt on Mr Durban's floor, even specks of blood, Kenneth's blood. He'd been allowed to keep the school shoes since his own no longer fitted. He walked them forward, bringing to the exit the huge feet for Mother to hate.

Papers, keys, signings. That's what the porter was doing at the reception hatch when he came. But now he was moving to the outer door, swinging it open, telling Bill not to come back. 'The gentleman's waiting for you in his car.'

An open door. The pillars, stone staircase. Outside. Nothing in between him and the swathe of grass behind the gravelled road. Air, sky, space.

. . .

It seems very bright, though it's cold and the sky's grey. Bill screws up his eyes, dazzled. A voice comes through the faint sunlight.

'Bill! Come on, lad, I'm here now.'

It sounds kind and it's familiar. So is the jacket. That comes nearer to him until he can touch it. Like a small child, he holds a piece. He's seeing whether it's real. Behind him, papers have been signed, official words spoken, but it doesn't matter because he's standing on the right side, the outside, with Mr Durban next to him. It really is Mr Durban. All that the Governor said had come true. Mr Durban is collecting him, giving him a home.

They walk to the gate. Mr Durban lights a cigarette. Bill breathes in the smoke hungrily, so very long since he's smelled it, Craven A. He swivels his eyes sideways, gets a view of his rescuer, his oldest friend.

Mr Durban's got a car now. It's black. He opens a door and touches Bill, pushes him into the passenger seat.

The smell of leather is overwhelming. The dashboard is familiar. The car's the same make and model as the woman's car that brought him here.

Mr Durban slides into the driving seat.

Bill hangs his head. How can he say a whole lifetime of Sorry? He chokes out, 'I'm really sorry.'

'It was my fault, Bill. Mine. I shouldn't have had it there, or left you alone with it in the house. I got into terrible trouble.'

He remembers, coming out of the Court, as he was put in a bare room, Dad's voice, raging, 'You never told me! If you'd said he was obsessed with the wretched thing, I could have dealt with him.'

'It was an accident,' Bill mutters, pathetic even to himself.

'I know. And Kenneth said. A terrible accident. But—'

There's the <u>but</u>. Bill's had time, months of hours on his own to think of the <u>but</u>. The magistrate sentenced on the basis of the <u>but</u>, the secret thought 'but I hated Kenneth at that moment. He was always taking everything, like my friends, Jill, the photo, Angela, and he was taking the shashka.'

It was the shashka that took the wounding thoughts and made the frightful incision. Bill can still play football, still take photographs, while Kenneth—

'What can I do, now?'

'To put it right?' Mr Durban takes a cloth and rubs the windscreen free of smears. 'Lead a good life. Your parents want that more than anything. You must be rehabilitated. I've got the responsibility for that now.'

'But Mrs Durban?'

'She's agreed and it's all been arranged with your family. You're to live with us.'

'In your house?' He'd imagined some bare room or two that Mr Durban would supervise, not a house. Not his house, the place where it happened! How could Mr Durban let him through the door again?

'You'll have the spare bedroom.'

'Angela—?' Angela would never want to see him again. That last look as she turned back to him before she left the bloodied lounge, following the stretcher with Kenneth on it. An image of her face, shocked beyond words, blasts him between the eyes.

'She's in Nottingham. An opportunity came up at the bank. We encouraged her to take it, her mother comes from there. So Angela won't be at home. When she wants to come back for a weekend, well, we shall have to see. Let's sort that out when it happens, not now.'

'But you shouldn't have to,' Bill's voice trails away.

Mr Durban puts his hand on Bill's, almost in it. It's the first gesture of affection Bill's had for over six months. He flinches.

'Remember, I always wanted a son. Remember, I told you when you were a nipper that I'd have liked a son just like you.'

Bill shakes his head, very slowly, as if confusion might flake away and lightly descend onto the car mats. 'Not like me.'

'Like you will be. Let's get you out of here.'

He starts the car and it moves away down the long, long road.

Bill turns and sees that from here there's no sign of what goes on in that fine building, Brigville School. Now the detail of detention is too far to be detected by the naked eye. He screws up his eyes hardly believing that he is being drawn away from it, further and further. He sees it glide into a distant perspective. The large gates and monstrous brick walls grow smaller. He keeps his eyes on them until they are just a black fleck on the grey horizon.

CHAPTER 37

Bill blinked hard. When the car was well clear of the Approved School environs, he could dare believe that this was not a dream. Mr Durban *had* come to rescue him.

The car slowed down and Bill saw woods and fields passing on either side. Although the sky was low and grey and the trees hardly one bud more than bare, the scene was as fresh as if he'd never seen countryside before. Mr Durban opened his window and Bill breathed in deeply. He smelled pine, flowers, grass. The field beside them stretched on and on until it reached a row of trees in the far distance.

'Is there anything you'd like to do before we get back? I know it's going to be difficult, seeing it all again.'

Bill had his hand on the door handle. 'I'd like to run.'

Mr Durban got out promptly. 'You mustn't…'

'I won't – I mean I'll come back.'

'…mustn't go far.'

He was out, into the field and running at full tilt, catching his breath and feeling his limbs stretch to their full extent, his shoes hitting the grass softly, rapidly. He felt like a cricket speeding along, invisible to any predator. He ran and ran until his lungs pained like thumps in his side, then he turned, held Mr Durban in view and loped back.

He got back into the car and said nothing.

Mr Durban drove straight to Fulham.

Bill couldn't avoid seeing the streets and buildings become more and more familiar. By the time they got back to the scene of his crime, he found it difficult to walk up the path let alone go through the door. It opened before he could back away and Mrs Durban stood there. His armpits dampened as a trickle of cold sweat made its way down his sides. What could he say? Slowly he approached her with his hand held out. He quite expected her to smack it away but then his brain reminded him that coming here had been arranged with her agreement. How long would he be staying for? Would he see his parents here? And what would happen to him afterwards?

Mrs Durban smiled at him. She said only a few words before taking him upstairs to the guest bedroom past Angela's slightly open door where flashes of pink gauze taunted him. It was only now that the question forced itself upwards. 'What was Kenneth doing visiting Angela that day?' How could he be stupid enough to speak that thought out loud!

'They were at the same evening class, English Literature. Don't you remember Angela had started them?'

But Kenneth didn't need evening classes. He had Literature at Dulwich College. Those evenings when he wetted his hair smooth, brushed his shoes, looked in the hall mirror, was it Angela he was going to meet! He shook his head. He couldn't cope with that idea as well as facing the enormity of moving in to live here.

Meanwhile, Mrs Durban had opened the guest room door. 'This is for you. I think you'll be comfortable in here.'

It looked blissful, a room with only one bed and no bars. 'Thank you,' was quite inadequate for how he felt.

The plain bed had a tartan blanket tucked tightly over the sheets. There were two Biggles books on the bedside table, and a lamp. A familiar suitcase stood on the floor. It was the one he'd taken into the front door of Primley Road when they first got back from evacuation. The suitcase must have been left here or passed to Mr Durban by Dad. It would have more clothes. He put his Brigville bag beside it and put his hand in his pocket. The piece of napkin was still safe.

'Look, Bill.' A cork board had been pinned on the wall. 'For your pictures, we thought,' said Mrs Durban. 'Your photos.'

She'd remembered his hobby!

They went downstairs, Bill silent, fearing sight of the snug. He was sick with the kind of fear he had when opening his eyes after nightmares to see whether the horror was real. But the Durbans had shut the snug door and it remained shut.

In the dining room they sat around a cheese and onion pie and a bowl of salad. It was the first time Bill had eaten off a plate since the accident. He felt awkward and clumsy, like the half-clothed vagrants had been at the vicarage where Mother had been billeted.

Mr and Mrs Durban spoke as if Bill was a full part of the conversation, about the journey, their relief at some sign of sun, the management of cooking times because of the electricity cuts, the roadworks approaching the bridge.

He had difficulty swallowing, yet every mouthful made him full of appreciation. The food was wonderfully different from the Approved School's. He finished the plateful.

Afterwards, they cleared the table together. Mrs Durban checked the onion soup that was simmering ready for lunch the next day. The aroma was strong enough to sting his eyes. She put on a half-lid and the sweaty smell followed them as they moved away to sit in the lounge.

Mr Durban lit up a cigarette. Bill breathed in the smoke, wanting to feel a part of that, floating away to safety. He knew this was a preparatory pause. He looked at Mrs Durban to see what was coming.

She spoke kindly. 'You're fifteen, Bill. School leaving age, although if nothing had happened you would have continued at St Werberg's until the summer of this year, if not longer. You will have missed getting your School Certificate. Perhaps the education at Brigville was limited?'

He nodded. Care of cats and travelling in Kurdistan didn't seem very useful.

'Perhaps you should attend school in Fulham.'

He hunched down in his chair. 'I can't.' Where would he tell teachers, boys, he had been at school?

'No? We must see.'

'No-one will have me now, Mrs Durban,' he muttered.

'You can call us Letty and Peter. We're going to treat you like a grown-up in the hope that you'll be one. A good one.' She looked at her husband, a comforting figure in his sports jacket and corduroys.

He puffed away, his smoke rising and twirling. 'The thing is, Bill, we're in loco parentis now. That's what's been agreed.'

His parents didn't want him home. He knew that. He wasn't going to ask what *in loco parentis* meant, it might be too awful. It sounded like one of Dad's sayings. *Loco* suggested being sent on a long train journey. How long was he allowed to stay here? What was Dad wanting him to do, where to go, after this? He kept hunched into his seat, as if the slightest movement of a muscle would make things more dangerous.

'You know I'm a long-standing friend of your father's. He's in a very difficult position. He has responsibilities to you, but also to Kenneth, in lieu of Frank.'

Mrs Durban added, 'Too difficult, the two of you in the same house.'

Bill nodded slowly. Dad had given him away; he could feel it. Mother had too. Although she wasn't Uncle Frank's blood, she preferred Kenneth. She'd never wanted a boy, not Bill's sort of boy and certainly not what he had become. She hadn't wanted one in the beginning when she was ready to have babies. She didn't want one now, but she could handle Kenneth's sort of boy, quiet, artistic. And now he was an invalid, needing to be quiet, he would not be like a boy at all.

'Dear, I don't think you're listening to me,' Mrs Durban – Letty – chided him. She'd carried on talking and he hadn't taken it in.

The thing was, he wasn't used to a woman's voice these days.

'Sorry.'

'I was saying that because it was in our house the awful thing happened, and it was Peter's sabre, we felt a long way responsible.'

Mr Durban said, 'We discussed this, coming here. As the magistrate pointed out, I was responsible.'

Responsible. Such a heavy word. But he, Bill, was the one who crashed the shashka down, no-one else.

Peter screwed out his cigarette into the wooden ashtray that had the big-beaked bird joined on one side. It looked down with disdain at the damaged stump of the cigarette. 'Try to pay attention. This is important, Bill. Now that you're here, you're safe. You've got us to stand beside you. What we're trying to say is that we have the task of setting you on your feet, and that means telling you everything that's happened since Juvenile Court. All right?'

'Yes, sir.'

'Don't "sir" me. Letty's said, you can call me Peter. This is all very hard, but before you go to bed tonight I want you to be completely clear about everything.'

Bill nodded, *Peter* not finding an easy way to his lips. He blinked, telling himself to pay attention, focus on what was being said. After all, there was no-one to shout things now. It did feel strange to be without the shouts, the orders, the clanging, the quantity of footsteps. There would be orders, though, there were bound to be.

Peter Durban began.

Bill was glad he didn't have to say anything. To avoid trouble, he had rarely talked more than the necessary sentence, the Yes, the No, the three bags full, for months. He didn't think his throat was up to much more. He was waiting for the bad news. There were bound to be bad things about Kenneth, about everything at home, things lying in wait for him, awful things that he was going to be forced to face. He must listen, it was important.

'You should still be at school, really, but I agree it's too difficult,' Peter was saying. 'Your parents feel your name is still too notorious for you to attend a school locally, even in Fulham. There is also Jill to think of.'

Jill! What would she be thinking? She'd never be allowed to see him again. His last sight of her had been a bewildered face, pushed behind Mother.

'It became terrible for her at school. The things children said to her, so they thought it best if Jill went to boarding school, away where no-one would know.'

A whispered 'No' escaped his lips. It wasn't fair that Jill had to go away. How she'd cried those first weeks at junior school, where at least she came home for tea, slept in her own bed. She would hate to be on her own. Who would tie her hair ribbons, find her skipping rope when she left it around? He slumped further into his chair.

Peter was saying that there had been a collection locally so that Kenneth could have private tuition until he could return to Dulwich College. It had funded a visiting tutor for Kenneth to catch up all the time he'd lost while in hospital. He had his Higher School Certificate to worry about. He needed that before the possibility of university could be considered. Individual school friends were helping with his study notes, for writing with his left hand was a slow and frustrating task, and he was having difficulty adapting emotionally—

Bill looked at his own hands, ones that could write any time he wanted.

'—to the damage to his eye and drawing hand,' Letty continued Peter's theme, 'so that he can't now be an artist.'

Bile rose to Bill's gullet. This was what he had forced himself not to think about, he just couldn't think about. He turned his head away from both of them.

Peter ended her point, 'Yes. So your father has to do his best to educate Kenneth for other things.'

Other things? Bill felt his neck where his Adam's apple had been poking out more and more, recently, and sometimes hurt badly, like now. What other things could there be? Kenneth loved Art.

'You're probably wondering why I say "your father" and don't include your aunt… weren't you?'

He hadn't been wondering. Aunty wasn't ever mentioned and he'd got used to that. Dad was always the one to decide things.

The small silence signalled that Peter wanted a reply. A couple of bicycle bells sounded outside on the road. Such a sound seemed so unusual that Bill started, his head lifting to the window then dropping. In the months and months since he'd heard a bicycle bell, ordinary life had been going on outside. He became aware that Peter was looking at him expectantly.

'Your father, not your aunt.'

He felt blank. Aunty.

'You need to know that she has taken all this very badly. She tried hard at first, when Kenneth came home, to do everything for him, look after him.'

Aunty. That awful cry 'His beautiful face!' shrilled through his brain. She would have worked really hard, looking after Kenneth. She would have been so upset by his bleeding, crying all the time at the sight of him. She'd no longer be the friend who had a soft spot for Bill. Her kindness would be gone.

'Look at me, Bill. It's best you know everything straight away. We all decided this. It's very hard, but you have to face it full on, and then go forward.'

Peter Durban paused and Bill could only see kindly concern in his face. He nodded his readiness.

'She had a nervous breakdown. What had happened to Kenneth wrecked the excitement of Dwaine's arrival.'

Dwaine! How had Bill forgotten he was on his way from America that fateful day. He would have arrived to find everything awful.

'When he arrived, your aunt collapsed and needed treatment. Dwaine was all for taking them both off back to the States, installing Doreen in his new house, getting Kenneth top treatment there at his own expense...'

Wondrous! Dwaine would fix everything, make Aunty happy, cure Kenneth, far, far away in America.

'...But Kenneth wasn't well enough to go. I think you knew that he didn't want his mother to marry Dwaine. He told her to go to America. Doreen couldn't cope with the problem. All the plans to go had been decided before Dwaine arrived, and then—'

'She really went to bits,' Letty put in before Peter's hand stilled her.

Bill had to look down, hiding his eyes which had filled. He'd so wanted Aunty to be happy when he introduced her to Dwaine.

'Dwaine had come with only enough time to arrange the passages to New York. Either Doreen had to go, or he had to go back alone. Your father thought Doreen would fare better with a man to look after her. With your parents already caring for Kenneth, and his hospital treatment under way, she decided to marry Dwaine, which meant leaving with him.' Peter paused. He looked over to Letty.

'It was arranged that Kenneth should remain with your parents. That's what he said he wanted, but he can join his mother in America whenever he chooses.'

Kenneth wouldn't choose that. He'd prefer to be in Bill's house, in Bill's room, with Bill's sister, Bill's parents. Bill clenched his fists beneath the curl of the armchair. Yes! And it was his own fault.

'Do you understand all this, dear?' Letty said, leaning forward to him. 'It's so much to take in, isn't it?'

So much. So awful, all of it. He took a deep breath. He could smell the onion soup, wafting from the kitchen, stale, sweaty, stinging. He managed to stammer out, 'Is Aunty all right now?'

'Dwaine's looking after her,' she said. 'Your father says he's a strong, kindly man. And she will be having a good life in America.'

'She's already gone!'

Letty nodded.

'But I didn't say Goodbye, I haven't... I mean I couldn't...'

'Say you're sorry properly? She'll know.' Peter rubbed one side of his face. 'Whatever else, they do all know that you didn't mean to do this. Even Kenneth says it was an accident.'

Bill desperately needed to be on his own. He wouldn't be able to hold back his tears much longer. He needed to cry and cry and cry out with his shame and misery for in all the months since it happened, he'd hardly shed a tear.

Peter said, 'We're nearly finished with all this and then you can go to bed. I can see you're really tired and overcome, but you need to know the whole picture so that you aren't left confused and without knowing the situation. Things are not all bad, Bill.'

He set his jaw and nodded. Surely he'd heard all the worst by now.

'Since your father has Kenneth's problems to manage, through no fault of his own, it's been decided that we will take on the responsibility for you. You will live here until you're ready for work. We will give you a new start in life, and you'll do your best to improve and rise to the challenge.'

'I will, I will.' Was that all he was going to be asked to do? Work, try hard? That was easy.

'And when you're on an even keel, in work, earning your keep, your father thinks it's only right that Kenneth should decide what retribution he wants.'

A shudder went through Bill despite himself. 'Retribution?'

'You don't know what that means, that word? It's like a correction, a putting things to rights. It used to mean a vengeance but that's not what your father meant, of course. He feels you owe Kenneth something you can do or provide that will improve his life: a small thing, if you think how it's been so terribly damaged.'

Bill understood. He nodded with the truth, the fairness of it. Dad knew what was right. He just didn't know Kenneth.

CHAPTER 38

Although Bill, heavily blanketed, had saturated the pillow slip with his tears for what felt like hours, he found he'd slept long and soundly. It must have been the comfort of the bed, the room all to himself. Church bells woke him, a comforting, pure sound. It was a Sunday.

Despite the awfulness of the information Peter and Letty had given him last night, it felt good to be here, the soft bed comforting him into a new stage of his life. He sat up and drank in the smell and sight of the fresh dew on the garden outside his window. A bedside clock informed that it was nearly nine. Goodness! He would have had breakfast, done PT and be ready for lessons back at Brigville.

He washed, and hurried down to breakfast and found a conversation going that was wonderfully trivial and normal. Peter and Letty smiled, nodded and continued their discussion of the prefabs going up near the common, the tasks of the day, the problem of wandering dogs in their garden. It was a comfortable discussion. Once it was clear that last night's subjects were not going to be raised again, his stomach began to relax.

He helped Letty clear the table. There was another painful thing he needed to know. He'd better get it over with, while she was busy with dishes and putting things away, not sitting looking at him.

'Letty, did Angela like Kenneth best?'

'She'll have liked him differently, Bill. They used to have a cup of tea after class, in the café opposite the Reading Rooms. She had told me that week that she thought Kenneth might ask her for a date.'

I was going to ask her that! he stopped himself from blurting out. Angela had never told him, all those times he'd photographed her, that she was seeing Kenneth. He made his words come slowly, 'Then, after – afterwards, did Angela visit him?' Would she even come back and start dating Kenneth as soon as he was well enough to go out?

'She didn't keep in touch after the first visit. She couldn't cope with the way he looked. She felt so bad about that, because she should have been one of his supports. But he had school friends, and soon afterwards, she met Vincent.' Her voice tailed away.

Vincent? Was he someone working in the same bank? Had he gone to Nottingham with Angela? It didn't matter now. Angela was a distant figure altogether.

Letty turned to him. 'Have you unpacked?'

He hadn't thought about it. He hadn't packed the suitcase himself and so it didn't feel like his own. He went upstairs. *Angela and Kenneth.* All that time, when Bill thought Kenneth was still avoiding the Durbans, he had begun a secret friendship. He'd been paying Bill back for that time he'd made him feel small, after the theft of the photo. It didn't matter to Kenneth how long after an event it was, he paid Bill back. And now, when what Bill had done was as serious as it could possibly be, how awful might the *retribution* be? And it might come after years. He would never feel safe.

It was no good panicking about it. He had to think of the *now*. The *now* was challenging enough. He was supposed to be unpacking.

The suitcase held clothes that smelled of Primley Road, clothes he needed. But under them it had his precious camera! He picked it up and hung it round his neck, back where it belonged. There was his photograph album tied safely in its box, his football boots – too small now – a couple of his favourite books and the Head Boy badge. Dad or Mother must have bothered to pack these for him. They had thought about what he might need or want. That small germ of thoughtfulness was a comfort.

He turned to his soft overnight case with its horrible memories of

Brigville. It had his photography manuals and the Dutch history book Dad had brought from the war zone. He emptied the case totally, and screwed it into the furthest corner of the wardrobe.

When everything looked tidy, he opened the bedroom window onto the garden where he and Angela had once run, where the Anderson had stood. He breathed in the sweet air. It smelled like spring and it would be spring next month.

Downstairs, Peter was moving towards the back door. He gestured for Bill to join him. They moved outside where it was chilly but bright. They strolled up the path as the church bells chimed. He said, 'I love Sundays. I had too many years when I still had to work on them, not to appreciate the leisure now. Home Guard duties and catching up with work or sleep, that's all over, thank goodness. But let's move on with your concerns.'

Bill fell into step with him. It wasn't difficult; they were much of a size.

'I don't know what we're going to do about friends for you. That is, your old friends. Your father thought it best you didn't contact anyone from St Werberg's.'

Bill nodded glumly.

'And it's not very helpful to stay in touch with any friends you've made at Brigville.'

'There aren't any, really.' He wouldn't tell Peter about the misery of isolation because of being different, the wariness between the boys, the hum of resentment and aggression in their movements, the viciousness ready to surface at any lapse in supervision, the knowledge that his false reputation as a swordsman, near murderer, was likely to shatter at the slightest confrontation. Some boys, like the Irish lad, were friendly enough for conversations or board games, but there were no real friends.

'So, you're not in touch with anyone from before?'

'I can be now! There's Alan!' Alan had said they'd be in contact as soon as he finished his sentence. 'Near Thornton Heath, Norwood, he lives. Alan's the friend I had in evacuation, we were billeted together. He knows about – what happened. I wrote to him from Brigville and he wrote back once. He will be all right, I think. His parents – I don't know whether they will have contacted my family.' He heard his own enthusiastic tone fade.

Peter stopped beside the garden shed and leant against it. 'We'll have to see if it's appropriate to see Alan; if it's not going to cause anyone any distress.'

Bill looked down, the heaviness of the previous evening returning. Mrs Routledge would probably have telephoned Mother early on, to sympathise. What would she think of him? How could she want Alan to stay his friend?

They went indoors and Bill asked for notepaper. He wrote to Alan, not saying too much about Brigville. The censoring couldn't be forgotten even though Bill knew that wasn't there anymore. Would Alan write back as he'd promised?

He sealed the envelope and looked at the notepaper's next blank page.

'Should I write to Aunty? Could I?'

'Write and wish her every happiness in her new life.'

Every happiness! *Some* happiness, more like. Unless he wrote *Sorry* five thousand times over every inch of the card, what else could he say? How stupid a thing to say, *Sorry*, knowing that her son could never be *un*damaged.

Alan wrote back. He said they'd get together in his school holidays. That was marvellous. But even after three weeks, no answer came from Aunty. He wasn't surprised. She'd never forgive him. Did she have some happiness? He imagined Dwaine escorting Aunty in his gentlemanly way to a large American car; or at home, opening the door of a huge refrigerator loaded with food. 'Let's eat, honey,' he'd say. Dwaine would make sure Aunty was all right.

Peter walked Bill down to the local football club on the Saturday. 'The juniors meet here at ten. I've explained to the coach that you're just back from boarding school and that you're keen to play in any position.'

Bill took a huge breath and felt it surge through his chest. It would be wonderful to play football properly after the constant fouls in the Brigville School games.

'You sign on with the juniors today, and who knows? Wouldn't it be superb if you managed to be selected to their training scheme? Fulham are working their way up to the first division. Think of that.'

Bill's thrill subsided at the words *sign on*. 'But Dad said everyone will avoid me once they know my name.'

Peter held his arm. 'There is something else important that Letty and I haven't discussed with you, yet. We thought it best to tell you in the context of something positive.'

What now? What else did he have to face? Had the whole bunch of junior footballers been warned about him?

'Because of that very difficulty, your name being in the newspaper, your father and I thought it was better if you were known as Bill Durban. We can't do that if you went to school or college, because of your birth certificate. But otherwise, shall we do that for the present? It saves you being bothered with any questions.'

It was like a thump in his stomach. Dad didn't want him to be a Wilson any more. A new surname. Whatever name they called him, he was the boy who dreadfully damaged his cousin.

CHAPTER 39

It would have been easier to stay in the Durbans' house and garden and not see anyone, but Letty said that the weekly football game and Wednesday evening training were important for him socially. She'd suggested Scouts, but he felt too old somehow. Fulham Scouts might want to check how he'd got his badges, and those would be under his real name.

He did play football enthusiastically, but didn't chat in the changing room or see the other boys in between training sessions and matches. He knew they thought him boring. He didn't mind. It was safer.

During the day he did some gardening and household jobs. Letty was out and left him to himself, which was what he needed. Sometimes, he went into the kitchen and watched her make soup or stews. He liked the cooking smells and it might be useful to know how to make some meals for himself. Suppose Letty got ill? He would be able to step in and help out.

In the evenings, after supper, Peter helped him with his studies. 'I'm not a mathematician but this is what you might need in the real world ahead of you; keeping accounts, devising a budget, knowing what things cost.'

Bill found he was expected to read the newspaper fully every day to keep up with what was happening in the world, as well as listening to the six o'clock news on the wireless.

Otherwise he wrote out information from Peter's books, luckily more interesting and comprehensive than what was available at Brigville. There was a whole set of encyclopaedias that Letty said had cost the earth. They had been a wedding present from her parents. Bill taught himself facts about countries, products, population, culture; and about animals. One day, under K in the encyclopaedia he saw something about knights. For the first time he could follow-up Alan's suggestion, as long as it didn't involve swords.

He soon found the code of chivalry, and he wrote it down twice, once in his notebook and once on separate paper. It felt important to have something to show Alan, even if it wasn't as good as a School Certificate.

Peter got textbooks in physics and chemistry from a second-hand bookshop. 'You can't do experiments but you must learn some of the things you've missed in your schooling. Chemistry's involved in photographic work, the processing.' That made sense to Bill so he took especial trouble to learn what he could.

When he'd finished all the study Peter had set, or in gaps during the daytime, Bill studied his photography manuals. The problem was, he needed film to practise what he was learning. He certainly couldn't ask Peter for film: the Durbans were doing so much for him already.

But then, the miracle. The post on a Tuesday brought a package from Alan. Inside there were two films and the Vacuee card game. They'd played that in evacuation. Because he was alone in the hall, he twizzled around twice. Film at last! Now he could put some of his study into practice. The Vacuee game was precious because it was like saying, *Remember those old times*. Alan would have meant something like that when he sent it. Mrs Routledge must have allowed him to. It was a great relief that she didn't want Alan to keep away from him. The best thing of all was knowing he was still a friend, whatever Bill had done. The Routledges would be very shocked by what had happened but they would know, surely they'd know, that Bill had never meant to damage Kenneth? He kicked at a ruck in the mat. He'd like to tell himself he never meant to hurt Kenneth, but in his heart he knew that he had wanted to hurt him – just not with the shashka, and certainly not seriously.

He took his treasures upstairs and found his camera, ready to wind in a film. He'd use it carefully, not waste a single snap. The chapter he'd reached in the manual was about photographing a person who was speaking, to avoid the posed effect. He'd like to photograph Alan, if he was going to see him.

He went back downstairs slowly. Peter was at work, but Letty was in the kitchen. Before he could think of visiting or meeting a friend, there were further things he had to face – those questions he'd never asked – because knowing the answers would have made Brigville unbearable. Now he'd better approach each question carefully. He'd found out why Kenneth was here that dreadful day. He'd found out about Angela. There was a worse question he hadn't asked yet. He was like a soldier testing for a bomb, risking that it would blow him to bits.

With Letty's back towards him as she stirred mince on the stove, he ventured the hope he could never quite put out of his mind: 'Letty, with the hospital treatment is Kenneth's hand... on the mend?'

She twisted around so rapidly that a strand of her hair flew sideways. 'On the mend? Bill! You surely know? They must have told you months ago.'

He shook his head.

She sat down at the table and waved him to sit opposite. 'Bill, I think you must have been told, either by your parents or the headmaster at Brigville.'

'Was I?'

'And you've somehow put it out of your mind. Kenneth's hand had to be amputated.'

His own hand flew to his mouth, the back of it pressed against his teeth. 'Cut off?'

She nodded.

No! The hand had been bleeding loads but the ambulance men would have bandaged it. He knew it was very badly damaged but surely it was still there, in its bandage, a sling perhaps.

Letty leant forward searching his face. 'Sometimes when we're very shocked we stop ourselves facing the truth. You know you damaged Kenneth very severely.'

'Yes.' He nodded, looked at the floor, looked up again. 'Yes, I know.'

'Well, Kenneth's hand is gone. He is being fitted for a prosthetic hand.' She said slowly, 'That means a false hand.'

False hand. He tried to imagine it. So far he'd thought of Kenneth not able to draw because of his hand in a sling, and hurting still, but not of having *no* hand. He felt terribly sick. He might have to dash to the cloakroom. But before he could do so, Letty went on.

'And his eye. You do know that his eye can't get better, don't you? He's lost the sight of that for good. There is no treatment that can repair the damage.'

He stared at the kitchen table so hard that it expanded and swayed in front of him.

She stood. 'I'll make you a strong sweet tea. You've had a shock.'

It was as if it had just happened. As if he'd come out of the snug with all the blood on the carpet and a doctor had said, *Look what you've done. Your cousin has no hand and his eye will never see again.* All he'd seen of Kenneth after the accident was that one time, in hospital, just a lump under the covers, silent. People had spoken of damage, pain, suffering, disaster, injuries, but they hadn't said what Letty had just told him. It was only now that he knew what he'd really done to Kenneth.

~

That night, he was slow to go to sleep. He heard the telephone's ting as Peter picked up the receiver to dial a number. Another Brigville boy had told him how to work out who was being telephoned: 9 9 9 was all of the clicks all of the way, three times – easy! And any number you could work out from counting the clicks after the first three, which would be the exchange name.

His door was not completely closed. He shouldn't listen, but he couldn't stop himself. He counted the clicks for the exchange name, then three, eight, one, one – home, his old home.

Peter's voice, muted, announcing himself. Something about a file and a new entry on the Court list, a pause, then, 'Yes, he's doing quite well.' Pause. 'Yes, the name problem appears to have been accepted. And what's the latest your end?'

A long pause. Peter tutting, 'Did he? With the same consultant? Yes, I see. Poor chap! Dreadful.'

Another wait; hm hmming. Then, 'The problem, this end, is that Bill hadn't realised the extent of it. Letty had to spell it out, unequivocally. Didn't you say, when he was at Brigville?'

Pause.

'You didn't? No, it doesn't seem that Brigville did. Or if they did, Bill must have been too traumatised to take it in. He certainly knows now. We've tried to be very direct with him from the start. The best way, don't you think?'

Pause.

'Yes, I agree. He is buckling down to things, but it's going to be a time before he's ready to go out into the world in any form.'

Bill slid back into bed. He'd been leaning out, listening. That wasn't what a decent sort of chap should do. How could he be any sort of decent chap ever again? He'd served the time the magistrate had ordered, but it hadn't put things right. It wasn't ever going to.

Next morning, Peter opened up the Kenneth subject over breakfast. 'Your father and I spoke on the telephone last night. He's off to Lincoln this morning, the assizes timetable, so we shan't see each other for a few weeks. I told him you're settling down, studying. I needed to ask him about the visits.

'Dad and Mother coming here?'

'No, their visit will be later.'

Letty passed him the toast rack. 'Better that visits are somewhere neutral, Bill.'

Peter said, 'I was meaning Kenneth's visits.'

All the bones in Bill's head felt they were expanding and pushing their way outwards. 'Kenneth!'

'Yes. Kenneth will decide when he wants to see you.'

'Not yet!'

'No, not yet. But it must be planned for.'

He hadn't planned, hadn't expected ever to visit Kenneth. He pushed the toast rack back to Letty. Toast would choke him.

It was later that week when Peter said the Routledges had agreed that Alan could meet Bill. 'It will lift your spirits, and get you another step back into the world.'

'Are you sure it's all right?' The thought of going to Norwood, just as he used to, was exciting but rather scary.

He felt nervous throughout the bus journey to Thornton Heath. It would be awkward at first. What was he going to talk about? He and Alan couldn't ignore what had happened.

Alan was waiting at the clock tower, like all those times before the trouble.

Bill went up to him slowly. 'Thanks ever so much for the film and the game.'

Alan said, 'I thought you might like them.' He led the way. 'Might as well go to the rec.'

The day was cloudy and grey. Once they would have run, but now they walked in unison, not speaking, past the pond and across the grass. They sat on the swings, since no-one else was there.

Bill gave a quick glance sideways at Alan. It had been a whole year since they'd seen each other. They'd never been so long apart. Now it was like looking at a before time, like going back to the village or like arriving in back Wandsworth after the evacuation.

'You look pretty well the same to me,' Alan said. 'Except for your clothes.'

'I grew out of most of them while I was inside. Letty, Mrs Durban, got me these. We had an awful uniform at the Approved School, short trousers, scratchy, colour of shit.' He paused. He'd never have used that word before Brigville. Now it felt like a normal word. They'd better get the subject over with. 'You'll say I deserved it.'

Alan was straight. 'Probably not. You've always said it was an accident. I suppose it could've happened to anyone if they were messing about with something lethal like that. You just shouldn't have been.'

'But it was Kenneth took it down from its place, pulled it out of the scabbard. I tried to stop him. He knows that.'

'I know you'd never have hurt someone on purpose, even Kenneth. But you were crazy to get hold of the shashka. Still, it was hard on you, sending you away. Perhaps a birching would've been easier.'

'Yes. Then it would have been over with. Whereas, you wouldn't normally speak to a boy from an Approved School.'

Alan shrugged. 'It doesn't stop us being friends. We always have been.'

'Thanks.' Bill's feet went forward a little way, starting his swing. Having his old friend back was a huge thing. Alan was someone who really knew him. He was the friend he'd had in evacuation with the kind of freedom you just couldn't have in London. Bill had been so long without any freedom. He threw his legs forward and made the swing go high. 'We two got through the whole war together,' he shouted. Do you remember that first night, when Mrs Y showed us the privy?'

Alan swung up to meet him, laughing. 'And that rotten tin potty under the bed!'

'And being hungry all the time!'

Alan grinned. 'There were good things, too. We made things better for Mrs Y, I reckon. Not just the billeting money, but playing games with Sally and Tim. That helped her. She said as much when I went down there.'

Bill swung higher, remembering the rope round the post in the road. 'Playing out' had been so shocking to his mother. And now, being at Approved School would be so shocking to Mrs Youldon and the Pawseys. As he and Alan passed mid-swing he said, 'They'd all want to forget me if they knew this stuff.'

'Never. Think of your bravery award.'

'Anyone would've done that.'

'I don't think so – not in freezing water, when you couldn't swim. Another person would have gone for help, like me. You were the Youldons' hero.' Alan stopped his swing. 'Especially Sally. She's waiting until you eventually go down.'

'Really!' That was a warming thought, that she remembered him as a hero. Bill brought his swing to a rest and turned to face Alan properly. Alan's letter had said that he'd just passed his School Certificate. 'Congratulations on the exam.'

'It's the school's doing, really.' Alan pointed to his blazer badge with its Latin words.

'Don't know Latin.'

'It means: *Good Education leads to Success.*'

'I'm going to have to succeed without,' said Bill. In the old days they would have drawn a Chad on his wall – *Wot, no education* – and rolled about laughing. It wasn't funny now.

'What are you doing about studying?'

'Peter sets me tasks, and there's the encyclopaedia. That's where I found this: The Code of Chivalry. There weren't many books at all at Brigville, so I couldn't follow up your hint about knights but I have been looking at Peter's. I don't understand all the words. It's from the Middle Ages. Look.' He pulled out the sheet he'd prepared.

To fear God and maintain His Church
To serve the liege lord in valour and faith
To protect the weak and defenceless
To give succour to widows and orphans
To refrain from the wanton giving of offence
To live by honour and for glory
To despise pecuniary reward
To fight for the welfare of all
To obey those placed in authority
To guard the honour of fellow knights
To eschew unfairness, meanness, deceit
To keep faith
At all times to speak the truth
To persevere to the end in any enterprise begun
To respect the honour of women
Never to refuse a challenge from an equal

Never to turn the back upon a foe

Alan looked impressed. 'Pretty strong advice. You can imagine the knights avowing it all, holding their chalices.'

'Who's the liege lord?'

'That'd be Peter, where you're living.'

'Wanton?'

'Careless.'

'Pecuniary?'

'Don't know. Look it up in the dictionary.'

'I have been trying to do some of those things listed.'

'You are a bit of a knight; I've always known that. Come on.' Alan led him to a cafe and ordered tea and buttered buns. He read the list again. 'It's good you found this. It's a bit beyond me, but well worth talking through with Peter.'

'Never turn the back upon a foe. That means, not neglecting Kenneth, doesn't it?'

The tea and buns came before Alan found an answer. He said, 'What do you reckon you'll do now?'

'I'm still going to be a photographer; I haven't changed my ideas. Tell your parents I've been studying that manual all the time, even at Brigville. Now you've sent me film I can try some of the things out, the techniques.'

'Such as?'

'I had been trying portraits before this happened.'

'Portraits?'

'Angela sat for me,' His stomach lurched. She never would again. 'And I didn't ever guess that she was seeing Kenneth every week after night school.'

Alan frowned. 'So there was something more behind what happened?'

'I've told you all about it. Peter says I must look to the future now. But I'm worried about it. I don't go to school, I won't have exams, I only go to football club and that's it. I'm just studying indoors.'

'Goodness, you've got to get out! I'll come over when I can, but

Higher School Cert has lots of homework. Look, have another bun. Let's eat up then have a kick around on the common for a bit. There's some chaps I know who'll likely be playing.'

Alan, and all he stood for, was like a tropical island; calm, in a raging sea.

CHAPTER 40

Bill slid into a deckchair glad that there was enough warmth to sit in the garden for a while after work. It was wearisome at Whitley's of Fulham and dark in its storeroom, but stacking the hardware in the back was about right for a strong lad with no school leaving exams and a bad record. He was lucky getting any sort of job considering the length of the queues outside the labour exchange.

He'd been working part-time there for five months. Would he still be doing this at sixteen, at seventeen, his high spot in the month meeting up with Alan, seeing his successes. Would football on Saturdays be his only weekly pleasure?

He looked up at the trees, remembering that time of the A-bombs, feeling lucky to see blue through the branches, that he wasn't in Japan when the A-bomb dropped, that he had a father who was a pacifist. He must hold onto Letty's advice to keep hold of his ambitions, and just use Whitley's as his first step into outside life.

He'd finished Alan's two films a long time ago, and was saving up for another. There was something in Chapter Eighteen of his photography manual that he wanted to try out: getting a transparent effect on objects. That was going to be a challenge.

Peter came out of the French doors, back from his Wednesday

evening club. 'Hallo, Bill. Brighten up, I think I've arranged you an apprenticeship.'

His deckchair wobbled as he stood up sharply. 'Instead of working at Whitley's?'

'Yes. Gibson, an arty type at the philosophy club has a photographic studio at Clapham. The chaps say he is well respected. I've told him of your passion, and he's going to give you a trial.'

'Does he know about–? Do I have to say?'

'No. And he wouldn't be interested. He's a philosopher more than a photographer.'

Bill almost danced into the house. The beginning of a proper career! 'Thank you so much, Peter. That's spiffing, simply spiffing! I'll give it my very best.'

'I know you will.'

Bill took the bus daily. Mr Gibson, in a ginger suit with a collarless green shirt beneath it, met him at the door of the studio. 'Hello, Bill Durban. I hear you're keen. Good. Two weeks' trial, okay? Eight thirty to five thirty, Monday to Saturday, except half day on Fridays, free from one p.m. Duties: number one, study my works of art,' he waved a square hand to the window display, 'and number two, just make yourself useful.'

The studio was a one-man affair. Passers-by mostly came in for a one-off portrait. Mr Gibson didn't do weddings. 'Can't stand the affairs. Having the happy couple in the studio is the nearest I'm going to get to marriage, thanks very much.'

He was a modest man. Looking through a range of the standard photographs, Bill saw the odd artistic study, such as a man at dusk, disappearing into the distance, just a small pool of light from the gaslight above. There was the occasional portrait that caught the eye, a child with an adult expression, a dog looking up at its master. Bill knew he'd be content learning photography here.

As Peter had indicated, Mr Gibson didn't bother him with any questions about school or past events. Bill made himself very useful, arranging the equipment so that it was easily to hand, bringing tea promptly between sittings, taking payments from customers, and giving change with no mistakes.

There was the front room where orders were taken and money paid; the studio with its big lights and camera set-up, and down below, the darkroom with open dishes on the table, bottles of chemicals, and negatives pegged on a line, rather like washing. He meant to learn every tiny thing he could.

They didn't work inside all the time. Even the first week they attended an important auction and an acrobatic performance at the theatre, both tremendously exciting after Bill's last year. It was Mr Gibson under the photographer's hood, of course, but Bill watched the techniques and asked questions when Mr Gibson was free.

Sometimes a customer brought an animal to be photographed. Bill might have to walk a dog around the block before it posed. Mostly, he had the clearing up to do and the sweeping. Afterwards he'd take the bus back home and could pepper the conversation over tea with something interesting for once.

After Bill had arrived punctually every day for the two-week trial and brought a cup of tea at regular intervals to the back studio, the trial ended with a two years' apprenticeship. 'There'll be a better wage in Year Two if you're competent by then.'

At last there was something to smile about. As Bill Durban, photographer's assistant, he could feel a different person, a worthier one.

Mr Gibson was appreciative. 'You make a mean cup of tea and don't keep me waiting for it. No, joking apart, I can see that you have a real passion for photography. I don't. This just earns me money sufficient for my passion – I collect Toby jugs; ugly, some say, but there's no greater excitement for me than finding the next one. I like going to auctions, wherever they are. You'll be the real photographer eventually. By the way, I shall provide all the film you need.'

'Gosh, really! That'll be a tremendous help.'

'Yes, you'll just show me all the photographs you take. That way, I can check your progress and guide you. You get free processing, of course. In fact, you'll be doing most of the processing for me once you've learned how to do it properly.'

Having film was a wonderful bonus. Bill could properly experiment without worry over the cost. He went back to Peter and Letty that evening with a lighter heart.

'Well done on completing the trial period,' said Peter.

'Things are moving forwards for you, you see,' Letty smiled as they settled into the comfort of the evening.

He nodded, feeling a rare grin spread his cheeks and he looked around at his new home as if he had only just moved in.

The carpet where they were sitting was cream with a green and maroon pattern that repeated itself only four times. Letty's shoes had a pattern of tiny holes and she had fastened them with a neat double knot. The cushion beside him was a tapestry pattern, and the walls were papered with pale green, with light beige flowers. It needed re-papering, but the pattern was gentle. All this had been around him for weeks, and he was only just noticing it.

Peter said, 'It's good to see you more confident. Now we must work out a budget with you.'

Bill's pay at Whitley's' had been so tiny that Peter told him to keep it, so that his empty pockets at least had bus fares.

'Now that I have a regular wage, I can give most of my pay packet for my keep.'

'We'll take some, and part must go to your father towards Kenneth's keep, but you must be left enough for essentials. When your earnings go up, you'll be able to contribute more.'

It was a relief to be paying his way and something towards Kenneth's costs. 'I'll feel better now. I ought to pay more. I know Aunty sends money for Kenneth, but there's Jill's school fees. She wouldn't be at that school if it wasn't for me.'

'Don't feel too bad,' Letty said. 'Your mother had been wanting Jill at a private school ever since she found that Dawn was attending one.'

Bill remembered all the tears when Jill started at the local primary, the shock about having forty-one children in her class. He squeezed his nails into the palms of his hands, praying that she was happier at her new school.

Peter said, 'This feels like a success for Letty and me, you know, starting you on a photographic career. We will gain great satisfaction over fledging you into the world as a useful citizen.'

There was a cosy silence as Bill took this in. There'd been a time, a long time, when he'd dreamed he'd inherit the shashka because he was Mr Durban's son. Now that he really was Bill Durban, the last thing he wanted was the shashka, and until this moment, all he'd felt was misery that Dad didn't want him as a Wilson anymore. That had hit hard, but being a Durban was very good. "Bill Durban" was his face for the world now.

'Could I make a telephone call?' He'd waited so long for this: a good time to phone Mr and Mrs Pawsey. He had some explaining to do, but he wouldn't lie. He could talk privately in the hall while Peter and Letty listened to the wireless. He watched Peter bend down to turn it on.

He didn't need to look up the number, it was in his heart as well as in his head. He dialled with a sweaty finger, praying Mrs Pawsey would be in to answer the ring. In his mind he could see the very phone in her hall, imagined it vibrating as it rang. When her voice sounded, he only managed to blurt out, 'Hallo, it's Bill.'

'Oh Lordy me.' She called out to Mr Pawsey. 'It's our Bill phoning, at long last. What a treat it is to hear you, that's for sure.'

'I have been wanting to phone for ages.'

'Isn't your voice so deep, my love?' she remarked in that way he remembered so well, a question instead of a statement. 'Let's see, are you still at school?'

'No. I'm nearly sixteen. I'm a working man.'

'Well, I'll be blowed.' She went on in a flurry of chat.

It was so wonderful to hear her delight and her string of questions that he could manage to say why he'd been out of touch for such a very long time. 'I did something really bad, and that stopped me telephoning before. I'm putting things right bit by bit.'

'That's good, Bill. Didn't I know there must be trouble?' She was too nice to ask awkward questions about it. 'And what are you doing now?'

'I'm going to be a photographer, and it's Mr Pawsey's camera that made it happen.'

'My, won't he be pleased?'

Soon it was his turn to ask questions. Having Mrs Pawsey talk about the village, giving the sense that everything was pretty much the same there, except the dogs had got too old and had died, and there were now two new ones – he could hear some barking.

'Aren't they going to love meeting you, tails a-wagging?'

He said, 'When I'm a real success, I'm coming down to see you.'

'Then I shall have to get your bed made up. Don't leave it too long. And let's have a letter, occasionally.'

Now he had the awkward task of telling her that his address, his very name was different. 'It's best I explain when I see you.'

She went quiet at that.

He went on, 'But will you tell Mrs Youldon I'm in contact, and give them all my love.'

'Won't I just, Bill. And we'll be waiting the day till we see you.'

He came back into the lounge just as *Twenty Questions* was finishing.

'I can see that was a good call from the smile on your face,' Peter said as he switched off. 'I'm glad. You need to keep your spirits up.' He rubbed his knuckles and leaned forwards. 'Now – a harder subject to consider.'

Things could never be nice too long! Bill tensed, and prepared himself.

'Seeing your parents.'

That hadn't been mentioned since the first day he'd moved in. He'd thought that at least Dad, Peter's friend, would come here; the families had often exchanged visits before the *event*. The last time he'd seen his parents had been at Brigville. If the atmosphere was the same, he could see that Letty wouldn't want that awkwardness in her comfortable home.

He pressed his fist into his other hand. 'How is it best for me to see them?'

It was clear from Peter's expression that a visit had already been arranged. Peter didn't look at him but into space, as if seeing the event at the cinema. 'Once a month, your parents will meet you at the Corner House, Oxford Street.'

Did he have to meet them there? He wasn't even used to going into the West End.

'It's easy enough to find.' Peter gave him clear directions.

Then he realised he had visited this Corner House, it seemed years ago now, when they were showing Dwaine the West End. They had gone inside, for Dwaine had been impressed by the decor and all the different restaurants on four or five floors, some with musicians. Kenneth had been thrilled by the lithographs on the walls. There'd been a picture of a pier at Herne Bay and Kenneth was excited because the artist, Mr Goss, had been born in Dulwich.

'It's such a grand place to go into on my own.' And then he'd have to face his parents as people from his past. It was as bad as suggesting he put on his old St Werberg's uniform and walk in as if he'd never left.

'A nice place where lots of people go. A meeting around tea, that's probably best. Your father's arranged to be free on the fourth Friday afternoon of every month.'

~

In the days that followed Bill found it difficult to keep his mind on his work. On the Friday, he set off after his half day at work. Every stitch he wore was clean on, and he'd been to the barber's in his lunch break the day before. Surely his parents would be pleased to see him now?

The bus inched along between the mess of blackened buildings. The ugliness of Stockwell, the sad and decrepit Elephant and Castle where there were so many grubby people in such dirty crowded roads. He wouldn't have liked to walk along them, especially in the dark. The men in ill-fitting clothes looked as if they were just waiting until they could get drunk. They hardly noticed the women with their battered prams overfull with children whose faces needed a thorough wash.

At last Hyde Park appeared with its welcome green swathe. He got off there so that he could take deep breaths of good air before walking alongside the car fumes to face his parents. At least he had progress to report. Last time they'd seen him he'd been in the Brigville uniform, humiliated to be back in short trousers so soon after the joy of his first long pair, the pair he'd worn to visit Angela in the hope of asking her for his first date.

People hurrying along Park Lane looked grey and preoccupied and that's how he felt. He checked Peter's written directions, turned into Oxford Street and walked along to the Corner House. Announcing itself in white paint and gold writing, it was a very fine building for his parents to see such a son. Why here? It was hardly to reward him? No. He understood. It was a big enough place, crowded enough for him not to be noticed; a place far enough away from Wandsworth to avoid anyone they knew; and it was a place that would emphasise his parents' dignity.

Inside, the choice of cafes and restaurants under the one roof was confusing. There were many people shopping at the counters, others ascending or descending the fine staircase. He wasn't sure which floor or doorway, but he had left enough time. Dad did expect punctuality.

The Mountview Café had many round tables with four chairs, padded for the small of the back and the seat. His parents were unmissable. They were the only people sitting stiffly at their white-clothed table without tea in front of them. As he sidled into the tea-room, so embarrassed and out of his depth, their static pose became even more rigid as though a joint paralysis had suddenly afflicted them. They had seen him, a young man who had once been their son.

Mother wore a neat hat that matched her green flecked jacket. Dad had removed his trilby. Otherwise, he was still the suited figure Bill had known as a child, who went away to work carrying his wig box.

Bill bent his upper half towards them. 'I'm here.' How stupid he sounded. He lowered himself into the third chair clasping his hands on his lap.

Mother looked at Bill warily. Did she think he'd jump up and thrash her? 'Are you well? You don't seem to have grown.'

Was that a compliment? She normally hated his size. 'Yes, thank you. I hope you're both well.'

Dad lifted his hand to summon the waitress, who came forward swiftly. Her formal cap, fitted black dress and frilly white apron made Bill feel oafish and clumsy. She glanced at him as if she knew he'd recently been eating from a tin dish in an Approved School.

Dad ordered tea and cakes as grimly as if the treat was prison refreshments.

Mother said, 'It's very nice here,' as the waitress departed with a swish of black skirt.

'It's been a while since we met,' Dad said. It was actually eight months. He didn't ask how Bill had settled. He'd be updated by Peter, of course, as often as he wanted, probably in the cloakroom at Chambers when no-one else was around to overhear the word *Bill.*

'You did receive the suitcase safely?'

'Yes. I have it. Thank you very much for packing it. Should I have brought it back?'

Dad waved a negative hand.

Mother said, 'We chose these tea-rooms. I enjoy the trio who play here.'

The waitress approached with her tray. No-one spoke during this arrival of tea paraphernalia. Bill had no words.

When the waitress left, Dad fingered his pipe, but placed it neatly in the glass ashtray. 'We must tell you about Kenneth's adaptations. He now has a bookstand for reading—'

The waitress came again and placed a cake-stand right in front of Bill. As though he could face eating cake! She whisked away to another table.

'—and the hospital have worked hard to get him a better prosthetic hand. He's still trying to use his left hand, but that isn't coming easily. Most fortunately, Dulwich College has been extremely sympathetic. When he cannot attend in person, tutors support Kenneth's studies.'

Mother cleared her throat, and fiddled with the tea things, arranging the cups, pouring milk and then stirring the tea in the teapot. 'Jill is doing quite well at boarding school. Sussex is far enough away for her to be protected from the fear of other girls knowing about you.' Her eyes raised to the highly decorated ceiling. 'The fees mean we have had to make many sacrifices.' She poured the tea into the cups, each three-quarters full, and passed them over.

Dad said, 'We do the best we can for Jill. She no longer has Dawn and Iris as playmates, of course. Their parents hardly nod to us should we cross paths.' He pushed the cake-stand forward. 'It can be difficult for her, occupying herself during the rather long holidays.'

'Perhaps I could help,' Bill said eagerly. 'I could take her out at the weekends.' Surely Jill would want to see him again?

Dad raised both eyebrows. 'Not appropriate. And Peter said you'd been asking about visiting your grandparents. We don't see how you can for quite a while.'

Mother took one dainty sip of her tea and placed her cup carefully onto its saucer. 'Best not to write, either. It was the most terrible, terrible shock for them.' Her eyes watered, an awful thing to see. 'Telling them what you'd done was the very worst thing I have been forced to do to my family.'

Dad took her elbow. Someone at the next table looked across. It must have looked as if Dad was preventing her from taking a cake.

She looked at Dad's hand, and then at the very white tablecloth. 'And now I'm so limited in the time I can give them.' She took another tiny sip of tea using her left hand and Dad released her other elbow.

'Is Colin—?' There wasn't any more Bill could say. His throat was too tight.

'What a blessing he's still there.' Dad waited for Mother to choose her cake and then he took the Eccles. He pushed the plate towards Bill.

Bill fiddled with his teacup, not taking either the slice of Madeira or the iced fancy.

'We've paid for them anyway,' said Mother, nodding at the cake-stand.

Was it best to waste the cake or ignore Mother's direction? He took the Madeira and crumbled a little edge into his mouth. He took a large gulp of tea to wash it down.

'None of your Brigville manners here, please,' said Dad, almost squirming.

'Sorry.' He concentrated on lifting the teacup to his mouth and replacing it carefully.

The three musicians took their places on a dais and played delicate music as they sipped their tea.

'Boccherini. How nice.' Mother nodded her head more or less in time. 'It makes a treat, a civilised tea like this, doesn't it?'

They enjoyed the rest of it without speaking.

As polite applause followed the music, Bill tried, 'I am assisting a photographer in Clapham, now.'

'Yes, we heard. That's good,' said Mother.

'Ensure you complete your apprenticeship with no blots on your service.' Dad raised the tip of his hand at the waitress, who hurried over with the bill.

Mother stood up, easing her jacket more securely onto her shoulders, sliding on her gloves.

Bill stood quickly and moved each of their chairs under the table, siting them as perfectly as the ones at the unoccupied tables.

Dad's coins chinked on the tiny silver tray in the waitress's hands. For the first time, she smiled before disappearing beyond the wooden screen. Dad reached down to his briefcase and brought out two books, *The Pilgrim's Progress* and *My Life in Jeopardy*. 'Improving texts, Bill. Something to read and think over until we see you next month.' He placed them into Bill's hands, where they weighed heavily.

'Thank you, Dad. Thank you for coming, Mother.' Should he shake hands?

But they had both said *Goodbye* while he was dithering, and turned away.

He watched his parents pass through the door and start down the staircase. The tea, the visit, was over.

He walked the first part of the journey back. It was still warm. He needed to stride down Park Lane to keep the greenness of Hyde Park in his mind before the bus took him the rest of the journey, past the dirty toothless mouths of buildings, back from being Wilson to being Durban.

CHAPTER 41

The apprenticeship was moving into its second year. By now Mr Gibson was treating Bill almost like a partner. Bill dealt with all the work of the darkroom. He'd learned to produce proofs long ago and sets of immaculate prints. As for his own attempts, his portraits were often praised and Mr Gibson displayed the best ones in the window alongside his own.

He had become chatty in slack moments and even asked Bill's opinion on his choice of ties if he was going out for the evening. These ranged from dark green with spots to light blue with spots, whereas the ginger jacket remained the same, corduroy and slightly dusty.

Mr Gibson took his tea strong, with two sugars, though goodness knows where he managed to get his supply. One morning, with no customer due, he sipped his tea and looked philosophical. 'Bill, you're a good apprentice but more than that, you show real talent. You can take a good portrait; you can snap an interesting scene. Now you need to realise the significance photographs can have. It's not just a record of the moment, as people think of it. They come in to get a picture of their loved ones, but the result is also history.'

'I know. In a hundred years, married couples will look different. Perhaps they'll wear black.'

'More appropriate, perhaps.' Peter called Mr Gibson a cynic. 'You must make sure their grandchildren value the photograph you've taken. It's a responsibility.'

'I'll remember that. But I like photographing outside. This week I did someone disappearing under an arch, and rain falling on a pile of rubbish.'

'Yes, I've seen those in the darkroom. Promising. Now, I'm going to let you do some of the booked portraits, the females.'

Bill felt a blush, although Mr Gibson would never know about his early attempts using Angela. 'Thank you.' It was a compliment that he was being trusted.

'We have to progress, Bill. Photography is an Art. And photography is where artifice becomes reality. These film stars, they look unbelievably beautiful or handsome because of photography. Remember this. It's the lighting, the angle, the speed of your capture,' he leaned forward, wiping his mouth, and said almost in a whisper, 'And your understanding of what's going on behind their faces.'

Bill hadn't thought of that. It wasn't something included in his manual. Had there been something going on behind Angela's face, her meetings with Kenneth at the Evening Institute? What other portraits had he done that he could look at in this way? He had a sudden thought. 'I did take a photograph that almost isn't of a face, but it's special. I took it when I was little but it worked by accident. I hate it, but I'm proud of it. I'd almost forgotten, I don't know how. I always wanted to show it to a proper photographer.'

'Bring it in tomorrow, I'm fascinated.'

After tea, he went up to his bedroom and took out his album, still tied into its own box. He hadn't opened it since before the accident. The photos of his favourite people and places would make him too sad, and his well of sadness was already over-full. He wouldn't look at it now, but would save it, like a treat or reward, to relish after he'd paid his retribution, once Kenneth had decided what that was to be. He would just take the envelope from the box and leave the album unopened.

He undid the ties and put his hand under the album. The envelope wasn't there. His hand went to his stomach as he felt the familiar thud. He took the album out completely but there was no envelope, nor any loose photograph. The album had been left tied up on the bookcase beside his bed at home. At some point, one-handed, Kenneth must have taken the photograph; the second time he'd stolen a photograph from Bill. This time it wasn't because he meant to give it to another person. This time it really was destined for the rubbish bin. Kenneth would have taken it to destroy it.

He didn't need to check whether the album photos were safe. Kenneth would only be interested in the one of himself. He packed the album away. The missing photo was another loss; something of a past time he could never get back, and his own piece of art gone forever. He'd so looked forward to sharing that photo with a photographer who would appreciate it. It wasn't something he could ever recreate like a portrait of a film star.

When had Kenneth taken it? Immediately he got out of hospital, or only when he knew Dad was about to pack Bill's suitcase?

He couldn't even be angry, because this time Kenneth had some right to a picture of himself. If you were the subject of a photo, did you own it? Kenneth would think it fair. He had asked Bill not to photograph him, and it was taken at a time he was grieving.

He put the album away. He'd have to tell Mr Gibson that sadly he had lost the special photo. Mr Gibson would shrug and say he could take plenty more. But this was the one that began his career and told Kenneth's story. Even if he did meet Kenneth, the very last thing he could imagine of such an awful event would be asking for the photo back.

~

At work, photography was what he was supposed to be doing. At home, photography was an excuse for escape. He could put the camera around his neck and go out without it seeming odd, whatever time of the day or evening. He used the excuse to visit a café where other young people met, one of them who played a guitar. He used it for awkward times in the Durban home. Like when Angela visited. How embarrassing, or worse, was that!

'We've visited Angela many times as you know, but this is her first trip home for two years. You must take a low profile, Bill,' Peter warned.

'She's going to have so much to tell me,' Letty said hesitantly. 'It's just not the same on the telephone.'

He said quickly, 'I thought I'd take my camera somewhere this weekend. A bus journey, probably, to find different subjects. I'm practising scenes in different lights, you know.'

'Thank you, Bill, but be here when she arrives. Angela does accept that you live here.'

It was going to be another hurdle he had to climb.

On the Friday night, Angela arrived in a great flurry of chatter, Peter and Letty rushing to the door as the taxi drew up. He could see how much they had missed her all the time she had been away. They drew her indoors, one on either side of her, each of them asking and answering questions.

Even if nothing had happened in between, Bill would have been breathless to see Angela. He hadn't looked at another girl since bringing her pin-up poster. Because of her, he'd never had a girlfriend. Yet, it could never have been her, as he'd stupidly hoped that dreadful day. She had really encouraged him to fall in love with her, but of course she'd never have dated a boy three years younger. In a large sealed envelope, he had a pile of portraits he had taken of her just before the event, when he was practising portraits using her as a model. Truth – liking the excuse to get near her. He hadn't looked at these nor wanted to show them to Mr Gibson.

He watched her from where he waited at the open door of the lounge. She was wearing a blue coat. Her hair was shorter, neater, her legs shiny in nylons. She must hate him being here, a reminder of an awful experience and a scene she needed to blot out. She'd hate that she'd ever made a fuss of him.

He saw Peter take her coat. This was the right moment to show himself. There was no polite opening that he could sensibly use, such as *Nice to see you again*. She could hardly reply with the same.

'Hello, Angela.'

'Hello.' She hardly looked at him, as if he was a disreputable porter at a strange railway station.

Accepting her chilly greeting, he took her creamy white suitcase with its soft lid and carried it upstairs. He placed it in the pink bedroom, averting his eyes from the bed where she'd once paraded her favourite dresses for him.

'Thank you, Bill.' She put her hand on the case, as a signal that she was waiting for him to leave.

'I hope you've been enjoying your new position at work.'

'I have. Thank you.'

He stepped out of her room. She was politely distant and wary, like Mother was, as if there was some beast in him that might leap out. His mother, he understood. He'd confirmed the worst of her fears when she produced a boy child, but Angela, his long-time friend, the person who had wanted to hug him –her attitude to him now was hard to bear. He made for his bedroom, the muscles in his face taut.

Letty was on the landing. She took his arm and stepped inside his room with him, whispering, 'Remember, she was fond of both of you. And she was there where it happened so soon afterwards.'

He all but crumpled, remembering that scream.

'Try to understand. She knows you were quarrelling about her. She feels responsible.' Letty squeezed his arm sympathetically then slid back to Angela's room.

But it was the shashka he and Kenneth were quarrelling about, wasn't it, not Angela?

"She feels responsible." *Responsible.* That horrible word was weighing everyone down around him. It was as if he'd slashed at all their lives with the one stroke of the shashka. Its old story flashed into his mind, the Cossack soldier's dying words, '...mind its path, protect it well. It will inflict the most terrible wounds.' And it had, it had. He hadn't remembered those words at the time Kenneth snatched it, he hadn't heeded the warning. It had been there all along. He was the only one who was responsible. He slumped down on his bed, his head in his hands. And despite everything that he was responsible for, more loathsomely still, he was *glad* Angela was not going out with Kenneth.

He stayed in his bedroom as long as he could justify. He stood by the window to take deep breaths of the air beyond his window. He kept his eye on the church tower. It was more imposing, less cosy than the squat one on the village church he missed so much. How much more manageable things had been back in evacuation! What did it actually mean *evacuate*? He searched in his dictionary. Fancy never looking before! It meant *to remove to a safer place*. He was evacuated here, then.

He picked up his camera, a new roll of film, and trod downstairs. It was time to go out. He pushed his arms into his mac. You never knew when it was going to rain.

CHAPTER 42

Months had gone by, marked by the Corner House teas. *Retribution* was always in his head, his whole being alert until the word left Dad's lips. The teas followed the same pattern: sitting near enough to the music for crucial words like *Approved School* to be masked; the neat waitress bringing a cake-stand bearing one iced cake with a cherry, one square sponge with a tiny blob of chocolate, one dry slice of sandy Madeira, one Eccles cake, and a pot of tea. Simmering in the teapot's steam each time was the question of when Bill would have to meet Kenneth.

Gradually, he dared ask about Kenneth in more than a general way. His parents told him that he hoped to study art history, that he spent a long time with his gramophone. He had managed to go back to choir and sang tenor.

Tenor! Before the accident, Bill had wanted to taunt Kenneth about still having a treble voice beyond the age of fourteen. His voice must have broken. Did it break at the moment of the accident? Was that Bill's fault too? But Kenneth would be eighteen next month.

Mother said, 'Kenneth's been given an upright piano. He practises the choral music, sounding out the notes with his left hand.'

Swallowing, Bill ventured, 'Is he getting used to the metal hand?'

Mother answered. 'Yes, but it often hurts where it joins the live flesh.' If Bill didn't shudder outwardly, his stomach did. Why did *live flesh* sound so awful?

Then Dad said the words, as if Bill's direct mention of the prosthetic had wreaked the evil magic. 'He'll probably choose to see you soon. Up to him of course, in his own time.'

Bill prayed for Kenneth's time to be long drawn out.

Art history didn't sound like a job. What work could someone as disabled as Kenneth do? Bill thought of his own work. He was so dependent upon his eye to the viewfinder, both hands to steady the sides of his camera. He couldn't imagine how he'd manage without one hand, let alone one eye. It was truly awful.

Little was spoken of, other than a request for Bill to outline his progress. He spoke of his study using the encyclopaedias, hoping this would please.

Dad nodded. *"The essence of knowledge is, having it, to apply it,"* Confucius.

He had tried to apply the knights' code, but he hadn't understood some of it, and Dad was not the person to ask.

Mother stood up, swinging a blue and grey scarf around her shoulders. Bill remembered it from long, long ago. He must have been only five years old, for the memory was how the scarf identified her from the other mothers waiting at the school gate, and by the time he was six he'd started walking home on his own. Dad should buy her a new scarf. Perhaps Bill could do so, or would she throw it away?

The piano trio were playing light popular music. *We'll meet again, don't know where, don't know when.*

'Herbert, are you ready?' she said.

Dad put both hands on the table, preparatory to standing. 'The thing is, we can't be doing this for ever.'

'No', said Bill, 'of course not.' He was too scared to ask whether Dad meant the Corner House teas or the caring of Kenneth. He watched his father stand, flex his shoulders, feel for his pipe. He never smoked at the table, Mother didn't like it.

'You'll recall there's the not so little matter of retribution.'

The word hit him, just as he had anticipated the trial of the tea had ended, and the thankful relaxation that always followed.

'Yes.' He hadn't really thought his pathetic sums of money went any way towards it.

'You realised when retribution was first mentioned, that it might well be appropriate later rather than sooner?' Dad must mean, *once you're earning more money.*

He nodded. The feeling of doom was more about having to see Kenneth and hear his choice of retribution than the loss of money.

...and I know we'll meet again, the music played on. Everyone knew the words to that Vera Lynn song. It was written for lovers parting, not for rivals renewing their conflict. Customers were humming along cosily as his parents sidled between tea tables to the exit, *some sunny day.*

'As long as you don't forget that.'

As if he could! He watched his parents walk down Oxford Street. They were going to choose some curtain material in John Lewis. The store was nearly rebuilt now after its bombing. Afterwards, they would go home. Would 'home' look much different these days? Had they got rid of the second bed, Bill's bed, in what was now Kenneth's bedroom? It must be difficult for Kenneth to climb to the top bunk, and now there would never be a time when Bill would occupy it.

Peter and Letty were always particularly warm when he got back after his monthly tea. He wiped his shoes and hung his mac beside theirs on the hallstand. Peter put his head round the dining room door. 'Glad you're back. We're eating early tonight. Go and tell Letty you're back.'

Letty was in the lounge, looking out of the French doors at the swathe of green lawn. 'Do you remember running up and down that with Angela when you were little?' She smiled.

'Rather! And your Anderson in the side garden. I remember lots of times being here. Often my parents didn't realise where I was.'

'Really? We were glad to have you visit. When Angela was a baby, I used to sit here with her and look out at the garden. I'd imagine her running around with a brother. I'd imagine a son playing cricket while she tended the flowers.' She laughed. 'Ridiculous fantasy.

Angela never got into gardening and we never got our son. It wasn't to be.'

He didn't know what to say. Did she mean to underline that he had never been like a son? Or was it that he couldn't be like one now?

He asked if he should lay the table.

'No, it's done. Let's go in and eat. I'm going out to a musical concert with some friends and leaving you two men to enjoy *Bandwagon* without me.'

She had prepared a Macaroni Cheese, one of Bill's favourite meals.

'TTFN,' Peter quipped as she left. He was deliberately trying to sound jolly because of where Bill had been. He knew it was the tensest moment in Bill's month.

They cleared the table and did the dishes together. Bill felt a glow of closeness. Then he sensed Peter preparing to speak. He could tell something was coming.

When they'd finished tidying up, Peter purposefully moved to open the snug door. It had been kept closed all these months, even when Angela was home. If they went into it at all, Peter and Letty must have waited until Bill was well out of the way.

He turned quickly away but Peter kept hold of the door. 'Come along, we can't have part of the house taboo for ever.'

Bill moved his feet forward until he was standing at the entrance. A shudder went through him.

'Face it, Bill. The room is all right now. We'll go in.' He took Bill's elbow, ushering him right inside.

The room was fully organized. Peter had finished the project. The military mementoes and photographs were arranged on the walls. The dreaded rug had been removed, ruined for sure, and now there was a neutral carpet almost reaching the sides of the small room. Slowly, he lifted his eyes until he took in the sight of the shashka fastened by clasps to the wall opposite the window.

Peter followed the direction of his eyes. 'Yes, I kept it. I did keep it. Whatever happened with it here, I can't part with it. It's just too important to me. And I contacted a history professor, a specialist in Russian literature. There is a book that is key to my shashka, apparently, but it's very difficult to get hold of in translation, and costs a great deal of money.'

Did Peter imagine Bill would still want to read about it? The opposite was true. He'd keep far away from the subject. That was safest. He concentrated his gaze on the clasps holding the shashka to the wall.

'Yes. I ordered these special wall clasps which are locked, so now no-one can just lift it down.'

'I wouldn't!' The thought of it was impossible. In a lower voice he said, 'I didn't.'

'We won't go into any of that, Bill. Leave the whole matter now. I just want you to get used to this part of the house again so that I can leave the door open as I want. I like to see my displays while I'm sitting in the lounge. I don't want the snug shut off. And you shouldn't shut off things. Everything is part of your life, part of you.'

'I wish it wasn't,' Bill said, cold to the root of his feet.

From then on, the door was left open. There were times when Bill saw Letty dusting in there and others when he saw Peter turning pages of a volume. Friends of Peter's now came and were taken to see his collection.

Bill didn't go in, but he could now manage to remain in the lounge with the snug door open.

He had just passed it without looking, when Peter took him aside and gave him a paper bag from Boots. 'Shaving kit. You need to start shaving. A few tips, let's go upstairs and I'll show you.'

Bill put a hand to his jaw. He had felt the down getting wirier but he still thought of himself as a child, and children don't shave.

Peter demonstrated the best technique to him in the bathroom. 'There you go! Now you'll have to do that regularly, and soon every day – the curse of the man,' Peter laughed.

Afterwards, feeling his smooth, though tingling upper lip and chin, Bill looked in the mirror to see the truth. The thing was, he hadn't really been looking in the mirror, hadn't done so for a long, long time. Had the last time been the day he smartened himself up to give Angela her pin-up picture?

THE day. That day. It had stopped everything. It had stopped him looking in the mirror, it had stopped him finishing school, being

Head Boy, Captain of the football team, as well as going round to help Nanny, helping to bring Ted back to his old self. How had they all been managing? He could have been there once a week, twice a week all this time if only…

And now he shaved and was a man.

He strode from his bedroom. It should be possible to make a few of his own decisions. He was a working man, being paid wages, paying his way.

He found Peter and Letty in the kitchen. 'Is it all right if I visit my grandparents on Sunday?' he said.

Peter and Letty exchanged glances. 'They haven't said not to, have they?'

'They haven't said anything. I haven't seen them since…'

'No. Well, it's not for us to say. Phone your parents if you think you should check.'

But he didn't think he would. He never telephoned his parents. His father had telephoned him twice, otherwise, messages came via Peter. That was safest. Mother and Dad had said it was better not to visit Nanny and Grandad for a while. A while had passed.

On Sunday he threw on a coat and took the bus to Wandsworth. He walked up the hill to the place he'd so loved all those Sundays of his childhood, before evacuation. He smiled, remembering Ted upside down, his trousers flapping. Now it was a new Sunday. Surely, they would be pleased to see him now he was on an upward path?

Ted opened the door. He wasn't as closely shaven as Bill, the stubble adding to the grey bony look of his face. 'Yes?'

'Ted. Uncle Ted, it's me.'

'Bill?' There was a pause as if Ted was remembering what to do. Then he clapped both hands on the tops of Bill's arms. The palms, the fingers felt light, hardly making a dent. 'Didn't recognise you at first. You're out, prisoner of war! They let you out. Long time.' He took Bill's elbow with a lean white hand and came out of the front door. He walked Bill round the side of the house. 'Where have you been?'

It wasn't clear what Ted knew, what he understood but it was clear there weren't going to be any handstands. He looked at Ted, wondering where to begin.

Ted put a hand to his hair. 'Oh yes, Sis did say you'd got out of the Approved School. But you've been sent somewhere else…'

'Only to a friend's house, Dad's friend. I'm not far away. Fulham. If Colin's not here anymore, I could come over and lend a hand.'

'Lend a hand, that's what Sis does every Saturday, when Bert takes Kenneth out.'

Dad hardly ever took Bill out. Why did he take Kenneth?

'And Colin is still here. He helps. He got me some work at the refrigerator factory in Streatham. Only a few hours a week, but still.'

Ted was looking better. Lean and still a little odd, but better. Did Bill look worse? Ted was still holding his arm. 'You've had your punishment. You had a sword fight, slash, slash, someone gets hurt.' He picked up the garden fork and waved it. 'We're taught to fight, then when we do, we get punished. I know that, Bill.'

He took the fork away from Ted and leant it against the fence. 'I was lucky, Ted. War's ended. I'm nearly seventeen now and I've had none of what you suffered.'

'A year's time or so, you'll have National Service.' He came forward to Bill and grasped his arm tightly. 'I don't want you to go to war.'

'No, all right.' He'd better not argue, but people did have to go to war to defend their country. Several of the lads at football were already on National Service. Even Dad had served in the war. 'Where's Nanny?'

'Kitchen.' Ted looked at his hands, brushed them together.

They went to the back door. Bill hesitated. He wasn't expected. Coming in this way might startle Nanny. He didn't want to alarm her. 'Wait, Ted.'

Ted called out, 'Mother! Bill's come over.'

Nanny came to the back door, but slowly.

She would have known all along, and so would Grandad, that the damage to Kenneth was an accident, a total accident.

She set eyes on him, watery eyes. There was a long pause.

'Bill,' she breathed heavily. 'Bill! We didn't know you were coming.' She breathed again. 'I'm glad to see you're all right. Quite a man, now. Let's go and sit down with Grandad. Ted, you go and dig that trench for the potatoes, there's a good lad.'

Ted had been relegated to a younger child's role. He wasn't normal, he needed looking after, telling what to do. He looked at Nanny vaguely, then returned to the garden.

Nanny took Bill's arm. 'It was a terrible thing, what you did.'

He started to speak.

She paused, rubbed her ear. 'What's that? I can't hear well.' She led him into the sitting room.

Grandad was sitting in his chair, just like last time, only lower, slumped, as though he'd been sitting all these months waiting for Bill. He looked up, blearily. 'Colin – bring me...' He stopped.

Nanny said, 'It's Bill. Bill, come to see us.' She brought him forward, pointed to a low chair padded with the cushions she had embroidered while pregnant with Mother in 1907.

Grandad watched Bill sit on the low chair with his large knees poking upwards. 'Well, well, here you are, Bill. We knew you would come, eventually, whatever they said. So you've come to explain the whole dreadful thing to your old folks?'

'It was an accident, Grandad. I didn't mean to hurt him at all. He was going to pick it up. I went to stop him, grab it.' The act was so far behind him. He could put an end to it now, surely. 'That's how it happened.'

Grandad looked unimpressed. 'Some accidents are actions in the mind of the aggressor first.'

Bill's mouth closed. Was Grandad going to quote things? Had he caught the habit off Dad? But then he realised these were Grandad's own words, words he really meant.

Nanny fed in, 'The trouble is, Bill, you were always jealous of your cousin. I know he was petted, with his looks and sweet ways. But you had your health, you could always do things.'

'Jealousy's a dreadful thing, leads to worse,' said Grandad.

Jealous? Bill wrestled with the cushions beside him. *He*, jealous? It was Kenneth always trying to get his stuff, his friends, his family, everyone and everything in his life. It was Kenneth who had his home now. He turned his face to Nanny, deliberately showing his confusion.

'Yes, you were jealous, you know, Bill. Your mother explained the situation ages ago. He had the pretty manners and got the praise, so you were always complaining that Kenneth had hurt you, taken something of yours. You found it difficult to share, even though you had far more than he did. You didn't like him moving in despite he'd had the great sadness of losing his father in that dreadful way. And then he got keen on the same girl as you, and that did it. That's what we heard. We read it in the paper.'

Bill pushed at his head with the heel of his hand. 'I'm trying to help make things better for Kenneth. I've been working, since I finished serving my time.'

There was a pause, Nanny looking down at her hands, Grandad nodding.

'I'm working at a photographic studio.'

Nanny said, 'It's only right that you do what you can for Kenneth.'

'Yes. And I thought I'd come over to see you, to see if I can help. Like I used to.'

Grandad sounded gruff, proud. 'We manage all right. Colin helps us in the evenings, keeps an eye on Ted and takes him around a bit. Your mother comes most Saturdays. She shows Ted what has to be done during the week. He can do things not too badly.'

'But I could do more, queue for your rations, cheer Ted up. I could visit you, ask your advice.' He paused, looking at them both, waiting. Nanny was silent.

Grandad stroked his chin. 'No. I'm a prisoner in this chair just as much as you were in your prison school. I haven't anything left these days, no energy, no talk, no advice, not on this scale.'

Nanny touched Bill's arm. 'We're old folk now, too old. We've had our time. It's nice you came to see us, but it's best you remember us how we were. And we'll always remember you how you were, like we do with Ted.' She stood up, the action and her words robbing her of her breath.

'That's for sure.' Grandad nodded slowly. 'We'll remember all the good things. All those Sundays. And if we've guided you at all in the past, you can remember that.' He leant forward as best he could on his wasted thighs. 'Off you go, Bill.'

Go! 'But, I just wanted to—'

'Try and lead a good life now.'

'I will, I am. I'm doing well. I'm going to be a photographer,' Bill's words spilled out.

'Yes, your mother did say. That's good. We'll be proud if you do well.' He sat back, as if his work on Bill's behalf was done.

Nanny asked, 'Would you like a drink before you go, Bill?'

He shook his head; he could hardly swallow as it was. 'No thank you,' he muttered.

She moved to the door.

'G'bye, Grandad,' he bent forward, low, hoping for a handshake or something. 'I can— I could come again, when you like.'

Grandad put a brown speckled hand on Bill's. 'Leave it, Bill. Let it be. Things are best as they are. You've shown you care, that's all that matters now.'

Nanny was still at the door, waiting. It was as if she couldn't bear for him to be there any longer. Bill gave her a hug, but she had no substance. He could feel bones where the cuddles used to be. He moved back, scared of crushing her.

They walked down the hall. He looked back to the garden door expectantly. One of the coloured panes in it was cracked.

'No good calling to Ted,' she said. 'He'll have forgotten you're here already. I've probably got to go and remind him what he was doing.'

'But I could...'

'He works a few hours a week now, under supervision. It's doing him good. And he amuses himself, collecting postcards, rearranging them. He listens to the wireless programmes, and all the repeats. He can do things for us, so don't you worry.'

Bill stepped across the threshold. Was it really for the last time?

Nanny blew him a kiss. 'You were a lovely little boy, whatever's happened since.' And then she closed the door.

CHAPTER 43

Bill stood at Nanny's gate for some moments. Had Mother known it would be like this and tried to protect him from the hurt? She had said it would be better not to visit. Now he had seen that for himself.

He walked down the sideway to the patch where he'd worked on the carrots, and then returned to the road where Ted had shuffled home from Dunkirk looking like a scarecrow. The war had done that, that's what wars did and why Ted and Dad both thought you shouldn't fight. But Grandad, Mr Durban, Churchill and everyone in the posters said you should fight to save what you loved.

What he'd done to Kenneth was after the war and wasn't to save anything except something he'd wanted. The shashka didn't need protecting. If he'd left it alone, Kenneth would have put it down, certainly hung it up again before Peter came home. And now Kenneth had lost what mattered most to him, his looks and being able to paint things and even how he saw things. No wonder Bill had lost his family. It was only fair. His eyes filled as he held the house in his gaze. Every part of it reminded him of the warmth and fun and love he'd had when he was little. He couldn't believe Nanny and Grandad weren't there for him now.

He walked to Wandsworth High Street for the first time since his crime. He looked in the shop windows, the same shops that he'd queued outside with Mother, the butchers where he'd picked up Nanny's meat ration. He walked past the common, the defunct shelter, the roads where direct hits had occurred, a row of prefabs where children played in their small patch of grass behind a picket fence. A woman, their mother, stood, her hands akimbo, her mouth moving. She was talking to a passer-by in a hat with a feather. 'And we've got a fridge,' she said, 'so some good came out of it.'

'A refrigerator! Well I never!' said the passer-by and the feather in her hat nodded.

A fridge, like the Americans. That's what he'd like to buy for Nanny, but she wouldn't want one. She'd say she was happy to have that wooden safe with the wire door. Joan Youldon would be over the moon to have one, and the electricity to run it. One day he'd do that, when he earned enough money.

But it was Kenneth he should be buying things for. Retribution. He should provide something that meant Kenneth could work, and go properly into the world Bill had ended for him. But what?

He walked on and on, past the common until he reached the slides and roundabouts that he'd played on while Dad sat and smoked his pipe the week Jill was born. Mr Durban had given him pipe cleaners, and Dad had shown him how to make little men with them. It was the only time he remembered Dad playing with him, those few minutes.

It was as if his life was unravelling like those old jumpers that had to be re-knitted into socks for soldiers. He remembered Mrs Pawsey's attempts and the wrinkly wool, the messy balls. Unravelled. That was just how he felt.

A man was coming towards the swings, so he walked slowly away, but the man followed, picked up speed and slapped him on the back. 'It's Bill, isn't it?'

'Colin!'

'Why haven't you been over?'

'I just have. Mother warned me not to. They don't want me to come. They've said it's better not to. I could help, but—'

'That's tough. Still, it's been a shock for them. The old folk were kids in Queen Victoria's time, things were different then.

People went wrong, and that was that. But Ted will still want to see you.'

'Yes, he was all right to me. It's good about him having that work at your firm.'

'It's done him good. Look, I can bring him over to the place you're staying.'

'Fulham, not far. That will be super, if you can.' Bill felt his whole body lift with hope. At least he'd have Ted. He paused. 'You should know, I'm called Bill Durban, these days. Dad decided.'

Colin raised his eyebrows. 'I see. That's quite a thing. Listen, let's go and have a bite somewhere. Got time?' He walked back towards Wandsworth High Street, and although he needed to go in the opposite direction, Bill wasn't going to pass up the chance to sit and chat with a friend who was helping his family.

Colin led him into the small cafe where they sold pies and mugs of tea. He bought one of each for them both and put them on a table. 'Here, tuck into this.' After the first few mouthfuls he said, 'I know you've had to be banged up, but I never believed you had it in you to be vicious. I told your grandparents that.'

'Thanks.'

'Listen! This'll cheer you up. Remember you asked me if I heard more about Ted's injury I was to let you know on the QT? Well, while I've been living there, Ted's come out with the odd mention of action in Italy. After all, I served there too, and sometimes I chat to the old man about it. He takes a keen interest in operations, anything about the war, see.'

Bill leant forward, his knife and fork crossed over the pie. 'What was it?'

'The reason Ted flipped his lid? His platoon had it particularly rough, the position they were trapped in. The enemy was attacking from the hill above them, and each dawn foray ended with more men lost. Ted only had one mate left out of the conscripts, the others were regulars. It had been pouring with rain for days so they were struggling along in thick mud. They were covered in it and moving around was a slow hell. Supplies had been held up as well as letters from home, so spirits were about as low as they could get. The next time they were under fire, Ted saw his mate fall. The mud stopped him getting a hold to drag him to safety, so he lay on top of him to protect him. That's when he got the bullet in his backside. It wasn't from trying to escape.'

Bill's heart seemed to swell under his chest. 'So Ted was a hero.'

'Sort of. Only when the firing stopped, he found his mate was dead, and that's what did his head in.'

They finished their pies while Bill took this all in. What Ted had suffered was awful, yet Bill felt a glow. Ted had acted bravely; he had put his friend first. 'My father believes Ted never recovered from the three days in the sea at Dunkirk, waiting for rescue. The troops were under fire while they waited.'

'I wasn't in that show. I've always counted myself lucky. Poor old Ted. But he's better, he's definitely better. He manages the part-time work, and there's some guy linked to the Resettlement Office that's started seeing him. A sort of doctor, I think, but they just talk.'

'I'm glad if there's any help for him.' Now he could talk freely to Peter about soldiers losing their nerve, for Ted had tried to protect his friend. His last friend. 'I'm glad Ted's got you, Colin.'

'Ah, and there's more news. I have a young lady, these days. We've been going steady this last year. The plan is we'll get married and your grandad has said we can live there. The stairs are too much for both of them, so they're going to move out of their bedroom and let us have it. We'll all eat in the kitchen and the old folks will use the dining room as their bedroom.'

Bill couldn't find an answer. It seemed very shocking that the house would be so turned around.

Then Colin said, 'Peggy, my wife-to-be, has worked up at the hospital assisting the nurses so she's picked up a lot. She's going to look after them both, see. Your nan won't have to worry about housework or cooking. The old folks will have all that done for them.'

'Really! How super. Mother will be glad.' The news helped lift away the heavy sadness of parting with Nanny and Grandad. He wrote his address and telephone number down for Colin on a back page of his diary, and set off for Fulham. 'Don't forget about bringing Ted over, will you?'

Peter was in the hall when he got in, folding piles of newspaper ready to tear into strips for the boiler. 'They say we're in for another vicious winter. That's nice to look forward to, isn't it.' He looked up at Bill. 'Not a good idea, to visit then?'

'No, not really. I can't go again.' He firmed his jaw. 'But there are some good things.' He told Peter about Colin and his wife-to-be. 'It will be so much better if Nanny doesn't have to worry about house-work and cooking. Colin says he'll bring Ted over to Fulham to see me. Can they come here; would you mind?'

Peter was glad for him and so there was something new to look forward to. No-one had visited him here so far. He went up to his bedroom and sat on his bed. From there he could see the tree next door, virtually leafless. It had seemed chilly lately, but perhaps worse was in store.

He opened his chest of drawers. There was one knitted V-neck, a relic of Aunty's handiwork, now too small for him. One jumper had been school uniform in those days when he'd been a prefect. He'd had a thicker one at Brigville but it had gone for rags, worn-out and out-grown. There was only one other jumper, rather a thin one. He wouldn't have enough to keep him warm this winter.

His bottle of shillings was half full. He always put in a shilling whenever he still had one left at the end of a week. Upending it, Bill found the contents came to twenty-seven shillings. He put thirteen on one side and fourteen on the other. He wasn't particularly super-stitious but he took the fourteen, not the thirteen, downstairs to Peter.

'Peter. I've been saving. This is for Kenneth, to help with his singing lessons. Can you pass this onto Dad, please?'

'That's the spirit, Bill. I'll do that.'

Bill would need the thirteen shillings for a warm jumper before the month was out and warmer trousers if it was going to get much colder. It was already a monthly problem getting his one pair of good trousers back from the cleaners in time for work on Monday.

Peter said, 'On a cheerful note, Bill, I saw Gibson at the club. He said that you're an asset. Business has looked up since you got your hand in. He's taken on a lot more bookings.'

It was true. Mr Gibson had also encouraged him to experiment and let him borrow equipment. The studio had some American magazines lying around and they were good for sparking new ideas.

As far as his career was concerned, things had got to the point where he'd stopped being frightened of the future, except for the one threat of doom. Retribution.

CHAPTER 44

When he heard that Angela was to spend Christmas and New Year with the Durbans, Bill wondered how he could possibly manage the awkwardness of the situation. Because he'd taken no holiday from work so far, Mr Gibson had given him from Christmas Eve until January 2nd off, so it would be difficult to escape the house. Luckily, Alan rescued him. On one of their many get-togethers after work, he invited Bill to stay for the entire holiday. Bill clapped him on the shoulder. 'You're such a topping friend. Thank you!'

Christmas was a good week. The Routledge parents were their usual kind and interested selves, as though Bill had never been a criminal. Somehow Major Routledge had found a ham, and there were vegetables from Alan's patch as well as trifle, and a cake and some dates that Mrs Routledge had been given at work. They played different board games during the week, and when the rain stopped, he and Alan worked on the garden borders, or went down to Thornton Heath for a kick-around with his friends.

The Routledges all wanted to see his photographs, his original album and all the loose ones, loads of them, that he'd taken since joining Gibson's studio. It was so good having people interested in his efforts.

The three of them had bought him a Christmas present: a large portfolio he could never have afforded himself, with padded covers and useful slits for the photograph corners.

Mrs Routledge painted a heading on the first page with white poster paint, 'New Year 1949', and suggested he put in photographs taken of them that day using the flash equipment Mr Gibson had lent him. His Christmas present to Bill had been four bulbs for the flash gun that attached to the camera, and it was exciting to try it out.

Although Bill timed each take carefully, Mrs Routledge couldn't help flinching when the flash went off, so he knew there'd likely be only one of the four that was any good. He threw the used bulbs away, wondering when he'd be able to afford some more. There were so many more possibilities with a flash gun, like night-time studies. He was going to try that next.

During the month of January, he compiled his best photographs and put them in his new portfolio. He ordered the pages carefully, presenting a full range of studies. He checked out whether Peter and Letty liked each one before including it. 'You can't trust your own judgment.'

By February, the album was full and organised, and he felt ready to show it to Mr Gibson. He took it to work in the large portfolio messenger bag that Peter and Letty had given him. It was second hand, of course, but was a super useful thing to have.

As he hurried towards the studio he could see that Mr Gibson was waiting at the entrance grasping a white envelope. Could it hold something about his past? 'Is something wrong, Mr Gibson?'

'No, something's right, very right.' He gave Bill an embarrassed hug. 'Your pic of brewery horses in the snow won the *Photographic Monthly* winter competition.'

Bill's breath left him, 'No!' He shook his coat off quickly and took the envelope.

'It's in the name of the studio of course, but I'll make sure you get full credit.'

He took the letter. He hadn't dare to hope that his photo would even be placed. He had actually won?

'I've already rung the local rag.'

Bill couldn't speak. The last time he'd been in the paper it had been for something truly awful. But that was in a different name.

Mr Gibson bounced on his feet as if he was about to start dancing. 'You've put my little studio on the map. I'll have the trophy to display in the window, thanks to you. But the fifty-pound prize, that's solely yours. Only fair.'

'Gosh!' That was an immense amount, half the fare to America.

'You're gobsmacked, aren't you? As for me, my studio will be listed in *Photographic Monthly* forever.'

He noticed the large album under Bill's arm. 'What's this, now?'

'I've put a portfolio together, as you suggested.'

Mr Gibson sat down. 'Go and make some tea while I look through it.'

When Bill brought back the tea, Mr Gibson closed the album and said, 'These are good. Some, very good. You're getting to the point where I've no more to teach you. When your apprenticeship ends, you don't have to go to a bigger studio to work. I'll make a job for you here. We'll take on corporate work, if you want to stay.'

'Definitely!' Bill couldn't imagine leaving. Where would he go?

'I can't increase your wage by much now, but I'll help you sell your work to magazines. That'll bump your income up. You could even think about having your own studio when you're twenty-one.'

'Really!'

'Yes, when it comes to it. Get your National Service over, save as much as you can, then set up on your own, as long as it's not in Clapham. I don't want you as competition! I already have *Jerome, branches everywhere!* to contend with.'

He laughed, and Bill laughed too, a well of excitement surging somewhere in his middle. His own studio! But it certainly wouldn't be in Clapham, not even in South London.

'You should make a plan. It's something to discuss with Peter. First of all, upgrade your equipment. I can help you with that. Then price out for a studio, materials, processing and charges for customers. Best to have a future ready, as soon as you get back from wherever you're sent to serve.'

He went home, not hearing or seeing anything around him, and reported back to Letty and Peter. Their delight at his win was almost as warming as his own. 'I don't know whether I can be a businessman, but it would be my dream to have my own studio.'

Peter grabbed a lined notebook and a pencil. 'Magnificent. You've stuck at your study and now it's paid off. Let's work out some figures. Stay with Gibson till you're eighteen. You could defer your National Service if you're on a course of study.'

'But I'm not, and I don't even have School Certificate.'

Peter sighed.

Letty said, 'Or you can claim a Conscientious Objection. Your father's a pacifist.'

'No. I shall serve. I want to do my bit.'

'Good man. Do your service, then. Get a good record, and after it's over, you can make your move.'

Bill clasped his hands tightly on his lap. It would mean a move in all senses. Something else to face; excitement and sadness mixed.

Peter lit a cigarette and blew the smoke towards the window. 'The photographic prize plus Mr Gibson's suggestion; very good news to give your parents tomorrow.'

'Yes,' Bill nodded. The following day was his monthly Corner House tea, and at last Dad and Mother had something that might make them proud of him. What would they say at the idea of his having his own studio?

His heart thumped a touch on the way. He was a little late as he passed the Brasserie and he leapt up the staircase, two at a time, to the usual tearoom. He sidled past the musicians who were just moving towards their dais, and looked for his parents' familiar backs. He spotted them. But there were three backs. There was no mistaking the curls. The back of the head was unchanged.

It had to happen, he'd known that, but they hadn't warned him. They should have. It wasn't fair. He paused and took a breath before stepping between the tables to show himself, and to see Kenneth face-on for the first time since the shashka had damaged it.

He managed a careful *Hello,* directing his gaze to the middle of the table.

'Bill.' His father spoke, but was too busy kneading his knuckles to look up.

'Kenneth thought he'd join us today,' Mother said, waving away the waitress for the moment.

The slight figure in the Dulwich College blazer leaned forward. His intent stare from his one eye made Bill's knees weaken. A satin eye patch covered the right eye. The reality of a familiar but damaged Kenneth was worse than his imaginings. The challenge in the stare was, this time, fully justified.

He sat down with a thump. Mother started, and he muttered, 'Sorry.'

It felt a lifetime since he'd seen Kenneth properly. The last time he'd been a hump in a hospital bed. He took in the eye patch, the wormof a red scar beneath it spoiling the peach-like face. He must keep the shock from his expression. He tightened his face muscles. Automatically he held out his hand.

With a wry smile, Kenneth held out his left hand and the two hands met over one side of the white tablecloth. It was like holding hands as a child instead of the formal gesture he'd intended. Instantly he felt a deep blush cover his face.

'I find people prefer the wrong hand to a metal one,' Kenneth said ironically, flicking back his right sleeve to show the ugly thing. Technicians must have made some attempt to humanize it, but it was still crude: a parody of Kenneth's sensitive white hand with its long fingers.

What could he say? It wasn't as if he'd never rehearsed his words. He'd dark-dreamed them often enough. But now no words would come.

Kenneth had less difficulty. 'Well, one of us hasn't changed much in the last three eventful years. You're still built like a football player. I suppose you still do play?'

Bill tried to nod calmly despite inwardly cringing.

Dad raised one hand, twitching his fingers to alert the waitress.

Mother cleared her throat and said in her highest voice, 'The singing lessons have gone really well, Bill. Kenneth's in great demand for solos as well as for his contribution to local choirs.'

'I just need transporting,' said Kenneth with a lift of his left eyebrow. Did the right one still work or was that damaged too? 'My health is still a little frail for public transport.'

'I hope to get a car soon,' said Dad. 'That will be a great help, as other choir members can't collect him every time. But it's a bit beyond me at present.'

Bill nodded and concentrated on the rise and fall of his stomach. He'd never been to sea, but it felt as though he was rocking to-and-fro on a see-sawing deck.

The waitress came for the order. They'd always had the same but this time Dad turned to Kenneth first and asked if he wanted anything special.

Kenneth turned his good eye upon him and considered. 'An egg sandwich would be so nice, Dad.'

The waitress was an older woman. She bent towards Kenneth solicitously. 'The sandwiches are meant to be the set variety, but I'll make sure there's an extra egg one for you, sir.'

Kenneth treated her to his dimples. He still had both of those.

There was a distant rustle as the trio took their places. Bill's applause was much more enthusiastic than before. He couldn't wait for the music to start. It would prevent the need for conversation. The violinist tuned up and a medley of romantic music began.

'Schubertiana,' said Kenneth.

'Delightful,' said Mother.

Dad was looking tense, or was it anxious? He couldn't be more so than Bill. What statement or demand would come at the end of the tea and cakes, or was this occasion merely that Kenneth felt ready to reacquaint himself with his attacker?

The waitress came with the tea, placing the pot by Mother and smiling at Kenneth who was humming along with Schubert's *Trout*. She returned with the food.

For once, the cake-stand would not have one of its four cakes left at the end, always the dry sandy Madeira. Bill kept his eyes on the safe yellow rectangle. It would be left to him to eat it. He waited to be proved right.

They began with the sandwiches. Bill handed them around, deliberately averting his eyes when Kenneth took his with a metallic click against the plate.

Mother, nibbling at an eggy triangle, said, 'Won't it be absolutely magnificent when there is butter again? War's well over but things seem to have got harder and harder.'

At that point Kenneth's metal hand clonked accidentally on the plate and his serviette fell to the floor. Before Bill had time to react, Dad had leapt up and retrieved it.

Instantly, Bill saw how things must be and understood the grey in his father's face.

Dad placed the serviette close to Kenneth's left hand. Then he leant towards Bill. 'For his new career, Kenneth is to be an art historian.'

Kenneth smile conveyed pain bravely borne, rather than pleasure. 'Prevented from creating Art myself, I am to analyse and appreciate the Art of others, masters of past work.'

Bill put his sandwich down. It was the meat paste one. How sensible a solution, for Kenneth to have a place in the artistic world without need to wield a brush; but how stinging a transcription of his situation.

Mother said, 'If his Higher School Certificate results are to expectation, he will undertake a BA course at the Courtauld Institute.'

There was a pause. Bill had never heard of it. As if in celebration, the trio began playing a march. Kenneth probably knew its name.

Dad continued the train of thought. 'A most prestigious institution. Anthony Blunt heads it, leaving his questionable politics behind, I trust. A great honour if Kenneth gains a place there.'

'It's quite near here, in fact,' Mother added. 'Portman Square. So convenient for Selfridges.'

'That's – super. Impressive,' said Bill, bemused. He had no idea why art historians or Kenneth needed Selfridges nearby.

Kenneth moistened his lips. 'Mama is delighted to hear this, of course. But the exams are yet to be faced. One mustn't count one's chickens.' He looked modestly at his second egg sandwich.

'If all goes well, he'll start in October. But he still needs physical support at home.' Mother added, 'When your father's away, it falls to me.' Her expression was pained.

In the following pause, Kenneth began to reach for the cake-stand and Dad quickly proffered it. After a mouthful of the lemon fancy, Kenneth explained. 'At the Courtauld, the note-taking during lectures will be beyond me. My left hand is very clumsy and my right,' he gave a tinkling laugh, 'will need a wealth of practice.'

What did that imply? Bill waited.

'For his course, he will need an amanuensis,' said Dad.

'Amanuensis? Is that something you buy?' Bill prepared himself for the price.

Kenneth smiled at Mother, the corners of his mouth turning up while his upper lip moved down in a way Bill remembered so well.

'It's a person, Bill, someone who takes notes from what you say,' Mother said. 'At school, the boys have taken it in turns to do this for Kenneth.'

Bill bit the inside of his cheek. If they were saying he had to take the notes, how could he go to work?

Dad corrected his guess. 'Kenneth will have to interview candidates for the amanuensis, a paid position.'

There was his fifty-pound prize. That should cover it. It would be the retribution Dad had suggested, something to really help Kenneth back into the world he wanted. He felt his stomach muscles soften. What a relief it would be to have the retribution sorted.

Kenneth was leaning forward. 'But enough about me. Let's hear what you're up to, our strong member of the family.'

Everything Kenneth said now would be laced with sarcasm or making a weighted point. How was it best to respond? It was like being a fencer with no lance.

'Yes, Bill, how is your progress at the photographic studio?' said Dad, the pinch of his nose suggesting a touch of interest.

The pianist was now taking the forefront of the performance, his arpeggios rippling away while the violinist and 'cellist merely gave the odd stroke to their strings, or so it looked to Bill.

He toyed with his pastry fork, its handle greasy with sweat. Mother had foisted an egg sandwich on him, sliding it onto his plate while the three of them continued with cake. He forked a piece of egg white, hoping it was soft enough to slide down his tense throat.

Kenneth's left hand was imitating the delicate tinkling of the solo piano part.

Bill had hurried here eager to tell of his win and the plan he'd worked out with Peter. But now, in Kenneth's presence, these achievements would feel like an insult.

Dad persisted. 'You must be progressing by now? Does the photographer let you use the equipment yourself?'

That stung. 'Yes! All the time! Mr Gibson, the boss, lets me take some of the portraits. He's put some in the window. Also, I won a competition with a photograph I took in my spare time. It will be on the front of *Photographers Monthly*.'

'A journal, is that?' Dad indicated that most people would never have heard of it.

'Front page?' said Kenneth.

'With your name beneath it?' said Dad.

Bill looked down. 'Inside the journal.'

Applause broke out in the tea-room. The trio had finished the selection. Kenneth fell quiet, unable to clap.

Mother's token tapping of her fingertips lasted only seconds. Then she joined Dad in asking more questions about Bill's work.

He answered, relieved to be on safer ground, and ended, 'Mr Gibson thinks I'll be good enough to set up my own studio before I'm twenty-one. After National Service, I plan to move on, live independently.'

'Live independently,' Kenneth repeated in a dreamy voice. 'How enviable.'

'Your own studio?' Dad queried. 'That sounds risky. But you'll probably think better of it by the time you've finished National Service.'

'Better to be employed by a known establishment,' said Mother.

Bill looked at them for signs of some satisfaction. Was *photographer* an acceptable occupation, one they could admit their son was following?

'I knew Peter would provide a sound guide and influence on you,' Dad summed up.

Mother's interest had waned. 'You haven't had your Madeira, Bill.'

'I thought Kenneth would like it,' he fenced.

Kenneth shook his head and wrinkled his nose.

The trio began 'The Skaters' Waltz', a piece he'd heard on the Routledge's gramophone.

'How I used to adore waltzing,' said Mother. 'I suppose those days will never come back for me.'

'I'm hardly in a position to take you, am I?' said Dad.

'If only I could,' said Kenneth regretfully.

Bill looked at the crumbs on his plate. It couldn't be long before Dad brought an end to this ordeal. Nothing definite had been said about what he was supposed to do or offer. There hadn't even been a quotation, only the talk of an amanuensis. Was that to be it, the retribution, or not?

Dad stood. 'I'll pay the bill. One day it may be you doing this, Bill, taking us to tea.'

Bill reached for his wallet that he knew held only two shillings. 'I can contribute.'

Dad waved a hand. 'Another time, perhaps.'

Mother moved her chair wide from the table, a too visible statement that otherwise Kenneth might bump into it as he moved from the table.

'Well, then,' said Dad. He rubbed his hands together as if ridding them of sand from the Madeira which finally he had been the one to eat, muttering, 'Waste not, want not.' *Ridding* was clearly in his mind for he went on, 'Now that Kenneth has met with you, I think this marks the last of our teas here. Kenneth can think about things before a new meeting.' Dad looked at Kenneth. 'Just the two of you, if he feels that's better.'

Kenneth inclined his head. He still hadn't said anything about retribution.

Dad picked up his rolled umbrella. 'You could come to the house, perhaps. What do you say to that, Kenneth? Just for a cup of tea, a conversation–'

Kenneth said, 'If Bill's not averse.'

Bill felt totally averse to it. Dad saying '*the house*' instead of '*home*' didn't help. He gave a nod, more in recognition of Kenneth's allowing it than in agreement with the idea, one he hoped would just melt away.

Dad took Mother's elbow. 'We'll let you know, Bill. *Tempus fugit.*

We must be off. I have to pack my files. Sessions in Winchester begin Monday.'

Bill read Mother's face as *'And I'm left to cope alone'*. He was so, so lucky that Peter had taken him in and he hadn't had to endure these things daily, not that he'd have been allowed home.

'I suppose that photography could be considered an art form,' conceded Kenneth as if his mind had remained in an earlier conversation. 'And one that pays, it seems.'

Bill made a minute raise of his shoulders, the nearest he could get to a non-committal acknowledgement. 'Goodbye,' he said, nodding to each of them. He tried not to show his great eagerness to escape but his feet betrayed him. 'Thank you for the tea, Dad. It's wonderful about your art history, Kenneth.'

He could have sworn that Kenneth made a regretful glance at the metal appendage where his drawing hand had been. Certainly the fingers twitched upwards in a gesture of some kind.

'March of the Toreador' accompanied Bill's eager strides to the staircase. He could still hear the strains as he negotiated the press of bodies around the food hall and squeezed thankfully to the exit.

CHAPTER 45

He'd been dreading the moment of facing Kenneth ever since Brigville. Now, even months after the final awful Corner House tea, he didn't feel he'd recovered from it. Since then, he'd concentrated on his work, and felt heartfelt gratitude each week that went by, that he wasn't having to endure another meeting.

He'd posted fifty pounds as soon as he'd received his prize, addressing the envelope to Dad to ensure that he would know Bill was paying for an amanuensis. As he watched the letter drop through the open mouth of the letterbox, he prayed that this would be accepted as retribution.

He had a plain postcard from Kenneth stating, 'Received £50, thank you.' He heard nothing more, and Dad had said nothing to Peter.

Then Mother telephoned. A telephone call from 'home' was a rare and tense event. Would it be a crisis, a demand or a belated acknowledgement of the money he'd sent as appropriate for Kenneth's retribution – what Alan called his Sword of Damocles?

'How are you, Bill?' she didn't wait for an answer. 'Kenneth feels ready to have you visit here, at the house.' The tone suggested that gratitude would be the appropriate response.

'Thank you.' How could he delay it? He tried, 'Would it be more convenient for you if I wait until Dad is back from Sessions?'

'Not necessarily.'

The years of separation from Mother were not long enough to miss the hidden command. She needed him to come now, for some reason. His instinct told him he should go immediately, his stomach felt differently. At that last Corner House meeting, Dad had said 'just for a cup of tea'. He would act on that.

'Shall I call by for a cup of tea after work on Friday, then, my half day?' Going soon would avoid agonizing about it for days and nights.

'Thursday would be better. I have friends on Friday.' Of course, Mother wouldn't want Bill seen, not in daylight especially.

'I'll come after work, then. It will be just before seven by the time I get there.'

'That's quite suitable for us. Until Thursday, then.'

He held onto the receiver after he'd rung off, as if that would delay his visit. It was going to be dreadful to see his old home. It was not far off three years since he'd set eyes on it. He visualised the door opening onto it all. What was familiar would underline his loss, and what was changed would underline his distance from his family. But he had to go.

He'd come home that Saturday of the last meeting muttering, 'Kenneth was there,' and Peter and Letty looked sympathetic. Bill never knew if they had additional information. Now he went into the lounge to tell them what he had to do after work on Thursday.

The day came, and heavy rain with it. Peter walked to the bus stop with him, holding his large umbrella over them both. They both travelled in the same direction to work but on different buses. The puddles splashed around their feet as they marched to the bus stop.

'You're a good soul, really, Bill. Believe that. Just have a cup of tea with your mother and Kenneth. It breaks the ice, you know. You needn't make more of it than that.'

Bill shook his lowered head. Peter was warning him that the invitation was not Mother's prelude to having him back home. 'I won't. But they have plans for me. I'm sure.'

Peter didn't seem to take that in. He pressed his hand on Bill's shoulder. 'Remember, despite all these difficulties you have to face, there are very good things ahead.'

Bill's bus came first, splattering them both with muddy water. 'Thanks, Peter.'

'Good luck. Stay positive.'

Once at the studio, Bill made an excuse to work in the darkroom all day. It avoided his tension showing itself to Mr Gibson, who remained completely unaware of Bill's life, an ignorance that was comfortable for them both.

When Bill emerged into the light of the street he felt like an unearthed mole. He was greeted by relentless rain. He started for the bus, but, suddenly disorientated, had to stop and think how to get to his old home. He'd never gone from this direction before. He recognised he'd need a different route and cast around for the right bus stop. There was no shelter so he was wet through by the time the bus came.

The rain had not lessened when he left the bus in Wandsworth. Without the protection of Peter's large umbrella he would have to rely on a handkerchief to dry off his face and hair when he arrived.

He approached his old road viewing it like the visitor he now was. Forty-three, Primley Road was still one of its kind. No colour on the gate or paintwork marked it out as different from the rest of the street, or as the kind of house where a couple might have a criminal son. He kept his head down and his coat collar up just in case neighbours might see him in the dusk, and hurried towards the gate. His shoes were suffering from the rain and the state of the pavements, ensuring a lessening of his welcome.

When he reached the front path, intending to dab himself dry, he pulled out his handkerchief and the precious piece of napkin fell out into a puddle. It felt like a bad omen. He picked the sodden fragment up and put it in his left pocket as he moved to the porch.

There'd been such a hurricane of events since he'd opened this front door with his own key. He certainly didn't have one now. Ding-dong, the bell chimed with ironic cheer. Mother answered and almost pulled him inside.

'Did anyone see you?'

'I don't think so.'

She took his raincoat and hung it on the peg next to Dad's trilby.

'You're soaked.'

'Yes, I'm sorry.'

'Best to leave your shoes here, then.' She went to the cloakroom and brought out the hand towel.

'Thank you,' he said, drying his face and hair. But the damp from the napkin seeped its reminder in whatever position he stood.

Mother looked him up and down, appraisingly. 'Of course, you're hardly a youth anymore, at least, no-one would think of you as one.'

He realised she was comparing him to his pre-criminal appearance, imagining how he'd appear to neighbours who had known him. 'You look like a working man now.'

'Well I am.'

'Yes. I'm sure you're very competent at what you do.'

'Would you like to see some of my latest work some time?' As soon as the words had left his mouth he knew they were ill-judged.

Mother's eyes closed briefly. 'Some time, yes.' She extended a half-hearted arm. 'Kenneth's in the garden room. I'll put this in the laundry.' She took the towel from him and went towards the kitchen.

Bill took the private moment to look around, breathing in the crushingly familiar smell of lavender polish. The stairs had a new carpet. It would be crass to comment upon it. Mother had gestured towards the garden room, so he moved towards it.

Inside the open door, he saw the bookcase that had once held a few *Readers' Digest* abridged novels, his annuals, an atlas and the set of Home Encyclopaedias. It now displayed a hard-backed series, *Gems from the Art World*. These books provided a safe enough place for his eyes to focus on as the next stage of his drama unfolded. His cousin was standing at the french doors, his back to Bill.

'Hello, Kenneth.'

Kenneth turned from his contemplation of the garden at night. The sight reminded Bill of a scene in a Noel Coward play. Peter had taken him to see it not long ago. Would Kenneth break into song?

'Bill. Welcome. Is Marcia making tea?' Kenneth asked, musically enough.

Marcia now. Bill supposed that figured; *Aunty* didn't sound sophisticated. 'I didn't ask her. How are you, Kenneth?'

'As well as can be expected. I struggle on.' With his good hand, he smoothed down his finely knitted jumper patterned in small jewels of colour, perhaps the first jumper he'd owned that wasn't hand-knitted by his mother. 'How does it feel to be here again?'

'As difficult as can be expected.' Bill jolly well wasn't going to pretend, and there were limits to what he would tolerate. Peter had advised him to draw a line under it somewhere.

'Will you want to look around?'

'Not really.'

'Ah.'

There was a pause.

Bill looked around the garden room while he could. It was more or less unchanged. 'How is the amanuensis?' He needed a clue to see if his fifty pounds had been an acceptable gesture of retribution.

'Still interviewing possibles. I've given one or two a trial. There's time before my course begins.'

Bill's heart sank. The gesture hadn't been large enough; the sword of Damocles was still raised at the ready.

'Shall we go into the front room? That's where we usually take tea.' Kenneth sounded like an old married man, or, perhaps, Dad.

It was a long way past tea-time. It was also a long time since Bill had had anything to eat. The likelihood of his being offered actual food was remote, and he might not feel like eating when this ordeal ended.

'Come.' Kenneth led on, his remaining eye showing the way. He'd adopted a tilt of the head as a way of operating one-eyed. Bill followed, the guest. The hero opened the front room door.

Yes, Kenneth wanted him to see that Aunty's furniture had gone. The pouffe and the chairs with their lacy arm covers were back just as they'd been before the war. With a jolt Bill remembered sitting in here the very first time he'd met Kenneth, the little boy with knife pleats on his shorts, pushed forward by terrifying Uncle Frank.

Kenneth sat in one chair and waited for Bill to take the other. Bill took his time, looking around before sitting down. The left side of his trousers was uncomfortably damp, and he shifted position.

He said, 'You must miss your mother, all her things.'

'One grows up. I could have gone to America, I could go now, any time, but I shan't.'

'That seems hard.'

'A lot of things are hard.' Kenneth waved the good hand. 'She telephones once a fortnight. They can afford it.'

A gust of wind, followed by an increased downpour against the window, filled the silence.

How long could Mother possibly be bringing tea, or was this lengthy interim deliberate?

'I miss Aunty,' he said voicing his thoughts unwittingly, then fabricated a cough to cover them.

'I doubt if the feeling's mutual. The youth who ruined her lovely boy!'

He swallowed his misery at the thought of Aunty's loathing. 'I'm really sorry she's gone.'

'I let her go; partly from kindness. She couldn't bear to see my injuries, my facing hospital stays or the aftermath of surgery. I thought I'd save her from witnessing it, over and over again. Anyway, you know very well that I didn't want to go to *A*-merica with *Duh*-waine.' His sarcasm died suddenly. He leant forward his jaw tense. 'My mother has been taken from me, as well as my eye and my hand. You also had a part in bringing her Dwaine, didn't you?'

Bill's breathing was hurting his chest like a runner who shouldn't tackle hills. If he had anything to say he hadn't breath to say it. At that point, thankfully, he heard footsteps.

Mother tripped in with the tea. 'Not too early for you, Kenneth?'

'Perfect, Marcia. Grateful as always. I shall have to find some little thank-you, later.'

Bill cringed. What might that involve? He kept his eyes on the tray of tea. Mother tweaked the tea cosy, ready to pour. He remembered Aunty knitting it during evacuation. She'd used the red and cream wool from a child's jumper that Kenneth had unravelled. He'd excelled at that.

Mother began a litany of Kenneth's events. He imagined her speaking to her Ladies' Circle in a similar way. 'Kenneth will be on his way to read History of Art at the Courtauld in September. He's been a soloist at Wandsworth's Choral Society on many occasions, and now he's been chosen to join the tenors for Bach's B minor Mass to be performed by the Southern England Philharmonic at Christmas. Such an honour!' Kenneth held up his good hand.

'Enough about me, Marcia. Bill won't have a clue about oratorio, collections or artistic movements. Mustn't bore the poor chap.' He turned to Bill, politely. 'Do you still play football, then?'

Bill nodded.

Mother shuddered. 'In rainy weather, all that mud. Your kit must be horrendous to wash.'

He nodded again, guilty as charged. She'd be so relieved it wasn't in her wash-load. 'I play Saturdays, left wing usually. We train Wednesday evenings.'

'How vigorous,' Kenneth said. He paused. 'I still go to watch my cricket team, in the summer.'

His voice trailed off, weary after emphasizing the *watch*. Mother's cup clinked gently on its saucer.

A horse and cart clattered past, *Any old rags 'n' bones, rags 'n' bones*. It was surely the same man who'd always come past at home times? The man had been old even then.

'Really!' exclaimed Mother. 'In the evening! And I wish he'd confine his calls to the main road.'

What should be said next? What was coming, if anything was coming? How long was long enough? When could he politely leave? He drank the rest of his tea.

'How are your prospects now?' said Mother.

'Good, Mother.' He started to tell her about the pictures that magazines had bought, the competition wins; his further plans. After the halting exchanges this topic was a relief, and his enthusiasm filtered through his reserve.

'I'm glad,' said Mother, 'you're making good. Your father will be pleased. Competiton wins...your name will be under your photographs, of course.' She paused, and as if he couldn't precisely follow her train of thought, 'Perhaps you should return to your own name in the future. William Wilson, the photographer.'

He didn't answer. Kenneth's legs stretched into the middle of the room, and he crossed one foot over the other. His smug expression emphasized the Wilson in him. Bill remembered his dismay when he first met Kenneth, discovering that he wasn't the only Wilson in the world.

Mother repeated, 'William Wilson?'

'Is that what Dad thinks my name should be?'

'He will. Now.'

He allowed a pause. 'It's best I keep to *Bill Durban*.' That was the name he'd generously been given. That was the man he'd become.

Mother's eyes widened. He sensed outrage. 'I shall have to tell your father that.'

In the silence, Mother was waiting for him to change his mind. He kept still.

Kenneth gave a small cough. 'So you're doing well as a photographer. Moving towards that *independence*,' his expression was thoughtful.

'Yes.'

Mother started gathering the cups. It was an appropriate time to leave. How wonderful! There wasn't to be a new demand.

Bill rose. 'Thank you for tea, Mother.'

'Was there anything you'd like to collect, while you're here?'

This was her way of saying this would be the only opportunity. There were things, and he hadn't known how to ask. His bravery medal was hidden behind Kenneth's picture; his letters in Dad's study. Should he admit to it, or chance losing his precious things forever?

'There is something I left in the bedroom,' he started carefully.

Kenneth smirked. 'Wouldn't I have noticed it? I passed over your bits when Dad packed your suitcase at the end of your sentence.'

Oh, what did it matter now if he revealed the hiding place? He'd never need it again. 'I hid something important.'

Kenneth's one eye gleamed. 'Ah. Tell me where, I'll get it.'

Bill didn't want to go up himself and see his bedroom changed into Kenneth's enclave. In any case, Kenneth would follow him and see the hiding place, so he stayed where he was. 'Thank you, Kenneth. If you could bring your picture down, the one Aunty framed for you, I'll show you.'

Kenneth disappeared upstairs. Bill turned quickly to Mother. 'There's something I hid in Dad's study, please.'

She raised her eyebrows. 'You had no right. Get it then.'

The study was unchanged, as he'd predicted, but now he was tall enough to reach up to the legal annals. With a shudder he remembered the last time he'd done this – to collect the fatal pin-up poster for Angela, that dreadful day. He removed his precious shashka story from the largest tome, and the letters, and rapidly slid them into his jacket pocket. Kenneth was coming downstairs. He moved into the hall before Kenneth reached the bottom stair, the bravery medal in his good hand. He dangled it from its ribbon. 'A treasure behind my picture! A touch of embarrassment, I suppose? But I admire your choice of hiding place.'

He didn't answer but stood at the bottom of the stairs, which prevented Kenneth coming further. Bill was angry now. Kenneth had asked for this. He took his medal from Kenneth and put it in his top pocket. 'There was one other thing.'

Mother was behind him and he turned, not wanting her to miss his words. 'An important photograph is missing from my album.'

'But your father packed your album when you first moved into Peter's.'

He turned back to face Kenneth. 'Yes. But the envelope with this particular photograph was no longer *under* the album, *inside* its box, which was still tightly tied.' He let his words fall out singly to ensure their import wasn't lost on Mother.

She said defensively, 'You must have so many photographs, Bill. The loss of one can't matter. Don't be self-important.'

'Was it a photograph of me?' said Kenneth, airily.

He resisted making the retort *You know it was.* He didn't want his old home to hold anger and bitterness as its last memory of him. He said in his most generous tone, 'Yes, it was, Kenneth.'

'Then we must aim to replace it.'

'There, you see,' Mother said with a triumphant flick of her shining hair, 'Kenneth is putting things to right.'

He took a step back and Kenneth descended the rest of the stairs. Hadn't Kenneth destroyed it after all? Did he genuinely mean to post it back to him? Bill had a surge of hope. It was one of his earliest photos, his first really good one, his own piece of art, even if it was from a sad and awkward time. The occluded light would interest Mr Gibson. 'Thank you, it would be really good to have it back.'

'Replaced,' said Kenneth. 'I shall have to let you know how. After all, we still have the ultimate to discuss.'

The sword of Damocles. How could he have imagined that it would not descend? And if Kenneth still had that photograph, wouldn't he just bring it out now?

Mother was moving down the hall with small steps and the two of them followed her, as if threaded together.

As a last thrust towards ownership Bill said, 'When will Dad be back? It's some time since I've seen him.' Now Mother would have to invite him again, surely?

'He's back on Sunday to a tremendously busy time. He says the court list is over-full with crimes committed by youths who've lacked discipline during the war years.'

Kenneth tutted quietly.

Bill's cheeks flamed. So, Mother would never forgive him, and she was revealing that Dad did not want to see him in this house. They were both conveying that this was no longer 'home'.

Kenneth raised his right hand, as if displaying the prosthesis for the first time. 'A thought, Bill. Mama has been asking for a recent photograph. I also want one for the alumni book at Dulwich College, to leave my mark, you might say. And now I need one to replace the one you lost.' He smiled sarcastically. 'So please arrange a sitting at Gibson's. Who better to take my portrait than my prize-winning photographer cousin?'

Touche. Bill stilled. Kenneth always delivered the most devious thrust. The suggestion had to be accepted. Bill couldn't refuse: it would be turning away Mr Gibson's business. Other Dulwich College school leavers might well follow Kenneth's lead, such photography a profitable avenue. His teeth clamped, he nodded at Kenneth, unable to find words.

'I am preoccupied now with preparations for my History of Art course. It may not be for a month or two, but I shall telephone Gibsons for an appointment. Ask him to get hold of a decent chair, will you? And a suitable backdrop. I want to set the right scene.'

Bill turned. 'I must go.'

Mother and Kenneth both stood by the front door as he opened it. It was totally dark outside.

'Your trousers seem wet,' said Kenneth indicating the growing patch on his thigh.

'My handkerchief fell onto the path.'

'How unfortunate. You must have been uncomfortable all through this visit.'

He wouldn't answer.

Mother handed him his raincoat. 'Your father will be in touch.'

The words hung heavily, as the drizzle of rain met his exit.

Kenneth peered out. 'Nasty rain. Shame you haven't an umbrella to keep the worst off.'

Bill lifted his collar and hunched his shoulders in preparation.

'You'll just have to walk briskly,' Mother added as she closed the door.

CHAPTER 46

Kenneth certainly took his time before telephoning the Gibson studio; two months in fact, but then requested the entire morning for his sitting. Mr Gibson borrowed two chairs from the neighbouring second-hand shop that stretched to the occasional antique. 'I trust one of these will suit,' he said, dragging a Windsor and a green velvet regency affair behind him.

Kenneth also requested a gramophone. 'I can only relax with music in the background, because of my condition. And make sure it's a fine model, to look fitting beside my chair. *His Master's Voice* would be good.'

'Fussy bugger, your cousin,' Mr Gibson said, after the phone call, 'if you don't mind my saying.'

'I don't.'

'Why don't you send him elsewhere to be photographed, save yourself the aggro?'

'This is something I have to do. It's—' How could he explain? Mr Gibson knew nothing about the accident. 'There may be quite a number of proofs, and several prints, some framed. I want to meet all the cost.'

'Are you sure?' Mr Gibson's eyebrows shot up, but he was not one to probe. 'Do you want me to stay when he comes, the Lord Muck?'

'Thanks, no. Best not. He has a metal hand; he might feel awkward about posing in front of anyone else.'

Mr Gibson immediately became understanding and on the day, made himself scarce, probably glad to have an entire morning free.

Bill prepared the scene: the books, the vase of dried flowers, the chairs, the gramophone standing on a rotating bookcase. He owed the second-hand shopkeeper a few favours now.

Mr Gibson owned three different backdrop screens: the romantic landscape, the library, the misty sea-scape. Otherwise he used a plain white, or the outside of the studio between surges of traffic. Kenneth was bound to choose the library backdrop.

Everything was ready. Bill waited by the door like an expectant shopkeeper. Would meeting the expense of these photographs satisfy Kenneth's need for retribution? After such a prolonged period of dread, it would be such a relief to go for National Service with none of that in his emotional kitbag. Whether his photographs could satisfy Kenneth, the ultimate in difficult customers, was anyone's guess.

He'd phoned Alan about it who'd advised: 'Prepare for the worst, be glad of anything less.'

The studio clock told him Kenneth was due. He watched a large cloud lower itself on the top of the buildings opposite and imagined Kenneth on a throne in its midst. But at that moment, a car drew up outside and an older lady in a neat suit and a fox fur opened her door, and tripped round to the passenger door where Kenneth was stepping out.

'Thank you so much for the lift, Violet,' he said, dipping his head to indicate appreciation. 'I'll see you at choir.'

Bill felt he was nurturing a star rather than a cousin. Kenneth's black velvet jacket, the matching eye patch, a cream silky shirt and a purple cravat suggested stardom. Was Kenneth really intending to turn up for his lectures in this garb? What could Bill say, apart from, 'Everything's ready, Kenneth. Come in.'

Kenneth had brought his own record to enhance the sitting. 'Some Gilbert and Sullivan will lighten the mood, I think. I assume you'll take a number of *shots*, is it called?'

'Not really.'

'A number of proofs from which I can choose, then. Choice is everything, don't you think?'

Bill showed him the three background screens, and Kenneth opted for the library one, as expected.

Bill displayed the chairs: the ordinary studio one, pillowed to support babies; the Windsor chair, the low velvet armchair, the high-back leather armchair, green and shiny.

'Take that velvet one away. Why would I want to sit so low? It has to be this one,' Kenneth grasped hold of the leather wing of the high-backed chair. 'I just love it.'

Bill moved the Windsor chair nearer him. 'Try this first. It's plain and won't argue with your clothing.'

'Hate the wooden arms.' Kenneth sighed and slid into it, placing his prosthetic hand heavily, so that it clanged a protest. He watched Bill move to the camera and disappear under the hood.

Bill didn't need to do so, but it avoided the awful situation for a few moments. How was he going to manage this: treat Kenneth like a film star or a cosseted patient, or ignore the affectations and risk some come-back? Goodness knows, he'd suffered enough from those in the past.

His deliberations were interrupted by the sound of Kenneth opening the lid of the gramophone, placing his record on the turntable. He wound the handle many times. There was a light click as the arm was lifted and placed down upon the record. *A wandering minstrel, I…*

His nerves raw, Bill heard it first as *A Wandering Minstrel Eye* and had to listen for several repetitions before he understood the words. He emerged from under the cloth. 'Are you ready, Kenneth? How would you like to sit?'

Kenneth was humming along with the melody. He placed his velvet covered arms on the wooden ones of the Windsor chair and closed his eyes briefly. 'You can try me on this, but I think we'll need to transfer to the wing chair.'

Bill arranged the lighting, highlighting Kenneth's good hand, its fingers extended delicately. He returned to his hood and took two pictures.

Kenneth stood and stretched, his good eye focussed on the green leather chair. It wouldn't set him off so well, but it pleased Kenneth.

Bill swapped the chairs' positions and motioned to Kenneth to sit down. He looked as if he might break into song. Did he want a photograph of himself singing? Anything was possible.

Our wonderful tenor, Bill imagined the mainstay of the choir saying, as she came to collect Kenneth every Tuesday and Thursday evening.

'A thing of shreds and patches…' Kenneth's tenor joined with the one on his record.

'Do you want the same pose or shall I take you from one side? If so, which side?'

Kenneth stopped singing. 'Now which side would that be? Can you possibly work that out, Bill?' He sat down in the green leather chair, sliding his legs to one side and then the other, his head inclined to match. 'Try this pose, will you?' He angled himself to one side, his legs partly stretched out.

Bill took the picture, but said, 'You hardly look relaxed.'

'*…A dreamy lullaby, da, da-di, di-da-diddy da,*' Kenneth continued. Was that intended to taunt?

'Just move around as you would at home. I'll take several and we'll see which ones work best. How about one standing, perhaps holding the back of the chair?'

'Ah yes, good idea. Follow my movements, then.' Kenneth stood, turned a touch to the left, posed to right, sat, rested back, and leant on his knees.

Bill adjusted the lights, then took photographs of all. 'That should do it, Kenneth.'

Kenneth stood up again, staring down imperiously at Bill, hunched near the camera's hood. He assumed Bill had finished but another press of the button, Bill's hand tucked behind him, captured the moment. *Me boss, you worker,* that was Kenneth's expression and Bill knew it was in his mind.

Kenneth hummed on, *'Da-diddy, da-diddy da.* I'll enjoy *The Mikado* while you work away. Just carry on if you need to take your frames to the darkroom.'

Some instinct stopped Bill from leaving Kenneth in the studio with all the expensive equipment while he went down to the darkroom. He would delay that until Kenneth had gone. He bustled about, tidying things a little, waiting.

When the record came to an end, Kenneth stood and lifted the gramophone's arm to put it gently on its rest. He removed the needle. 'Past its best. Throw this away, will you?'

Bill took it over to the waste bin. It wasn't all he'd love to throw away. He had finished all the fiddling about he could reasonably make. He felt anxious, queasy. More than the awfulness of having Kenneth as a sitter, he needed Kenneth to just go. It was dreadfully uncomfortable having him in this territory, territory that wasn't even his.

Suddenly he located the discomfort. The last time he'd been left in charge of a premises with Kenneth present, it had been the *event* itself. He stepped forward. 'I shall do my very best with these photographs. Obviously I want Aunty to have one that she'll really treasure, and I want you to be satisfied too.'

'And I want you to have a replacement for the one you lost,' Kenneth said with an irony he meant Bill to absorb.

'Can I just check, Kenneth. Do you have any objection to possible public display of your photograph?' Mr Gibson might choose to display one, and what went into the windows was his decision.

'Will it say who I am, that I'm studying at the Courtauld?'

'It certainly can.'

Kenneth nodded, his tongue exploring the side of his mouth and then his lower lip, apparently with great satisfaction. 'I'm meeting Marcia at Arding and Hobbs now. The proofs?'

'They'll all be posted to you for your consideration.' Bill moved items swiftly from camera, table, desk and chair hoping to prompt Kenneth to leave.

'No hurry whatsoever. Quality before speed, wouldn't you say?' Kenneth registered Bill's agitation. As if to underline the point, he strolled slowly towards the door, flexing his neck and shoulders.

Bill screwed his fingers into fists. He must make an arrangement for finalising this matter, once and for all. 'I'll meet you at Fullers for tea when the prints are ready.'

'The ultimate discussion over tea. Yes, very civilised. Don't worry about calling a taxi, I'll walk.'

CHAPTER 47

'Absolutely smashing!' Bill came off the phone to Alan, grinning. 'Alan's father has pulled strings so that Alan and I can do our National Service together.'

'That is a bonus,' Letty said, as she handed him a pile of ironed clothes. 'He's got his Higher School Cert, then?'

'Yes, but hasn't decided what to do after National Service.' It was the one matter that made Bill feel he was ahead of Alan.

This good news about National Service with Alan was one of the plus things in a plus and minus month. Since he'd received his call-up papers, he'd been busy trying to leave everything in good order. There were a lot of things to settle, some extremely unpleasant.

Mr Gibson had given him photographic equipment small enough and suitable to take in his kit. 'Insure it! And I'll look after all the rest of your gear until you get back and set up your studio. Maybe the army will make use of your talent and you'll take military photos one day.' He gave Bill a week's paid holiday. 'You've earned it. I'll do anything that's unfinished.'

Bill gladly left him with the task of preparing Kenneth's proofs. He hadn't the stomach for looking at the negatives and used the excuse that Kenneth wasn't in a hurry because he was busy preparing for his Art History course.

'The awkward cousin! I'd better send off the proofs wrapped in gold,' Mr Gibson grinned. 'Lucky you won't be here if he isn't satisfied.'

It was a terrible wrench for Bill to move out of his room at the Durbans, worse to know that he wouldn't be back, not to live. He knew the move came at the right time. Angela was moving back home. She and her fiancé, Vincent, planned to marry in the spring. Finding somewhere to live would be difficult initially; meantime they could live with her parents. Bill would be over twenty when he came back, nearly an adult. Anyone would expect him to find his own accommodation then.

Peter and Letty went over the figures again for setting up his own studio. Peter had seen a likely premises in Stockwell. Bill didn't reveal that South London was not where he'd settle for he knew they'd assume he would want to live near them.

When he changed his name by deed poll, it was like a christening. Letty and Peter emphasized he was like a son in their eyes. They'd celebrated with dinner at a venue only known to the barristers Peter worked with. 'This event has caused a chilly atmosphere between your father and myself, but he accepts that originally it was his own wish for you to lose *Wilson* so he can't object if you decide to stay *Durban* now.'

Bill was very happy to be a Durban. He knew it was on Peter's minds that the name would otherwise have been lost when Angela married. He felt like Caesar! He imagined Angela having a son and the item he would inherit, and how the Durbans would protect him from it until he was adult, warning him of its heritage, using the dreadful story of Bill and Kenneth.

It was a relief, now, that he wouldn't ever own the shashka himself. He didn't need its imaginary power. The inner power Peter Durban had given him was infinitely more valuable.

There was one thing he could do related to the shashka. It would be appropriate and also of real benefit to the shashka heritage. This item was very expensive, as Peter had predicted, but Bill had managed to track it down: the copy of the ancient book, the traditional Cossack tale the professor of Russian history had told Peter about.

Bill had telephoned first and now, in the Charing Cross Road shop, the bookseller brought the dark covered volume out. Bill no longer wanted to know its contents, only that it was the story Peter needed. He put his own book on the counter for part exchange, the Dutch history. The book-seller examined it closely. His raised eyebrows and slight smile revealed his satisfaction.

How strange the thrill, discovering that when Kenneth had opted to have the German grammar, he'd left Bill with the treasure! And Dad had given his own son the prize, even if unintentionally. Now Bill was exchanging that prize to achieve something otherwise unattainable.

He left the shop with a glow. He wrapped his treasure up carefully, adding only a small card to tuck inside the front cover. *Thank you both for ALL you've done for me.* He couldn't put into words how much this was. Perhaps he wouldn't even know the extent until he was a father himself, if then. Once Bill had moved into the barracks, Peter would find the present in the snug where it would belong.

Colin brought Ted to see him before he left. They sat on the Durbans' sofa, drinking tea.

Colin jerked his head towards Ted, whose face was nearly as long as it had been after Dunkirk. 'He doesn't want you to do your National Service, Bill.'

'You know what I said, Bill. You could go for deferment. Don't let them take you to war. You might have to fight in Korea.'

Bill put his arm on Ted's shoulder. 'I don't like war either, but I want to serve my country. So far, I haven't any qualifications, but after this I'll have a record of service and I'll make sure it's a creditable one. You understand, Colin, don't you?'

'Yep. But I'm not your uncle.'

Ted was pulling Bill's sleeve. 'Listen to me. Don't go.'

'Ted! Think how your job has helped put you back to rights? Well, doing National Service will achieve that for me. I'll feel I've made myself acceptable.'

A few days later, he made his goodbyes to his parents. 'Are you sure about this?' said Dad. *This*, as Bill knew, referred to everything from doing his military service, through photography as an occupation, to changing his name.

Mother said, 'You'll be a man when you get back. National Service is supposed to be very character-building.' She made a move towards him he momentarily thought was going to be a kiss, but she just corrected his cuff that had turned itself back a little. It was her moment of warmth; the amount she could spare. 'Look after yourself,' she said. Hadn't she conveyed that instruction, years ago?

He'd first looked after himself on a journey to the country where he'd found people who'd made him feel like a prince. And that's where he went next, half-expecting it all to be a myth in his mind, but it wasn't.

It was totally dark when he passed the chicken hutch and tapped on the door he'd last seen as a twelve-year-old, heart-broken to be leaving. He had something to return, the remains of a napkin, the missing one of its set. He had a lot of missing gaps to talk about, and now he could be totally frank.

It didn't take a day to confirm that, whatever he'd done and might do, Bill's secure place remained in the Pawseys' hearts.

Mr Pawsey waved his glasses. 'You'd better not leave it longer before popping down to the Youldons, Bill. They'll all be waiting for you. They're so excited! And come straight back afterwards. The missus has made up your bed ready.'

His heart jolted as he got to the dim lane of little cottages and saw the door where Mrs Youldon had taken him in when no other housewife would. He peered down the side of the cottage. Only a sliver of moon helped him pick out the fence, the outline of the privy, the trees behind the cottages. It was the view he'd had that very first night away from home, a lonely, scared child, sharing the space with Alan, another evacuee feeling the same way. His hands found their way onto his stomach, just as they had done those years ago. He couldn't get back to that state of innocence, a time when he'd never done anything worse than make noise in his mother's back yard, but he had made changes in himself enough to return here. He knocked.

Tim opened the door with one brawny arm. His face went first blank then it flushed with delight. He said nothing, but turned to his mother and sister, opening the door wider. The two women looked up and behind them Bill saw the photograph, one of his first efforts, the children as they had been then, Sally giggling and hanging on to Tim.

Joan Youldon came forward. 'Bill? *Bill!*'

Sally, now the same height as her mother, stayed sitting, wisps of hair hiding her eyes but not her joy. 'Hello, Bill,' she said quietly, her mouth quirking upwards at the sides.

He moved behind her and placed his hands upon her shoulders, feeling the slight bones under his fingers. The sensation reminded him of how he'd once held her tiny figure up from the icy water.

'How are you all? How have you been?'

'I can't believe you're here, Bill.' Joan Youldon held both hands to her neck, gaping up at hime. 'You're so – fine.'

'No!' He gave a gusty laugh. 'Hardly! Remember, I said I'd come. You don't know how long I've been longing to. Years!'

'Mum never believed you'd manage to,' Sally said, as though they'd discussed it many times, 'but I did.'

Bill's four days with the Pawseys and the Youldons confirmed his plan to set up his studio in the county town there. 'Two years service,' he said to them all, 'and I'll be back, this time for good.'

'We'll be waiting for you,' Mrs Youldon said. 'Really.'

Then he turned to Sally. Whatever women he met in the future, none would have the look in Sally's eyes as she said Goodbye. This village was where his future belonged. He let them know.

And that evening, he let the Pawseys know. Their joyful faces he'd hold in his mind if National Service got grim. 'I am coming back to live near you. Believe it.'

'God willing, we'll still be here when you get back, Bill. And if you get leave, you spend it here, mind.'

He'd disclosed his plans here. Otherwise, it would only be Alan he'd tell until well after National Service.

He left Kenneth until last. There was no question that he and Kenneth had the most to settle.

He checked the finished photographs at the studio briefly. Mr Gibson had prioritized the work and sent off the proofs. To Bill's surprise, they'd all met Kenneth's satisfaction. He wanted prints of all of them. Mr Gibson had enlarged and framed three.

One was for Aunty. It would prepare her for the reality of Kenneth as he was now, before she came over in May for the Festival of Britain. Afterwards, would Kenneth return with her and sample the much more comfortable life that Dwaine could provide? Kenneth's first love, Art, would surely mean he remained, at least until the end of his studies at the Courtauld. But with Kenneth, nothing could be predicted. As he'd said, having a choice was good.

As Bill approached Fuller's restaurant, a bright green scarf and the velvet eye patch identified Kenneth in the crowd . The Corner House teas had established the habit of a dainty tea-table in a neutral environment as the most fitting place to settle heavy matters. In such a place, raised voices, conflict, aggression would be unimaginable.

He ushered Kenneth to the rear-most table where they would benefit from more privacy. Until the waitress took their order, they discussed the course at the Courtauld and Kenneth's arrangements for study, including the amanuensis Bill had financed.

'I've settled for a very nice girl. Attentive, and not too much to say. She'll suit my needs well. I use my left hand between times, but the writing's so poor that I'm getting her to take the pages home to rewrite. She doesn't seem to mind the extra chore. She has a good craven attitude.'

Bill said nothing. He didn't envy the girl.

The waitress brought tea, and the coffee walnut cake Kenneth favoured.

Bill said, 'I'm glad you approve of all the proofs, Kenneth. The prints will arrive tomorrow, including the framed ones, so I hope you'll be at home to receive them—'

Kenneth nodded, looking pleased.

'—because I shall be away. I'm due to start my training, as you know.'

'National Service. I haven't been called up, of course.' His prosthetic hand lifted slightly. 'What a shame I can't serve.' He dropped his sarcastic tone. 'Perhaps I should be grateful that you've saved me from the experience. Square-bashing, wielding an instrument – it's hardly me, is it?'

Bill looked at his hands. 'I hope I'll the instrument I'll be wielding will be a camera. However.' He must get things entirely settled. 'The whole set of proofs and prints, I hope they're a suitable gesture towards – everything.'

Kenneth took another slice of cake. 'My compensation? I had intended something more retributive, but now you're off to National Service, perhaps to be killed or maimed in war, perhaps I should be satisfied.'

'Killed or maimed? Is that what you hope for?'

Kenneth closed his eyes briefly. 'You could have deferred, even claimed to be a conscientious objector. I would.'

'No, I won't. I will be serving for both of us, Kenneth. That seems only fair.'

'You'll take that risk?'

Bill felt stronger, the heavy dread of retribution dissipating like used tea-leaves. 'I'm sure we'll both have a good future.'

'As we both have a past,' Kenneth took the napkin and wiped the coffee cream from the white fingers of his left hand, 'if not a good one.'

Could Kenneth be referring to his own mean acts as well? Bill stood up. He'd had enough. He moved away from the tea table and in order to shake Kenneth's good hand, held out his left hand.

Kenneth looked at it, and then shook it with his own good hand, a firm shake. His face lost its sardonic expression. 'Come back safe. Whatever else, you're the closest I have to a brother.' He flicked his green scarf over the shoulder of his velvet jacket and left, the eyes of every customer following him to the door.

Bill was so stunned by Kenneth's words that the waitress had to ask him twice to pay the bill before he heard her. If he never saw Kenneth again, he would never lose the memory of his dramatic presence.

Some instinct made him hurry back to Gibson's studio to ensure the prints had been packaged and sent.

Mr Gibson had not yet gone home for the night. 'Bill! A most propitious swansong! I've sent off the prints, all very good. But *this* photograph is unlikely to be surpassed by anything in your future portfolio.' He brought out the picture Bill had taken when Kenneth had assumed the sitting was finished.

The nonchalant stance defined the black patch as signifying a fashion statement. Everything in the picture screamed a drama: the imperious expression, the quizzical remaining eye under a raised eyebrow, the black velvet jacket and bright cravat, the delicate artist's hand outstretched on the back of the green leather chair, the prosthetic one hanging limply in front.

'This will be on the front cover of *Hidden Power* in November.'

'*Hidden Power*?'

'Yes, it's the new, most prestigious London magazine for the Art world.' He held out a copy. 'This is August's issue. Any photographer would give his right hand to get a pic in this mag.'

A shudder ran through Bill's body.

Mr Gibson raced on enthusiastically, oblivious to his gaffe. 'I knew it was a winner as soon as I saw the negative. I nearly rang Peter's, but remembered you'd already moved out. What a stunner!' He waved the photo in front of Bill's face.

Bill flinched.

'Super work! One look, and the reader's full of questions. I sent it off directly it was printed and they snapped it up. Quite a stunt to hit the front page, just as you're off to National Service!' He struck the journal's front. 'Just imagine your stunner right here!'

Bill took the current issue of *Hidden Power* and turned its shiny pages.

'Now you have to pen a paragraph about the sitter.'

'Paragraph?'

'To write the background to the picture.'

The journal slipped from Bill's fingers and he bent to pick it up. 'I'm not a writer.'

'He's your cousin, eh? There'll be so much you can write. His whole stance shouts for explanations. I tell you, when you're famous, it will always be this photograph that everyone remembers.'

Bill sat down heavily.

Wherever he went, Kenneth, and the question of his injuries, would always be with him. Kenneth had manoeuvred a lasting retribution.

TO THE READER

This ends the trilogy, A RELATIVE INVASION, but if you are curious about what happened before Bill and Kenneth were even born, I have written a **Prequel.** In this, the adults tell their tale in their own voices.

I also plan to write about Bill and Kenneth again. With Bill about to begin his National Service and Kenneth to attempt a career despite his disablements, what career and family success will they have, and can they manage to keep their lives apart?

Thank you for reading about Bill and his world. If you've enjoyed the read, please consider reviewing this book online, however briefly. Writers are always very grateful for reviews.

If you like my character-driven writing, you might like to try my books in other genres, all available in ebook and paperback.

A contemporary psychological suspense series, Uncommon Relations. *A disenchanted young married man chances across his double. He's excited at the opportunity of a brighter lifestyle, but finds himself trapped in a labyrinth of hidden identities and dark secrets.*

A pair of short story collections where the oddities of women (Me-Time Tales) are matched by those of the men(Curious Men). Witty tales with a dark edge. Good for commuting or neat meaningful gifts!

To learn more, do join my READERS LIST for the Newsletter with inside information, exclusive snippets and advance information of forthcoming books. You will find a free offer when you join up. See it on the Rosalind Minett website

Also, check out my Characterful Writer blog and please follow me on Bookbub.

Printed in Great Britain
by Amazon

17244367R10434